*PRAISE FOR THE MODERN LIBRARY*
*EDITION OF* IN SEARCH OF LOST TIME

"Twice amended to bring it to documentary decorum and the kind of textual completion Proust himself could never achieve, the C. K. Scott Moncrieff translation of the *Search*, buffed, rebuffed, lightened, tightened, and in the abstergent sense, brightened, constitutes a monument which is also a medium—THE medium by which to gain access to the book, the books, even the apocrypha of modern scripture. A triumph of tone, of a single (and singular) vision, this ultimate revision of the primary version affords the surest sled over the ice fields as well as the most sinuous surfboard over the breakers of Proustian prose, an invaluable and inescapable text."

—RICHARD HOWARD

# IN SEARCH OF
# LOST TIME

# MARCEL PROUST

# IN SEARCH OF LOST TIME

## VOLUME VI

### TIME REGAINED

*Translated by*
*Andreas Mayor and Terence Kilmartin*

*Revised by D. J. Enright*

### A GUIDE TO PROUST

*Compiled by Terence Kilmartin*
*Revised by Joanna Kilmartin*

THE MODERN LIBRARY

NEW YORK

This edition was originally published in hardcover in Great Britain by Chatto
& Windus in 1992 and in the United States by Modern Library in 1993.

This translation is a revised edition of the 1981 translation of *The Past
Recaptured* by Andreas Mayor and Terence Kilmartin, published in the
United States by Random House, Inc., and in Great Britain by
Chatto & Windus. Revisions by D. J. Enright.

LIBRARY OF CONGRESS CATALOGING-IN-PUBLICATION DATA
Proust, Marcel, 1871–1922.
[Temps retrouvé. English]
Time regained/Marcel Proust; translated by Andreas Mayor and
Terence Kilmartin; revised by D. J. Enright. A guide to Proust/compiled by
Terence Kilmartin; revised by Joanna Kilmartin.
p.    cm.—(In search of lost time; 6)
Includes bibliographical references.
ISBN 0-375-75312-5
I. Mayor, Andreas.    II. Kilmartin, Terence.    III. Enright, D. J. (Dennis
Joseph), 1920– .    IV. Kilmartin, Terence. Guide to Proust. 1993.    V. Title.
VI. Series: Proust, Marcel, 1871–1922. À la recherche du temps perdu.
English; v. 6.
PQ2631.R63T413 1993
843'.912—dc20            93-3628

Modern Library website address: www.modernlibrary.com

Printed in the United States of America

8  9  7

# MARCEL PROUST

Marcel Proust was born in the Parisian suburb of Auteuil on July 10, 1871. His father, Adrien Proust, was a doctor celebrated for his work in epidemiology; his mother, Jeanne Weil, was a stockbroker's daughter of Jewish descent. He lived as a child in the family home on Boulevard Malesherbes in Paris, but spent vacations with his aunt and uncle in the town of Illiers near Chartres, where the Prousts had lived for generations and which became the model for the Combray of his great novel. (In recent years it was officially renamed Illiers-Combray.) Sickly from birth, Marcel was subject from the age of nine to violent attacks of asthma, and although he did a year of military service as a young man and studied law and political science, his invalidism disqualified him from an active professional life.

During the 1890s Proust contributed sketches to *Le Figaro* and to a short-lived magazine, *Le Banquet,* founded by some of his school friends in 1892. *Pleasures and Days,* a collection of his stories, essays, and poems, was published in 1896. In his youth Proust led an active social life, penetrating the highest circles of wealth and aristocracy. Artistically and intellectually, his influences included the aesthetic criticism of John Ruskin, the philosophy of Henri Bergson, the music of Wagner, and the fiction of Anatole France (on whom he modeled his character Bergotte). An affair begun in 1894 with the composer and pianist Reynaldo Hahn marked the beginning of Proust's often anguished acknowledgment of his homosexuality. Following the publication of Emile Zola's letter in defense of Colonel Dreyfus in 1898, Proust became "the first Dreyfusard," as he later phrased it. By the time Dreyfus was finally vindicated of charges of treason, Proust's social circles had been torn apart by the anti-Semitism and political hatreds stirred up by the affair.

Proust was very attached to his mother, and after her death in 1905 he spent some time in a sanatorium. His health worsened progressively, and he withdrew almost completely from society and devoted himself to writing. Proust's early work had done nothing to establish his reputation as a major writer. In an unfinished novel, *Jean Santeuil* (not published until 1952), he laid some of the groundwork for *In Search of Lost Time*, and in *Against Sainte-Beuve*, written in 1908–9, he stated as his aesthetic credo: "A book is the product of a different self from the one we manifest in our habits, in society, in our vices. If we mean to try to understand this self it is only in our inmost depths, by endeavoring to reconstruct it there, that the quest can be achieved." He appears to have begun work on his long masterpiece sometime around 1908, and the first volume, *Swann's Way*, was published in 1913. In 1919 the second volume, *Within a Budding Grove*, won the Goncourt Prize, bringing Proust great and instantaneous fame. Two subsequent sections—*The Guermantes Way* (1920–21) and *Sodom and Gomorrah* (1921)—appeared in his lifetime. (Of the depiction of homosexuality in the latter, his friend André Gide complained: "Will you never portray this form of Eros for us in the aspect of youth and beauty?") The remaining volumes were published following Proust's death on November 18, 1922: *The Captive* in 1923, *The Fugitive* in 1925, and *Time Regained* in 1927.

# CONTENTS

## TIME REGAINED
### 1

## A GUIDE TO PROUST

*Numerals in the text refer the reader to explanatory notes, which follow the text.*

# A Note on the Translation
## (1981)

### Terence Kilmartin

C. K. Scott Moncrieff's version of *À la recherche du temps perdu* has in the past fifty years earned a reputation as one of the great English translations, almost as a masterpiece in its own right. Why then should it need revision? Why tamper with a work that has been enjoyed and admired, not to say revered, by several generations of readers throughout the English-speaking world?

The answer is that the original French edition from which Scott Moncrieff worked (the "abominable" edition of the *Nouvelle Revue Française,* as Samuel Beckett described it in a marvellous short study of Proust which he published in 1931) was notoriously imperfect. This was not so much the fault of the publishers and printers as of Proust's methods of composition. Only the first volume (*Du côté de chez Swann*) of the novel as originally conceived—and indeed written—was published before the 1914–1918 war. The second volume was set up in type, but publication was delayed, and moreover by that time Proust had already begun to reconsider the scale of the novel; the remaining eight years of his life (1914–1922) were spent in expanding it from its original 500,000 words to more than a million and a quarter. The margins of proofs and typescripts were covered with scribbled corrections and insertions, often overflowing on to additional sheets which were glued to the galleys or to one another to form interminable strips—what Françoise in the novel calls the narrator's *"paperoles."* The unravelling and deciphering of these copious additions cannot have been an enviable task for editors and printers.

Furthermore, the last three sections of the novel (*La prisonnière*, *La fugitive*—originally called *Albertine disparue*—and *Le temps retrouvé*) had not yet been published at the time of Proust's death in November 1922 (he was still correcting a typed copy of *La prisonnière* on his deathbed). Here the original editors had to take it upon themselves to prepare a coherent text from a manuscript littered with sometimes hasty corrections, revisions and afterthoughts and leaving a number of unresolved contradictions, obscurities and chronological inconsistencies. As a result of all this the original editions—even of the volumes published in Proust's lifetime—pullulate with errors, misreadings and omissions.

In 1954 a revised three-volume edition of *À la recherche* was published in Gallimard's Bibliothèque de la Pléiade. The editors, M. Pierre Clarac and M. André Ferré, had been charged by Proust's heirs with the task of "establishing a text of his novel as faithful as possible to his intentions." With infinite care and patience they examined all the relevant material—manuscripts, notebooks, typescripts, proofs, as well as the original edition—and produced what is generally agreed to be a virtually impeccable transcription of Proust's text. They scrupulously avoided the arbitrary emendations, the touchings-up, the wholesale reshufflings of paragraphs in which the original editors indulged, confining themselves to clarifying the text wherever necessary, correcting errors due to haste or inadvertence, eliminating careless repetitions and rationalising the punctuation (an area where Proust was notoriously casual). They justify and explain their editorial decisions in detailed critical notes, occupying some 200 pages over the three volumes, and print all the significant variants as well as a number of passages that Proust did not have time to work into his book.

The Pléiade text differs from that of the original edition, mostly in minor though none the less significant ways, throughout the novel. In the last three sections (the third Pléiade volume) the differences are sometimes considerable. In particular, MM. Clarac and Ferré have included a number of passages, sometimes of a paragraph or two, sometimes of several pages, which the original editors omitted for no good reason.

The present translation is a reworking, on the basis of the Pléiade edition, of Scott Moncrieff's version of the first six sections of *À la recherche*—or the first eleven volumes of the twelve-volume English edition. A post-Pléiade version of the final volume, *Le temps retrouvé* (originally translated by Stephen Hudson after Scott Moncrieff's death in 1930), was produced by the late Andreas Mayor and published in 1970; with some minor emendations, it is incorporated in this edition. There being no indication in Proust's manuscript as to where *La fugitive* should end and *Le temps retrouvé* begin, I have followed the Pléiade editors in introducing the break some pages earlier than in the previous editions, both French and English—at the beginning of the account of the Tansonville episode.

The need to revise the existing translation in the light of the Pléiade edition has also provided an opportunity of correcting mistakes and misinterpretations in Scott Moncrieff's version. Translation, almost by definition, is imperfect; there is always "room for improvement," and it is only too easy for the latecomer to assume the *beau rôle*. I have refrained from officious tinkering for its own sake, but a translator's

loyalty is to the original author, and in trying to be faithful
to Proust's meaning and tone of voice I have been obliged,
here and there, to make extensive alterations.

A general criticism that might be levelled against Scott
Moncrieff is that his prose tends to the purple and the
precious—or that this is how he interpreted the tone of the
original: whereas the truth is that, complicated, dense, over-
loaded though it often is, Proust's style is essentially natural
and unaffected, quite free of preciosity, archaism or self-
conscious elegance. Another pervasive weakness of Scott
Moncrieff's is perhaps the defect of a virtue. Contrary to
a widely held view, he stuck very closely to the original
(he is seldom guilty of short-cuts, omissions or loose para-
phrases), and in his efforts to reproduce the structure of
those elaborate sentences with their spiralling subordinate
clauses, not only does he sometimes lose the thread but he
wrenches his syntax into oddly unEnglish shapes: a whiff
of Gallicism clings to some of the longer periods, obscur-
ing the sense and falsifying the tone. A corollary to this is
a tendency to translate French idioms and turns of phrase
literally, thus making them sound weirder, more outland-
ish, than they would to a French reader. In endeavouring to
rectify these weaknesses, I hope I have preserved the un-
doubted felicity of much of Scott Moncrieff while doing the
fullest possible justice to Proust.

I should like to thank Professor J. G. Weightman for his
generous help and advice and Mr D. J. Enright for his patient and percipient editing.

# A Note on the Revised Translation (1992)

## D. J. Enright

Terence Kilmartin intended to make further changes to the translation as published in 1981 under the title *Remembrance of Things Past*. But, as Proust's narrator observed while reflecting on the work he had yet to do, when the fortress of the body is besieged on all sides the mind must at length succumb. "It was precisely when the thought of death had become a matter of indifference to me that I was beginning once more to fear death . . . as a threat not to myself but to my book."

C. K. Scott Moncrieff excelled in description, notably of landscape and architecture, but he was less adroit in translating dialogue of an informal, idiomatic nature. At ease with intellectual and artistic discourse and the finer feelings, and alert to sallies of humorous fantasy, he was not always comfortable with workaday matters and the less elevated aspects of human behaviour. It was left to Kilmartin to elucidate the significance of Albertine's incomplete but alarming outburst—". . . *me faire casser* . . ."—in *The Captive*, a passage Scott Moncrieff rendered totally incomprehensible, perhaps through squeamishness, perhaps through ignorance of low slang. Other misunderstandings of colloquialisms and failures to spot secondary meanings remained to be rectified. And some further intervention was prompted by Scott Moncrieff's tendency to spell out things for the benefit of the English reader: an admirable intention (shared by Arthur Waley in his *Tale of Genji*), though the effect could be to clog Proust's flow and make his drift harder to follow.

The present revision or re-revision has taken into account the second Pléiade edition of *À la recherche du temps perdu*, published in four volumes between 1987 and 1989 under the direction of Jean-Yves Tadié. This both adds, chiefly in the form of drafts and variants, and relocates material: not always helpfully from the viewpoint of the common (as distinct from specialist) reader, who may be surprised to encounter virtually the same passage in two different locations when there was doubt as to where Proust would finally have placed it. But the new edition clears up some long-standing misreadings: for example, in correcting Cambremer's admiring "niece" in *Time Regained* to his "mother," an identification which accords with a mention some thousand pages earlier in the novel.

Kilmartin notes that it is only too easy for the latecomer, tempted to make his mark by "officious tinkering," to "assume the *beau rôle*." The caveat, so delicately worded, is one to take to heart. I am much indebted to my wife, Madeleine, without whose collaboration I would never have dared to assume a role that is melancholy rather than (in any sense) *beau*.

# TIME REGAINED

I should have no occasion to dwell upon this visit which I paid to the neighbourhood of Combray at perhaps the moment in my life when I thought least about Combray, had it not, precisely for that reason, brought me what was at least a provisional confirmation of certain ideas which I had first conceived along the Guermantes way, and also of certain other ideas which I had conceived on the Méséglise way. I repeated every evening, in the opposite direction, the walks which we used to take at Combray, in the afternoon, when we went the Méséglise way. One dined now at Tansonville at an hour at which in the past one had long been asleep at Combray. And because of the seasonal heat, and also because Gilberte spent the afternoon painting in the chapel attached to the house, we did not go out for our walk until about two hours before dinner. The pleasure of those earlier walks, which was that of seeing, on the way home, the crimson sky framing the calvary or mirroring itself in the Vivonne, was now replaced by the pleasure of setting forth at nightfall, when one encountered nothing in the village but the blue-grey, irregular and shifting triangle of a flock of sheep being driven home. Over one half of the fields the sun had already set; above the other half the moon was already alight and would soon bathe them in their entirety. It sometimes happened that Gilberte let me go without her, and I set off, trailing my shadow behind me, like a boat gliding across enchanted waters. But as a rule Gilberte came with

me. The walks that we took thus together were very often
those that I used to take as a child: how then could I help
but feel much more acutely even than in the past on the
Guermantes way the conviction that I would never be
able to write, reinforced by the conviction that my imagination and my sensibility had weakened, when I found
how incurious I was about Combray? I was distressed to
see how little I relived my early years. I found the
Vivonne narrow and ugly alongside the towpath. Not that
I noticed any great physical discrepancies from what I remembered. But, separated as I was by a whole lifetime
from places I now happened to be passing through again,
there was lacking between them and me that contiguity
from which is born, even before we have perceived it, the
immediate, delicious and total deflagration of memory.
Having doubtless no very clear conception of its nature, I
was saddened by the thought that my faculty of feeling
and imagining things must have diminished since I no
longer took any pleasure in these walks. Gilberte herself,
who understood me even less than I understood myself,
increased my melancholy by sharing my astonishment.
"What," she would say, "you feel no excitement when
you turn into this little footpath which you used to
climb?" And she herself had changed so much that I no
longer thought her beautiful, that she was no longer beautiful at all. As we walked, I saw the landscape change; we
had to climb hills, followed by downward slopes. We
chatted—very agreeably for me. Not without difficulty,
however. In so many people there are different strata
which are not alike: the character of the father, then of the
mother; one traverses first one, then the other. But, next
day, the order of their superimposition is reversed. And

finally one does not know who will decide between the contestants, to whom one is to appeal for the verdict. Gilberte was like one of those countries with which one dare not form an alliance because of their too frequent changes of government. But in reality this is a mistake. The memory of the most multiple person establishes a sort of identity in him and makes him reluctant to go back on promises which he remembers, even if he has not countersigned them. As for intelligence, Gilberte's, in spite of certain absurdities inherited from her mother, was very acute. But, quite unrelated to this, I remember that, in the course of our conversations during these walks, on several occasions she surprised me a great deal. The first time was when she said to me: "If you were not too hungry and if it was not so late, by taking that road to the left and then turning to the right, in less than a quarter of an hour we should be at Guermantes." It was as though she had said to me: "Turn to the left, then bear right, and you will touch the intangible, you will reach the inaccessibly remote tracts of which one never knows anything on this earth except the direction, except" (what I thought long ago to be all that I could ever know of Guermantes, and perhaps in a sense I had not been mistaken) "the 'way.'" One of my other surprises was that of seeing the "source of the Vivonne," which I imagined as something as extra-terrestrial as the Gates of Hell, and which was merely a sort of rectangular basin in which bubbles rose to the surface. And the third occasion was when Gilberte said to me: "If you like, we might after all go out one afternoon and then we can go to Guermantes, taking the road by Méséglise, which is the nicest way," a sentence which upset all the ideas of my childhood by informing me that the two "ways" were not as irreconcilable as I had supposed. But what struck me most forcibly was how little, during this stay, I relived my childhood years, how little I desired to see Combray, how narrow and ugly I thought the Vivonne. But where Gilberte corroborated some of my childhood imaginings along the Méséglise way was during one of those walks which were more or less nocturnal even though they occurred before dinner— for she dined so late. Before descending into the mystery of a deep and flawless valley carpeted with moonlight, we stopped for a moment like two insects about to plunge into the blue calyx of a flower. Gilberte then uttered, per- haps simply out of the politeness of a hostess who is sorry you are going away so soon and would have liked to show you more of a countryside which you seem to appreciate, an avowal of the sort in which her practice as a woman of the world skilled in putting to the best advantage silence, simplicity, sobriety in the expression of her feelings, makes you believe that you occupy a place in her life which no one else could fill. Opening my heart to her suddenly with a tenderness born of the exquisite air, the fragrant evening breeze, I said to her: "You were speaking the other day of the little footpath. How I loved you then!" She replied: "Why didn't you tell me? I had no idea. I loved you too. In fact I flung myself twice at your head." "When?" "The first time at Tansonville. You were going for a walk with your family, and I was on my way home, I'd never seen such a pretty little boy. I was in the habit," she went on with a vaguely bashful air, "of going to play with little boys I knew in the ruins of the keep of Roussainville. And you will tell me that I was a very naughty girl, for there were girls and boys there of all sorts who took advantage of the darkness. The altar-boy from Combray church, Théodore, who, I must admit, was very nice indeed (goodness, how handsome he was!) and who has become quite ugly (he's the chemist now at Méséglise), used to amuse himself with all the peasant girls of the district. As I was allowed to go out by myself, whenever I was able to get away, I used to rush over there. I can't tell you how I longed for you to come there too; I remember quite well that, as I had only a moment in which to make you understand what I wanted, at the risk of being seen by your people and mine, I signalled to you so vulgarly that I'm ashamed of it to this day. But you stared at me so crossly that I saw that you didn't want to."

And suddenly I thought to myself that the true Gilberte, the true Albertine, were perhaps those who had at the first moment yielded themselves with their eyes, one through the hedge of pink hawthorn, the other on the beach. And it was I who, having been incapable of under-standing this, having failed to recapture the impression until much later in my memory after an interval in which, as a result of my conversation, a dividing hedge of senti-ment had made them afraid to be as frank as in the first moments, had ruined everything by my clumsiness. I had "botched it" more completely than had Saint-Loup with Rachel—although in fact the relative failure with them was less absurd—and for the same reasons.

"And the second time," Gilberte went on, "was years later when I passed you in the doorway of your house, the day before I met you again at my aunt Oriane's. I didn't recognise you at first, or rather I did unconsciously recognise you because I felt the same attraction as I had felt at Tansonville."

"But in the meantime there'd been, after all, the Champs-Elysées."

"Yes, but there you were too fond of me. I felt you were prying into everything I did."

I did not think to ask her who the young man was with whom she had been walking along the Avenue des Champs-Elysées on the day when I had set out to call on her again, when I might have been reconciled with her while there was still time, that day which would perhaps have changed the whole course of my life, if I had not caught sight of those two shadowy figures strolling side by side in the dusk. If I had asked her, she would perhaps have confessed the truth, as would Albertine had she been restored to life. And indeed when we meet again after many years women whom we no longer love, is there not the abyss of death between them and us, quite as much as if they were no longer of this world, since the fact that our love exists no longer makes the people that they were or the person that we were then as good as dead? Perhaps, too, she might not have remembered, or she might have lied. In any case I was no longer interested to know, since my heart had changed even more than Gilberte's face. This face gave me little pleasure, but above all I was no longer unhappy, and I should have been incapable of conceiving, had I thought about it again, that I could have been so unhappy at the sight of Gilberte tripping along by the side of a young man that I had said to myself: "It's all over, I shall never attempt to see her again." Of the state of mind which, in that far-off year, had been tantamount to a long-drawn-out torture for me, nothing survived. For in this world of ours where everything withers, everything perishes, there is a thing that decays, that crumbles into dust even more completely, leaving behind still fewer traces of itself, than beauty: namely grief.

And so I am not surprised that I did not ask her then with whom she had been walking in the Champs-Elysées, for I had already seen too many examples of the incuriosity that is brought about by Time, but I am a little surprised that I did not tell her that before I saw her that evening I had sold a Chinese porcelain bowl in order to buy her flowers. It had indeed, during the gloomy period that followed, been my sole consolation to think that one day I should be able with impunity to tell her of so tender an intention. More than a year later, if I saw another carriage about to crash into mine, my sole reason for wishing not to die was that I might be able to tell this to Gilberte. I consoled myself with the thought: "There's no hurry, I have a whole lifetime in which to tell her." And for this reason I was anxious not to lose my life. Now it would have seemed to me an unseemly, almost ridiculous thing to say, and a thing that would "involve consequences."

I did not ask then with whom she had been walking that evening. (I asked her later. It was Léa dressed as a man. Gilberte was aware that she knew Albertine, but could tell me nothing more. Thus it is that certain persons always reappear in one's life to herald one's pleasures or one's griefs.) What reality there had been beneath the appearance on that occasion had become quite immaterial to me. And yet for how many days and nights had I not tormented myself with wondering who it had been, had I not been obliged, even more perhaps than in the effort not to go downstairs to say good-night to Mamma in this very Combray, to control the beating of my heart! It is said, and this is what accounts for the gradual disappearance of certain nervous affections, that our nervous system grows old. This is true not merely of our permanent self, which continues throughout the whole duration of our life, but of all our successive selves which, after all, to a certain extent compose it.

"Moreover," Gilberte went on, "even on the day when I passed you in the doorway, you were still just the same as at Combray; if you only knew how little you'd changed!"

I pictured Gilberte again in my memory. I could have drawn the rectangle of light which the sun cast through the hawthorns, the spade which the little girl was holding in her hand, the slow gaze that she fastened on me. Only I had supposed, because of the coarse gesture that accompanied it, that it was a contemptuous gaze because what I longed for it to mean seemed to me to be a thing that little girls did not know about and did only in my imagination, during my hours of solitary desire. Still less could I have supposed that so casually, so rapidly, almost under the eyes of my grandfather, one of them would have had the audacity to suggest it.

And so I was obliged, after an interval of so many years, to touch up a picture which I recalled so well—an operation which made me quite happy by showing me that the impassable gulf which I had then supposed to exist between myself and a certain type of little girl with golden hair was as imaginary as Pascal's gulf, and which I thought poetic because of the long sequence of years at the end of which I was called upon to perform it. I felt a

stab of desire and regret when I thought of the dungeons
of Roussainville. And yet I was glad to be able to tell myself that the pleasure towards which I used to strain every
nerve in those days, and which nothing could restore to
me now, had indeed existed elsewhere than in my mind,
in fact so close at hand, in that Roussainville of which I
used to speak so often, and which I could see from the
window of the orris-scented closet. And I had known
nothing! In short, the image of Gilberte summed up everything that I had desired during my walks to the point
of being unable to make up my mind to return home,
seeming to see the tree-trunks part asunder and take human form. What I had so feverishly longed for then she
had been ready, if only I had been able to understand and
to meet her again, to let me taste in my boyhood. More
completely even than I had supposed, Gilberte had been
in those days truly part of the Méséglise way.

And even on the day when I had passed her in a
doorway, although she was not Mlle de l'Orgeville, the
girl whom Robert had met in houses of assignation (and
what an absurd coincidence that it should have been to
her future husband that I had applied for information
about her), I had not been altogether mistaken as to the
meaning of her glance, nor as to the sort of woman that
she was and confessed to me now that she had been. "All
that is a long time ago," she said to me, "I've never given
a thought to anyone but Robert since the day of our engagement. And even so, you see, it's not those childish
whims that I feel most guilty about."[1]

All day long, in that slightly too countrified house
which seemed no more than a place for a rest between

walks or during a sudden downpour, one of those houses
in which all the sitting-rooms look like arbours and, on
the wall-paper in the bedrooms, here the roses from the
garden, there the birds from the trees outside join you
and keep you company, isolated from the world—for it
was old wall-paper on which every rose was so distinct
that, had it been alive, you could have picked it, every
bird you could have put in a cage and tamed, quite different from those grandiose bedroom decorations of today
where, on a silver background, all the apple-trees of Normandy display their outlines in the Japanese style to hal-
lucinate the hours you spend in bed—all day long I
remained in my room which looked over the fine greenery
of the park and the lilacs at the entrance, over the green
leaves of the tall trees by the edge of the lake, sparkling in
the sun, and the forest of Méséglise. Yet I looked at all
this with pleasure only because I said to myself: "How
nice to be able to see so much greenery from my bedroom
window," until the moment when, in the vast verdant picture, I recognised, painted in a contrasting dark blue simply because it was further away, the steeple of Combray
church. Not a representation of the steeple, but the
steeple itself, which, putting in visible form a distance of
miles and of years, had come, intruding its discordant
tone into the midst of the luminous verdure—a tone so
colourless that it seemed little more than a preliminary
sketch—and engraved itself upon my window-pane. And
if I left my room for a moment, I saw at the end of the
corridor, in a little sitting-room which faced in another direction, what seemed to be a band of scarlet—for this
room was hung with a plain silk, but a red one, ready to
burst into flames if a ray of sun fell upon it.

The love of Albertine had disappeared from my memory. But it seems that there exists too an involuntary memory of the limbs, a pale and sterile imitation of the other but longer-lived, just as there are animals or vegetables without intelligence which are longer-lived than man. Our legs and our arms are full of torpid memories. And once, when I had said good-night to Gilberte rather early, I woke up in the middle of the night in my room at Tansonville and, still half-asleep, called out: "Albertine!" It was not that I had thought of her or dreamt of her, nor that I was confusing her with Gilberte, but a memory in my arm, opening like a flower, had made me fumble behind my back for the bell, as though I had been in my bedroom in Paris. And not finding it, I had called out: "Albertine!", thinking that my dead mistress was lying by my side, as she had often done in the evening, and that we were both dropping off to sleep, and reckoning, as I woke up, that, because of the time it would take Françoise to reach my room, Albertine might without imprudence pull the bell which I could not find.

During our walks Gilberte intimated to me that Robert was turning away from her, but only in order to run after other women. And it is true that many women encumbered his life, yet always these associations, like certain masculine friendships in the lives of men who love women, had that quality of ineffectual resistance, of purposelessly filling an empty space that often in a house may be seen in objects which are not there to be used.

He came several times to Tansonville while I was there and I found him very different from the man I had known. His life had not coarsened him or slowed him down, as had happened with M. de Charlus; on the contrary, working in him an inverse change, it had given him, in a degree in which he had never had it before—and this although he had resigned his commission on his marriage—the grace and ease of a cavalry officer. Gradually, just as M. de Charlus had grown heavier, Robert (it is true that he was very much younger, but one felt that with age he would only get nearer and nearer to this ideal), had, like those women who resolutely sacrifice their faces to their figures and after a certain moment never stir from Marienbad (they realise that they cannot preserve more than one kind of youth and think that a youthful figure will serve best to represent youth in general), become slimmer and taken to moving more rapidly, a contrary effect of an identical vice. This swiftness of movement had, moreover, various psychological causes, the fear of being seen, the wish to conceal that fear, the feverishness which is generated by self-dissatisfaction and boredom. He was in the habit of visiting certain low haunts into which, as he did not wish to be seen going in or coming out, he would hurl himself in such a way as to present the smallest possible target to the unfriendly glances of possible passers-by, like a soldier going into an attack.[2] And this manner of moving like a gust of wind had become a habit. Perhaps also it symbolised the superficial intrepidity of a man who wants to show that he is not afraid and does not want to give himself time to think. We must mention too, if our account is to be complete, a desire, the older he grew, to appear young, and also the impatience characteristic of those perpetually bored and perpetually cynical men that people inevitably turn into when they are too intelligent for the relatively idle lives they lead, in which their faculties do not have full play. No doubt idleness, in these men as in others, may express itself in inertia. But in these days especially, when physical exercise is so much in favour, there exists also, even outside the actual hours of sport, an athletic form of idleness which finds expression not in inertia but in a feverish vivacity that hopes to leave boredom neither time nor space to develop in.

Becoming—at any rate during this tiresome phase—much harder in his manner, towards his friends, towards for example myself, he now exhibited scarcely any trace of sensibility. Towards Gilberte on the other hand he behaved with an affectation of sentiment carried to the point of theatricality, which was most disagreeable. Not that he was in fact indifferent to her. No, he loved her. But he lied to her all the time and his untruthfulness, if not the actual purpose of his lies, was invariably detected; and then he thought that the only way to extricate himself was to exaggerate to a ridiculous degree the genuine distress which he felt at having hurt her. He would arrive at Tansonville, obliged, he said, to leave again the next morning because of some business with a certain neighbouring landowner who was supposed to be waiting for him in Paris; but the neighbour, when they happened to meet him near Combray the same evening, would unintentionally expose the lie, of which Robert had neglected to inform him, by saying that he had come to the country for a month's rest and would not be going back to Paris during his stay. Robert would blush, would observe Gilberte's melancholy and knowing smile, get rid of the blundering friend with a few sharp words, go home before his wife, send her a desperate note saying that he had told this lie in order not to hurt her, so that she should not think, when she saw him go off for a reason which he could not avow to her, that he did not love her (and all this, though Robert thought that he was lying when he wrote it, was in substance true), and then would ask permission to come to her room and there—part genuine distress, part the nervous strain of the life he led, part a pretence which became every day more brazen—would sob, plunge his head into cold water, talk about his imminent death, sometimes throw himself on the floor as though he had been taken ill. Gilberte did not know how far she should believe him, supposed that in each particular case he was lying but that in a general way he loved her, and was worried by this presentiment of an imminent death, thinking that he perhaps had some illness she did not know of, so that for that reason she did not dare to thwart him or ask him to give up his travels. All this, however, did not help me to understand why Robert insisted on Morel's being accepted as the son of the house—as much a part of it as Bergotte,[3] wherever the Saint-Loups were, in Paris or at Tansonville. Morel imitated Bergotte marvellously. It was even unnecessary, after a while, to ask him for an impersonation. Like those hysterics whom one doesn't have to hypnotise to make them become such or such a person, he entered spontaneously and immediately into the character.

Françoise, who had seen all that M. de Charlus had done for Jupien and saw now all that Robert de Saint-Loup was doing for Morel, did not conclude that this was a characteristic which reappeared from generation to generation in the Guermantes family. She, who was so moral and so full of prejudices, had come rather to believe—as Legrandin too was so kind to Théodore—that this was a custom rendered respectable by its universality. She would say of a young man, whether Morel or Théodore: "He has found a gentleman who takes an interest in him and has done a great deal to help him." And as in such cases it is the protectors who love and suffer and forgive, Françoise, faced with a choice between the "gentlemen" and the youths whom they seduced, did not hesitate to award her sympathy to the seducers, to decide that it was they who "really had hearts." She blamed Théodore for all the tricks he played on Legrandin—and yet it seemed scarcely possible that she could have any doubt about the nature of their relations, for she would add: "Then the boy realised that it was his turn to make a move and said: 'Take me with you, I will love you, I will do my best to please you,' and upon my word the gentleman has such a heart that I'm sure Théodore is sure to do well with him. Perhaps much better than he deserves, for he's a proper madcap, but the gentleman is so good that I've often said to Jeannette (Théodore's fiancée): 'My girl, if ever you're in trouble, go to the gentleman. He'd give you his bed rather than let you sleep on the floor. He's been too fond of that lad (Théodore) to turn him out. You can be sure he'll never desert him.'" Out of politeness I inquired what was the surname of Théodore, who was now living somewhere in the south of France, and she told me that it was Sanilon. "Then that's who it was," I exclaimed, "who wrote to me about my article in *Le Figaro*."

In the same way Françoise had a higher esteem for Saint-Loup than for Morel and gave it as her opinion that, in spite of all the tricks the lad (Morel) had played, the Marquis would always come to his rescue if he were in trouble, for he was a man with a real heart—or if he didn't, it would only be because he himself had suffered some great disaster.

Saint-Loup insisted that I should stay on at Tansonville and once, although he never now visibly sought to give me pleasure, let slip the remark that my coming had been so great a joy to his wife that it had caused her, as she had told him, a transport of happiness which lasted a whole evening, an evening when she had been feeling so miserable that my unexpected arrival had miraculously saved her from despair, "Perhaps from something worse," he added. He asked me to try to persuade her that he loved her and told me that, though he loved another woman, he loved her less than his wife and would soon break with her. "And yet," he continued, with such self-satisfaction and such an evident need to confide that there were moments when I thought the name of Charlie would, for all Robert's efforts, "come up" like a number in a lottery, "I had something to be proud of. This woman who has given me so many proofs of her affection and whom I am about to sacrifice to Gilberte, had never looked at a man before, she even thought herself incapable of falling in love. I am the first man in her life. I knew that she had refused offers right and left, so that when I received the marvellous letter in which she told me that there would be no happiness for her except with me, I just could not get over it. Obviously, there would be something here for me to lose my head about, were it not that the thought of seeing poor Gilberte in tears is intolerable to me. Don't you see something of Rachel in her?" he went on. And indeed I had been struck by a vague resemblance which one could, if one tried, now find between them. Perhaps it was due to a real similarity of certain features (owing possibly to the Jewish origin of both, though of this there was little evidence in Gilberte) which had caused Robert, when his family had insisted that he should marry, to feel himself more attracted to Gilberte than to any other girl who was equally rich. But it was due also to the fact that Gilberte, having come across some hidden photographs of Rachel, whose name even had been unknown to her, tried to please Robert by imitating certain habits dear to the actress, such as always wearing a red ribbon in her hair and a black velvet ribbon on her arm, and by dyeing her hair in order to look dark. Then, feeling that her unhappiness was spoiling her looks, she tried to do something about it. Sometimes she went a great deal too far. One day, when Robert was coming to Tansonville for a single night, I was astounded to see her take her place at table looking so strangely different, not merely from what she had been in the past, but from her present self of every day, that I sat dumbfounded as if I had before my eyes an actress, a sort of Empress Theodora. I felt that in spite of myself I was staring at her, so curious was I to know what it was that was changed. My curiosity was soon satisfied when she blew her nose—in spite of all the precautions with which she did this. For from the many colours which were left on her handkerchief, turning it into a sumptuous palette, I saw that she was heavily made up. This it was that gave her that blood-red mouth which she tried hard to control into laughter in the belief that it was becoming to her, while the thought that the time of her husband's train was approaching and still she did not know whether he would really come or whether he would send one of those telegrams of which M. de Guermantes had wittily fixed the formula: "Cannot come, lie follows," turned her cheeks pale beneath the violet sweat of her grease-paint and drew dark rings round her eyes.

"Ah! don't you see?" he would say to me—in an artificially affectionate manner which contrasted painfully with his spontaneous affection of the old days, with the voice of an alcoholic and an actor's intonations—"Gilberte happy, there is nothing I would not give to see that. She has done so much for me. You can't possibly know." And the most disagreeable part of all this was once again his vanity, for he was flattered at being loved by Gilberte and, without daring to say that it was Charlie whom he loved, gave, nevertheless, of the love which the violinist was supposed to feel for him, details which he, the Saint-Loup from whom Charlie every day demanded more and more money, knew to be wildly exaggerated if not invented from start to finish. And so, entrusting Gilberte to my care, he would go off to Paris again. In Paris (to anticipate a little, for I am still at Tansonville) I once had an opportunity of observing him at a party and from a distance and on this occasion, though the way in which he spoke was still alive and charming and enabled me to rediscover the past, I was struck by the great changes taking place in him. More and more he resembled his mother: the haughtily elegant manner which he had inherited from her and which she, by means of the most elaborate training, had perfected in him was now freezing into exaggeration; the penetrating glance proper to him as a Guermantes gave him the air of inspecting every place in which he happened to be, but of doing this in an almost unconscious fashion, as though from habit, in obedience to a sort of animal characteristic. Even when he was at rest, the colouring which he possessed in a greater degree than any other Guermantes—that air of being merely the solidified sunniness of a golden day—gave him as it seemed a plumage so strange, made of him a species so rare and so precious, that one would have liked to acquire him for an ornithological collection; but when, in addition, this ray of light, metamorphosed into a bird, set itself in motion, when for instance I saw Robert de Saint-Loup enter this evening party at which I was present, the way in which he tossed back his head, so silkily and proudly crested with the golden tuft of his slightly moulting hair, and moved his neck from side to side, was so much more supple, so much more aloof and yet more delicate than anything to be expected of a human being that, fired by the sight with curiosity and wonder, half social and half zoological, one asked oneself whether one was really in the Faubourg Saint-Germain and not rather in the Zoological Gardens, whether one was watching the passage of a great nobleman through a drawing-room or a bird pacing its cage. And if one was prepared to exercise a little imagination, the twittering lent itself just as well to this second interpretation as the plumage. For he was beginning to use phrases which he thought redolent of the age of Louis XIV, and though in this he was simply imitating the manners of the Guermantes, in him some indefinable nuance was turning them into the manners of M. de Charlus. "I must leave you for a moment," he said to me for instance, at this party, at which Mme de Marsantes was standing a little way away from us. "I have to pay my respects to my mother."

To return to this "love," of which he could not stop talking to me, it was not only love for Charlie, although this was the only one that counted for him. Whatever the nature of a man's loves, one always makes mistakes as to the number of people with whom he has affairs, partly from wrongly interpreting friendships as love affairs, an error which exaggerates the total, but also through believing that one proved love affair excludes another, which is an error of a contrary kind. Two people may say: "X's mistress, yes, I know her," they may pronounce two different names and neither of them may be mistaken. A woman whom we love seldom satisfies all our needs and we deceive her with a woman whom we do not love. As to the species of loves that Saint-Loup had inherited from M. de Charlus, a husband who is that way inclined usually makes his wife happy. This is a general rule to which the Guermantes contrived to be an exception, because those of them who had this taste wanted it to be believed that on the contrary they were fond of women. So they made themselves conspicuous with one woman or another and drove their own wives to despair. The Courvoisiers were more sensible. The young Vicomte de Courvoisier thought he was the only man alive, perhaps the only man since the beginning of the world, to be tempted by someone of his own sex. Supposing this inclination to come to him from the devil, he struggled against it, married an extremely pretty wife and had children by her. Then one of his cousins taught him that the tendency is fairly widespread and was even so kind as to take him to places where he could indulge it. M. de Courvoisier became fonder than ever of his wife and redoubled his philoprogenitive zeal, and he and she were quoted as the happiest couple in Paris. That could not possibly be said of the Saint-Loups, because Robert, instead of being content with inversion, made his wife ill with jealousy by keeping mistresses without pleasure to himself.

It is possible that Morel, being excessively dark, was necessary to Saint-Loup in the way that shadow is necessary to the sunbeam. Can one not imagine some golden-haired aristocrat sprung from an ancient family such as his, intelligent and endowed with every kind of prestige, concealing within him, unbeknown to all his friends, a secret taste for negroes?

Robert never allowed the conversation to touch upon his own species of loves. If I said a word about it, "Oh! I don't know," he would reply, with a detachment so profound that it caused him to drop his monocle, "I am utterly ignorant about those things. If you want information about them, my dear boy, I advise you to go elsewhere. I am a soldier, that's all I can say for myself. The things you speak of leave me cold. What I *am* interested in, passionately, is the course of the Balkan war. That sort of thing interested you too once, the 'etymology' of battles. I told you in those days that we should see again, even in greatly changed circumstances, battles conforming to certain types, for example the great exercise in lateral envelopment, the battle of Ulm. Well! However special these Balkan wars may be, Lüleburgaz is Ulm all over again: lateral envelopment. These are the subjects you can talk to me about. As for the sort of thing you allude to, it means about as much to me as Sanskrit."

While Robert thus expressed his disdain for the subject, Gilberte on the contrary, after he had left, was very willing to raise it in the conversation which I had with her. Not with reference to her husband certainly, for she knew, or pretended to know, nothing. But she liked to discuss it at length in so far as other men were concerned, whether because she saw in this a sort of indirect excuse for Robert or because he, divided like his uncle between an austere silence with regard to the subject and a need to let himself go and talk slander, had opened her eyes in many directions. M. de Charlus was one of those who were not spared, doubtless because Robert, without mentioning Charlie to Gilberte, could not help, when he was with her, repeating in one form or another what the violinist had told him; and the latter pursued his former benefactor with unrelenting hate. These conversations, and Gilberte's evident liking for them, gave me a chance to ask her whether, in a parallel category, Albertine, whose name I had first heard from Gilberte herself when they were attending the same classes, had comparable tastes. Gilberte could not give me any information on this point. And in any case it had long ceased to be of interest to me. But I continued to make inquiries mechanically, as an old man with a failing memory from time to time asks for news of the son he has lost.

What is odd, though I cannot here enlarge upon the topic, is the degree to which, at that time, all the people whom Albertine loved, all those who might have been able to persuade her to do what they wanted, asked, entreated, I will even say begged to be allowed to have, if not my friendship, at least some sort of acquaintance with me. No longer should I have had to offer money to Mme Bontemps as an inducement to send Albertine back to me. But this turn of fortune's wheel, taking place when it was no longer of the slightest use, merely saddened me profoundly, not because of Albertine, whom I would have received without pleasure had she been brought back not from Touraine but from the other world, but because of a young woman with whom I was in love and whom I could not contrive to meet. I told myself that, if she died, or if I no longer loved her, all those who might have brought us together would suddenly be at my feet. Meanwhile, I tried in vain to work upon them, not having been cured by experience, which ought to have taught me—if ever it taught anybody anything—that loving is like an evil spell in a fairy-story against which one is powerless until the enchantment has passed.

"As a matter of fact the book I'm reading at the moment talks about that sort of thing," Gilberte said to me. "It is an old Balzac which I am swotting up so as to be as well-informed as my uncles, *La Fille aux Yeux d'Or*. But it is absurd, improbable, nightmarish. For one thing, I suppose a woman might be kept under surveillance in that way by another woman, but surely not by a man." "You are wrong, I once knew a woman who was loved by a man who in the end literally imprisoned her; she was never allowed to see anybody, she could only go out with trusted servants." "Well, you who are so kind must be horrified at the idea. By the way, we were saying, Robert and I, that you ought to get married. Your wife would improve your health and you would make her happy." "No, I have too bad a character." "How absurd!" "I mean it. Besides, I was engaged once. But I couldn't quite make up my mind to marry the girl—and anyhow she thought better of it herself, because of my undecided and cantankerous character." This was, in fact, the excessively simple light in which I regarded my adventure with Albertine, now that I saw it only from outside.

Back in my bedroom again, I thought sadly that I had

not once been back to revisit Combray church, which seemed to be waiting for me amidst green foliage in a violet-tinted window. "Never mind," I said to myself, "that can wait for another year, if I don't die in the meanwhile," seeing no other possible obstacle but my own death and not envisaging that of the church which must, as I supposed, endure for centuries after my death as it had for centuries before my birth.

One day I spoke to Gilberte about Albertine, and asked her whether Albertine loved women. "Not in the least!" "But you used to say that you didn't approve of her." "I said that? No, I'm sure you're mistaken. In any case, if I said it—but you're wrong about that—what I was referring to was flirtations with young men. And anyhow, at her age, it probably didn't go very far." Did Gilberte say this in order to conceal from me that she herself—or so Albertine had told me—loved women and had made advances to Albertine? Or did she (for other people are often better informed about our life than we think) know that I had loved and been jealous of Albertine, and did she (since, though others may know more of the truth about us than we think, they may also stretch it too far and fall into the error of supposing too much, whereas we had hoped that they made the mistake of supposing nothing at all) imagine that this was still the case, was she, out of kindness, placing over my eyes that bandage with which we are always ready to blindfold the jealous? In any case, Gilberte's remarks, from the "disapproval" of the old days to the present certificate of respectability, were pursuing an opposite course to the statements of Albertine, who in the end had almost admitted some sort of relations with Gilbert. In this Albertine had astonished me, just as I had been astonished by what Andrée had told me, for with all the girls in the little band, if I had at first believed, before knowing them, in their perversity, I had come round to the view that my suspicions were false, as must often happen when one finds a virtuous girl, almost ignorant of the facts of love, in surroundings which one had wrongly supposed to be extremely depraved. Then later I had travelled the same road in the opposite direction, back to a belief in the truth of my original suspicions. But perhaps Albertine had told me this because she wanted to appear more experienced than she was and to dazzle me in Paris with the prestige of her depravity, as on the earlier occasion at Balbec with that of her virtue; or quite simply, when I had talked about women who loved women, had not wanted to appear not to know what I meant, just as, if Fourier or Tobolsk is mentioned in a conversation, one tries to look as if one understood even if one has no idea what they are. She had perhaps lived, though in proximity to Mlle Vinteuil's friend and to Andrée, yet separated from them by a watertight partition, so that they thought that she was "not one," and had perhaps only got to know about the subject later—in the spirit of a woman who marries a man of letters and tries to improve her mind—in order to please me by making herself capable of answering my questions, until the day when she realised that the questions were inspired by jealousy, when she had hastily gone into reverse. Unless it was Gilberte who was lying to me. It even occurred to me that it was because he had learnt from Gilberte, while flirting with her with an eye all the while on his real interests, that she did not altogether dislike women, that Robert had married her, hoping for pleasures which, since he now went elsewhere for them, he must have failed to obtain from her. None of these hypotheses was absurd, for with women like Odette's daughter or the girls of the little band there is such a diversity, such an accumulation of alternating if not actually simultaneous tastes, that they pass easily from an affair with a woman to a great love for a man, so that to define the real and dominating taste must always be difficult.

I did not want to borrow Gilberte's copy of *La Fille aux Yeux d'Or* as she was reading it herself. But she lent me to read in bed, on that last evening of my stay with her, a book which produced on me a strong but mixed impression, which did not, however, prove to be lasting. It was a newly published volume of the Journal of the Goncourts. And when, before putting out my candle, I read the passage which I am about to transcribe, my lack of talent for literature, of which I had had a presentiment long ago on the Guermantes way and which had been confirmed during the stay of which this was the last evening—one of those evenings before a departure when we emerge from the torpor of habits about to be broken and attempt to judge ourselves—struck me as something less to be regretted, since literature, if I was to trust the evidence of this book, had no very profound truths to reveal: and at the same time it seemed to me sad that literature was not what I had thought it to be. At the same time, the state of ill-health which was soon to shut me up in a sanatorium seemed to me also less to be regretted, if the beautiful things of which books speak were not more beautiful than what I had seen myself. And yet, by an odd contradiction, now that they were being spoken of in this book I had a desire to see them. Here are the pages that I read before fatigue closed my eyes . . .

"The day before yesterday Verdurin drops in here to carry me off to dine with him—Verdurin, former critic of the *Revue*, author of that book on Whistler in which the workmanship, the painterly colouration, of the American eccentric is interpreted sometimes with great delicacy by the lover of all the refinements, all the *prettinesses* of the painted canvas, that Verdurin is. And while I am getting dressed to accompany him, he treats me to a long narrative, almost at moments a timidly stammered confession, about his renunciation of writing immediately after his marriage to Fromentin's 'Madeleine,' a renunciation brought about, he says, by his addiction to morphine and which had the result, according to Verdurin, that most of the frequenters of his wife's drawing-room did not even know that her husband had ever been a writer and spoke to him of Charles Blanc, of Saint-Victor, of Sainte-Beuve, of Burty, as individuals to whom they considered him, Verdurin, altogether inferior. 'Now, you Goncourts, you know—and Gautier knew too—that my *Salons* were on a different plane from those pitiful *Maîtres d'Autrefois* which are deemed a masterpiece in my wife's family.' Then, through a dusk in which, as we pass the towers of the Trocadéro, the last glimmer of a gleam of daylight makes them positively resemble those towers of red-currant jelly that pastry-cooks used to make, the conversation continues in the carriage on its way to the Quai Conti, where their mansion is, which its owner claims was once the mansion of the Venetian ambassadors and in which there is a room used as a smoking-room which Verdurin tells me was transported lock, stock and barrel, as in a tale of the *Arabian Nights*, from a celebrated *palazzo* whose name I forget, a *palazzo* boasting a well-head decorated with a Coronation of the Virgin which Verdurin maintains is positively one of Sansovino's finest things and which now, he says, their guests find useful as a receptacle for cigar-ash. And upon my word, when we arrive, in the watery shimmer of a moonlight really just like that in which the paintings of the great age enwraps Venice, against which the silhouetted dome of the Institute makes one think of the Salute in Guardi's pictures, I have almost the illusion of looking out over the Grand Canal. And the illusion is preserved by the way in which the house is built so that from the first floor one cannot see the quay, and by the evocative remark of its owner, who affirms that the name of the Rue du Bac—the devil if ever I'd thought of it—comes from the ferry which once upon a time used to take an order of nuns, the Miramiones, across to attend services in Notre-Dame. A whole quarter which my childhood used idly to explore when my aunt de Courmont lived there, and which I am inspired to *re-love* by rediscovering, almost next door to the Verdurin mansion, the sign of 'Little Dunkirk,' one of the rare shops surviving elsewhere than in the crayon and wash vignettes of Gabriel de Saint-Aubin, to which the eighteenth-century connoisseur would come to pass a few leisure moments in cheapening trinkets French and foreign and 'all the newest products of the arts,' as an invoice of this Little Dunkirk puts it, an invoice of which we two, Verdurin and myself, are, I believe, alone in possessing copies, one of those flimsy masterpieces of engraved paper upon which the

reign of Louis XV made out its accounts, with a head-
piece representing a billowy sea laden with vessels, a sea
of billows which might be an illustration, in the Fermiers
Généraux La Fontaine, to 'The Oyster and the Litigants.'
The mistress of the house, who has placed me next to her
at dinner, graciously tells me before we go in that she has
decked out her table with nothing but Japanese chrysanthemums—but chrysanthemums displayed in vases which
are the rarest masterpieces, one in particular of bronze on
which petals of red-gold copper seem to have been shed
by the living flower. Cottard, the doctor, is there, his
wife, the Polish sculptor Viradobetski, Swann the collector, and an aristocratic Russian lady, a princess with a
name ending in -off which I fail to catch (Cottard whis-
pers in my ear that she is the woman who is supposed to
have fired point-blank at the Archduke Rudolf), according
to whom in Galicia and the whole of the north of Poland
my reputation stands extraordinarily high, no young girl
ever giving her consent to an offer of marriage without
first ascertaining whether her fiancé is an admirer of *La
Faustin*. 'You cannot understand that, you western Euro-
peans'—this is thrown in as a sort of coda by the
Princess, who, upon my word, strikes me as a person of a
really superior intelligence—'that penetration by a writer
of a woman's most intimate feelings.' A man with a close-
shaven chin and lip and the side-whiskers of a butler,
rolling out in a condescending tone the witticisms of a
fifth-form schoolmaster unbending among his prize pupils
on the feast of St Charlemagne—this is Brichot, of the
university. I am introduced to him by Verdurin but he
utters not a word of reference to our books, and I am
filled with a mixture of discouragement and anger at this

conspiracy organised against us by the Sorbonne, which
brings even into this pleasant dwelling where I am received as an honoured guest the contradiction, the hostility, of deliberate silence. We go in to dinner, and there
follows an extraordinary cavalcade of plates which are
nothing less than masterpieces of the porcelainist's art,
that artist whose chatter, during an exquisite meal, is
heard with more pleasure than any fellow-guest's by the
titillated attention of the connoisseur—Yung-cheng plates
with nasturtium-coloured borders and purple-blue irises,
leafless and tumid, and those supremely decorative flights
of kingfishers and cranes trailing across a dawn sky, a
dawn that has just the early-morning tones glimpsed daily
from Boulevard Montmorency by my awakening eyes—
Dresden plates daintier and of more graceful workmanship, with drowsy, bloodless roses fading into violet, with
ragged-edged tulips the colour of wine-lees, with the ro-
coco elegance of a pink or a forget-me-not—Sèvres plates
meshed with the close guilloche of their white fluting,
whorled in gold, or knotted with a golden ribbon that
stands in gallant relief upon the creamy smoothness of the
paste—finally a whole service of silver plate arabesqued
with those myrtles of Luciennes that were not unknown
to the du Barry. And what is perhaps equally rare is the
truly quite remarkable quality of the things served upon
these plates, a meal most subtly concocted, a real spread
such as Parisians, one cannot say it too emphatically,
never have at their really grand dinner-parties and which
reminds me of certain prize dishes of Jean d'Heurs. Even
the foie gras bears no resemblance to the insipid mousse
customarily served under that name; and I do not know
many places in which a simple potato salad is made as it

is here with potatoes firm as Japanese ivory buttons and patina'd like those little ivory spoons with which Chinese women sprinkle water over their new-caught fish. Into the Venetian glass which I have before me is poured, like a rich cascade of red jewels, an extraordinary Léoville bought at M. Montalivet's sale, and it is a delight to the imagination of the eye and also, I am not afraid to say it, of what used to be called the gullet, to see a brill placed before us which has nothing in common with those anything but fresh brills that are served at the most luxurious tables, which in the slow course of their journey from the sea have had the pattern of their bones imprinted upon their backs; a brill that is served not with the sticky paste prepared under the name of white sauce by so many chefs in great houses, but with a genuine white sauce, made with butter that costs five francs a pound; to see this brill brought in on a wonderful Chinese dish streaked with the purple rays of a sun setting above a sea upon which ludicrously sails a flotilla of large lobsters, their spiky stippling rendered with such extraordinary skill that they seem to have been moulded from living shells, with a border too depicting a little Chinese who plays with rod and line a fish whose silver and azure belly makes it a marvel of iridescent colour. When I remark to Verdurin what an exquisite pleasure it must be for him to eat this choice grub off a collection such as no prince today possesses in his show cases: 'It is easy to see that you don't know him,' gloomily interjects the mistress of the house. And she speaks to me of her husband as of an original and a crank, indifferent to all these dainties, 'a crank,' she repeats, 'yes, that is the only word for it,' a crank who would get more enjoyment from a bottle of cider drunk in

the somewhat plebeian coolness of a Normandy farm.
And this charming woman, whose speech betrays her positive adoration of local colouring, talks with overflowing
enthusiasm of the Normandy in which they once lived, a
Normandy, so she says, like an immense English park,
with the fragrance of tall woodlands that Lawrence might
have painted, with the cryptomeria-coloured velvet of natural lawns bordered with the porcelain of pink hy-
drangeas, with crumpled sulphur-roses which, as they
cascade over a cottage-door, above which the incrustation
of two entwined pear-trees has the effect of a purely decorative sign over a shop, make one think of the free
arabesque of a flowery branch of bronze in a candle-
bracket by Gouthière, a Normandy absolutely unsuspected by the Parisian holiday-makers, protected by the
iron gates of each of its little properties, gates which the
Verdurins confessed to me that they did not scruple to
open one and all. At the end of the day, in the drowsy ex-
tinguishment of all colours, when the only light was from
an almost curdled sea, blue-white like whey ('No, not in
the least like the sea you know,' frantically protests my
neighbour, when I start to tell her that Flaubert once took
us, my brother and me, to Trouville, 'not the slightest bit,
you must come with me, otherwise you will never find
out'), they would go home, through the forests—absolute
forests abloom with pink tulle—of the great rhododen-
drons, quite drunk with the smell of the sardine fisheries
which gave her husband terrible attacks of asthma—'Yes,'
she insists, 'I mean it, real attacks of asthma.' Thereupon,
the following summer, they returned, lodging a whole
colony of artists in an old cloister which they rented for
next to nothing, and which made an admirable mediaeval

abode. And upon my word, as I listen to this woman who, in passing through so many social circles of real distinction, has nevertheless preserved in her speech a little of the freshness and freedom of language of a woman of the people, a language which shows you things with the colour which your imagination sees in them, my mouth waters at the life which she avows to me they lived down there, each one working in his cell and the whole party assembling before luncheon, in a drawing-room so vast that it had two fireplaces, for really intelligent conversation interspersed with parlour games, a life which makes me think of the one we read of in that masterpiece of Diderot, the *Lettres à Mademoiselle Volland*. Then, after luncheon, they would all go out, even on the days when the weather was unsettled, in a brief burst of sunshine or the diffused radiance of a shower, a shower whose filtered light sharpened the knotted outlines of a magnificent avenue of century-old beeches which began just behind the house and brought almost up to the iron grill that vegetable embodiment of "the beautiful" so dear to eighteenth-century taste, and of the ornamental trees which held suspended in their branches not buds about to flower but drops of rain. They would stop to listen to the delicate splish-splash of a bullfinch, enamoured of coolness, bathing itself in the tiny dainty Nymphenburg bath made for it by the corolla of a white rose. And when I mention to Mme Verdurin Elstir's delicate pastel sketches of the landscapes and the flowers of that coast: 'But it is through me that he discovered all those things,' she bursts out, with an angry toss of the head, 'all of them, yes, all, make no mistake about it, the interesting spots, every one of his subjects—I threw it in his teeth when he left us, didn't I,

Gustave?—every one of the subjects he has painted. *Things* he has always known about, there one must be fair, one must admit that. But as for flowers, he had never seen any, he couldn't tell a mallow from a hollyhock. It was I who taught him—you won't believe this—to recognise jasmine.' And one must admit that it is a curious thought that the artist who is cited by connoisseurs today as our leading flower-painter, superior even to Fantin-Latour, would perhaps never, without the help of the woman sitting beside me, have known how to paint jasmine. 'Yes, honestly, jasmine. And all the roses he has done have been painted in my house, or else it was I who took them to him. Among us he was always known simply as Monsieur Tiche; ask Cottard, ask Brichot, ask anybody here, whether we treated him as a great man. He would have laughed at the idea himself. I taught him to arrange his flowers; at first he couldn't manage it at all. He never learnt how to make a bouquet. He had no natural taste in selecting, I had to say to him: "No, don't paint that, that's no good, paint this." Ah! if he had listened to us about the arrangement of his life as he did about the arrangement of his flowers, and hadn't made that vile marriage!' And of a sudden, her eyes feverish from her absorption in thoughts of the past, plucking nervously at the silk sleeves of her bodice as she frenziedly tenses her fingers, she presents, in the distortion of her grief-stricken pose, an admirable picture which has, I think, never been painted, a picture in which one would see portrayed all the restrained revolt, all the passionate susceptibilities of a female friend outraged in the delicate feelings, the modesty of a woman. Thereupon she talks about the admirable portrait which Elstir did for her, the portrait of the Cottard family, which she gave to the Luxembourg at the time of her quarrel with the painter, confessing that it was she who gave him the idea of painting the man in dress clothes in order to get all that splendid ebullition of fine linen, and she who chose the woman's velvet gown which forms a solid mass amid all the glitter of the bright tones of the carpets, the flowers, the fruit, the little girls' muslin dresses that look like dancers' tutus. It was she too, she tells me, who gave him the idea of the woman brushing her hair, an idea for which the artist was subsequently much praised and which consisted simply in painting her not as if she were on show but surprised in the intimacy of her everyday life. ' "In a woman doing her hair," I used to say to him, "or wiping her face, or warming her feet, when she thinks she is not observed, there is a multitude of interesting movements, movements of a grace and charm that are positively Leonardesque!" ' But at a sign from Verdurin indicating that the revival of these old indignations is dangerous for the health of his wife, who is really a mass of nerves, Swann points out to me the wonderful necklace of black pearls which the mistress of the house is wearing, which she bought, as a necklace of white pearls, at the sale of a descendant of Mme de La Fayette, to whom they were given by Henrietta of England, and which became black as the result of a fire which destroyed part of a house which the Verdurins had in a street whose name I do not remember, after which fire the casket containing these pearls was found, with the pearls completely black inside it. 'And I know the portrait of these pearls, on the shoulders of Mme de La Fayette herself, yes, positively their portrait,' insists Swann, checking the exclamations of the somewhat dumbfounded guests, 'their authentic portrait, in the collection of the Duc de Guermantes.' A collection which has not its equal in the world, proclaims Swann, and which I ought to go and see, a collection inherited by the celebrated Duke, who was her favourite nephew, from his aunt Mme de Beausergent, who afterwards became Mme d'Hatzfeldt and was the sister of the Marquise de Villeparisis and of the Princess of Hanover, in whose house years ago my brother and I became so fond of him under the guise of the charming infant known as Basin, which is indeed the Duke's first name. Thereupon Doctor Cottard, with that keen intelligence which shows him to be a man of real distinction, harks back to the story of the pearls and informs us that catastrophes of this kind can produce changes in people's brains which are just like those that may be observed in inanimate matter, and, discoursing in a philosophical vein well beyond the powers of most doctors, quotes as an example Mme Verdurin's own valet, who from the terrible shock of this fire in which he very nearly lost his life became a changed man, with a handwriting so altered that when his master and mistress, then in Normandy, first received a letter from him with the news of the fire, they thought that someone was playing a practical joke upon them. And not only an altered handwriting, according to Cottard, who maintains that this man, hitherto always sober, became such an abominable sot that Mme Verdurin was obliged to get rid of him. And the Doctor's stimulating dissertation passes, upon a gracious sign from the mistress of the house, from the dining-room to the Venetian smoking-room, where he tells us that he has witnessed cases of what can only be called dual personality, citing as an instance one of his pa-

tients, whom he is so kind as to offer to bring to my
house, whose temples he only has to touch, so he says, to
awaken him to a second life, a life during which he remembers nothing of his first life and so different that,
while he behaves most respectably in the first, he has
more than once been arrested for thefts committed in the
second, in which he is nothing more nor less than an
abominable scoundrel. Whereupon Mme Verdurin acutely
observes that medical science could provide the theatre
with truer themes than those now in favour, themes in
which the comicality of the plot would be based upon
misunderstandings of a pathological kind, and this, by a
natural transition, leads Mme Cottard to say that a very
similar subject has been employed by a story-teller who is
her children's favourite at bedtime, the Scotsman Stevenson, a name which brings from Swann the peremptory
statement: 'But he is a really great writer, Stevenson, I assure you, M. de Goncourt, a very great writer, equal to
the greatest.' Next, after I have admired the ceiling of the
room where we are smoking, with its escutcheoned coffers
from the old Barberini palace, when I intimate my regret
at the progressive blackening of a certain stone basin by
the ash of our 'Havanas' and Swann remarks that similar
stains on books from the library of Napoleon which are
now, despite his anti-Bonapartist opinions, in the possession of the Duc de Guermantes, bear witness to the fact
that the Emperor chewed tobacco, Cottard, who evinces a
truly penetrating curiosity in all things, declares that the
stains do not come from that at all—'No, no, no, not at
all,' he insists with authority—but from the habit the
Emperor had of always, even on the field of battle,
clutching in his hand the liquorice tablets which he took

to relieve the pain in his liver. 'For he had a disease of the liver and that is what he died of,' concludes the Doctor."

There I stopped, for I was leaving the next morning; and besides it was the hour at which I was habitually summoned by that other master in whose service we spend, every day, a part of our time. The task which he assigns to us we accomplish with our eyes closed. Every morning he hands us back to the master who shares us with him, knowing that, unless he did so, we should be remiss in his own service. Curious, when our intelligence reopens its eyes, to know what we can have done under this master who first makes his slaves lie down and then puts them to work at full speed, the most artful among us try, the moment their task is finished, to take a covert glance. But sleep is racing against them to obliterate the traces of what they would like to see. And after all these centuries we still know very little about the matter.

I closed the Journal of the Goncourts. Prestige of literature! I wished I could have seen the Cottards again, asked them all sorts of details about Elstir, gone to look at the shop called Little Dunkirk, if it still existed, asked permission to visit the Verdurin mansion where I had once dined. But I felt vaguely depressed. Certainly, I had never concealed from myself that I knew neither how to listen nor, once I was not alone, how to look. My eyes were blind to the sort of necklace an old woman might be wearing, and the things I might be told about her pearls never entered my ears. All the same, I had known these people in daily life, I had dined with them often, they were simply the Verdurins and the Duc de Guermantes and the Cottards, and each one of them I had found just as commonplace as my grandmother had found that Basin of whom she had no suspicion that he was the darling nephew, the enchanting young hero, of Mme de Beausergent, each one of them had seemed to me insipid; I could remember the vulgarities without number of which each of them was composed . . .

And that all this should make a star in the night![4]

But provisionally I decided to ignore the objections against literature raised in my mind by the pages of Goncourt which I had read on the evening before I left Tansonville. Even without taking into account the manifest naïvety of this particular diarist, I could in any case reassure myself on various counts. First, in so far as my own character was concerned, my incapacity for looking and listening, which the passage from the Journal had so painfully illustrated to me, was nevertheless not total. There was in me a personage who knew more or less how to look, but it was an intermittent personage, coming to life only in the presence of some general essence common to a number of things, these essences being its nourishment and its joy. Then the personage looked and listened, but at a certain depth only, without my powers of superficial observation being enhanced. Just as a geometer, stripping things of their sensible qualities, sees only the linear substratum beneath them, so the stories that people told escaped me, for what interested me was not what they were trying to say but the manner in which they said it and the way in which this manner revealed their character or their foibles; or rather I was interested in what had always, because it gave me specific pleasure, been more particularly the goal of my investigations: the point that was common to one being and another. As soon as I perceived this my intelligence—until that moment slumbering, even if sometimes the apparent animation of my talk might disguise from others a profound intellectual torpor—at once set off joyously in pursuit, but its quarry then, for instance the identity of the Verdurin drawing-room in various places and at various times, was situated in the middle distance, behind actual appearances, in a zone that was rather more withdrawn. So the apparent, copiable charm of things and people escaped me, because I had not the ability to stop short there—I was like a surgeon who beneath the smooth surface of a woman's belly sees the internal disease which is devouring it. If I went to a dinner-party I did not see the guests: when I thought I was looking at them, I was in fact examining them with X-rays.

The result was that, when all the observations I had succeeded in making about the guests during the party were linked together, the pattern of the lines I had traced took the form of a collection of psychological laws in which the actual purport of the remarks of each guest occupied but a very small space. But did this take away all merit from my portraits, which in fact I did not intend as such? If, in the realm of painting, one portrait makes manifest certain truths concerning volume, light, movement, does that mean that it is necessarily inferior to another completely different portrait of the same person, in which a thousand details omitted in the first are minutely transcribed, from which second portrait one would conclude that the model was ravishingly beautiful while from the first one would have thought him or her ugly, a fact which may be of documentary, even of historical importance, but is not necessarily an artistic truth?

Furthermore my frivolity, the moment I was not alone, made me eager to please, more eager to amuse by chattering than to acquire knowledge by listening, unless it happened that I had gone out into society in search of information about some particular artistic question or some jealous suspicion which my mind had previously been revolving. Always I was incapable of seeing anything for which a desire had not already been roused in me by something I had read, anything of which I had not myself traced in advance a sketch which I wanted now to confront with reality. How often—and I was well aware of this even without being apprised of it by these pages of Goncourt—have I remained incapable of bestowing my attention upon things or people that later, once their image has been presented to me in solitude by an artist, I would have travelled many miles, risked death to find again! Then and then only has my imagination been set in motion, has it begun to paint. And of something which a year before had made me yawn I have said to myself with anguish, longingly contemplating it in advance: "Shall I really be unable to see this thing? I would give anything for a sight of it!"

When one reads articles about people, perhaps mere fashionable people, who are described as "the last representatives of a society of which no eye-witness now exists," one may of course exclaim: "Fancy using such extravagant language about so insignificant a creature! This is what I should have lamented never having known if I had only read the newspapers and the monthly reviews and had not met the man!" But I was tempted rather, when I read such pages in the newspapers, to think: "How unfortunate that in those days when I was solely preoccupied with meeting Gilberte or Albertine again I did not pay more attention to this gentleman! I took him for a society bore, a mere dummy. On the contrary he was a Distinguished Figure!" The pages of Goncourt which I had read made me regret this tendency of mine. For though I might have inferred from them that life teaches us to cheapen the value of a book, and shows us that what a writer extols was in fact worth very little, it was equally possible for me to come to the contrary conclusion, that reading teaches us to take a more exalted view of the value of life, a value at the time we did not know how to appreciate and of whose magnitude we have only become aware through the book. We may, without too much difficulty, console ourselves for having taken little pleasure in the society of a Vinteuil, a Bergotte. But the prudish respectability of the one, the intolerable defects of the other, even the pretentious vulgarity of an Elstir in his early days—for I had discovered from the Goncourt Journal that he was none other than the "Monsieur Tiche" whose twaddle had once exasperated Swann in the Verdurins' drawing-room—prove nothing against them: their genius is manifested in their works. What man of genius has not in his conversation adopted the irritating mannerisms of the artists of his set, before attaining (as Elstir had eventually done, though this does not always happen) to a good taste that rises above them? Are not Balzac's letters, for instance, strewn with vulgar expressions which Swann would have suffered a thousand deaths rather than employ? Yet can one doubt that Swann, finely intelligent as he was, purged of all odious absurdities, would have been incapable of writing *La Cousine Bette* or *Le Curé de Tours*? As for the Vinteuils, the Bergottes, the Elstirs, the question whether it is we or the writers of memoirs who are at fault when they represent the society of these men as charming whereas we found it disagreeable, it is a question of slight importance, since even if our estimate were the correct one, this would be no argument against the value of a life that can produce such geniuses.

Right at the other pole of experience, when I saw that the most piquant anecdotes, which form the inexhaustible material of the Goncourt Journal and provide the reader with entertainment for many solitary evenings, had been related to the writer by these people whom he had met at dinner and who, though on the evidence of his pages we should certainly have wanted to meet them, had in my mind left no trace of any interesting recollection, that too was not altogether difficult to explain. In spite of the naïvety of Goncourt, who inferred from the interest of these anecdotes the probable distinction of the man who related them, it might well be that commonplace men had seen during their lives, or heard related, remarkable things which they in their turn had described. Goncourt knew how to listen, just as he knew how to see; I did not. Besides, all these facts needed to be considered and judged separately. Certainly M. de Guermantes had not given me the impression of that adorable model of the youthful graces which my grandmother so wished she had known and which she set before me, in the Memoirs of Mme de Beausergent, as an inimitable example. But one must remember that Basin was then seven years old, that the writer was his aunt, and that even a husband who within a few months will be suing for divorce will praise his wife to the skies. In one of his most delightful poems Sainte-Beuve describes an apparition beside a fountain—a little girl crowned with every gift and every grace, young Mlle de Champlâtreux, whose age at the time cannot have been ten. And in spite of all the affectionate respect which the poet of genius who is the Comtesse de Noailles bore for her husband's mother, the Duchesse de Noailles *née* Champlâtreux, one wonders whether, had she had occasion to portray her, the result might not have contrasted rather sharply with the portrait drawn by Sainte-Beuve fifty years earlier.

More puzzling perhaps were the people in between the two extremes, those in whom what the writer says of them implies more than a memory which has succeeded in retaining a piquant anecdote, with whom, nevertheless, one has not, as with the Vinteuils, the Bergottes, the resource of judging them on their work, for they have created none: they have only—to the great astonishment of us who found them so commonplace—inspired the work of others. I could, it is true, understand how the drawing-room which, seen on the walls of a museum, will give a greater impression of elegance than anything since the great paintings of the Renaissance, might be that of the ridiculous middle-class woman whom, had I not known her, I would have longed, as I stood before the picture, to be able to approach in reality, hoping to learn from her the most precious secrets of the painter's art which his canvas did not reveal to me, and how her lace and her stately train of velvet might have become a piece of painting as lovely as anything in Titian. For I had already realised long ago that it is not the man with the liveliest

mind, the most well-informed, the best supplied with
friends and acquaintances, but the one who knows how to
become a mirror and in this way can reflect his life, commonplace though it may be, who becomes a Bergotte
(even if his contemporaries once thought him less witty
than Swann, less erudite than Bréauté), and could one not
say as much, and with better reason, of a painter's models? The artist may paint anything in the world that he
chooses, but when beauty is awakened within him, the
model for that elegance in which he will find themes of
beauty will be provided for him by people a little richer
than he is himself, in whose house he will find what is
not normally to be seen in the studio of an unrecognised
man of genius selling his canvases for fifty francs: a drawing-room with chairs and sofas covered in old brocades,
an abundance of lamps, beautiful flowers, beautiful fruit,
beautiful dresses—people in a relatively modest position,
or who would seem to be so to people of real social brilliance (who are not even aware of their existence), but
who, for that reason, are more within reach of the obscure
artist's acquaintance, more likely to appreciate him, to invite him, to buy his pictures, than men and women of the
aristocracy who, like the Pope and Heads of State, get
themselves painted by academicians. Will not posterity,
when it looks at our time, find the poetry of an elegant
home and beautifully dressed women in the drawing-room
of the publisher Charpentier as painted by Renoir, rather
than in the portraits of the Princesse de Sagan or the
Comtesse de La Rochefoucauld by Cot or Chaplin? The
artists who have given us the most splendid visions of elegance have gathered the materials for them from among
people who were rarely the leaders of fashion in their age,

for the leaders of fashion rarely commission pictures from
the unknown bearer of a new type of beauty which they
are unable to distinguish in his canvases, concealed as it is
by the interposition of that formula of hackneyed charm
which floats in the eye of the public like the subjective visions which a sick man supposes really to exist before his
eyes. This, I say, I could understand; but that these commonplace models whom I had known should in addition
have inspired and advised certain arrangements which had
enchanted me, that the presence of one or another of them
in a painting should be not merely that of a model but of
a friend whom an artist wants to put into his pictures,
this made me ask myself whether all the people whom we
regret not having known because Balzac depicted them in
his novels or dedicated books to them in homage and admiration, the people about whom Sainte-Beuve or Baudelaire wrote their loveliest poems, still more whether all the
Récamiers, all the Pompadours, would not have seemed to
me insignificant creatures, either owing to an infirmity of
my nature, which, if it were so, made me furious at being
ill and therefore unable to go back and see again all the
people whom I had misjudged, or because they owed their
prestige only to an illusory magic of literature, in which
case I had been barking up the wrong tree and need not
repine at being obliged almost any day now by the steady
deterioration of my health to break with society, renounce
travel and museums, and go to a sanatorium for treatment.

These ideas, tending on the one hand to diminish,
and on the other to increase, my regret that I had no gift
for literature, were entirely absent from my mind during

the long years—in which I had in any case completely renounced the project of writing—which I spent far from
Paris receiving treatment in a sanatorium, until there
came a time, at the beginning of 1916, when it could no
longer get medical staff. I then returned to a Paris very
different from the city to which, as we shall see presently,
I had come back once before in August 1914 for a medical consultation, after which I had withdrawn again to my
sanatorium.

On one of the first evenings of my second return, in
1916, wanting to hear people talk about the only thing
that interested me at the time, the war, I went out after
dinner to call on Mme Verdurin, who was, with Mme
Bontemps, one of the queens of this wartime Paris which
made one think of the Directory. As if by the germination
of a tiny quantity of yeast, apparently of spontaneous generation, young women now went about all day with tall
cylindrical turbans on their heads, as a contemporary of
Mme Tallien's might have done, and from a sense of patriotic duty wore Egyptian tunics, straight and dark and
very "war," over very short skirts; they wore thonged
footwear recalling the buskin as worn by Talma, or else
long gaiters recalling those of our dear boys at the front; it
was, so they said, because they did not forget that it was
their duty to rejoice the eyes of these "boys at the front,"
that they still decked themselves of an evening not only in
flowing dresses, but in jewellery which suggested the
army by its choice of decorative themes, when indeed the
actual material from which it was made did not come
from, had not been wrought in the army; for instead of
Egyptian ornaments recalling the campaign in Egypt, the
fashion now was for rings or bracelets made out of frag-

ments of exploded shells or copper bands from 75 millimetre ammunition, and for cigarette-lighters constructed
out of two English pennies to which a soldier, in his dug-
out, had succeeded in giving a patina so beautiful that the
profile of Queen Victoria looked as if it had been drawn
by the hand of Pisanello; and it was also because they
never stopped thinking of the dear boys, so they said, that
when one of their own kin fell they scarcely wore mourning for him, on the pretext that "their grief was mingled
with pride," which permitted them to wear a bonnet of
white English crêpe (a bonnet with the most charming effect, "authorising every hope" and "inspired by an invin-
cible confidence in final victory") and to replace the
cashmere of former days by satin and chiffon, and even to
keep their pearls, "while observing the tact and propriety
of which there is no need to remind Frenchwomen."

The Louvre and all the other museums were closed,
and when one saw at the head of an article in a newspaper
the words: "A sensational exhibition," one could be sure
that the exhibition in question was not one of paintings
but of dresses, of dresses moreover which aimed at reviv-
ing "those refined joys of art of which the women of Paris
have for too long been deprived." So it was that fashion
and pleasure had returned, fashion, in the absence of the
arts, apologising for its survival as the arts had done in
1793, in which year the artists exhibiting in the revolutionary Salon proclaimed that, though "stern Republicans
might find it strange that we should occupy ourselves
with the arts when Europe united in coalition is besieging
the soil of liberty," they would be wrong. The same sort
of thing was said in 1916 by the dressmakers, who, with

the self-conscious pride of artists, affirmed that "to create
something new, to get away from banality, to assert an individual character, to prepare for victory, to evolve for the
post-war generations a new formula of beauty, such was
the ambition that tormented them, the chimera that they
pursued, as would be apparent to anyone who cared to
visit their salons, delightfully installed in the Rue de
la . . . , where to efface by a note of luminous gaiety the
heavy sadness of the hour seems to be the watchword,
with the discretion, naturally, that circumstances impose."

"The sadness of the hour"—it was true—"might
prove too strong for feminine energies, were it not that we
have so many lofty examples of courage and endurance to
contemplate. So, as we think of our warriors dreaming in
their trenches of more comfort and more pretty things for
the girl they have left behind them, we shall not pause in
our ever more strenuous efforts to create dresses that answer to the needs of the moment. The vogue"—and what
could be more natural?—"is for the fashion-houses of our
English allies, and the rage this year is the barrel-dress,
which, with its charming informality, gives us all an
amusing little cachet of rare distinction. We may even say
that one of the happiest consequences of this sad war will
be," added the delightful chronicler (and one expected:
"the return of our lost provinces" or "the reawakening of
national sentiment")—"one of the happiest consequences
of this sad war will be that we have achieved some charming results in the realm of fashion, without ill-considered
and unseemly luxury, with the simplest materials, that we
have created prettiness out of mere nothings. To the
dresses of the great designers, reproduced in a number of

copies, women prefer just now dresses made at home, which affirm the intelligence, the taste and the personal preferences of the individual."

As for charity, the thought of all the miseries that had sprung from the invasion, of all the wounded and disabled, meant naturally that it was obliged to develop forms "more ingenious than ever before," and this meant that the ladies in tall turbans were obliged to spend the latter part of the afternoon at "teas" round a bridge table, discussing the news from the "front," while their cars waited at the door with a handsome soldier in the driver's seat who chatted to the footman. It was, moreover, not only the headdresses with their strange cylinders towering above the ladies' faces that were new. The faces were new themselves. These ladies in new-fangled hats were young women who had come one did not quite know from where and had been the flower of fashion, some for six months, others for two years, others for four. And these differences were of as much importance for them as had been, at the time when I took my first steps in society, for two families like the Guermantes and the La Rochefoucaulds a difference of three or four centuries of proven antiquity. The lady who had known the Guermantes since 1914 looked upon the lady who had been introduced to them in 1916 as an upstart, greeted her with the air of a dowager, quizzed her with her lorgnette, and admitted with a little grimace that no one even knew for certain whether or no she was married. "It is all rather nauseating," concluded the lady of 1914, who would have liked the cycle of new admissions to have come to a halt after herself. These new ladies, whom the young men found pretty ancient and whom, also, certain elderly men, who had not moved exclusively in the best circles, thought that they recognised as being not so new as all that, did not merely recommend themselves to society by offering it its favourite amusements of political conversation and music in intimate surroundings; part of their appeal was that it was *they* who offered these amenities, for in order that things should appear new even if they are old—and indeed even if they are new—there must in art, as in medicine and in fashion, be new names. (New names indeed there were in certain spheres. For instance, Mme Verdurin had visited Venice during the war, but—like those people who cannot bear sad talk or display of personal feelings—when she said that "it" was "marvellous" she was referring not to Venice, or St Mark's, or the palaces, all that I had so loved and she thought so unimportant, but to the effect of the searchlights in the sky, of which searchlights she could give you a detailed account supported by statistics. So from age to age is reborn a certain realism which reacts against what the previous age has admired.)

The Saint-Euverte salon was a faded banner now, and the presence beneath it of the greatest artists, the most influential ministers, would have attracted nobody. But people would run to listen to the secretary of one of these same artists or a subordinate official of one of the ministers holding forth in the houses of the new turbaned ladies whose winged and chattering invasion filled Paris. The ladies of the first Directory had a queen who was young and beautiful and was called Mme Tallien. Those of the second had two, who were old and ugly and were called Mme Verdurin and Mme Bontemps. Who could now hold it against Mme Bontemps that in the Dreyfus

Affair her husband had played a role which the *Echo de Paris* had sharply criticised? The whole Chamber having at a certain moment become revisionist, it was inevitably from among former revisionists—and also from among former socialists—that the party of social order, of religious tolerance, of military preparedness, had been obliged to enlist its recruits. Time was when M. Bontemps would have been abominated, because then the antipatriots bore the name of Dreyfusards. But presently this name had been forgotten and replaced by that of "opponent of the law of three years' military service." M. Bontemps, far from being its opponent, was one of the sponsors of this law; consequently he was a patriot.

In society (and this social phenomenon is merely a particular case of a much more general psychological law) novelties, whether blameworthy or not, excite horror only so long as they have not been assimilated and enveloped by reassuring elements. It was the same with Dreyfusism as with that marriage between Saint-Loup and the daughter of Odette which had at first produced such an outcry. Now that "everybody one knew" was seen at the parties given by the Saint-Loups, Gilberte might have had the morals of Odette herself but people would have "gone there" just the same and would have thought it quite right that she should disapprove like a dowager of any moral novelties that had not been assimilated. Dreyfusism was now integrated in a scheme of respectable and familiar things. As for asking oneself whether intrinsically it was good or bad, the idea no more entered anybody's head, now when it was accepted, than in the past when it was condemned. It was no longer *shocking* and that was all that mattered. People hardly remembered that it had once been thought so, just as, when a certain time has elapsed, they no longer know whether a girl's father was a thief or not. One can always say, if the subject crops up: "No, it's the brother-in-law, or someone else with the same name, that you're thinking of. There has never been a breath of scandal about her father." In the same way, there had undeniably been Dreyfusism and Dreyfusism, and a man who was received by the Duchesse de Montmorency and was helping to pass the three years law could not be bad. And then, as the saying goes, no sin but should find mercy. If Dreyfusism was accorded an amnesty, so, *a fortiori*, were Dreyfusards. In fact, there no longer were Dreyfusards in politics, since at one moment every politician had been one if he wanted to belong to the government, even those who represented the contrary of what at the time of its shocking novelty—the time when Saint-Loup had been getting into bad ways—Dreyfusism had incarnated: anti-patriotism, irreligion, anarchy, etc. So the Dreyfusism of M. Bontemps, invisible and constitutional like that of every other politician, was no more apparent than the bones beneath the skin. No one troubled to remember that he had been a Dreyfusard, for people in society are scatterbrained and forgetful and, besides, all *that* had been a very long time ago, a "time" which these people affected to think longer than it was, for one of the ideas most in vogue was that the pre-war days were separated from the war by something as profound, something of apparently as long a duration, as a geological period, and Brichot himself, that great nationalist, when he alluded to the Dreyfus case now talked of "those prehistoric days."

(The truth is that this profound change wrought by

the war was in inverse ratio to the quality of the minds
which it affected, at least above a certain level. At the
very bottom of the scale the really stupid people, who
lived only for pleasure, did not bother about the fact that
there was a war. But, at the other end of the scale too,
people who have made for themselves a circumambient
interior life usually pay small regard to the importance of
events. What profoundly modifies their system of thought
is much more likely to be something that in itself seems
to have no importance, something that reverses the order
of time for them by making them contemporaneous with
another epoch in their lives. And that this is so we may
see in practice from the beauty of the writing which is inspired in this particular way: the song of a bird in the
park at Montboissier, or a breeze laden with the scent of
mignonette, are obviously phenomena of less consequence
than the great events of the Revolution and the Empire;
but they inspired Chateaubriand to write pages of infinitely greater value in his *Mémoires d'Outre-tombe*.) The
words Dreyfusard and anti-Dreyfusard no longer had any
meaning then. But the very people who said this would
have been dumbfounded and horrified if one had told
them that probably in a few centuries, or perhaps even
sooner, the word Boche would have only the curiosity
value of such words as *sans-culotte, chouan* and *bleu*.

Things had altered so little that people still found it
quite natural to use the old catchwords "right-minded"
and "not right-minded." And yet change of a kind there
was, for, just as former partisans of the Commune had at
a later date been against a retrial, so now the most extreme Dreyfusards of the old days wanted to shoot people
right and left, and the generals supported them in this

policy just as they had supported Galliffet's opponents at
the time of the Affair.

M. Bontemps did not want there to be any question
of peace until Germany had been broken up into tiny
states as it had been in the Middle Ages, the fall of the
House of Hohenzollern pronounced, and the Kaiser stood
up against a wall and shot. In a word he was what Brichot
called a *jusqu'au-boutiste*, and this was the highest certificate of patriotism that could be conferred upon him.
Doubtless for the first three days Mme Bontemps had
been a little bewildered in the midst of the people who
had asked Mme Verdurin to introduce them to her, and it
was in a tone of some slight asperity that Mme Verdurin
had replied: "No, my dear, the Comte," when Mme Bontemps said to her, "That was the Duc d'Haussonville you
introduced to me just now, wasn't it?", either out of total
ignorance and failure to associate the name Haussonville
with any title whatsoever or, on the contrary, from excess
of information and an association of ideas with the "Party
of the Dukes," to which she had been told that in the
Academy M. d'Haussonville belonged. But by the fourth
day she had begun to be firmly installed in the Faubourg
Saint-Germain. Sometimes there could still be seen
around her the nameless fragments of a world that one
did not know, which, in those who knew the egg from
which Mme Bontemps had emerged, evoked no more surprise than the debris of shell around a chick. But after a
fortnight she had shaken them off, and before the end of
the first month, when she said: "I am going to the
Lévis'," everybody understood, without her having to explain herself, that it was the Lévis-Mirepoix she meant,
and not a duchess would have gone to bed without having

inquired of Mme Bontemps or Mme Verdurin, at least by telephone, what there had been in the evening communiqué, what had been deliberately left out, how the Greek situation was developing, what offensive was being prepared, in a word all the news that the public would know only on the following day or later but of which the two ladies staged the equivalent of a dressmaker's private view. In conversation, when she was announcing news, Mme Verdurin would say "we" when she meant France. "Now listen: we demand of the King of Greece that he should withdraw from the Peloponnese, etc.; we send him, etc." And in all her stories there was constant mention of GHQ ("I telephoned to GHQ"), an abbreviation which gave her, as it fell from her lips, the pleasure that in former days women who did not know the Prince d'Agrigente had got from asking with a smile, when his name was mentioned, so as to show that they were in the swim: "Grigri?", a pleasure which in untroubled times is confined to the fashionable world but in great crises comes within the reach of the lower classes. Our butler, for instance, if the King of Greece was mentioned, was able, thanks to the newspapers, to say like the Kaiser Wilhelm: "Tino?", whereas hitherto his familiarity with kings had been of his own invention and of a more plebeian kind, as when at one time he had been in the habit of referring to the King of Spain as "Fonfonse." Another noticeable change was that, as more and more smart people made advances to Mme Verdurin, inversely the number of those whom she dubbed "bores" diminished. By a sort of magical transformation, every bore who had come to call on her and asked to be invited to her parties immediately became a charming and intelligent person. In short, at the end of a year, the number of bores had dwindled to such an extent that "the fear and awfulness of being bored," which had filled so large a place in the conversation and played so great a role in the life of Mme Verdurin, had almost entirely disappeared. In her latter days, it seemed, this awfulness of being bored (which anyhow, as she had formerly assured people, she had not known in her early youth) afflicted her less, just as certain kinds of migraine, certain nervous asthmatic conditions lose their force as one grows older. And the terror of being bored would doubtless, for want of bores, have entirely abandoned Mme Verdurin had she not, in some slight degree, replaced the vanishing bores by others recruited from the ranks of the former faithful.

Be that as it may, to conclude the subject of the duchesses who now frequented Mme Verdurin's house, they came, though they did not realise this, in search of exactly the same thing as the Dreyfusards had sought there in the old days, that is to say a social pleasure so compounded that their enjoyment of it at the same time assuaged their political curiosities and satisfied their need to discuss with others like themselves the incidents about which they had read in the newspapers. Mme Verdurin said: "Come at 5 o'clock to talk about the war" as she would have said in the past: "Come and talk about the Affair," or at an intermediate period: "Come to hear Morel."

Morel, incidentally, ought not to have been there, for the reason that he had not, as was supposed, been invalided out of the army. He had simply failed to rejoin his regiment and was a deserter, but nobody knew this.

One of the stars of the salon was "I'm a wash-out,"

who in spite of his sportive tastes had got himself exempted and whom I now thought of mainly as the author of remarkable works of art which were constantly in my thoughts. To such an extent had he assumed for me this new character that it was only by chance, when from time to time I established a transverse current linking two series of memories, that it crossed my mind that he was also the person who had brought about the departure of Albertine from my house. And even this transverse current ended, as far as these vestigial memories of Albertine were concerned, in a channel which petered out completely at a distance of several years from the present. For I never thought of her now. That was a channel of memories, a route, which I had quite ceased to take. Whereas the works of "I'm a wash-out" were recent and this route of memory was one perpetually visited and used by my mind.

I ought to say that the acquaintance of Andrée's husband was neither very easy nor very agreeable to make, and that any attempt to make friends with him was destined to numerous disappointments. He was, in fact, at this time already seriously ill and spared himself all fatigues except those which he thought likely to give him pleasure. Now in this category he included only meetings with people whom he did not yet know, whom his ardent imagination represented to him doubtless as being possibly different from others. When it came to people he was already acquainted with, he knew too well what they were like and what they would be like again and they no longer seemed to him worth the trouble of a fatigue that would be dangerous and might even be fatal to him. In short, he was a very poor friend. And perhaps in his taste for new

people there was still something to be found of the frenzied daring which he had shown in the old days at Balbec,
in sport, in gambling, in excesses of eating and drinking.

Whenever Andrée and I were there together Mme
Verdurin tried to introduce me to her, being unable to accept the fact that we were already acquainted. Andrée did
not often come with her husband, but she at least was an
admirable and sincere friend to me. Faithful to the aesthetic ideas of her husband, who had reacted against the
Russian Ballet, she was always saying of the Marquis de
Polignac: "He's had his house decorated by Bakst. How
can one sleep with all that round one? I would rather have
Dubuffe." The Verdurins, too, swept along by the fatal
progress of aestheticism which ends by eating its own tail,
said now that they could not endure *art nouveau* (besides,
it came from Munich) or white rooms; they cared only for
old French furniture in a sombre colour-scheme.

I saw a lot of Andrée at this time. We did not know
what to say to each other, and once there came into my
mind that name, Juliette, which had risen from the depths
of Albertine's memory like a mysterious flower. Mysterious then, but now it no longer stirred any feeling in me:
many subjects that were indifferent to me I discussed but
on this subject I was silent; not that it meant less to me
than others, but a sort of supersaturation takes place when
one has thought about a thing too much. Perhaps the
epoch in my life when I saw so many mysteries in that
name was the true one. But as these epochs will not last
for ever, it is a mistake for a man to sacrifice his health
and his fortune to the elucidation of mysteries which one
day will no longer interest him.

Now that Mme Verdurin could get anyone she

wanted to come to her house, people were very surprised to see her make indirect advances to someone she had completely lost sight of, Odette, the general opinion being that Odette could add nothing to the brilliant set that the little group had become. But a prolonged separation, which has the effect of appeasing resentments, in some cases also reawakens feelings of friendship. And then too the phenomenon of the dying man who pronounces none but familiar names from the past, or the old man who finds pleasure in his childhood memories, has its social equivalent. To succeed in the project of making Odette return to her, Mme Verdurin employed, naturally, not the "ultras" but the less faithful members of the group who had kept a foot in each of the two drawing-rooms. "I can't think why we no longer see her here," she said to them. "She may have fallen out with me, I haven't with her. After all, what harm have I done her? It was in my house that she met both her husbands. If she wants to come back, let her know that the door is open." These words, which would have involved a sacrifice of pride for the Mistress if they had not been dictated to her by her imagination, were passed on, but without success. Mme Verdurin waited in vain for Odette, until events which will come to our notice later brought about, for entirely different reasons, what the intercession of the "deserters," for all their zeal, had been unable to achieve. So rarely do we meet either with easy success or with irreversible defeat.

To these parties Mme Verdurin used to invite a few ladies of rather recent origin, known for their good works, who at first came magnificently dressed, with great pearl necklaces that Odette, who had a necklace just as beauti-

ful the display of which she had herself formerly over-
done, regarded, now that she was "dressed for war" in
imitation of the ladies of the Faubourg, with some sever-
ity. But women know how to adapt themselves. After
three or four appearances they realised that the clothes
which they had thought smart were precisely the ones
proscribed by people who were smart; they laid aside their
gold dresses and resigned themselves to simplicity.

"It is too bad," Mme Verdurin would say. "I must
telephone to Bontemps to get things put right for tomorrow, they have *blue-pencilled* the whole of the end of Norpois's article and just because he hinted that Percin had
been *bowler-hatted*." For the idiocy of the times caused
people to pride themselves on using the expressions of the
times; in this way they hoped to show that they were in
the fashion, like the middle-class woman who says, when
MM. de Bréauté or d'Agrigente or de Charlus is mentioned: "You mean Babal de Bréauté? Grigri? Mémé de
Charlus?" As a matter of fact duchesses do this too, and
duchesses felt the same pleasure in saying "bowler-
hatted," for it is in their names that these ladies—for the
commoner with a poetical imagination—are exceptional;
in their language and their ideas they conform to the intellectual category to which they belong and to which also
belong a vast number of middle-class people. The classes
of the intellect take no account of birth.

All this telephoning that Mme Verdurin did was not,
however, without its disadvantages. Although we have
forgotten to mention the fact, the Verdurin "salon," if it
continued to exist in spirit and in all essentials, had been
temporarily transferred to one of the largest hotels in
Paris, the lack of coal and light making it too difficult for

the Verdurins to entertain in the former mansion of the
Venetian ambassadors, which was extremely damp. But
the new drawing-room was not altogether disagreeable.
Just as, in Venice, the restrictions that water imposes
upon a site dictate the shape of a palace, and in Paris a
scrap of garden is more ravishing than a whole park in the
country, so the narrow dining-room that Mme Verdurin
had in the hotel, with the dazzling white walls of its irregular quadrilateral, made a sort of screen upon which fig-
ured every Wednesday, indeed almost every day of the
week, all the most interesting men of every kind, all the
smartest women in Paris, only too delighted to avail
themselves of the luxury of the Verdurins, which went on
increasing, with their wealth, at a time when other very
rich people were economising, because part of their income was frozen. In their altered form the receptions had
not ceased to enchant Brichot, who, as the circle of the
Verdurins' acquaintance grew wider and wider, found in
their parties ever new pleasures, packed tight together in a
tiny space like surprises in a Christmas stocking. On some
days the guests were so numerous that the dining-room of
the private suite was too small and the dinner was given
in the huge dining-room downstairs, where the faithful, if
they feigned a hypocritical regret for the intimacy of upstairs, were at heart delighted—while keeping themselves
to themselves, as in the old days on the little train—to be
a spectacle and an object of envy for neighbouring tables.
Doubtless, under normal peacetime conditions, a "society"
note surreptitiously sent to *Le Figaro* or *Le Gaulois* would
have informed a larger public than could be contained in
the dining-room of the Majestic that Brichot had dined
with the Duchesse de Duras. But since the war, the social

reporters having suppressed this type of news (they made up for it, however, in funerals, "mentions in despatches" and Franco-American banquets), publicity could only be attained through a more embryonic, a more restricted medium, worthy of primitive ages and anterior to the discovery of Gutenberg: one had actually to be seen at Mme Verdurin's table. After dinner the guests went upstairs to the Mistress's reception rooms, and then the telephoning began. But many large hotels were at this period peopled with spies, who duly noted the news announced over the telephone by Bontemps with an indiscretion which might have had serious consequences but for a fortunate lack of accuracy in his reports, which invariably were contradicted by events.

Before the hour at which the afternoon tea-parties came to an end, at the close of the day, in the still light sky one saw, far off, little brown dots which one might have taken, in the blue evening, for midges or birds. In the same way, when one sees a mountain at a great distance one can imagine it to be a cloud. But because one knows that this "cloud" is huge, solid and resistant one's emotions are stirred. And I too was moved by the thought that the brown dot in the summer sky was neither midge nor bird but an aeroplane with a crew of men keeping guard over Paris. (The memory of the aeroplanes which I had seen with Albertine on our last drive, near Versailles, played no part in this emotion, for the memory of that drive had become indifferent to me.)

When the time came for dinner, the restaurants were full; and if, passing in the street, I saw a wretched soldier on leave, escaped for six days from the constant danger of

death and about to return to the trenches, halt his gaze
for a moment upon the illuminated windows, I suffered as
I had in the hotel at Balbec when fishermen used to watch
us at dinner, but I suffered more now because I knew that
the misery of the soldier is greater than that of the poor,
since it combines in itself all miseries, and more touching
still because more resigned, more noble, and because it
was with a philosophical shake of the head, without hatred, that on the eve of setting out again for the war the
soldier would say to himself, as he saw the shirkers
jostling one another in their efforts to secure a table:
"You'd never know there was a war on here." Then at
half past nine, before anyone had had time to finish dinner, the lights were all suddenly turned out because of the
police regulations, so that at nine thirty-five the second
jostling of shirkers snatching their overcoats from the
page-boys of the restaurant where I had dined with Saint-
Loup one evening when he was on leave took place in a
mysterious half-darkness which might have been that of a
room in which slides are being shown on a magic lantern,
or of the auditorium, during the exhibition of a film, of
one of those cinemas towards which the men and women
who had been dining would presently rush.

But at any later hour for those who, like myself on
the evening which I am going to describe, had had dinner
at home and were going out to see friends, Paris, at least
in certain quarters, was even blacker than had been the
Combray of my childhood; the visits that people paid one
another were like the visits of country neighbours. Ah! if
Albertine had been alive, how delightful it would have
been, on the evenings when I had dined out, to arrange to
meet her out of doors, under the arcades! At first I should

have seen nothing, I should have had the pang of thinking that she had failed to turn up, when suddenly I should have seen one of her beloved grey dresses emerge from the black wall, then her smiling eyes which had already seen me, and we could have walked along with our arms round each other without any fear of being recognised or disturbed, and then at length gone home. But alas, I was alone and I felt as if I was setting out to pay a neighbourly visit in the country, like those that Swann used to pay us after dinner, without meeting more people on his way through the darkness of Tansonville, along the little tow-path and as far as the Rue du Saint-Esprit, than I now met in the streets, transformed into winding rustic lanes, between Sainte-Clotilde and the Rue Bonaparte. Or again—since the effect of those fragments of landscape which travel in obedience to the moods of the weather was no longer nullified by surroundings which had become invisible—on evenings when the wind was chasing an icy shower of rain I had, now, much more strongly the impression of being on the shore of that raging sea of which I had once so longingly dreamed than I had had when I was actually at Balbec; and other natural features also, which had not existed in Paris hitherto, helped to create the illusion that one had just got out of the train and arrived to spend a holiday in the depth of the country: for example the contrast of light and shadow on the ground that one had all round one on evenings when the moon was shining. There were effects of moonlight normally unknown in towns, sometimes in the middle of winter even, when the rays of the moon lay outpoured upon the snow on the Boulevard Haussmann, untouched now by the broom of any sweeper, as they would have

lain upon a glacier in the Alps. Against this snow of
bluish gold the silhouettes of the trees were outlined clear
and pure, with the delicacy that they have in certain
Japanese paintings or in certain backgrounds of Raphael;
and on the ground at the foot of the tree itself there was
stretched out its shadow as often one sees trees' shadows
in the country as sunset, when the light inundates and
polishes to the smoothness of a mirror some meadow in
which they are planted at regular intervals. But by a refinement of exquisite delicacy the meadow upon which
were displayed these shadows of trees, light as souls, was
a meadow of paradise, not green but of a whiteness so
dazzling because of the moonlight shining upon the jade-
like snow that it might have been a meadow woven entirely from petals of flowering pear-trees. And in the
squares the divinities of the public fountains, holding a jet
of ice in their hand, looked like statues wrought in two
different materials by a sculptor who had decided to
marry pure bronze to pure crystal. On these exceptional
days all the houses were black. But in the spring, on the
contrary, here and there, defying the regulations of the
police, a private house, or simply one floor of a house, or
even simply one room of one floor, had failed to close its
shutters and appeared, mysteriously supported by dark
impalpable shadows, to be no more than a projection of
light, an apparition without substance. And the woman
whom, if one raised one's eyes high above the street, one
could distinguish in this golden penumbra, assumed, in
this night in which one was oneself lost and in which she
too seemed to be hidden away, the mysterious and veiled
charm of an oriental vision. Then one passed on and

nothing more interrupted the rustic tramp, wholesome and monotonous, of one's feet through the darkness.

I reflected that it was a long time since I had seen any of the personages who have been mentioned in this work. In 1914, it was true, during the two months that I had spent in Paris, I had caught a glimpse of M. de Charlus and seen something of Bloch and Saint-Loup, the latter only twice. The second occasion was certainly that on which he had been most himself; he had quite effaced that disagreeable impression of insincerity which he had made on me during the stay at Tansonville that I have described, and I had once more recognised in him all the fine qualities of his earlier days. On the earlier occasion, which was less than a week after the declaration of war, while Bloch made a display of the most chauvinistic sentiments, Saint-Loup, once Bloch had left us, was unashamedly cynical about the fact that he himself had not joined his regiment, and I had been almost shocked at the violence of his tone.

Saint-Loup had just come back from Balbec. I learnt later, indirectly, that he had made unsuccessful advances to the manager of the restaurant. The latter owed his position to the money he had inherited from M. Nissim Bernard. He was, in fact, none other than the young waiter whom in the past Bloch's uncle had "protected." But wealth in his case had brought with it virtue and it was in vain that Saint-Loup had attempted to seduce him. Thus, by a process of compensation, while virtuous young men abandon themselves in their later years to the passions of which they have at length become conscious, promiscuous youths turn into men of principle from whom any Charlus who turns up too late on the strength of old stories will get an unpleasant rebuff. It is all a question of chronology.

"No," he exclaimed, gaily and with force, "if a man doesn't fight, whatever reason he may give, it is because he doesn't want to be killed, because he is *afraid*." And with the same affirming gesture, even more energetic than that which he had used to underline the fear of others, he added: "And that goes for me too. If I haven't rejoined my regiment, it is quite simply from *fear*—so there!" I had already observed in more than one person that the affectation of praiseworthy sentiments is not the only method of covering bad ones; another less obvious method is to make a display of these bad sentiments, so that at least one does not appear to be unaware of them. Moreover, in Saint-Loup this tendency was strengthened by his habit, when he had committed an indiscretion or made a blunder for which he expected to be blamed, of proclaiming it aloud and saying that it had been done on purpose. A habit which, I believe, must have come to him from some instructor at the Ecole de Guerre whom he had known well and greatly admired. I had, therefore, no hesitation in interpreting this outburst as the verbal confirmation of a sentiment which, since it had dictated the conduct of Saint-Loup and his non-participation in the war now beginning, he preferred to proclaim aloud.

"Have you heard the rumour," he asked, as he left me, "that my aunt Oriane is going to get a divorce? Personally I know nothing about it whatsoever. There have been rumours of the kind from time to time, and I have so often heard that it's imminent that I shall wait until it happens before I believe it. I must admit, it would be very understandable. My uncle is a charming man, not only socially but as a friend and in the family. He even, in a way, has much more heart than my aunt, who is a saint but makes him terribly aware of it. Only he is a dreadful husband, who has never ceased to be unfaithful to his wife, to insult her, to bully her, to keep her short of money. It would be so natural for her to leave him that that is a reason for the story to be true, but also a reason why it may not be true—the idea occurs to people and inevitably they talk about it. And then she has put up with him for so long! Of course I know quite well that there are lots of things which are reported falsely, and then denied, but later do become true." This put it into my head to ask him whether there had ever been any question of his marrying Mlle de Guermantes. He seemed amazed and assured me that there had not, that it was merely one of those rumours of the fashionable world which arise from time to time one does not know why and vanish in the same way, without their falsity causing those who believed them to be any more cautious when a new rumour arises, of an engagement or a divorce, or a political rumour, in giving credence to it and spreading it.

Forty-eight hours had not elapsed before certain facts which I learnt proved to me that I had been absolutely wrong in my interpretation of Robert's words: "If a man is not at the front, it is because he is afraid." Saint-Loup had said this in order to shine in conversation, to appear in the role of an original psychologist, so long as he was not sure that his own enlistment would be accepted. But meanwhile he was moving heaven and earth to bring this about and showing himself in this less "original," in the meaning that he thought it necessary to give to the word, but more profoundly a Frenchman of Saint-André-des-Champs, more in conformity with all that at this moment was best in the Frenchmen of Saint-André-des-Champs, lords, citizens and serfs—feudally respectful serfs and serfs in revolt, those two divisions, both equally French, of the same family, the Françoise branch and the Morel branch, from which two arrows were now converging upon a common target, the frontier. Bloch had been enchanted to hear a confession of cowardice from a nationalist (who was, as a matter of fact, so little of a nationalist) and when Saint-Loup had asked him whether he himself would soon be off, had assumed a high-priestly air and replied: "Short-sighted."

But Bloch had completely changed his mind about the war a few days later, when he came to see me in a state of frenzy. Although short-sighted, he had been passed fit for service. I was accompanying him home when we met Saint-Loup, who was on his way to an interview at the Ministry of War with a colonel to whom he was to be introduced by a retired officer—"M. de Cambremer," he said to me, and added: "Oh! but of course, he is an old acquaintance of yours. You know Cancan as well as I do." I replied that I did indeed know him and his wife too, and that I didn't have a particularly high opinion of them. But I was so much in the habit, ever since I had first met them, of considering the wife as in her way a remarkable woman, who knew her Schopenhauer and at least had access to an intellectual sphere which was closed to her boorish husband, that I was at first astonished to hear Saint-Loup reply: "His wife is idiotic, I won't try to defend her. But *he* is an excellent man—he was talented once and is still a very pleasant person." By the "idiocy" of the wife, Saint-Loup meant no doubt her desperate desire to move in grand society, which is the thing that grand society judges most severely; by the good qualities of the husband, he meant perhaps something of the qualities that were recognised in him by his mother when she declared that he was the best of the family. He, at least, did not worry about duchesses, though this it must be admitted is a form of "intelligence" which differs as much from the intelligence that characterises thinkers as the "intelligence" admired by the public in this or that rich man who has "been clever enough to make a fortune." However, Saint-Loup's words did not displease me, because they reminded me that pretentiousness is near akin to stupidity and that simplicity has a flavour which though it lies beneath the surface is agreeable. I had, it is true, had no opportunity to savour that of M. de Cambremer. But this was merely an instance of the law that a person is many different persons according to who is judging him, quite apart from the different standards by which different people judge. In the case of M. de Cambremer, I had known only the rind. His flavour, therefore, though avouched to me by others, was to me personally unknown.

Bloch left us outside his house, overflowing with bitterness against Saint-Loup and saying to his face that men of his sort, privileged dandies who strutted about at headquarters, ran no risks and that he, as a plain private soldier, had no wish to "get a hole in his skin just because of William." "It seems that the Emperor William is seriously ill," replied Saint-Loup. Bloch, like everybody connected with the Stock Exchange, was more than usually credulous of sensational reports. "Yes," he said, "there is even a strong rumour that he is dead." In Stock Exchange circles every monarch who is ill, whether it be Edward VII or William II, is dead, every town which is about to be besieged has already been captured. "It is only being kept secret," added Bloch, "in order not to damage the morale of the Boches. But he died the night before last. My father has it from an absolutely first-class source." Absolutely first-class sources were the only ones to which M. Bloch senior paid any attention, and it was always with such a source that thanks to his "important connexions" he was fortunate enough to be in touch, when he heard before anyone else that Foreign Bonds were going to go up or that De Beers were going to fall. However, if just at that moment De Beers had a rise or Foreign Bonds "came on offer," if the market in the former was "firm and active" and that in the latter "hesitant and weak, with a note of caution," the first-class source did not, for that reason, cease to be a first-class source. So Bloch informed us of the death of the Kaiser with an air of mystery and self-importance, but also of fury. He was exasperated beyond measure at hearing Robert say: "the Emperor William." I believe that under the blade of the guillotine Saint-Loup and M. de Guermantes could not have spoken otherwise. Two men of "society," surviving alone on a desert island where they would have nobody to impress by a display of good manners, would recognise each other by these little signs of breeding, just as two Latinists in the same circumstances would continue to quote Virgil correctly. Saint-Loup, even under torture at the hands of the Germans, could never have used any other expression than "the Emperor William." And this good breeding, whatever else one may think of it, is a symptom of formidable mental shackles. The man who cannot throw them off can never be more than a man of the world. However, his elegant mediocrity—particularly when it is allied, as is often the case, with hidden generosity and un-expressed heroism—is a delightful quality in comparison with the vulgarity of Bloch, at once coward and braggart, who started now to scream at Saint-Loup: "Can't you simply say William? The trouble is you've got the wind up. Even in Paris you crawl on your belly before him! Pooh! we're going to have some fine soldiers at the fron-tier, they'll lick the boots of the Boches. You and your friends in fancy uniforms, you're fit to parade in a tourna-ment and that's about all."

"Poor Bloch is absolutely determined that I am to do nothing but strut about on parade," said Saint-Loup to me with a smile, when we had left our friend. And I sensed that this was not at all what Robert wished to do, although at the time I did not realise what his intentions were as clearly as I did later when, as the cavalry re-mained inactive, he got leave to serve as an officer in the infantry and then in the light infantry, or when, later still, there came the sequel which the reader will learn in due course. But Robert's patriotism was something that Bloch was unaware of simply because Robert chose not to dis-play it. If Bloch had treated us to a viciously anti-militarist profession of faith once he had been passed as "fit," he had previously made the most chauvinistic state-ments when he thought that he would be discharged on the grounds of short sight. But Saint-Loup would have been incapable of making these statements; in the first place from that sort of moral delicacy which prevents people

from expressing sentiments that lie too deep within them
and that seem to them quite natural. My mother, in the
past, would not only not have hesitated for a second to
die for my grandmother, but would have suffered horribly
if anyone had prevented her from doing so. Nevertheless,
I cannot retrospectively imagine on her lips any such
phrase as "I would give my life for my mother." And the
same reticence, in his love of France, was displayed by
Robert, who at this moment seemed to me much more
Saint-Loup (in so far as I could form a picture of his father) than Guermantes. And then Robert would also have
been saved from expressing the chauvinistic sentiments of
Bloch by the fact that his intelligence was in itself to some
extent a moral quality. Among intelligent and genuinely
serious workers there is a certain aversion for those who
make literature out of the subject they are engaged on,
those who use it for self-display. Robert and I had not
been at the Lycée or at the Sorbonne together, but we had
attended, independently, certain courses of lectures by the
same teachers, and I remember the smile he had for the
ones who—as happens sometimes when a man is giving a
remarkable series of lectures—tried to pass themselves off
as geniuses by giving their theories an ambitious name.
We only had to mention them for Robert to burst out
laughing. Our personal and instinctive preference was,
naturally, not for the Cottards or the Brichots, but we had
nevertheless a certain respect for any man with a really
thorough knowledge of Greek or medicine who did not
for that reason think himself entitled to behave as a char-
latan. I have said that, if in the past all Mamma's actions
had as their basis the sentiment that she would have given
her life for her mother, she had yet never formulated this

sentiment to herself, and that in any case it would have
seemed to her not merely unnecessary and ridiculous but
shocking and shameful to express it to others; in the same
way it was impossible for me to imagine on the lips of
Saint-Loup—talking to me about his equipment, the
things he had to do in Paris, our chances of victory, the
weakness of the Russian army, how England would act—
it is impossible for me to imagine on his lips even the
most eloquent phrase that even the most deservedly popular minister might have addressed to a wildly cheering
Chamber of Deputies. I cannot, however, say that in this
negativeness which checked him from expressing the noble sentiments that he felt, he was not to some extent influenced by the "Guermantes spirit," of which we have
seen so many similar instances in Swann. For, if I found
him more Saint-Loup than anything else, he was, nevertheless, also Guermantes, and consequently, among the
numerous motives which animated his courage, there were
some which did not exist for his friends of Doncières,
those young men enamoured of their profession with
whom I had dined night after night and of whom so
many went to their deaths at the battle of the Marne or
elsewhere, leading their men into action.

As for the young socialists who were at Doncières
when I was there but whom I did not get to know because they did not belong to the same set as Saint-Loup,
they could see now for themselves that the officers of that
set were by no means "nobs," with the implications of
haughty pride and base self-indulgence which the "plebs,"
the ex-ranker officers, the freemasons attached to that
word. And conversely, this same patriotism was found by
the officers of aristocratic birth to exist in full measure

among the socialists whom I had heard them accuse, while I was at Doncières at the height of the Dreyfus case, of being "men without a country." The patriotism of the military caste, as sincere and profound as any other, had assumed a fixed form which the members of that caste regarded as sacrosanct and which they were infuriated to see heaped with "opprobrium," but the radical-socialists, who were independent and to some extent unconscious patriots without any fixed patriotic religion, had failed to perceive the profound and living reality that lay behind what they thought were empty and malignant formulas.

No doubt, like his friends, Saint-Loup had formed the habit of inwardly cultivating, as the truest part of himself, the search for and the elaboration of the best possible manoeuvres which would lead to the greatest strategic and tactical successes, so that, for him as for them, the life of the body was something relatively unimportant which could easily be sacrificed to this inner part of the self, the real vital core within them, around which their personal existence was of value only as a protective outer skin. But in Saint-Loup's courage there were also more individual elements, and amongst these it would have been easy to recognise the generosity which in its early days had constituted the charm of our friendship, and also the hereditary vice which had later awoken from dormancy in him and which, at the particular intellectual level which he had not been able to transcend, caused him not only to admire courage but to exaggerate his horror of effeminacy into a sort of intoxication at any contact with virility. He derived, chastely no doubt, from spending days and nights in the open with Senegalese soldiers who might at any moment be called upon to sacrifice their lives, a cerebral gratification of desire into which there entered a vigorous contempt for "little scented gentlemen" and which, however contrary it might seem, was not so very different from that which he had obtained from the cocaine in which he had indulged excessively at Tansonville and of which heroism—one drug taking the place of another—was now curing him. And another essential part of his courage was that double habit of courtesy which, on the one hand, caused him to bestow praise on others but where he himself was concerned made him content to do what had to be done and say nothing about it—the opposite of a Bloch, who had said to him just now "You—of course you'd funk it," and yet was doing nothing himself—and on the other hand impelled him to hold as of no value the things that he himself possessed, his fortune, his rank, and even his life, so that he was ready to give them away: in a word, the true nobility of his nature.

"Are we in for a long war?" I said to Saint-Loup. "No, I believe it will be very short," he replied. But here, as always, his arguments were bookish. "Bearing in mind the prophecies of Moltke, re-read," he said to me, as if I had already read it, "the decree of the 28th October, 1913, about the command of large formations; you will see that the replacement of peacetime reserves has not been organised or even foreseen, a thing which the authorities could not have failed to do if the war were likely to be a long one." It seemed to me that the decree in question could be interpreted not as a proof that the war would be short, but as a failure on the part of its authors to foresee that it would be long, and what kind of war it would be, the truth being that they suspected neither the appalling wastage of material of every kind that would take place in a war of stable fronts nor the interdependence of different theatres of operations.

Outside the limits of homosexuality, among the men who are most opposed by nature to homosexuality, there exists a certain conventional idea of virility, which the homosexual finding at his disposal proceeds, unless he is a man of unusual intelligence, to distort. This ideal—to be seen in certain professional soldiers, certain diplomats—can be singularly exasperating. In its crudest form it is simply the gruffness of the man with the heart of gold who is determined not to show his emotions, the man who at the moment of parting from a friend who may very possibly be killed has a secret desire to weep, which no one suspects because he conceals it beneath a mounting anger which culminates, at the actual moment of farewell, in a sort of explosion: "Well, now, damn it! Shake hands with me, you old ruffian, and take this purse, it's no use to me, don't be an idiot." The diplomat, the officer, the man who believes that nothing counts except a great task in the service of the nation but who was fond nevertheless of the "poor boy" in his legation or his battalion who has died from a fever or a bullet exhibits the same taste for virility in a form that is less clumsy, and more sophisticated, but at bottom just as odious. He does not want to mourn for the "poor boy," he knows that soon he and everybody else will forget him, just as a kind-hearted surgeon soon forgets though, for a whole evening after some little girl has died in an epidemic, he feels a grief which he does not express. Should the diplomat be a writer and describe this death, he will not say that he felt grief. No—first from "manly reticence," secondly from that skilled artistry which arouses emotion by dissembling it. With one of his colleagues he will watch by the side of the dying man. Not for one second will they say that they feel grief. They will talk of the affairs of the legation or the battalion and their remarks may be even more terse than usual: "B. said to me: 'Don't forget we have the general's inspection tomorrow. See to it that your men are well turned out.' Habitually so gentle, he spoke in a sharper tone than usual. I noticed that he avoided looking at me, I too felt myself to be overwrought." And the reader understands that this "sharp tone" is simply grief showing itself in men who do not want to appear to feel grief, an attitude which might be ridiculous and nothing more but is in fact also wretched and ugly, because it is the manner of feeling grief of those who think that grief does not matter, that there are more serious things in life than being parted from one's friends, etc., so that when someone dies they give the same impression of falsehood, of nothingness, as on New Year's Day the gentleman who hands you a present of marrons glacés and just manages to say with a titter: "With the compliments of the season!"

To conclude the narrative of the officer or the diplomat watching at the deathbed, his head covered because the wounded or sick man has been carried out of doors, the moment comes when all is over. " 'I must go back and get my kit cleaned,' I thought. But I do not know why, at the moment when the doctor let go the pulse, simultaneously B. and I, without any sign passing between us—the sun was beating vertically down, perhaps we were hot standing beside the bed—removed our caps." And the reader knows that it was not because of the heat of the sun but from emotion in the presence of the majesty of death that the two virile men, on whose lips the words grief and affection were almost unknown, now bared their heads.

In homosexuals like Saint-Loup the ideal of virility is not the same, but it is just as conventional and just as false. The falsehood consists for them in the fact that they do not want to admit to themselves that physical desire lies at the root of the sentiments to which they ascribe another origin. M. de Charlus had detested effeminacy. Saint-Loup admired the courage of young men, the intoxication of cavalry charges, the intellectual and moral nobility of friendships between man and man, entirely pure friendships, in which each is prepared to sacrifice his life for the other. War, which turns capital cities, where only women remain, into an abomination for homosexuals, is at the same time a story of passionate adventure for homosexuals if they are intelligent enough to concoct dream figures, and not intelligent enough to see through them, to recognise their origin, to pass judgment on themselves. So that while some young men were enlisting simply in order to join in the latest sport—in the spirit in which one year everybody plays diabolo—for Saint-Loup, on the other hand, war was the very ideal which he imagined himself to be pursuing in his desires (which were in fact much more concrete but were clouded by ideology), an ideal which he could serve in common with those whom he preferred to all others, in a purely masculine order of chivalry, far from women, where he would be able to risk his life to save his orderly and die inspiring a fanatical love in his men. And thus, though there were many ele-

ments in his courage, the fact that he was a great nobleman was one of them, and another, in an unrecognisable
and idealised form, was M. de Charlus's dogma that it
was of the essence of a man to have nothing effeminate
about him. But just as in philosophy and in art ideas acquire their value only from the manner in which they are
developed, and two analogous ones may differ greatly according to whether they have been expounded by
Xenophon or by Plato, so, while I recognise how much, in
his behaviour, the one has in common with the other, I
admire Saint-Loup, for asking to be sent to the point of
greatest danger, infinitely more than I do M. de Charlus
for refusing to wear brightly coloured cravats.

I spoke to Saint-Loup about my friend the manager
of the Grand Hotel at Balbec, who, it seems, had alleged
that at the beginning of the war there had been in certain
French regiments defections, which he called "defectuosi-
ties," and had accused what he called the "Prussian mili-
tariat" of having provoked them; he had even, at one
moment, believed in a simultaneous landing by the
Japanese, the Germans and the Cossacks at Rivebelle as
threatening Balbec, and had said that the only thing to do
was to "decramp." He also thought that the departure of
the government and the ministries for Bordeaux was a little precipitate and declared that they were wrong to "decramp" so soon. This German-hater would say with a
laugh of his brother: "He is in the trenches, twenty-five
yards away from the Boches," until the authorities, having
discovered that he was a "Boche" himself, put him in a
concentration camp. "Talking of Balbec, do you remember the lift-boy who used to be in the hotel?" said Saint-
Loup as he left me, in a tone suggesting that he did not

quite know who the lift-boy was and was counting on me for enlightenment. "He is joining up and has written to ask me to get him into the flying corps." No doubt the young man was tired of going up in the captive cage of the lift, and the heights of the staircase of the Grand Hotel no longer sufficed him. He was going to "get his stripes" otherwise than by becoming a hall-porter, for our destiny is not always what we had supposed. "I shall certainly support his application," said Saint-Loup. "I was saying to Gilberte only this morning, we shall never have enough aeroplanes. It is aeroplanes that will enable us to see what the enemy is preparing, and aeroplanes that will rob him of the greatest advantage of attack, which is surprise. The best army will be, perhaps, the army with the best eyes."

(I had met this lift-boy airman a few days earlier. He had spoken to me about Balbec, and, curious to know what he would say about Saint-Loup, I brought the conversation round to the subject by asking whether it was true, as I had heard, that towards young men M. de Charlus had . . . etc. The lift-boy seemed surprised, he knew absolutely nothing about it. But on the other hand he made accusations against the rich young man, the one who lived with a mistress and three friends. As he seemed to lump all of them together, and as I knew from M. de Charlus who, it will be remembered, had informed me in front of Brichot that it was not so, I told the lift-boy that he must be mistaken. He met my doubts with the firmest avowals. It was the girlfriend of the rich man who had the job of picking up young men, and they all took their pleasure together. Thus M. de Charlus, the best-informed of men on the subject, had been entirely wrong, so fragmentary, secret, unpredictable is the truth. Afraid of reasoning like a bourgeois, and of seeing Charlusism where it was not, he had missed the fact that the woman was flushing out the game. "She came often enough to find me," said the lift-boy. "But she saw at once who it was she was dealing with. I refused categorically, I don't go in for that sort of monkey business. I told her I found it wholly objectionable. It's enough for one person to talk, word gets around, and you can't find another place anywhere." These last reasons weakened the virtuous declarations with which the lift-boy had begun, for they implied that he would have obliged had he been assured of discretion. Such must not have been the case where Saint-Loup was concerned. It is probable that even the rich man and his mistress and friends had been luckier, since the lift-boy quoted many conversations between him and them, held at various times, something that happens rarely when one has declined so categorically. For instance, the rich man's mistress had come to him to make the acquaintance of a page with whom he was close friends. "I don't think you know him, you weren't here then. Victor, they called him. Of course," the lift-boy added with the air of referring to inviolable and faintly secret laws, "you can't say no to a comrade who isn't well off." I remembered the invitation the rich man's noble friend had extended to me a few days before I left Balbec. But most likely this had nothing to do with it, and was dictated purely by amiability.)

"And tell me about poor Françoise, has she succeeded in getting her nephew exempted?" But Françoise, who for a long time had been making every effort to achieve this, and who, when she had been offered through the Guermantes a recommendation to General de Saint-Joseph, had replied in a tone of despair: "Oh no, that would be quite useless, there's nothing to be got from that old fogy, he's as bad as could be, he's patriotic," Françoise, as soon as there had been any question of war, however much she suffered at the thought of it, was of the opinion that it would be wrong to abandon the "poor Russians" since we were "allianced" to them. The butler, who in any case was convinced that the war would only last ten days and would end in a brilliant victory for France, would not have dared, for fear of being contradicted by events—and would not even have had enough imagination—to predict a long and indecisive war. But from this complete and immediate victory he tried at least to extract in advance the maximum of suffering for Françoise. "Things may well take an ugly turn, because it seems there are lots who refuse to march, boys of sixteen in floods of tears." And this habit of telling her disagreeable things in order to "vex" her was what he called "putting the wind up her," "making her flesh creep," "giving her a bit of a jolt." "Sixteen, Holy Mother!" said Françoise, and then suspicious for a moment: "But they said they only took them at twenty, at sixteen they're still children." "Naturally the papers have been told to say nothing about it. Anyhow, the young men, one and all, will be off to the front and there won't be many to come back. In one way it'll do some good. A good blood-letting, you know, is useful now and again. And then it will help trade. And I promise you, if there are any lads who are a bit soft and think twice about it, they'll be for the firing-squad, bang, bang, bang! I suppose it has to be done. And then, the officers, what does it matter to them? They get paid their screw, that's all they ask." Françoise turned so pale whenever one of these conversations took place that we were afraid the butler might cause her death from a heart attack.

But this did not mean that she had lost her old faults. Whenever I had a visit from a girl, however much her old servant's legs might be hurting her, if I happened to leave my room for a moment there she was at the top of a step-ladder in the dressing-room, searching, so she said, for some overcoat of mine to see if the moths had got into it, but really in order to eavesdrop. And she still, in spite of all my complaints, had her insidious manner of asking questions in an indirect way, the phrase she now used for this purpose being "because of course." Not daring to say to me: "Has this lady her own house?" she would say, her eyes timidly raised like the eyes of a good dog: "Because of course this lady has her own house . . . ," avoiding a blatant interrogative not so much in order to be polite as in order not to seem too curious. Then again, as the servants whom we love most—and this is particularly true when they have almost ceased to give us either the service or the respect proper to their employment—remain, unfortunately, servants and only make more clear the limitations of their caste, which we ourselves would like to do away with, when they imagine that they are penetrating most successfully into ours, Françoise often addressed me ("to get under my skin," as the butler would have said) with odd remarks which someone of my own class could not have made: for instance, with a joy carefully dissembled but as profound as if she had detected a serious illness, she would say to me if I was hot and there were beads of sweat which I had not noticed on my forehead: "But you're absolutely dripping," looking astonished as though this were some strange phenomenon and at the same time with that little smile of contempt with which we greet an impropriety ("Are you going out? You know you've forgotten to put your tie on") and also with the anxious voice which we assume when we want to alarm someone about the state of his health. One would have thought that no one in the world had ever been "dripping" before. Finally, she no longer spoke good French as she had in the past. For in her humility, in her affectionate admiration for people infinitely inferior to herself, she had come to adopt their ugly habits of speech. Her daughter having complained to me about her and having used the words (I do not know where she had heard them): "She's always finding fault with me because I don't shut the doors properly and *patatipatali* and *patatatipatala*," Françoise clearly thought that only her imperfect education had deprived her until now of this beautiful idiom. And from those lips which I had once seen bloom with the purest French I heard several times a day: "And *patatipatali* and *patatatipatala*." It is indeed curious how little not only the expressions but also the ideas of an individual vary. The butler, having got into the habit of declaring that M. Poincaré was a wicked man, not because he was after money but because he had been absolutely determined to have a war, repeated this seven or eight times a day to an audience which was always the same and always just as interested. Not a word was altered, not a gesture or an intonation. The performance only lasted two minutes, but it was unvarying, like that of an actor. And his faulty French was quite as much to blame as that of her daughter for corrupting the language of Françoise. He thought that what M. de Rambuteau had been so annoyed one day to hear the Duc de Guermantes call "Rambuteau shelters" were called "rinals." No doubt in his childhood he had failed to hear the "u" and had never realised his mistake, so every time he used the word—and he used it frequently—he mispronounced it. Françoise, embarrassed at first, ended by using it too, and liked to complain that the same sort of thing did not exist for women as well as for men. But as a result of her humility and her admiration for the butler she never said "urinals" but—with a slight concession to customary usage—"arinals."

She no longer slept, no longer ate. Every day she insisted on the bulletins, of which she understood nothing, being read to her by the butler who understood hardly more of them than she did, and in whom the desire to torment Françoise was frequently dominated by a patriotic cheerfulness: he would say, with a sympathetic laugh, referring to the Germans: "Things are hotting up for them, it won't be long before old Joffre puts salt on the tail of the comet." Françoise had no idea what comet he was alluding to, but this strengthened her conviction that the phrase was one of those amiable and original extravagances to which a well-bred person is required by the laws of courtesy to respond good-humouredly, so gaily shrugging her shoulders as if to say: "He's always the same," she tempered her tears with a smile. At least she was happy that her new butcher's boy, who in spite of his trade was anything but courageous (his first job nevertheless had been in the slaughterhouses), was not old enough to be called up. Otherwise she would have been quite capable of going to see the Minister of War to get him exempted.

The butler had not enough imagination to realise that the bulletins were not excellent and that we were not advancing towards Berlin, since he kept reading: "We have repulsed with heavy enemy losses, etc.," actions which he celebrated as a succession of victories. I, however, was alarmed at the speed with which the scene of these victories was approaching Paris, and was astonished that even the butler, having seen in one bulletin that an engagement had taken place near Lens, was not disturbed to read in the newspaper next day that it had been followed by satisfactory operations in the neighbourhood of Jouy-le-Vicomte, of which the approaches were firmly in our hands. Now the butler knew Jouy-le-Vicomte well by name, for it was not so very far from Combray. But we read the newspapers as we love, blindfold. We do not try to understand the facts. We listen to the soothing words of the editor as we listen to the words of our mistress. We are "beaten and happy" because we believe that we are not beaten but victorious.

I had, in any case, not remained long in Paris but had returned very soon to my sanatorium. Although in principle the doctor's treatment consisted in isolation, I had been allowed to receive, at different times, a letter from Gilberte and a letter from Robert. Gilberte wrote (this was in about September 1914) that, however much she would have liked to stay in Paris in order to get news of Robert more easily, the constant Taube raids on the city had caused her such alarm, particularly for her little girl, that she had fled by the last train to leave for Combray, that the train had not even got as far as Combray, and that it was only thanks to a peasant's cart, on which she had had an appalling journey of ten hours, that she had succeeded in reaching Tansonville! "And there, imagine what awaited your old friend," she concluded her letter. "I had left Paris to escape from the German aeroplanes, supposing that at Tansonville I should be perfectly safe. Before I had been there two days you will never imagine what turned up: the Germans, who having defeated our troops near La Fère, were overrunning the district. A German headquarters staff, with a regiment just behind it, presented itself at the gates of Tansonville and I was obliged to take them in, and not a hope of getting away, no more trains, nothing." Whether the German staff had really behaved well, or whether it was right to detect in Gilberte's letter the influence, by contagion, of the spirit of those Guermantes who were of Bavarian stock and related to the highest aristocracy of Germany, she was lavish in her praise of the perfect breeding of the staff-officers, and even of the soldiers who had only asked her for "permission to pick a few of the forget-me-nots growing near the pond," a good breeding which she contrasted with the disorderly violence of the fleeing French troops, who had pillaged everything as they crossed the property before the arrival of the German generals. In any case, if Gilberte's letter was in some ways impregnated with the spirit of the Guermantes—others would say the spirit of Jewish internationalism, which would probably have been unfair to her, as we shall see—the letter which I received several months later from Robert was, on the other hand, much more Saint-Loup than Guermantes and reflected in addition all the liberal culture which he had acquired. Altogether, it was a delightful letter. Unfortunately, he did not talk about strategy as he had in our conversations at Doncières, nor did he tell me to what ex-

tent he considered that the war confirmed or invalidated
the principles which he had then expounded to me.

All he said was that since 1914 there had in reality
been a series of wars, the lessons of each one influencing
the conduct of the one that followed. For example, the
theory of the "break-through" had been supplemented by
a new idea: that it was necessary, before breaking through,
for the ground held by the enemy to be completely devas-
tated by the artillery. But then it had been found that on
the contrary this devastation made it impossible for the
infantry and the artillery to advance over ground in which
thousands of shell-holes created as many obstacles.
"War," he wrote, "does not escape the laws of our old
friend Hegel. It is in a state of perpetual becoming."

This was meagre in comparison with what I should
have liked to know. But what was still more annoying was
that he was forbidden to mention the names of generals.
And anyhow, according to the little that the newspapers
told me, the generals as to whom at Doncières I had been
so eager to know which among them would prove most
effective and courageous in a war, were not the ones who
were now in command. Geslin de Bourgogne, Galliffet,
Négrier were dead. Pau had retired from active service almost at the beginning of the war. Of Joffre, of Foch, of
Castelnau, of Pétain, Robert and I had never spoken.
"My dear boy," he wrote, "I recognise that expressions
like *passeront pas* and *on les aura* are not agreeable; they
have always set my teeth on edge as much as *poilu* and
the rest, and of course it is tiresome to be composing an
epic with words and phrases which are—worse than an
error of grammar or of taste—an appalling contradiction
in terms, a vulgar affectation and pretension of the kind

that you and I abominate, as bad as when people think it clever to say 'coco' instead of 'cocaine.' But if you could see everybody here, particularly the men of the humbler classes, working men and small shopkeepers, who did not suspect what heroism they concealed within them and might have died in their beds without suspecting it—if you could see them running under fire to help a comrade or carry off a wounded officer and then, when they have been hit themselves, smiling a few moments before they die because the medical officer has told them that the trench has been recaptured from the Germans, I assure you, my dear boy, it gives you a magnificent idea of the French people, makes you begin to understand those great periods in history which seemed to us a little extraordinary when we learned about them as students. The epic is so magnificent that you would find, as I do, that words no longer matter. Cannot Rodin or Maillol create a masterpiece from some hideous raw material which he transforms out of all recognition? At the touch of such greatness, the word *poilu* has for me become something of which I no more feel that it may originally have contained an allusion or a joke than one does, for instance, when one reads about the *chouans*. But I do know that *poilu* is already waiting for great poets, like other words, 'deluge,' or 'Christ,' or 'barbarians,' which were already instinct with greatness before Hugo, Vigny and the rest made use of them. As I say, the people, the working men, are the best of all, but everybody is splendid. Poor young Vaugoubert, the Ambassador's son, was wounded seven times before he was killed, and each time he came back from a raid without having 'copped it' he seemed to want to apologise and to say that it was not his fault. He was a charming creature. We had become close friends. His parents were given permission to come to the funeral, on condition that they did not wear mourning and only stayed five minutes because of the shelling. The mother, a great horse of a woman whom I dare say you know, was no doubt deeply moved but showed no sign of it. But the poor father was in such a state that I assure you that I, who am now totally unfeeling because I have got used to seeing the head of the comrade who is talking to me suddenly ripped open by a landmine or even severed from its trunk, I could not contain myself when I saw the collapse of poor Vaugoubert, who was an utter wreck. The general tried to tell him that it was for France, that his son had behaved like a hero, but it was no use, this only redoubled the sobs of the poor man, who could not tear himself away from his son's body. The fact is, and that is why we must learn to put up with *passeront pas*, it is men like these, like my poor valet, like Vaugoubert, who have prevented the Germans from 'passing.' You may think we are not advancing much, but logic is beside the point, there is a secret inner feeling which tells an army that it is victorious—or a dying man that he is finished. We know that victory will be ours and we are determined that it shall be, so that we can dictate a just peace, I don't mean 'just' simply for ourselves, but truly just, just to the French and just to the Germans."

I do not wish to imply that the "calamity" had raised Saint-Loup's intelligence to a new level. But just as soldier heroes with commonplace and trivial minds, if they happened to write poems during their convalescence, placed themselves, in order to describe the war, at the level not of events, which in themselves are nothing, but of the commonplace aesthetic whose rules they had obeyed in the past, and talked, as they would have ten years earlier, of the "blood-stained dawn," "victory's tremulous wings," and so on, so Saint-Loup, by nature much more intelligent and much more of an artist, remained intelligent and an artist, and it was with the greatest good taste that he now recorded for my benefit the observations of landscape which he made if he had to halt at the edge of a marshy forest, very much as he would have done if he had been out duck-shooting. To help me to understand certain contrasts of light and shade which had been "the enchantment of his morning," he alluded in his letter to certain paintings which we both loved and was not afraid to cite a passage of Romain Rolland, or even of Nietzsche, with the independent spirit of the man at the front, who had not the civilian's terror of pronouncing a German name, and also—in thus quoting an enemy—with a touch of coquetry, like Colonel du Paty de Clam who, waiting among the witnesses at Zola's trial and chancing to pass Pierre Quillard, the violently Dreyfusard poet, whom he did not even know, recited some lines from his symbolist play, *La Fille aux Mains Coupées*. In the same way if Saint-Loup had occasion in a letter to mention a song by Schumann, he never gave any but the German title, nor did he use any periphrasis to tell me that, when at dawn on the edge of the forest he had heard the first twittering of a bird, his rapture had been as great as though he had been addressed by the bird in that "sublime *Siegfried*" which he so looked forward to hearing after the war.

And now, on my second return to Paris, I had received, the day after I arrived, another letter from

Gilberte, who had doubtless forgotten, or at least forgotten what she had said in, the letter I have described, for
in this new letter her departure from Paris at the end of
1914 was presented retrospectively in a very different
light. "Perhaps you do not know, my dear friend," she
wrote, "that I have now been at Tansonville for nearly
two years. I arrived here at the same time as the Germans. Everybody had tried to prevent me from leaving. I
was regarded as mad. 'What,' my friends said, 'here you
are safe in Paris and you want to go off to enemy-
occupied territory just when everybody is trying to escape
from it.' I was quite aware of the strength of this argument. But I can't help it; if I have one good quality, it is
that I am not a coward, or perhaps I should say, I am
loyal, and when I knew that my beloved Tansonville was
threatened, I simply could not leave our old bailiff to defend it alone. I felt that my place was by his side. And it
was, in fact, thanks to this decision that I succeeded in
more or less saving the house when all the other big
houses in the neighbourhood, abandoned by their panic-
stricken owners, were almost without exception reduced to
ruins—and in saving not only the house but the valuable
collections too, which dear Papa was so fond of." In a
word, Gilberte was now persuaded that she had gone to
Tansonville not, as she had written to me in 1914, in order to escape from the Germans and be in a safe place,
but on the contrary in order to face them and defend her
house against them. They had, as a matter of fact, not
stayed long at Tansonville, but since then the house had
witnessed a constant coming and going of soldiers, far
more intensive than that marching up and down the
streets of Combray which had once drawn tears to the

eyes of Françoise, and Gilberte had not ceased, as she said, this time quite truly, to live the life of the front. So that the newspapers spoke with the highest praise of her wonderful conduct and there was some question of giving her a decoration. The end of the letter was absolutely truthful. "You have no idea what this war is like, my dear friend, or of the importance that a road, a bridge, a height can assume. How often have I thought of you, of those walks of ours together which you made so delightful, through all this now ravaged countryside, where vast battles are fought to gain possession of some path, some slope which you once loved and which we so often explored together! Probably, like me, you did not imagine that obscure Roussainville and boring Méséglise, where our letters used to be brought from and where the doctor was once fetched when you were ill, would ever be famous places. Well, my dear friend, they have become for ever a part of history, with the same claim to glory as Austerlitz or Valmy. The battle of Méséglise lasted for more than eight months; the Germans lost in it more than six hundred thousand men, they destroyed Méséglise, but they did not capture it. As for the short cut up the hill which you were so fond of and which we used to call the hawthorn path, where you claim that as a small child you fell in love with me (whereas I assure you in all truthfulness it was I who was in love with you), I cannot tell you how important it has become. The huge field of corn upon which it emerges is the famous Hill 307, which you must have seen mentioned again and again in the bulletins. The French blew up the little bridge over the Vivonne which you said did not remind you of your childhood as much as you would have wished, and the

Germans have thrown other bridges across the river. For a year and a half they held one half of Combray and the French the other."

The day after I received this letter, that is to say two days before the evening on which, as I have described, I made my way through the dark streets with the sound of my footsteps in my ears and all these memories revolving in my mind, Saint-Loup, arrived from the front and very shortly to return to it, had come to see me for a few moments only, and the mere announcement of his visit had violently moved me. Françoise had been tempted to fling herself upon him, in the hope that he could obtain an exemption for the timid butcher's boy whose class was to be called up the following year. But she had been checked, without my saying anything to her, by the thought of the futility of this endeavour, for the timid slaughterer of animals had moved to another butcher's some time previously. And whether our butcher's wife was afraid of losing our custom, or whether she was telling the truth, she declared to Françoise that she did not know where the boy—who, in any case, would never make a good butcher—was working. Françoise had searched everywhere. But Paris is large and butcher's shops are numerous, and although she had visited a great many she had never succeeded in finding the timid and blood-stained young man.

When Saint-Loup came into my room I had gone up to him with that feeling of shyness, that impression of something supernatural which was in fact induced by all soldiers on leave and which one feels when one enters the presence of a man suffering from a fatal disease, who still, nevertheless, leaves his bed, gets dressed, goes for walks.

It seemed (above all it had seemed at first, for upon those who had not lived, as I had, at a distance from Paris, there had descended Habit, which cuts off from things which we have witnessed a number of times the root of profound impression and of thought which gives them their real meaning), it seemed almost that there was something cruel in these leaves granted to the men at the front. When they first came on leave, one said to oneself: "They will refuse to go back, they will desert." And indeed they came not merely from places which seemed to us unreal, because we had only heard them spoken of in the newspapers and could not conceive how a man was able to take part in these titanic battles and emerge with nothing worse than a bruise on his shoulder; it was from the shores of death, whither they would soon return, that they came to spend a few moments in our midst, incomprehensible to us, filling us with tenderness and terror and a feeling of mystery, like phantoms whom we summon from the dead, who appear to us for a second, whom we dare not question, and who could, in any case, only reply: "You cannot possibly imagine." For it is extraordinary how, in the survivors of battle, which is what soldiers on leave are, or in living men hypnotised or dead men summoned by a medium, the only effect of contact with mystery is to increase, if that be possible, the insignificance of the things people say. Such were my feelings when I greeted Robert, who still had a scar on his forehead, more august and more mysterious in my eyes than the imprint left upon the earth by a giant's foot. And I had not dared to put a single question to him and he had made only the simplest remarks to me. Remarks that even differed very little from the ones he might have made before the war, as though people, in spite of the war, continued to be what they were; the tone of conversation was the same, only the subject-matter differed—and even that not so very much!

I guessed from what he told me that in the army he had found opportunities which had gradually made him forget that Morel had behaved as badly towards him as towards his uncle. However, he still felt a great affection for him and was seized by sudden cravings to see him again, though he always postponed doing this. I thought it kinder to Gilberte not to inform Robert that to find Morel he had only to pay a call on Mme Verdurin.

I remarked apologetically to Robert how little one felt the war in Paris. He replied that even in Paris it was sometimes "pretty extraordinary." This was an allusion to a Zeppelin raid which had taken place the previous night and he went on to ask me if I had had a good view, very much as in the old days he might have questioned me about some spectacle of great aesthetic beauty. At the front, I could see, there might be a sort of bravado in saying: "Isn't it marvellous? What a pink! And that pale green!" when at any moment you might be killed, but here in Paris there could be no question of any such pose in Saint-Loup's way of speaking about an insignificant raid, which had in fact looked marvellously beautiful from our balcony when the silence of the night was broken by a display which was more than a display because it was real, with fireworks that were purposeful and protective and bugle-calls that did more than summon on parade. I spoke of the beauty of the aeroplanes climbing up into the night. "And perhaps they are even more beautiful when they come down," he said. "I grant that it is a magnificent moment when they climb, when they fly off in *constellation*, in obedience to laws as precise as those that govern the constellations of the stars—for what seems to you a mere spectacle is the rallying of the squadrons, then the orders they receive, their departure in pursuit, etc. But don't you prefer the moment, when, just as you have got used to thinking of them as stars, they break away to pursue an enemy or to return to the ground after the all-clear, the moment of *apocalypse*, when even the stars are hurled from their courses? And then the sirens, could they have been more Wagnerian, and what could be more appropriate as a salute to the arrival of the Germans?—it might have been the national anthem, with the Crown Prince and the Princesses in the imperial box, the *Wacht am Rhein*; one had to ask oneself whether they were indeed pilots and not Valkyries who were sailing upwards." He seemed to be delighted with this comparison of the pilots to Valkyries, and went on to explain it on purely musical grounds: "That's it, the music of the sirens was a 'Ride of the Valkyries'! There's no doubt about it, the Germans have to arrive before you can hear Wagner in Paris." In some ways the simile was not misleading. The town from being a black shapeless mass seemed suddenly to rise out of the abyss and the night into the luminous sky, where one after another the pilots soared upwards in answer to the heart-rending appeal of the sirens, while with a movement slower but more insidious, more alarming—for their gaze made one think of the object, still invisible but perhaps already very near, which it sought—the searchlights strayed ceaselessly to and fro, scenting the enemy, encircling him with their beams until the moment when the aeroplanes should be unleashed to bound after him in pursuit and seize him. And squadron after squadron, each pilot, as he soared thus above the town, itself now transported into the sky, resembled indeed a Valkyrie. Meanwhile on ground-level, at the height of the houses, there were also scraps of illumination, and I told Saint-Loup that, if he had been at home the previous evening, he might, while contemplating the apocalypse in the sky, at the same time have watched on the ground (as in El Greco's *Burial of Count Orgaz*, in which the two planes are distinct and parallel) a first-rate farce acted by characters in night attire, whose famous names merited a report to some successor of that Ferrari whose society paragraphs had so often provided amusement to the two of us, Saint-Loup and myself, that we used also to amuse ourselves by inventing imaginary ones. And that is what we did once more on the day I am describing, just as though we were not in the middle of a war, although our theme, the fear of the Zeppelins, was very much a "war" one: "Seen about town: the Duchesse de Guermantes magnificent in a night-dress, the Duc de Guermantes indescribable in pink pyjamas and a bath-robe, etc."

"I am sure," he said, "that in all the large hotels you would have seen American Jewesses in their night-dresses, hugging to their ravaged bosoms the pearl necklaces which will enable them to marry a ruined duke. The Ritz, on these evenings when the Zeppelins are overhead, must look like Feydeau's *Hôtel du libre échange*."

"Do you remember," I said to him, "our conversations at Doncières?"

"Ah! those were the days! What a gulf separates us from them! Will those happy times ever re-emerge

from the abyss forbidden to our plummets,
As suns rejuvenated climb the heavens,
Having washed themselves on deep sea-beds?"[5]


"But don't let's think about those conversations simply in order to remind ourselves how delightful they
were," I said. "I was attempting in them to arrive at a
certain kind of truth. What do you think, does the present war, which has thrown everything into confusion—
and most of all, so you say, the idea of war—does it
render null and void what you used to tell me then about
the types of battle, the battles of Napoleon, for instance,
which would be imitated in the wars of the future?"

"Not in the least," he said, "the Napoleonic battle
still exists, particularly in this war, since Hindenburg is
imbued with the Napoleonic spirit. His rapid movements
of troops, his feints—the device, for instance, of leaving
only a small covering force opposite one of his enemies,
while he falls with his united strength upon the other
(Napoleon in 1814) or the other stratagem of pressing
home a diversion so strongly that the enemy is compelled
to keep up his strength on a front which is not the really
important one (for example, Hindenburg's feint before
Warsaw, which tricked the Russians into concentrating
their resistance there and brought about their defeat at the
Mazurian Lakes)—his tactical withdrawals, analogous to
those with which Austerlitz, Arcola, Eckmühl began, everything in Hindenburg is Napoleonic, and we haven't
seen the end of him. I must add that if, when we are no
longer together, you try, as the war proceeds, to interpret
its events, you should not rely too exclusively on this par-

ticular aspect of Hindenburg to reveal to you the meaning of what he is doing and the key to what he is about to do. A general is like a writer who sets out to write a certain play, a certain book, and then the book itself, with the unexpected potentialities which it reveals here, the impassable obstacles which it presents there, makes him deviate to an enormous degree from his preconceived plan. You know, for instance, that a diversion should only be made against a position which is itself of considerable importance; well, suppose the diversion succeeds beyond all expectation, while the principal operation results in a deadlock: the diversion may then become the principal operation. But there is one type of Napoleonic battle which I am waiting to see Hindenburg attempt, and that is the one which consists in driving a wedge between two allies, in this case the English and ourselves."

I have said that the war had not altered the stature of Saint-Loup's intelligence, but I ought to add that this intelligence, developing in accordance with laws in which heredity counted for much, had acquired a brilliancy which I had never seen in him before. What a difference between the fair-haired boy who had once been run after by smart women or women who were hoping to become smart, and the voluble talker, the theorist who never stopped juggling with words! In another generation, grafted upon another stock, like an actor re-interpreting a part played years ago by Bressant or Delaunay, he was like a successor—pink, fair and golden, whereas the other had been half and half very dark and quite white—of M. de Charlus. It was true that he did not agree with his uncle about the war, since he had ranged himself with that section of the aristocracy which put France above everything else in the world while M. de Charlus was at heart defeatist, but nevertheless he could demonstrate to anyone who had not seen the "creator of the part" what a success could be made in the role of verbal acrobat.

"It seems that Hindenburg is a revelation," I said to him.

"An old revelation," he retorted instantly, "or a future revolution. Instead of being soft with the enemy, we should have supported Mangin in his offensive, then we might have smashed Austria and Germany and europeanised Turkey instead of balkanising France."

"But soon we shall have the help of the United States," I said.

"Meanwhile, I see here only the spectacle of the disunited states. Why refuse to make more generous concessions to Italy for fear of dechristianising France?"

"How shocked your uncle Charlus would be to hear you!" I said. "The fact is that you would be only too pleased to give the Pope another slap in the face, while your uncle is in despair at the thought of the damage that may be done to the throne of Franz Josef. And in this he says that he is in the tradition of Talleyrand and the Congress of Vienna."

"The age of the Congress of Vienna is dead and gone," he replied; "the old secret diplomacy must be replaced by concrete diplomacy. My uncle is at heart an impenitent monarchist, who can be made to swallow carps like Mme Molé and scamps like Arthur Meyer provided that both carps and scamps are *à la Chambord*. He so hates the tricolour flag that I believe he would rather

serve under the duster of the Red Bonnet, which he
would take in good faith for the white flag of the Monar-
chists."

Admittedly, this was mere play on words and Saint-
Loup was far from possessing the sometimes profound
originality of his uncle. But he was as affable and agreeable in character as the other was jealous and suspicious.
And he had remained charming and pink as he had been
at Balbec beneath his shock of golden hair. And one family characteristic he possessed in at least as high a degree
as his uncle, that attitude of mind of the Faubourg Saint-
Germain which remains deeply implanted in the men of
that world who fancy that they have most completely detached themselves from it, the attitude which combines
respect for clever men who are not of good family (a respect which flourishes, truly, only among the aristocracy,
and which makes revolutions so unjust) with a fatuous
satisfaction with themselves. Through this mixture of humility and pride, of acquired intellectual curiosity and
innate authority, M. de Charlus and Saint-Loup, by different paths, and with opposite opinions, had become,
with the gap of a generation between them, intellectuals
whom every new idea interested and talkers whom no interruption could silence. So that a not very intelligent person might, according to the humour in which he
happened to be, have found both the one and the other
either dazzling or insufferably tedious.

I had gone on walking as I turned over in my mind
this recent meeting with Saint-Loup and had come a long
way out of my way; I was almost at the Pont des Invalides. The lamps (there were very few of them, on ac-

count of the Gothas) had already been lit, a little too early
because "the clocks had been put forward" a little too
early, when the night still came rather quickly, the time
having been "changed" once and for all for the whole of
the summer just as a central heating system is turned on
or off once and for all on a fixed date; and above the city
with its nocturnal illumination, in one whole quarter of
the sky—the sky that knew nothing of summer time and
winter time and did not deign to recognise that half past
eight had become half past nine—in one whole quarter of
the sky from which the blue had not vanished there was
still a little daylight. Over that whole portion of the city
which is dominated by the towers of the Trocadéro the
sky looked like a vast sea the colour of turquoise, from
which gradually there emerged, as it ebbed, a whole line
of little black rocks, which might even have been nothing
more than a row of fishermen's nets and which were in
fact small clouds—a sea at that moment the colour of
turquoise, sweeping along with it, without their noticing,
the whole human race in the wake of the vast revolution
of the earth, that earth upon which they are mad enough
to continue their own revolutions, their futile wars, like
the war which at this very moment was staining France
crimson with blood. But if one looked for long at the sky,
this lazy, too beautiful sky which did not condescend to
change its timetable and above the city, where the lamps
had been lit, indolently prolonged its lingering day in
these bluish tones, one was seized with giddiness: it was
no longer a flat expanse of sea but a vertically stepped series of blue glaciers. And the towers of the Trocadéro
which seemed so near to the turquoise steps must, one realised, be infinitely remote from them, like the twin tow-

ers of certain towns in Switzerland which at a distance one
would suppose to be near neighbours of the upper mountain slopes.

I retraced my steps, but once I had left the Pont des
Invalides there was no longer any trace of day in the sky
and there was practically no light in the town, so that
stumbling here and there against dustbins and mistaking
one direction for another, I found to my surprise that, by
mechanically following a labyrinth of dark streets, I had
arrived on the boulevards. There, the impression of an
oriental vision which I had had earlier in the evening
came to me again, and I thought too of the Paris of an
earlier age, not now so much of the Paris of the Directory
as of the Paris of 1815. As in 1815 there was a march past
of allied troops in the most variegated uniforms; and
among them, the Africans in their red divided skirts, the
Indians in their white turbans were enough to transform
for me this Paris through which I was walking into a
whole imaginary exotic city, an oriental scene which was
at once meticulously accurate with respect to the costumes
and the colours of the faces and arbitrarily fanciful when
it came to the background, just as out of the town in
which he lived Carpaccio made a Jerusalem or a Con-
stantinople by assembling in its streets a crowd whose
marvellous motley was not more rich in colour than that
of the crowd around me. Walking close behind two
zouaves who seemed hardly to be aware of him, I noticed
a tall, stout man in a soft felt hat and a long heavy overcoat, to whose purplish face I hesitated whether I should
give the name of an actor or a painter, both equally notorious for innumerable sodomist scandals. I was certain in
any case that I was not acquainted with him; so I was not

a little surprised, when his glance met mine, to see that he appeared to be embarrassed and deliberately stopped and came towards me like a man who wants to prove that you have not surprised him in an occupation which he would prefer to remain secret. For a second I asked myself who it was that was greeting me: it was M. de Charlus. One may say that for him the evolution of his malady or the revolution of his vice had reached the extreme point at which the tiny original personality of the individual, the specific qualities he has inherited from his ancestors, are entirely eclipsed by the transit across them of some generic defect or malady which is their satellite. M. de Charlus had travelled as far as was possible from himself, or rather he was himself but so perfectly masked by what he had become, by what belonged not to him alone but to many other inverts, that for a moment I had taken him for some other invert, as he walked behind these zouaves down the wide pavement of the boulevard, for some other invert who was not M. de Charlus, who was not a great nobleman or a man of imagination and intelligence, and whose only point of resemblance to the Baron was the look that was common to them all, which in him now, at least until one had taken the trouble to observe him carefully, concealed every other quality from view.

Thus it was that, having intended to call on Mme Verdurin, I had met M. de Charlus. And certainly I should not now as in the past have found him in her drawing-room; their quarrel had grown steadily more bitter and Mme Verdurin even took advantage of present events to discredit him further. Having said for years that she found him stale, finished, more out of date in his professed audacities than the dullest philistine, she now

summed up this condemnation in such a way as to make
him an object of general aversion, by saying that he was
"pre-war." The war had set between him and the present,
so the little clan declared, an abyss which left him
stranded in the deadest of dead pasts. Besides—and this
was addressed particularly to the political world, which
was less well informed—she made him out to be just as
"bogus," just as much an "outsider" from the point of
view of social position as from that of intellectual merit.
"He sees nobody, nobody invites him," she said to
M. Bontemps, whom she easily convinced. Anyhow, there
was an element of truth in these words. The position of
M. de Charlus had changed. Caring less and less about
society, having quarrelled, because of his cantankerous
character, and having disdained, because of his high opinion of his own social importance, to reconcile himself with
most of the men and women who were the flower of society, he lived in a relative isolation which was not caused,
like that in which Mme de Villeparisis had died, by the
fact that the aristocracy had ostracised him, but which
nevertheless in the eyes of the public for two reasons appeared to be worse. The bad reputation which M. de
Charlus was now known to enjoy made ill-informed people think that it was for this reason that his company was
not sought by people whom in fact he himself made a
point of refusing to see. So that what was really the result
of his own spleen seemed to be due to the contempt of
the people upon whom he vented it. Secondly, Mme de
Villeparisis had had one great bulwark: the family. But
between his family and himself M. de Charlus had multi-
plied quarrels. His family in any case—particularly the
"old Faubourg" side of it, the Courvoisier side—had al-

ways seemed to him uninteresting. And he was far from suspecting, he who, from a spirit of opposition to the Courvoisiers, had made such audacious advances in the direction of art, that the feature in him which would most have interested, for example, a Bergotte, was precisely his kinship with the whole of this old Faubourg which he despised, and the descriptions he could have given of the almost provincial life led by his female cousins, in that district bounded by the Rue de la Chaise and the Place du Palais-Bourbon in one direction and the Rue Garancière in the other.

And then, considering the question from another point of view, less transcendent and more practical, Mme Verdurin affected to believe that he was not French. "What is his nationality exactly, isn't he an Austrian?" M. Verdurin would ask innocently. "No, certainly not," Comtesse Molé would reply, her first reaction being one rather of common sense than of resentment. "No, he is Prussian," the Mistress would say. "Yes, I know what I am talking about, he has told us countless times that he is a hereditary member of the Prussian Chamber of Peers and a Durchlaucht." "Still, the Queen of Naples told me . . ." "You know she is a dreadful spy," screamed Mme Verdurin, who had not forgotten how the fallen sovereign had behaved in her house one evening. "I know—there is absolutely no question about it—that that is what she has been living on. If we had a more energetic government, she and her kind ought all to be in a concentration camp. I mean it! In any case, you will be wise not to receive visits from that charming set, because I know that the Minister of the Interior has his eye on them, your house would be watched. I have not the slightest doubt

that for two years Charlus did nothing but spy on us all."
And thinking probably that there might be some doubt as
to the interest that the German government would show
in even the most circumstantial reports on the organisation of the little clan, Mme Verdurin went on, with a
mild and perspicacious air, like someone who knows that
the value of what she is saying will only seem greater if
she does not raise her voice: "Let me tell you, I said to
my husband the very first day: 'I don't like the way that
man wormed his way into my house. There's something
shady here.' We had a property which stood on very high
ground, looking down over a bay. Quite obviously he had
been sent by the Germans to prepare a base for their sub-
marines. There were many things which surprised me at
the time, but which I understand now. For instance, at
first, he would not come by the train with my other regular guests. I was so kind as to offer to put him up in the
house. But no, he preferred to stay at Doncières, which
was swarming with soldiers. All this stank to high heaven
of espionage."

About the first of the charges brought against the
Baron de Charlus, that of being out of date, fashionable
people were only too ready to agree with Mme Verdurin.
In this they were ungrateful, for M. de Charlus was to
some extent their poet, the man who had been able to extract from the world of fashion a sort of essential poetry,
which had in it elements of history, of beauty, of the picturesque, of the comic, of frivolous elegance. But people
in society, incapable of understanding this poetry, did not
see that it existed in their own lives; they sought for it
rather elsewhere, and placed on an infinitely higher peak
than M. de Charlus men who were much stupider than

him but who professed to despise "society" and liked instead to hold forth about sociology and political economy. M. de Charlus, for instance, took a delight in repeating unconsciously characteristic remarks of the Duchesse de Montmorency and in describing the studied charm of her clothes, and spoke of her as if she were something sublime, but this merely gave him the reputation of an utter idiot in the eyes of the sort of society women who thought that the Duchesse de Montmorency was an uninteresting fool, and that dresses are made to be worn but without the wearer appearing to give them a moment's attention, and who meanwhile gave proof of their own superior intelligence by running to hear lectures at the Sorbonne or Deschanel speak in the Chamber.

In short, people in society had become disillusioned about M. de Charlus, not from having penetrated too far, but without having penetrated at all, his rare intellectual merit. The reason why he was found to be "pre-war," old-fashioned, was that the people who are least capable of judging the worth of individuals are also the most inclined to adopt fashion as a principle by which to classify them; they have not exhausted, or even grazed the surface of, the talented men of one generation, when suddenly they are obliged to condemn them all *en bloc*, for here is a new generation with a new label which will be no better understood than its predecessor.

As for the second accusation, that of being pro-German, fashionable people because of their dislike of extreme views tended to reject it, but the charge had an unwearying and particularly cruel advocate in Morel, who, having managed to retain in the newspapers and even in society the position which M. de Charlus had first

achieved for him and then tried equally hard, but without
success, to undermine, pursued the Baron with a hatred
that was all the more infamous since, whatever the precise
relations between them had been, Morel had seen and
known the side of him that he concealed from so many
people: his profound kindness. M. de Charlus had shown
such generosity, such delicacy towards the violinist, had
been so scrupulous about fulfilling his promises to him
that, when Charlie left him, the image of the Baron that
remained in his mind was not at all that of a vicious man
(at most he regarded the Baron's vice as a disease) but of
a man with loftier ideas than any other he had ever
known, a man with extraordinary capacity for feeling, a
kind of saint. So little disposed was he to deny this that
even after the quarrel he would say in all sincerity to a
young man's parents: "You can trust your son to him, he
can only have the most excellent influence on him." And
so when by his articles in the papers he tried to make him
suffer, it was in his imagination not vice but virtue incarnate that he was scourging. Not long before the war there
had begun to appear short "pieces," transparent to the so-
called initiated, in which M. de Charlus was most monstrously libelled. Of one, entitled *The Misfortunes of a
Dowager ending in -us or the Latter Days of the Baroness*,
Mme Verdurin had bought fifty copies in order to be able
to lend it to her acquaintances and M. Verdurin, declaring
that Voltaire himself did not write better, took to reading
it aloud. Since the war the tone of these pieces had
changed. Not only was the Baron's inversion denounced,
but also his alleged Germanic nationality: "Frau Bosch,"
"Frau von den Bosch" were the names habitually used to
designate M. de Charlus. A little composition of a poetic

nature appeared with the title—borrowed from some of Beethoven's dances—*Une Allemande*. Finally two short stories, *The Uncle from America and the Aunt from Frankfurt* and *The Jolly Rear Admiral*, read in proof in the little clan, had delighted even Brichot himself, who exclaimed: "So long as the most high and puissant Lady Censorship does not blue-pencil us!" The articles themselves were cleverer than their ridiculous titles. Their style derived from Bergotte but in a way which, for the reason that follows, perhaps no one but myself perceived. Bergotte's *writings* had had not the slightest influence on Morel. The fertilisation had been effected in a most unusual way, which I record here only because of its rarity. I have described earlier the very special manner which Bergotte had, when he spoke, of choosing and pronouncing his words. Morel, who for a long time had been in the habit of meeting him at the Saint-Loups', had at that period done "imitations" of him, in which he exactly mimicked his voice, using just the words that Bergotte would have chosen. And now that he had taken to writing, Morel used to transcribe passages of "spoken Bergotte," but without first transposing them in the way which would have turned them into "written Bergotte." Not many people having known Bergotte as a talker, the tone of his voice was not recognised, since it differed from the style of his pen. This oral fertilisation is so rare that I have thought it worth mentioning here. The flowers that it produces are, however, always sterile.

Morel, who was in the Press Office, found after a while, his French blood boiling in his veins like the juice of the grapes of Combray, that there was not much to be said for being in an office during the war, and he ended by joining up, although Mme Verdurin did everything she could to persuade him to stay in Paris. Admittedly she was indignant that M. de Cambremer, at his age, should be on the general staff, and of every man who did not come to her parties she would say: "I can't think where the wretch has managed to hide himself all this time," and if someone assured her that the wretch had been in the front line since the first day, would reply, without any scruple about telling a lie or perhaps just because she was so used to getting things wrong: "Not at all, he has not budged from Paris, he's doing something about as danger-ous as taking a minister for walks, I know what I am talk-ing about, you can take my word for it, I was told by someone who has seen him at it"; but where the faithful were concerned it was not the same thing, she did not want to let them go off to the war, and looked upon it as a great "bore" that caused them to defect. And so she pulled every possible string to keep them in Paris, which would give her the double pleasure of having them at her dinner-parties and at the same time, before they arrived or after they left, making scathing remarks about their in-activity. However, the faithful in each case had to be made to agree to the soft job she had found for them and she was bitterly distressed to find Morel recalcitrant; in vain had she said to him over and over again: "But don't you see, you are *serving* in your office, and serving more than you would be at the front. The important thing is to be useful, to be really part of the war, to be in it. There are those who are in it, and there are the shirkers. Now you, you're in it, you have nothing to worry about, every-body knows this, nobody's going to throw stones at you." In the same way, in different circumstances, although men were at that time not so scarce and she had not been, as she was now, obliged to have a preponderance of women, if a man had lost his mother she had not hesitated to try and convince him that there was no objection to his continuing to come to her parties. "Grief is worn in the heart. If you wanted to go to a dance" (she never gave one) "I should be the first to advise you not to do it, but here, at my little Wednesdays, or in a box, nobody will be in the least surprised. We all know you have had a great grief . . ." Men were scarcer now and mourning more frequent though no longer needed to prevent men from going to parties, the war itself having put a stop to that. Mme Verdurin hung on to the survivors. She tried to persuade them that they were more useful to France if they stayed in Paris, just as in the past she would have assured them that the deceased would have been happy to see them enjoying themselves. In spite of all her efforts she did not have many men; perhaps sometimes she regretted that between herself and M. de Charlus she had brought about a rupture which left no hope of a return to their former relations.

But, if M. de Charlus and Mme Verdurin no longer saw one another, they continued nevertheless, Mme Verdurin to entertain, M. de Charlus to pursue his pleasures, very much as if nothing had changed. A few little differences there were, but of no great importance: Cottard, for instance, was now to be seen at Mme Verdurin's parties in a colonel's uniform which might have come out of Loti's *Ile du Rêve* (it bore a striking resemblance to that of a Haitian admiral and at the same time, with its broad sky-blue ribbon, recalled that of the "Children of Mary"); and M. de Charlus, finding himself in a town from which

the mature men for whom he had hitherto had a taste had
vanished, followed the example of those Frenchmen who,
after being womanisers in France, go to live in the
colonies: from necessity he had acquired first the habit of
and then the taste for little boys.

But the first of these newly acquired characteristics
was not in evidence for long: Cottard soon died "facing
the enemy," so the newspapers said, though he had never
left Paris—but it was true that he had exerted himself too
much for his age—and he was soon followed by M. Verdurin, whose death caused grief to one person only and
that, strangely enough, was Elstir. For whereas I had been
able to study Elstir's work from a point of view which
was to some extent objective, the painter himself, particularly as he grew older, linked it superstitiously to the society which had provided him with models and which had
also, after thus transforming itself within him through the
alchemy of impressions into a work of art, given him his
public, his spectators. More and more he was inclined to
believe materialistically that a not inconsiderable part of
beauty is inherent in objects, and just as, at the beginning, he had adored in Mme Elstir the archetype of that
rather heavy beauty which he had pursued and caressed in
his paintings and in tapestries, so now in the death of
M. Verdurin he saw the disappearance of one of the last
relics of the social framework, the perishable framework—
as swift to crumble away as the very fashions in clothes
which form part of it—which supports an art and certifies
its authenticity, and he was as saddened and distressed by
this event as a painter of *fêtes galantes* might have been by
the Revolution which destroyed the elegances of the eighteenth century, or Renoir by the disappearance of Mont-

martre and the Moulin de la Galette; but more than this, with M. Verdurin he saw disappear the eyes, the brain, which had had the truest vision of his painting, in which, in the form of a cherished memory, his painting was to some extent inherent. No doubt young men had come along who also loved painting, but painting of another kind; they had not, like Swann, like M. Verdurin, received lessons in taste from Whistler, lessons in truth from Monet, lessons which alone would have qualified them to judge Elstir with justice. So the death of M. Verdurin left Elstir feeling lonelier, although they had not been on speaking terms for a great many years: it was for him as though a little of the beauty of his own work had been eclipsed, since there had perished a little of the universe's sum total of awareness of its special beauty.

As for the change which had overtaken the pleasures of M. de Charlus, this was no more than intermittent: by maintaining a correspondence with numerous soldiers at the front, who sometimes came on leave, he did not altogether lack the company of mature men.

At the time when I believed what people said I should have been tempted, hearing Germany, or later Bulgaria or Greece, protest their pacific intentions, to give credence to these statements. But since life with Albertine and with Françoise had accustomed me to suspect in them thoughts and projects which they did not disclose, I now allowed no pronouncement, however specious, of William II or Ferdinand of Bulgaria or Constantine of Greece, to deceive my instinct and prevent it from divining what each one of them was plotting. Of course my quarrels with Françoise or with Albertine had been merely private quarrels, of interest only to the life of that little cell, en-

dowed with mind, that a human being is. But just as
there are animal bodies and human bodies, each one of
which is an assemblage of cells as large in relation to a
single cell as Mont Blanc, so there exist huge organised
accumulations of individuals which are called nations:
their life does no more than repeat on a larger scale the
lives of their constituent cells, and anybody who is incapable of comprehending the mystery, the reactions, the
laws of these smaller lives, will only make futile pronouncements when he talks about struggles between nations. But if he is master of the psychology of individuals,
then these colossal masses of conglomerated individuals
will assume in his eyes, as they confront one another, a
beauty more potent than that of the struggle which arises
from a mere conflict between two characters; and they
will seem to him as huge as the body of a tall man would
seem to the infusoria of which more than ten thousand
would be required to fill the space of a cubic millimetre.
So it had been now for some time past: the huge irregular
geometric figure France, filled to its perimeter with millions of little polygons of various shapes, and another figure filled with an even greater number of polygons,
Germany, had been engaged in one of these quarrels. And
considered from this point of view, the body Germany
and the body France, and the allied and enemy bodies,
were behaving to some extent like individuals, and the
blows which they were exchanging were governed by the
innumerable rules of that art of boxing which Saint-Loup
had expounded to me; but since, even if one chose to consider them as individuals, they were at the same time
giant assemblages of individuals, the quarrel took on immense and magnificent forms, like the surge of a million-

waved ocean which tries to shatter an age-old line of cliffs, or like gigantic glaciers which with their slow destructive oscillations attempt to break down the frame of mountains which surrounds them.

But in spite of this, life continued almost unchanged for many of these who have played a part in this story, and not least for M. de Charlus and the Verdurins, just as if the Germans had not been as near them as they were, since the threat of a danger momentarily checked but permanently alive leaves us absolutely indifferent if we do not picture it to ourselves. People, as they go about their pleasures, do not normally stop to think that, if certain moderating and weakening influences should happen to be suspended, the proliferation of infusoria would attain its maximum theoretical rate and after a very few days the organisms that might have been contained in a cubic millimetre would take a leap of many millions of miles and become a mass a million times greater than the sun, having in the process destroyed all our oxygen and all the substances on which we live, so that there would exist neither humanity nor animals nor earth, nor do they reflect that an irremediable and by no means improbable catastrophe may one day be generated in the ether by the incessant and frenzied activity which lies behind the apparent immutability of the sun; they busy themselves with their own affairs without thinking about these two worlds, the one too small, the other too large for us to be aware of the cosmic menaces with which they envelop us.

So it was that the Verdurins gave dinner-parties (then, after a time, Mme Verdurin gave them alone, for M. Verdurin died) and M. de Charlus went about his pleasures and hardly ever stopped to reflect that the Germans—immobilised, it is true, by a bloody barrier perpetually renewed—were only an hour by car from Paris. The Verdurins, one would imagine, did think about this fact, since they had a political salon in which every evening they and their friends discussed the situation not only of the armies but of the fleets. They thought certainly of these hecatombs of regiments annihilated and passengers swallowed by the waves; but there is a law of inverse proportion which multiplies to such an extent anything that concerns our own welfare and divides by such a formidable figure anything that does not concern it, that the death of unknown millions is felt by us as the most insignificant of sensations, hardly even as disagreeable as a draught. Mme Verdurin, who suffered even more from her headaches now that she could no longer get croissants to dip in her breakfast coffee, had eventually obtained a prescription from Cottard permitting her to have them specially made in a certain restaurant of which we have spoken. This had been almost as difficult to wangle with the authorities as the appointment of a general. The first of these special croissants arrived on the morning on which the newspapers reported the sinking of the *Lusitania*. As she dipped it in her coffee and gave a series of little flicks to her newspaper with one hand so as to make it stay open without her having to remove her other hand from the cup, "How horrible!" she said. "This is something more horrible than the most terrible stage tragedy." But the death of all these drowned people must have been reduced a thousand million times before it impinged upon her, for even as, with her mouth full, she made these distressful observations, the expression which spread over her face, brought there (one must suppose) by the savour of that so precious remedy against headaches, the croissant, was in fact one of satisfaction and pleasure.

As for M. de Charlus, his case was a little different, but worse even, for he went beyond not passionately desiring the victory of France: he desired rather, without admitting it to himself, that Germany should, if not triumph, at least not be crushed as everybody hoped she would be. And for this attitude of his the reason was, again, that the great collections of individuals called nations themselves behave to some extent like individuals. The logic that governs them is an inner logic, wrought and perpetually re-wrought by passions, like that of men and women at grips with one another in an amorous or domestic quarrel, the quarrel of a son with his father, or of a cook with her mistress, or a wife with her husband. The party who is in the wrong believes nevertheless that he is in the right—this was so in the case of Germany—and the party who is in the right sometimes supports his excellent cause with arguments which appear to him to be irrefutable only because they answer to his own passionate feelings. In these quarrels of individuals, the surest way of being convinced of the excellence of the cause of one party or the other is actually to be that party: a spectator will never to the same extent give his unqualified approval. Now within a nation the individual, if he is truly part of the nation, is simply a cell of the nation-individual. It is ridiculous to talk about the power of propaganda. Had the French been told that they were going to be beaten, no single Frenchman would have given way to despair any more than he would if he had been told that he was going to be killed by the Berthas. The real propaganda is what—if we are genuinely a living member of a nation—we tell ourselves because we have hope, hope being a symbol of a nation's instinct of self-preservation. To remain blind to the unjustness of the cause of the individual "Germany," to recognise at every moment the justness of the cause of the individual "France," the surest way was not for a German to be without judgment, or for a Frenchman to possess it, it was, both for the one and for the other, to be possessed of patriotism. M. de Charlus, who had rare moral qualities, who was susceptible to pity, generous, capable of affection and devotion, on the other hand for various reasons—among which the fact that his mother had been a Duchess of Bavaria may have played a part—did not have patriotism. He belonged, in consequence, no more to the body France than to the body Germany. Even I myself, had I been devoid of patriotism, had I not felt myself to be one of the cells of the body France, could not, it seems to me, have judged the quarrel in the manner in which I might have judged it in the past. In my adolescence, when I believed word for word what I was told, I should no doubt, hearing the German government protest its good faith, have been tempted to believe that this good faith existed; but I had learned long ago that our thoughts do not always accord with our words; not only had I one day, from the window on the staircase, discovered a Charlus whose existence I did not suspect; more important, in Françoise, and then, alas, in Albertine, I had seen the formation of opinions and projects so contrary to their words that now, even in the role of mere spectator, I should not have allowed any of the pronouncements of the Kaiser or the King of Bulgaria to deceive my instinct. But after all I can only conjecture what I might have done if I had not been an actor in the drama, if I had not been a part of the actor France in the same way as, in my quarrels with Albertine, my sad gaze and the choking feeling in my throat had been parts of the individual "me" who was passionately interested in my cause; I could not arrive at detachment. That of M. de Charlus was complete. And given that he was nothing more than a spectator, and that, without being genuinely French, he was living in France, there was every reason why he was likely to be pro-German. In the first place, he was very intelligent and in every country fools form the bulk of the population; no doubt, had he lived in Germany, the German fools defending foolishly and with passion an unjust cause would have irritated him; but living as he did in France, the French fools defending foolishly and with passion a just cause irritated him quite as much. The logic of passion, even if it happens to be in the service of the best possible cause, is never irrefutable for the man who is not himself passionate. Inevitably M. de Charlus with his critical intelligence seized on every weak point in the reasoning of the patriots. And then the complacency that an imbecile derives from the excellence of his cause, and the certainty of victory, are particularly irritating phenomena. Inevitably M. de Charlus was irritated by the triumphant optimism of people who did not know Germany and Germany's strength as he did, who believed every month in a crushing victory for the following month, and at the end of the year were as confident in making fresh predictions as though they had never, with equal confidence, made false ones—which they had, however, forgotten, saying, if they were reminded of them, that it "was not the same thing." (Yet M. de Charlus, profound as his intelligence was in some directions, would perhaps have failed to see that in art "This is not the same thing" is what the detractors of Manet return to those who tell them "People said the same thing about Delacroix."

Then again, M. de Charlus was merciful, the idea of a vanquished opponent caused him pain, he was always on the side of the underdog, he refrained from reading the law reports in the newspapers in order not to have to suffer in his own flesh from the anguish of the condemned man and from the impossibility of assassinating the judge, the executioner and the crowd that stood gloating to see "justice done." He was certain in any case that France could not be defeated now, and he knew on the other hand that the Germans were suffering from famine and would be obliged sooner or later to surrender unconditionally. And this idea too he more particularly disliked owing to the fact that he was living in France. His memories of Germany, after all, were distant, while the French who spoke of the crushing defeat of Germany with a joy which disgusted him, were people whose defects were known to him, their personalities unsympathetic. In such circumstances we pity more readily those whom we do not know, whom we merely imagine, than those who are near us in the vulgarity of daily life, unless—once again—we ourselves altogether are the latter and form but one flesh with them, since patriotism accomplishes the miracle that we are "for" our country as in a quarrel between lovers we are "for" ourself.

So the war for M. de Charlus was an extraordinarily fertile breeding-ground of those hatreds he was prone to which sprang up in him in a moment and had only a very brief existence, during which, however, he would have abandoned himself to any violent impulse. When he read the newspapers, the air of triumph with which day after day the journalists portrayed Germany as beaten—"the Beast at bay, reduced to impotence"—while the contrary was only too true, their cheerful and savage stupidity, intoxicated him with rage. The newspapers at this moment were written partly by well-known men who found this a means of "serving their country again," men such as Brichot, Norpois, Morel even, and Legrandin. M. de Charlus longed to meet them, to heap the most bitter sarcasms on their heads. Always particularly well-informed about sexual irregularities, he knew of some in individuals who, believing their own to be unknown, complacently denounced such things in the sovereigns of the "Empires of Prey," in Wagner, etc. He had a furious desire to find himself face to face with these men, to rub their noses in their own vice before the eyes of the world and leave them, these insulters of a vanquished opponent, dishonoured and gasping for breath.

Finally, M. de Charlus had also more particular reasons for being the pro-German that he was. One was that, himself a man of the world, he had lived much among men of the world, honourable men and men of honour, men who will not shake hands with a scoundrel; he was acquainted with their scruples and also with their hardness, he knew them to be insensible to the tears of a man whom they expel from a club or with whom they refuse to fight a duel, even if this act of "moral hygiene" should bring about the death of the black sheep's mother. And so in spite of himself, whatever admiration he might feel for England and for the admirable fashion in which she entered the war, nevertheless this impeccable England—in-

capable of falsehood but forbidding the entry of wheat
and milk into Germany—was in his eyes a little too much
the man of honour among nations, the professional second
in duels, the arbiter of affairs of honour, whereas his experience told him that men of a different type, men with a
blot upon their reputation, scoundrels like some of Dostoievsky's characters, may in fact be better—though I
have never been able to understand why he identified the
Germans with such men, since falsehood and deceit are in
themselves no evidence of a kind heart, which is something the Germans do not seem to have displayed.

One last trait must be mentioned to complete this account of the pro-Germanism of M. de Charlus: he owed
it, and through a most bizarre reaction, to his "Charlusism." He found the Germans very ugly, perhaps because they were rather too near to his own blood—it was
the Moroccans he was mad about and even more the
Anglo-Saxons, in whom he saw living statues by Phidias.
Now in him pleasure was not unaccompanied by a certain
idea of cruelty of which I had not at that time learned the
full force: the man whom he loved appeared to him in the
guise of a delightful torturer. In taking sides against the
Germans he would have seemed to himself to be acting as
he did only in his hours of physical pleasure, to be acting,
that is, in a manner contrary to his merciful nature, fired
with passion for seductive evil and helping to crush virtuous ugliness. This too was his reaction at the time of the
murder of Rasputin, an event which, happening as it did
at a supper-party à la Dostoievsky, caused a general surprise because people found in it so strong a Russian
flavour (this impression would have been stronger still
had the public not been unaware of aspects of the case

that were perfectly well known to M. de Charlus), because life disappoints us so often that in the end we come to believe that literature bears no relation to it and we are therefore astounded when we see the precious ideas that literature has revealed to us display themselves, without fear of getting spoiled, gratuitously, naturally, in the midst of daily life, when we see, for instance, that a supper-party and a murder taking place in Russia actually have something Russian about them.

The war dragged on indefinitely and those who, already several years earlier, had reported on good authority that negotiations for peace had been begun, even specifying the clauses of the treaty, were at no pains now, when they talked to you, to make excuses for their previous false rumours. They had forgotten them and were ready in all sincerity to propagate others which they would forget just as quickly. It was the period when there were constant Gotha raids; the air was perpetually buzzing with the vibration, vigilant and sonorous, of French aeroplanes. But at intervals the siren rang out like the heart-rending scream of a Valkyrie—the only German music to have been heard since the war—until the moment when the fire-engines announced that the alert was over, while beside them, like an invisible street-urchin, the all-clear at regular intervals commented on the good news and hurled its cry of joy into the air.

M. de Charlus was astonished to see that even men like Brichot who before the war had been militarists and had never ceased to reproach France for her lack of military preparedness, were not content now with reproaching Germany for the excesses of her militarism, but criticised even her admiration of the army. No doubt they ex-

pressed quite different opinions the moment there was
any danger of slowing down the war against Germany and
continued, for the best reasons, to denounce the pacifists
of their own country. But Brichot, for example, having
consented, in spite of his bad eyesight, to discuss in some
lectures certain works which had appeared in neutral
countries, gave high praise to a novel by a Swiss author
which has a satirical passage about two children—militarists in embryo—who are struck dumb with symbolic
admiration at the sight of a dragoon. There were other
reasons why this satire was likely to displease M. de
Charlus, who deemed that a dragoon may be a very beautiful thing. But above all he did not understand Brichot's
admiration, if not for the book, which the Baron had not
read, at least for its spirit, so different from that which
had animated Brichot himself before the war. At that time
everything that a military man did was right, even the irregularities of General de Boisdeffre, the disguises and
strategies of Colonel du Paty de Clam, the forgery of
Colonel Henry. By what extraordinary volte-face (it was
in reality merely another aspect of the same very noble
passion, the passion of patriotism, which, from being militarist when it was struggling against Dreyfusism, a phenomenon of anti-militarist tendencies, had been obliged
itself to become almost anti-militarist now that the struggle was against the hyper-militaristic Germany) had Brichot come to exclaim: "O marvellous and mighty
spectacle, fit lure for the youth of an age that is all brutality and knows only the cult of force: a dragoon! Well may
one judge what the base soldiery will be of a generation
reared in the cult of these manifestations of brutal force."
He approved too of another Swiss novelist, Spitteler, who

"wanting something to oppose to the hideous conception of the sword supreme, symbolically exiled to the depths of the forests the dreamy figure, mocked, calumniated and solitary, whom he calls the Mad Student, his delightful incarnation of the sweetness—unfashionable, alas, and perhaps soon to be forgotten if the grim rule of the ancient god of the militarists is not destroyed—the adorable sweetness of the times of peace."

"Now tell me," M. de Charlus said to me, "you know Cottard and you know Cambremer. Every time I see them, they talk to me about Germany's extraordinary lack of psychology. But between ourselves, do you think that hitherto they have cared much about psychology, or that even now they are capable of giving proof of any skill in it? You may be sure that I am not exaggerating. Even if he is talking about the very greatest of Germans, about Nietzsche or Goethe himself, you will hear Cottard say: 'with the habitual lack of psychology which characterises the Teutonic race.' Naturally there are things in the war which cause me greater distress, but you must admit that this is exasperating. Norpois is more intelligent, I grant you, although since the beginning of the war he has on every occasion been wrong. But what can one say of these articles of Brichot's which are arousing universal enthusiasm? You know as well as I do, my dear sir, the merit of the man, whom I like very much, even after the schism which has cut me off from his little church, which causes me to see much less of him than I used to. But still I have a certain regard for this usher with the gift of the gab and a vast amount of learning, and I confess that it is very touching that at his age—and with his strength failing as it clearly has been failing for some years past—he should, as he says, have taken it upon himself to 'serve again.' But after all, good intentions are one thing, talent is another, and talent Brichot has never had. I admit that I share his admiration for certain elements of greatness in the present war. I do, however, find it strange that a blind partisan of antiquity like Brichot, who could not be sarcastic enough about Zola for discovering more poetry in a working-class home or a coal-mine than in the famous palaces of history, or about Goncourt for elevating Diderot above Homer and Watteau above Raphael, should incessantly drum into our ears that Thermopylae and even Austerlitz were nothing compared with Vauquois. And this time, to make things worse, the public, after resisting the modernists of literature and art, is falling into line with the modernists of war, because it is an accepted fashion to think like this and also because little minds are crushed, not by the beauty, but by the hugeness of the action. It is true that *kolossal* is now spelt only with a *k*, but fundamentally, what people are bowing the knee to is simply the colossal. By the way, talking of Brichot, have you seen Morel? I am told that he wants to see me again. He has only to take the first step. I am the older man, it is not for me to make a move."

Unfortunately only the next day, to anticipate a little, M. de Charlus found himself face to face with Morel in the street; Morel, to inflame his jealousy, took him by the arm and told him various tales which were more or less true and which agitated M. de Charlus and made him feel that he needed Morel's presence beside him that evening, that he must not be allowed to go anywhere else. But the young man, catching sight of a friend of his own age, quickly said good-bye to M. de Charlus, whereupon the

Baron, hoping that this threat—which naturally he would never carry out—would make Morel stay, said to him: "Take care, I shall have my revenge." Morel, however, went off with a laugh, giving his astonished young friend a pat on the neck and putting his arm round his waist.

No doubt the remark which M. de Charlus had just made to me about Morel's wishing to see him was proof of the extent to which love—and that of the Baron must have been extremely persistent—while it makes a man more imaginative and quicker to take offence, at the same time makes him more credulous and less proud. But when M. de Charlus went on: "He is a boy who is mad about women and thinks of nothing else," his words were truer than he thought. He said this out of vanity and out of love, so that people might suppose that Morel's attachment to him had not been followed by others of the same nature. I certainly did not believe a word of it, I who had seen, what M. de Charlus still did not know, that for fifty francs Morel had once given himself to the Prince de Guermantes for a night. And if, when he saw M. de Charlus pass in the street, Morel (except on the days when, from a need to confess, he would bump into him so as to have the opportunity to say gloomily: "Oh! I am so sorry, I quite see that I have behaved disgustingly towards you"), seated at a café on the pavement with his friends, would join them in noisily pointing at the Baron and making those little clucking noises with which people make fun of an old invert, I was persuaded that this was in order to conceal his own activities; and that likewise, taken aside by the Baron, each one of these public accusers would have done everything that the latter asked of him. I was wrong. If a strange development had brought

to inversion—and in every social class—men like Saint-
Loup who were furthest removed from it, a movement in
the contrary direction had detached from these practices
those in whom they were most habitual. In some the
change had been wrought by tardy religious scruples, by
the emotion they had felt when certain scandals had
blazed into publicity, or by the fear of non-existent dis-
eases in which they had been made to believe either, in all
sincerity, by a relative who was often a concierge or a
valet, or, disingenuously, by a jealous lover who had
thought that in this way he would keep for himself alone
a young man whom he had, on the contrary, succeeded in
detaching from himself as well as from others. Thus it
was that the former lift-boy at Balbec would now not
have accepted for silver or gold propositions which he had
come to regard as no less criminal than treasonable pro-
posals from the enemy. In the case of Morel, however, his
refusal of all offers without exception, as to which M. de
Charlus had unwittingly spoken a truth which at one and
the same time justified his illusions and destroyed his
hopes, came from the fact that, two years after having left
M. de Charlus, he had fallen in love with a woman whom
he now lived with and that she, having the stronger will
of the two, had managed to impose upon him an absolute
fidelity. So that Morel, who at the time when M. de
Charlus was showering so much money upon him had
given a night to the Prince de Guermantes for fifty francs,
would not now have accepted from the latter or from any
other man whatever an offer even of fifty thousand. In
default of honour and disinterestedness, his mistress had
inculcated in him some concern for people's opinion of
him, which made him not averse even to demonstrating,

with a show of bravado, that all the money in the world meant nothing to him when it was offered on certain conditions. Thus, in the flowering of the human species, the interplay of different psychological laws operates always in such a way as to compensate for any process that might otherwise, in one direction or the other, through plethora or through rarefaction, bring about the annihilation of the race. And thus, too, among flowers, a similar wisdom, which Darwin was the first to bring to light, governs their different modes of fertilisation, opposing them successively one to another.

"It is a strange thing," M. de Charlus went on, in the shrill little voice with which he sometimes spoke, "I hear people who appear to be perfectly happy all day long and enjoy their cocktails, declare that they will never last until the end of the war, that their hearts won't stand it, that they can think of nothing else, that they will quite suddenly die. And what is really extraordinary is that this does in fact happen! How curious it is! Is it a question of nourishment, because the food they eat is all so badly prepared now, or is it because, to prove their zeal, they harness themselves to tasks which are useless but destroy the mode of life which kept them alive? Anyhow, I have noted an astonishing number of these strange premature deaths, premature at least from the point of view of the deceased. I forget what I was saying to you just now, about Norpois and his admiration for the war. But what a singular manner he has of writing about it! First, have you noticed the pullulation in his articles of new expressions which, when they have eventually worn themselves out by dint of being employed day after day—for really Norpois is indefatigable, I think the death of my aunt

Villeparisis must have given him a second youth—are immediately replaced by yet other commonplaces? In the old
days I remember you used to amuse yourself by recording
the fashionable phrases which appeared and had their
vogue and then disappeared: 'he who sows the wind reaps
the whirlwind'; 'the dogs bark, but the caravan moves on';
'give me a good policy and I will give you good finances,
as Baron Louis said'; 'these are symptoms which it would
be exaggerated to take tragically but wise to take seriously'; 'to work for the King of Prussia' (this last, inevitably, has come to life again). Well, since then, alas,
how many of the species have I seen born and die! We
have had 'the scrap of paper,' 'the Empires of Prey,' 'the
famous *Kultur* which consists in massacring defenceless
women and children,' 'victory belongs, as the Japanese
say, to the side which can hold out for a quarter of an
hour longer than the other,' 'the Germano-Turanians,'
'scientific barbarism,' 'if we want to win the war, as Mr
Lloyd George has forcibly said' (but that's out of date
now), and 'the fighting spirit of our troops' or 'the pluck
of our troops.' Even the syntax of the excellent Norpois
has undergone in consequence of the war as profound a
change as the baking of bread or the speed of transport.
Have you observed that the excellent man, wanting to
proclaim his own desires as a truth on the verge of being
realised, does not dare nevertheless to employ the future
pure and simple, since this would run the risk of being
contradicted by events, but has adopted as a sign of future tense the verb 'to know'?"

I confessed to M. de Charlus that I did not quite understand what he meant.

(I ought to mention here that the Duc de Guermantes

by no means shared his brother's pessimism. Further-more, he was as anglophile as M. de Charlus was anglo-phobe. And he regarded M. Caillaux as a traitor who deserved a thousand times over to be shot. When his brother asked him for proofs of the man's treason, M. de Guermantes replied that, if we were only to convict peo-ple who signed a statement saying "I am a traitor," the crime of treason would never be punished. But in case I should not have occasion to return to the subject, I will mention also that a few years later, when Caillaux was on trial, the Duc de Guermantes, animated as he was by the purest anti-Caillautism, met an English military attaché and his wife, an exceptionally cultivated couple with whom he made friends, as he had done at the time of the Dreyfus case with the three charming ladies; that on the first day of the acquaintance he was astounded, talking of Caillaux, whom he regarded as obviously guilty and cer-tain to be convicted, to hear the cultivated and charming couple say: "But he will probably be acquitted, there is absolutely no evidence against him." M. de Guermantes tried to argue that M. de Norpois, in the witness box, had fixed the unhappy Caillaux with his gaze and said to him: "You are the Giolitti of France, yes, Monsieur Caillaux, you are the Giolitti of France." But the cultivated and charming couple had smiled, made fun of M. de Norpois, cited proofs of his senility and concluded that, though Le Figaro might have said that he had addressed these words to "the unhappy M. Caillaux," he had probably in fact addressed them to a highly amused M. Caillaux. The Duc de Guermantes lost no time in changing his opinions. That this change could be brought about by the influence of an Englishwoman is not so extraordinary as one might have supposed had it been foretold even as late as 1919, when the English still spoke of the Germans only as "the Huns" and demanded savage penalties for the guilty. For their opinions too had changed and now—less than a year later—they approved every decision which was likely to distress France and be of help to Germany.)

To return to M. de Charlus: "Yes," he said, in reply to my confession that I did not quite understand. "I mean exactly what I say: 'to know,' in the articles of Norpois, indicates the future, it indicates, that is to say, the desires of Norpois, and indeed the desires of us all," he added, perhaps without complete sincerity. "I am sure you will agree with me. If 'to know' had not become simply a sign of the future tense, one might just find it intelligible for the subject of this verb to be a country. For instance, every time Norpois says: 'America would not know how to remain indifferent to these repeated violations of international law,' 'the Dual Monarchy would not know how to fail to come to its senses,' it is clear that such phrases express the desires of Norpois (they are also mine, and yours)—but here nevertheless the verb can still just retain its original meaning, for a country can 'know,' America can 'know,' the Dual Monarchy itself can 'know' (in spite of its eternal 'lack of psychology'). But when Norpois writes: 'These systematic devastations would not know how to persuade the neutrals,' 'the region of the Lakes would not know how to fail to fall speedily into the hands of the Allies,' 'the results of these neutralist elections would not know how to reflect the opinion of the vast majority of the country,' there is no longer any possibility of doubt. For it is certain that these devastations, these regions, these electoral results are inanimate things which cannot 'know.' And in using this formula Norpois is simply addressing to the neutrals an injunction (which, I regret to say, they do not appear to be obeying) to abandon their neutrality, or to the region of the Lakes an injunction no longer to belong to the 'Boches' " (M. de Charlus gave the impression of having to pluck up courage to pronounce the word "Boche," very much as in the past, in the "tram" at Balbec, he had when he had talked about men whose taste is not for women).

"And then, have you noticed the wily fashion in which, ever since 1914, Norpois has begun his articles to the neutrals? He starts by declaring that of course it is not for France to interfere in the politics of Italy (or of Romania or Bulgaria or whatever country it may be). These powers alone must decide, in full independence and with only their own national interests in view, whether or no it is their duty to abandon neutrality. But if these opening statements of the article (what would once have been called the exordium) are disinterested, the sequel is generally much less so. 'Nevertheless'—this is the gist of what Norpois goes on to say—'it is quite clear that only those nations will derive a material benefit from the struggle which have ranged themselves on the side of Law and Justice. It cannot be expected that the Allies should reward, by bestowing upon them the territories which for centuries have resounded with the groans of their oppressed brethren, those peoples who, taking the line of least resistance, have not drawn their sword in the service of the Allies.' Once he has taken this first step towards a counsel of intervention, there is no holding Norpois, it is not only the principles but the moment of intervention as to which, with less and less attempt at disguise, he delivers advice. 'Certainly,' he says, sailing, as he himself would say, under false colours, 'it is for Italy, for Romania alone to decide when the hour has come to strike and what form their intervention shall take. They cannot, however, be unaware that, if they protract their tergiversations, they run the risk of losing their opportunity. Already the hoofs of the Russian cavalry are sending a shiver of unspeakable panic through the trapped millions of Germany. It must be evident that the peoples who have done nothing more than fly to the help of that victory of which already we see the resplendent dawn, will have no right or title to the reward that they may still, if they hasten, etc.' It is like the notices you see at the theatre: 'Book now. The last remaining seats will soon be sold.' And what makes this reasoning all the stupider is that Norpois has to revise it every six months, saying to Romania at regular intervals: 'The hour has come for Romania to determine whether or no she wishes to realise her national aspirations. Any further delay and it may be too late.' But though he has been saying this for three years, not only has the 'too late' not yet come, the offers that are made to Romania are constantly being improved. In the same way he invites France, etc., to intervene in Greece by virtue of her status as a protective power because the treaty that bound Greece to Serbia has not been observed. But, candidly, if France were not at war and did not desire the assistance or the benevolent neutrality of Greece, would she take it into her head to intervene as a protective power? Those moral sentiments which make France raise her voice in horror because Greece has not kept her engagements towards Serbia, are they not silent the moment it is a question of the equally flagrant viola-

tion of treaties by Romania or Italy, which countries—
rightly I think, and the same is true of Greece—have
failed to carry out their obligations (though these are less
imperative and less far-reaching than they are said to be)
as allies of Germany? The truth is that people see everything through the medium of their newspaper, and what
else could they do, seeing that they are not personally acquainted with the men or the events under discussion? At
the time of the Affair in which you took so passionate and
so bizarre an interest, in that epoch from which it is now
the convention to say that we are separated by centuries—
for the philosophers of the war have spread the doctrine
that all links with the past are broken—I was shocked to
see men and women of my family express high esteem for
anti-clericals with a Communard past whom their newspaper represented to them as anti-Dreyfusards, and at the
same time severe disapproval of a Catholic general of
good family who was in favour of a retrial. I am no less
shocked now to see all Frenchmen execrate that same Emperor Franz Josef whom once they venerated—and
rightly, I may say, I who have known him well and whom
he is gracious enough to treat as his cousin. Ah! I haven't
written to him since the war," he added, as if he were
boldly confessing a fault for which he knew quite well he
could not be blamed. "No, the first year I did write, but
once only. But what would you have me do? My respect
for him is unaltered, but I have many young relatives here
fighting in our lines who would, I know, be most displeased were I to carry on a regular correspondence with
the head of a nation that is at war with us. How could I?
Criticise me who will," he continued, and again he
seemed bravely to invite my reproaches, "but in these

times I have not wanted a letter signed Charlus to arrive in Vienna. There is only one point in the conduct of the old monarch that I would wish to criticise at all severely, and that is that a nobleman of his rank, head of one of the most ancient and illustrious houses of Europe, should have allowed himself to be led astray by a petty landowner—a very intelligent man, of course, but still a complete upstart—like William of Hohenzollern. It is one of the more shocking anomalies of this war."

And as, the moment he returned to considerations of genealogy and precedence, which for him fundamentally dominated all others, M. de Charlus became capable of extraordinary childishness, he said to me, in the tone that he might have used in speaking of the Marne or Verdun, that there were important and extremely curious things which ought not to be omitted by anyone who came to write the history of this war. "For instance," he said, "everybody is so ignorant that no one has bothered to point out this very striking fact: the Grand Master of the Order of Malta, who is a pure Boche, continues none the less to live in Rome where, as Grand Master of our order, he enjoys the privilege of extraterritoriality. Most interesting," he added significantly, as if to say: "You see that you have not wasted your evening by meeting me." I thanked him, and he assumed the modest air of one who asks no reward for services rendered.

M. de Charlus still retained all his respect and all his affection for certain great ladies who were accused of defeatism, just as he had in the past for others who had been accused of Dreyfusism. He regretted only that by stooping to meddle in politics they had given a handle to the "polemics of the journalists." In his own attitude to them nothing had changed. So systematic was his frivolity that for him birth, combined with beauty and with other sources of prestige, was the durable thing and the war, like the Dreyfus case, merely a vulgar and fugitive fashion. Had the Duchesse de Guermantes been shot for trying to make a separate peace with Austria, he would still have considered her no less noble than before, no more dishonoured by this mischance than is Marie-Antoinette in our eyes from having been condemned to the guillotine. He was speaking seriously now and for a brief instant, with the noble air of a Saint-Vallier or a Saint-Mégrin, erect and stiff and solemn, he was free of all those mannerisms by which men of his sort betray themselves. And yet, why is it that not one of these men can ever have a voice which hits absolutely the right note? Even at this moment, when M. de Charlus's voice was so very near to solemnity, its pitch was still false, it still needed the tuning-fork to correct it. "Now, what was I saying to you?" he went on. "Ah! yes, that people hate Franz Josef now, because they take their cue from their newspaper. As for King Constantine of Greece and the Tsar of Bulgaria, the public has oscillated more than once between aversion and sympathy, according as it has been said turn and turn about that they would join the side of the Entente or of what Brichot calls the Central Empires. Brichot, by the way, is telling us at every moment that 'the hour of Venizelos will strike.' Now I do not doubt that M. Venizelos is a statesman of great capabilities, but who says that the Greeks are so particularly eager to have him? We are told that he wanted Greece to keep her engagements towards Serbia. Even so, it would be as well to know what these engagements were and whether they

were more far-reaching than those which Italy and Romania did not scruple to violate. We display for the manner
in which Greece implements her treaties and respects her
constitution an anxiety which we certainly would not display were it not in our interest to do so. Had there been
no war, do you think the 'guarantor' powers would even
have noticed the dissolution of the Chambers? What I see
is simply that one by one the supports of the King of
Greece are being withdrawn from him, so that when the
day arrives when he no longer has an army to defend him
he can be thrown out of the country or put into prison. I
was saying just now that the public judges the King of
Greece and the King of the Bulgars only as it is told to
judge them by the newspapers. But here again, what opinion of these monarchs could people have except that of
their newspapers, seeing that they are not acquainted with
them? I personally have seen a great deal of them both, I
knew Constantine of Greece very well indeed when he
was Diadoch, he is a really splendid man. I have always
thought that the Emperor Nicholas had a great affection
for him. Of course I mean to imply nothing dishon-
ourable. Princess Christian used to talk openly about it,
but she is a terrible scandalmonger. As for the Tsar of the
Bulgars, he is an out-and-out nancy and a monstrous liar,
but very intelligent, a remarkable man. He likes me very
much."

M. de Charlus, who could be so delightful, became
horrid when he touched on these subjects. He brought to
them that same sort of complacency which we find so exasperating in the invalid who keeps drawing attention to
his good health. I have often thought that in the "twister"
of Balbec, the faithful who so longed to hear the admis-

sion which he avoided making, would in fact have been unable to endure any real display of his mania; ill at ease, breathing with difficulty as one does in a sick-room or in the presence of a morphine addict who takes out his syringe in public, they would themselves have put a stop to the confidences which they imagined they desired. It was, indeed, exasperating to hear the whole world accused, and often without any semblance of proof, by someone who omitted himself from the special category to which one knew perfectly well that he belonged and in which he so readily included others. In spite of all his intelligence, he had in this context fabricated for himself a narrow little philosophy (at the bottom of which there was perhaps just a spark of that interest in the curiousness of life which Swann had felt) which explained everything by reference to these special causes and in which, as always happens when a man stoops to the level of his own vice, he was not only unworthy of himself but exceptionally satisfied with himself. Thus it was that this dignified and noble man put on the most imbecile smile to complete the following little speech: "As there are strong presumptions of the same kind as for Ferdinand of Coburg in the case of the Emperor William, this may well be the reason why Tsar Ferdinand has joined the side of the 'Empires of Prey.' After all, it is very understandable, one is indulgent to a *sister*, one refuses her nothing. To my mind that would be a very pretty explanation of Bulgaria's alliance with Germany." And at this stupid explanation M. de Charlus pealed with laughter as though he really found it most ingenious—an explanation which, even had it been based upon true facts, was in the same puerile category as the observations which M. de Charlus made about the war when he judged it from the point of view of a feudal lord or a Knight of St John of Jerusalem. He ended with a more sensible remark: "What is astonishing," he said, "is that this public which judges the men and events of the war solely from the newspapers, is persuaded that it forms its own opinions."

In this M. de Charlus was right. I have been told that it was fascinating to see the moments of silence and hesitation, so exactly like those that are necessary not merely to the pronouncement but to the formation of a personal opinion, which Mme de Forcheville used to have before declaring, as though it were a heartfelt sentiment: "No, I do not think they will take Warsaw"; "I have the impression that it cannot last another winter"; "the worst thing that could happen is a patched-up peace"; "what alarms me, if you want to know, is the Chamber"; "yes, I believe all the same that we shall succeed in breaking through." And to make these statements Odette assumed a simpering air which became even more exaggerated when she said: "I don't say the German armies do not fight well, but they lack what is called pluck." In pronouncing the word "pluck" (and it was the same when she merely said "fighting spirit") she executed with her hand the sculptural gesture, and with her eyes the wink, of an art student employing a technical term of the studios. Her language now, however, even more than in the past bore witness to her admiration for the English, whom she was no longer obliged to call, as formerly, merely "our neighbours across the Channel," or at most "our friends the English": they were "our loyal allies." Needless to say she never failed, relevant or not, to quote the expression *fair play* (and to point out that in the eyes of the English the

Germans were unfair players) and also: "the important thing is to win the war, as our brave allies say." She even had an unfortunate habit of associating the name of her son-in-law with the subject of English soldiers and of referring to the pleasure which he derived from living cheek by jowl with Australians and Scotsmen, New Zealanders and Canadians. "My son-in-law Saint-Loup has learned the slang of all the brave *tommies*, he can make himself understood by the ones from the most distant *dominions*— and I don't mean just the general in command of the base, he fraternises with the humblest *private*."

May this parenthesis on Mme de Forcheville serve as my excuse, while I am strolling along the boulevards side by side with M. de Charlus, for embarking upon another, of greater length but useful as an illustration of this era, on the relations of Mme Verdurin with Brichot. The truth is that if, as we have seen, poor Brichot was judged without indulgence by M. de Charlus (because the latter was both extremely intelligent and more or less unconsciously pro-German), he was treated still worse by the Verdurins. They no doubt were chauvinistic, and this ought to have made them appreciate Brichot's articles, which were in any case quite as good as many pieces of writing which delighted Mme Verdurin. But first, the reader may remember that already at La Raspelière Brichot had become for the Verdurins, instead of the great man that he had once been in their eyes, if not actually a scapegoat like Saniette at any rate a target for their scarcely disguised ridicule. Still, at that period he remained a faithful of the faithful and thus was entitled to a share in the advantages tacitly conferred by the statutes upon all the founding or associate members of the little group. But while, under

cover of the war perhaps, or through the rapid crystallisation of a long-delayed social prestige, of which in fact all
the necessary elements had for a long time existed in it,
invisible and in a state of saturation, the drawing-room of
the Verdurins had been opening itself to a new world and
the faithful, at first the baits to attract this new world,
had ended by being invited less and less themselves, at
the same time a parallel phenomenon had been taking
place in the life of Brichot. In spite of the Sorbonne, in
spite of the *Institut*, before the war he had been a celebrity
only inside the Verdurin drawing-room. But when he began to write, almost every day, articles adorned with that
second-rate brilliance which we have so often seen him
scatter open-handed in the presence of the faithful, yet
enriched too with a perfectly genuine learning which, like
a true man of the Sorbonne, he made no attempt to conceal however he might clothe it in agreeable forms, the
"great world" was literally dazzled. And for once it had
bestowed its favour upon someone who was far from being a nonentity, upon a man who could hold the attention
of an audience by the fertility of his intelligence and the
resources of his memory. So that now, while three
duchesses spent the evening with Mme Verdurin, three
other duchesses contested the honour of having the great
man at their dinner table, and one of these invitations the
great man usually accepted, feeling all the freer to do this
since Mme Verdurin, exasperated by the success of his articles with the Faubourg Saint-Germain, was careful never
to ask him to her house when some smart woman was to
be there whom he did not yet know and who would lose
no time in luring him away. Thus journalism (into which
he was really doing no more than pour belatedly, with ap-

plause and in return for a magnificent financial reward, what all his life he had squandered incognito and for nothing in the Verdurin drawing-room—for his articles, since he had so much knowledge and wrote with such ease, cost him no more trouble than his conversation) might have led, indeed at one moment seemed to be leading Brichot to an indefeasible glory, had it not been for Mme Verdurin. Admittedly, these articles were far from being as remarkable as fashionable people supposed. The vulgarity of the man was apparent in every line beneath the pedantry of the scholar. And side by side with images which had absolutely no meaning ("the Germans will no longer be able to look Beethoven's statue in the face; Schiller must have shuddered in his tomb; the ink which had guaranteed the neutrality of Belgium was scarcely dry; Lenin speaks, but his words are scattered on the winds of the steppe") there were trivialities such as: "twenty thousand prisoners, that is indeed a figure; our command will know how to keep a weather eye open; we mean to win, that sums it up in a nutshell." Yet mixed with all this, how much knowledge, how much intelligence, what just reasoning! Mme Verdurin, however, never began an article by Brichot without first dwelling upon the enjoyable thought that she was going to find ridiculous things in it, and she read it with the most sustained attention in order to be certain of not letting them escape her. And unfortunately it could not be denied that ridiculous things there were. But the faithful did not even wait until they had found them. The most felicitous quotation from an author who was really very little known, at least in the work to which Brichot referred, was seized upon as proof of the most insufferable pedantry, and

Mme Verdurin could hardly wait for the hour of dinner
when she would unloose the torrential laughter of her
guests. "Well, what do you say to tonight's Brichot? I
thought of you when I read the quotation from Cuvier. I
honestly think the man is going mad." "I haven't read it
yet," Cottard would say. "What, you haven't read it yet?
But you don't know what delights you are missing. I
promise you you will die of laughter." And pleased at
heart that someone had not yet read the latest Brichot,
since this meant that she herself could call attention to the
ludicrous things in it, Mme Verdurin would tell the butler
to bring Le Temps and would herself read the article
aloud, lingering with emphasis on the most simple
phrases. After dinner, for the whole of the evening, the
anti-Brichot campaign would continue, but with hypocritical reservations. "I won't say it too loud because I am
afraid that over there," she would say, indicating
Comtesse Molé, "there is a good deal of admiration for
this stuff. Fashionable people are more foolish than is
generally supposed." In saying this she did her best, by
speaking just loud enough, to let Mme Molé hear that she
was being talked about, and at the same time to convey to
her, by occasionally lowering her voice, that she did not
want her to hear what she was saying. Mme Molé was
cowardly enough to disown Brichot, whom in fact she
thought the equal of Michelet. She said that of course
Mme Verdurin was right, and so as to end by nevertheless saying something which seemed to her incontestably
true, added: "What one must allow him, is that it is well
written." "You call that well written?" said Mme Verdurin. "Personally, I consider that it might have been
written by a pig"—an audacity which always made her

fashionable guests laugh, particularly as Mme Verdurin, as though she herself were frightened by the word "pig," uttered it in a whisper, holding her hand to her lips. Her rage against Brichot was still further increased by the naïve fashion in which he displayed his pleasure at his success, in spite of the fits of ill-humour provoked in him by the censorship every time that it—as he expressed it, for he liked to employ new words in order to show that he was not too donnish—"blue-pencilled" part of his article. In his presence, however, Mme Verdurin did not reveal too clearly, save by a certain grumpiness which might have been a warning to a more perspicacious man, the poor opinion which she had of the writings of "Chochotte." Only once did she criticise him, for using the word "I" too often. And it was true that he was in the habit of using it continually, firstly because, with his professorial habits, he was constantly employing phrases like "I grant that" and even (in the sense of "I am willing to admit that") "I am willing that," as for instance: "I am willing that the vast development of the fronts should necessitate, etc.," but principally because, as a militant anti-Dreyfusard of the old days who had had suspicions of German preparations long before the war, he had frequently had occasion to write: "Since 1897 I have been denouncing"; "I pointed out in 1901"; "In my little pamphlet, of the greatest rarity today (*habent sua fata libelli*) I drew attention," and the habit, once formed, had remained with him. He turned crimson at Mme Verdurin's remark, which had been made with acerbity. "You are right, Madame. A man who had no more love for the Jesuits than M. Combes—although he never had the honour of a preface from our sweet master of delicious

scepticism, Anatole France, who was, if I am not mistaken, my adversary . . . before the Flood—observed
that the first person singular is always odious."⁶ From that
moment Brichot replaced "I" by "one," but *one* did not
prevent the reader from seeing that the author was speaking of himself, indeed it permitted him to speak of himself more frequently than ever, to comment on the most
insignificant of his own phrases, to build a whole article
round a single negative statement, always behind the protective screen of *one*. If for example Brichot had said, in
another article perhaps, that the German armies had lost
some of their strength, he would begin thus: "One does
not camouflage the truth here. One has said that the German armies have lost some of their strength. One has not
said that they do not still possess great strength. Still less
will one write that the ground gained, if it is not, etc." In
short, simply by enunciating all that he would not say and
by recalling all that he had said some years ago and all
that Clausewitz, Jomini, Ovid, Apollonius of Tyana and
others had said in the more recent or more remote past,
Brichot could easily have put together the material for a
solid volume. It is to be regretted that he did not publish
one, for these erudite articles are now difficult to come by.
The Faubourg Saint-Germain, admonished by Mme Verdurin, began by laughing at Brichot in her drawing-room,
but continued, after departing from the little clan, to admire him. Then after a while it became the fashion to
scoff at him as it had previously been to admire him, and
even those ladies who continued to find him dazzling in
secret while they were actually reading his articles,
checked themselves and mocked as soon as they were no
longer alone, so as not to appear less clever than their

friends. Never was Brichot so much discussed in the little clan as at this period, but in a spirit of derision. The criterion for judging the intelligence of a newcomer was simply his opinion of Brichot's articles, and if the first time he gave the wrong reply no pains were spared to instruct him how it was that you were recognised to be foolish or clever.

"Well, my poor friend," M. de Charlus went on, "all this is very dreadful, and tedious articles are not the only things we have to deplore. We hear talk of vandalism, of the destruction of statues. But the destruction of so many marvellous young men, who while they lived were incomparable polychrome statues, is that not also vandalism? Will not a town which has lost all its beautiful men be like a town of which all the sculpture has been smashed to pieces? What pleasure can I get from dining in a restaurant where I am served by moth-eaten old buffoons who look like Father Didon, if not by hags in mob-caps who make me think I have strayed into one of Duval's soup-kitchens? Yes, it's as bad as that, my boy, and I think I have the right to say these things, because beauty is still beauty when it exists in a living material. How delightful to be served by rachitic creatures with spectacles on their noses and the reason for their exemption from military service written all over their faces! In these changed times, if you wish to rest your eyes on someone nice-looking in a restaurant, you must look not among the waiters who are serving you but among the customers who are eating and drinking. And then in the old days one could always see a waiter a second time, although they frequently changed, but with some English lieutenant who has perhaps never been to the restaurant before and may well be killed tomorrow, what hope is there of finding out who he is and when he will return? When Augustus of Poland, as we are told by the charming Morand, the delightful author of *Clarisse*, exchanged one of his regiments for a collection of Chinese porcelain, it is my opinion that he made a bad bargain. To think that all those huge footmen six foot tall and more, who used to adorn the monumental staircases of the lovely hostesses whose houses we visited, have one and all been killed, and that most of them joined up because it was dinned into them that the war would last two months! Ah! they did not know as I do the strength of Germany, the courage of the Prussian race," he said, forgetting himself. And then, realising that he had revealed too much of his point of view, he went on: "It is not so much Germany that I fear for France as the war itself. People away from the front imagine that the war is no more than a gigantic boxing match, of which, thanks to the newspapers, they are spectators at a comfortable distance. But it is nothing of the sort. It is an illness which, when it seems to have been defeated at one point, returns at another. Today Noyon will be recovered from the enemy, tomorrow there will be no bread or chocolate, the next day the man who thought he was safe and was prepared, if necessary, to face death on the battlefield because he had not imagined it, will be panic-stricken to read in the newspapers that his class has been called up. As for monuments, it is not so much the quality as the quantity of the destruction that appals me, I am less horrified at the disappearance of a unique monument like Rheims than at that of all the living entities which once made the smallest village in France instructive and charming."

My mind turned immediately to Combray, but in the past I had thought that I would lower myself in the eyes of Mme de Guermantes by confessing to the humble position which my family occupied there. I wondered now whether the facts had not been revealed to the Guermantes and to M. de Charlus, either by Legrandin or by Swann or Saint-Loup or Morel, and I said nothing, even this silence being less painful to me than a retrospective explanation. I only hoped that M. de Charlus would not mention Combray.

"I do not wish to speak ill of the Americans, Monsieur," he went on, "it seems that they are inexhaustibly generous, and as there has been nobody to conduct the orchestra in this war, as each performer has joined in a long time after the one before and the Americans only began when we had almost finished, they may possibly have an ardour which in us four years of war have succeeded in damping. Even before the war they were fond of our country and our art, they paid high prices for our masterpieces. They have taken many home with them. But this uprooted art, as M. Barrès would call it, is precisely the opposite of what once formed the delicious charm of France. The château explained the church, which itself, because it had been a place of pilgrimage, explained the *chanson de geste*. I need not dwell upon the illustriousness of my family and my connexions, which in any case is not the subject that concerns us. But recently I had occasion, to settle a matter of business, and in spite of a certain coolness that exists between the young couple and myself, to visit my niece Saint-Loup who lives at Combray. Combray was simply a small town like hundreds of others. But the ancestors of my family were portrayed as donors in some of the windows in the church, and in others our armorial bearings were depicted. We had our chapel there, and our tombs. And now this church has been destroyed by the French and the English because it served as an observation-post to the Germans. All that mixture of art and still-living history that was France is being destroyed, and we have not seen the end of the process yet. Of course I am not so absurd as to compare, for family reasons, the destruction of the church of Combray with that of the cathedral of Rheims, that miracle of a Gothic cathedral which seemed, somehow naturally, to have rediscovered the purity of antique sculpture, or of the cathedral of Amiens. I do not know whether the raised arm of St Firmin is still intact today or whether it has been broken. If so, the loftiest affirmation of faith and energy ever made has disappeared from this world."

"You mean its symbol, Monsieur," I interrupted. "And I adore certain symbols no less than you do. But it would be absurd to sacrifice to the symbol the reality that it symbolises. Cathedrals are to be adored until the day when, to preserve them, it would be necessary to deny the truths which they teach. The raised arm of St Firmin said, with an almost military gesture of command: 'Let us be broken, if honour requires.' Do not sacrifice men to stones whose beauty comes precisely from their having for a moment given fixed form to human truths."

"I understand what you mean," M. de Charlus replied, "and M. Barrès, who has sent us, alas, on too many pilgrimages to the statue of Strasbourg and the tomb of M. Déroulède, was both moving and graceful when he wrote that the cathedral of Rheims itself was less dear to us than the lives of our infantrymen. An assertion which makes nonsense of the wrath of our newspapers against the German general in command there who said that the cathedral of Rheims was less precious to him than the life of one German soldier. Indeed, the exasperating and depressing thing is that each country says the same. The reasons for which the industrialists of Germany declare the possession of Belfort indispensable for safeguarding their nation against our ideas of revenge, are the very same reasons as those which Barrès gives for demanding Mainz as a protection against the recurrent urge to invade which possesses the Boches. Why is it that the recovery of Alsace-Lorraine seemed to France an insufficient motive for embarking on a war, yet a sufficient motive for continuing one, for redeclaring it afresh year after year? You appear to believe that nothing can rob France of victory now and with all my heart I hope that you are right, you may be quite sure of that. But is it not a fact that since, rightly or wrongly, the Allies have come to believe that they are sure to win (for my part naturally I should be enchanted by this outcome, but what I see is mostly a profusion of victories on paper, Pyrrhic victories whose cost is not revealed to us) and the Boches no longer believe that they are sure to win, we see Germany striving to make peace quickly and France to prolong the war, France which is a just nation and does right to pronounce words of justice but is also sweet, gentle France and ought to pronounce words of mercy, were it only in order to spare her own children and to allow the flowers which bloom with each new spring to shed their lustre on other things than tombs? Be honest, my friend, you yourself once propounded a theory to me about things existing only in virtue of a creation which is perpetually renewed.

The creation of the world did not take place once and for all, you said, it is, of necessity, taking place every day. Well, if you are sincere, you cannot except war from this theory. Never mind if the excellent Norpois has written (trotting out one of those oratorical phrases which are as dear to him as 'the dawn of victory' and 'General Winter'): 'Now that Germany has determined on war, the die is cast,' the truth is that every morning war is declared afresh. And the men who wish to continue it are as guilty as the men who began it, more guilty perhaps, for the latter perhaps did not foresee all its horrors.

"Besides, can we be sure that a war thus prolonged, even if it must eventually end in victory, is without danger? It is difficult to speak of things which have no precedent and of the repercussions upon an organism of an operation which is being attempted for the first time. Generally, it is true, novelties which people find alarming pass off very well. The most prudent republicans thought that it was mad to separate the Church from the State. It was as easy as sending a letter through the post. Dreyfus was rehabilitated, Picquart was made Minister of War, and nobody uttered a murmur. Yet what may we not fear from the stress and strain of a war which has continued without pause for several years? What will men do when they return from it? Will fatigue have broken them or will it have driven them mad? All this could have grave results, if not for France, at least for the government, perhaps even for the present form of government. You once made me read Maurras's excellent novel *Aimée de Coigny*. The original Aimée, you remember, was waiting for the collapse of the Empire to ensue from the war that it was waging in 1812, and I should be surprised if she has not her counterpart today. If a present-day Aimée de Coigny exists, will her hopes with regard to the Republic be fulfilled? I wouldn't want that.

"But to return to the war itself, can we say that the man who first began it was the Emperor William? I am very doubtful about that. And if it was, what has he done that Napoleon, for instance, did not do—something that I certainly find abominable, but that I am astonished to see also inspiring such horror in those who burn incense before Napoleon, those who on the day that war was declared exclaimed like General Pau: 'I have been waiting forty years for this day. It is the most glorious day of my life.' Heaven knows whether anyone protested with greater energy than myself at the time when a deference out of all proportion was paid by society to the nationalists and the military men, when every friend of the arts was accused of occupying himself with things of baleful import to France and all civilisation of an unwarlike nature was thought to be pernicious! In those days an authentic member of the best society hardly counted compared with a general. Some madwoman came within an inch of presenting *me* to M. Syveton, as if *I* were *his* inferior. You will tell me that the rules I was striving to maintain were merely social ones. But for all their apparent frivolity they might have prevented many excesses. I have always honoured the defenders of grammar or logic. We realise fifty years later that they have averted serious dangers. Today our nationalists are the most anti-German of men, the most determined to persevere to the bitter end. But in the last fifteen years their philosophy has completely changed. It is true that they are pressing for the continuation of the war. But they are doing this only in order to exterminate a warlike race, they are doing it from love of peace. The idea of a martial civilisation, which fifteen years ago they thought so beautiful, now fills them with horror; not only do they reproach the Prussians for having allowed the military element to predominate in their state, they claim that throughout the ages military civilisations have been destructive of all that they now hold precious, not only of the arts but also of chivalry towards women. And if any critic of their views is converted to nationalism he at the same moment becomes a friend of peace. He is persuaded that in all martial civilisations women have been humiliated and crushed. One dare not reply that the 'lady' of a knight in the Middle Ages or Dante's Beatrice was perhaps placed upon a throne as elevated as the heroines of M. Becque. Any day now I expect to see myself placed at table beneath a Russian revolutionary or simply beneath one of these generals of ours who wage war out of horror of war and in order to punish a people for cultivating an ideal which fifteen years ago they themselves regarded as the only one that could invigorate a nation. It is not many months since the unhappy Tsar was honoured for his part in assembling the conference at The Hague. But now that people hail the advent of a free Russia they forget his claim to glory. So turns the wheel of the world. Meanwhile Germany uses expressions so similar to those of France that one can hardly believe she is not quoting her, she never tires of saying that she is 'struggling for existence.' When I read: 'We shall struggle against an implacable and cruel enemy until we have obtained a peace which will give us guarantees for the future against all aggression and ensure that the blood of our brave soldiers shall not have flowed in vain,' or: 'he who is not for us is against us,' I do not know whether the words are the Emperor William's or M. Poincaré's, for they have both of them, with a few trifling differences, pronounced such phrases twenty times, although to be truthful I must admit that in this instance it is the Emperor who has copied the President of the Republic. France would perhaps have been less eager to prolong the war if she had remained weak, and Germany certainly would have been in less of a hurry to end it if she had not ceased to be strong. I should say, to be as strong as she was; for strong, as you will see, she still is."

He had got into the habit of talking at the top of his voice, from excitability, from the need to find an outlet for impressions of which, never having cultivated any art, he needed to unburden himself—as an airman unloads his bombs, if necessary in open country—even where his words could impinge upon nobody, particularly in society, where they fell completely at random and where people listened to him out of snobbishness, uncritically and (to such an extent did he tyrannise his audience) one may say under compulsion and even from fear. On the boulevards this loud harangue of his was also a mark of contempt for the passers-by, for whom he no more lowered his voice than he would have stepped aside to avoid them. But it struck a discordant note there and caused astonishment and, worse than that, rendered audible to the people who turned round to look at us remarks which might well have made them take us for defeatists. I pointed this out to M. de Charlus but succeeded only in arousing his mirth. "You must admit that that would be most amusing," he said. "After all, one never knows, every evening each one of us runs the risk of being part of the next day's news. Is there really any reason why I should not be shot in a ditch at Vincennes? That is what happened to my great-uncle the Duc d'Enghien. The thirst for noble blood maddens a certain rabble—and here they show a greater fastidiousness than lions, for those beasts, as you know, would throw themselves even upon Mme Verdurin if she had so much as a scratch upon her nose. Upon what in my youth we would have called her boko!" And he began to roar with laughter as if we had been alone in a room.

At moments, seeing suspicious-looking individuals drawn out of the shadows by the passage of M. de Charlus conglomerate at a little distance from him, I wondered whether it would be more agreeable to him if I left him alone or remained with him. In the same way, if you meet an old man who is subject to frequent epileptic fits and see from the incoherence of his gait that an attack is probably imminent, you may ask yourself whether your company is more desired by him as a support or dreaded as that of a witness from whom he would prefer to conceal the attack and whose mere presence may perhaps suffice to bring it on, whereas absolute calm might succeed in averting it. But in the case of the sick man the possibility of the event upon which you are uncertain whether or no you ought to turn your back is revealed by his walking in circles as if he were drunk; while in that of M. de Charlus the divagations—sign of a possible incident as to which I did not know whether he desired or feared that my presence should prevent its occurrence—were transferred, as in an ingenious stage production, from the Baron himself, who was walking straight ahead, to a whole circle of supernumerary actors. All the same, it is my belief that he preferred to avoid the encounter, for he dragged me down a side-street, darker than the boulevard but into which nevertheless the latter was incessantly discharging—or else like a tributary stream they were flowing towards it— soldiers of every arm and of every nation, a rising youthful tide, compensatory and consoling for M. de Charlus, the reverse of that ebb-tide of all men towards the frontier which in the first days of mobilisation had made a vacuum in the capital. At every moment M. de Charlus expressed his admiration for the brilliant uniforms which passed before us, which made of Paris a town as cosmopolitan as a port, as unreal as a stage setting designed by a painter who has simply put up a few scraps of architecture as an excuse for assembling the most variegated and glittering costumes.

Literally he did not know which way to turn his head; often he raised it, regretting that he did not have a pair of field-glasses (which would in fact have been of very little use to him), since because of the Zeppelin raid of two days earlier, which had caused the authorities to redouble their precautions, there were soldiers in greater numbers than usual even in the sky. The aeroplanes which a few hours earlier I had seen, like insects, as brown dots upon the surface of the blue evening, now passed like blazing fire-ships through the darkness of the night, which was made darker still by the partial extinction of the street lamps. And perhaps the greatest impression of beauty that these human shooting stars made us feel came simply from their forcing us to look at the sky, towards which normally we so seldom raise our eyes. In this Paris, whose beauty in 1914 I had seen awaiting almost defenceless the threat of the approaching enemy, there was certainly, as there had been then, the ancient unalterable splendour of a moon cruelly and mysteriously serene, which poured down its useless beauty upon the still untouched buildings of the capital; but as in 1914, and more now than in 1914, there was also something else, there were lights from a different source, intermittent beams which, whether they came from the aeroplanes or from the searchlights of the Eiffel Tower, one knew to be directed by an intelligent will, by a friendly vigilance which gave one the same kind of emotion, inspired the same sort of gratitude and calm that I had felt in Saint-Loup's room at Doncières, in the cell of that military cloister where so many fervent and disciplined hearts were exercising themselves in readiness for the day when, without hesitation, in the midst of their youth, they would consummate their sacrifice.

After the raid of two days earlier, when it had been more full of movement than the earth, the sky had become calm again as the sea becomes calm after a storm. But like the sea after a storm, it had not yet recovered absolute tranquillity. Aeroplanes were still mounting like rockets to the level of the stars, and searchlights, as they quartered the sky, swept slowly across it what looked like a pale dust of stars, of errant milky ways. Meanwhile the aeroplanes took their places among the constellations and seeing these "new stars" one might well have supposed oneself to be in another hemisphere.

M. de Charlus spoke to me of his admiration for these airmen of ours, and went on, since he was no more capable of checking the flow of his pro-German feelings than of his other inclinations, even though at the same time he denied both the one and the other tendency: "I must add of course that I have just as much admiration

for the Germans who go up in the Gothas. And when it
comes to the Zeppelins, think of the courage that is
needed! They are heroes, there is no other word for it.
What difference can it make that they are attacking civilians, if guns are firing at them? Are you afraid of the
Gothas and the bombardment?" I admitted that I was
not, but perhaps I was wrong. No doubt, my idleness
having given me the habit, when it was a question of my
work, of putting it off from one day to another, I imagined that death too might be postponed in the same fashion. How should one be afraid of a bombardment when
one is convinced that one will not be hit today? Anyhow,
formed in isolation, the idea of bombs being dropped, the
idea of the possibility of death, had added nothing tragic
to the image which I had in my mind of the German flying machines, until from one of them, storm-tossed and
partly hidden from my sight by the thick billowing mists
of an agitated sky, from an aeroplane which, though I
knew it to be murderous, I imagined only as stellar and
celestial, I had one evening seen the gesture of a bomb
dropped upon us. For the novel reality of a danger is perceived only through the medium of that new thing, not
assimilable to anything that we already know, to which we
give the name "an impression" and which is often, as in
the present case, epitomised in a line, a line which defines
an intention and possesses the latent potentiality of the
action which has given it its particular form, like the invisible line described by this falling bomb or those other
lines which I had seen at the same time from the Pont de
la Concorde, on all sides of the threatening, hunted aeroplane, as though they had been reflexions in the clouds of
the fountains of the Champs-Elysées and the Place de la

Concorde and the Tuileries: the beams of the searchlights travelling through the sky like luminous jets of water, which also were lines full of intention, full of the provident and protective intentions of men of power and wisdom to whom, as on that night in the barracks at Doncières, I felt grateful for condescending to employ their strength, with this so beautiful precision, in watching over our safety.

The night was as beautiful as in 1914, and the threat to Paris was as great. The moonlight was like a soft and steady magnesium flare, by the light of which some camera might, for the last time, have been recording nocturnal images of those lovely groups of buildings like the Place Vendôme and the Place de la Concorde, to which my fear of the shells that were perhaps about to destroy them imparted by contrast, as they stood in their still intact beauty, a sort of plenitude, as if they were bending forward and freely offering their defenceless architecture to the blows that might fall. "You are not afraid?" M. de Charlus repeated. "The people of Paris don't realise the situation. I am told that Mme Verdurin gives parties every day. I know it only from hearsay, personally I know absolutely nothing about them, I have completely broken off relations," he added, lowering not only his eyes as if a telegraph boy had passed, but also his head and his shoulders and raising his arm with the gesture that signifies, if not "I wash my hands of them" at any rate "I can tell you nothing about them" (not that I had asked him anything). "I know that Morel still goes there a lot," he went on (it was the first time that he had mentioned him again). "It is rumoured that he much regrets the past and would like to make it up with me," he continued, exhibiting at one

and the same time the credulity of a man of the Faubourg
who says: "People say that there are more talks than ever
going on between France and Germany, and even that negotiations have been started," and that of the lover whom
the most cruel rebuffs are unable to convince. "In any
case, if he wants it, he only has to say so. I am older than
he, it is not for me to take the first step." And certainly
there was no need to say this, so evident was it. But it
was not even sincere, and this made one very embarrassed
for M. de Charlus, for one felt that, by saying that it was
not for him to take the first step, he was in fact making
one and was waiting for me to offer to undertake a reconciliation.

Naturally I was familiar with the credulity, naïve or
feigned, of people who love someone, or simply are not
invited to someone's house, and attribute to that someone
a desire of which, in fact, in spite of wearisome solicita-
tions, he has given no hint. But from the sudden tremor
of the voice with which M. de Charlus pronounced these
words, from the anxious look which flickered in the
depths of his eyes, I got the impression that there was
something more here than an ordinary attempt at bluff. I
was not mistaken, and I will relate straight away the two
facts which proved subsequently that I was right. (I take a
leap of many years for the second of these incidents,
which was posterior to the death of M. de Charlus, who
was not to die until a much later period and whom we
shall have occasion to see again a number of times, greatly
changed from what we have known him to be, particularly
the last time of all, when he had come to forget Morel
completely.) The first of these incidents took place only
two or three years after the evening on which I walked

down the boulevards with M. de Charlus. About two years after this evening, I met Morel. I thought immediately of M. de Charlus, of the pleasure it would give him to see the violinist again, and I urged Morel to go and see him, even if it were only once. "He has been good to you," I said, "he is an old man now, he may die, you should settle old scores and obliterate all trace of your quarrel." Morel appeared to be entirely of my opinion as to the desirability of making peace, but he none the less refused categorically to visit M. de Charlus even once. "You are wrong," I said. "Is it from obstinacy, from indolence, from spite, from misplaced vanity, from concern for your virtue (you may be sure that it will not be attacked), from coquettishness?" At this point the violinist, twisting his features as he forced himself to make an admission which no doubt was extremely painful, replied with a shudder: "No, it is from none of all those things. As for virtue, I don't give a damn for it. Spite? On the contrary, I am beginning to pity him. It is not from coquettishness, which could serve no purpose. It is not from having too much to do, for there are whole days when I stay at home and twiddle my thumbs. No, it is not for any of these reasons. It is—but never say this to anybody, I am mad to tell you—it is, it is . . . from fear!" He began to tremble in every limb. I confessed that I did not understand him. "No, don't ask me, don't let's talk about it, you do not know him as I do, I may say that you do not know him at all." "But what harm can he do you? In any case, he won't want to harm you if you put an end to the bitterness that exists between you. And then, you know that at heart he is very kind." "Good heavens, yes! I know he is kind. And wonderfully considerate, and honest. But let me alone, don't let's talk about it, I beseech you—it's a shameful admission, but I am afraid!"

The second incident dates from after the death of M. de Charlus. I was brought one or two things which he had left me as mementoes, and also a letter enclosed in three envelopes, which he had written at least ten years before his death. He had been seriously ill at the time and had put all his affairs in order, but then had recovered, only to fall later into the condition in which we shall see him on the day of an afternoon party given by the Princesse de Guermantes—and the letter, put aside in a strong-box with the objects which he was bequeathing to a few friends, had remained there for seven years, seven years during which he had completely forgotten Morel. It was written in a firm and delicate hand-writing and was couched in the following terms:

"My dear friend, the ways of Providence are inscrutable. Sometimes a fault in a very ordinary man is made to serve its purposes by helping one of the just not to slip from his lofty eminence. You know Morel, you know the humbleness of his origin and the height (my own level, no less) to which I wished to raise him. You are aware that he preferred to return not to the dust and ashes from which every man—for man surely is the true phoenix—may be born again, but to the slime in which the viper crawls. He fell, and in so doing he saved me from falling from where I belong. You know that my arms contain the device of Our Lord himself: *Inculcabis super leonem et aspidem*, with the crest of a man having beneath the soles of his feet, as heraldic supporters, a lion and a serpent. Well, if I have succeeded as I have in crushing the lion proper that I am, it is thanks to the serpent and his prudence, which just now I was thoughtless enough to call a fault, for the profound wisdom of the Gospel makes a virtue of it, a virtue at least for other people. Our serpent, of the once harmonious and well-modulated hisses, was, when he had a charmer—a charmer charmed, moreover—not merely musical and reptilian, he had, to the point of cowardice, that virtue, prudence, which I now hold to be divine. This divine prudence it was that made him resist the appeals to come back and see me which I conveyed to him, and I shall have no peace in this world or hope of forgiveness in the next if I do not confess the truth to you. He was, in resisting my appeals, the instrument of divine wisdom, for I was resolved, had he come, that he should not leave my house alive. One of us two had to disappear. I had decided to kill him. God counselled him prudence to preserve me from crime. I do not doubt that the intercession of the Archangel Michael, my patron saint, played a great part in this and I beseech him to pardon me for having so neglected him over many years and for having so ill responded to the innumerable favours which he has conferred upon me, especially in my struggle against evil. I owe it to this Servant of God—I say the words in the plenitude of my faith and my understanding—that the heavenly Father inspired Morel not to come. And so it is I who am now about to die.

> Your faithfully devoted, *Semper idem*,
> P. G. Charlus.

Reading these words I understood Morel's fear. Certainly there was in the letter more than a small element of pride and of literature. But the confession was true. And Morel had known better than I that the "practically mad side" of her brother-in-law's character which Mme de Guermantes used to hint at was not confined, as until this revelation I had supposed, to his momentary exhibitions of superficial and ineffective rage.

But I must return to my narrative. I am walking down the boulevards by the side of M. de Charlus, who has just made a vague attempt to use me as an intermediary for overtures of peace between himself and Morel.

Seeing that I made no reply, "Anyhow," he went on, "I do not know why it is that he no longer gives concerts. There is no music now on the pretext that there is a war on, but people dance and go out to dinner and women invent something called Ambrine for their skin. Social amusements fill what may prove, if the Germans continue to advance, to be the last days of our Pompeii. And if the city is indeed doomed, that in itself will save it from frivolity. The lava of some German Vesuvius—and their naval guns are no less terrible than a volcano—has only to surprise these good people at their toilet and to eternise their gestures by interrupting them, and in days to come it will be part of a child's education to look at pictures in his school-books of Mme Molé about to put on a last layer of powder before going out to dine with a sister-in-law, or Sosthène de Guermantes adding the final touches to his false eyebrows; these things will be the subject of lectures by the Brichots of the future, for the frivolity of an age, when ten centuries have passed over it, is matter for the gravest erudition, particularly if it has been embalmed by a volcanic eruption or by the substances akin to lava which a bombardment projects. What documents for the future historian if asphyxiating gases, like the fumes of Vesuvius, and the collapse of a whole city, like the catastrophe which buried Pompeii, should preserve intact all the imprudent dowagers who have not yet sent off their paintings and their statues to safety in Bayonne! And indeed, for the last year, have we not already seen fragments of Pompeii every evening: people burying themselves in their cellars, not in order to emerge with some old bottle of Mouton Rothschild or Saint-Emilion, but to conceal along with themselves their most treasured belongings, like the priests of Herculaneum whom death surprised in the act of carrying away the sacred vessels? Attachment to an object always brings death to its possessor. True, Paris was not, like Herculaneum, founded by Hercules. But how many points of resemblance leap to the eye! And this lucid vision that is given to us is not unique to ourselves, it has been granted to every age. If I reflect that tomorrow we may suffer the fate of the cities of Vesuvius, these in their turn sensed that they were threatened with the doom of the accursed cities of the Bible. On the wall of a house in Pompeii has been found the revealing inscription: *Sodoma, Gomora.*"

Perhaps it was this name of Sodom and the ideas that it evoked in him, or possibly the idea of the bombardment, that made M. de Charlus for an instant raise his eyes to heaven, but soon he brought them back to earth. "I admire all the heroes of this war," he said. "Why, my dear boy, those English soldiers whom at the beginning I rather thoughtlessly dismissed as mere football players presumptuous enough to measure themselves against professionals—and what professionals!—well, purely from the aesthetic point of view they are quite simply Greek athletes, you understand me, my boy, Greek athletes, they are the young men of Plato, or rather they are Spartans. I have a friend who has been to Rouen where their base is, he has seen marvels, marvels almost unimaginable. It is not Rouen any longer, it is another town. Of course the old Rouen still exists, with the emaciated saints of the cathedral. And naturally, that is beautiful too, but it is something quite different. And our *poilus!* I cannot tell you how deliciously full of character I find our *poilus,* the young Parisian boys, like that one there, for instance, who is passing us, with his knowing expression, his alert and humorous face. I often stop them for one reason or another and we chat for a moment or two, and what subtlety, what good sense! And the boys from the provinces, how amusing and nice they are, with the way they roll their *r*'s and their regional dialects! I have always lived a lot in the country, I have slept in farms, I know how to talk to them. Still, our admiration for the French must not make us depreciate our enemies, that would only be to disparage ourselves. And you don't know what a soldier the German soldier is; you haven't seen him, as I have, march past on parade, doing the goose-step, *unter den Linden.*"

And returning to that ideal of virility which he had outlined to me at Balbec and which, with time, had assumed a more philosophical form in his mind, but using also absurd arguments which at moments, even just after he had said something out of the ordinary, gave his hearer a glimpse of the flimsiness of mental fabric of a mere society gentleman, albeit an intelligent one: "You see," he said to me, "that splendid sturdy fellow the Boche soldier is strong and healthy and thinks only of the greatness of his country, *Deutschland über Alles*, which is not so stupid as you might think, whereas we, while they were preparing themselves in a virile fashion, were hopelessly sunk in dilettantism." This word probably signified for M. de Charlus something analogous to literature, for immediately, remembering no doubt that I was fond of literature and had at one time intended to devote myself to it, he slapped me on the shoulder (taking the opportunity to lean so heavily upon me that the blow hurt as much as, in the days when I was doing my military service, the recoil of a "76" against my shoulder-blade) and said, as if to soften the reproach: "Yes, we were sunk in dilettantism, all of us, you too, you may remember. Like me you may say your *mea culpa*. We have been too dilettante." From astonishment at this reproach, from lack of readiness in repartee, from deference towards my interlocutor, and also because I was touched by his friendly kindness, I replied as though I too, as he suggested, had cause to beat my breast—an idiotic reaction, for I could not be accused of the slightest suggestion of dilettantism. "Well," he said to me, "I must leave you here" (the group which had escorted him at a distance had finally abandoned us), "I am going off to bed like a very old gentleman, particularly as, so it seems, the war has changed all our habits—isn't that one of the imbecile aphorisms which Norpois is so fond of?" I knew, as a matter of fact, that when he went home at night M. de Charlus did not cease to be surrounded by soldiers, for he had turned his house into a military hospital and had done this, I believe, in obedience to the dictates much less of his imagination than of his kind heart.

It was a transparent and breathless night; I imagined that the Seine, flowing between the twin semicircles of the span and the reflection of its bridges, must look like the Bosporus. And—a symbol perhaps of the invasion foretold by the defeatism of M. de Charlus, or else of the co-operation of our Muslim brothers with the armies of France—the moon, narrow and curved like a sequin, seemed to have placed the sky of Paris beneath the oriental sign of the crescent.

M. de Charlus lingered a few moments more, while he said good-bye to me with a shake of my hand powerful enough to crush it to pieces—a Germanic peculiarity to be found in those who think like the Baron. For several seconds he continued, as Cottard would have said, to "knead" my hand, as if he had wished to restore to my joints a suppleness which they had never lost. In certain blind men the sense of touch makes good to a certain extent the lack of sight. I do not exactly know what sense it was taking the place of here. Perhaps he thought that he was merely shaking my hand, as no doubt he thought that he was merely seeing a Senegalese soldier who passed in the darkness without deigning to notice that he was being admired. But in each case the Baron was mistaken, the intensity of contact and of gaze was greater than propriety permitted. "Don't you see all the Orient of Decamps and Fromentin and Ingres and Delacroix in this scene?" he asked me, still immobilised by the passage of the Senegalese. "As you know, I for my part am interested in things and in people only as a painter, a philosopher. Besides, I am too old. But how unfortunate that to complete the picture one of us two is not an odalisque!"

It was not the Orient of Decamps or even of Delacroix that began to haunt my imagination when the Baron had left me, but the old Orient of those *Arabian Nights* which I had been so fond of; losing myself gradually in the network of these dark streets, I thought of the Caliph Harun al-Rashid going in search of adventures in the hidden quarters of Baghdad. The weather was warm and my walk had made me hot and thirsty, but the bars had all closed long ago and, because of the scarcity of petrol, the rare taxis which I met, driven by Levantines or negroes, did not even take the trouble to respond to my signs. The only place where I might have been able to get something to drink and rest until I felt strong enough to walk home would have been a hotel. But in the street, rather remote from the centre of the town, to which I had penetrated, every hotel, since the Gothas had begun to drop their bombs on Paris, had closed. The same was true of almost all the shops, the shopkeepers, either owing to lack of staff or because they had taken fright themselves, having fled to the country and left on their door a hand-written notice announcing in some conventional phrase that they would re-open at a distant date (though even that seemed problematical). The few establishments which had managed to survive announced in the same fashion that they were open only twice a week. One felt that poverty, dereliction, fear inhabited the whole quarter. I was all the more surprised, therefore, to see that among these abandoned houses there was one in which life seemed, on the contrary, to have been victorious and ter-ror and bankruptcy to have yielded to activity and wealth. Behind the closed shutters of each window the lights, dimmed on account of police regulations, revealed never-theless a complete disregard for economy. And at every moment the door opened to allow some fresh visitor to enter or leave. It was a hotel which, because of the money its proprietors must be making, could not fail to have aroused the envy of all the neighbouring tradespeople; and I too became curious when, at a distance of fifteen yards, that is to say too far off for me to be able to make him out clearly in the profound darkness, I saw an officer come out and walk rapidly away.

Something, however, struck me: not his face, which I did not see, nor his uniform, which was disguised by a heavy greatcoat, but the extraordinary disproportion be-

tween the number of different points which his body successively occupied and the very small number of seconds
within which he made good this departure which had almost the air of a sortie from a besieged town. So that my
mind turned, if I did not explicitly recognise him—I will
not say even to the build, nor to the slimness or the carriage or the swift movements of Saint-Loup—but to the
sort of ubiquity which was so special to him. This military man with the ability to occupy so many different positions in space in such a short time disappeared down a
side-street without seeing me, and I was left wondering
whether it would be wise to enter a hotel whose modest
appearance made me think that it could hardly have been
Saint-Loup who had emerged. And yet I recalled involuntarily that he had—unjustly—been involved in a case of
espionage because his name had been found in some letters captured on a German officer. He had, of course,
been completely exonerated by the military authorities.
But in spite of myself I associated this recollection with
what I now saw. Was this hotel being used as a meeting-
place of spies?

The officer had only just disappeared when I saw
some private soldiers of various arms go in, which further
strengthened my suspicions. I was now, however, extremely thirsty. I should probably be able to get something to drink inside and at the same time I might
attempt, although I felt nervous at the prospect, to assuage my curiosity. And so, but not, I think, primarily
from curiosity about the officer I had seen, I hesitated no
longer but climbed the little staircase at the top of which
the door of a sort of hall stood open, no doubt on account
of the heat. I thought at first that I might fail to discover

very much, for from the staircase, where I remained in
shadow, I saw several people come and ask for a room
and receive the answer that there were absolutely none
left. The objection to these people, I guessed, was simply
that they did not belong to the nest of espionage, for a
moment later a common sailor presented himself and was
promptly given room No. 28. From where I stood in the
darkness I could, without being seen, observe a few soldiers and two men of the working classes who were chat-
ting tranquilly in a stiflingly hot little room, gaudily
decorated with coloured pictures of women cut from illustrated magazines and reviews.

These men, as they chatted quietly together, were expounding patriotic ideas: "After all, you've got to do what
the other blokes do," said one. "Well, you can be jolly
sure I don't mean to get killed," was the reply of another,
who evidently was going off the next day to a dangerous
post, to some expression of good wishes which I had not
heard. "I reckon, at twenty-two, after only doing six
months, it would be a bit hard," he exclaimed in a voice
in which could be heard, even more plainly than the desire to go on living, the assurance that his reasoning was
correct, as though the fact that he was only twenty-two
could not fail to give him a better chance of survival, as
though it were out of the question that he should be
killed. "It's terrific in Paris," said another; "you'd never
know there's a war on. How about you, Julot, d'you still
mean to join up?" "Of course I do, I can't wait to take a
pot-shot or two at these filthy Boches." "This Joffre, you
know, he's just a man who sleeps with the politicians'
wives, he's never done a thing himself." "That's a dreadful way to talk," said a slightly older man, an airman, and

then, turning to the workman who had just made the statement: "I should advise you not to talk like that in the front line, the *poilus* would soon do you in." The banality of these scraps of conversation did not inspire me with any great wish to hear more, and I was about to make my entrance or go back down the stairs when I was jolted out of my indifference by hearing a series of remarks which made me shudder: "I'm amazed the boss isn't back yet, damn it, at this hour of the night I don't know where he's going to find any chains." "Anyhow, the chap's already tied up." "Tied up? Well, he is and he isn't. Tie me up like that and I'd soon untie myself." "But the padlock's closed." "Of course it's closed, but it's not so impossible to open it. The trouble is the chains aren't long enough. Don't you try and tell me, I was beating the stuffing out of him all last night until my hands were covered with blood." "Are you doing the beating tonight?" "No. It's not me, it's Maurice. But it'll be me on Sunday, the boss promised me." I understood now why the strong arm of the sailor had been needed. If peaceable citizens had been turned away, it was not because the hotel was a nest of spies. An appalling crime was about to be committed, unless someone arrived in time to discover it and have the criminals arrested. And yet the whole scene, in the midst of this peaceful and threatened night, was like a dream or a fairy-tale, so that it was at once with the pride of an emissary of justice and the rapture of a poet that I at length, my mind made up, entered the hotel.

I touched my hat lightly and the people in the room, without rising to their feet, replied more or less civilly to the greeting. "Can you tell me who is in charge here? I should like a room and something to drink sent up to it."

"Will you wait a minute, the boss has gone out."
"There's the director, he's upstairs," suggested one of the
men who had taken part in the conversation. "But you
know he can't be disturbed." "Do you think they will
give me a room?" "Expect so." "43 must be free," said
the young man who was sure he would not be killed because he was twenty-two years old. And he moved a little
way along the sofa to make room for me. "Suppose we
open the window a bit, you can cut the smoke with a
knife in here!" said the airman; and indeed they all had
their pipe or their cigarette. "Yes, but in that case close
the shutters first, you know it's forbidden to show any
light because of the Zeppelins." "We've finished with the
Zeppelins. There's even been something in the papers
about their having all been shot down." "We've finished
with this, we've finished with that, what d'you know
about it? When you've done fifteen months at the front,
as I have, and shot down your fifth Boche aeroplane,
you'll be able to talk. What d'you want to believe the papers for? They were over Compiègne yesterday, they
killed a mother and two children." "A mother and two
children!" said the young man who hoped not to be
killed, with blazing eyes and a look of profound compassion upon his energetic and open countenance, which I
found very likeable. "There's been no news of big Julot
lately. His 'godmother' hasn't had a letter from him for
eight days, and it's the first time he's been so long without writing." "Who is she, his 'godmother'?" "The
woman who looks after the toilets just beyond the
Olympia." "Do they sleep together?" "What an idea!
She's a married woman, she couldn't be more respectable.
She sends him money every week out of pure kindness of

heart. She's a real good sort." "Do you know him then, big Julot?" "Do I know him!" retorted scornfully the young man of twenty-two. "He's a close friend of mine and one of the best. There's not many I think as highly of as I do of him: a real pal, always ready to do you a good turn. Yes, it would be a catastrophe all right if anything had happened to him." Someone proposed a game of dice and, from the feverish haste with which the young man of twenty-two shook them and cried out the results, with his eyes starting out of his head, it was easy to see that he had the gambler's temperament. I did not quite catch the next remark that someone made to him, but he exclaimed with a note of profound pity in his voice: "Julot a ponce! You mean he *says* he's a ponce. But he's no more a ponce than I am. I've seen him with my own eyes paying his woman, yes, paying her. That's to say, I don't say Jeanne l'Algérienne didn't give him a little something now and then, but it was never more than five francs, and what's that from a woman in a brothel earning more than fifty francs a day? A present of five francs! Some men are just too stupid to live. And now she's at the front, well, her life may be hard, I grant you, but she can earn as much as she wants—and she sends him nothing. Bah, that chap a ponce? There's plenty who could call themselves a ponce at that rate. Not only is he not a ponce, in my opinion he's an imbecile." The oldest of the group, whom the boss had no doubt for that reason put in charge of the others, with instructions to make them behave with a certain restraint, had been to the lavatory for a moment and heard only the end of this conversation. But he could not help looking in my direction and seemed visibly upset at the impression such talk must have made on me. Without addressing himself specially to the young man of twenty-two, though it was he who had been expounding this theory of venal love, he said, in a general manner: "You're talking too much and too loud, the window is open, there are people asleep at this hour. You know quite well that if the boss came back and heard you talking like that, he wouldn't be at all pleased."

At that very moment the door was heard to open and everyone was silent, thinking it was the boss, but it was only a foreign chauffeur who was welcomed as an old friend by everybody in the room. But seeing a magnificent watchchain displayed upon the chauffeur's jacket, the young man of twenty-two threw him a questioning and amused glance, followed by a frown and a severe wink in my direction. I understood that the first look meant: "What's that, did you steal it? My congratulations." And the second: "Don't say anything, because of this fellow we don't know." Suddenly the boss came in, carrying several yards of heavy iron chains—sufficient to secure quite a number of convicts—and sweating. "What a weight!" he said. "If you weren't all so idle, I shouldn't be obliged to fetch them myself." I told him that I wanted a room. "Just for a few hours. I can't find a cab and I am rather unwell. But I should like something to drink sent up." "Pierrot, go and fetch some *cassis* from the cellar and tell them to get No. 43 ready. There's 7 ringing again. They say they're ill. Ill my foot, I wouldn't be surprised if they'd been doping themselves, they look half cracked, it's time they were shown the door. Has anybody put a pair of sheets in 22? Good! There goes 7 again, run and see what it is. Well, Maurice, what are you standing there for? You know someone's waiting for you, go up to 14b.

And get a move on." And Maurice hurried out after the boss, who seemed a little annoyed that I had seen his chains and disappeared carrying them with him. "How is it you're so late?" the young man of twenty-two asked the chauffeur. "What do you mean, late? I'm an hour early. But it's too hot in the streets. My appointment's not till midnight." "Who have you come for then?" "Pretty Pamela," said the dark-skinned chauffeur, whose laugh uncovered a set of fine white teeth. "Ah!" said the young man of twenty-two.

Presently I was taken up to Room 43, but it was so unpleasantly stuffy and my curiosity was so great that, having drunk my *cassis*, I started to go downstairs again, then, changing my mind, turned round and went up past the floor of Room 43 to the top of the building. Suddenly from a room situated by itself at the end of a corridor, I thought I heard stifled groans. I walked rapidly towards the sounds and put my ear to the door. "I beseech you, mercy, have pity, untie me, don't beat me so hard," said a voice. "I kiss your feet, I abase myself, I promise not to offend again. Have pity on me." "No, you filthy brute," replied another voice, "and if you yell and drag yourself about on your knees like that, you'll be tied to the bed, no mercy for you," and I heard the noise of the crack of a whip, which I guessed to be reinforced with nails, for it was followed by cries of pain. At this moment I noticed that there was a small oval window opening from the room on to the corridor and that the curtain had not been drawn across it; stealthily in the darkness I crept as far as this window and there in the room, chained to a bed like Prometheus to his rock, receiving the blows that Maurice rained upon him with a whip which was in fact studded

with nails, I saw, with blood already flowing from him
and covered with bruises which proved that the chastise-
ment was not taking place for the first time—I saw before
me M. de Charlus.

Suddenly the door opened and a man came in who
fortunately did not see me. It was Jupien. He went up to
the Baron with an air of respect and a smile of understanding: "Well, you don't need me, do you?" The Baron
asked Jupien to send Maurice out of the room for a moment. Jupien did so with perfect unconcern. "We can't be
heard, can we?" said the Baron to Jupien, who assured
him that this was the case. The Baron knew that Jupien,
with an intelligence worthy of a man of letters, was yet
quite lacking in practical sense and constantly talked
about people in their presence with innuendoes which de-
ceived nobody and nicknames which everybody understood.

"Just a second," interrupted Jupien, who had heard a
bell ring in Room No. 3. It was a deputy of the Liberal
Action party, who was about to leave. Jupien did not need
to look at the bell-board, for he recognised the man's ring.
Indeed the deputy came every day after lunch, but today
he had been obliged to re-arrange his timetable, for at
twelve o'clock he had given away his daughter in marriage
at the church of Saint-Pierre-de-Chaillot. So he had come
in the evening but was anxious to leave early on account
of his wife, who very easily became nervous if he was late
in getting home, particularly in these days of bombardment. Jupien always liked to accompany him downstairs
in order to show his deference for the status of "honourable," and in this he was quite disinterested. For although this deputy (who repudiated the exaggerations of

*L'Action Française* and would in any case have been incapable of understanding a line of Charles Maurras or Léon
Daudet) stood well with the ministers, whom he flattered
by inviting them to his shooting-parties, Jupien would not
have dared to ask him for the slightest support in his difficulties with the police. He knew that, had he ventured to
mention that subject to the affluent and apprehensive leg-
islator, he would not have saved himself even the most
harmless "raid" but would immediately have lost the most
generous of his clients. After having escorted the deputy
as far as the door, from which he set off with his hat
pulled down over his eyes and his collar turned up and
with a rapid gliding movement not unlike the style of his
electoral manifestos, by which devices he hoped to render
his face invisible, Jupien went upstairs again to M. de
Charlus. "It was Monsieur Eugène," he said to him. In
Jupien's establishment, as in a sanatorium, people were
referred to only by their Christian names, though their
real names, either to satisfy the curiosity of the visitor or
to enhance the prestige of the house, were invariably
added in a whisper. Sometimes, however, Jupien was unaware of the real identity of a client and imagined and
said that he was some well-known financier or nobleman
or artist—fleeting errors not without charm for the man
to whom the wrong name was attached—and in the end
had to resign himself to the idea that he still did not know
who Monsieur Victor was. Sometimes too, to please the
Baron, he was in the habit of inverting the procedure that
is customary on certain social occasions ("Let me introduce you to M. Lebrun," then a whisper: "He wants to
be called M. Lebrun but he is really Grand Duke X——
of Russia"). Jupien on the other hand felt that it was not

quite sufficient to introduce M. de Charlus to a young milkman. He would murmur to him with a wink: "He's a milkman but he's also one of the most dangerous thugs in Belleville" (and it was with a superbly salacious note in his voice that Jupien uttered the word "thug"). And as if this recommendation were not sufficient, he would try to add one or two further "citations." "He has had several convictions for theft and burglary, he was in Fresnes for assaulting" (the same salacious note in his voice) "and practically murdering people in the street, and he's been in a punishment battalion in Africa. He killed his sergeant."

The Baron was slightly cross with Jupien for his lack of prudence, for he knew that in this house which he had instructed his factotum to purchase for him and to manage through a subordinate, everybody, thanks to the blunders of Mlle d'Oloron's uncle, was more or less aware of his identity and his name (many, however, thought that it was not a title but a nickname, and mispronounced and distorted it, so that their own stupidity and not the discretion of Jupien had served to protect the Baron). But he found it simpler to let himself be reassured by Jupien's assurances, and now, relieved to know that they could not be heard, he said to him: "I did not want to speak in front of that boy, who is very nice and does his best. But I don't find him sufficiently brutal. He has a charming face, but when he calls me a filthy brute he might be just repeating a lesson." "I assure you, nobody has said a word to him," replied Jupien, without perceiving how improbable this statement was. "And besides, he was involved in the murder of a concierge in La Villette." "Ah! that is extremely interesting," said the Baron with a smile.

"But I'll tell you who I have here: the killer of oxen, the man of the slaughter-houses, who is so like this boy; he happened to be passing. Would you care to try him?" "Yes, certainly I should." I saw the man of the slaughter-houses enter the room; he was indeed a little like Maurice, but—and this was odder—they both had in them something of a type which I had never myself consciously observed in Morel's face but which I now clearly saw to exist there; they bore a resemblance, if not to Morel as I had seen him, at least to a certain countenance which eyes seeing Morel otherwise than I did might have constructed out of his features. No sooner had I, out of features borrowed from my recollections of Morel, privately made for myself this rough model of what he might represent to somebody else, than I realised that the two young men, one of whom was a jeweller's assistant while the other worked in a hotel, were in a vague way substitutes for Morel. Was I to conclude that M. de Charlus, at least in a certain aspect of his loves, was always faithful to a particular type and that the desire which had made him select these two young men one after the other was the identical desire which had made him accost Morel on the platform at Doncières station; that all three resembled a little the ephebe whose form, engraved in the sapphire-like eyes of M. de Charlus, gave to his glance that strange quality which had alarmed me the first day at Balbec? Or that, his love for Morel having modified the type which he pursued, to console himself for Morel's absence he sought men who resembled him? A third hypothesis which occurred to me was that perhaps, in spite of appearances, there had never existed between him and Morel anything more than relations of friendship, and

that M. de Charlus caused young men who resembled
Morel to come to Jupien's establishment so that he might
have the illusion, while he was with them, of enjoying
pleasure with Morel himself. It is true that, if one thought
of everything that M. de Charlus had done for Morel, this
hypothesis was bound to seem most unlikely, did one not
know that love drives us not only to the greatest sacrifices
on behalf of the person we love, but sometimes even to
the sacrifice of our desire itself, a desire which in any case
we find all the harder to gratify if the loved person is
aware of the strength of our love.

Something else that makes this hypothesis less unlikely than at first sight it appears (though probably it
does not correspond to the reality) lies in the nervous
temperament, in the profoundly passionate character of
M. de Charlus—in this resembling Saint-Loup—which
in the early days of his relations with Morel might have
played the same part, in a more decent and negative way,
as it did at the beginning of his nephew's relations with
Rachel. A man's relations with a woman whom he loves
(and the same may be true of love for a young man) may
remain platonic for a reason which is neither the woman's
virtue nor a lack of sensuality in the love which she inspires. The reason may be that the lover, too impatient
from the very excess of his love, does not know how to
wait with a sufficient show of indifference for the moment
when he will obtain what he desires. Over and over again
he returns to the charge, he writes incessantly to the
woman, he tries constantly to see her, she refuses, he is in
despair. Henceforth she understands that if she accords
him her company, her friendship, this happiness in itself
will seem so considerable to the man who thought he had

lost it, that she may spare herself the trouble of giving him anything more and may take advantage of a moment when he can no longer endure not to see her, when he is determined at any price to end the war, to impose upon him a peace of which the first condition will be the platonic nature of their relations. In any case, during the period which preceded this treaty, the lover, always anxious, hoping all the time for a letter, a glance, has given up thinking of physical possession, which at first had been the object of the desire which had tormented him; that desire has withered away with waiting and its place has been taken by needs of another order, needs which can, however, if they remain unsatisfied, cause him yet greater pain. So that the pleasure which at the beginning he had hoped to obtain from caresses, he receives later not in its natural form but instead from friendly words, from mere promises of the loved woman's presence, which after the effects of uncertainty—sometimes after a single look, black with a heavy cloud of disdain, which has withdrawn her to such a distance that he thinks he will never see her again—bring with them a delicious relief from tension. A woman divines these things and knows that she can afford the luxury of never giving herself to a man who, because he has been too agitated to conceal it during the first few days, has allowed her to become aware of his incurable desire for her. She is only too pleased to receive, without giving anything in return, much more than she is accustomed to be given when she gives herself. Men with a nervous temperament believe therefore in the virtue of their idol. And the halo which they place round her is a product, but as we have seen an indirect one, of their excessive love. The woman then finds herself very much in the position—though she of course is conscious, while they are not—of those unwittingly crafty drugs like sleeping-draughts and morphine. It is not to the people to whom they bring the pleasure of sleep or a genuine well-being that these drugs are an absolute necessity; it is not by such people as these that they would be bought at any price, bartered against all the sick man's possessions, but by that other class of sick men (who may perhaps be the same individuals but become different with the passage of a few years), those whom the medicine does not send to sleep, to whom it gives no thrill of pleasure, but who, so long as they are without it, are prey to an agitation which at any price, even the price of their own death, they need desperately to end.

In the case of M. de Charlus, which on the whole, with slight discrepancies due to the identity of sex, accords very well with the general laws of love, for all that he belonged to a family more ancient than the Capets, that he was rich and vainly sought after by fashionable society while Morel was nobody, he would have got nowhere by saying to Morel, as he had once said to me: "I am a prince, I want to help you"—it was still Morel who had the upper hand so long as he refused to surrender. And for him to persist in this refusal, it was perhaps enough that he should feel himself to be loved. The horror that grand people have for the snobs who move heaven and earth to make their acquaintance is felt also by the virile man for the invert, by a woman for every man who is too much in love with her. M. de Charlus possessed, and would have offered Morel a share in, immense advantages. But it is possible that all this might have hurled itself in vain against a determined will. And in that case, M. de Charlus would have suffered the same fate as the Germans—in whose ranks in fact his ancestry placed him—who in the war at that moment taking its course were indeed, as the Baron was a little too fond of repeating, victorious on every front. But of what use were their victories, since after every one they found the Allies yet more firmly resolved to refuse them the one thing that they, the Germans, wanted: peace and reconciliation? Napoleon too, as he advanced into Russia, had again and again magnanimously invited the authorities to meet him. But nobody came.

I made my way downstairs and went back into the little ante-room where Maurice, uncertain whether he would be sent for again (he had been told by Jupien to wait just in case), was engaged in a game of cards with one of his friends. There was a lot of excitement about a *croix de guerre* which had been found lying on the ground—nobody knew who had lost it and to whom it ought to be returned so that the owner should not be punished. Then there was talk of the generosity of an officer who had been killed trying to save his batman. "All the same, there are some good blokes among the rich. I'd gladly get myself killed for a chap like that," said Maurice, who evidently performed his terrible fustigations of the Baron simply from mechanical habit, as a result of a neglected education, from need of money and from a certain preference for making it in a manner which was supposed to be less trouble, and was perhaps really more trouble, than ordinary work. But as M. de Charlus had feared, he was perhaps really very kind-hearted and certainly, so it seemed, a young man of exemplary courage. He almost had tears in his eyes as he spoke of the death of this officer, and the young man of twenty-two was no less moved. "Yes, indeed, they're fine blokes. For poor chaps like us there's not much to lose, but when it's a toff who has a whole troop of flunkeys and can go to posh bars every night of his life, it's really terrific! You can scoff as much as you like, but when you see blokes like that dying, it really does something to you. Rich people like that, God shouldn't let them die—for one thing they're too useful to the working man. A death like that makes you want to kill every Boche to the last man. And then look what they did at Louvain, and cutting off the hands of little children! No, I don't know, I'm no better than the next man, but I'd rather face the music and be shot to bits than give in to barbarians like that; they're not men, they're real barbarians, don't you try and tell me anything else." All these young men were patriots at heart. One only, who had been slightly wounded in the arm but was soon going to have to return to the front, did not rise to the level of the others. "Darn it," he said, "it wasn't the right sort of wound" (the kind that gets you invalided out), very much as in the past Mme Swann would have said: "Somehow or other I've caught this most tiresome influenza."

The door opened to re-admit the chauffeur, who had been taking the air for a moment. "What, finished already? You weren't long," he said, catching sight of Maurice, whom he supposed to be still engaged in beating the individual whom, in allusion to a newspaper which was appearing at that time, they had nicknamed "the Man in Chains." "It may not have seemed long to you out in the fresh air," replied Maurice, vexed that the others should see that he had failed to give satisfaction upstairs. "But if you'd been obliged to wallop away with all your might in this heat, like me! If it wasn't for the fifty francs he gives . . ." "And then, he's a man who talks well; you can see he's educated. Does he say it will soon be over?" "He says we'll never beat them, it will end without either side really winning." "Bloody hell, if he says that he must be a Boche . . ." "I've already told you you're talking too loud," said the oldest of the group to the others, seeing that I had returned, and then to me: "Have you finished with your room?" "Shut your trap, you're not the boss here." "Yes, I've finished, and I've come to pay." "It would be better if you paid the *patron*. Maurice, go and fetch him." "But I don't want to bother you." "It's no trouble." Maurice went upstairs, and came back saying: "The *patron* will be down in a second." I gave him two francs for his pains. He blushed with pleasure. "Oh! thank you very much. I'll send it to my brother who's a prisoner. No, he doesn't have a bad time. It depends a lot on the camp you're in."

Meanwhile, two very smart clients, in white tie and tails and wearing overcoats—two Russians, as I guessed from the very slight accent with which they spoke—were standing in the doorway and deliberating whether they should enter. It was visibly the first time that they had been to the place, to which no doubt they had come on somebody's recommendation, and they appeared torn between desire, temptation and extreme fright. One of the two—a good-looking young man—kept repeating every ten seconds to the other, with a smile that was half a question and half an attempt at persuasion: "Well! After all, what do we care?" But though no doubt he meant by this that after all they did not care about the conse-

quences, it is probable that he cared rather more than he
implied, for the remark was not followed by any movement to cross the threshold but by a further glance at his
companion, followed by the same smile and the same
"After all, what do we care?" And in this "After all, what
do we care?" I saw a perfect example of that portentous
language, so unlike the language we habitually speak, in
which emotion deflects what we had intended to say and
causes to emerge in its place an entirely different phrase,
issued from an unknown lake wherein dwell these expressions alien to our thoughts which by virtue of that very
fact reveal them. I remember an occasion when Françoise,
whose approach we had not heard, was about to come
into the room while Albertine was completely naked in
my arms, and Albertine, wanting to warn me, blurted out:
"Good heavens, here's the beautiful Françoise!" Françoise, whose sight was no longer very good and who
was merely going to cross the room at some distance from
us, would no doubt have noticed nothing. But the un-
precedented phrase "the beautiful Françoise," which Albertine had never uttered before in her life, was in itself
enough to betray its origin; Françoise sensed that the
words had been plucked at random by emotion and had
no need to look to understand what was happening; she
went out muttering in her dialect the word *poutana*. On
another occasion, many years later, after Bloch had become the father of a family and had married off one of his
daughters to a Catholic, an ill-mannered gentleman said
to the young woman that he thought he had heard that
her father was a Jew and asked what his name was.
Whereupon she, who had been Mlle Bloch with a *k*
sound from the day she was born, replied "Bloch" with

the Teutonic *ch* which the Duc de Guermantes would have used.

The *patron*, to return to the scene in the hotel (into which the two Russians had decided to penetrate—"After all, what do we care?"), had still not arrived when Jupien came in to say that they were talking too loud and that the neighbours would complain. But seeing me he was rooted to the spot in amazement. "Go out on to the landing, all of you." They were all rising to their feet when I said to him: "It would be simpler if these young men stayed where they are and you and I went outside for a moment." He followed me, very agitated. I explained to him why I had come. Clients could be heard inquiring of the *patron* whether he could introduce them to a footman, a choir-boy, a negro chauffeur. Every profession interested these old lunatics, every branch of the armed forces, every one of the allied nations. Some asked particularly for Canadians, influenced perhaps unconsciously by the charm of an accent so slight that one does not know whether it comes from the France of the past or from England. The Scots too, because of their kilts and because dreams of a landscape with lakes are often associated with these desires, were at a premium. And as every form of madness is, if not in every case aggravated by circumstances, at least imprinted by them with particular characteristics, an old man in whom curiosity of every kind had no doubt been satisfied was asking insistently to be introduced to a disabled soldier. Slow footsteps were heard on the stairs. With the indiscretion that was natural to him, Jupien could not refrain from telling me that it was the Baron who was coming down, and at all costs he must not see me, but that if I liked to go into the bedroom adjoin-

ing the ante-room where the young men were, he would
open the ventilator, a device which he had fixed up so
that the Baron could see and hear without being seen, and
which he said he would use in my favour against him.
"Only don't move." And pushing me into the dark, he
left me. In any case he had no other room to give me, his
hotel, in spite of the war, being full. The one which I had
just left had been taken by the Vicomte de Courvoisier
who, having got away from the Red Cross at X—for two
days, had come to Paris for an hour's entertainment before going on to the Château de Courvoisier to be reunited with his wife, to whom he would explain that he
had not been able to catch the fast train. He had no suspicion that M. de Charlus was a few yards away from
him, and the latter would have been equally surprised to
know that his cousin was there, never having met him in
the establishment of Jupien, who was himself ignorant of
the Vicomte's carefully concealed identity.

The Baron soon entered the ante-room, walking with
difficulty on account of his injuries, though doubtless he
must have been used to them. Although his pleasure was
at an end and he had only come in to give Maurice the
money which he owed him, he directed at the young men
a tender and curious glance which travelled round the
whole circle, promising himself with each of them the
pleasure of a moment's chat, platonic but amorously prolonged. And in the sprightly frivolity which he exhibited
before this harem which appeared almost to intimidate
him, I recognised those jerky movements of the body and
the head, those languishing glances which had struck me
on the evening of his first visit to La Raspelière, graces
inherited from some grandmother whom I had not

known, which in ordinary life were disguised by more virile expressions on his face but which from time to time
were made to blossom there coquettishly, when circumstances made him anxious to please an inferior audience,
by the desire to appear a great lady.

Jupien had recommended the young men to the
Baron's favour by swearing that they were all pimps from
Belleville and would sell you their own sisters for a few
francs. And in this he was at the same time lying and
telling the truth. Better, more soft-hearted than he made
them out to be, they did not belong to a race of savages.
But the clients who believed them to be thugs spoke to
them nevertheless with complete truthfulness, a truthfulness which they imagined these terrible beings to share.
For a man given to sadistic pleasures may believe that he
is talking to a murderer but this will not alter his own purity of heart, he will still be astounded by the mendacity
of his companion, who is not a murderer at all but wants
to earn a little easy money and whose father or mother or
sister alternately die, come to life, and die again as he
contradicts himself in his conversation with the client
whom he is attempting to please. The client, in his
naïvety, is astounded, for with his arbitrary conception of
the gigolo, while he gets a thrill of delight from the numerous murders of which he believes him to be guilty, he
is horrified by any simple contradiction or lie which he
detects in his words.

Everybody in the room seemed to know him, and
M. de Charlus stopped for a long time before each one,
talking to them in what he thought was their language,
both from a pretentious affectation of local colour and because he got a sadistic pleasure from contact with a life of

depravity. "You're disgusting, you are, I saw you outside
the Olympia with two tarts. After a bit of brass, no
doubt. Just shows how faithful you are to me." Luckily
for the man to whom these remarks were addressed, he
did not have time to declare that he would never have accepted "brass" from a woman, a claim which would have
damped the Baron's ardour, but reserved his protest for
the final phrase, which he answered by saying: "But of
course I'm faithful to you." This remark gave M. de
Charlus a lively pleasure, and as, in spite of himself, the
kind of intelligence that was natural to him showed
through the character which he affected, he turned to
Jupien: "How nice of him to say that! And how well he
says it! One would really think it was true. And after all,
what does it matter whether it is true or not since he
manages to make me believe it? What charming little eyes
he has! There, I'm going to give you two big kisses for
your trouble, my dear boy. You will think of me in the
trenches. Things are not too bad there?" "Whew, there
are some days, when a grenade just misses you . . ."
And the young man proceeded to imitate the noise of the
grenade, the aeroplanes, etc. "But one's got to do what
the others do, and you can be absolutely sure that we will
go on to the end." "To the end! If one only knew to what
end!" said the Baron in a melancholy manner, giving rein
to his "pessimism." "You haven't seen what Sarah Bernhardt said in the papers: 'France will go on to the end. If
necessary, the French will let themselves be killed to the
last man.'" "I do not doubt for a single moment that the
French would bravely let themselves be killed to the last
man," said M. de Charlus, as if this were the simplest
thing in the world and although he himself had no inten-

tion of doing anything whatsoever, hoping by this remark
to correct the impression of pacifism which he gave when
he forgot himself. "That I do not doubt, but I ask myself
to what extent *Madame* Sarah Bernhardt is qualified to
speak in the name of France . . . But I don't think I have
made the acquaintance of this charming, this delightful
young man," he added, spying another whom he did not
recognise or perhaps had not seen before. He greeted him
as he would have greeted a prince at Versailles, and making the most of this opportunity to have a supplementary
pleasure for nothing—just as, when I was little and my
mother had finished giving an order at Boissier's or
Gouache's, I would accept the offer of a sweet which one
of the ladies behind the counter would invite me to select
from those glass bowls over which she and her colleagues
held sway—he took the hand of the charming young man
and gave it a long squeeze, in the Prussian manner, smil-
ingly fixing him with his eyes for the interminable time
which photographers used to take to pose you when the
light was bad. "Sir, I am charmed, I am enchanted to
make your acquaintance. What pretty hair he has!" he
said, turning to Jupien. Next he went up to Maurice to
give him his fifty francs, but first, putting his arm round
his waist: "You never told me that you had knifed an old
hag of a concierge in Belleville." And M. de Charlus
shrieked with ecstatic laughter and brought his face close
to that of Maurice. "Oh! Monsieur le Baron," said the
gigolo, who had not been warned, "how can you believe
such a thing?" Whether the report was in fact false, or
whether it was true and the perpetrator of the deed nevertheless thought it abominable and one of those things that
it is better to deny, he went on: "Me touch a fellow-

creature? A Boche, yes, because that's war, but a woman, and an old woman at that!" This declaration of virtuous principles had the effect of a douche of cold water upon the Baron, who brusquely moved away from Maurice, having first handed him his money, but with the disgusted air of someone who has been cheated, who pays because he does not want to make a fuss but is far from pleased. The bad impression made upon the Baron was accentuated by the manner in which the recipient thanked him, with the words: "I shall send this to the old folks and keep a bit for my brother at the front as well." By these touching sentiments M. de Charlus was almost as gravely disappointed as he was irritated by the rather conventional peasant's language in which they were expressed. Occasionally Jupien warned the young men that they ought to be more perverse. Then one of them, as if he were confessing to something diabolical, would hazard: "I say, Baron, you won't believe me, but when I was a kid I used to watch my parents making love through the key-hole. Pretty vicious, wasn't it? You look as if you think that's a cock and bull story, but I swear it's the truth." And M. de Charlus was driven at once to despair and to exasperation by this factitious attempt at perversity, the result of which was only to reveal such depths both of stupidity and of innocence. Yet even the most determined thief or murderer would not have satisfied him, for that sort of man does not talk about his crimes; and besides there exists in the sadist—however kind he may be, in fact all the more the kinder he is—a thirst for evil which wicked men, doing what they do not because it is wicked but from other motives, are unable to assuage.

The young man realised his mistake and tried to repair it by saying that he loathed the sight of a copper and by daringly inquiring of the Baron: "How about a date?"—but it was too late, the charm was dispelled. One had a distinct feeling of sham, as with the books of authors who force themselves to write slang. It was in vain that the young man described in detail all the "filthy things" that he did with his wife; M. de Charlus merely reflected that these "filthy things" amounted to very little. And in this he was not simply being insincere. Nothing is more limited than pleasure and vice. In that sense one may say truly, altering slightly the meaning of the phrase, that we revolve always in the same vicious circle.

If M. de Charlus was believed to be not a baron but a prince, there was, conversely, general regret in the establishment for the death of someone of whom the gigolos said: "I don't know his name, but it seems that he is a baron," and who was none other than the Prince de Foix (the father of Saint-Loup's friend). Supposed by his wife to spend a lot of time at his club, in reality he would sit for hours at Jupien's, retailing fashionable gossip to an audience from the underworld. Like his son, he was tall and good-looking. M. de Charlus, no doubt because he had always known him in society, remained strangely ignorant that the Prince shared his own tastes, to such a degree that he was even said to have had designs at one time upon his own son, Saint-Loup's friend, then still at school. This was probably untrue: on the contrary, excellently informed about activities whose existence many do not suspect, he watched with care over the company kept by his son. One day a man—and a man not of exalted origin—followed the young Prince de Foix as far as his father's house, where he threw a note in at the window, which the father picked up. But the follower, though genealogically this was not the case, from another point of view belonged to the same world as M. de Foix the father. He therefore had no difficulty in finding among those who shared their common secrets an intermediary who silenced M. de Foix by proving to him that it was his son who had himself provoked this rash act of an elderly man. And this was quite possible. For the Prince de Foix had succeeded in preserving his son from the external influence of bad company but not from heredity. The young Prince de Foix, however, remained, like his father, in this respect unknown to his social equals, although in a different world his behaviour was wild in the extreme.

"How simple he is! You would never say he was a baron," said some of the frequenters of the establishment when M. de Charlus had left, after being escorted to the street door by Jupien, to whom he did not fail to complain of the young man's virtuousness. From the air of annoyance of Jupien, whose duty it was to have trained the young man in advance, it was clear that the fictitious murderer would presently get a terrific dressing-down. "The truth is exactly the opposite of what you told me," added the Baron, so that Jupien might profit by the lesson for another time. "He seems most good-natured, he expresses sentiments of respect for his family." "Still, he's on bad terms with his father," Jupien objected. "It's true they live together, but they work in different bars." Obviously this was not much of a crime compared with murder, but Jupien had been caught unprepared with an answer. The Baron said no more, for, if he wanted others to prepare his pleasures for him, he wanted to give himself the illusion that they were unprepared. "He is a real crook, he said all that to mislead you, you are too gullible," Jupien went on, in an attempt to exculpate himself which succeeded only in wounding the vanity of M. de Charlus.

"It seems that he has a million francs a day to spend," said the young man of twenty-two, who saw no improbability in this statement. The car which had come to fetch M. de Charlus was now heard to drive away. At the same moment there entered the room with a slow step, by the side of a soldier who had evidently emerged with her from a neighbouring bedroom, what appeared to me to be an elderly lady in a black skirt. I soon realised my mistake: it was a priest—that thing so rare, and in France altogether exceptional, a bad priest. Evidently the soldier was teasing his companion about the discrepancy between his conduct and his habit, for the other with a serious air, raising a finger towards his hideous face with the gesture of a doctor of theology, said sententiously: "What do you expect? I am not" (I expected him to say "a saint") "a good girl." He was, however, ready to depart and he said good-bye to Jupien, who had just come upstairs again after seeing the Baron to the door. But absentmindedly the bad priest had forgotten to pay for his room. Jupien, who had always a ready wit, shook the collecting box in which he placed the contribution of each client and said, as he made it clink: "For the expenses of the church, Monsieur l'Abbé!" The horrid creature apologised, put in his coin and disappeared.

Jupien came to fetch me from the cave of darkness in which I had been standing without daring to move. "Come into the hall for a moment where my young men are sitting, while I go upstairs and lock up the bedroom;

since you have taken a room, it's quite natural." The *pa-tron* was there, so I paid him. At that moment a young man in a dinner-jacket came in and asked the *patron* with an air of authority: "Will I be able to have Léon at a quarter to eleven instead of eleven tomorrow morning, as I have a luncheon engagement?" "That will depend," replied the *patron*, "on how long the Abbé keeps him." This reply appeared not to satisfy the young man in a dinner-jacket, who seemed to be on the point of launching into abuse of the Abbé, but his fury was diverted when he caught sight of me. Going straight up to the *patron*: "Who is this? What does this mean?" he muttered in a quiet but angry voice. The *patron*, very put out, explained that my presence was quite harmless, that I had taken a room. The young man in a dinner-jacket appeared to be not in the slightest degree pacified by this explanation. He kept repeating: "This is extremely unpleasant, things of this sort ought not to happen, you know I detest them, if you are not careful I will never set foot here again." The execution of this threat did not, however, appear to be imminent, for he went off in a rage, but not without ask-ing that Léon should try to be free at a quarter to eleven, or better still half past ten. Jupien came back to fetch me and we went downstairs together and out into the street.

"I do not want you to misjudge me," he said to me. "This house does not bring me in as much profit as you might think. I am obliged to let rooms to respectable peo-ple, though of course if they were my only customers I should simply be throwing money down the drain. Here, contrary to the doctrine of the Carmelites, it is thanks to vice that virtue is able to live. No, if I took this house, or rather if I got the manager whom you have seen to take it,

it was purely and simply in order to render a service to
the Baron and amuse his old age." Jupien was here referring not merely to scenes of sadism like those which I had
witnessed and to the actual vicious practices of the Baron.
The latter, even for conversation, for company, for a game
of cards, now only enjoyed the society of lower-class people who exploited him. No doubt the snobbery of the gutter may be understood as easily as snobbery of the other
kind. The two had in fact long been united, alternating
one with the other, in M. de Charlus, who thought no
one was smart enough to be numbered among his social
acquaintances, no one sufficiently a ruffian to be worth
knowing in other ways. "I detest the intermediate style,"
he would say. "Bourgeois comedy is stiff and affected. Let
me have either the princesses of classical tragedy or broad
farce. No half-way houses—either *Phèdre* or *Les Saltim-
banques*." But in the end the balance between the two
forms of snobbery had been broken. Perhaps because he
was an old man and tired, perhaps because sensuality had
come to enter into even his trivial relationships, the Baron
now lived only among his "inferiors," thus unintentionally
taking his place as the successor of more than one among
his great ancestors, the Duc de La Rochefoucauld, the
Prince d'Harcourt, the Duc de Berry, whom we see in the
pages of Saint-Simon passing their lives in the midst of
their lackeys, who extracted enormous sums from them,
and sharing their amusements, to such an extent that people who had to visit them were embarrassed, for their
sakes, to find these great noblemen familiarly engaged in a
game of cards or a drinking-bout with their domestic servants. "And above all," Jupien went on, "it is to keep him
out of trouble, because the Baron, you know, is a big

baby. Even now that he has here everything that he can desire, he still wanders about in search of sordid adventures. And with his generosity, that sort of thing could have disagreeable consequences in these days. Only the other day there was a page-boy from a hotel who was absolutely terrified because of all the money the Baron offered him if he would go to his house! (To his house, what imprudence!) The boy, who in fact only cares about women, was reassured when he understood what was wanted of him. Hearing all these promises of money, he had taken the Baron for a spy. And he was greatly relieved when he realised that he was being asked to sell not his country but his body, which is possibly not a more moral thing to do, but less dangerous and in any case easier." And listening to Jupien, I said to myself: "How unfortunate it is that M. de Charlus is not a novelist or a poet! Not merely so that he could describe what he sees, but because the position in which a Charlus finds himself with respect to desire causes scandals to spring up around him, and compels him to take life seriously, to load pleasure with a weight of emotion. He cannot get stuck in an ironical and superficial view of things because a current of pain is perpetually reawakened within him. Almost every time he makes a declaration of love he is violently snubbed, if he does not run the risk of being sent to prison." A slap in the face or a box on the ear helps to educate not only children but poets. If M. de Charlus had been a novelist, the house which Jupien had set up for him, by reducing so greatly the risks—at least (for a raid by the police was always a possibility) the risk emanating from an individual casually encountered in the street, of whose inclinations the Baron could not have felt certain—

would have been a misfortune for him. But in the sphere of art M. de Charlus was no more than a dilettante, who never dreamt of writing and had no gift for it.

"Besides, I may as well admit to you," Jupien continued, "that I have very few scruples about making money in this way. The actual thing that is done here is—I can no longer conceal the fact from you—something that I like, it is what I have a taste for myself. Well, is it forbidden to receive payment for things that one does not regard as wickedness? You are better educated than I am, and you will tell me no doubt that Socrates was of the opinion that he could not accept money for his lessons. But in our age professors of philosophy do not hold that view, nor do doctors or painters or playwrights or theatrical producers. Do not imagine that this trade of mine brings me into contact only with the dregs of society. No doubt the director of an establishment of this kind, like a great courtesan, receives only men, but he receives men who are conspicuous in every walk of life and who are generally, on their own level, among the most intelligent, the most sensitive, the most agreeable of their profession. In no time at all, I assure you, this house could be transformed into an information bureau or a school of wit." Nevertheless, I was still under the impression of the blows which I had seen inflicted upon M. de Charlus.

And the truth is that, when one knew M. de Charlus well—his pride, his satiety with social pleasures, his fancies which changed easily into passions for men of the lowest class and the worst character—one could very easily understand that the possession of a huge fortune, the charm of which, had he been an upstart, would have been that it enabled him to marry his daughter to a duke and invite Highnesses to his shooting-parties, pleased him simply because it allowed him to have at his disposal in this way one or perhaps several establishments with a permanent supply of young men whose company he enjoyed. And perhaps this might have come to pass even without his special vice, heir as he was to so many great noblemen, dukes or princes of the blood, of whom Saint-Simon tells us that they never associated with anybody "who could boast a name."

"Meanwhile," I said to Jupien, "this house is anything but what you say it might become. It is worse than a madhouse, since the mad fancies of the lunatics who inhabit it are played out as actual, visible drama—it is a veritable pandemonium. I thought that I had arrived, like the Caliph in the *Arabian Nights*, in the nick of time to rescue a man who was being beaten, and in fact it was a different tale from the *Arabian Nights* which I saw enacted before me, the one in which a woman who has been turned into a dog willingly submits to being beaten in order to recover her former shape." Jupien appeared to be very upset by my words, for he realised that I had seen the Baron being beaten. He was silent for a moment, while I stopped a cab which was passing; then suddenly, with that pretty wit which had so often struck me in this self-educated man when in the courtyard of our house he had greeted me or Françoise with some graceful phrase: "You have mentioned one or two of the tales in the *Arabian Nights*," he said. "But there is another I know of, not unrelated to the title of a book which I think I have seen at the Baron's" (he was alluding to a translation of Ruskin's *Sesame and Lilies* which I had sent M. de Charlus). "If ever you are curious, one evening, to see, I will not say forty but a dozen thieves, you have only to come here; to know whether I am in the house you have only to look up at that window; if I leave my little window open with a light visible it means that I am in the house and you may come in; it is my private Sesame. I say only Sesame. As for Lilies, if they are what you seek I advise you to go elsewhere." And with a somewhat offhand gesture of farewell—for an aristocratic clientele and the habit of ruling like a pirate chief over a gang of young men had imparted a certain lordliness to his manners—he was about to take his leave of me when the noise of an explosion—a bomb which had fallen before the sirens could give warning—made him advise me to stay with him for a moment. Soon the anti-aircraft barrage began, and with such violence that one could sense very near, just above our heads, the presence of the German aeroplane.

In an instant the streets became totally black. At moments only, an enemy aeroplane flying very low lit up the spot upon which it wished to drop a bomb. I set off, but very soon I was lost. I thought of that day when, on my way to La Raspelière, I had met an aeroplane and my horse had reared as at the apparition of a god. Now, I thought, it would be a different meeting—with the god of evil, who would kill me. I started to walk faster in order to escape, like a traveller pursued by a tidal wave; I groped my way round dark squares from which I could find no way out. At last the flames of a blazing building showed me where I was and I got back on to the right road, while all the time the shells burst noisily above my head. But my thoughts had turned to another subject. I was thinking of Jupien's house, perhaps by now reduced to ashes, for a bomb had fallen very near me just after I had left it—that house upon which M. de Charlus might prophetically have written *Sodoma*, as the unknown inhabitant of Pompeii had done, with no less prescience or perhaps when the volcano had already started to erupt and the catastrophe had begun. But what mattered sirens and Gothas to the men who had come to seek their pleasure? The social setting or the natural scene which surrounds our love-making barely impinges upon our thoughts. The tempest may rage over the sea, the ship roll and plunge in every direction, the sky pour down avalanches convulsed by the wind, and at most we bestow the attention of a single second, forced from us by physical discomfort, upon this immense scenic background against which we ourselves are so insignificant, both we and the body which we long to approach. The siren with its warning of bombs troubled Jupien's visitors no more than an iceberg would have done. Indeed, the threat of physical danger delivered them from the fear which for long had morbidly harassed them. For it is wrong to suppose that the scale of our fears corresponds to that of the dangers by which they are inspired. A man may be afraid of not sleeping and not in the least afraid of a serious duel, afraid of a rat and not of a lion. For a few hours now the police would have their hands full looking after something as trivial as the lives of the city's inhabitants and their reputations were temporarily in no danger. But if some, their fears allayed, remained in Jupien's establishment, others were tempted not so much by the thought of recovering their moral liberty as by the darkness which had suddenly settled upon the streets. Some of these, like the Pompeians upon whom the fire from heaven was already raining, descended into the passages of the Métro, black as catacombs. They knew that they would not be alone there. And darkness, which envelops all things like a new element, has the effect, irresistibly tempting for certain people, of suppressing the first halt on the road to pleasure—it permits us to enter without impediment into a region of caresses to which normally we gain access only after a certain delay. Whether the coveted object is a woman or a man, supposing even that the first approach is easy and that there is no need of the gallant speeches which in a drawing-room might run on for ever (at any rate in daylight), on a normal evening, even in the most dimly lit street, there is at least a preamble in which the eyes alone feed on the unripe fruit, and fear of passers-by, fear even of the coveted being, prevents us from doing more than look and speak. In the darkness this time-honoured ritual is instantly abolished—hands, lips, bodies may go into action at once. There is always the excuse of darkness, and of the mistakes that darkness engenders, if we are not well received. And if we are, this immediate response of a body which does not withdraw but approaches, gives us of the woman (or the man) whom we have selected the idea that she is without prejudices and full of vice, which adds an extra pleasure to the happiness of having bitten straight into the fruit without first coveting it with our eyes and without asking permission. Meanwhile the darkness persisted; plunged into the new element, imagining that they had travelled to a distant country and were witnessing a natural phenomenon like a tidal wave or an eclipse, that they were enjoying not an artificially prepared, sedentary pleasure but a chance encounter in the unknown, the men who had come away from Jupien's house celebrated, while the bombs mimicked the rumbling of a volcano, deep in the earth as in a Pompeian house of ill fame, their secret rites in the shadows of the catacombs.

The Pompeian paintings of Jupien's house were admirably suited, recalling as they did the later days of the Revolution, to the age so similar to the Directory which was about to begin. Already, without waiting for peace, concealing themselves in the darkness so as not too openly to infringe the regulations of the police, everywhere new-fangled dances were being evolved and frenziedly danced by their devotees throughout the night. And at the same time certain artistic opinions less anti-German in tone than those of the first years of the war were coming into vogue, allowing suffocated minds to breathe once more— but still before you dared to present these ideas you needed to produce a certificate of your patriotism. A professor might write a remarkable book on Schiller and it would be reviewed in the newspapers. But before discussing the author of the book they would record, as a sort of *imprimatur*, that he had been at the Marne or Verdun, that he had been mentioned in despatches five times or had two sons killed. Then and then only did they praise the lucidity, the depth of his work on Schiller, whom it was permissible to describe as "great" provided that he was called not "that great German" but "that great Boche." This was the pass-word, and having passed this test the article was allowed to proceed.

The clients who had not wished to leave had collected together in one room in Jupien's house. They were not acquainted with one another, but one could see that they all belonged nevertheless roughly to the same world, rich and aristocratic. The appearance of each one had in it

something repugnant, a reflexion, I presumed, of their
failure to resist degrading pleasures. One, an enormous
man, had a face covered with red blotches like a drunkard. I was told that formerly he had not drunk much himself but had merely enjoyed making young men drunk.
But, terrified at the idea of being called up (although he
seemed to be in his fifties) and being very stout, he had
started to drink without stopping in order to get his
weight above a hundred kilos, as nobody over this limit
was accepted for the army. And now, this calculation having transformed itself into a passion, the moment that he
was left alone, wherever it might be, he would disappear
and be found again in a wine-shop. But as soon as he
spoke I saw that, though his intelligence was commonplace, he was a man with a good deal of knowledge, education and culture. Another man came in, very young and
of great physical distinction. This one, who clearly belonged to the best society, had as yet it is true no external
marks of vice, but—and this was more disturbing—the
interior signs were there. Very tall, with a charming face,
his speech revealed an intelligence of quite a different order from that of his alcoholic neighbour, an intelligence
that might without exaggeration be called really outstand-
ing. But to everything that he said there was added a facial expression which would have suited a different
phrase. As though, while possessing the whole treasure-
house of the expressions of the human countenance, he
lived in some world of his own, he displayed these expressions in the wrong order, appearing to scatter smiles and
glances at random without any connexion with the remarks that were being addressed to him. I hope for his
sake—if, as he certainly is, he is still alive—that he was

the victim not of a lasting malady but of a brief intoxication. Probably, had one asked all these men for their visiting cards, one would have been surprised to see that they belonged to an exalted social class. But some vice or other, and that greatest of all vices, the lack of will-power which prevents a man from resisting any vice in particular, brought them together in this place, in isolated rooms it is true, but evening after evening so I was told, so that, though their names might be known to fashionable hostesses, the latter had gradually lost sight of their faces and no longer ever received their visits. Invitations might still be sent to them, but habit brought them back to their composite haunt of depravity. They made, moreover, little attempt at concealment, unlike the page-boys, young workmen, etc., who ministered to their pleasures. And this fact, for which a number of reasons could be given, is best explained by this one: for a man with a job, whether in industry or in domestic service, to go to Jupien's was much the same as for a woman supposed respectable to go to a house of assignation; some, while ready to admit that they had gone there, denied having gone more than once, and Jupien himself, lying to protect their reputations or to discourage competition, would declare: "Oh, no, he doesn't come to my establishment, he wouldn't go *there*." For men with a social position it was not so serious, particularly as other men with a social position who do not go *there* know nothing about the place and do not concern themselves with your life. But in an aeroplane factory, for instance, if one or two fitters have gone *there*, their comrades, who have spied on them, would not dream of following their example for fear of being found out.

As I made my way home, I reflected upon the speed

with which conscience ceases to be a partner in our habits, which she allows to develop freely without bothering herself about them, and upon the astonishing picture which may consequently present itself to us if we observe simply from without, and in the belief that they engage the whole of the individual, the actions of men whose moral or intellectual virtues may at the same time be developing independently in an entirely different direction. Clearly it was a gross fault in their education, or a complete absence of education, combined with a propensity for making money in the way which, if not the least painful (for there were many forms of work which must in the long run be pleasanter—but then does not an invalid in the same way fabricate for himself, with fads, privations and remedies, an existence much more painful than the one imposed upon him by the often trivial disease against which he imagines himself to be fighting by these methods?), was at least less laborious than any other, which had led these ordinary young men to do, quite innocently one may almost say and for a very moderate reward, things which caused them no pleasure and which must in the beginning have inspired in them a lively disgust. On this evidence one might have supposed them to be fundamentally bad, but not only were they in the war splendid soldiers, men of incomparable courage, in civil life too they had often been kind-hearted and sometimes wholly admirable people. They had long ceased to speculate upon the morality or immorality of the life they led, because it was the life that was led by everybody round them. So it is that, when we study certain periods of ancient history, we are astonished to see men and women individually good participate without scruple in mass assassinations or human sacrifices which probably seemed to them natural things. And our own age no doubt, when its history is read two thousand years hence, will seem to an equal degree to have bathed men of pure and tender conscience in a vital element which will strike the future reader as monstrously pernicious, but to which at the time these men adapted themselves without difficulty. Similarly, I knew few men, I may even say I knew none, who in point of intelligence and sensibility were as gifted as Jupien; for the store of knowledge which gave such a delightful quality of wit to his conversation came to him not from that instruction at school or that liberal education at a university which might have made him indeed a remarkable man, but from which many fashionable youths derive no profit. It was simply his innate good sense, his natural taste, which had enabled him, from a few books read at random, without a guide, at odd moments, to construct that correct and elegant manner of speaking in which all the symmetries of language were revealed and their beauty displayed. Yet the trade that he followed might with good reason be regarded, though certainly as one of the most lucrative, as the lowest of all. As for M. de Charlus, whatever disdain his aristocratic pride may have given him for the thought of what people would say, how was it that some feeling of personal dignity and self-respect had not forced him to refuse his sensuality certain satisfactions for which the only imaginable excuse might seem to be complete insanity? But in him, as in Jupien, the practice of separating morality from a whole order of actions (and this is something that must also often happen to men who have public duties to perform, those of a judge for instance or a statesman and many others as well) must have been so long established that Habit, no longer asking Moral Sentiment for its opinion, had grown stronger from day to day until at last this consenting Prometheus had had himself nailed by Force to the rock of Pure Matter.

No doubt, as I saw clearly enough, a new stage had been reached in the malady of M. de Charlus, which since I had first observed it had, to judge from the diverse phases which had presented themselves to my vision, pursued its development with ever-increasing speed. The poor Baron could not now be very far from the malady's final term, from death itself, though this possibly would be preceded, in accordance with the predictions and prayers of Mme Verdurin, by an imprisonment which at his age could only hasten its coming. Yet I have perhaps been inaccurate in speaking of the rock of Pure Matter. In this Pure Matter it is possible that a small quantum of Mind still survived. This madman knew, in spite of everything, that he was the victim of a form of madness and during his mad moments he nevertheless was playing a part, since he knew quite well that the young man who was beating him was not more wicked than the little boy who in a game of war is chosen by lot to be "the Prussian," upon whom all the others hurl themselves in a fury of genuine patriotism and pretended hate. The victim of a madness, yet a madness into which there entered nevertheless a little of the personality of M. de Charlus. Even in these aberrations (and this is true also of our loves or our travels), human nature still betrays its need for belief by its insistent demands for truth. Françoise, if I spoke to her about a church in Milan, a town which she would probably never visit, or about the cathedral of Rheims—

or even merely that of Arras!—which she would not be able to see since they had been more or less destroyed, spoke enviously of the rich who can afford to visit such treasures or else exclaimed with nostalgic regret: "Ah! how lovely it must have been!" although, after all these years that she had lived in Paris, she had never had the curiosity to go and see Notre-Dame. For Notre-Dame is part of Paris and Paris was the town in which the daily life of Françoise took its course, the town, in consequence, in which it was difficult for our old servant—as it would have been for me had not the study of architecture corrected in me at certain points the instincts of Combray— to situate the objects of her dreams. In the people whom we love, there is, immanent, a certain dream which we cannot always clearly discern but which we pursue. It was my belief in Bergotte and in Swann which had made me love Gilberte, my belief in Gilbert the Bad which had made me love Mme de Guermantes. And what a vast expanse of sea had been hidden away in my love—the most full of suffering, the most jealous, seemingly the most individual of all my loves—for Albertine! In any case, just because we are furiously pursuing a dream in a succession of individuals, our loves for people cannot fail to be more or less of an aberration. (And are not even the maladies of the body, at least those that are at all closely connected with the nervous system, in the nature of special tastes or special fears acquired by our organs or our joints, which indicate in this manner that they have conceived for certain climates a horror as inexplicable and as obstinate as the fondness which certain men betray for, it might be, women with an eye-glass or women on horseback? Who can say to what long-lived and unconscious dream is

linked the desire that never fails to re-awaken at the sight
of a woman on horseback, an unconscious dream as mysterious as is, for example, for a man who has suffered all
his life from asthma, the influence of a certain town, in
appearance no different from any other town, in which for
the first time he breathes freely?) And if there is something of aberration or perversion in all our loves, perver-
sions in the narrower sense of the word are like loves in
which the germ of disease has spread victoriously to every
part. Even in the maddest of them love may still be
recognised. If M. de Charlus insisted that his hands and
feet should be bound with chains of proven strength, if he
asked repeatedly for the "bar of justice" and, so Jupien
told me, for other ferocious instruments which it was almost impossible to obtain even from sailors—for they
served to inflict punishments which have been abolished
even on board ship where discipline is more rigorous than
anywhere else—at the bottom of all this there persisted in
M. de Charlus his dream of virility, to be attested if need
be by acts of brutality, and all that inner radiance, invisible to us but projecting in this manner a little reflected
light, with which his mediaeval imagination adorned
crosses of judgment and feudal tortures. It was the same
sentiment that made him, every time he arrived, say to
Jupien: "I hope there will be no alert this evening, for already I see myself consumed by this fire from heaven like
an inhabitant of Sodom." And he affected to be nervous
of the Gothas, not that they caused him the slightest
shadow of fear, but so as to have a pretext, as soon as the
sirens sounded, to rush into the shelters in the Métro,
where he hoped for pleasure from brief contact with un-
seen figures, accompanied by vague dreams of mediaeval

dungeons and oubliettes. In short his desire to be bound in chains and beaten, with all its ugliness, betrayed a dream as poetical as, in other men, the longing to go to Venice or to keep ballet-dancers. And M. de Charlus was so determined that this dream should give him the illusion of reality that Jupien was obliged to sell the wooden bed which was in Room 43 and replace it by an iron bed which went better with the chains.

The all-clear sounded at last as I was approaching my house. A little boy in the street told me what a noise the fire-engines had made. I met Françoise coming up from the cellar with the butler. She thought that I had been killed. She told me that Saint-Loup had looked in, with apologies, to see whether he had not, in the course of the visit he had paid me during the morning, dropped his *croix de guerre*. For he had just noticed that he had lost it, and as he had to rejoin his regiment the following morning he had wanted to see whether it was in our flat. He had searched everywhere with Françoise and had found nothing. Françoise thought that he must have lost it before coming to see me, for, she said, she was almost sure, in fact she could have sworn that he was not wearing it when she saw him. In this she was mistaken. So much for the value of evidence and memory! In any case it was of no great importance. Saint-Loup was as much esteemed by his officers as loved by his men, and the matter could easily be arranged.

However, I sensed immediately, from the unenthusiastic manner in which they spoke of him, that Saint-Loup had made a poor impression on Françoise and on the butler. True, whereas the butler's son and Françoise's nephew had made every effort to get themselves into safe jobs, Saint-Loup had made efforts of the opposite kind, and with success, to be sent to as dangerous a post as possible. But this, because they judged from their own natures, was something that Françoise and the butler were incapable of believing. They were convinced that the rich are always put where there is no danger. In any case, had they known the truth concerning the heroic courage of Robert, it would have left them unmoved. He did not say "Boches," he had praised the valour of the Germans, he did not attribute to treachery the fact that we had not been victorious from the first day. That is what they would have liked to hear, that is what would have seemed to them a sign of courage. So although they continued to search for the *croix de guerre*, I found them chilly on the subject of Robert. Having my suspicions as to where the cross had been forgotten, I advised Françoise and the butler to go to bed. (However, if Saint-Loup had amused himself that evening in the fashion which I suspected, it was only to pass the time of waiting, for he had been seized once more by the desire to see Morel and had made use of all his military connexions to find out in what regiment he was serving, so that he could go and see him, but so far had only received hundreds of contradictory answers.) But the butler was never in a hurry to leave Françoise now that, thanks to the war, he had found a means of torturing her even more efficacious than the expulsion of the nuns or the Dreyfus case. That evening, and every time I went near them during the few more days that I spent in Paris before leaving to go to a new sanatorium, I heard the butler say to a terrified Françoise: "They're not in a hurry of course, they're biding their time, but when the time is ripe they will take Paris, and on that day we shall see no mercy!" "Heavens above, Mother of God," cried Françoise, "aren't they satisfied to have conquered poor Belgium? She suffered enough, that one, at the time of her innovation." "Belgium, Françoise? What they did in Belgium will be nothing compared to this!" And as the war had flooded the conversation of working-class people with a quantity of terms with which they had become acquainted through their eyes alone, by reading the newspapers, and which they consequently did not know how to pronounce, the butler went on to say: "I cannot understand how everybody can be so stupid. You will see, Françoise, they are preparing a new attack with a wider *scoop* than all the others." At this I rebelled, if not in the name of pity for Françoise and strategic common sense, at least in that of grammar, and declared that the word should be pronounced "scope," but succeeded only in causing the terrible phrase to be repeated to Françoise every time I entered the kitchen, for to the butler the pleasure of alarming his companion was scarcely greater than that of showing his master that, though he had once been a gardener at Combray and was a mere butler, he was nevertheless a good Frenchman according to the rule of Saint-André-des-Champs and possessed, by virtue of the Declaration of the Rights of Man, the right to use the pronunciation "scoop" in full independence and not to let himself be dictated to on a point which formed no part of his service and upon which in consequence, since the Revolution had made us all equals, he need listen to nobody.

To my annoyance, therefore, I had to listen to him talking to Françoise about an operation of wide "scoop" with an emphasis which was intended to prove to me that this pronunciation was the result not of ignorance but of an act of will following upon ripe reflexion. He confounded the government and the newspapers in a single "they" full of mistrust, saying: "They tell us about the losses of the Boches, they don't tell us about our own, it seems that they are ten times as big. They tell us that the enemy are at the end of their tether, that they have nothing to eat, personally I believe they are a hundred times better off than we are for food. It's no use stuffing us with lies. If the enemy had nothing to eat, they wouldn't fight as they did the other day when they killed a hundred thousand of our young men not twenty years old." Thus at every moment he exaggerated the triumphs of the Germans, as in the past he had those of the Radicals; and at the same time he recounted their atrocities in order that these triumphs might be yet more painful to Françoise, who never stopped saying: "Ah! Holy Mother of the Angels! Ah! Mary, Mother of God!", and sometimes, in order to be disagreeable to her in a different way, he said: "Anyhow, we are no better than they are, what we're doing in Greece is no prettier than what they have done in Belgium. You will see that we shall turn everybody against us, we shall find ourselves fighting every nation in the world," whereas the truth was exactly the opposite. On days when the news was good he destroyed its effect by assuring Françoise that the war would last thirty-five years, and if there was talk of the possibility of an armistice, he declared that peace would not last more than a few months and would be followed by battles which would make the present ones look like child's play, such battles that after them there would be nothing left of France.

The victory of the Allies seemed, if not near at hand, at least more or less certain, and it must unfortunately be admitted that the butler was greatly distressed at the prospect. For he had reduced the "world" war, like everything else, to the war which he was secretly waging against Françoise (of whom, nevertheless, he was fond, just as one may be fond of the person whom one enjoys infuriating every day by beating him at dominoes) and victory in his eyes took the shape of the first conversation in which he would have the pain of hearing Françoise say: "Well, it's over at last, and they'll have to give us more than we gave them in '70." He believed, nevertheless, that this fatal day of reckoning was perpetually about to arrive, for an unconscious patriotism made him suppose, like all Frenchmen, victims of the same mirage as myself since my illness, that victory—like my recovery—was just round the corner. This event he anticipated by announcing to Françoise that victory might perhaps come, but that his heart bled at the thought, for revolution would follow hard on its heels and then invasion. "Ah! this blooming war, the Boches will be the only ones to recover from it quickly, Françoise. They have already made hundreds of thousands of millions out of it. But as for their coughing up a *sou* to us, what nonsense! They will print that in the newspapers perhaps," he added out of prudence and so as to be ready for any eventuality, "in order to appease the people, just as for three years now they have been saying that the war will be over tomorrow." Françoise was only too easily disturbed by these words, because, having at first believed the optimists rather than the butler, she saw now that the war, which she had thought would end in a fortnight in spite of "the *innova-*

*tion* of poor Belgium," was indeed still going on, that we were not advancing (the phenomenon of fixed front warfare was beyond her comprehension) and that, according to one of the innumerable "godsons" to whom she gave everything that she earned with us, "they" were concealing various awkward facts. "It's the working man who will have to pay," concluded the butler. "They will take your field away from you, Françoise." "Ah! God in Heaven!" But to these distant misfortunes he preferred nearer ones and devoured the newspapers in the hope of being able to announce a defeat to Françoise. He waited for pieces of bad news as eagerly as if they had been Easter eggs, hoping that things would go badly enough to terrify Françoise but not badly enough to cause him any material suffering. Thus the prospect of a Zeppelin raid enchanted him: he would have the spectacle of Françoise hiding in the cellars, and at the same time he was persuaded that in a town as large as Paris the bombs would never happen to fall just on our house.

Françoise meanwhile was beginning at moments to return to her Combray pacifism. She almost had doubts about the "German atrocities." "When the war started we were told that the Germans were murderers, brigands, real bandits, Bbboches . . ." (If she gave several *b*'s to Boche, it was because the accusation that the Germans were murderers seemed to her quite plausible, but the idea that they were Boches, because of the enormity of the accusation, improbable in the extreme. Only it was not at all easy to understand what mysteriously terrifying sense Françoise gave to the word Boche, since the period she was talking about was the very beginning of the war, and also on account of the air of doubt with which she pronounced the word. For a doubt whether the Germans were criminals might be ill-founded in fact but did not contain in itself, from the point of view of logic, any contradiction. But how was it possible to doubt that they were Boches, since the word, in the popular language, means nothing more nor less than German? Perhaps she was simply repeating in an indirect fashion the violent remarks she had heard at the time, in which the word Boche was emphasised with particular energy.) "I believed all that," she went on, "but I am wondering now whether we are not every bit as scoundrelly as they are." This blasphemous thought had been slyly prepared in Françoise's mind by the butler, who, seeing that she had a certain fondness for King Constantine of Greece, had not ceased to represent him to her as literally starved by us until the day when he would yield. So the abdication of this monarch had aroused strong feelings in Françoise, who went so far as to declare: "We are no better than they are. If we were in Germany, we would do just the same."

I saw little of her, in any case, during these few days, for she spent much time at the house of those cousins of whom Mamma had said to me one day: "But you know that they are richer than you are." These cousins had given an example of that beautiful conduct which was very frequent at this period throughout the country and which would bear witness, if there were a historian to perpetuate its memory, to the greatness of France, her greatness of soul, her greatness after the fashion of Saint-André-des-Champs, a kind of conduct displayed as much by thousands of civilians living in safety far from the front as by the soldiers who fell at the Marne. There had been killed at Berry-au-Bac a nephew of Françoise who was also a nephew of the millionaire cousins, former proprietors of a large café who had retired long since after making their fortune. The young man who was killed had been the owner of a very small café and quite poor; he had gone off, twenty-five years old, when the army was mobilised, leaving his young wife alone to look after the little bar to which he hoped to return in a few months. He had been killed. And then this is what happened. The millionaire cousins of Françoise, who were not related by blood to the young woman who was their nephew's widow, had left the home in the country to which they had retired ten years earlier and had set to work again as café proprietors, without putting a sou into their own pockets; every morning at six the millionairess, a real lady, was up and dressed together with Mademoiselle her daughter, ready to help their niece and cousin by marriage. And for nearly three years now they had been washing glasses and serving drinks from early morning until half past nine at night, without a day's rest. In this book in which there is not a single incident which is not fictitious, not a single character who is a real person in disguise, in which everything has been invented by me in accordance with the requirements of my theme, I owe it to the credit of my country to say that only the millionaire cousins of Françoise who came out of retirement to help their niece when she was left without support, only they are real people who exist. And persuaded as I am that I shall not offend their modesty, for the reason that they will never read this book, it is both with childish pleasure and with a profound emotion that, being unable to record the names of so many others who undoubtedly acted in the same way, to all of whom France owes her survival, I transcribe here the real name of this family: they are called—and what name could be more French?—Larivière. If there were a few vile shirkers like the arrogant young man in a dinner-jacket whom I had seen in Jupien's establishment, whose only concern was to know whether he could have Léon at half past ten "as he had a luncheon engagement," they are redeemed by the innumerable throng of all the Frenchmen of Saint-André-des-Champs, by all the sublime soldiers and by those whom I rank as their equals, the Larivières.

The butler, to sharpen the fears of Françoise, showed her an old copy of *Lectures pour tous* which he had found, with a picture on its cover (it dated from before the war) of the "imperial family of Germany." "There's our lord and master to be," said the butler to Françoise, showing her "William." She goggled, then pointed to the feminine personage who stood by his side and said: "And there's the Williamess!"

My departure from Paris was delayed by a piece of news which caused me such grief that I was for some time rendered incapable of travelling. This was the death of Robert de Saint-Loup, killed two days after his return to the front while covering the retreat of his men. Never had any man felt less hatred for a nation than he (and as for the Emperor, for particular reasons, very possibly incorrect, he thought that William II had tried rather to prevent the war than to bring it about). Nor had he hated Germanism; the last words which I had heard on his lips, six days before he died, were the opening words of a Schumann song which he had started to hum in German on my staircase, until I had made him desist because of the neighbours. Accustomed by supreme good breeding to eliminate from his conduct all trace of apology or invective, all rhetoric, he had avoided in face of the enemy, as he had at the time of mobilisation, the actions which would have ensured his survival, through that tendency to efface himself before others of which all his behaviour was symbolic, down to his manner of coming out into the street bare-headed to close the door of my cab, every time I visited him. For several days I remained shut up in my room, thinking of him. I recalled his arrival the first time at Balbec, when, in an almost white suit, with his eyes greenish and mobile like the waves, he had crossed the hall adjoining the great dining-room whose windows gave on to the sea. I recalled the very special being that he had then seemed to me to be, the being for whose friendship I had so greatly wished. That wish had been realised beyond the limits of what I should ever have thought possible, without, however, at the time giving me more than a very slight pleasure; and then later I had come to understand the many great virtues and something else as well which lay concealed behind his elegant appearance. All this, the good as well as the bad, he had given without counting the cost, every day, as much on the last day when he advanced to attack a trench, out of generosity and because it was his habit to place at the service of others all that he possessed, as on that evening when he had run along the backs of the seats in the restaurant in order not to disturb me. And the fact that I had seen him really so little but against such varied backgrounds, in circumstances so diverse and separated by so many intervals—in that hall at Balbec, in the café at Rivebelle, in the cavalry barracks and at the military dinners in Doncières, at the theatre where he had slapped the face of the journalist, in the house of the Princesse de Guermantes—only had the effect of giving me, of his life, pictures more striking and more sharply defined and for his death a grief more lucid than we are likely to have in the case of people whom we have loved more, but with whom our association has been so nearly continuous that the image we retain of them is no more than a sort of vague average between an infinity of imperceptibly different images and our affection, satiated, has not, as with those whom we have seen only for brief moments, during meetings prematurely ended against their wish and ours, the illusion that there was possible between us a still greater affection of which circumstances alone have defrauded us. A few days after the day on which I had seen him pursuing his monocle and supposed him to be so haughty, in that hall at Balbec, there was another living form which I had seen for the first time on the beach at Balbec and which now, like his, no longer existed except in the state of memory: Albertine, making her progress along the sand that first evening, indifferent to everybody around her, a marine creature, like a seagull. For her my love had come so swiftly that, in order to be free to go out with her every day, I had never during my stay at Balbec gone over to Doncières to see Saint-Loup. And yet the history of my relations with him bore witness also to the fact that at one period I had ceased to love Albertine, since if later I had installed myself for a while near Robert at Doncières, the reason lay in my unhappiness at seeing that the feeling which I had for Mme de Guermantes was not returned. His life and Albertine's, so late made known to me, both at Balbec, and so swiftly concluded, had scarcely crossed, though it was he, I told myself, perceiving that the nimble shuttles of the years weave links between those of our memories which seem at first most independent of each other, it was he whom I had sent to see Mme Bontemps after Albertine had left me. And then it had turned out that their two lives had each of them a parallel secret, which I had not suspected. Saint-Loup's secret caused me now more sadness perhaps than that of Albertine, whose life had become so alien to me. But I felt an inconsolable regret that her life as well as his had been so short. They had often said to me, both of them: "You who are ill . . . ," they had looked after me. And yet it was they who were dead, while I, both of the one and of the other, could set side by side, separated by an interval which after all was really not very long, the final image—before the trench, in the river-bed—and the first image, which even in the case of Albertine I valued now only because it was associated in my mind with that of the sun setting over the sea.

Saint-Loup's death was received by Françoise with more compassion than that of Albertine. Immediately she assumed her role of hired mourner and descanted upon the memory of the dead man with frenzied threnodies and lamentations. She paraded her grief and only put on an unfeeling expression, at the same time averting her head, when in spite of myself I betrayed mine, which she wished to appear not to have seen. For like many emotional people, she was exasperated by the emotions of others, which bore no doubt too great a resemblance to her own. She loved now to draw attention to her slightest rheumatic twinge, to a fit of giddiness, to a bump. But if I referred to one of my symptoms, in an instant she was

stoical and grave again and pretended not to have heard.
"Poor Marquis," she said, although she continued to believe that he would have done anything in the world in
order not to go to the front and, once there, in order to
run away from danger. "Poor lady," she said, thinking of
Mme de Marsantes, "how she must have cried when she
heard about her boy's death! If at least she had been able
to see him again! But perhaps it's better that she didn't,
because his nose was cut in two, he was completely dis-
faced." And the eyes of Françoise filled with tears, behind
which, however, there was perceptible the cruel curiosity
of the peasant woman. No doubt Françoise pitied the sorrow of Mme de Marsantes with all her heart, but she regretted not knowing the form which this sorrow had taken
and not being able to enjoy the afflicting spectacle of it.
And as she would dearly have loved to cry and to be seen
by me to cry, she said, in order to work herself up: "This
has really done something to me!" In me too she sought
to detect the traces of grief, with an avidity which caused
me to feign a certain indifference when I spoke of Robert.
And, largely no doubt out of a spirit of imitation and because she had heard the phrase used—for there are
clichés in the servants' hall as well as in social coteries—
she kept repeating, not however without a poor man's
smugness in her voice: "All his riches did not save him
from dying like anybody else, and what use are they to
him now?" The butler took advantage of the occasion to
say to Françoise that of course it was sad, but that it
hardly counted beside the millions of men who fell every
day in spite of all the efforts which the government made
to conceal the fact. But this time the butler did not succeed in augmenting the sorrow of Françoise as he had

hoped. For she replied: "It is true that they also die for France, but they are nobodies; it is always more interesting when it is somebody whom one knows." And Françoise, who enjoyed crying, went on to add: "You must be sure to let me know if they talk about the death of the Marquis in the newspaper."

Robert had often said to me sadly, long before the war: "Oh! my life, don't let's talk about it, I am a condemned man from the start." Was he alluding to the vice which he had succeeded hitherto in concealing from the world, but of which he was himself aware and whose seriousness he perhaps exaggerated, just as children who make love for the first time, or merely before that age seek solitary pleasure, imagine themselves to be like a plant which cannot scatter its pollen without dying immediately afterwards? Perhaps this exaggeration, for Saint-Loup as for the children, came partly from the still unfamiliar idea of sin, partly from the fact that an entirely novel sensation has an almost terrible force which later will gradually diminish; or had he really, justifying it if need be by the death of his father at an early age, a presentiment of his own premature end? Such a presentiment would seem, no doubt, to be impossible. Yet death appears to be obedient to certain laws. Often for instance, one gets the impression that children of parents who have died very old or very young are almost compelled to disappear at the same age, the former protracting until their hundredth year their incurable miseries and ailments, the latter, in spite of a happy and healthy existence, swept away at the premature but inevitable date by an illness so opportune and so accidental (whatever deep roots it may have in the victim's temperament) that it appears to be merely the formality necessary for the realisation of death. And may it not be possible that accidental death too— like that of Saint-Loup, which was perhaps in any case linked to his character in more ways than I have thought it necessary to describe—is somehow recorded in advance, known only to the gods, invisible to men, but revealed by a peculiar sadness, half unconscious, half conscious (and even, insofar as it is conscious, proclaimed to others with that complete sincerity with which we foretell misfortunes which in our heart of hearts we believe we shall escape but which will nevertheless take place) to the man who bears and forever sees within himself, as though it were some heraldic device, a fatal date?

He must have been truly magnificent in those last hours. This man who throughout his life, even when sitting down, even when walking across a drawing-room, had seemed to be restraining an impulse to charge, while with a smile he dissembled the indomitable will which dwelt within his triangular head, at last had charged. Freed from the books which encumbered it, the feudal turret had become military once more. And this Guermantes had died more himself than ever before, or rather more a member of his race, into which slowly he dissolved until he became nothing more than a Guermantes, as was symbolically visible at his burial in the church of Saint-Hilaire at Combray, completely hung for the occasion with black draperies upon which stood out in red, beneath the closed circle of the coronet, without initials or Christian names or titles, the G of the Guermantes that he had again in death become.

Even before going to this burial, which did not take place immediately, I wrote to Gilberte. I ought perhaps to have written to the Duchesse de Guermantes, but I told myself that she would receive the death of Robert with the same indifference which I had seen her display towards the deaths of so many others who had seemed to be closely linked to her life, and that she would perhaps even, with her Guermantes wit, try to show that she did not share the superstition about ties of blood. And I was too unwell to write to everybody. In the past I had believed that she and Robert were fond of each other in the sense in which that phrase is used in society, that is to say that, when they were together, they said to each other tender things which at the moment they truly felt. But away from her, he did not hesitate to declare that she was an idiot, and if she sometimes derived an egotistical pleasure from seeing him, I had observed her on the other hand to be incapable of taking the slightest trouble, of making even the smallest use of her credit in order to render him a service or even to spare him an unpleasantness. Her unkindness in refusing to give Robert a recommendation to General de Saint-Joseph, at the time when he wanted to avoid returning to Morocco, proved surely that the devoted help which she had given him on the occasion of his marriage was no more than a sort of atonement which cost her almost nothing. So I was very astonished to hear—she was unwell at the moment when Robert was killed—that in order to spare her the shock which the news would cause her her family had thought it necessary to conceal from her for several days, under the most fallacious pretexts, the newspapers which would have informed her of his death. And my surprise increased when I heard that, after they had at last been obliged to tell her the truth, the Duchess wept for a whole day, fell sick and

for a long time—more than a week, which was a long
time for her—was inconsolable. When I heard of her
grief, I was touched. It enabled society to say, and it enables me to vouch for the truth of the statement, that a
great friendship existed between them. But then when I
recall all the little malicious utterances, all the ill-natured
refusals to help each other which this friendship had not
excluded, I cannot help reflecting that in society a great
friendship does not amount to much.

However, a little later, in circumstances which, if they
touched my heart less, were historically more important,
Mme de Guermantes showed herself, to my mind, in a
yet more favourable light. This woman who as a girl, as
the reader may remember, had behaved with such audacious impertinence towards the imperial family of Russia,
and who after her marriage had addressed them always
with a freedom which sometimes caused her to be charged
with lack of tact, was perhaps alone, after the Russian
Revolution, in giving proofs of a limitless devotion to the
Grand Duchesses and the Grand Dukes. Only the year
before the war she had not a little annoyed the Grand
Duchess Vladimir by persistently referring to Countess
Hohenfelsen, the morganatic wife of the Grand Duke Paul,
as "the Grand Duchess Paul." Nevertheless, no sooner had
the Russian Revolution broken out than our ambassador in
St Petersburg, M. Paléologue ("Paléo" in diplomatic society, which like society at large has its supposedly witty
abbreviations), was plagued with telegrams from the Duchesse de Guermantes asking for news of the Grand Duchess
Maria Pavlovna. And for a long time the only marks of
sympathy and respect which this Princess received came to

her regularly and exclusively from Mme de Guermantes.

To various individuals Saint-Loup caused not so much by his death as by what he had done in the preceding weeks a distress greater than that which afflicted the Duchess. What happened was that, only the day after the evening on which I had seen him, and two days after the Baron had said to Morel, "I will have my revenge," the inquiries which Saint-Loup had made about the whereabouts of Morel were successful; they succeeded, that is to say, in bringing to the notice of the general under whose command Morel should have been the fact that he was a deserter, whereupon the general had him searched for and arrested and, to apologise to Saint-Loup for the punishment which he was obliged to inflict upon someone in whom he took an interest, wrote to inform him how the matter stood. Morel did not doubt that his arrest had been brought about by the rancour of M. de Charlus. He remembered the words "I will have my revenge," thought that this was the threatened revenge, and asked to be allowed to make some disclosures. "It is quite true," he declared, "that I am a deserter. But if I have been led astray, is it altogether my fault?" He then told apropos of M. de Charlus and M. d'Argencourt, with whom also he had quarrelled, stories in which he had not in fact himself been directly involved, but which they, with the double expansiveness of lovers and of inverts, had related to him, and the result was the immediate arrest of both these gentlemen. But each of them suffered less perhaps at being arrested than at learning—what neither of them had known—that the other was his rival, and the judicial examination revealed that they had an enormous number of other obscure, quotidian rivals, picked up in the street. M. de Charlus and M. d'Argencourt were soon released. So was Morel, because the general's letter to Saint-Loup was returned to him with the information: "Deceased, killed in action." Out of respect for the dead man the general so arranged things that Morel was merely sent to the front. He conducted himself bravely there, survived every danger and returned, when the war was over, with the cross which M. de Charlus had in the past vainly solicited for him and which in this indirect fashion was procured for him by the death of Saint-Loup.

I have often thought since then, remembering the *croix de guerre* which went astray in Jupien's establishment, that if Saint-Loup had lived, he could easily have got himself elected a deputy in the elections which followed the armistice, thanks to the scum of universal fatuousness which the war left in its wake and the halo which still adhered to military glory. For at that time, if the loss of a finger could abolish centuries of prejudice and allow a man of humble birth to make a brilliant marriage into an aristocratic family, the *croix de guerre*, even one won by sitting in an office, sufficed for a triumphal election to the Chamber of Deputies, if not to the Académie Française. The election of Saint-Loup, because of his "holy family," would have caused M. Arthur Meyer to pour out floods of tears and ink. But perhaps he was too sincerely fond of the people to be good at winning their votes, although on account of his quarterings of nobility they would probably have forgiven him his democratic ideas. These he would no doubt have expounded with success before a Chamber composed of aviators. Certainly these heroes would have understood him, and a few other exceptionally intelligent

and high-minded men. But thanks to the platitudinous
mentality of the National Bloc, the old lags of politics
who are invariably re-elected had also turned up again,
and such of them as failed to enter a Chamber of aviators
solicited, so that they might at least get into the Académie
Française, the suffrages of the Marshals, of the President
of the Republic, the President of the Chamber, etc. These
men would have looked with less favour upon Saint-Loup
than they did upon another of Jupien's habitués, the
deputy of Liberal Action, who was once more returned
unopposed and who continued to wear the uniform of a
territorial officer long after the war had been over. His
election was hailed with joy by all the newspapers which
had agreed to put his name forward, as well as by the noble and wealthy ladies who now dressed only in rags from
feelings of propriety and from fear of taxes, while the gentlemen of the Bourse never stopped buying diamonds, not
for their wives but because, having lost all confidence in
the credit of any nation, they were seeking refuge in this
tangible wealth and as a result sending up the price of De
Beers by a thousand francs. All this tomfoolery was not
exactly popular, but there was less disposition to blame
the National Bloc when suddenly there appeared on the
scene the victims of bolshevism, those Grand Duchesses
in tatters whose husbands had been assassinated in carts,
while their sons after being left to starve and then forced
to work in the midst of abuse, had finally been thrown
into wells and buried beneath stones because it was believed that they had the plague and might pass it on.
Those of them who succeeded in escaping suddenly
turned up in Paris.

\*       \*       \*

The new sanatorium to which I withdrew was no more successful in curing me than the first one, and many years passed before I came away. During the train journey which eventually took me back to Paris, the thought of my lack of talent for literature—a defect which I had first discovered, so I supposed, long ago on the Guermantes way, which I had again recognised, and been still more saddened by, in the course of the daily walks that I had taken with Gilberte before returning to dine very late at night at Tansonville, and which on the eve of my departure from that house I had come very near to identifying, after reading some pages of the Goncourt Journal, with the vanity, the falsehood of literature—this thought, less painful perhaps but more melancholy still if I referred it not to a private infirmity of my own but to the nonexistence of the ideal in which I had believed, this thought, which for a very long time had not entered my mind, struck me afresh and with a force more painful than ever before. The train had stopped, I remember, in open country. The sun was shining on a row of trees that followed the railway line, flooding the upper halves of their trunks with light. "Trees," I thought, "you no longer have anything to say to me. My heart has grown cold and no longer hears you. I am in the midst of nature. Well, it is with indifference, with boredom that my eyes register the line which separates your radiant foreheads from your shadowy trunks. If ever I thought of myself as a poet, I know now that I am not one. Perhaps in the new, the so desiccated part of my life which is about to begin, human beings may yet inspire in me what nature can no longer say. But the years in which I might have been able to sing *her* praise will never return." But in thus consoling myself with the thought that the observation of humanity might possibly come to take the place of an unattainable inspiration, I knew that I was merely seeking to console myself, I knew that I knew myself to be worthless. If I really had the soul of an artist, surely I would be feeling pleasure at the sight of this curtain of trees lit by the setting sun, these little flowers on the bank which lifted themselves almost to the level of the steps of my compartment, flowers whose petals I was able to count but whose colour I would not, like many a worthy man of letters, attempt to describe, for can one hope to transmit to the reader a pleasure that one has not felt? A little later I had noticed with the same absence of emotion the glitter of gold and orange which the sun splashed upon the windows of a house; and finally, as the evening advanced, I had seen another house which appeared to be built out of a strange pink substance. But I had made these various observations with the same absolute indifference as if, walking in a garden with a lady, I had seen a pane of glass, and a little further on an object of an alabaster-like material, the unusual colour of which had failed to draw me out of the most languorous boredom, but as if, nevertheless, out of politeness towards the lady, in order to say something and also in order to show that I had noticed these colours, I had pointed in passing to the tinted glass and the fragment of stucco. In the same way, to satisfy my conscience, I indicated to myself now as to someone who was travelling with me and might be able to extract from them more pleasure than I, the flame-like reflexions in the windows and the pink transparency of the house. But the companion whose attention I had drawn to these curious effects was evidently of a less enthusiastic nature than

many more sympathetically disposed persons who are enraptured by such sights, for he had taken cognisance of
the colours without any kind of joy.

My long absence from Paris had not prevented old
friends from continuing, as my name remained on their
lists, faithfully to send me invitations, and when on my
return I found—together with one to a tea-party given by
Berma for her daughter and her son-in-law—another to
an afternoon party with music which was to take place the
following day at the house of the Prince de Guermantes,
the gloomy reflexions which had passed through my mind
in the train were not the least of the motives which urged
me to accept. Really, I said to myself, what point is there
in forgoing the pleasures of social life if, as seems to be
the case, the famous "work" which for so long I have
been hoping every day to start the next day, is something
I am not, or am no longer, made for and perhaps does not
even correspond to any reality. This reasoning was, it is
true, completely negative and merely deprived of their
force those other reasons which might have dissuaded me
from going to this fashionable concert. The positive reason that made me decide to go was the name of Guermantes, absent long enough from my mind to be able,
when I read it upon the invitation card, to re-awaken a
ray of my attention, to draw up from the depths of my
memory a sort of section of the past of the Guermantes,
attended by all the images of seigniorial forest and tall
flowers which at that earlier time of my life had accompanied it, and to reassume for me the charm and the significance which I had found in it at Combray when, passing
along the Rue de l'Oiseau on my way home, I used to see
from outside, like some dark lacquer, the window of

Gilbert the Bad, Lord of Guermantes. For a moment the Guermantes had once more seemed to me to be totally different from people in society, comparable neither with them nor with any living being, even a reigning prince, creatures begotten of the union of the sharp and windy air of the dark town of Combray in which my childhood had been spent with the past which could be sensed there, in the little street, at the height of the stained-glass window. I had had a longing to go to the Guermantes party as if in going there I must have been brought nearer to my childhood and to the depths of my memory where my childhood dwelt. And I had continued to read and re-read the invitation until in the end, rising in revolt, the letters which composed this name at once so familiar and so mysterious, like that of Combray itself, resumed their independence and outlined before my tired eyes a name that I seemed never to have seen before. (Mamma happened to be going to a little tea-party of Mme Sazerat's which she knew beforehand she would find extremely boring, so I had no scruples about going to the Princesse de Guermantes's.)

I took a cab to go to the Prince de Guermantes's house, which was no longer his former home but a magnificent mansion that he had recently built in the Avenue du Bois. One of the mistakes of society people is not to realise that, if they want us to believe in them, it is first necessary that they should believe in themselves, or at least should respect the essential elements of our belief. At the time when I believed, even if I knew the contrary to be true, that the Guermantes lived in this or that grand house in virtue of a hereditary right, to penetrate into the palace of the sorcerer or the fairy, to compel to open be-

fore me the doors which yield only when one has pronounced the magic formula, seemed to me as difficult as
to obtain an interview with the sorcerer or the fairy themselves. To persuade myself that the old manservant engaged twenty-four hours earlier or supplied by Potel and
Chabot was the son, the grandson, the scion of a whole
line of menials who had been in the family's service since
long before the Revolution was the easiest thing in the
world, and I was only too happy to take for an ancestral
portrait some painting which had been bought the previous month from Bernheim Jeune. But enchantment cannot be decanted from one vessel to another, memories are
indivisible, and of the Prince de Guermantes, now that he
had himself shattered the illusions of my belief by going
to live in the Avenue du Bois, nothing much was left.
The ceilings which I had once feared to see collapse upon
the announcement of my name, those ceilings under
which, for me, there would still have floated something of
the enchantment and the fears of those early days, now
looked down upon the parties of an American hostess in
whom I took not the slightest interest. Intrinsically, material objects have in themselves no power, but, since it is
our practice to bestow power upon them, doubtless at this
moment some middle-class schoolboy was feeling, in front
of the house in the Avenue du Bois, the same sentiments
that I had once felt as I stood before the house where the
Prince de Guermantes had lived in my youth. He, this
schoolboy, was still at the age of beliefs, but I had passed
beyond it, I had lost that privilege, just as after one's first
years one loses the ability that a baby has to break up the
milk which he ingests into digestible fragments, so that
the prudent adult will drink milk only in small quantities

whereas babies can continue to suck it in indefinitely without pausing for breath. But at least the Prince de Guermantes's change of residence had this advantage for me, that the cab which had come to fetch me and in which, as it took me to the party, I was making these reflexions, was obliged to traverse the streets which lead to the Champs-Elysées. They were very badly paved at this time, but the moment I found myself in them I was, none the less, detached from my thoughts by that sensation of extraordinary physical comfort which one has when suddenly a car in which one is travelling rolls more easily, more softly, without noise, because the gates of a park have been opened and one is gliding over alleys covered with fine sand or dead leaves; materially nothing of the sort had happened, but I felt suddenly that all external obstacles had been eliminated, simply because I no longer had to make that effort of adaptation or attention which we make, sometimes without being conscious of it, in the presence of new things: the streets through which I was passing at this moment were those, so long forgotten, which I used once upon a time to take with Françoise when we went to the Champs-Elysées. The solid earth knew of its own accord where it had to go; its resistance was vanquished. And like an airman who hitherto has progressed laboriously along the ground, abruptly "taking off" I soared slowly towards the silent heights of memory. Among all the streets of Paris these streets will always stand out for me, as though they were made of a different substance from the others. When we reached the corner of the Rue Royale where once had stood the open-air vendor of the photographs beloved by Françoise, it seemed to me that the cab, feeling the pull of hundreds of former turns, could not do otherwise than turn of its own accord. I was not traversing the same streets as the people who were walking about the town that day, I was traversing a past, gliding, sad and sweet; a past which was moreover compounded of so many different pasts that it was difficult for me to recognise the cause of my melancholy, to know whether it was due to those walks in which the hope of meeting Gilberte had co-existed with the fear that she would not come, to the proximity of a certain house to which I had been told that Albertine had gone with Andrée, or to that vanity of all things which seems to be the significance of a route which one has followed a thousand times in a state of passion which has disappeared and which has borne no fruit, like the route which I used to take on those expeditions of feverish haste after luncheon to see, with the paste still damp upon them, the posters of *Phèdre* and *Le Domino noir*.

The cab turned into the Champs-Elysées and, as I did not particularly want to hear the whole of the concert which was being given at the Guermantes party, I stopped it and was preparing to get out in order to walk a few yards when I was struck by the spectacle presented by another cab which was also stopping. A man with staring eyes and hunched figure was placed rather than seated in the back, and was making, to keep himself upright, the efforts that might have been made by a child who has been told to be good. But his straw hat failed to conceal an unruly forest of hair which was entirely white, and a white beard, like those which snow forms on the statues of river-gods in public gardens, flowed from his chin. It was—side by side with Jupien, who was unremitting in his attentions to him—M. de Charlus, now convalescent

after an attack of apoplexy of which I had had no knowledge (I had only been told that he had lost his sight, but
in fact this trouble had been purely temporary and he
could now see quite well again) and which, unless the
truth was that hitherto he had dyed his hair and that he
had now been forbidden to continue so fatiguing a practice, had had the effect, as in a sort of chemical precipita-
tion, of rendering visible and brilliant all that saturation of
metal which the locks of his hair and his beard, pure silver now, shot forth like so many geysers, so that upon the
old fallen prince this latest illness had conferred the
Shakespearian majesty of a King Lear. His eyes had not
remained unaffected by this total convulsion, this metal-
lurgical transformation of his head, but had, by an inverse
phenomenon, lost all their brightness. But what was most
moving was that one felt that this lost brightness was
identical with his moral pride, and that somehow the
physical and even the intellectual life of M. de Charlus
had survived the eclipse of that aristocratic haughtiness
which had in the past seemed indissolubly linked to them.
To confirm this, at the moment which I am describing,
there passed in a victoria, no doubt also on her way to the
reception of the Prince de Guermantes, Mme de Saint-
Euverte, whom formerly the Baron had not considered elegant enough for him. Jupien, who tended him like a
child, whispered in his ear that it was someone with
whom he was acquainted, Mme de Saint-Euverte. And
immediately, with infinite laboriousness but with all the
concentration of a sick man determined to show that he is
capable of all the movements which are still difficult for
him, M. de Charlus lifted his hat, bowed, and greeted
Mme de Saint-Euverte as respectfully as if she had been

the Queen of France or as if he had been a small child
coming timidly in obedience to his mother's command to
say "How do you do?" to a grown-up person. For a child,
but without a child's pride, was what he had once more
become. Perhaps the very difficulty that M. de Charlus
had in making these gestures was in itself a reason for
him to make them, in the knowledge that he would create
a greater effect by an action which, painful for an invalid,
became thereby doubly meritorious on the part of the
man who performed it and doubly flattering to the individual to whom it was addressed, invalids, like kings,
practising exaggerated civility. Perhaps also there was in
the movements of the Baron that lack of co-ordination
which follows upon maladies of the spinal column and the
brain, so that his gestures went beyond anything that he
intended. What I myself saw in them was above all a sort
of gentleness, an almost physical gentleness, and of detachment from the realities of life, phenomena so strik-
ingly apparent in those whom death has already drawn
within its shadow. And the exposure of the veins of silver
in his hair was less indicative of profound alterations than
this unconscious humility which turned all social relations
upside down and abased before Mme de Saint-Euverte—
as it would have abased before the most vulgar of American hostesses (who at last would have been able to
congratulate herself on the hitherto unattainable politeness
of the Baron)—what had seemed to be the proudest snobbishness of all. For the Baron still lived, still thought; his
intellect was not impaired. And more than any chorus of
Sophocles on the humbled pride of Oedipus, more than
death itself or any funeral oration on the subject of death,
the humble greeting, full of effort to please, which the

Baron addressed to Mme de Saint-Euverte proclaimed the fragile and perishable nature of the love of earthly greatness and all human pride. M. de Charlus, who until this moment would never have consented to dine with Mme de Saint-Euverte, now bowed to the ground in her honour. To receive the homage of M. de Charlus had been, for her, the highest ambition of snobbery, just as, for the Baron, the central principle of snobbery had been to be rude to her. And now this inaccessible and precious essence which he had succeeded in making Mme de Saint-Euverte believe to be part of his nature, had at a single stroke been annihilated by M. de Charlus, by the earnest timidity, the apprehensive zeal with which he raised a hat from beneath which, all the while that his head remained deferentially uncovered, there streamed with the eloquence of a Bossuet the torrents of his silvery hair. Jupien helped the Baron to descend and I greeted him. He spoke to me very rapidly, in a voice so inaudible that I could not distinguish what he was saying, which wrung from him, when for the third time I made him repeat his remarks, a gesture of impatience that astonished me by its contrast with the impassivity which his face had at first displayed, which was no doubt an after-effect of his stroke. But when after a while I had grown accustomed to this pianissimo of whispered words, I perceived that the sick man retained the use of his intelligence absolutely intact.

There were, however, two M. de Charluses, not to mention any others. Of the two, one, the intellectual one, passed his time in complaining that he suffered from progressive aphasia, that he constantly pronounced one word, one letter by mistake for another. But as soon as he actually made such a mistake, the other M. de Charlus, the

subconscious one, who was as desirous of admiration as
the first was of pity and out of vanity did things that the
first would have despised, immediately, like a conductor
whose orchestra has blundered, checked the phrase which
he had started and with infinite ingenuity made the end
of his sentence follow coherently from the word which he
had in fact uttered by mistake for another but which he
thus appeared to have chosen. Even his memory was intact, and from it his vanity impelled him, not without the
fatigue of the most laborious concentration, to drag forth
this or that ancient recollection, of no importance, which
concerned myself and which would demonstrate to me
that he had preserved or recovered all his lucidity of
mind. Without moving his head or his eyes, and without
varying in the slightest degree the modulation of his
voice, he said to me, for instance: "Look, there's a poster
on that telegraph-pole like the one which I was standing
near when I saw you for the first time at Avranches—no,
I am mistaken, at Balbec." And it was in fact an advertisement for the same product.

I had found it difficult at first to understand what he
was saying, just as one begins by seeing absolutely nothing in a room of which all the curtains are closed. But like
one's eyes in half-darkness, my ears soon accustomed
themselves to this pianissimo. The sound had in any case,
I think, gradually grown in volume while the Baron was
speaking, perhaps because the weakness of his voice was
due in part to a nervous apprehension which was dispelled
when he was distracted by the presence of another person
and ceased to think about it, though possibly, on the
other hand, the feeble voice corresponded to the real state
of his health and the momentary strength with which he

spoke in conversation was the result of an artificial, tran-
sient and even dangerous excitement, which might make
strangers say: "He is much better, he must stop thinking
about his illness," but in fact only aggravated the illness,
which lost no time in resuming its sway. Whatever the
explanation may be, the Baron at this moment (even making allowances for the improvement in my own hearing)
was flinging down his words with greater force, as the
tide, on days of bad weather, flings down its little con-
torted waves. And the traces of his recent attack caused
one to hear at the back of his words a noise like that of
pebbles dragged by the sea. Continuing to speak to me
about the past, no doubt to prove to me that he had not
lost his memory, he evoked it now—in a funereal fashion
but without sadness—by reciting an endless list of all the
people belonging to his family or his world who were no
longer alive, less, it seemed, with any emotion of grief
that they were dead than with satisfaction at having survived them. He appeared indeed, as he recalled their extinction, to enjoy a clearer perception of his own return
towards health and it was with an almost triumphal stern-
ness that he repeated, in a monotonous tone, stammering
slightly and with a dull sepulchral resonance: "Hannibal
de Bréauté, dead! Antoine de Mouchy, dead! Charles
Swann, dead! Adalbert de Montmorency, dead! Boson de
Talleyrand, dead! Sosthène de Doudeauville, dead!" And
every time he uttered it, the word "dead" seemed to fall
upon his departed friends like a spadeful of earth each
heavier than the last, thrown by a grave-digger grimly determined to immure them yet more closely within the
tomb.

The Duchesse de Létourville, who was not going to

the Princesse de Guermantes's reception because she had just recovered from a long illness, passed near us at that moment on foot, and seeing the Baron, of whose recent attack she knew nothing, stopped to say good-day to him. But the effect of her own illness was to make her not more understanding but more impatient—with a nervous ill-humour that was nevertheless perhaps not without a large element of compassion—of the illnesses of others. Hearing the Baron pronounce certain words with difficulty and incorrectly and seeing the painful effort he had to make to move his arm, she cast her eyes first upon Jupien and then upon myself as though to demand an explanation of so shocking a phenomenon. As we said nothing, it was to M. de Charlus himself that she addressed a long look full of sadness but also of reproach. She seemed to think it very wrong of him to be out of doors and in her company in a condition as unusual as if he had come out without a tie or without shoes. And when yet another error in pronunciation was perpetrated by the Baron, augmenting both the distress and the indignation of the Duchess, she cried out to him: "Palamède!" in the interrogative and exasperated tone of those nervous people who cannot bear to be kept waiting for a single moment and will say to you sharply, if you let them come into your room before you are ready (with a word of apology for being still engaged upon your toilet), not so as to excuse themselves but in order to accuse you: "Oh, I'm disturbing you, am I?" as if it was your fault that you were being disturbed. Finally she left us, looking crosser and crosser and saying to the Baron: "Really, you ought to go home."

M. de Charlus said he would like to sit down on a

chair to rest while Jupien and I went for a little walk, and with some difficulty pulled out of his pocket a book which looked to me like a prayer-book. I was not displeased to have an opportunity to learn from Jupien various details of the Baron's state of health. "I am very glad to talk to you, sir," said Jupien, "but we won't go further than the Rond-Point. Thank heaven, the Baron is better now, but I dare not leave him alone for long, he is always the same, he is too kind-hearted, he would give away everything he possesses: and then that's not the only thing, he still tries to pick people up as if he was a young man, and I have to keep my eyes open." "Particularly as he has recovered the use of his own eyes," I replied; "I was very distressed when I was told that he had lost his sight." "Yes, it's true that his eyes were affected by his stroke. For a time he could see nothing at all. Just imagine, during the cure, which as a matter of fact did him a great deal of good, he was for several months unable to see more than a man born blind." "At least that must have made your surveillance largely unnecessary?" "Not at all, no sooner had he arrived in a hotel than he would ask me what this or that individual on the staff was like. I used to assure him that they were all horrors. But he realised that that couldn't be universally true, that I must sometimes be lying. Little rascal that he is! And then he was extraordinarily good at guessing, from the voice perhaps, I don't know. He used to contrive to send me on urgent errands. One day—you will excuse my telling you this, but you came once by chance to the Temple of Shamelessness and I have nothing to hide from you" (in fact, it was a disagreeable feature of his character that he seemed always to enjoy revealing secrets in his possession)—"I was return-

ing from one of these supposedly urgent errands, all the
faster because I guessed it to have been arranged on purpose, when as I approached the Baron's room I heard a
voice saying: 'What?' and the Baron reply: 'You don't
mean that this has never happened to you before?' I went
into the room without knocking, and imagine my terror!
The Baron, misled by a voice which was in fact deeper
than is usual at that age (remember that at this period he
was completely blind and in the old days, as you know,
he had always been partial to men who were not quite
young), was with a little boy who could not have been ten
years old."

I have been told since that at that time he suffered almost every day from severe fits of mental depression, during which, though his mind was not actually wandering,
he used to proclaim aloud before people whose presence
or whose strict views he forgot opinions which normally
he concealed, his pro-Germanism for instance. The war
had long since ended, but still he groaned over the defeat
of the Germans, amongst whose number he counted himself, and would say proudly: "And yet, inevitably, we
shall have our revenge. For we have proved that we are
the nation with the greatest capacity for resistance, and
the best organisation too." Or else his confidences would
take another direction, and he would cry out angrily:
"Lord X—— (or the Prince de XX——) had better not
dare repeat what he said yesterday, it was all I could do
not to reply: 'You know you're just as much one as I
am.' " Needless to say, when, at the moments when he
was "not quite all there," M. de Charlus made these
avowals of his pro-German or other tendencies, anybody
from his immediate circle who might be with him,

whether it were Jupien or the Duchesse de Guermantes, would interrupt the imprudent remarks and interpret them for the benefit of others less intimately acquainted with the Baron and less discreet in a far-fetched but honourable sense.

"But, good heavens!" cried Jupien, "I was right not to want us to go too far. Look! He's already managed to get into conversation with a gardener's boy. I had better say good-bye to you, sir, I must not leave my invalid alone for a second, he is really just a big baby now."

I got out of my cab a second time just before it reached the house of the Princesse de Guermantes and I began once more to reflect upon the mood of lassitude and boredom in which I had attempted, the previous day, to note the characteristics of that line which, in a countryside reputed one of the loveliest of France, had separated upon the trunks of the trees the shadow from the light. Certainly the reasoned conclusions which I had drawn at the time did not cause me so much pain today. They were unchanged; but at this moment, as on every occasion when I found myself torn from my habits—in a new place, or going out at an unaccustomed hour—I was feeling a lively pleasure. The pleasure seemed to me today a purely frivolous one, that of going to an afternoon party given by Mme de Guermantes. But since I knew now that I could hope for nothing of greater value than frivolous pleasures, what point was there in depriving myself of them? I told myself again that I had felt, in attempting the description, not a spark of that enthusiasm which, if it is not the sole, is a primary criterion of talent. I tried next to draw from my memory other "snapshots," those in particular which it had taken in Venice, but the mere word "snapshot" made Venice seem to me as boring as an exhibition of photographs, and I felt that I had no more taste, no more talent for describing now what I had seen in the past, than I had had yesterday for describing what at that very moment I was, with a meticulous and melancholy eye, actually observing. In a few minutes a host of friends whom I had not seen for years would probably ask me to give up being a recluse and devote my days to them. And what reason had I to refuse their request, now that I possessed the proof that I was useless and that literature could no longer give me any joy whatever, whether this was my fault, through my not having enough talent, or the fault of literature itself, if it were true that literature was less charged with reality than I had once supposed?

When I thought of what Bergotte had said to me: "You are ill, but one cannot pity you for you have the joys of the mind," how mistaken he had been about me! How little joy there was in this sterile lucidity! Even if sometimes perhaps I had pleasures (not of the mind), I sacrificed them always to one woman after another; so that, had fate granted me another hundred years of life and sound health as well, it would merely have added a series of extensions to an already tedious existence, which there seemed to be no point in prolonging at all, still less for any great length of time. As for the "joys of the intelligence," could I call by that name those cold observations which my clairvoyant eye or my power of accurate ratiocination made without any pleasure and which remained always infertile?

But it is sometimes just at the moment when we think that everything is lost that the intimation arrives which may save us; one has knocked at all the doors which lead nowhere, and then one stumbles without knowing it on the only door through which one can enter—which one might have sought in vain for a hundred years—and it opens of its own accord.

Revolving the gloomy thoughts which I have just recorded, I had entered the courtyard of the Guermantes mansion and in my absent-minded state I had failed to see a car which was coming towards me; the chauffeur gave a shout and I just had time to step out of the way, but as I moved sharply backwards I tripped against the uneven paving-stones in front of the coach-house. And at the moment when, recovering my balance, I put my foot on a stone which was slightly lower than its neighbour, all my discouragement vanished and in its place was that same happiness which at various epochs of my life had been given to me by the sight of trees which I had thought that I recognised in the course of a drive near Balbec, by the sight of the twin steeples of Martinville, by the flavour of a madeleine dipped in tea, and by all those other sensations of which I have spoken and of which the last works of Vinteuil had seemed to me to combine the quintessential character. Just as, at the moment when I tasted the madeleine, all anxiety about the future, all intellectual doubts had disappeared, so now those that a few seconds ago had assailed me on the subject of the reality of my literary gifts, the reality even of literature, were removed as if by magic.

I had followed no new train of reasoning, discovered no decisive argument, but the difficulties which had seemed insoluble a moment ago had lost all importance. The happiness which I had just felt was unquestionably the same as that which I had felt when I tasted the madeleine soaked in tea. But if on that occasion I had put off the task of searching for the profounder causes of my emotion, this time I was determined not to resign myself to a failure to understand them. The emotion was the same; the difference, purely material, lay in the images evoked: a profound azure intoxicated my eyes, impressions of coolness, of dazzling light, swirled round me and in my desire to seize them—as afraid to move as I had been on the earlier occasion when I had continued to savour the taste of the madeleine while I tried to draw into my consciousness whatever it was that it recalled to me—I continued, ignoring the evident amusement of the great crowd of chauffeurs, to stagger as I had staggered a few seconds ago, with one foot on the higher paving-stone and the other on the lower. Every time that I merely repeated this physical movement, I achieved nothing; but if I succeeded, forgetting the Guermantes party, in recapturing what I had felt when I first placed my feet on the ground in this way, again the dazzling and indistinct vision fluttered near me, as if to say: "Seize me as I pass if you can, and try to solve the riddle of happiness which I set you." And almost at once I recognised the vision: it was Venice, of which my efforts to describe it and the supposed snapshots taken by my memory had never told me anything, but which the sensation which I had once experienced as I stood upon two uneven stones in the baptistery of St Mark's had, recurring a moment ago, restored to me complete with all the other sensations linked on that day to that particular sensation, all of which had been waiting in their place—from which with imperious suddenness a chance happening had caused them to emerge—in the series of forgotten days. In the same way the taste of the little madeleine had recalled Combray to me. But why had the images of Combray and of Venice, at these two different moments, given me a joy which was like a certainty and which sufficed, without any other proof, to make death a matter of indifference to me?

Still asking myself this question, and determined to-day to find the answer to it, I entered the Guermantes mansion, because always we give precedence over the inner task that we have to perform to the outward role which we are playing, which was, for me at this moment, that of guest. But when I had gone upstairs, a butler requested me to wait for a few minutes in a little sitting-room used as a library, next to the room where the refreshments were being served, until the end of the piece of music which was being played, the Princess having given orders for the doors to be kept shut during its performance. And at that very moment a second intimation came to reinforce the one which had been given to me by the two uneven paving-stones and to exhort me to persevere in my task. A servant, trying unsuccessfully not to make a noise, chanced to knock a spoon against a plate and again that same species of happiness which had come to me from the uneven paving-stones poured into me; the sensation was again of great heat, but entirely different: heat combined with a whiff of smoke and relieved by the cool smell of a forest background; and I recognised that what seemed to me now so delightful was that same row of trees which I had found tedious both to observe and to describe but which I had just now for a moment, in a sort of daze—I seemed to be in the railway carriage again, opening a bottle of beer—supposed to be before my eyes, so forcibly had the identical noise of the spoon knocking

against the plate given me, until I had had time to remember where I was, the illusion of the noise of the hammer with which a railwayman had done something to a
wheel of the train while we stopped near the little wood.
And then it seemed as though the signs which were to
bring me, on this day of all days, out of my disheartened
state and restore to me my faith in literature, were
thronging eagerly about me, for, a butler who had long
been in the service of the Prince de Guermantes having
recognised me and brought to me in the library where I
was waiting, so that I might not have to go to the buffet,
a selection of petits fours and a glass of orangeade, I
wiped my mouth with the napkin which he had given me;
and instantly, as though I had been the character in the
*Arabian Nights* who unwittingly accomplishes the very rite
which can cause to appear, visible to him alone, a docile
genie ready to convey him to a great distance, a new vision of azure passed before my eyes, but an azure that
this time was pure and saline and swelled into blue and
bosomy undulations, and so strong was this impression
that the moment to which I was transported seemed to
me to be the present moment: more bemused than on the
day when I had wondered whether I was really going to
be received by the Princesse de Guermantes or whether
everything round me would not collapse, I thought that
the servant had just opened the window on to the beach
and that all things invited me to go down and stroll along
the promenade while the tide was high, for the napkin
which I had used to wipe my mouth had precisely the
same degree of stiffness and starchedness as the towel
with which I had found it so awkward to dry my face as I
stood in front of the window on the first day of my arrival

at Balbec, and this napkin now, in the library of the Prince de Guermantes's house, unfolded for me—concealed within its smooth surfaces and its folds—the plumage of an ocean green and blue like the tail of a peacock. And what I found myself enjoying was not merely these colours but a whole instant of my life on whose summit they rested, an instant which had been no doubt an aspiration towards them and which some feeling of fatigue or sadness had perhaps prevented me from enjoying at Balbec but which now, freed from what is necessarily imperfect in external perception, pure and disembodied, caused me to swell with happiness.

The piece of music which was being played might end at any moment, and I might be obliged to enter the drawing-room. So I forced myself to try as quickly as possible to discern the essence of the identical pleasures which I had just experienced three times within the space of a few minutes, and having done so to extract the lesson which they might be made to yield. The thought that there is a vast difference between the real impression which we have had of a thing and the artificial impression of it which we form for ourselves when we attempt by an act of will to imagine it did not long detain me. Remembering with what relative indifference Swann years ago had been able to speak of the days when he had been loved, because what he saw beneath the words was not in fact those days but something else, and on the other hand the sudden pain which he had been caused by the little phrase of Vinteuil when it gave him back the days themselves, just as they were when he had felt them in the past, I understood clearly that what the sensation of the uneven paving-stones, the stiffness of the napkin, the taste

of the madeleine had reawakened in me had no connexion
with what I frequently tried to recall to myself of Venice,
Balbec, Combray, with the help of an undifferentiated
memory; and I understood that the reason why life may
be judged to be trivial although at certain moments it
seems to us so beautiful is that we form our judgment, ordinarily, on the evidence not of life itself but of those
quite different images which preserve nothing of life—
and therefore we judge it disparagingly. At most I noticed
cursorily that the differences which exist between every
one of our real impressions—differences which explain
why a uniform depiction of life cannot bear much resemblance to the reality—derive probably from the following
cause: the slightest word that we have said, the most insignificant action that we have performed at any one
epoch of our life was surrounded by, and coloured by the
reflexion of, things which logically had no connexion with
it and which later have been separated from it by our intellect which could make nothing of them for its own rational purposes, things, however, in the midst of
which—here the pink reflexion of the evening upon the
flower-covered wall of a country restaurant, a feeling of
hunger, the desire for women, the pleasure of luxury;
there the blue volutes of the morning sea and, enveloped
in them, phrases of music half emerging like the shoulders
of water-nymphs—the simplest act or gesture remains
immured as within a thousand sealed vessels, each one of
them filled with things of a colour, a scent, a temperature
that are absolutely different one from another, vessels,
moreover, which being disposed over the whole range of
our years, during which we have never ceased to change if
only in our dreams and our thoughts, are situated at the

most various moral altitudes and give us the sensation of
extraordinarily diverse atmospheres. It is true that we
have accomplished these changes imperceptibly; but between the memory which brusquely returns to us and our
present state, and no less between two memories of different years, places, hours, the distance is such that it alone,
even without any specific originality, would make it impossible to compare one with the other. Yes: if, owing to
the work of oblivion, the returning memory can throw no
bridge, form no connecting link between itself and the
present minute, if it remains in the context of its own
place and date, if it keeps its distance, its isolation in the
hollow of a valley or upon the highest peak of a mountain
summit, for this very reason it causes us suddenly to
breathe a new air, an air which is new precisely because
we have breathed it in the past, that purer air which the
poets have vainly tried to situate in paradise and which
could induce so profound a sensation of renewal only if it
had been breathed before, since the true paradises are the
paradises that we have lost.

And I observed in passing that for the work of art
which I now, though I had not yet reached a conscious
resolution, felt myself ready to undertake, this distinctness
of different events would entail very considerable difficulties. For I should have to execute the successive parts of
my work in a succession of different materials; what
would be suitable for mornings beside the sea or afternoons in Venice would be quite wrong if I wanted to depict those evenings at Rivebelle when, in the dining-room
that opened on to the garden, the heat began to resolve
into fragments and sink back into the ground, while a
sunset glimmer still illumined the roses on the walls of

the restaurant and the last water-colours of the day were still visible in the sky—this would be a new and distinct material, of a transparency and a sonority that were special, compact, cool after warmth, rose-pink.

Over all these thoughts I skimmed rapidly, for another inquiry demanded my attention more imperiously, the inquiry, which on previous occasions I had postponed, into the cause of this felicity which I had just experienced, into the character of the certitude with which it imposed itself. And this cause I began to divine as I compared these diverse happy impressions, diverse yet with this in common, that I experienced them at the present moment and at the same time in the context of a distant moment, so that the past was made to encroach upon the present and I was made to doubt whether I was in the one or the other. The truth surely was that the being within me which had enjoyed these impressions had enjoyed them because they had in them something that was common to a day long past and to the present, because in some way they were extra-temporal, and this being made its appearance only when, through one of these identifications of the present with the past, it was likely to find itself in the one and only medium in which it could exist and enjoy the essence of things, that is to say: outside time. This explained why it was that my anxiety on the subject of my death had ceased at the moment when I had unconsciously recognised the taste of the little madeleine, since the being which at that moment I had been was an extra-temporal being and therefore unalarmed by the vicissitudes of the future. This being had only come to me, only manifested itself outside of activity and immediate enjoyment, on those rare occasions when the miracle of an analogy had made me escape from the present. And only this being had the power to perform that task which had always defeated the efforts of my memory and my intellect, the power to make me rediscover days that were long past, the Time that was Lost.

And perhaps, if just now I had been disposed to think Bergotte wrong when he spoke of the life of the mind and its joys, it was because what I thought of at that moment as "the life of the mind" was a species of logical reasoning which had no connexion with it or with what existed in me at this moment—an error like the one which had made me find society and life itself tedious because I judged them on the evidence of untrue recollections, whereas now, now that three times in succession there had been reborn within me a veritable moment of the past, my appetite for life was immense.

A moment of the past, did I say? Was it not perhaps very much more: something that, common both to the past and to the present, is much more essential than either of them? So often, in the course of my life, reality had disappointed me because at the instant when my senses perceived it my imagination, which was the only organ that I possessed for the enjoyment of beauty, could not apply itself to it, in virtue of that ineluctable law which ordains that we can only imagine what is absent. And now, suddenly, the effect of this harsh law had been neutralised, temporarily annulled, by a marvellous expedient of nature which had caused a sensation—the noise made both by the spoon and by the hammer, for instance—to be mirrored at one and the same time in the past, so that my imagination was permitted to savour it, and in the present, where the actual shock to my senses of the noise, the touch of the linen napkin, or whatever it might be, had added to the dreams of the imagination the concept of "existence" which they usually lack, and through this subterfuge had made it possible for my being to secure, to isolate, to immobilise—for a moment brief as a flash of lightning—what normally it never apprehends: a fragment of time in the pure state. The being which had been re-born in me when with a sudden shudder of happiness I had heard the noise that was common to the spoon touching the plate and the hammer striking the wheel, or had felt, beneath my feet, the unevenness that was common to the paving-stones of the Guermantes courtyard and to those of the baptistery of St Mark's, this being is nourished only by the essences of things, in these alone does it find its sustenance and delight. In the observation of the present, where the senses cannot feed it with this food, it languishes, as it does in the consideration of a past made arid by the intellect or in the anticipation of a future which the will constructs with fragments of the present and the past, fragments whose reality it still further reduces by preserving of them only what is suitable for the utilitarian, narrowly human purpose for which it intends them. But let a noise or a scent, once heard or once smelt, be heard or smelt again in the present and at the same time in the past, real without being actual, ideal without being abstract, and immediately the permanent and habitually concealed essence of things is liberated and our true self, which seemed—had perhaps for long years seemed—to be dead but was not altogether dead, is awakened and reanimated as it receives the celestial nourishment that is brought to it. A minute freed from the order of time has re-created in us, to feel it, the man freed from the order of time. And one can understand that this man should have confidence in his joy, even if the simple taste of a madeleine does not seem logically to contain within it the reasons for this joy, one can understand that the word "death" should have no meaning for him; situated outside time, why should he fear the future?

But this species of optical illusion, which placed beside me a moment of the past that was incompatible with the present, could not last for long. The images presented to us by the voluntary memory can, it is true, be prolonged at will, for the voluntary memory requires no more exertion on our part than turning over the pages of a picture-book. On the day, for instance, long ago, when I was to visit the Princesse de Guermantes for the first time, I had from the sun-drenched courtyard of our house in Paris idly regarded, according to my whim, now the Place de l'Eglise at Combray, now the beach at Balbec, as if I had been choosing illustrations for that particular day from an album of water-colours depicting the various places where I had been; and with the egotistical pleasure of a collector, I had said to myself as I catalogued these illustrations stored in my memory: "At least I have seen some lovely things in my life." And of course my memory had affirmed that each one of these sensations was quite unlike the others, though in fact all it was doing was to make varied patterns out of elements that were homogeneous. But my recent experience of the three memories was something utterly different. These, on the contrary, instead of giving me a more flattering idea of myself, had almost caused me to doubt the reality, the existence of that self. And just as on the day when I had dipped the madeleine in the hot tea, in the setting of the place where

I happened at the time to be—on that first day my room in Paris, today at this moment the library of the Prince de Guermantes, a few minutes earlier the courtyard of his house—there had been, inside me and irradiating a little area outside me, a sensation (the taste of the madeleine dipped in the tea, a metallic sound, a step of a certain kind) which was common both to my actual surroundings and also to another place (my aunt Léonie's bedroom, the railway carriage, the baptistery of St Mark's). And now again, at the very moment when I was making these re-flexions, the shrill noise of water running through a pipe, a noise exactly like those long-drawn-out whistles which sometimes on summer evenings one heard the pleasure-steamers emit as they approached Balbec from the sea, made me feel—what I had once before been made to feel in Paris, in a big restaurant, by the sight of a luxurious dining-room, half-empty, summery and hot—something that was not merely a sensation similar to the one I used to have at the end of the afternoon in Balbec when, the tables already laid and glittering with linen and silver, the vast window-bays still open from one end to the other on to the esplanade without a single interruption, a single solid surface of glass or stone, while the sun slowly de-scended upon the sea and the steamers in the bay began to emit their cries, I had, if I had wished to join Albertine and her friends who were walking on the front, merely to step over the low wooden frame not much higher than my ankle, into a groove in which the whole continuous range of windows had been wound down so that the air could come into the hotel. (The painful recollection of having loved Albertine was, however, absent from my present sensation. Painful recollections are always of the dead.

And the dead decompose rapidly, and there remains even in the proximity of their tombs nothing but the beauty of nature, silence, the purity of the air.) Besides, it was not only an echo, a duplicate of a past sensation that I was made to feel by the noise of the water in the pipe, it was that past sensation itself. And in this case as in all the others, the sensation common to past and present had sought to re-create the former scene around itself, while the actual scene which had taken the former one's place opposed with all the resistance of material inertia this incursion into a house in Paris of a Normandy beach or a railway embankment. The marine dining-room of Balbec, with its damask linen prepared like so many altar-cloths to receive the setting sun, had sought to shatter the solidity of the Guermantes mansion, to force open its doors, and for an instant had made the sofas around me sway and tremble as on another occasion it had done to the tables of the restaurant in Paris. Always, when these resurrections took place, the distant scene engendered around the common sensation had for a moment grappled, like a wrestler, with the present scene. Always the present scene had come off victorious, and always the vanquished one had appeared to me the more beautiful of the two, so beautiful that I had remained in a state of ecstasy on the uneven paving-stones or before the cup of tea, endeavouring to prolong or to reproduce the momentary appearances of the Combray or the Balbec or the Venice which invaded only to be driven back, which rose up only at once to abandon me in the midst of the new scene which somehow, nevertheless, the past had been able to permeate. And if the present scene had not very quickly been victorious, I believe that I should have lost consciousness;

for so complete are these resurrections of the past during the second that they last, that they not only oblige our eyes to cease to see the room which is near them in order to look instead at the railway bordered with trees or the rising tide, they even force our nostrils to breathe the air of places which are in fact a great distance away, and our will to choose between the various projects which those distant places suggest to us, they force our whole self to believe that it is surrounded by these places or at least to waver doubtfully between them and the places where we now are, in a dazed uncertainty such as we feel sometimes when an indescribably beautiful vision presents itself to us at the moment of our falling asleep.

Fragments of existence withdrawn from Time: these then were perhaps what the being three times, four times brought back to life within me had just now tasted, but the contemplation, though it was of eternity, had been fugitive. And yet I was vaguely aware that the pleasure which this contemplation had, at rare intervals, given me in my life, was the only genuine and fruitful pleasure that I had known. The unreality of the others is indicated clearly enough—is it not?—either by their inability to satisfy us, as is the case with social pleasures, the only consequence of which is likely to be the discomfort provoked by the ingestion of unwholesome food, or with friendship, which is a simulacrum, since, for whatever moral reasons he may do it, the artist who gives up an hour of work for an hour of conversation with a friend knows that he is sacrificing a reality for something that does not exist (our friends being friends only in the light of an agreeable folly which travels with us through life and to which we readily accommodate ourselves, but which at the bottom of our hearts we know to be no more reasonable than the delusion of the man who talks to the furniture because he believes that it is alive), or else by the sadness which follows their satisfaction, a sadness which I had felt, for instance, on the day when I had been introduced to Albertine, at having taken pains (not even in fact very great pains) in order to achieve something— getting to know this girl—which seemed to me trivial simply because I had achieved it. And even a more profound pleasure, like the pleasure which I might have hoped to feel when I was in love with Albertine, was in fact only experienced inversely, through the anguish which I felt when she was not there, for when I was sure that she would soon be with me, as on the day when she had returned from the Trocadéro, I had seemed to experience no more than a vague dissatisfaction, whereas my exaltation and my joy grew steadily greater as I probed more and more deeply into the noise of the spoon on the plate or the taste of the tea which had brought into my bedroom in Paris the bedroom of my aunt Léonie and in its train all Combray and the two ways of our walks.

To this contemplation of the essence of things I had decided therefore that in future I must attach myself, so as somehow to immobilise it. But how, by what means, was I to do this? Naturally, at the moment when the stiffness of the napkin had restored Balbec to me and for an instant caressed my imagination not only with the sight of the sea as it had been that morning but with the smell of my room, the speed of the wind, the sensation of looking forward to lunch, of wondering which of the different walks I should take (all this being attached to the feel of the linen like those thousand wings of the angels which

revolve a thousand times in a minute), or at the moment
when the unevenness of the two paving-stones had extended in every direction and dimension the desiccated
and insubstantial images which I normally had of Venice
and St Mark's and of all the sensations which I had felt
there, reuniting the piazza to the cathedral, the landing-
stage to the piazza, the canal to the landing-stage, and to
all that the eyes see the world of desires which is seen
only by the mind—naturally at those moments I had
been tempted, if not, because of the time of the year, to
go and walk once more through the watery streets of
Venice which for me were above all associated with the
spring, at least to return to Balbec. But this thought did
not for an instant detain me. I knew for one thing that
countries were not such as their names painted them to
my imagination, so that now it was scarcely ever except in
my dreams, while I was asleep, that a place could lie
spread before me wrought in that pure matter which is
entirely distinct from the matter of the common things
that we see and touch but of which, when I had imagined
these common things without ever having seen them, they
too had seemed to me to be composed: and I knew also
that the same was true of that other species of image
which is formed by the memory, so that not only had I
failed to discover the beauty of Balbec as I had imagined
it when I had gone there for the first time, I had failed
also when I went back the second time to rediscover the
remembered beauty which that first visit had left me. Experience had taught me only too well the impossibility of
attaining in the real world to what lay deep within myself;
I knew that Lost Time was not to be found again on the
piazza of St Mark's any more than I had found it again on

my second visit to Balbec or on my return to Tansonville
to see Gilberte, and that travel, which merely dangled
once more before me the illusion that these vanished impressions existed outside myself, could not be the means
which I sought. And I did not want to let myself be side-
tracked once more, for the task before me was to discover
at long last whether or no it was possible to attain to
what—disappointed as I had always been by the actuality
of places and people—I had, although once the septet of
Vinteuil had seemed to point to the contrary conclusion,
come to think of as unrealisable. I did not intend, then, to
make yet another experiment in a direction which I had
long known could lead nowhere. Impressions such as
those to which I wished to give permanence could not but
vanish at the touch of a direct enjoyment which had been
powerless to engender them. The only way to savour
them more fully was to try to get to know them more
completely in the medium in which they existed, that is to
say within myself, to try to make them translucid even to
their very depths. I had not known pleasure at Balbec any
more than I had known pleasure when I lived with Albertine, for the pleasure of living with her had been perceptible to me only in retrospect. When I recapitulated the
disappointments of my life as a lived life, disappointments
which made me believe that its reality must reside elsewhere than in action, what I was doing was not merely to
link different disappointments together in a purely fortuitous manner and in following the circumstances of my
personal existence. I saw clearly that the disappointment
of travel and the disappointment of love were not different disappointments at all but the varied aspects which
are assumed, according to the particular circumstances

which bring it into play, by our inherent powerlessness to realise ourselves in material enjoyment or in effective action. And thinking again of the extra-temporal joy which I had been made to feel by the sound of the spoon or the taste of the madeleine, I said to myself: "Was this perhaps that happiness which the little phrase of the sonata promised to Swann and which he, because he was unable to find it in artistic creation, mistakenly assimilated to the pleasures of love, was this the happiness of which long ago I was given a presentiment—as something more supraterrestrial even than the mood evoked by the little phrase of the sonata—by the call, the mysterious, rubescent call of that septet which Swann was never privileged to hear, having died like so many others before the truth that was made for him had been revealed? A truth that in any case he could not have used, for though the phrase perhaps symbolised a call, it was incapable of creating new powers and making Swann the writer that he was not."

And then, after I had dwelt for some little time upon these resurrections of the memory, the thought came to me that in another fashion certain obscure impressions, already even at Combray on the Guermantes way, had solicited my attention in a fashion somewhat similar to these reminiscences, except that they concealed within them not a sensation dating from an earlier time, but a new truth, a precious image which I had sought to uncover by efforts of the same kind as those that we make to recall something that we have forgotten, as if our finest ideas were like tunes which, as it were, come back to us although we have never heard them before and which we have to make an effort to hear and to transcribe. I remembered—with pleasure because it showed me that already in those days I had been the same and that this type of experience sprang from a fundamental trait in my character, but with sadness also when I thought that since that time I had never progressed—that already at Combray I used to fix before my mind for its attention some image which had compelled me to look at it, a cloud, a triangle, a church spire, a flower, a stone, because I had the feeling that perhaps beneath these signs there lay something of a quite different kind which I must try to discover, some thought which they translated after the fashion of those hieroglyphic characters which at first one might suppose to represent only material objects. No doubt the process of decipherment was difficult, but only by accomplishing it could one arrive at whatever truth there was to read. For the truths which the intellect apprehends directly in the world of full and unimpeded light have something less profound, less necessary than those which life communicates to us against our will in an impression which is material because it enters us through the senses but yet has a spiritual meaning which it is possible for us to extract. In fact, both in the one case and in the other, whether I was concerned with impressions like the one which I had received from the sight of the steeples of Martinville or with reminiscences like that of the unevenness of the two steps or the taste of the madeleine, the task was to interpret the given sensations as signs of so many laws and ideas, by trying to think—that is to say, to draw forth from the shadow—what I had merely felt, by trying to convert it into its spiritual equivalent. And this method, which seemed to me the sole method, what was it but the creation of a work of art? Already the consequences came flooding into my mind: first, whether I considered reminiscences of the kind evoked by the noise of the spoon or the taste of the madeleine, or those truths written with the aid of shapes for whose meaning I searched in my brain, where—church steeples or wild grass growing in a wall— they composed a magical scrawl, complex and elaborate, their essential character was that I was not free to choose them, that such as they were they were given to me. And I realised that this must be the mark of their authenticity. I had not gone in search of the two uneven paving-stones of the courtyard upon which I had stumbled. But it was precisely the fortuitous and inevitable fashion in which this and the other sensations had been encountered that proved the trueness of the past which they brought back to life, of the images which they released, since we feel, with these sensations, the effort that they make to climb back towards the light, feel in ourselves the joy of rediscovering what is real. And here too was the proof of the trueness of the whole picture formed out of those contemporaneous impressions which the first sensation brings back in its train, with those unerring proportions of light and shade, emphasis and omission, memory and forgetfulness to which conscious recollection and conscious observation will never know how to attain.

As for the inner book of unknown symbols (symbols carved in relief they might have been, which my attention, as it explored my unconscious, groped for and stumbled against and followed the contours of, like a diver exploring the ocean-bed), if I tried to read them no one could help me with any rules, for to read them was an act of creation in which no one can do our work for us or even collaborate with us. How many for this reason turn aside from writing! What tasks do men not take upon themselves in order to evade this task! Every public event, be it the Dreyfus case, be it the war, furnishes the writer with a fresh excuse for not attempting to decipher this book: he wants to ensure the triumph of justice, he wants to restore the moral unity of the nation, he has no time to think of literature. But these are mere excuses, the truth being that he has not or no longer has genius, that is to say instinct. For instinct dictates our duty and the intellect supplies us with pretexts for evading it. But excuses have no place in art and intentions count for nothing: at every moment the artist has to listen to his instinct, and it is this that makes art the most real of all things, the most austere school of life, the true last judgment. This book, more laborious to decipher than any other, is also the only one which has been dictated to us by reality, the only one of which the "impression" has been printed in us by reality itself. When an idea—an idea of any kind—is left in us by life, its material pattern, the outline of the impression that it made upon us, remains behind as the token of its necessary truth. The ideas formed by the pure intelligence have no more than a logical, a possible truth, they are arbitrarily chosen. The book whose hieroglyphs are patterns not traced by us is the only book that really belongs to us. Not that the ideas which we form for ourselves cannot be correct in logic; that they may well be, but we cannot know whether they are true. Only the impression, however trivial its material may seem to be, however faint its traces, is a criterion of truth and deserves for that reason to be apprehended by the mind, for the mind, if it succeeds in extracting this truth, can by the impression and by nothing else be brought to a state of greater perfection and given a pure joy. The impression is for the writer what experiment is for the scientist, with the difference that in the scientist the work of the intelligence precedes the experiment and in the writer it comes after the impression. What we have not had to decipher, to elucidate by our own efforts, what was clear before we looked at it, is not ours. From ourselves comes only that which we drag forth from the obscurity which lies within us, that which to others is unknown.

(A level ray of the setting sun recalls to me instantaneously an episode in my early childhood to which I had never since that time given a thought: my aunt Léonie had a fever which Doctor Percepied feared might be typhoid and for a week I was made to sleep in Eulalie's little room looking out on the Place de l'Eglise, which had nothing but rush mats on the floor and over the window a muslin curtain that was always buzzing with a sunshine to which I was not accustomed. And seeing how the recollection of this little old-fashioned servant's bedroom suddenly added to my past life a long stretch of time so different from the rest and so delicious, I thought by contrast of the nullity of the impressions which had been contributed to it by the most sumptuous entertainments in the most princely mansions. The only thing at all sad about this room of Eulalie's was that at night, because the viaduct was so near, one heard the hooting of the trains. But as I knew that these were bellowings produced by machines under human control, they did not terrify me as, in a prehistoric age, I might have been terrified by the ululations of a neighbouring mammoth taking a free and unco-ordinated stroll.)

I had arrived then at the conclusion that in fashioning

a work of art we are by no means free, that we do not choose how we shall make it but that it pre-exists us and therefore we are obliged, since it is both necessary and hidden, to do what we should have to do if it were a law of nature—to discover it. But this discovery which art obliges us to make, is it not, I thought, really the discovery of what, though it ought to be more precious to us than anything in the world, yet remains ordinarily for ever unknown to us, the discovery of our true life, of reality as we have felt it to be, which differs so greatly from what we think it is that when a chance happening brings us an authentic memory of it we are filled with an immense happiness? In this conclusion I was confirmed by the thought of the falseness of so-called realist art, which would not be so untruthful if we had not in life acquired the habit of giving to what we feel a form of expression which differs so much from, and which we nevertheless after a little time take to be, reality itself. I began to perceive that I should not have to trouble myself with the various literary theories which had at moments perplexed me—notably those which practitioners of criticism had developed at the time of the Dreyfus case and had taken up again during the war, according to which "the artist must be made to leave his ivory tower" and the themes chosen by the writer ought to be not frivolous or sentimental but rather such things as great working-class movements or—in default of crowds—at least no longer as in the past unimportant men of leisure ("I must confess that the depiction of these useless characters rather bores me," Bloch had been fond of saying), but noble intellectuals or men of heroic stature.

In any case, quite apart from what I might think of

the logical propositions which they contained, these theories seemed to me to indicate very clearly the inferiority of those who upheld them—my reaction was that of the truly well-brought-up child who, lunching in a strange house and hearing his hosts say: "We are frank, we don't hide our light under a bushel here," feels that the remark indicates a moral quality inferior to right conduct pure and simple, which says nothing. Authentic art has no use for proclamations of this kind, it accomplishes its work in silence. Moreover, those who theorised in this way used hackneyed phrases which had a curious resemblance to those of the idiots whom they denounced. And it is perhaps as much by the quality of his language as by the species of aesthetic theory which he advances that one may judge of the level to which a writer has attained in the moral and intellectual part of his work. Quality of language, however, is something the critical theorists think that they can do without, and those who admire them are easily persuaded that it is no proof of intellectual merit, for this is a thing which they cannot infer from the beauty of an image but can recognise only when they see it directly expressed. Hence the temptation for the writer to write intellectual works—a gross impropriety. A work in which there are theories is like an object which still has its price-tag on it. (And as to the choice of theme, a frivolous theme will serve as well as a serious one for a study of the laws of character, in the same way that a prosector can study the laws of anatomy as well in the body of an imbecile as in that of a man of talent, since the great moral laws, like the laws of the circulation of the blood or of renal elimination, vary scarcely at all with the intellectual merit of individuals.) A writer reasons, that is to say he goes astray, only when he has not the strength to force himself to make an impression pass through all the successive states which will culminate in its fixation, its expression. The reality that he has to express resides, as I now began to understand, not in the superficial appearance of his subject but at a depth at which that appearance matters little; this truth had been symbolised for me by that clink of a spoon against a plate, that starched stiffness of a napkin, which had been of more value to me for my spiritual renewal than innumerable conversations of a humanitarian or patriotic or internationalist or metaphysical kind. "Enough of style," had been the cry, "enough of literature, let us have life!" And one may well imagine how since the beginning of the war even the simple theories of M. de Norpois, his denunciations of the "flute-players," had enjoyed a second vogue. For plenty of people who lack the artistic sense, who lack, that is to say, the faculty of submitting to the reality within themselves, may yet possess the ability to expatiate upon the theory of art until the crack of doom. And if they happen to be diplomats or financiers to boot, involved in the "realities" of the present age, they are likely to believe that literature is an intellectual game destined in the future to be progressively eliminated. (Some critics now liked to regard the novel as a sort of procession of things upon the screen of a cinematograph. This comparison was absurd. Nothing is further from what we have really perceived than the vision that the cinematograph presents.)

The idea of a popular art, like that of a patriotic art, if not actually dangerous seemed to me ridiculous. If the intention was to make art accessible to the people by sacrificing refinements of form, on the ground that they are "all right for the idle rich" but not for anybody else, I had seen enough of fashionable society to know that it is there that one finds real illiteracy and not, let us say, among electricians. In fact, an art that was "popular" so far as form was concerned would have been better suited to the members of the Jockey Club than to those of the General Confederation of Labour—and as for subject, the working classes are as bored by novels of popular life as children are by the books which are written specially for them. When one reads, one likes to be transported into a new world, and working men have as much curiosity about princes as princes about working men. At the beginning of the war M. Barrès had said that the artist (he happened to be talking about Titian) must first and foremost serve the glory of his country. But this he can do only by being an artist, which means only on condition that, while in his own sphere he is studying laws, conducting experiments, making discoveries which are as delicate as those of science, he shall think of nothing—not even his country— but the truth which is before him. Let us not imitate the revolutionaries who out of "civic sense" despised, if they did not destroy, the works of Watteau and La Tour, painters who have brought more honour upon France than all those of the Revolution. Anatomy is not perhaps the occupation that a kind-hearted man would choose, if he or any artist had the possibility of choice, and certainly it was not the kindness of a virtuous heart (though he was a truly kind man) that made Choderlos de Laclos write *Les Liaisons dangereuses*, nor was it any affection for the lower or upper bourgeoisie that made Flaubert choose the themes of *Madame Bovary* and *L'Education sentimentale*— but this is no valid criticism of the work of these writers.

Some people were also saying that the art of an age of haste would be brief, just as many people before the war had predicted that it would be short. The railway, according to this mode of thinking, was destined to kill contemplation and there was no sense in regretting the age of the diligence. But in fact the car has taken over its function and once more deposits tourists outside forgotten churches.

As I entered the library where I had been pursuing this train of thought I had remembered what the Goncourts say about the magnificent first editions which it contains and I had promised myself that I would look at them while I was waiting. And all this while, without paying very much attention to what I was doing, I had been taking first one and then another of the precious volumes from the shelves, when suddenly, at the moment when I carelessly opened one of them—it was George Sand's *François le Champi*—I felt myself unpleasantly struck by an impression which seemed at first to be utterly out of harmony with the thoughts that were passing through my mind, until a moment later, with an emotion so strong that tears came to my eyes, I recognised how very much in harmony with them it was. Imagine a room in which a man has died, a man who has rendered great services to his country; the undertaker's men are getting ready to take the coffin downstairs and the dead man's son is holding out his hand to the last friends who are filing past it; suddenly the silence is broken by a flourish of trumpets beneath the windows and he feels outraged, thinking that this must be some plot to mock and insult his grief; but presently this man who until this moment has mastered his emotions dissolves into tears, for he re-

alises that what he hears is the band of a regiment which
has come to share in his mourning and to pay honour to
his father's corpse. Like this dead man's son, I had just
recognised how completely in harmony with the thoughts
in my mind was the painful impression which I had experienced when I had seen this title on the cover of a book
in the library of the Prince de Guermantes, for it was a title which after a moment's hesitation had given me the
idea that literature did really offer us that world of mystery which I had ceased to find in it. And yet the book
was not a very extraordinary one, it was *François le
Champi*. But that name, like the name Guermantes, was
for me unlike the names which I had heard for the first
time only in later life. The memory of what had seemed
to me too deep for understanding in the subject of
*François le Champi* when my mother long ago had read
the book aloud to me, had been reawakened by the title,
and just as the name of Guermantes, after a long period
during which I had not seen the Guermantes, contained
for me the essence of the feudal age, so *François le
Champi* contained the essence of the novel, and for a second this memory substituted itself for the quite commonplace idea of "one of George Sand's novels about Berry."
At a dinner-party, where thought always remains superficial, I might no doubt have been able to talk about
*François le Champi* and the Guermantes without either the
novel or the family being what they had been to me at
Combray. But alone, as I was at this moment, I was
plunged by these names to a greater depth. At such moments the idea that some woman whom I had met at parties was a cousin of Mme de Guermantes, a cousin that is
to say of a personage of the magic lantern, seemed to me

incomprehensible, and equally incomprehensible was the
idea that the best books I had ever read might be—I will
not say superior to, though that is in fact of course what
they were—but even equal to this extraordinary *François
le Champi*. This was a very deeply buried impression that
I had just encountered, one in which memories of childhood and family were tenderly intermingled and which I
had not immediately recognised. My first reaction had
been to ask myself, angrily, who this stranger was who
was coming to trouble me. The stranger was none other
than myself, the child I had been at that time, brought to
life within me by the book, which knowing nothing of me
except this child had instantly summoned him to its presence, wanting to be seen only by his eyes, to be loved
only by his heart, to speak only to him. And this book
which my mother had read aloud to me at Combray until
the early hours of the morning had kept for me all the
charm of that night. Admittedly the "pen" of George
Sand, to borrow a phrase from Brichot, who was so fond
of saying that a book was written with a "lively pen," no
longer seemed to me, as for so long it had seemed to my
mother before she had gradually come to model her literary tastes upon mine, in the least a magic pen. But it was
a pen which, unintentionally, like a schoolboy amusing
himself with a real pen, I had charged with electricity,
and now a thousand trifling details of Combray which for
years had not entered my mind came lightly and spontaneously leaping, in follow-my-leader fashion, to suspend
themselves from the magnetised nib in an interminable
and trembling chain of memories.

Certain people, whose minds are prone to mystery,
like to believe that objects retain something of the eyes

which have looked at them, that old buildings and pictures appear to us not as they originally were but beneath
a perceptible veil woven for them over the centuries by
the love and contemplation of millions of admirers. This
fantasy, if you transpose it into the domain of what is for
each one of us the sole reality, the domain of his own sensibility, becomes the truth. In that sense and in that sense
alone (but it is a far more important one than the other), a
thing which we have looked at in the past brings back to
us, if we see it again, not only the eyes with which we
looked at it but all the images with which at the time
those eyes were filled. For things—and among them a
book in a red binding—as soon as we have perceived
them are transformed within us into something immaterial, something of the same nature as all our preoccupations and sensations of that particular time, with which,
indissolubly, they blend. A name read long ago in a book
contains within its syllables the strong wind and brilliant
sunshine that prevailed while we were reading it. And this
is why the kind of literature which contents itself with
"describing things," with giving of them merely a miserable abstract of lines and surfaces, is in fact, though it
calls itself realist, the furthest removed from reality and
has more than any other the effect of saddening and im-
poverishing us, since it abruptly severs all communication
of our present self both with the past, the essence of
which is preserved in things, and with the future, in
which things incite us to enjoy the essence of the past a
second time. Yet it is precisely this essence that an art
worthy of the name must seek to express; then at least, if
it fails, there is a lesson to be drawn from its impotence
(whereas from the successes of realism there is nothing to

be learnt), the lesson that this essence is, in part, subjective and incommunicable.

Nor is this all. A thing which we saw, a book which we read at a certain period does not merely remain for ever conjoined to what existed then around us; it remains also faithfully united to what we ourselves then were and thereafter it can be handled only by the sensibility, the personality that were then ours. If, even in thought, I pick from the bookshelf *François le Champi*, immediately there rises within me a child who takes my place, who alone has the right to spell out the title *François le Champi*, and who reads it as he read it once before, with the same impression of what the weather was like then in the garden, the same dreams that were then shaping themselves in his mind about the different countries and about life, the same anguish about the next day. Or if I see something which dates from another period, it is a young man who comes to life. So that my personality of today may be compared to an abandoned quarry, which supposes everything it contains to be uniform and monotonous, but from which memory, selecting here and there, can, like some sculptor of genius, extract innumerable different statues. And this is true of everything that we see again after a lapse of time, books in this respect behaving just like other things: the way in which the covers of a binding open, the grain of a particular paper, may have preserved in itself as vivid a memory of the fashion in which I once imagined Venice and of the desire that I had to go there as the actual phrases of a book. An even more vivid memory perhaps, for phrases sometimes are an obstruction, just as sometimes when we look at a photograph of a person we recollect him less clearly than we do when we are

merely thinking about him. Certainly, there are many
books which I read in my childhood, including even, I am
sorry to say, some of those of Bergotte himself, which
now, if I happen to be tired one evening, I take up merely
in the spirit in which I might go for a train journey, with
the hope, that is, of resting myself by the sight of objects
that I do not see every day and by breathing the atmosphere of an earlier time. But it can happen that this deliberate attempt at evocation is actually thwarted by the
prolonged reading of the book. There is, for instance, a
book by Bergotte (there was a copy in the Prince's library,
with a dedication both sycophantic and platitudinous in
the extreme), which I read years ago one winter day when
I was unable to see Gilberte and which I now search in
vain for the phrases which I then thought wonderful. Certain words almost make me believe that I have found
them, but it cannot be so, for of the beauty that I once
saw in them there is no trace. But the volume itself still
glistens with the snow that covered the Champs-Elysées
on the day when I first read it—I open its pages and the
scene is before my eyes.

So it is that, if I had been tempted to become a bibliophile like the Prince de Guermantes, I should only have
been one in my own peculiar fashion, though I should not
have despised that beauty, independent of the intrinsic
value of a book, which is attached to it in the eyes of col-
lectors by their knowing the libraries through which it has
passed, knowing for instance that it was given by such
and such a sovereign, on the occasion of such and such an
event, to such and such a famous man, by their having
followed it from sale to sale through the course of its
life—that beauty, which is in a certain sense the historic

beauty of a book, would not be lost upon me. But it is rather in the history of my own life, and not simply as a connoisseur of the past in general, that I should seek this beauty; and I should attach it often not to a particular copy but to the work itself, to *François le Champi*, for instance, first contemplated by me in my little bedroom at Combray, during the night that was perhaps the sweetest and the saddest of my life, when I had alas! (at a time when the Guermantes still seemed to me mysterious and inaccessible) won from my parents that first abdication of their authority from which, later, I was to date the decline of my health and my will, and my renunciation, each day disastrously confirmed, of a task that daily became more difficult—and rediscovered by me today, in the library of these same Guermantes, on this most wonderful of all days which had suddenly illuminated for me not only the old groping movements of my thought, but even the whole purpose of my life and perhaps of art itself. As for particular copies of books, I should have been able to take an interest in them too, but in a living sense. The first edition of a work would have been more precious in my eyes than any other, but by this term I should have understood the edition in which I read it for the first time. I should seek out original editions, those, that is to say, in which I once received an original impression of a book. For the impressions that one has later are no longer original. In the case of novels I should collect old-fashioned bindings, those of the period when I read my first novels, those that so often heard Papa say to me: "Sit up straight!" Like the dress which a woman was wearing when we saw her for the first time, they would help me to rediscover the love that I then had, the beauty on which I have since superimposed so many less and less loved images, they would help me to find that first image again, even though I am no longer the "I" who first beheld it, even though I must make way for the "I" that I then was if that "I" summons the thing that it once knew and that the "I" of today does not know.

The library which I should thus assemble would contain volumes of an even greater value; for the books which I read in the past at Combray or in Venice, enriched now by my memory with vast illuminations representing the church of Saint-Hilaire or the gondola moored at the foot of San Giorgio Maggiore and the Grand Canal incrusted with sparkling sapphires, would have become the equals of those ancient "picture books"—illustrated bibles or books of hours—which the collector nowadays opens not to read their text but to savour once more the enchantment of the colours which some rival of Foucquet has added to it and which make these volumes the treasures that they are. And yet, even to open these books for the purpose merely of looking at the pictures with which, when I read them long ago, they were not yet adorned, would seem to me in itself so dangerous that, even in the sense which I have described, which is the only one that I can understand, I should not, I think, be tempted to become a bibliophile. I know very well how easily these images, deposited by the mind, can be effaced by the mind. For the old images it substitutes new ones which no longer have the same power of resurrection. And if I still possessed the *François le Champi* which Mamma unpacked one evening from the parcel of books which my grandmother was to have given me for my birthday, I should never look at it; I should be too afraid that I might gradually insinuate into it my impressions of today and smother my original impressions beneath them, that I might see it become so far a thing of the present that, when I asked it to evoke once more the child who spelt out its title in the little bedroom at Combray, the child, not recognising its voice, would no longer reply to its summons and would remain for ever buried in oblivion.

An image presented to us by life brings with it, in a single moment, sensations which are in fact multiple and heterogeneous. The sight, for instance, of the binding of a book once read may weave into the characters of its title the moonlight of a distant summer night. The taste of our breakfast coffee brings with it that vague hope of fine weather which so often long ago, as with the day still intact and full before us, we were drinking it out of a bowl of white porcelain, creamy and fluted and itself looking almost like vitrified milk, suddenly smiled upon us in the pale uncertainty of the dawn. An hour is not merely an hour, it is a vase full of scents and sounds and projects and climates, and what we call reality is a certain connexion between these immediate sensations and the memories which envelop us simultaneously with them—a connexion that is suppressed in a simple cinematographic vision, which just because it professes to confine itself to the truth in fact departs widely from it—a unique connexion which the writer has to rediscover in order to link for ever in his phrase the two sets of phenomena which reality joins together. He can describe a scene by describing one after another the innumerable objects which at a given moment were present at a particular place, but truth will be attained by him only when he takes two different objects, states the connexion between them—a connexion analogous in the world of art to the unique connexion which in the world of science is provided by the law of causality—and encloses them in the necessary links of a well-wrought style; truth—and life too—can be attained by us only when, by comparing a quality common to two sensations, we succeed in extracting their common essence and in reuniting them to each other, liberated from the contingencies of time, within a metaphor. Had not nature herself—if one considered the matter from this point of view—placed me on the path of art, was she not herself a beginning of art, she who, often, had allowed me to become aware of the beauty of one thing only in another thing, of the beauty, for instance, of noon at Combray in the sound of its bells, of that of the mornings at Doncières in the hiccups of our central heating? The link may be uninteresting, the objects trivial, the style bad, but unless this process has taken place the description is worthless.

But my train of thought led me yet further. If reality were indeed a sort of waste product of experience, more or less identical for each one of us, since when we speak of bad weather, a war, a taxi rank, a brightly lit restaurant, a garden full of flowers, everybody knows what we mean, if reality were no more than this, no doubt a sort of cinematograph film of these things would be sufficient and the "style," the "literature" that departed from the simple data that they provide would be superfluous and artificial. But was it true that reality was no more than this? If I tried to understand what actually happens at the moment when a thing makes some particular impression upon one—on the day, for instance, when as I crossed the bridge over the Vivonne the shadow of a cloud upon the water had made me cry: "Gosh!" and jump for joy; or the occasion when, hearing a phrase of Bergotte's, all that I had disengaged from my impression was the not specially relevant remark: "How splendid!"; or the words I had once heard Bloch use in exasperation at some piece of bad behaviour, words quite inappropriate to a very commonplace incident: "I must say that that sort of conduct seems to me absolutely fffantastic!"; or that evening when, flattered at the politeness which the Guermantes had shown to me as their guest and also a little intoxicated by the wines which I had drunk in their house, I could not help saying to myself half aloud as I came away alone: "They really are delightful people and I should be happy to see them every day of my life"—I realised that the words in each case were a long way removed from the impressions that I or Bloch had in fact received. So that the essential, the only true book, though in the ordinary sense of the word it does not have to be "invented" by a great writer—for it exists already in each one of us—has to be translated by him. The function and the task of a writer are those of a translator.

And if in some cases—where we are dealing, for instance, with the inaccurate language of our own vanity— the rectification of an oblique interior discourse (which deviates gradually more and more widely from the first and central impression) until it merges with the straight line which the impression ought to have produced is a laborious undertaking which our idleness would prefer to shirk, there are other circumstances—for example, where love is involved—in which this same process is actually painful. Here all our feigned indifferences, all our indignation at the lies of whoever it is whom we love (lies which

are so natural and so like those that we perpetrate ourselves), in a word all that we have not ceased, whenever
we are unhappy or betrayed, not only to say to the loved
one but, while we are waiting for a meeting with her, to
repeat endlessly to ourselves, sometimes aloud in the silence of our room, which we disturb with remarks like:
"No, really, this sort of behaviour is intolerable," and: "I
have consented to see you once more, for the last time,
and I don't deny that it hurts me," all this can only be
brought back into conformity with the felt truth from
which it has so widely diverged by the abolition of all that
we have set most store by, all that in our solitude, in our
feverish projects of letters and schemes, has been the substance of our passionate dialogue with ourselves.

Even where the joys of art are concerned, although we
seek and value them for the sake of the impression that
they give us, we contrive as quickly as possible to set
aside, as being inexpressible, precisely that element in
them which is the impression that we sought, and we concentrate instead upon that other ingredient in aesthetic
emotion which allows us to savour its pleasure without
penetrating its essence and lets us suppose that we are
sharing it with other art-lovers, with whom we find it
possible to converse just because, the personal root of our
own impression having been suppressed, we are discussing
with them a thing which is the same for them and for us.
Even in those moments when we are the most disinterested spectators of nature, or of society or of love or of art
itself, since every impression is double and the one half
which is sheathed in the object is prolonged in ourselves
by another half which we alone can know, we speedily
find means to neglect this second half, which is the one

on which we ought to concentrate, and to pay attention only to the first half which, as it is external and therefore cannot be intimately explored, will occasion us no fatigue. To try to perceive the little furrow which the sight of a hawthorn bush or of a church has traced in us is a task that we find too difficult. But we play a symphony over and over again, we go back repeatedly to see a church un- til—in that flight to get away from our own life (which we have not the courage to look at) which goes by the name of erudition—we know them, the symphony and the church, as well as and in the same fashion as the most knowledgeable connoisseur of music or archaeology. And how many art-lovers stop there, without extracting any- thing from their impression, so that they grow old useless and unsatisfied, like celibates of Art! They suffer, but their sufferings, like the sufferings of virgins and of lazy people, are of a kind that fecundity or work would cure. They get more excited about works of art than real artists, because for them their excitement is not the object of a la- borious and inward-directed study but a force which bursts outwards, which heats their conversations and em- purples their cheeks; at concerts they will shout "Bravo, bravo" till they are hoarse at the end of a work they ad- mire and imagine as they do so that they are discharging a duty. But demonstrations of this kind do not oblige them to clarify the nature of their admiration and of this they remain in ignorance. Meanwhile, like a stream which can find no useful channel, their love of art flows over into even their calmest conversations, so that they make wild gestures and grimace and toss their heads whenever they mention the subject. "I was at a concert the other day. They played the first piece and I must say it left me cold.

Then they started on the quartet. By Jove, what a difference!" (At this moment the face of the music-lover expresses a sudden anxiety, as if he were thinking: "Don't I
see sparks? And I smell burning! Something's on fire.")
"It's the most exasperating thing I've ever heard, damn it!
It's not exactly a good composition, but it's stunning, it's
something quite out of the ordinary." And yet, ludicrous
though they may be, such people are not altogether to be
despised. They are the first attempts of nature in her
struggle to create the artist, experiments as misshapen, as
unviable as those first animals that came before the
species of today and were so constituted that they could
not survive for long. And, with their sterile velleities, the
art-lovers are as touching to contemplate as those early
machines which tried to leave the ground and could not,
but which yet held within them, if not the secret, the still
to be discovered means, at least the desire of flight. "You
know, old boy," goes on the music-lover, as he takes you
by the elbow, "this is the eighth time I've heard it, and I
promise you it won't be the last." And indeed, since they
fail to assimilate what is truly nourishing in art, they need
artistic pleasures all the time, they are victims of a morbid
hunger which is never satisfied. So they go to concert after concert to applaud the same work and think that they
have a duty to put in an appearance whenever it is performed just as other people think they have a duty to attend a board meeting or a funeral. Then presently,
whether it be in music or in literature or in painting,
other works come along, works that may even be the very
opposite of the ones which they supersede. For the ability
to launch ideas and systems—and still more of course the
ability to assimilate them—has always been much com-

moner than genuine taste, even among those who themselves produce works of art, and with the multiplication of reviews and literary journals (and with them of factitious vocations as writer or artist) has become very much more widespread. Not so long ago, for instance, the best part of the younger generation, the most intelligent and the most disinterested of them, through a change of fashion admired nothing but works with a lofty moral and sociological, and even religious, significance. This they imagined to be the criterion of a work's value, renewing the old error of David and Chenavard and Brunetière and all those who in the past thought like them. Bergotte, whose prettiest phrases had in fact demanded much deeper reflexion on the part of the reader, was rated lower now than writers who seemed more profound simply because they wrote less well. The intricacy of his style was all right for fashionable people but not for anybody else, said democratic critics, paying to fashionable people a tribute which they did not deserve. The truth is that as soon as the reasoning intelligence takes upon itself to judge works of art, nothing is any longer fixed or certain: you can prove anything you wish to prove. Whereas the reality of talent is something universal, whether it be a gift or an acquirement, and the first thing that a reader has to do is to find out whether this reality is present beneath a writer's superficial mannerisms of thought and style, it is upon just these superficial mannerisms that criticism seizes when it sets out to classify authors. Because he has a peremptory tone, because he parades his contempt for the school that preceded him, criticism hails as a prophet a writer who in fact has no message that is new. And so frequent are these aberrations of criticism that a writer might almost with reason prefer to be judged by the general public (were not the public incapable even of understanding what an artist has attempted in a realm of discovery which is outside its experience). For there is a closer analogy between the instinctive life of the public and the talent of a great writer, which is simply an instinct religiously listened to in the midst of a silence imposed upon all other voices, an instinct made perfect and understood, than between this same talent and the superficial verbiage and changing criteria of the established judges of literature. From decade to decade their wordy battles are renewed, for it is not only social groups that are kaleidoscopic but ideas too about society and politics and religion; refracted through large bodies they can assume a momentary amplitude but their life-span is the brief one of ideas which owe their success to their novelty and gain the adherence only of such minds as are not particular about proof. So it is that parties and schools follow upon one another's heels, attaching to themselves always the same minds, those men of moderate intelligence who are an easy prey to the successive enthusiasms into which others more scrupulous and less easily satisfied in the matter of proof will decline to plunge. And unfortunately, just because those in the first category are no more than half-minds, they need to buttress themselves in action, with the result that, being more active than the better minds, they draw the crowd after them and create around them not only inflated reputations and victims of undeserved contempt but wars too, both civil and foreign, which a little self-examination of an old-fashioned Jansenist kind might well have prevented.

As for the enjoyment which is derived by a really dis-

cerning mind and a truly living heart from a thought
beautifully expressed in the writings of a great writer, this
is no doubt an entirely wholesome enjoyment, but, precious though the men may be who are truly capable of
enjoying this pleasure—and how many of them are there
in a generation?—they are nevertheless in the very process reduced to being no more than the full consciousness
of another. If, for instance, a man of this type has done
everything in his power to make himself loved by a
woman who could only have made him unhappy, but has
not even succeeded, in spite of efforts redoubled over the
years, in persuading her to meet him in private, instead of
seeking to express his sufferings and the danger from
which he has escaped, he reads over and over again, ap-
pending to it "a million words" and the most moving
memories of his own life, this observation of La Bruyère:
"Men often want to love where they cannot hope to succeed; they seek their own undoing without being able to
compass it, and, if I may put it thus, they are forced
against their will to remain free." Whether or no this is
the meaning that the aphorism had for the man who
wrote it (to give it this meaning, which would make it
finer, he should have said "to be loved" instead of "to
love"), there is no doubt that, with this meaning, the sensitive lover of literature reanimates it and swells it with
meaning until it is ready to burst, he cannot repeat it to
himself without overflowing with joy, so true and beautiful does he find it—but in spite of all this he has added
to it nothing, it remains merely an observation of La
Bruyère.

   How could the literature of description possibly have
any value, when it is only beneath the surface of the little

things which such a literature describes that reality has its
hidden existence (grandeur, for example, in the distant
sound of an aeroplane or the outline of the steeple of
Saint-Hilaire, the past in the taste of a madeleine, and so
on) and when the things in themselves are without significance until it has been extracted from them? Gradually,
thanks to its preservation by our memory, the chain of all
those inaccurate expressions in which there survives nothing of what we have really experienced comes to consti-
tute for us our thought, our life, our "reality," and this lie
is all that can be reproduced by the art that styles itself
"true to life," an art that is as simple as life, without
beauty, a mere vain and tedious duplication of what our
eyes see and our intellect records, so vain and so tedious
that one wonders where the writer who devotes himself to
it can have found the joyous and impulsive spark that was
capable of setting him in motion and making him advance
in his task. The greatness, on the other hand, of true art,
of the art which M. de Norpois would have called a dilettante's pastime, lay, I had come to see, elsewhere: we have
to rediscover, to reapprehend, to make ourselves fully
aware of that reality, remote from our daily preoccupations, from which we separate ourselves by an ever greater
gulf as the conventional knowledge which we substitute
for it grows thicker and more impermeable, that reality
which it is very easy for us to die without ever having
known and which is, quite simply, our life. Real life, life
at last laid bare and illuminated—the only life in consequence which can be said to be really lived—is literature,
and life thus defined is in a sense all the time immanent
in ordinary men no less than in the artist. But most men
do not see it because they do not seek to shed light upon

it. And therefore their past is like a photographic dark-room encumbered with innumerable negatives which remain useless because the intellect has not developed them. But art, if it means awareness of our own life, means also awareness of the lives of other people—for style for the writer, no less than colour for the painter, is a question not of technique but of vision: it is the revelation, which by direct and conscious methods would be impossible, of the qualitative difference, the uniqueness of the fashion in which the world appears to each one of us, a difference which, if there were no art, would remain for ever the secret of every individual. Through art alone are we able to emerge from ourselves, to know what another person sees of a universe which is not the same as our own and of which, without art, the landscapes would remain as unknown to us as those that may exist on the moon. Thanks to art, instead of seeing one world only, our own, we see that world multiply itself and we have at our disposal as many worlds as there are original artists, worlds more different one from the other than those which revolve in infinite space, worlds which, centuries after the extinction of the fire from which their light first emanated, whether it is called Rembrandt or Vermeer, send us still each one its special radiance.

This work of the artist, this struggle to discern beneath matter, beneath experience, beneath words, something that is different from them, is a process exactly the reverse of that which, in those everyday lives which we live with our gaze averted from ourselves, is at every moment being accomplished by vanity and passion and the intellect, and habit too, when they smother our true impressions, so as entirely to conceal them from us, beneath a whole heap of verbal concepts and practical goals which we falsely call life. In short, this art which is so complicated is in fact the only living art. It alone expresses for others and renders visible to ourselves that life of ours which cannot effectually observe itself and of which the observable manifestations need to be translated and, often, to be read backwards and laboriously deciphered. Our vanity, our passions, our spirit of imitation, our abstract intelligence, our habits have long been at work, and it is the task of art to undo this work of theirs, making us travel back in the direction from which we have come to the depths where what has really existed lies unknown within us. And surely this was a most tempting prospect, this task of re-creating one's true life, of rejuvenating one's impressions. But it required courage of many kinds, including the courage of one's emotions. For above all it meant the abrogation of one's dearest illusions, it meant giving up one's belief in the objectivity of what one had oneself elaborated, so that now, instead of soothing oneself for the hundredth time with the words: "She was very sweet," one would have to transpose the phrase so that it read: "I experienced pleasure when I kissed her." Certainly, what I had felt in my hours of love is what all men feel. One feels, yes, but what one feels is like a negative which shows only blackness until one has placed it near a special lamp and which must also be looked at in reverse. So with one's feelings: until one has brought them within range of the intellect one does not know what they represent. Then only, when the intellect has shed light upon them, has intellectualised them, does one distinguish, and with what difficulty, the lineaments of what one felt.

But I realised also that the suffering caused by the

thought that our love does not belong to the person who
inspires it, a suffering which I had first known in connexion with Gilberte, is for two reasons salutary. The first
and the less important is that, brief though our life may
be, it is only while we are suffering that we see certain
things which at other times are hidden from us—we are,
as it were, posted at a window, badly placed but looking
out over an expanse of sea, and only during a storm,
when our thoughts are agitated by perpetually changing
movements, do they elevate to a level at which we can see
it the whole law-governed immensity which normally,
when the calm weather of happiness leaves it smooth, lies
beneath our line of vision; perhaps only for a few great
geniuses does this movement of thought exist all the time,
uncontingent upon the agitations of personal grief, yet can
we be sure, when we contemplate the ample and regular
development of their joyous creations, that we may not
too readily infer from the joyousness of their work that
there was joy also in their lives, which perhaps on the
contrary were almost continuously unhappy? But the principal reason is that, if our love is not only the love of a
Gilberte (and this fact is what we find so painful), the
reason is not that it is also the love of an Albertine but
that it is a portion of our mind more durable than the
various selves which successively die within us and which
would, in their egoism, like to keep it to themselves, a
portion of our mind which must, however much it hurts
us (and the pain may in fact be beneficial), detach itself
from individuals so that we can comprehend and restore
to it its generality and give this love, the understanding of
this love, to all, to the universal spirit, and not merely
first to one woman and then to another with whom first

one and then another of the selves that we have successively been has desired to be united.

I was surrounded by symbols (Guermantes, Albertine, Gilberte, Saint-Loup, Balbec, etc.) and to the least of
these I had to restore the meaning which habit had caused
them to lose for me. Nor was that all. When we have arrived at reality, we must, to express it and preserve it,
prevent the intrusion of all those extraneous elements
which at every moment the gathered speed of habit lays at
our feet. Above all I should have to be on my guard
against those phrases which are chosen rather by the lips
than by the mind, those humorous phrases such as we utter in conversation and continue at the end of a long conversation with other people to address, factitiously, to
ourselves although they merely fill our mind with lies—
those, so to speak, purely physical remarks, which, in the
writer who stoops so low as to transcribe them, are accompanied always by, for instance, the little smile, the little grimace which at every turn disfigures the spoken
phrase of a Sainte-Beuve, whereas real books should be
the offspring not of daylight and casual talk but of darkness and silence. And as art exactly reconstitutes life,
around the truths to which we have attained inside ourselves there will always float an atmosphere of poetry, the
soft charm of a mystery which is merely a vestige of the
shadow which we have had to traverse, the indication, as
precise as the markings of an altimeter, of the depth of a
work. (For the quality of depth is not inherent in certain
subjects, as those novelists believe who are spiritually
minded only in a materialistic way: they cannot penetrate
beneath the world of appearances and all their noble intentions, like the endless virtuous tirades of certain people

who are incapable of the smallest act of kindness, should not blind us to the fact that they have lacked even the strength of mind to rid themselves of those banalities of form which are acquired through imitation.)

As for the truths which the intellectual faculty—even that of the greatest minds—gathers in the open, the truths that lie in its path in full daylight, their value may be very great, but they are like drawings with a hard outline and no perspective; they have no depth because no depths have had to be traversed in order to reach them, because they have not been re-created. Yet it happens to many writers that after a certain age, when more mysterious truths no longer emerge from their innermost being, they write only with their intellect, which has grown steadily in strength, and then the books of their riper years will have, for this reason, greater force than those of their youth but not the same bloom.

I felt, however, that these truths which the intellect educes directly from reality were not altogether to be despised, for they might be able to enshrine within a matter less pure indeed but still imbued with mind those impressions which are conveyed to us outside time by the essences that are common to the sensations of the past and of the present, but which, just because they are more precious, are also too rare for a work of art to be constructed exclusively from them. And—capable of being used for this purpose—I felt jostling each other within me a whole host of truths concerning human passions and character and conduct. The perception of these truths caused me joy; and yet I seemed to remember that more than one of them had been discovered by me in suffering, and others in very trivial pleasures (every individual who makes us suffer can be attached by us to a divinity of which he or she is a mere fragmentary reflexion, the lowest step in the ascent that leads to it, a divinity or an Idea which, if we turn to contemplate it, immediately gives us joy instead of the pain which we were feeling before—indeed the whole art of living is to make use of the individuals through whom we suffer as a step enabling us to draw nearer to the divine form which they reflect and thus joyously to people our life with divinities). And then a new light, less dazzling, no doubt, than that other illumination which had made me perceive that the work of art was the sole means of rediscovering Lost Time, shone suddenly within me. And I understood that all these materials for a work of literature were simply my past life; I understood that they had come to me, in frivolous pleasures, in indolence, in tenderness, in unhappiness, and that I had stored them up without divining the purpose for which they were destined or even their continued existence any more than a seed does when it forms within itself a reserve of all the nutritious substances from which it will feed a plant. Like the seed, I should be able to die once the plant had developed and I began to perceive that I had lived for the sake of the plant without knowing it, without ever realising that my life needed to come into contact with those books which I had wanted to write and for which, when in the past I had sat down at my table to begin, I had been unable to find a subject. And thus my whole life up to the present day might and yet might not have been summed up under the title: A Vocation. Insofar as literature had played no part in my life the title would not have been accurate. And yet it would have been accurate because this life of mine, the memories of its sadnesses and its joys, formed a reserve which fulfilled the same function as the albumen lodged in the germ-cell of a plant, from which that cell starts to draw the nourishment which will transform it into a seed long before there is any outward sign that the embryo of a plant is developing, though already within the cell there are taking place chemical and respiratory changes, secret but extremely active. In the same way my life was linked to what, eventually, would bring about its maturation, but those who would one day draw nourishment from it would remain ignorant, as most of us do when we eat those grains that are human food, that the rich substances which they contain were made for the nourishment not of mankind but of the grain itself and have had first to nourish its seed and allow it to ripen.

In this context, certain comparisons which are false if we start from them as premises may well be true if we arrive at them as conclusions. The man of letters envies the painter, he would like to take notes and make sketches, but it is disastrous for him to do so. Yet when he writes, there is not a single gesture of his characters, not a trick of behaviour, not a tone of voice which has not been supplied to his inspiration by his memory; beneath the name of every character of his invention he can put sixty names of characters that he has seen, one of whom has posed for the grimaces, another for the monocle, another for the fits of temper, another for the swaggering movement of the arm, etc. And in the end the writer realises that if his dream of being a sort of painter was not in a conscious and intentional manner capable of fulfilment, it has nevertheless been fulfilled and that he too, for his work as a writer, has unconsciously made use of a sketch-book. For, impelled by the instinct that was in him, the writer, long before he thought that he would one day become one, regularly omitted to look at a great many things which other people notice, with the result that he was accused by others of being absent-minded and by himself of not knowing how to listen or look, but all this time he was instructing his eyes and his ears to retain for ever what seemed to others puerile trivialities, the tone of voice in which a certain remark had been made, or the facial expression and the movement of the shoulders which he had seen at a certain moment, many years ago, in somebody of whom perhaps he knows nothing else whatsoever, simply because this tone of voice was one that he had heard before or felt that he might hear again, because it was something renewable, durable. There is a feeling for generality which, in the future writer, itself picks out what is general and can for that reason one day enter into a work of art. And this has made him listen to people only when, stupid or absurd though they may have been, they have turned themselves, by repeating like parrots what other people of similar character are in the habit of saying, into birds of augury, mouthpieces of a psychological law. He remembers only things that are general. By such tones of voice, such variations in the physiognomy, seen perhaps in his earliest childhood, has the life of other people been represented for him and when, later, he becomes a writer, it is from these observations that he composes his human figures, grafting on to a movement of the shoulders common to a number of people—a movement as truthfully delineated as though it had been recorded in an anatomist's note-book, though the truth which he uses it to express is of a psychological order—a movement of the neck made by someone else, each of many individuals having posed for a moment as his model.

(It may be that, for the creation of a work of literature, imagination and sensibility are interchangeable qualities and that the latter may with no great harm be substituted for the former, just as in people whose stomach is incapable of digesting this function is relegated to the intestine. A man born with sensibility but without imagination might, in spite of this deficiency, be able to write admirable novels. For the suffering inflicted upon him by other people, his own efforts to ward it off, the long conflict between his unhappiness and another person's cruelty, all this, interpreted by the intellect, might furnish the material for a book not merely as beautiful as one that was imagined, invented, but also in as great a degree exterior to the day-dreams that the author would have had if he had been left to his own devices and happy, and as astonishing to himself, therefore, and as accidental as a fortuitous caprice of the imagination.)

The stupidest people, in their gestures, their remarks, the sentiments which they involuntarily express, manifest laws which they do not themselves perceive but which the artist surprises in them. Because he makes observations of this kind the writer is popularly believed to be ill-natured. But this belief is false: in an instance of ridiculous behaviour the artist sees a beautiful generality, and he no more condemns on this account the individual in whom he observes it than a surgeon would despise a patient for suffering from some quite common disorder of the circulation; the writer, in fact, is the least inclined of all men to scoff at folly. Unhappily, he is more unhappy than ill-natured: when it concerns his own passions, while well aware of their universality, he frees himself less easily from the personal sufferings which they cause. Naturally, when some insolent fellow insults us, we would rather he had paid us a compliment, and *a fortiori*, when a woman whom we adore betrays us, what would we not give for this not to have happened! But then the pain of an affront, the anguish of abandonment, would have been lands which we should never know, lands whose discovery, painful though it may be for the man, is nevertheless invaluable for the artist. And so, though it is neither his wish nor theirs, the ill-natured and the ungrateful find their place in his work. The writer who writes a pamphlet involuntarily associates with his glory the riff-raff whom he castigates in it, and in every work of art one can recognise those whom the artist has most hated and also, alas! those whom he has most loved. They indeed have quite simply been posing for the artist at the very moment when, much against his will, they made him suffer most. When I was in love with Albertine, I had realised very clearly that she did not love me and I had had to resign myself to the thought that through her I could gain nothing more than the experience of what it is to suffer and to love, and even, at the beginning, to be happy.

And when we seek to extract from our grief the generality that lies within it, to write about it, we are perhaps to some extent consoled for yet another reason apart from those that I have mentioned, which is that to think in terms of general truths, to write, is for the writer a wholesome and necessary function the fulfilment of which makes him happy, it does for him what is done for men of a more physical nature by exercise, perspiration, baths. This conclusion, I must admit, I was a little reluctant to accept. I was ready to believe that the supreme truth of life resides in art, and I could see, too, that I was no more capable by an effort of memory of being still in love with Albertine than I was of continuing to mourn my grandmother's death, and yet I asked myself whether a work of art of which they would not be conscious could really for them, for the destiny of these two poor dead creatures, be a fulfilment. My grandmother, whom with so little feeling I had seen agonise and die beside me! I longed that in expiation, when my work should be finished, I might, incurably stricken, suffer for long hours, abandoned by all, and then die! And there were others less dear to me, or for whom I had cared nothing at all, for whom I felt an infinite pity, all those whose sufferings, or merely whose follies, my thought, in its effort to understand their destinies, had used for its own selfish purpose. All those men and women who had revealed some truth to me and who were now no more, appeared again before me, and it seemed as though they had lived a life which had profited only myself, as though they had died for me. Saddening too was the thought that my love, to which I had clung so tenaciously, would in my book be so detached from any individual that different readers would apply it, even in detail, to what they had felt for other women. But had I a right to be shocked at this posthumous infidelity, shocked that strangers should find new and alien objects for my feelings in unknown women, when this infidelity, this division of love between a number of women, had begun in my lifetime and even before I had started to write? It was true that I had suffered successively for Gilberte, for Mme de Guermantes, for Albertine. But successively I had also forgotten them, and only the love which I dedi-

cated to different women had been lasting. The profana-
tion of one of my memories by unknown readers was a
crime that I had myself committed before them. I felt
something near to horror at myself, the self-horror that
some nationalist party might come to feel after a long war
fought in its name, from which it alone had profited and
in which many noble victims had suffered and succumbed
without ever knowing (and for my grandmother at least
what a recompense this would have been!) what the outcome of the struggle would be. And my only consolation
for the thought that she did not know that at last I was
getting down to work was (such is the lot of the dead)
that, if she could not enjoy my progress, she had at least
long ceased to be conscious of my inactivity, of my
wasted life, which had been such an unhappiness to her.
And certainly there were others besides my grandmother
and Albertine, there were many from whom I had been
able to assimilate a single phrase or look although as individual human beings I had no recollection of them; a
book is a huge cemetery in which on the majority of the
tombs the names are effaced and can no longer be read.
Sometimes on the other hand we remember a name well
enough but do not know whether anything of the individual who bore it survives in our pages. That girl with the
very deep-set eyes and the drawling voice, is she here?
and if she is, in what part of the ground does she lie? we
no longer know, and how are we to find her beneath the
flowers? But since we live at a great distance from other
human beings, since even our strongest feelings—and in
this class had been my love for my grandmother and for
Albertine—at the end of a few years have vanished from
our hearts and become for us merely a word which we do

not understand, since we can talk casually of these dead people with fashionable acquaintances whose houses we still visit with pleasure though all that we loved has died, surely then, if there exists a method by which we can learn to understand these forgotten words once more, is it not our duty to make use of it, even if this means transcribing them first into a language which is universal but which for that very reason will at least be permanent, a language which may make out of those who are no more, in their truest essence, a lasting acquisition for the minds of all mankind? And as for that law of change which made these loved words unintelligible to us, if we succeed at least in explaining it, is not even our infirmity transformed into strength of a new kind?

And so I had to resign myself, since nothing has the power to survive unless it can become general and since the mind's own past is dead to its present consciousness, to the idea that even the people who were once most dear to the writer have in the long run done no more than pose for him like models for a painter.

When we turn to our own future, the work in which our unhappiness has collaborated may be interpreted both as an ominous sign of suffering and as an auspicious sign of consolation. For, when we say that the loves and griefs of a poet have been useful to him, have helped him to construct his work, that the unknown women who had not the least idea what they were doing, have—one through her cruelty to him, another through her mockery—brought each their stone for the building of the monument which they will never see, we do not sufficiently reflect that the life of the writer does not come to an end with this particular work, that the same nature which caused him to have certain sufferings, which then entered into his work, will continue to live after the work has been concluded and will cause him to love other women in conditions which would be similar, were they not made slightly to differ by the modifications that time brings about in circumstances, in the subject himself, in his appetite for love and in his resistance to pain. And from this point of view this first work of his must be considered simply as an unhappy love which fatally presages others of the kind: his life will resemble his work and in future the poet will scarcely need to write, for he will be able to find in what he has already written the anticipatory outline of what will then be happening. Thus it was that my love for Albertine, however different the two might be, was already inscribed in my love for Gilberte, in the midst of the happy days of which, for the first time, I had heard the name of Albertine pronounced and her character described by her aunt, without suspecting that this insignificant seed would develop and would one day overshadow the whole of my life.

But from another point of view the work is a promise of happiness, because it shows us that in every love the particular and the general lie side by side and it teaches us to pass from one to the other by a species of gymnastic which fortifies us against unhappiness by making us neglect its particular cause in order to gain a more profound understanding of its essence. Indeed—as I was to experience in the sequel—even at a time when we are in love and suffer, if our vocation has at last been realised, we feel so strongly during the hours in which we are at work that the individual whom we love is being dissolved into a vaster reality that at moments we succeed in forgetting her and we come to suffer from our love merely as we might from some purely physical disease in which the loved one played no part, some kind of malady of the heart. It is true that this only happens at a certain stage of our love and that if the work comes a little later its effect may appear to be the opposite. For when once the women whom we love, through their cruelty or their triviality, have succeeded in spite of us in destroying our illusions, have reduced themselves to nothing and become detached from the amorous chimera which we had fabricated in our imagination—if at this point we set ourselves to work, our mind will exalt them once more and identify them, for the purposes of our self-analysis, with objects of our love, and in this case literature, recommencing the ruined work of amorous illusion, will give a sort of second life to sentiments which have ceased to exist. And certainly we are obliged to re-live our individual suffering, with the courage of the doctor who over and over again practises on his own person some dangerous injection. But at the same time we have to conceptualise it in a general form which will in some measure enable us to escape from its embrace, which will turn all mankind into sharers in our pain, and which is even able to yield us a certain joy. Where life immures, the intelligence cuts a way out, for if there exists no remedy for a love that is not shared, the awareness of a state of suffering is something from which we can extricate ourselves, if only by deducing the consequences which it entails. The intelligence knows nothing of those closed situations of life from which there is no escape.

Sometimes, when a painful passage has remained in an inchoate state, a mere rough draft, a new tenderness and a new suffering come our way which enable us to complete it, to fill it out. And on the score of these great but useful unhappinesses we have little ground for complaint: they are plentiful and we seldom have to wait long for them. (In love, our fortunate rival, which is as much as to say our enemy, is our benefactor. To a woman who previously excited in us a mere paltry physical desire he instantly adds an immense value, foreign to her but confounded by us with her. If we had no rivals, pleasure would not transform itself into love. If we had none, or if we believed that we had none. For it is not necessary that rivals should really exist. The progress of our work requires only that they should have that illusory life which is conferred upon non-existent rivals by our suspicion, our jealousy.) Nevertheless one must make haste to take advantage of them when they come, for they do not last very long: either one consoles oneself or else, when they are too severe, if one's heart is no longer very robust one dies. For if unhappiness develops the forces of the mind, happiness alone is salutary to the body. But unhappiness, even if it did not on every occasion reveal to us some new law, would nevertheless be indispensable, since through its means alone we are brought back time after time to a perception of the truth and forced to take things seriously, tearing up each new crop of the weeds of habit and scepticism and levity and indifference. Yet it is true that truth, which is not compatible with happiness or with physical health, is not always compatible even with life. Unhappiness ends by killing. At every new torment which is too hard to bear we feel yet another vein protrude, to unroll its sinuous and deadly length along our temples or beneath our eyes. And thus gradually are formed those terrible ravaged faces, of the old Rembrandt, the old Beethoven, at whom the whole world mocked. And the pockets under the eyes and the wrinkled forehead would not matter much were there not also the suffering of the heart. But since strength of one kind can change into a strength of another kind, since heat which is stored up can become light and the electricity in a flash of lightning can cause a photograph to be taken, since the dull pain in our heart can hoist above itself like a banner the visible permanence of an image for every new grief, let us accept the physical injury which is done to us for the sake of the spiritual knowledge which grief brings; let us submit to the disintegration of our body, since each new fragment which breaks away from it returns in a luminous and significant form to add itself to our work, to complete it at the price of sufferings of which others more richly endowed have no need, to make our work at least more solid as our life crumbles away beneath the corrosive action of our emotions. Ideas come to us as the substitutes for griefs, and griefs, at the moment when they change into ideas, lose some part of their power to injure our heart; the transformation itself, even, for an instant, releases suddenly a little joy. But substitutes only in the order of time, for the primary element, it seems, is the idea, and grief is merely the mode in which certain ideas make their first entry into us. But within the tribe of ideas there are various families and some of them from the very first moment are joys.

These reflexions enabled me to give a stronger and more precise meaning to the truth which I had often dimly perceived, particularly when Mme de Cambremer had expressed surprise that I could give up seeing a remarkable man like Elstir for the sake of Albertine. Even from an intellectual point of view I had felt that she was wrong, but I did not know what it was that she had failed to understand: the nature of the lessons through which one serves one's apprenticeship as a man of letters. In this process the objective value of the arts counts for little; what we have to bring to light and make known to ourselves is our feelings, our passions, that is to say the passions and feelings of all mankind. A woman whom we need and who makes us suffer elicits from us a whole gamut of feelings far more profound and more vital than does a man of genius who interests us. It is for us later to decide, according to the plane upon which we are living, whether an infidelity through which some woman has made us suffer is of little or great account beside the truths which it has revealed to us and which the woman who exulted in our suffering would hardly have been able to understand. In any case these infidelities are not likely to be wanting. A writer need have no anxieties on that score when he embarks upon a long labour. Let his intellect begin the work and as he proceeds he will meet with griefs, enough or more than enough, which will undertake to finish it. As for happiness, that is really useful to us in one way only, by making unhappiness possible. It is necessary for us to form in happiness ties of confidence and attachment that are both sweet and strong in order that their rupture may cause us the heart-rending but so valuable agony which is called unhappiness. Had we not been happy, if only in hope, the unhappinesses that befall us would be without cruelty and therefore without fruit.

And more even than the painter, the writer, in order to achieve volume and substance, in order to attain to generality and, so far as literature can, to reality, needs to have seen many churches in order to paint one church and for the portrayal of a single sentiment requires many individuals. For if art is long and life is short, we may on the other hand say that, if inspiration is short, the sentiments which it has to portray are not of much longer duration. It is our passions which draw the outline of our books, the ensuing intervals of repose which write them. And when inspiration is born again, when we are able to resume our work, the woman who was posing for us to illustrate a sentiment no longer has the power to make us feel it. We must continue to paint the sentiment from another model, and if this means infidelity towards the individual, from a literary point of view, thanks to the similarity of our feelings for the two women, which makes a work at the same time a recollection of our past loves and a prophecy of our new ones, there is no great harm in these substitutions. And this is one reason for the futility of those critical essays which try to guess who it is that an author is talking about. A work, even one that is directly autobiographical, is at the very least put together out of several intercalated episodes in the life of the author— earlier episodes which have inspired the work and later ones which resemble it just as much, the later loves being traced after the pattern of the earlier. For to the woman whom we have loved most in our life we are not so faithful as we are to ourself, and sooner or later we forget her in order—since this is one of the characteristics of that self—to be able to begin to love again. At most our faculty of loving has received from this woman whom we so loved a particular stamp, which will cause us to be faithful to her even in our infidelity. We shall need, with the

woman who succeeds her, those same morning walks or
the same practice of taking her home every evening or
giving her a hundred times too much money. (A curious
thing, this circulation of the money which we give to
women who because of that make us unhappy, that is to
say are the cause of our writing books: it almost seems as
though a writer's works, like the water in an artesian well,
mount to a height which is in proportion to the depth to
which suffering has penetrated his heart.) These substitutions add then to our work something that is disinterested
and more general and they convey also the austere lesson
that it is not to individuals that we should attach ourselves, that it is not individuals who really exist and are,
in consequence, capable of being expressed, but ideas.
Nevertheless, while we have these models at our disposal
we must make haste and lose no time; for those who pose
for us as "happiness" can in general spare us only a few
sittings, and the same may be true alas!—since grief, yes,
grief too passes so quickly—of those who pose as "grief."
Yet grief, even when it does not, by revealing it to us,
provide the raw material of our writing, is valuable to us
as an incitement to work. The imagination, the reflective
faculty may be admirable machines in themselves but
they may also be inert. Suffering sets them in motion.
And then at least the woman who poses for us as grief
favours us with an abundance of sittings, in that studio
which we enter only in these periods and which lies deep
within us. And they are, these periods, like an image of
our life with its different griefs. For they too contain different griefs within themselves, and at the very moment
when we thought that all had become calm a new one
makes its appearance. New in every sense of the word:

perhaps because an unforeseen situation forces us to enter more profoundly into contact with ourself, these painful dilemmas which love is constantly putting in our way teach us and reveal to us, layer after layer, the material of which we are made. So when Françoise, seeing that Albertine had the run of the flat and passed in and out of all the rooms like a dog creating disorder everywhere and that she was ruining me and causing me unhappiness of every kind, used to say (for at that time I had already written some articles and done a few translations): "Ah! if only, instead of this girl who makes him waste all his time, Monsieur had got himself a nicely brought up young secretary who could have sorted all Monsieur's paperies for him!", I had perhaps been wrong in thinking that she spoke wisely. By making me waste my time, by causing me unhappiness, Albertine had perhaps been more useful to me, even from a literary point of view, than a secretary who would have arranged my "paperies." But all the same, when a living creature is so faultily constituted (and perhaps, if such a creature exists in nature, it is man) that he cannot love without suffering, and that he has to suffer in order to apprehend truths, the life of such a creature becomes in the end extremely wearisome. The happy years are the lost, the wasted years, one must wait for suffering before one can work. And then the idea of the preliminary suffering becomes associated with the idea of work and one is afraid of each new literary undertaking because one thinks of the pain one will first have to endure in order to imagine it. And once one understands that suffering is the best thing that one can hope to encounter in life, one thinks without terror, and almost as of a deliverance, of death.

If I had had to admit, albeit I found the idea some-what repugnant, that the writer plays with life and ex-ploits other people for the purpose of his books, I could not fail to observe also that this is sometimes very far from being the case. The history and the circumstances of Werther, the noble Werther, had not alas! been mine. Without for a moment believing in Albertine's love I had twenty times wanted to kill myself for her, I had ruined myself, I had destroyed my health for her. For when it is a question of writing, one is scrupulous, one examines things meticulously, one rejects all that is not truth. But when it is merely a question of life, one ruins oneself, makes oneself ill, kills oneself all for lies. It is true that these lies are a lode from which, if one has passed the age for writing poetry, one can at least extract a little truth. Sorrows are servants, obscure and detested, against whom one struggles, beneath whose dominion one more and more completely falls, dire and dreadful servants whom it is impossible to replace and who by subterranean paths lead us towards truth and death. Happy are those who have first come face to face with truth, those for whom, near though the one may be to the other, the hour of truth has struck before the hour of death!

When I considered my past life, I understood also that its slightest episodes had contributed towards giving me the lesson in idealism from which I was going to profit today. My meetings with M. de Charlus, for in-stance, had they not, even before his pro-German tenden-cies taught me the same lesson, demonstrated to me, even better than my love for Mme de Guermantes or for Al-bertine, or Saint-Loup's love for Rachel, the truth of the axiom that matter is indifferent and that anything can be

grafted upon it by thought; an axiom which in the phenomenon, so ill-understood and so needlessly condemned,
of sexual inversion is seen to be of even greater scope than
in that, in itself so instructive, of love? For love shows us
Beauty fleeing from the woman whom we no longer love,
and coming to take up her abode in a face which anybody
else would find hideous and which to ourselves too might
have seemed, as one day it will seem, unpleasing: but
even more striking is the spectacle of the goddess, taking
with her the reverent homage of a great nobleman who
thereupon instantly abandons a beautiful princess, migrat-
ing to a new perch beneath the cap of an omnibus conductor. And my astonishment every time I had seen after
an interval, in the Champs-Elysées or in the street or on
the beach, the face of Gilberte or of Mme de Guermantes
or of Albertine, was this not a proof that a memory is
prolonged only in a direction which diverges from the impression with which originally it coincided but from
which gradually it further and further departs?

The writer must not be indignant if the invert who
reads his book gives to his heroines a masculine countenance. For only by the indulgence of this slightly aberrant
peculiarity can the invert give to what he is reading its
full general import. Racine himself was obliged, as a first
step towards giving her a universal validity, for a moment
to turn the antique figure of Phèdre into a Jansenist; and
if M. de Charlus had not bestowed upon the "traitress"
for whom Musset weeps in La Nuit d'Octobre or Souvenir
the features of Morel, he would neither have wept nor
have understood, since it was only along this path, narrow
and indirect, that he had access to the verities of love. For
it is only out of habit, a habit contracted from the insin-

cere language of prefaces and dedications, that the writer speaks of "my reader." In reality every reader is, while he is reading, the reader of his own self. The writer's work is merely a kind of optical instrument which he offers to the reader to enable him to discern what, without this book, he would perhaps never have perceived in himself. And the recognition by the reader in his own self of what the book says is the proof of its veracity, the contrary also being true, at least to a certain extent, for the difference between the two texts may sometimes be imputed less to the author than to the reader. Besides, the book may be too learned, too obscure for a simple reader, and may therefore present to him a clouded glass through which he cannot read. And other peculiarities can have the same effect as inversion. In order to read with understanding many readers require to read in their own particular fashion, and the author must not be indignant at this; on the contrary, he must leave the reader all possible liberty, saying to him: "Look for yourself, and try whether you see best with this lens or that one or this other one."

If I had always taken so great an interest in dreams, was this not because, making up for lack of duration by their potency, they help us better to understand the subjective element in, for instance, love through the simple fact that they reproduce—but with miraculous swiftness—the process vulgarly known as getting a woman under one's skin, so effectively that within a sleep of a few minutes we can fall passionately in love with an ugly woman, a thing which in real life could only happen after years of habit and intimacy—as though they were intravenous injections of love discovered by some wonderworking doctor, of love and sometimes also of suffering?

With the same speed the amorous suggestions which they have instilled into us are dissipated, and sometimes, when the loving nocturnal visitant has vanished from our sight and reappeared in her familiar shape of an ugly woman, there vanishes with her something more precious, a whole ravishing landscape of feelings of tenderness, of voluptuous pleasure, of vaguely blurred regrets, a whole embarkation for the Cythera of passion, of which we should like to note, for our waking state, the subtle and deliciously lifelike gradations of tone, but which fades away like a discoloured canvas that can no longer be restored. And it was perhaps also because of the extraordinary effects which they achieve with Time that dreams had fascinated me. Have we not often seen in a single night, in a single minute of a night, remote periods, relegated to those enormous distances at which we can no longer distinguish anything of the sentiments which we felt in them, come rushing upon us with almost the speed of light as though they were giant aeroplanes instead of the pale stars which we had supposed them to be, blinding us with their brilliance and bringing back to our vision all that they had once contained for us, giving us the emotion, the shock, the brilliance of their immediate proximity, only, once we are awake, to resume their position on the far side of the gulf which they had miraculously traversed, so that we are tempted to believe—wrongly, however—that they are one of the modes of rediscovering Lost Time?

I had realised before now that it is only a clumsy and erroneous form of perception which places everything in the object, when really everything is in the mind; I had lost my grandmother in reality many months after I had lost her in fact, and I had seen people present various aspects according to the idea that I or others possessed of them, a single individual being several different people for different observers (Swann, for instance, for my family and for his friends in society, the Princesse de Luxembourg for the judge at Balbec and for those who knew her identity) or even for the same observer at different periods over the years (the name of Guermantes, and the different Swanns, for me). I had seen that love places in a person who is loved what exists only in the person who loves, indeed I could hardly have failed to become aware of this when I had seen stretched to its maximum the distance between objective reality and love (in Rachel, for instance, as she appeared to Saint-Loup and to me, in Albertine as she appeared to me and to Saint-Loup, in Morel or the omnibus conductor as they appeared to other people and to M. de Charlus, who in spite of this showered delicate attentions upon them, recited Musset's poems to them, etc.). Finally, to a certain extent, the Germanophilia of M. de Charlus (like the expression on the face of Saint-Loup when he had looked at the photograph of Albertine) had helped me to free myself for a moment, if not from my Germanophobia, at least from my belief in the pure objectivity of this feeling, had helped to make me think that perhaps what applied to love applied also to hate and that, in the terrible judgment which at this time France passed on Germany—that she was a nation outside the pale of humanity—the most important element was an objectification of feelings as subjective as those which had caused Rachel and Albertine to appear so precious, the one to Saint-Loup and the other to me. What, in fact, made it possible that this perversity was not entirely in-

trinsic to Germany was that, just as I as an individual had
had successive loves and at the end of each one its object
had appeared to me valueless, so I had already seen in my
country successive hates which had, for example, at one
time condemned as traitors—a thousand times worse than
the Germans into whose hands they were delivering
France—those very Dreyfusards such as Reinach with
whom today patriotic Frenchmen were collaborating
against a race whose every member was of necessity a liar,
a savage beast, a madman, excepting only those Germans
who, like the King of Romania, the King of the Belgians,
or the Empress of Russia, had embraced the French
cause. It is true that the anti-Dreyfusards would have
replied to me: "But it is not the same thing." But then it
never is the same thing, any more than it is the same person with whom after an interval we fall in love; otherwise,
faced with the same phenomenon as before, someone who
was a second time taken in by it would have no alternative but to blame his own subjective condition, he could
not again believe that the qualities or the defects resided
in the object. And so, since the phenomenon, outwardly,
is not the same, the intellect has no difficulty in basing
upon each set of circumstances a new theory (that it is
against nature to have schools directed by the religious orders, as the radicals believe, or that it is impossible for the
Jewish race to be assimilated into a nation, or that there
exists an undying hatred between the Teutonic and the
Latin races, the yellow race having been temporarily rehabilitated). This subjective element in the situation struck
one forcibly if one had any conversation with neutrals,
since the pro-Germans among them had, for instance, the
faculty of ceasing for a moment to understand and even to

listen when one spoke to them about the German atrocities in Belgium. (And yet they were real, these atrocities:
the subjective element that I had observed to exist in hatred as in vision itself did not imply that an object could
not possess real qualities or defects and in no way tended
to make reality vanish into pure relativism.) And if, after
so many years had slipped away and so much time had
been lost, I felt this influence to be dominant even in the
sphere of international relations, had I not already had
some notion of its existence right at the beginning of my
life, when I was reading in the garden at Combray one of
those novels by Bergotte which, even today, if I chance to
turn over a few of its forgotten pages where I see the
wiles of some villain described, I cannot put down until I
have assured myself, by skipping a hundred pages, that
towards the end this same villain is humiliated as he deserves to be and lives long enough to learn that his sinis-
ter schemes have failed? For I no longer have any clear
recollection of what happened to these characters, though
in this respect they are scarcely to be distinguished from
the men and women who were present this afternoon at
Mme de Guermantes's party and whose past life, in many
cases at least, was as vague in my mind as if I had read it
in a half-forgotten novel. The Prince d'Agrigente, for instance: had he ended by marrying Mlle X——? Or was it
rather the brother of Mlle X—— who might have married
the sister of the Prince d'Agrigente? Or was I confusing it
all with something that I had read long ago or recently
dreamed?

Dreams were another of the facts of my life which
had always most profoundly impressed me and had done
most to convince me of the purely mental character of re-

ality, and in the composition of my work I would not scorn their aid. At a time when I was still living, in a rather less disinterested fashion, for love of one kind or another, a dream would come to me, bringing strangely close, across vast distances of lost time, my grandmother, or Albertine, whom briefly I began to love again because in my sleep she had given me a version, highly diluted, of the episode with the laundry-girl in Touraine. And I thought that in the same way dreams would bring sometimes within my grasp truths or impressions which my efforts alone and even the contingencies of nature failed to present to me; that they would re-awaken in me something of the desire, the regret for certain non-existent things which is the necessary condition for working, for freeing oneself from the dominion of habit, for detaching oneself from the concrete. And therefore I would not disdain this second muse, this nocturnal muse who might sometimes do duty for the other one.

I had seen aristocrats turn into vulgar people when their intelligence was vulgar. ("Make yourself at home," for instance the Duc de Guermantes would say, using an expression that Cottard might have used.) I had seen everybody believe, during the Dreyfus Affair or during the war, and in medicine too, that truth is a particular piece of knowledge which cabinet ministers and doctors possess, a Yes or No which requires no interpretation, thanks to the possession of which the men in power *knew* whether Dreyfus was guilty or not and *knew*, without having to send Roques to make an inquiry on the spot, whether Sarrail in Salonika had or had not the resources to launch an offensive at the same time as the Russians, in the same way that an X-ray photograph is supposed to indicate without any need for interpretation the exact nature of a patient's disease.

It occurred to me, as I thought about it, that the raw material of my experience, which would also be the raw material of my book, came to me from Swann, not merely because so much of it concerned Swann himself and Gilberte, but because it was Swann who from the days of Combray had inspired in me the wish to go to Balbec, where otherwise my parents would never have had the idea of sending me, and but for this I should never have known Albertine. Certainly, it was to her face, as I had seen it for the first time beside the sea, that I traced back certain things which I should no doubt include in my book. And in a sense I was right to trace them back to her, for if I had not walked on the front that day, if I had not got to know her, all these ideas would never have been developed (unless they had been developed by some other woman). But I was wrong too, for this pleasure which generates something within us and which, retrospectively, we seek to place in a beautiful feminine face, comes from our senses: but the pages I would write were something that Albertine, particularly the Albertine of those days, would quite certainly never have understood. It was, however, for this very reason (and this shows that we ought not to live in too intellectual an atmosphere), for the reason that she was so different from me, that she had fertilised me through unhappiness and even, at the beginning, through the simple effort which I had had to make to imagine something different from myself. Had she been capable of understanding my pages, she would, for that very reason, not have inspired them. But Swann had been of primary importance, for had I not gone to Balbec I

should never have known the Guermantes either, since
my grandmother would not have renewed her friendship
with Mme de Villeparisis nor should I have made the acquaintance of Saint-Loup and M. de Charlus and thus got
to know the Duchesse de Guermantes and through her
her cousin, so that even my presence at this very moment
in the house of the Prince de Guermantes, where out of
the blue the idea for my work had just come to me (and
this meant that I owed to Swann not only the material but
also the decision), came to me from Swann. A rather slender stalk, perhaps, to support thus the whole development
of my life, for the "Guermantes way" too, on this interpretation, had emanated from "Swann's way." But often
this begetter of all the various aspects of a man's life is
someone very much inferior to Swann, someone utterly
insignificant. Suppose some schoolfriend who meant nothing to me had described an attractive girl who was to be
enjoyed there (whom probably I should not in fact have
met), would not that have been enough to send me to
Balbec? Often, meeting years later some friend of our
youth whom we never particularly liked, we scarcely trouble to shake hands with him, and yet, did we but think of
it, it is from a casual remark which he made to us, "You
ought to come to Balbec" or something of the kind, that
our whole life and our work have originated. But if it does
not occur to us to thank him, this is no proof of ingratitude. For when he uttered those words he had no thought
of the huge consequences which they would have for us.
It is our sensibility and our intelligence which have exploited the circumstances, which, once he has given them
their first impulse, have engendered one another as
cause and effect without his having been able to foresee

either—to return to my own story—my living with Albertine or the masked ball given by the Guermantes or anything else that had happened. No doubt the impulsion that he gave was necessary, and on that account the external form of our life and even the material which we shall use in our work derive from him. Without Swann, as I have said, my parents would never have had the idea of sending me to Balbec. (Yet Swann was not for this reason responsible for the sufferings which he himself had indirectly caused me: they sprang from my weakness, just as his own weakness had made him suffer through Odette.) But whoever it is who has thus determined the course of our life has, in so doing, excluded all the lives which we might have led instead of our actual life. If Swann had not talked to me about Balbec, I should not have known Albertine, the dining-room of the hotel, the Guermantes. I should have gone to some other town, I should have known other people, my memory and my books would be filled with quite different scenes, which I cannot even imagine and the novelty of which, their unknownness, I find so seductive that I almost regret that I was not directed instead towards them and that Albertine and the beach of Balbec and Rivebelle and the Guermantes did not for ever remain unknown to me.

Jealousy is a good recruiting-sergeant who, when there is a gap in our picture, goes out into the street and brings us in the desirable woman who was needed to fill it. Perhaps in our eyes she had ceased to be a beauty? She has become one again, for we are jealous of her and therefore she will fill the gap. Once we are dead, we shall have no joy that our picture was completed in this fashion. But this consideration does not in the least discourage us. We feel merely that life is a little more complicated than it is said to be, and circumstances too. And it is absolutely necessary that we should portray this complexity. The jealousy that is so useful is not necessarily born of a look, or an anecdote, or a retroflexion. It may be found, ready to sting us, between the leaves of a directory—what for Paris is called *Tout-Paris* and for the country the *Annuaire des Châteaux*. We had heard, for instance, but without paying any attention, some beauty to whom we have become indifferent say that she would have to go and see her sister for a few days in the Pas-de-Calais, near Dunkirk; we had also, in the past, but again without paying any attention, thought that perhaps the beauty had formerly been pursued by Monsieur E——, whom she had ceased to see, since she had ceased to go to the bar where she used to meet him. What could her sister be? A housemaid perhaps? Out of tact, we had never asked. And now suddenly, opening the *Annuaire des Châteaux* at random we find that Monsieur E—— has his country-house in the Pas-de-Calais, near Dunkirk. At once all is clear: to oblige the beauty he has taken her sister into his employment as a housemaid, and if the beauty no longer sees him in the bar, the reason is that he gets her to come and see him at home, either in Paris, where he lives most of the year, or in the Pas-de-Calais, since he cannot do without her even for the few weeks that he is there. Drunk with rage and love, we paint furiously away at the picture. And yet, suppose we are wrong? May not the truth be that Monsieur E—— no longer sees the beauty but, wanting to help her, has recommended her sister to a brother of his who lives all the year round in the Pas-de-Calais? And in that case she is going, perhaps quite by chance, to see her sister at a time when Monsieur E—— is not there, for they are no longer interested in each other. And then there is another possibility, that the sister is not a housemaid in the house near Dunkirk or anywhere else, but has relations in the Pas-de-Calais. Our anguish of the first moment gives way before these last hypotheses, which calm our jealousy. But it makes no difference. Jealousy, concealed between the leaves of the *Annuaire des Châteaux*, came at the right moment, and now the space that stood empty in our canvas is filled to abundance. And the whole composition takes shape, thanks to the presence, evoked by jealousy, of the beauty of whom already we are no longer jealous and whom we no longer love.

At this moment the butler came in to tell me that the first piece of music was finished, so that I could leave the library and go into the rooms where the party was taking place. And thereupon I remembered where I was. But I was not in the least disturbed in the train of thought upon which I had embarked by the fact that a fashionable gathering, my return to society, had provided me with that point of departure for a new life which I had been unable to find in solitude. There was nothing extraordinary about this fact, there was no reason why an impression with the power to resuscitate the timeless man within me should be linked to solitude rather than to society (as I had once supposed and as had perhaps once been the case for me, and perhaps ought still to have been the case, had I developed harmoniously instead of going through this long standstill which seemed only now to be coming to an end). For, as this impression of beauty came to me only

when, an immediate sensation—no matter how insignificant—having been thrust upon my consciousness by
chance, a similar sensation, spontaneously born again
within me, somehow in a single moment diffused the first
sensation over different periods of my life and succeeded
in filling with a general essence the empty space which
particular sensations never failed to leave in my mind, as
this was how I came to experience beauty I might just as
well receive sensations of the appropriate kind in a social
as in a natural environment, since they are supplied by
chance, aided no doubt by that special kind of excitement
which, on the days when we happen to be jolted out of
the normal routine of our lives, causes even the simplest
things to begin once again to give us those sensations
which habit, in its economical way, ordinarily begrudges
our nervous system. Why it was that precisely and
uniquely this kind of sensation should lead to the production of a work of art was a question to which I proposed
to try and find an objective answer, by following up the
thoughts which had come to me, linked in a continuous
chain, in the library, and I felt that the impulse given to
the intellectual life within me was so vigorous now that I
should be able to pursue these thoughts just as well in the
drawing-room, in the midst of the guests, as alone in the
library; it seemed to me that, from this point of view,
even in the midst of a numerous gathering I should be
able to maintain my solitude. For just as great events that
impinge upon us from without fail to influence the powers
of our mind, so that a mediocre writer who lives in a
heroic age does not cease to be a mediocre writer, for the
same reason, I realised, what is dangerous in social life is
merely the social and worldly inclinations with which one

approaches it. In itself it can no more turn one into a mediocre writer than an epic war can turn a bad poet into a sublime one. In any case, whether or no it was a good plan, theoretically, for a work of art to be constructed in this fashion, and whatever might be the result of the examination of this point which I intended to make, I could not deny that, so far as I was concerned, whenever genuinely aesthetic impressions had come to me, they had always followed upon sensations of this kind. It is true that such impressions had been rather rare in my life, but they dominated it, and I could still rediscover in the past some of these peaks which I had unwisely lost sight of (a mistake I would be careful not to make again). And already I could say that this characteristic, though it might, in the exclusive importance that it assumed in my thinking, be personal to me, was nevertheless, as I was reassured to find, akin to characteristics, less marked but still perceptible and at bottom not at all dissimilar, of certain well-known writers. Is it not from a sensation of the same species as that of the madeleine that Chateaubriand suspends the loveliest episode in the *Mémoires d'Outre-tombe*: "Yesterday evening I was walking alone . . . I was roused from my reflexions by the warbling of a thrush perched upon the highest branch of a birch tree. Instantaneously the magic sound caused my father's estate to reappear before my eyes; I forgot the catastrophes of which I had recently been the witness and, transported suddenly into the past, I saw again those country scenes in which I had so often heard the fluting notes of the thrush." And of all the lovely sentences in those memoirs are not these some of the loveliest: "A sweet and subtle scent of heliotrope was exhaled by a little patch of beans that were in flower;

it was brought to us not by a breeze from our own country but by a wild Newfoundland wind, unrelated to the exiled plant, without sympathy of shared memory or pleasure. In this perfume, not breathed by beauty, not cleansed in her bosom, not scattered where she had walked, in this perfume of a changed sky and tillage and world there was all the diverse melancholy of regret and absence and youth." And in one of the masterpieces of French literature, Gérard de Nerval's *Sylvie*, just as in the book of the *Mémoires d'Outre-tombe* which describes Combourg, there figures a sensation of the same species as the taste of the madeleine and the warbling of the thrush. Above all in Baudelaire, where they are more numerous still, reminiscences of this kind are clearly less fortuitous and therefore, to my mind, unmistakable in their significance. Here the poet himself, with something of a slow and indolent choice, deliberately seeks, in the perfume of a woman, for instance, of her hair and her breast, the analogies which will inspire him and evoke for him

the azure of the sky immense and round

and

a harbour full of masts and pennants.

I was about to search in my memory for the passages in Baudelaire at the heart of which one may find this kind of transposed sensation, in order once and for all to establish my place in so noble a line of descent and thus to give myself the assurance that the work which I no longer had any hesitation in undertaking was worthy of the pains which I should have to bestow upon it, when, having arrived at the foot of the flight of stairs which led down from the library, I found myself suddenly in the main drawing-room, in the middle of a party which, as I soon discovered, was to seem to me very different from those that I had attended in the past, and was to assume a special character in my eyes and take on a novel significance. In fact, as soon as I entered the crowded room, although I did not falter in the project which I had gone so far towards formulating within me, I was witness of a spectacular and dramatic effect which threatened to raise against my enterprise the gravest of all objections. An objection which I should manage no doubt to surmount, but which, while I continued silently to reflect upon the conditions that are necessary to a work of art, could not fail, by presenting to my gaze in a hundred different forms a consideration more likely than any other to make me hesitate, constantly to interrupt my train of thought.

For a few seconds I did not understand why it was that I had difficulty in recognising the master of the house and the guests and why everyone in the room appeared to have put on a disguise—in most cases a powdered wig—which changed him completely. The Prince himself, as he stood receiving his guests, still had that genial look of a king in a fairy-story which I had remarked in him the first time I had been to his house, but today, as though he too felt bound to comply with the rules for fancy dress which he had sent out with the invitations, he had got himself up with a white beard and dragged his feet along the ground as though they were weighted with soles of lead, so that he gave the impression of trying to imper-sonate one of the "Ages of Man." (His moustaches were

white too, as though the hoar-frost of Hop o' my
Thumb's forest still lay thick upon them. They seemed to
get in the way of his mouth, which he had difficulty in
moving, and one felt that having made his effect he ought
to have taken them off.) So successful was this disguise
that I recognised him only by a process of logical deduc-
tion, by inferring from the mere resemblance of certain
features the identity of the figure before me. I do not
know what young Fezensac had put on his face, but,
while others had whitened either half their beard or
merely their moustache, he had not bothered to use a dye
like the rest but had found some means of covering his
features with wrinkles and making his eyebrows sprout
with bristles; and all this did not suit him in the least, it
had the effect of making his face look hardened, bronzed,
rigid and solemn, and aged him to such an extent that one
would no longer have said he was a young man at all. Still
greater was my surprise when a moment later I heard the
name Duc de Châtellerault applied to a little elderly man
with the silvery moustaches of an ambassador, in whom,
thanks to a tiny fragment which still survived of the look
that I remembered, I was just able to recognise the youth
whom I had once met at Mme de Villeparisis's tea-party.
The first time that I thus succeeded in identifying somebody, by trying to dismiss from my mind the effects of
his disguise and building up, through an effort of memory, a whole familiar face round those features which had
remained unaltered, my first thought ought to have
been—and perhaps for a fraction of a second was—to
congratulate him on having made himself up with such
wonderful skill that one had initially, before recognising
him, that hesitation which a great actor, appearing in a

role in which he is unlike himself, can cause an audience to feel when he first comes on to the stage, so that knowing from the programme what to expect, it yet, for a moment, remains silent and puzzled before bursting into applause.

From the point of view of disguise, the most extraordinary of all the guests, the real star turn of the afternoon, was my personal enemy, M. d'Argencourt. Not only had he concealed his real beard, which was hardly even pepper-and-salt in colour, beneath a fantastic bushy growth of a quite improbable whiteness, but altogether (such is the power of small physical changes to shrink or enlarge a human figure and, even more, to alter the apparent character, the personality of an individual) he had turned into a contemptible old beggarman, and the diplomat whose solemn demeanour and starched rigidity were still present to my memory acted his part of old dotard with such verisimilitude that his limbs were all of a tremble and the features of what had once been a haughty countenance were permanently relaxed in an expression of smiling idiocy. Disguise, carried to this extent, ceases to be a mere art, it becomes a total transformation of the personality. And indeed, although certain details assured me that it was really Argencourt who presented this ludicrous and picturesque spectacle, I had to traverse an almost infinite number of successive states of a single face if I wished to rediscover that of the Argencourt whom I had known and who was now, though he had had no other materials than his own body with which to effect the change, so different from himself. Clearly this was the last extremity to which that body could be brought without suffering utter disintegration; already the immobile face and the proudly arched chest were no more than a bundle of rags, twitching and convulsed. With difficulty, by recalling certain smiles with which in the past Argencourt had sometimes for a moment tempered his disdain, was I able to see in the man before me the Argencourt whom I had once known, to understand that this smile of a doddering old-clothes-man existed potentially in the correct gentleman of an earlier day. But even supposing that the same intention lay behind Argencourt's smile now as in the past, because of the prodigious transformation of his face the actual physical matter of the eye through which he had to express this intention was so different that the smile which resulted was entirely new and even appeared to belong to a new person. I was tempted to laugh aloud at the sight of this sublime old gaffer, as senile in his amiable caricature of himself as was, in a more tragic vein, M. de Charlus thunderstruck into humble politeness. M. d'Argencourt, in his impersonation of an aged man in a farce by Regnard rewritten in an exaggerated fashion by Labiche, was as easy of access, as affable as M. de Charlus in the role of King Lear, punctiliously doffing his hat to the most unimportant passer-by. Yet it did not occur to me to tell him how impressed I was by the extraordinary vision which he offered to my eyes. And this was not because of any survival of my old feeling of antipathy, for indeed he had so far become unlike himself that I had the illusion of being in the presence of a different person, as gentle, as kindly, as inoffensive as the other Argencourt had been hostile, overbearing, and dangerous. So far a different person that the sight of this hoary clown with his ludicrous grin, this snowman looking like General Dourakine[7] in his second childhood, made me think that it must be possible for human personality to undergo metamorphoses as total as those of certain insects. I had the impression that I was looking into a glass-case in a museum of natural history at an instructive example of a later phase in the life-cycle of what had once been the swiftest and surest of predatory insects, and before this flabby chrysalis, more subject to vibration than capable of movement, I could not feel the sentiments which in the past M. d'Argencourt had always inspired in me. However, I was silent, I refrained from congratulating him on presenting a spectacle which seemed to extend the boundaries within which the transformations of the human body can take place.

For whereas at a fancy-dress ball or behind the scenes at a theatre civility leads one, if anything, to exaggerate the difficulty—to talk even of the impossibility—of recognising the person beneath the disguise, here on the contrary an instinct had warned me to do just the contrary; I felt that the success of the disguise was no longer in any way flattering because the transformation was not intentional. And I realised something that I had not suspected when I entered the room a few minutes earlier: that every party, grand or simple, which takes place after a long interval in which one has ceased to go into society, provided that it brings together some of the people whom one knew in the past, gives one the impression of a masquerade, a masquerade which is more successful than any that one has ever been to and at which one is most genuinely "intrigued" by the identity of the other guests, but with the novel feature that the disguises, which were assumed long ago against their wearers' will, cannot, when the party is over, be wiped off with the make-up. Intrigued, did I say, by the identity of the other guests? No more, alas, than they are intrigued by one's own. For the difficulty which I experienced in putting a name to the faces before me was shared evidently by all those who, when they happened to catch sight of mine, paid no more attention to it than if they had never seen it before or else laboriously sought to extract from my present appearance a very different recollection.

In performing this extraordinary "number," this brilliant study in caricature which offered certainly the most striking vision which I was likely to retain of him, M. d'Argencourt might be likened to an actor who at the end of a play makes a final appearance on the stage before the curtain falls for the last time in the midst of a storm of laughter. And if I no longer felt any ill will towards him, it was because in this man who had rediscovered the innocence of childhood there was no longer any recollection of the contemptuous notions which he might once have had of me, no longer any memory of having seen M. de Charlus suddenly drop my arm, either because these sentiments had ceased to exist in him or because in order to arrive at me they were obliged to pass through physical refractors which so distorted them that in the course of their journey they completely changed their meaning, so that M. d'Argencourt appeared to be kind for want of the physical means of expressing that he was still unkind, from inability to repress his unfailingly friendly mirth. I have compared him to an actor, but in fact, unencumbered as he was by any conscious soul, it was rather as a puppet, a trembling puppet with a beard of white wool, that I saw him being shakily put through his paces up and down this drawing-room, in a puppet-show which was both scientific and philosophical and in which he served—as though it had been at the same time a funeral oration and a lecture at the Sorbonne—both as a text for a sermon on the vanity of all things and as an object lesson in natural history.

A puppet-show, yes, but one in which, in order to identify the puppets with the people whom one had known in the past, it was necessary to read what was written on several planes at once, planes that lay behind the visible aspect of the puppets and gave them depth and forced one, as one looked at these aged marionettes, to make a strenuous intellectual effort; one was obliged to study them at the same time with one's eyes and with one's memory. These were puppets bathed in the immaterial colours of the years, puppets which exteriorised Time, Time which by habit is made invisible and to become visible seeks bodies, which, wherever it finds them, it seizes upon, to display its magic lantern upon them. As immaterial now as Golo long ago on the doorknob of my room at Combray, the new, the unrecognisable Argencourt was there before me as the revelation of Time, which by his agency was rendered partially visible, for in the new elements which went to compose his face and his personality one could decipher a number which told one the years of his age, one could recognise the hieroglyph of life—of life not as it appears to us, that is to say permanent, but as it really is: an atmosphere so swiftly changing that at the end of the day the proud nobleman is portrayed, in caricature, as a dealer in old clothes.

There were other people in the room in whom these changes, these veritable alienations seemed to belong rather to the realm of human psychology than of natural history, so that one was astonished, when one heard cer-

tain names, to learn that the same individual could present, not like M. d'Argencourt the characteristics of a new
and different species, but the external features of a different personality. From this young girl, for instance, as
from M. d'Argencourt, time had extracted possibilities
that one could never have suspected, but these possibilities, though it was through her physiognomy or her body
that they had expressed themselves, seemed to be of a
moral order. The features of the face, if they change, if
they group themselves differently, if their oscillations take
on a slower rhythm, assume with a different aspect a different significance. In a woman, for instance, whom one
had known as stiff and prim, an enlargement out of all
recognition of the cheeks, an unpredictable arching of the
nose, caused one the same surprise—and often it was an
agreeable surprise—as one would have felt at some sensitive and profound remark, some noble and courageous action that one would never have expected of her. On either
side of this nose, this new nose, one saw opening out
horizons which one would not have dared to hope for.
With these cheeks kindness and delicate affection, once
out of the question, had become possible. And in the
presence of this chin one could utter sentiments that one
would never have dreamed of voicing when confronted
with its predecessor. All these new features of the face
implied new features also of the character; the thin, severe
girl had turned into a vast and indulgent dowager. And
no longer in a zoological sense, as with M. d'Argencourt,
but in a social and moral sense one could say of her that
she was a different person.

For all these reasons a party like this at which I found
myself was something much more valuable than an image

of the past: it offered me as it were all the successive images—which I had never seen—which separated the past
from the present, better still it showed me the relationship
that existed between the present and the past; it was like
an old-fashioned peepshow, but a peepshow of the years,
the vision not of a moment but of a person situated in the
distorting perspective of Time.

As for the woman whose lover M. d'Argencourt had
been, considering the length of time that had elapsed she
had not changed very much, that is to say her face was
not too utterly demolished for the face of a human creature subject, as we all are, to deformation at every moment of her trajectory into the abyss towards which she
had been launched, that abyss whose direction we can express only by means of comparisons that are all equally
invalid, since we can borrow them only from the world of
space and their sole merit, whether we give them the ori-
entation of height, length or depth, is to make us feel that
this inconceivable yet apprehensible dimension exists. To
find a name for the faces before me I had been obliged, in
effect, to follow the course of the years back towards their
source, and this forced me, by a necessary consequence, to
re-establish, to give their real place to those years whose
passage I had hardly noticed. And from this point of
view, freeing me from the illusions produced in us by the
apparent sameness of space, the totally changed aspect of,
for instance, M. d'Argencourt was a striking revelation to
me of that chronological reality which under normal conditions is no more than an abstract conception to us, just
as the first sight of some strange dwarf tree or giant
baobab apprises us that we have arrived in a new latitude.
Life at such moments seems to us like a theatrical

pageant in which from one act to another we see the baby turn into a youth and the youth into a mature man, who in the next act totters towards the grave. And as it is through endless small changes that we feel that these beings, who enter our field of vision only at long intervals, can have become so different, we feel that we ourselves must have followed the same law in virtue of which they have been so totally transformed that, without having ceased to exist, indeed just because they have never ceased to exist, they no longer in any way resemble what we observed them to be in the past.

A young woman whom I had known long ago, white-haired now and compressed into a little old witch, seemed to suggest that it is necessary, in the final scene of a theatrical entertainment, for the characters to be disguised beyond all recognition. But her brother was still so straight-backed, so like himself, that one was surprised on his youthful face to see a bristling moustache dyed white. Indeed everywhere the patches of white in beards and moustaches hitherto entirely black lent a note of melancholy to the human landscape of the party, as do the first yellow leaves on the trees when one is still looking forward to a long summer, when before one has begun to enjoy the hot weather one sees that the autumn has arrived. So that at last I, who from childhood had lived from day to day and had received, of myself and of others, impressions which I regarded as definitive, became aware as I had never been before—by an inevitable inference from the metamorphoses which had taken place in all the people around me—of the time which had passed for them, a notion which brought with it the overwhelming revelation that it had passed also for me. And their old age, in itself a matter of indifference to me, froze my blood by announcing to me the approach of my own. At this point, as though to proclaim the lesson aloud and drive it home, there came to my ears at brief intervals a series of remarks which struck them like the trump of the Last Judgment. The first of these was made by the Duchesse de Guermantes; I had just caught sight of her, passing between a double hedge of curious onlookers, who, not fully aware of the marvellous artifices of toilet and aesthetic which evoked these responses within them, yet feeling themselves moved by the sight of this fair, reddish head, this salmon-pink body almost concealed by its fins of black lace and throttled by jewels, gazed at it, with its hereditary sinuosity of line, as they might have gazed at some archaic sacred fish, loaded with precious stones, in which was incarnate the protective genius of the Guermantes family. "Ah! how wonderful to see you," she said to me, "you, my oldest friend!" And though the vanity of the sometime young man from Combray who had never for a moment thought that he might become one of her friends, really participating in the real mysterious life that went on in the houses of the Guermantes, with the same title to her friendship as M. de Bréauté or M. de Forestelle or Swann or all those others who were now dead, might well have been flattered by these words, more than anything I was saddened by them. "Her oldest friend!" I said to myself. "Surely she exaggerates. One of the oldest perhaps, but can I really be . . ." At that moment a nephew of the Prince came up to me: "You, as a veteran Parisian . . ." he said to me, and while he was still speaking I was handed a note. Outside the house I had made the acquaintance of a young Létourville, who was related in some way which I had forgotten to the Duchess but who knew at least who I was. He had just left Saint-Cyr, and, telling myself that he would be a nice friend for me, like Saint-Loup, who could initiate me into military matters and explain the changes which had taken place in the army, I had told him that I would see him again at the party and that we might arrange to have dinner together one evening, and for this he had thanked me very civilly. But I had stayed too long lost in thought in the library and the note which he had left for me was to tell me that he had not been able to wait, and to leave me his address. The letter of this imagined comrade ended thus: "With the respectful wishes of your young friend, Létourville." "Young friend!" That was how in the past I had written to men thirty years older than myself, to Legrandin, for example. And now this second lieutenant, whom in my mind's eye I saw as my comrade after the fashion of Saint-Loup, called himself my "young friend"! Since the days of Doncières, it seemed, it was not only military methods that had changed; from this M. de Létourville, with whom I imagined myself sharing the pleasures of a youthful comradeship—and why not, since I appeared to myself to be youthful?—I was separated, it seemed, by an arc traced by an invisible compass whose existence I had not suspected, which removed me so far from the boyish second lieutenant that in the eyes of this "young friend" I was an old gentleman.

Almost immediately afterwards, hearing someone mention the name of Bloch, I asked whether he meant young Bloch or his father (who, though I was not aware of this, had died during the war, from grief, it was said, at seeing France invaded). "I didn't know he had any children," said the Prince, "I didn't even know he was married. But clearly it is the father we are talking about. He is not in the least like a young Bloch," he added with a laugh. "He is quite old enough to have grown-up sons." And I realised that it was my former schoolfriend who was being discussed. A moment later he came into the room. And indeed superimposed upon the features of Bloch I saw the mild but didactic countenance, the frail movements of the head quickly coming to rest like a piece of clockwork, in which I should have recognised the learned weariness of some amiable old man if at the same time I had not recognised my friend standing before me, so that at once my memories animated him with an uninterrupted flow of youthful enthusiasm which he now no longer seemed to possess. For me, who had known him on the threshold of life and had never ceased to see him thus, he was the friend of my boyhood, an adolescent whose youth I measured by the youth which unconsciously, not believing that I had lived since that time, I attributed to myself. I heard someone say that he quite looked his age, and I was astonished to observe on his face some of those signs which are indeed characteristic of men who are old. Then I understood that this was because he was in fact old and that adolescents who survive for a sufficient number of years are the material out of which life makes old men.

Someone, hearing that I had not been well, asked me whether I was not afraid of catching the influenza of which there was an epidemic at that moment, whereupon another well-wisher reassured me by saying: "Oh! no, it's usually only the young who get it. A man of your age has very little to fear." I was assured also that some of the

servants had recognised me. They had whispered my
name, and had even, as a lady informed me ("You know
the expressions they use"), been heard by her to say:
"Look, there's father . . ." (and then my surname), and
as I had no children this could only be an allusion to my
age.

"What do you mean, did I know the Marshal?" said
the Duchess to me. "But I knew figures far more typical
of the period: the Duchesse de Galliera, Pauline de Périgord, Monsignor Dupanloup." Hearing her, I naïvely regretted that I had not known what she described as relics
of an earlier time. I ought to have reflected that what one
calls an earlier time is the period of which one has oneself
known only the end: things that we see on the horizon assume a mysterious grandeur and seem to us to be closing
over a world which we shall not behold again; but meanwhile we are advancing, and very soon it is we ourselves
who are on the horizon for the generations that come after
us; all the while the horizon retreats into the distance, and
the world, which seemed to be finished, begins again. "I
even, when I was a girl," Mme de Guermantes went on,
"once saw the Duchesse de Dino. But then, you know I'm
no longer a chicken." These last words upset me. "She
shouldn't have said that," I thought, "that's the way for
an old woman to talk." And immediately I reflected that
in fact she was an old woman. "As for you," she continued, "you are always the same, you never seem to
change." And this remark I found almost more painful
than if she had told me that I had changed, for it
proved—if it was so extraordinary that there was so little
sign of change in me—that a long time had elapsed.
"Yes," she said, "you are astonishing, you look as young

as ever," another melancholy remark, which can only
mean that in fact, if not in appearance, we have grown
old. There was worse to come, for she added: "I have always regretted that you never married. But, who knows,
perhaps after all it is fortunate. You would have been old
enough to have sons in the war, and if they had been
killed, like poor Robert (I still often think of him), sensitive as you are, how would you ever have survived their
loss?" And I was able to see myself, as though in the first
truthful mirror which I had ever encountered, reflected in
the eyes of old people, still young in their own opinion as
I in mine, who, when I spoke of "an old man like myself"
in the hope of being contradicted, showed in their answering looks, which saw me not as they saw themselves but
as I saw them, not a glimmer of protest. For we failed to
see our own appearance, our own age, but each one of us,
as though it were a mirror that faced him, saw those of
the others. And no doubt the discovery that they have
grown old causes less sadness to many people than it did
to me. But in the first place old age, in this respect, is like
death. Some men confront them both with indifference,
not because they have more courage than others but because they have less imagination. And then, a man who
from his childhood on has aimed at one single idea and
who, from idleness and perhaps also because of poor
health, has perpetually put off its realisation, every
evening striking out as though it had never existed the
day that has slipped away and is lost, so that the illness
which hastens the ageing of his body retards that of his
mind, such a man is more surprised and more appalled to
see that all the while he has been living in Time than one
who lives little inside himself and, regulating his activities

by the calendar, does not in a single horrifying moment discover the total of the years whose mounting sum he has followed day by day. But there was a more serious reason for my distress: I had made the discovery of this destructive action of Time at the very moment when I had conceived the ambition to make visible, to intellectualise in a work of art, realities that were outside Time.

In some of the guests at the party the successive replacement, accomplished in my absence, of each cell by other cells, had brought about a change so complete, a metamorphosis so entire that I could have dined opposite them in a restaurant a hundred times without suspecting that I had known them in the past any more than I would have guessed the royal identity of a sovereign travelling incognito or the hidden vice of a stranger. And even this comparison is hardly adequate to the cases in which I had heard the name of the person before me, for it is perhaps not so extraordinary that a stranger sitting opposite one should be a criminal or a king, but these were people whom I had once known, or rather I had known people who bore the same name and yet were so different that I could not believe that they were the same. Nevertheless, just as I would have tried to introduce into the stranger the idea of royalty or of vice, which in a very short time can give a new face to the unknown person towards whom one might so easily, when one's eyes were still blindfolded, have committed the gaffe of behaving with inappropriate insolence or civility, and in whose unchanged features, once one knows who he is, one discerns traces of distinction or of guilt, so now I set to work to introduce into the face of the unknown, utterly unknown, woman before me the idea that she was, let us say, Mme Sazerat, and I succeeded eventually in restoring the meaning that I had once known to reside in her face, which would, however, have remained for me utterly alienated from its owner—as much the face of another person, wanting in all the human attributes which I had once known it to possess, as that of a man turned back into a monkey—if the name and the affirmation of identity had not, in spite of the arduous nature of the problem, set me on the path of its solution. Sometimes, however, the old image came to light again in my mind with such precision that I was able to essay a confrontation; and then, like a witness brought face to face with a suspect, I was obliged, so great was the difference, to say: "No, I do not recognise this person."

But was I right to tell myself that these special characteristics of individuals would die? I had always considered each one of us to be a sort of multiple organism or polyp, not only at a given moment of time—so that when a speck of dust passes it, the eye, an associated but independent organ, blinks without having received an order from the mind, and the intestine, like an embedded parasite, can fall victim to an infection without the mind knowing anything about it—but also, similarly, where the personality is concerned and its duration through life, I had thought of this as a sequence of juxtaposed but distinct "I's" which would die one after the other or even come to life alternately, like those which at Combray took one another's place within me when evening approached. But I had seen also that these moral cells of which an individual is composed are more durable than the individual himself. I had seen the vices and the courage of the Guermantes recur in Saint-Loup, as also at different times in

his life his own strange and ephemeral defects of character, and as in Swann his Semitism. And now I could observe the same phenomenon in Bloch. He had lost his
father some years previously, and when I had written to
him at the time, he had at first been unable to answer my
letter, for, quite apart from the strong family sentiments
which often exist in Jewish families, the idea that his father was an altogether exceptional man had imparted to
his affection the character of a cult. He had found his loss
unbearable and had had to take refuge in a sanatorium,
where he stayed for nearly a year. To my condolences he
replied in a tone of profound grief which was at the same
time almost haughty, so enviable in his eyes was the privilege which I had enjoyed of approaching this exceptional
man whose very ordinary two-horse carriage he would
have liked to present to some historical museum. And
now, as he sat at table in the midst of his family, he was
animated by the same wrath against his father-in-law as
had animated his own father against M. Nissim Bernard
and even interrupted his meals to deliver the same tirades
against him. So that just as, in listening to the conversation of Cottard and Brichot and so many others, I had felt
that, through the influence of culture and fashion, a single
undulation propagates identical mannerisms of speech and
thought through a whole vast extent of space, it seemed to
me now that throughout the whole duration of time great
cataclysmic waves lift up from the depths of the ages the
same rages, the same sadnesses, the same heroisms, the
same obsessions, through one superimposed generation after another, and that each geological section cut through
several individuals of the same series offers the repetition,
as of shadows thrown upon a succession of screens, of a

picture as unchanged—though often not so insignificant—as that of Bloch exchanging angry words with his father-in-law, M. Bloch the elder doing the same in the same fashion with M. Nissim Bernard, and many other pairs of disputants whom I had myself never known.

Gilberte de Saint-Loup[8] said to me: "Shall we go and dine together by ourselves in a restaurant?" and I replied: "Yes, if you don't find it compromising to dine alone with a young man." As I said this, I heard everybody round me laugh, and I hastily added: "or rather, with an old man." I felt that the phrase which had made people laugh was one of those which my mother might have used in speaking of me, my mother for whom I was still a child. And I realised that I judged myself from the same point of view as she did. If in the end I had registered, as she had, certain changes which had taken place since my early childhood, these were, nevertheless, changes which were now very remote. I had not advanced beyond the particular one which, long ago, almost before the remark corresponded with the facts, had made people say: "He's almost a grown-up man now." I still thought that was what I was, but by now the description was absurdly out of date. I did not realise how much I had changed. And indeed, though these people just now had burst out laughing, what was it that made them so sure of the change? I had not a single grey hair, my moustache was black. I should have liked to ask them what the evidence was which revealed the terrible fact.

And now I began to understand what old age was— old age, which perhaps of all the realities is the one of which we preserve for longest in our life a purely abstract conception, looking at calendars, dating our letters, seeing our friends marry and then in their turn the children of our friends, and yet, either from fear or from sloth, not understanding what all this means, until the day when we behold an unknown silhouette, like that of M. d'Argencourt, which teaches us that we are living in a new world; until the day when a grandson of a woman we once knew, a young man whom instinctively we treat as a contemporary of ours, smiles as though we were making fun of him because to him it seems that we are old enough to be his grandfather—and I began to understand too what death meant and love and the joys of the spiritual life, the usefulness of suffering, a vocation, etc. For if names had lost most of their individuality for me, words on the other hand now began to reveal their full significance. The beauty of images is situated in front of things, that of ideas behind them. So that the first sort of beauty ceases to astonish us as soon as we have reached the things themselves, but the second is something that we understand only when we have passed beyond them.

The cruel discovery which I had just made could not fail to be of service to me so far as the actual material of my book was concerned. For I had decided that this could not consist uniquely of the full and plenary impressions that were outside time, and amongst those other truths in which I intended to set, like jewels, those of the first order, the ones relating to Time, to Time in which, as in some transforming fluid, men and societies and nations are immersed, would play an important part. I should pay particular attention to those changes which the aspect of living things undergoes, of which every minute I had fresh examples before me, for, whilst all the while think-

ing of my work, which I now felt to be launched with
such momentum that no passing distractions could check
its advance, I continued to greet old acquaintances and to
enter into conversation with them. The process of ageing,
I found, was not marked in them all by signs of the same
sort. I saw someone who was inquiring after my name,
and I was told that it was M. de Cambremer. He came up
to me and to show that he had recognised me, "Do you
still have your fits of breathlessness?" he asked, and, upon
my replying in the affirmative, went on: "Well, at least
you see that it is no bar to longevity," as if I were already
a centenarian. While speaking to him, I fixed my eyes on
two or three features which I was able, by an effort of
thought, to reintegrate into that complex of my recollections—totally different though it was—which I called his
personality. But for a brief moment he turned his head
aside. And then I saw that he had been made unrecognisable by the attachment of enormous red pouches to his
cheeks, which prevented him from opening his mouth or
his eyes completely, and the sight of these startled me
into silence, since I did not dare to look at what I took to
be some form of anthrax which it seemed more polite not
to refer to unless he mentioned it first. However, like a
courageous invalid, he made no allusion to his malady but
talked and laughed, and I feared to appear lacking in sympathy if I did not ask, no less than in tact if I did ask,
what was its nature. "But surely they have become less
frequent with age?" he continued, still on the subject of
my fits of breathlessness. I replied that they had not.
"Oh! but my sister has them much less than she used to,"
he said, in a tone of contradiction, as though what was
true of his sister must also be true of me, and as though

age were one of a number of remedies which had helped Mme de Gaucourt and which, therefore, he was quite certain must be beneficial to me. Mme de Cambremer-Legrandin joined us and I became more and more afraid that they must think me callous for failing to deplore the symptoms which I observed on her husband's face, yet still I could not pluck up courage to broach the subject myself. "I expect you're glad to see him again," she said. "Yes, but how is he?" I replied, as though doubtful what answer I should receive. "Why, pretty well, as you can see for yourself." She had not noticed the disfigurement which offended my eyes and which was merely one of the masks in the collection of Time, a mask which Time had fastened to the face of the Marquis, but gradually, adding layer to layer so slowly that his wife had perceived nothing. When M. de Cambremer had finished his questions about my breathlessness, it was my turn to inquire in a low voice of someone standing near whether the Marquis's mother was still alive. And now I was beginning to discover that, in the appreciation of the passage of time, the first step is the hardest. At first one finds it extremely difficult to imagine that so much time has elapsed, later the difficulty is to understand how the lapse can have been so slight. Similarly, when one first suddenly becomes aware of the distance separating the thirteenth century from the present, it is difficult to believe that churches built in that age can still exist—but in fact they are to be found all over France. Within a few minutes I had developed, though very much more rapidly, in the same fashion as those who, after finding it hard to believe that somebody they knew in their youth has reached the age of sixty, are very much more surprised fifteen years later to learn that the same person is still alive and is only seventy-five. Having been assured that M. de Cambremer's mother had not died, I asked him how she was. "She is wonderful still," he said, using to describe her an adjective which in certain families—by contrast with those tribes where aged parents are treated without pity—is applied to old people in whom the continued exercise of the most rudimentary and unspiritual faculties, such as hearing, going to mass on foot, sustaining the demise of their relatives with insensibility, is endowed in the eyes of their children with an extraordinary moral beauty.

If some of the women in the room had acknowledged the arrival of old age by starting to paint their faces, it was also manifested in a contrary fashion by the absence of make-up on the features of certain men, where I had never consciously observed it in the past and who yet seemed to me greatly changed since they had given up the hopeless attempt to please and ceased to use it. One of these was Legrandin. The suppression of the pink, which I had never suspected of being artificial, upon his lips and his cheeks gave to his countenance the greyish tinge and also the sculptural precision of stone, so that with his long-drawn and gloomy features he was like some Egyptian god. Or perhaps less like a god than a ghost. He no longer had the heart either to paint himself or to smile, to make his eyes sparkle, to elaborate his ingenious speeches. One was astonished to see him so pale and so dejected, opening his mouth only at rare intervals to make remarks as trivial as those uttered by the spirits of the dead when we summon them to our presence. One wondered what could be the cause that prevented him from being lively, eloquent, charming, as one does when a medium, putting questions that call for long and fascinating answers to the "double" of a man who in his life-time was brilliant, elicits from him only the most uninteresting replies. And one told oneself that this cause, which had substituted for a Legrandin of rapid movements and rich colour a pale and melancholy phantom Legrandin, was old age.

There were some people whose hair had not turned white. I recognised for instance, when he came up to say a word to his master, the old valet of the Prince de Guermantes. The coarse hairs which bristled all over his cheeks as well as on his skull were still of a red that verged upon pink, yet one could hardly suspect him of using dye like the Duchesse de Guermantes. Nevertheless, he appeared old. One felt merely that in the human race there exist species, like the mosses and the lichens and a great many others in the vegetable kingdom, which do not change at the approach of winter.

Others again had preserved their faces intact and seemed merely to walk with difficulty; at first one supposed that they had something wrong with their legs; only later did one realise that age had fastened its soles of lead to their feet. A few, of whom the Prince d'Agrigente was one, seemed actually to have been embellished by age. His tall, thin figure, with its lacklustre eye and hair that seemed destined to remain a carroty red for all eternity, had turned, through a metamorphosis more appropriate to an insect, into an entirely different old man, whose red hair, too long exposed to view, had been taken out of service like a table-cloth too long in use and replaced by white. His chest had acquired a new corpulence, robust and almost military, which must have necessitated a positive explosion of the fragile chrysalis that I had known; a

conscious gravity flooded his eyes, which were tinged also
with a new kindliness which made him bow to right and
left. And as, in spite of his altered appearance, a certain
resemblance could be detected between the puissant
prince before me and the portrait preserved in my memory, I marvelled at the power to renew in fresh forms that
is possessed by Time, which can thus, while respecting
the unity of the individual and the laws of life, effect a
change of scene and introduce bold contrasts into two
successive aspects of a single person; for many of these
people could be identified immediately, but only as rather
bad portraits of themselves hanging side by side in an exhibition in which an inaccurate and spiteful artist has
hardened the features of one sitter, robbed another of her
fresh complexion and her slender figure, spread a gloom
over the countenance of a third. Comparing these effigies
with those that the eyes of my memory could show me, I
preferred the latter. Just as often, when asked by a friend
to choose a photograph, one finds the one he offers less
good than some other and would like to refuse it, so to
each of these people, presented with the new image which
they showed me of themselves, I should have liked to say:
"No, not this one, it is not so good of you, it's not really
like you." I would not have dared to add: "Instead of
your own straight and handsome nose, it has given you
your father's crooked nose, which I have never seen on
you." And yet this was what had happened: the nose was
new, but it was a family nose. If this was a portrait-
gallery, Time, the artist, had made of all the sitters portraits that were recognisable; yet they were not likenesses,
and this was not because he had flattered them but because he had aged them. He was an artist, moreover, who

worked very slowly. That replica of Odette's face, for instance, which I had seen as the merest outline of a sketch in Gilberte's face on the day on which I first met Bergotte, Time had at long last now wrought into the most perfect likeness; he was one of those painters who keep a work by them for half a lifetime, adding to it year after year until it is completed.

In some of the guests I recognised after a while not merely themselves but themselves as they had been in the past. Ski, for instance, was no more altered than a flower or a fruit which had been dried. Aged but still immature, one of those first attempts which nature abandons in the rough, he was a living confirmation of the theory which I had been formulating about the bachelor devotees of art. "Marvellous!" he said, taking me by the arm. "I have heard it eight times . . ." There were others, too, who had not ripened with age, not only art-lovers like Ski but men who had spent their lives in society. Their faces might be surrounded with a first circle of wrinkles and a sweep of white hair but they were still the same babyish faces, with the naïve enthusiasm of an eighteen-year-old. They were not old men, they were very young men in an advanced stage of withering. The marks of life were not deeply scored here, and death, when it came, would find it as easy to restore to these features their youthfulness as it is to clean a portrait which only a little surface dirt prevents from shining with its original brilliance. These men made me think that we are victims of an illusion when, hearing talk of a celebrated old man, we instantly make up our minds that he is kind and just and gentle; for I felt that, forty years earlier, these elderly men had been ruthless young men and that there was no reason to suppose

that they had not preserved their youthful arrogance and
their vanity, their duplicity and their guile.

And yet, in complete contrast with these, I had the
surprise of talking to men and women whom I remembered as unendurable and who had now, I found, lost almost every one of their defects, possibly because life, by
disappointing or by gratifying their desires, had rid them
of most of their conceit or their bitterness. A rich marriage, with the consequence that struggle and ostentation
had ceased to be necessary, the influence perhaps of the
wife herself, the slowly acquired knowledge of values beyond those that had formed the whole creed of a frivolous
youth, had allowed them to relax the tensions in their
character and to display their good qualities. Growing old,
they seemed to have acquired a different personality, like
those trees whose essential nature appears to be changed
by the autumn which alters their colours; the essential
marks of old age were manifested in them, but old age,
here, was a moral phenomenon. In others, it was almost
entirely physical, and so strange were its effects that a
person (Mme d'Arpajon, for instance) seemed to me at
the same time unknown and familiar. Unknown, for it
was impossible to suspect that it was she and in spite of
every effort I could not help showing signs, as I responded to her salutation, of the mental activity which
made me hesitate between three or four individuals, not
one of whom was Mme d'Arpajon and any one of whom I
thought that I might be greeting, and greeting with a fer-
vour which must have astonished her, for, fearing in my
uncertainty to appear too chilly should she turn out to be
an old and close friend, I had made up for the doubtful
expression of my eyes by the warmth of my hand-shake

and my smile. And yet, in a way, her new appearance was not unfamiliar to me. It was the appearance, often seen by me in the course of my life, of certain stout, elderly women, of whom at the time I had never suspected that, many years earlier, they could have looked like Mme d'Arpajon. So different was she to look at from the woman I had known that one was tempted to think of her as a creature condemned, like a character in a pantomime, to appear first as a young girl, then as a stout matron, with no doubt a final appearance still to come as a quavering, bent old crone. Like a swimmer in difficulties almost out of sight of the shore, she seemed with infinite effort scarcely to move through the waves of time which beat upon her and threatened to submerge her. Yet gradually, as I studied her face, hesitant and uncertain like a failing memory which has begun to lose the images of the past, I succeeded in rediscovering something of the face which I had known, by playing a little game of eliminating the squares and the hexagons which age had added to her cheeks. For in her case the material which the years had superimposed consisted of geometrical shapes, though on the cheeks of other women it might be of quite a different character. On those, for instance, of Mme de Guermantes, in many respects so little changed and yet composite now like a bar of nougat, I could distinguish traces here and there of verdigris, a small pink patch of fragmentary shell-work, and a little growth of an indefinable character, smaller than a mistletoe berry and less transparent than a glass bead.

Some men walked with a limp, and one was aware that this was the result not of a motor accident but of a first stroke: they had already, as the saying is, one foot in the grave. There were women too whose graves were waiting open to receive them: half paralysed, they could not quite disentangle their dress from the tombstone in which it had got stuck, so that they were unable to stand up straight but remained bent towards the ground, with their head lowered, in a curve which seemed an apt symbol of their own position on the trajectory from life to death, with the final vertical plunge not far away. Nothing now could check the momentum of this parabola upon which they were launched; they trembled all over if they attempted to straighten themselves, and their fingers let fall whatever they tried to grasp.

Certain faces, beneath their hood of white hair, had already the rigidity, the sealed eyelids of those who are about to die, and their lips, shaken by an incessant tremor, seemed to be muttering a last prayer. A countenance of which every line was unchanged needed only the substitution of white hair for black or fair to look totally different, for, as theatrical costumiers know, a powdered wig is in itself an adequate disguise which will make its wearer unrecognisable. The Marquis de Beausergent, whom I had seen, as a young lieutenant, in Mme de Cambremer's box on the day on which Mme de Guermantes had been with her cousin in hers, still had the same perfectly regular features, indeed they had become even more regular, since the pathological rigidity brought about by arteriosclerosis had even further exaggerated the impassive rectitude of his dandy's physiognomy and given to his features the intense hardness of outline, almost grimacing in its immobility, that they might have had in a study by Mantegna or Michelangelo. His complexion, once almost ribaldly red, was now solemnly pale; silvery hair, a slight portliness, the dignity of a Doge, an air of fatigue, even of somnolence, all combined to give him a new and premonitory impression of doomed majesty. The square light brown beard had gone and in its place was a square white beard, of the same trim proportions, which so totally transformed his appearance that, noticing that the second lieutenant whom I remembered now had five bands of braid on his sleeve, my first thought was to congratulate him, not on having been promoted colonel but on looking so well in the part of colonel, a disguise for which he seemed to have borrowed, together with the uniform, the lugubrious gravity of the senior officer that his father had been. But there was another guest whose face, in spite of the substitution of a white for a fair beard, had remained lively, smiling and boyish, so that the change of beard merely made him appear more rubicund and more pugnacious and enhanced the sparkle in his eye, giving to the still youthful man about town the inspired air of a prophet.

The transformations effected, in the women particularly, by white hair and by other new features, would not have held my attention so forcibly had they been merely changes of colour, which can be charming to behold; too often they were changes of personality, registered not by the eye but, disturbingly, by the mind. For to "recognise" someone, and, *a fortiori*, to learn someone's identity after having failed to recognise him, is to predicate two contradictory things of a single subject, it is to admit that what was here, the person whom one remembers, no longer exists, and also that what is now here is a person whom one did not know to exist; and to do this we have to apprehend a mystery almost as disturbing as that of death, of which it is, indeed, as it were the preface and the harbinger. I knew what these changes meant, I knew what they were the prelude to, and that is why the white hair of these women, along with all the other changes, profoundly disquieted me. I was told a name and I was dumbfounded to think that it could be used to describe both the fair-haired girl, the marvellous waltzer, whom I had known in the past, and the massive white-haired lady making her way through the room with elephantine tread. Along with a certain rosiness of complexion, the name was perhaps the only thing common to these two women, the girl in my memory and the lady at the Guermantes party, who were more unlike one another than an *ingénue* and a dowager in a play. To have succeeded in giving to the waltzer this huge body, in encumbering and retarding her movements by the adjustment of an invisible metronome, in substituting—with perhaps as sole common factor the cheeks, larger certainly now than in youth but already in those days blotched with red—for the feather-light fair girl this ventripotent old campaigner, it must have been necessary for life to accomplish a vaster work of dismantlement and reconstruction than is involved in the replacement of a steeple by a dome, and when one considered that this work had been effected not with tractable inorganic matter but with living flesh which can only change imperceptibly, the overwhelming contrast between the apparition before me and the creature that I remembered pushed back the existence of the latter into a past that was more than remote, that was almost unimaginable. One was terrified, because it made one think of the vast periods which must have elapsed before such a revolution could be accomplished in the geology of a face, to see what erosions had taken place all the way along the nose, what huge alluvial deposits at the edge of the cheeks surrounded the whole face with their opaque and refractory masses. It was difficult to find a link between the two figures, past and present, to think of the two individuals as possessing the same name; for just as one has difficulty in thinking that a dead person was once alive or that a person who was alive is now dead, so one has difficulty, almost as great and of the same kind (for the extinction of youth, the destruction of a person full of energy and high spirits, is already a kind of annihilation), in conceiving that she who was once a girl is now an old woman when the juxtaposition of the two appearances, the old and the young, seems so totally to exclude the possibility of their belonging to the same person that alternately it is the old woman and then the girl and then again the old woman who seems to one to be a dream, so that one might well refuse to believe that *this* can ever have been *that*, that the material of *that* has not taken refuge elsewhere but has itself, thanks to the subtle manipulations of Time, turned into *this*, that it is the same matter incorporated in the same body, were it not for the evidence of the similar name and the corroborative testimony of friends, to which an appearance of verisimilitude is given only by the pink upon the cheeks, once a small patch surrounded by the golden corn of fair hair, now a broad expanse beneath the snow.

And often these fair-haired dancers had acquired, along with a wig of white hair, the friendship of duchesses whom in the past they had not known. Nor was this all: having in their youth done nothing but dance, they had been "touched" by art as once a noble lady might have been touched by grace. And as the seventeenth-century lady, when this happened, withdrew into a life of religion, so now her descendant lived in an apartment filled with cubist paintings, a cubist painter worked for her alone and she lived only for him.

As in a snowy landscape, the degree of whiteness attained by a person's hair seemed in general to be an indication of the depth of time through which he or she had lived, just as in a range of mountains the higher peaks, even though they appear to the eye to be on the same level as the rest, nevertheless reveal their greater altitude by the intensity of their snowy whiteness. But there were exceptions to this rule, particularly among the women. Thus the tresses of the Princesse de Guermantes, which, when they were grey and had the lustre of silk, seemed to surround her bulging temples with silver, having in the process of turning white acquired the mattness of wool or tow, seemed now on the contrary, for that reason, to be grey, like snow which has become dirty and lost its brilliance.

Some of the old men whose features had changed tried nevertheless to preserve, fixed upon them in a state of permanency, one of those fugitive expressions which one assumes for a second when posing for a photograph, either in order to show off some good point in one's appearance to the best effect or to conceal a deformity; they seemed to have become, once and for all, snapshots of themselves insusceptible of change.

All these people had taken so much time putting on their disguises that generally these passed unobserved by the men and women who saw them every day. Often they had even been granted a reprieve, thanks to which up to a very late hour they were able to remain themselves. But in these cases the disguise, when it finally came, was assumed more rapidly; for disguise, one way or another, was unavoidable. Mme X——, for instance, had never seemed to me to bear any resemblance to her mother, whom I had known only as an old woman, looking like a little hunched Turk. The daughter, on the other hand, I had always known as a charming woman with an upright carriage, and this for many years she had continued to be, for too many years, in fact, for like someone who must not forget, before night falls, to put on his Turkish disguise, she had left things late and had then been obliged precipitately, almost instantaneously, to hunch herself up so as faithfully to reproduce the appearance of an old Turkish woman that had once been presented by her mother.

Someone offered to re-introduce me to a friend of my youth, whom for ten years I had seen almost every day. As I went up to him he said, in a voice which I recognised very well: "How delightful to see you again after all these years!" But if he was delighted, I was astonished. The familiar voice seemed to be emitted by a gramophone more perfect than any I had ever heard, for, though it was the voice of my friend, it issued from the mouth of a corpulent gentleman with greying hair whom I did not know, and I could only suppose that somehow artificially, by a mechanical device, the voice of my old comrade had been lodged in the frame of this stout elderly man who might have been anybody. And yet I knew that this was my friend; the man who had re-introduced us after all these years was not someone one could suspect of playing a practical joke. My friend himself declared that I had not changed, and I realised that in his own eyes he had not changed. I looked at him more closely. And in fact, except that he had grown so much stouter, he had preserved many features of his former self. And yet I could not take it in that it was he. Then I made an effort to remember. In his youth he had had blue eyes, always laughing and perpetually mobile, in search evidently of something the nature of which I had not asked myself, but something no doubt entirely disinterested, Truth perhaps, pursued in perpetual uncertainty, with a sort of boyish irresponsibility and yet with a wavering respect for all the friends of his family. And now that he had become an important politician, able and masterful, his blue eyes, which in any case had not found what they were seeking, had lost their mobility, and this gave them a look of narrow concentration, as though the brow above them were constantly frowning. His expression was no longer one of gaiety, innocence and spontaneity but of guile and dissimulation. Decidedly, I thought, this must be somebody else, but then suddenly I heard, evoked by something that I had said, his laugh, his old loud, unforced laugh, the one that went with the perpetual gay mobility of his glance. Experienced concert-goers find that orchestrated by X—— the music of Z—— becomes absolutely different, a somewhat subtle distinction which the ignorant public does not comprehend—but to hear the wild, choking laugh of a boy emerge from beneath a look which was as pointed as a well-sharpened blue pencil though set slightly crooked in the face, was more than a mere difference of orchestration. He stopped laughing; I should have liked to recognise my friend, but, like Ulysses in the *Odyssey* when he rushes forward to embrace his dead mother, like the spiritualist who tries in vain to elicit from a ghost an answer which will reveal its identity, like the visitor at an exhibition of electricity who cannot believe that the voice which the gramophone restores unaltered to life is not a voice spontaneously emitted by a human being, I was obliged to give up the attempt.

Nobody was exempt from change, but I had to qualify this statement with the observation that for certain people the tempo of Time itself may be accelerated or retarded. By chance I had met in the street, some four or five years earlier, the Vicomtesse de Saint-Fiacre (the daughter-in-law of the one who had been a friend of the Guermantes). Her sculptural features seemed to assure her of eternal youth, and indeed she was still young. But I was quite unable to recognise her now, in spite of her smiles and her greetings, in the lady before me whose features were so eroded that the original lines of her face could no longer be restored. For three years she had been taking cocaine and other drugs. Her eyes, deeply ringed with black, were almost frantic, and her mouth opened in a ghastly grin. She spent months on end now, I was told, without leaving her bed or her *chaise longue*, and had got up just for this party. Time has, it seems, special express trains which bring their passengers swiftly to a premature old age. But on the parallel track trains almost as rapid may be moving in the opposite direction. I took M. de Courgivaux for his son, for he looked the younger of the two—though he must have been more than fifty, he seemed younger than he had when he was thirty. He had found an intelligent doctor and given up alcohol and salt, and the result was that he had returned to his early thirties and on this particular day looked even younger still, for the reason that, that very morning, he had had his hair cut.

A curious thing was that the phenomenon of old age seemed, in its different modes, to take into account particular social habits. Thus certain great noblemen, who had always worn the plainest alpaca cloth and on their heads old straw hats which a man of the lower middle class would have refused to put on, had aged in the same fashion as the gardeners and the peasants in whose society they had spent their lives. Patches of brown had begun to spread over their cheeks and their faces had turned yellower and darker like the pages of an old book.

I thought also of all those who were not at the party because they were too weak or too ill to be there, those whom their secretary, seeking to give the illusion of their survival, had excused by one of those telegrams which from time to time were handed to the Princess, those invalids, moribund for years, who no longer leave their beds, no longer move, and even in the midst of the frivolous attentions of visitors, drawn to them by the curiosity of a tourist or the pious hopes of a pilgrim, with their eyes closed and their rosaries clutched in hands which feebly push back the sheet that is already a mortuary shroud, are like monumental figures, carved by illness until the skeleton is barely covered by a flesh which is white and rigid as marble, lying stretched upon a tomb.

There were men in the room whom I knew to be related to each other without it ever having crossed my mind that they had a feature in common. In admiring, for instance, the old hermit with white hair who was Legrandin in a new guise, I suddenly observed, with the satisfaction almost of a zoologist when he makes a scien-

tific discovery, in the transitions between the planes of his
cheeks the same construction as in the cheeks of his
young nephew, Léonor de Cambremer, who appeared
nevertheless to bear no resemblance to him; and to this
first common feature I added another which I had never
yet noticed in Léonor de Cambremer, and then again others, none of which was included in the youthful synthesis
of the nephew which habitually presented itself to me, until soon I had of him a caricature which was truer and
more profound for not being a literal representation: his
uncle now seemed to me simply a young Cambremer who
to amuse himself had assumed the countenance of the old
man that he would in fact one day be, so that now it was
not merely what had become of the young men of my
own youth but what would one day become of those of
today that impressed upon me with such force the sensation of Time.

The women sought to remain in contact with whatever had been most individual in their charm, but often
the new matter of their face no longer lent itself to this
purpose. Those features upon which had been engraved,
if not their youth, at least their beauty, had disappeared,
and they had endeavoured, with the face that remained to
them, to construct a new beauty for themselves. Displacing, if not the centre of gravity, at least the central point
of the perspective of their face, and grouping their features around it in a new pattern, they began at the age of
fifty to display a beauty of a new type, in the same way
that late in life a man may embark on a new profession or
a piece of ground which has become useless as a vineyard
may be turned over to the production of sugar beet. And
in the midst of these new features a second youth was

made to bloom. The only women who failed to adjust themselves to this kind of transformation were the ones who were either too beautiful or too ugly. The former were like some block of marble, the lines in which, once it has been carved, are final and admit of no change; ageing, they merely crumbled away like a statue. The others, those who had some deformity of face, actually had certain advantages over the beautiful women. In the first place they were the only women whom one instantly recognised. One knew, for example, that in the whole of Paris there could only be one mouth like *that*, so that at this party, where I failed to recognise almost everybody, I could at least put a name to the possessor of the mouth. And then they did not even appear to have aged. Old age is something human; these were monsters, and they no more seemed to have "changed" than whales.

Others too, both men and women, seemed not to have aged; their figures were just as slim, their faces as young. But if, to speak to them, one approached rather near to the face with the smooth skin and the delicate contours it then appeared quite different, like the surface of a plant or a drop of water or blood when you look at it under a microscope. At close quarters I could distinguish numerous greasy patches on the skin which I had supposed to be smooth and which now, because of these marks, I found repulsive. Nor could the lines of the face stand up to this magnification. That of the nose was seen now to be broken and rounded, its regularity marred by the same oily patches as the rest of the face; and the eyes at short range retreated behind pockets of flesh which destroyed the resemblance of the person before me to the one whom I had known in the past and thought that I had met again. So that these particular guests were young when seen at a distance but their age increased with the enlargement of the face and the possibility of studying its different planes; it was dependent upon the spectator, who to see them as young had to place himself correctly and to view them only with that distant inspection which diminishes its object like the lens selected by an oculist for a long-sighted elderly person; old age here, like the presence of infusoria in a drop of water, was made apparent not so much by the advance of the years as by a greater degree of accuracy in the scale of the observer's vision.

Some women no doubt were still easily recognisable: their faces had remained almost the same and they had merely, out of propriety and in harmony with the season, put on the grey hair which was their autumn attire. But there were others, and there were men too, whose metamorphosis was so complete, their identity so impossible to establish—that old monk, for instance, in a corner of the room and the notorious rake whom one remembered, were they the same person?—that it was of the art not so much of the actor as of certain prodigiously gifted mimes, of whom the supreme example is Fregoli, that these fabulous transformations reminded one. The old woman whose charm had resided in her indefinable and melancholy smile would have liked to weep, at first, when she realised that this smile could no longer break through with its radiance to the surface of the plaster mask with which age had covered her face. Then suddenly, weary of trying to please and finding it more intelligent, more amusing to resign herself to the inevitable, she had started to use it like a mask in the theatre, as a way of making people laugh. But with few exceptions the women strained every nerve in a ceaseless struggle against old age and held out the mirror of their features towards beauty, as it receded, as to a setting sun whose last rays they longed passionately to preserve. To achieve this end some of them tried to plane away all the irregularities of their face, to enlarge its smooth, white surface, renouncing the piquancy of dimples that had not long to live, the archness of a smile condemned and already half disarmed, while others, seeing that beauty had vanished beyond recall and taking refuge perforce in expression, like an actress whose skill in the art of diction makes up for the loss of her voice, clung desperately to a pout, to a pretty crow's-foot, to a dreamy glance, to a smile sometimes which, because of the incoordination of muscles that no longer obeyed the brain, made them look as though they were in tears.

Even in the case of the men who had changed very little—those, for instance, whose moustaches had merely turned white—one felt that the changes were not strictly speaking material. One might have been looking at these men through a vapour which imparted its own colour to them, or through a tinted optical glass which altered the appearance of their faces and above all, by making them slightly blurred, showed one that what it enabled us to see "life-size" was in reality a long way away, separated from us, it is true, by a distance other than spatial but from the depths of which, nevertheless, as from a further shore, we felt that they had as much difficulty in recognising us as we them. Only perhaps Mme de Forcheville, as though she had been injected with some liquid, some sort of paraffin with the property of inflating the skin but protecting it from change, might have been an old-fashioned cocotte "stuffed" for the benefit of posterity. Setting out from the idea that people have remained unchanged, one finds them old. But once one starts with the idea that they are old, meeting them again one does not think that they look too bad. In the case of Odette one could say much more than this; her appearance, once one knew her age and expected to see an old woman, seemed a defiance of the laws of chronology, more miraculous even than the defiance of the laws of nature by the conservation of radium. If I failed at first to recognise her, this was, uniquely, not because she had but because she had not changed. I had learnt in the last hour to take into account the new items that are added to people by Time and that had to be subtracted by me if I wanted to find my friends again as I had known them in the past, and I now rapidly made this calculation, adding to the former Odette the number of years which had passed over her; but the result at which I arrived was a person who could not, it seemed, be the one before me, precisely because she, the woman at the party, was so like the Odette of old days. In part, of course, this effect was achieved by rouge and dye. Beneath her flat golden hair—a little like the ruffled chignon of a big mechanical doll, above a face with a fixed expression of surprise which might also have belonged to a doll—on top of which rested a straw hat that was also flat, she might well have been "The Exhibition of 1878" (of which she would without a doubt, above all had she then been as old as she was today, have been the most fantastic marvel) coming forward on to the stage to speak her two lines in a New Year revue, but the Exhibition of 1878 played by an actress who was still young.

Another figure from the same period, who had been a minister before the era of Boulangism and was now in the

government again, passed beside us, wafting to the ladies
a tremulous and remote smile, but with the air of being
imprisoned in a thousand chains of the past, like a little
phantom paraded up and down by an invisible hand or—
diminished in stature and altered in substance—a reduced version of himself in pumice stone. This former
Prime Minister, now so well received in the Faubourg
Saint-Germain, had at one time been the object of criminal proceedings, and had been execrated both by society
and by the people. But thanks to the renewal of the individuals who compose these two bodies and to the renewal,
within the surviving individuals, of passions and even of
memories, nobody now knew this and he was held in high
honour. For the fact is that there is no humiliation so
great that one should not accept it with unconcern, knowing that at the end of a few years our misdeeds will be no
more than an invisible dust buried beneath the smiling
and blooming peace of nature. The man whose reputation
is momentarily under a cloud will soon find himself,
thanks to the balancing mechanism of Time, caught and
held between two new social levels which will have for
him nothing but deference and admiration. But Time
alone will achieve this result and at the moment of his
downfall nothing can console him for the fact that the
young dairy-maid across the street heard the crowd shout
"Bribery and corruption!" at him and saw them shake
their fists as he climbed into the Black Maria—for the
dairy-maid does not see things in the perspective of Time
and does not know that the men who receive the incense
of praise from this morning's newspapers were yesterday
in disgrace and that the fallen politician, who at this moment feels the shadow of prison bars upon him and yet

perhaps, as he thinks of the dairy-maid, cannot find
within himself the humble words which might win her
sympathy, will one day be extolled by the press and
sought after by duchesses. And Time in the same way
makes family quarrels recede into the distance. At the
Princesse de Guermantes's party, for instance, there was a
couple, husband and wife, who were respectively nephew
and niece of two men, now dead, who had once come to
blows and—worse still—one of them, still further to hu-
miliate the other, had sent him as seconds his concierge
and his butler, indicating that in his judgment gentlemen
would have been too good for him. But these stories
slumbered in the pages of the newspapers of thirty years
ago and nobody now remembered them. And thus the
drawing-room of the Princesse de Guermantes—illuminated, oblivious, flowery—was like a peaceful cemetery.
Time in this room had done more than decompose the
living creatures of a former age, it had rendered possible,
had created new associations.

To return to the politician, in spite of his change of
physical substance, just as profound as the transformation
of the moral ideas which his name now connoted to the
public, in spite (to say the same thing more simply) of the
lapse of so many years since he had been Prime Minister,
he was once again a member of the Cabinet, whose leader
had given him a portfolio in the recent re-shuffle rather in
the way that a theatrical producer gives a part to an old
actress friend long since retired, whom he judges nevertheless to be, even now, better able to interpret a part
with subtlety than any of her younger successors and
whom he knows, also, to be in financial straits, and who
in the event, at the age of nearly eighty, exhibits once

more to the public almost the fullness of her talent, with
that continued vitality which one is later astonished to
have observed up to the very threshold of death.

But if the politician was extraordinary, Mme de
Forcheville was so miraculous that one could not even say
that she had grown young again—it was more as though,
with all her carmines and her russets, she had bloomed
for a second time. Even more than the embodiment of the
Universal Exhibition of 1878, she might have been the
principal rarity and attraction of a flower show of today.
And indeed, for me she seemed to say, not so much: "I
am the Exhibition of 1878" as: "I am the Allée des Acacias of 1892." That was where, it seemed, she still might
have been. And just because she had not changed she
seemed scarcely to be alive. She looked like a rose that has
been sterilised. I greeted her and her eyes travelled for a
while over my face, searching for my name as a schoolboy
searches on the face of his examiner for the answer that
he might more easily have found in his own head. Then I
told her who I was and at once, as though the sound of
my name had broken a spell and I had lost the look of an
arbutus tree or a kangaroo which age no doubt had given
me, she recognised me and started to talk to me in that
strangely individual voice which people who had admired
her acting in some little theatre were astonished, when
they were invited to meet her at a luncheon party, to find
again, throughout the whole conversation, for as long as
they cared to listen, in each one of her remarks. It was a
voice that had not changed, exaggeratedly warm, caress-
ing, with a trace of an English accent. And yet, just as her
eyes appeared to be looking at me from a distant shore,
her voice was sad, almost suppliant, like the voice of the

shades in the *Odyssey*. Odette would still have been able to act. I complimented her on her youthfulness. "How nice of you, *my dear*," she said, "thank you," and, as it was difficult for her to express a sentiment, even the most sincere, in a manner that was not rendered artificial by her anxiety to be what she supposed was smart, she repeated several times: "Thank you *so* much, thank you *so* much." I meanwhile, who had once walked miles to see her pass in the Bois, who the first time that I had visited her house had listened to the sound of her voice as it fell from her lips as though it were some priceless treasure, now found the minutes that I was obliged to pass in her company interminable simply because I did not know what on earth to say to her, and I withdrew, thinking to myself that not only had Gilberte's remark, "You take me for my mother" been true[9] but that the likeness could only be flattering to the daughter.

Gilberte, for that matter, was by no means the only guest at the party in whom family features had become apparent which hitherto had remained as invisible in their faces as the coiled and hidden parts of a seed which one day will burst out into growth in a manner that it is impossible to foresee. Thus, in this woman or that man, at about the age of fifty an enormous maternal hook had arrived to transform a nose which until then had been straight and pure. And the complexion of another woman, a banker's daughter, from being as fresh as that of a milkmaid grew first russet and then coppery and finally assumed as it were a reflexion of the gold which her father had so lovingly handled. Some people had even in the end come to resemble the district in which they lived, bearing on their faces a sort of replica of the Rue de l'Arcade or the Avenue du Bois or the Rue de l'Elysée. But most commonly they reproduced the features of their parents.

Alas, Mme de Forcheville's second flowering was not to last for ever. Less than three years later I was to see her at an evening party given by Gilberte, not quite in her dotage but showing signs of senility and grown incapable of concealing beneath a mask of immobility what she was thinking, or rather (for thinking is too elevated a term) what she was passively experiencing, nodding her head, compressing her lips, shaking her shoulders in response to every impression that she felt, like a drunkard or a small child or those poets who, unaware of their surroundings and seized by inspiration, compose verses in the midst of a social occasion and frown and pout as they proceed to the dinner-table with an astonished lady on their arm. The impressions of Mme de Forcheville—except that single sentiment which was the cause of her presence at the party: her tender affection for her beloved daughter and her pride that she should be giving so brilliant a party, a pride which, in the mother, could not disguise the melancholy of being herself now nothing—these impressions were not joyful, their message was merely that she must not relax her defence against the snubs which were showered upon her, a defence, however, as timorous as that of a child. On all sides one heard people say: "I don't know whether Mme de Forcheville recognises me, perhaps I ought to get someone to introduce me to her again." "You may as well spare yourself the trouble," a booming voice would reply, its owner not suspecting that Gilberte's mother could hear every word—or perhaps not caring if she could. "It's quite unnecessary. You wouldn't find her at all amusing! She's best left alone in her corner. She's a bit gaga, you know." Furtively Mme de Forcheville shot a glance from her eyes which had remained so beautiful at the authors of these offensive remarks, then swiftly withdrew it for fear of having been rude, but was distressed nevertheless by the insult, and though she smothered her feeble indignation one saw her head shake and her breast heave until presently another glance was shot at another guest who had expressed himself just as discourteously— yet nothing of all this seemed to surprise her very much, for having felt extremely unwell for several days, she had covertly suggested to her daughter that she should put off her party, but her daughter had refused. Mme de Forcheville did not love her any the less: the sight of all the duchesses entering the room, the admiration of all the guests for the large new house, flooded her heart with joy, and when finally the Marquise de Sabran was announced, who was at that moment the lady at whom one arrived after laboriously ascending the topmost rungs of the social ladder, Mme de Forcheville felt that she had been a good and far-sighted mother and that her maternal task was accomplished. New guests arrived to titter at her and again she shot her glances and spoke to herself, if a mute language expressed only in gesture can be described as speech. Beautiful still, she had become—what she had never been in the past—infinitely pathetic; she who had been unfaithful to Swann and to everybody found now that the entire universe was unfaithful to her, and so weak had she become that, the roles being reversed, she no longer dared to defend herself even against men. And soon she would not defend herself even against death. But we have anticipated, and let us now go back three years, to the afternoon party which is being given by the Princesse de Guermantes.

I had difficulty in recognising my friend Bloch, who was now in fact no longer Bloch since he had adopted, not merely as a pseudonym but as a name, the style of Jacques du Rozier, beneath which it would have needed my grandfather's flair to detect the "sweet vale of Hebron" and those "chains of Israel" which my old schoolmate seemed definitively to have broken. Indeed an English chic had completely transformed his appearance and smoothed away, as with a plane, everything in it that was susceptible of such treatment. The once curly hair, now brushed flat, with a parting in the middle, glistened with brilliantine. His nose remained large and red, but seemed now to owe its tumescence to a sort of permanent cold which served also to explain the nasal intonation with which he languidly delivered his studied sentences, for just as he had found a way of doing his hair which suited his complexion, so he had found a voice which suited his pronunciation and which gave to his old nasal twang the air of a disdainful refusal to articulate that was in keeping with his inflamed nostrils. And thanks to the way in which he brushed his hair, to the suppression of his moustache, to the elegance of his whole figure—thanks, that is to say, to his determination—his Jewish nose was now scarcely more visible than is the deformity of a hunchbacked woman who skilfully arranges her appearance. But above all—and one saw this the moment one set eyes on him—the significance of his physiognomy had been altered by a formidable monocle. By introducing an element of machinery into Bloch's face this monocle ab-

solved it of all those difficult duties which a human face is
normally called upon to discharge, such as being beautiful
or expressing intelligence or kindliness or effort. The
monocle's mere presence even absolved an interlocutor, in
the first place, from asking himself whether the face was
pleasant to look at or not, just as, when a shop-assistant
has told you that some object imported from England is
"the last word in chic," you no longer dare to ask yourself
whether you really like it. In any case, behind the lens of
this monocle Bloch was now installed in a position as
lofty, as remote and as comfortable as if it had been the
glass partition of a limousine and, so that his face should
match the smooth hair and the monocle, his features
never now expressed anything at all.

Bloch asked me to introduce him to the Prince de
Guermantes, and this operation raised for me not a
shadow of those difficulties which I had come up against
on the day when I went to an evening party at his house
for the first time, difficulties which had then seemed to
me a part of the natural order, whereas now I found it the
simplest thing in the world to introduce to the Prince a
guest whom he had invited himself and I should even
have ventured, without warning, to bring to his party and
introduce to him someone whom he had not invited. Was
this because, since that distant era, I had become an intimate member, though for a long time now a forgotten
one, of that fashionable world in which I had then been
so new? Was it, on the contrary, because I did not really
belong to that world, so that all the imaginary difficulties
which beset people in society no longer existed for me
once my shyness had vanished? Was it because, having
gradually come to see what lay behind the first (and often

the second and even the third) artificial appearance of others, I sensed behind the haughty disdain of the Prince a great human avidity to know people, to make the acquaintance even of those whom he affected to despise? Was it also because the Prince himself had changed, like so many men in whom the arrogance of their youth and of their middle years is tempered by the gentleness of old age—particularly as the new men and the unknown ideas whose progress they had once resisted are now familiar to them, at least by sight, and they see that they are accepted all round them in society—a change which takes place more effectually if old age is assisted in its task by some good quality or some vice in the individual which enlarges the circle of his acquaintance, or by the revolution wrought by a political conversion such as that of the Prince to Dreyfusism?

Bloch started to question me, as years ago, when I first began to go to parties, I had questioned others—a habit which I had not quite lost—about the people whom I had known in society in the old days and who were as remote, as unlike anybody else, as those inhabitants of the world of Combray whom I had often sought to "place" exactly. But Combray for me had a shape so distinctive, so impossible to confuse with anything else, that it might have been a piece of a jigsaw puzzle which I could never succeed in fitting into the map of France. "So the Prince de Guermantes can give me no idea either of Swann or of M. de Charlus?" asked Bloch, whose manner of speaking I had borrowed long ago and who now frequently imitated mine. "None at all." "But what was so different about them?" "To know that, you would have had to hear them talk yourself. But that is impossible. Swann is dead and M. de Charlus is as good as dead. But the differences were enormous." And seeing Bloch's eyes shine at the thought of what these marvellous personages must have been, I wondered whether I was not exaggerating the pleasure which I had got from their company, since pleasure was something that I had never felt except when I was alone and the real differentiation of impressions takes place only in our imagination. Bloch seemed to guess what I was thinking. "Perhaps you make it out to be more wonderful than it really was," he said; "our hostess today, for instance, the Princesse de Guermantes, I know she is no longer young, still it is not so many years since you were telling me about her incomparable charm, her marvellous beauty. Well, I grant you she has a certain splendour, and she certainly has those extraordinary eyes you used to talk about, but I can't say I find her so fantastically beautiful. Of course, one sees that she is a real aristocrat, but still . . ." I was obliged to tell Bloch that the woman I had described to him was not the one he was talking about. The Princesse de Guermantes had died and the present wife of the Prince, who had been ruined by the collapse of Germany, was the former Mme Verdurin. "That can't be right, I looked in this year's Gotha," Bloch naïvely confessed to me, "and I found the Prince de Guermantes, living at this address where we are now and married to someone of the utmost grandeur, let me try to remember, yes, married to Sidonie, Duchesse de Duras, née des Baux." This was correct. Mme Verdurin, shortly after the death of her husband, had married the aged and impoverished Duc de Duras, who had made her a cousin of the Prince de Guermantes and had died after two years of marriage. He had served as a useful transition for Mme

Verdurin, who now, by a third marriage, had become
Princesse de Guermantes and occupied in the Faubourg
Saint-Germain a lofty position which would have caused
much astonishment at Combray, where the ladies of the
Rue de l'Oiseau, Mme Goupil's daughter and Mme Sazerat's step-daughter, had during these last years, before
she married for the third time, spoken with a sneer of
"the Duchesse de Duras" as though this were a role
which had been allotted to Mme Verdurin in a play. In
fact, the Combray principle of caste requiring that she
should die, as she had lived, as Mme Verdurin, her title,
which was not deemed to confer upon her any new power
in society, did not so much enhance as damage her reputation. For "to make tongues wag," that phrase which in
every sphere of life is applied to a woman who has a
lover, could be used also in the Faubourg Saint-Germain
of women who write books and in the respectable society
of Combray of those who make marriages which, for
better or for worse, are "unsuitable." After the twice-
widowed lady had married the Prince de Guermantes, the
only possible comment was that he was a false Guermantes, an impostor. For me, in this purely nominal identity, in the fact that there was once again a Princesse de
Guermantes and that she had absolutely nothing in common with the one who had cast her spell upon me, who
now no longer existed and had been robbed of name and
title like a defenceless woman of her jewels, there was
something as profoundly sad as in seeing the material objects which the Princess Hedwige had once possessed—
her country house and everything that had been
hers—pass into the possession and enjoyment of another
woman. The succession of a new individual to a name is

melancholy, as is all succession, all usurpation of property; and yet for ever and ever, without interruption, there
would come, sweeping on, a flood of new Princesses de
Guermantes—or rather, centuries old, replaced from age
to age by a series of different women, of different actresses playing the same part and then each in her turn
sinking from sight beneath the unvarying and immemorial
placidity of the name, one single Princesse de Guermantes, ignorant of death and indifferent to all that
changes and wounds our mortal hearts.

Of course, even these external changes in the figures
whom I had known were no more than symbols of an internal change which had been effected day by day. Perhaps these people had continued to perform the same
actions, but gradually the idea which they entertained
both of their own activities and of their acquaintances had
slightly altered its shape, so that at the end of a few years,
though the names were unchanged, the activities that they
enjoyed and the people whom they loved had become different and, as they themselves had become different individuals, it was hardly surprising that they should have
new faces.

But there were also guests whom I failed to recognise
for the reason that I had never known them, for in this
drawing-room, as well as upon individuals the chemistry
of Time had been at work upon society. This coterie,
within the specific nature of which, delimited as it was by
certain affinities that attracted to it all the great princely
names of Europe and by forces of an opposite kind which
repelled from it anything that was not aristocratic, I had
found, I thought, a sort of corporeal refuge for the name
of Guermantes, this coterie, which had seemed to confer

upon that name its ultimate reality, had itself, in its inner-most and as I had thought stable constitution, undergone a profound transformation. The presence of people whom I had seen in quite different social settings and whom I would never have expected to penetrate into this one, as-tonished me less than the intimate familiarity with which they were now received in it, on Christian name terms; a certain complex of aristocratic prejudices, of snobbery, which in the past automatically maintained a barrier be-tween the name of Guermantes and all that did not har-monise with it, had ceased to function. Enfeebled or broken, the springs of the machine could no longer per-form their task of keeping out the crowd; a thousand alien elements made their way in and all homogeneity, all con-sistency of form and colour was lost. The Faubourg Saint-Germain was like some senile dowager now, who replies only with timid smiles to the insolent servants who invade her drawing-rooms, drink her orangeade, present their mistresses to her. However, the sensation of time having slipped away and of the annihilation of a small part of my own past was conveyed to me less vividly by the de-struction of that coherent whole which the Guermantes drawing-room had once been than by the annihilation of even the knowledge of the thousand reasons, the thousand subtle distinctions thanks to which one man who was still to be found in that drawing-room today was clearly in his natural and proper place there while another, who rubbed shoulders with him, wore in these surroundings an aspect of dubious novelty. And this ignorance was not merely ig-norance of society, but of politics, of everything. For memory was of shorter duration in individuals than life, and besides, the very young, who had never possessed the recollections which had vanished from the minds of their elders, now formed part of society (and with perfect legitimacy, even in the genealogical sense of the word), and the origins of the people whom they saw there being forgotten or unknown, they accepted them at the particular point of their elevation or their fall at which they found them, supposing that things had always been as they were today, that the social position of Mme Swann and the Princesse de Guermantes and Bloch had always been very great, that Clemenceau and Viviani had always been conservatives. And as certain facts have a greater power of survival than others, the detested memory of the Dreyfus case persisting vaguely in these young people thanks to what they had heard their fathers say, if one told them that Clemenceau had been a Dreyfusard, they replied: "Impossible, you are making a confusion, he is absolutely on the other side of the fence." Ministers with a tarnished reputation and women who had started life as prostitutes were now held to be paragons of virtue. (Among the guests was a distinguished man who had recently, in a famous lawsuit, made a deposition of which the sole value resided in the lofty moral character of the witness, in the face of which both judge and counsel had bowed their heads, with the result that two people had been convicted. Consequently, when he entered the room there was a stir of curiosity and of deference. This man was Morel. I was perhaps the only person present who knew that he had once been kept by Saint-Loup and at the same time by a friend of Saint-Loup. In spite of these recollections he greeted me with pleasure, though with a certain reserve. He remembered the time when we had seen each other at Balbec, and these recollections had for him the poetry and the melancholy of youth.) Someone having inquired of a young man of the best possible family whether Gilberte's mother had not formerly been the subject of scandal, the young nobleman replied that it was true that in the earlier part of her life she had been married to an adventurer of the name of Swann, but that subsequently she had married one of the most prominent men in society, the Comte de Forcheville. No doubt there were still a few people in the room—the Duchesse de Guermantes was one—who would have smiled at this assertion (which, in its denial of Swann's position as a man of fashion, seemed to me monstrous, although I myself, long ago at Combray, had shared my great-aunt's belief that Swann could not be acquainted with "princesses"), and others also not in the room, women who might have been there had they not almost ceased to leave their homes, the Duchesses of Montmorency and Mouchy and Sagan, who had been close friends of Swann and had never set eyes on this man Forcheville, who was not received in society at the time when they went to parties. But it could not be denied that the society of those days, like the faces now drastically altered and the fair hair replaced by white, existed now only in the memories of individuals whose number was diminishing day by day. During the war Bloch had given up going out socially, had ceased to visit the houses which he had once frequented and where he had cut anything but a brilliant figure. On the other hand, he had published a whole series of works full of those absurd sophistical arguments which, so as not to be inhibited by them myself, I was struggling to demolish today, works without originality but which gave to young men and to many society women the impression of a rare and lofty intellect, a sort of genius. And so it was after a complete break between his earlier social existence and this later one that he had, in a society itself reconstituted, embarked upon a new phase of his life, honoured and glorious, in which he played the role of a great man. Young people naturally did not know that at his somewhat advanced age he was in fact making his first appearance on the social scene, particularly as, by sprinkling his conversation with the few names which he had retained from his acquaintance with Saint-Loup, he was able to impart to his prestige of the moment a sort of indefinite recession in depth. In any case he was regarded as one of those men of talent who in every epoch have flourished in the highest society, and nobody thought that he had ever frequented any other.

Survivors of the older generation assured me that society had completely changed and now opened its doors to people who in their day would never have been received, and this comment was both true and untrue. On the one hand it was untrue, because those who made it failed to take into account the curve of time which caused the society of the present to see these newly received people at their point of arrival, whilst they, the older generation, remembered them at their point of departure. And this was nothing new, for in the same way, when they themselves had first entered society, there were people in it who had just arrived and whose lowly origins others remembered. In society as it exists today a single generation suffices for the change which formerly over a period of centuries transformed a middle-class name like Colbert into an aristocratic one. And yet, from another point of view there was a certain truth in the comments; for, if the social position of individuals is liable to change (like the fortunes

and the alliances and the hatreds of nations), so too are
the most deeply rooted ideas and customs and among
them even the idea that you cannot receive anybody who
is not chic. Not only does snobbishness change in form, it
might one day altogether disappear—like war itself—and
radicals and Jews might become members of the Jockey.
Some people, who in my own early days in society, giving
grand dinner-parties with only such guests as the
Princesse de Guermantes, the Duchesse de Guermantes
and the Princesse de Parme, and themselves being entertained by these ladies with every show of respect, had
been regarded, perhaps correctly, as among the most
unimpeachable social figures of the time, yet they had
passed away without leaving any trace behind them. Possibly they were foreign diplomats, formerly *en poste* in
Paris and now returned to their own countries. Perhaps a
scandal, a suicide, an elopement had made it impossible
for them to reappear in society; perhaps they were merely
Germans. But their name owed its lustre only to their
own vanished social position and was no longer borne by
anyone in the fashionable world: if I mentioned them nobody knew whom I was talking about, if I spelt out the
name the general assumption was that they were some
sort of adventurers. People, on the other hand, who according to the social code with which I had been familiar
ought not to have been at this party, were now to my
great astonishment on terms of close friendship with
women of the very best families and the latter had only
submitted to the boredom of appearing at the Princesse de
Guermantes's party for the sake of these new friends. For
the most characteristic feature of this new society was the

prodigious ease with which individuals moved up or down the social scale.

If in the eyes of the younger generations the Duchesse de Guermantes seemed to be of little account because she was acquainted with actresses and such people, the elder, the now old ladies of her family, still considered her to be an extraordinary personage, partly because they knew and appreciated her birth, her heraldic pre-eminence, her intimate friendships with what Mme de Forcheville would have called *royalties*, but even more because she despised the parties given by the family and was bored at them and her cousins knew that they could never count upon her attendance. Her connexions with the theatrical and political worlds, in any case only vaguely known in the family, merely had the effect of enhancing her rarity and therefore her prestige. So that while in political and artistic society she was regarded as a creature whom it was hard to define, a sort of unfrocked priestess of the Faubourg Saint-Germain who consorted with Under-Secretaries of State and stars of the theatre, in the Faubourg Saint-Germain itself if one was giving an important evening party one would say: "Is it worth while even asking Oriane? She won't come. Perhaps one should, just for form's sake, but one knows what to expect." And if, at about half past ten, in a dazzling costume and with a hard glint in her eyes which bore witness to her contempt for all her female cousins, Oriane made her entrance, pausing first on the threshold with a sort of majestic disdain, and remained for a whole hour, this was even more of a treat for the old and noble lady who was giving the party than it would have been in the past for a theatrical manager who had obtained a vague promise from Sarah Bernhardt that she would contribute something to a programme, had the great actress, contrary to all expectation, turned up and recited, in the most unaffected and obliging way, not the piece which she had promised but twenty others. For although all the women there were among the smartest in Paris, the presence of this Oriane who was addressed in a condescending manner by Under-Secretaries and continued none the less ("intelligence governs the world") to try to make the acquaintance of more and more of them, had had the effect which nothing could have achieved without her, of placing the dowager's evening party in a class apart from and above all the other dowagers' evening parties of the same *season* (to use another of those English expressions of which Mme de Forcheville was so fond) which she, Oriane, had not taken the trouble to attend.

As soon as I had finished talking to the Prince de Guermantes, Bloch seized hold of me and introduced me to a young woman who had heard a lot about me from the Duchesse de Guermantes and who was one of the most fashionable women of the day. Not only was her name entirely unknown to me, but it appeared that those of the various branches of the Guermantes family could not be very familiar to her, for she inquired of an American woman how it was that Mme de Saint-Loup seemed to be on such intimate terms with all the most aristocratic people in the room. Now the American was married to the Comte de Farcy, an obscure cousin of the Forchevilles, for whom Forcheville was the grandest name in the world. So she replied ingenuously: "Well, isn't she a Forcheville by birth? And what could be grander than that?" But at least Mme de Farcy, though she naïvely be-

lieved the name of Forcheville to be superior to that of
Saint-Loup, knew something about the latter. But to the
charming lady who was a friend of Bloch and the
Duchesse de Guermantes it was utterly unknown, and,
being somewhat muddle-headed, she replied in all good
faith to a young girl who asked her how Mme de Saint-
Loup was related to their host, the Prince de Guermantes:
"Through the Forchevilles," a piece of information which
the girl passed on as if she had known it all her life to one
of her friends, a bad-tempered and nervous girl, who
turned as red as a turkeycock the first time a gentleman
said to her that it was not through the Forchevilles that
Gilberte was connected with the Guermantes, with the result that the gentleman supposed that he had made a mistake, adopted the erroneous explanation himself and lost
no time in propagating it. For the American woman
dinner-parties and fashionable entertainments were a sort
of Berlitz School. She heard the names and she repeated
them, without having first learnt their precise value and
significance. To someone who asked whether Tansonville
had come to Gilberte from her father M. de Forcheville I
heard the explanation given that, on the contrary, it was a
property in her husband's family, that Tansonville was a
neighbouring estate to Guermantes and had belonged to
Mme de Marsantes, that it had been heavily mortgaged
and the mortgage paid off with Gilberte's dowry. And finally, a veteran of the old guard having exchanged memories with me of Swann, friend of the Sagans and the
Mouchys, and Bloch's American friend having asked me
how I had known Swann, the old man declared that this
must have been in the house of Mme de Guermantes, not
suspecting that what Swann represented for me was a

country neighbour and a young friend of my grandfather. Mistakes of this kind have been made by the most distinguished men and are regarded as particularly serious in any society of a conservative temper. Saint-Simon, wishing to show that Louis XIV was of an ignorance which "sometimes made him fall, in public, into the most gross absurdities," gives of this ignorance only two examples, which are that the King, not knowing either that Renel belonged to the family of Clermont-Gallerande or that Saint-Herem belonged to that of Montmorin, treated these two men as though they were of low extraction. But at least, in so far as concerns Saint-Herem, we have the consolation of knowing that the King did not die in error, for "very late in life" he was disabused by M. de La Rochefoucauld. "Even then," adds Saint-Simon with a touch of pity, "it was necessary to explain to him what these houses were, for their names conveyed nothing to him."

This forgetfulness, which with its vigorous growth covers so rapidly even the most recent past, this encroaching ignorance, creates as its own counter-agent a minor species of erudition, all the more precious for being rare, which is concerned with genealogies, the true social position of people, the reasons of love or money or some other kind for which they have allied or misallied themselves in marriage with this family or that, an erudition which is highly prized in all societies where a conservative spirit rules, which my grandfather possessed in the highest degree with regard to the middle classes of Combray and of Paris and which Saint-Simon valued so highly that when he comes to celebrate the marvellous intelligence of the Prince de Conti, before speaking of the recognised branches of knowledge, or rather as though this were the first of them all, he praises him as "a man of a very fine mind, enlightened, just, exact, wide-ranging; vastly well read and of a retentive memory; skilled in genealogies, their chimeras and their realities; of a politeness variously accommodated to rank and merit, rendering all those courtesies that the princes of the blood owe but no longer render and even explaining why he acted as he did and how the other princes exceeded their rights. The knowledge which he had gained from books and from conversation afforded him material for the most obliging comments possible upon the birth, the offices, etc." In a less exalted sphere, in all that pertained to the bourgeois society of Combray and Paris, my grandfather possessed this same knowledge with no less exactitude and savoured it with no less relish. The epicures, the connoisseurs who knew that Gilberte was not a Forcheville, that Mme de Cambremer had not been born a Méséglise nor her nephew's young wife a Valentinois, were already reduced in number. Reduced in number and perhaps not even recruited from among the highest aristocracy (it is not necessarily among devout believers, or even among Catholics of any kind, that you will find those who are most learned on the subject of the *Golden Legend* or the stained glass of the thirteenth century), but often from a minor aristocracy, whose scions have a keener appetite for the high society which they themselves can seldom approach and which the little time that they spend in it leaves them all the more leisure to study. Still, they meet together from time to time and enjoy making each other's acquaintance and giving succulent corporate dinners, like those of the Society of Bibliophiles or the Friends of Rheims, at which

the items on the menu are genealogies. To these feasts
wives are not admitted, but the husbands, when they get
home, remark: "A most interesting dinner. There was a
M. de La Raspelière there who kept us spell-bound with
his explanation of how that Mme de Saint-Loup with the
pretty daughter is not really a Forcheville at all. It was as
good as a novel."

The friend of Bloch and of the Duchesse de Guermantes was not only beautifully dressed and charming,
she was also intelligent and conversation with her was
agreeable, but for me rendered difficult by the novelty to
my ears of the names not only of my interlocutress herself
but also of most of the people she talked about, although
they were the very people who formed the core of society
today. The converse also was true: at her request I related
various anecdotes of the past, and many of the names
which I pronounced meant absolutely nothing to her, they
had all sunk into oblivion (all those at least which had
shone only with the individual brilliance of a single person and were not the surname, permanent and generic, of
some famous aristocratic family, whose exact title even so
the young woman seldom knew, having perhaps recently
misheard a name at a dinner-party and proceeded to form
quite wrong ideas about its pedigree) and she had for the
most part never heard them mentioned, having, not
merely because she was young but because she had not
lived in France for long and when she first arrived had
known nobody, only started to go into society some years
after I myself had withdrawn from it. So that though for
ordinary speech she and I used the same language, when
it came to names our vocabularies had nothing in common. The name of Mme Leroi happened to fall from my

lips, and by chance, thanks to some elderly admirer, himself an old friend of Mme de Guermantes, my interlocutress had heard of her. But only vaguely and inaccurately, as I saw from the contemptuous tone in which this snobbish young woman replied to me: "Yes, I know who you mean by Mme Leroi, an old friend of Bergotte's, I believe," a tone which barely concealed the comment: "a woman whom I should never have wished to have in my house." I realised at once that the old friend of Mme de Guermantes, as a perfect man of the world imbued with the Guermantes spirit, one of the essential elements of which was not to appear to attach too much importance to aristocratic friendships, had thought it too stupid, too anti-Guermantes to say: "Mme Leroi, who was a friend of every Royalty and Duchess in Paris," and had preferred to say: "She could be quite amusing. Let me tell you the retort she made to Bergotte one day." But for people who are not already in the know information gleaned in this way from conversation is equivalent only to that which is doled out to the masses by the press and which makes them believe alternatively, depending upon the views of their newspaper, either that M. Loubet and M. Reinach are brigands or that they are great patriots. In the eyes of my interlocutress Mme Leroi had been something like Mme Verdurin as she was before her social transformation, but with less brilliance and with a little clan consisting of one member only, Bergotte. But at least this young woman, by pure chance, had heard the name of Mme Leroi, and she is one of the last of whom so much can be said. Today that name is utterly forgotten, nor is there any good reason why it should be remembered. It does not figure even in the index to the post-

humous memoirs of Mme de Villeparisis, whose mind
was so much occupied with the lady who bore it. And if
the Marquise has omitted to mention Mme Leroi, this is
less because in her lifetime that lady had been less than
friendly towards her than because, once she was dead, no
one was likely to take any interest in her, it is a silence
dictated less by the social resentment of a woman than by
the literary tact of an author. My conversation with
Bloch's fashionable friend was delightful, for she was an
intelligent young woman; but this difference which I have
described between our two vocabularies made it at the
same time both awkward and instructive. For although we
know that the years pass, that youth gives way to old age,
that fortunes and thrones crumble (even the most solid
among them) and that fame is transitory, the manner in
which—by means of a sort of snapshot—we take cognisance of this moving universe whirled along by Time, has
the contrary effect of immobilising it. And the result is
that we see as always young the men and women whom
we have known young, that those whom we have known
old we retrospectively endow in the past with the virtues
of old age, that we trust unreservedly in the credit of a
millionaire and the influence of a reigning monarch,
knowing with our reason, though we do not actually believe, that tomorrow both the one and the other may be
fugitives stripped of all power. In a more restricted field,
one that is purely social—as in a simpler problem which
initiates a student into difficulties that are more complex
but of the same order—the unintelligibility which, in my
conversation with the young woman, resulted from the
fact that the two of us had lived in the same world but
with an interval of twenty-five years between us, gave me

the impression, and might have strengthened within me the sense, of History.

And indeed this ignorance of people's true social position which every ten years causes the new fashionable elect to arise in all the glory of the moment as though the past had never existed, which makes it impossible for an American woman just landed in Europe to see that in an age when Bloch was nobody M. de Charlus was socially supreme in Paris and that Swann, who put himself out to please M. Bontemps, had himself been treated with every mark of friendship by the Prince of Wales, this ignorance, which exists not only in new arrivals but also in those who have always frequented adjacent but distinct regions of society, is itself also invariably an effect—but an effect operative not so much upon a whole social stratum as within individuals—of Time. No doubt we ourselves may change our social habitat and our manner of life and yet our memory, clinging still to the thread of our personal identity, will continue to attach to itself at successive epochs the recollection of the various societies in which, even if it be forty years earlier, we have lived. Bloch the guest of the Prince de Guermantes remembered perfectly well the humble Jewish environment in which he had lived at the age of eighteen, and Swann, when he was no longer in love with Mme Swann but with a waitress at that same Colombin's where at one time Mme Swann had thought it smart to go and drink tea (as she did also at the tea-room in the Rue Royale), Swann was very well aware of his own social value—he remembered Twickenham and had no doubt in his mind about the reasons for which he chose to go to Colombin's rather than to call on the Duchesse de Broglie, and he knew also that, had he been a thousand times less "smart" than he was, he would not have become the slightest bit smarter by frequenting Colombin's or the Ritz, since anybody can go to these places who pays. And no doubt the friends, too, of Bloch or of Swann remembered the little Jewish coterie or the invitations to Twickenham and thus, as though they, the friends, were other not very clearly defined "I's" of the two men, made no division in their memories between the fashionable Bloch of today and the sordid Bloch of the past, between the Swann who in his latter days could be seen at Colombin's and the Swann of Buckingham Palace. But these friends were to some extent Swann's neighbours in life, their own lives had developed along lines near enough to his own for their memories to be fairly full of him, whereas other men who were more remote from Swann—at a greater distance measured not perhaps socially but in terms of intimacy, which caused their knowledge of him to be vaguer and their meetings with him rarer—possessed of him recollections that were less numerous and in consequence conceptions that were less fixed. And after thirty years a comparative stranger of this kind no longer has any precise recollection with the power to change the value of the person whom he has before his eyes by prolonging him into the past. In the last years of Swann's life I had heard people, even people in society, say when his name was mentioned, as though this had been his title to fame: "You mean the Swann who goes to Colombin's?" And now, with reference to Bloch, even those who ought to have known better might be heard to inquire: "The Guermantes Bloch? The Bloch who is such a friend of the Guermantes?" These errors which split a life in two and, by isolating his present from his past, turn some man whom one is talking about into another, a different man, a creation of yesterday, a man who is no more than the condensation of his current habits (whereas the real man bears within himself an awareness, linking him to the past, of the continuity of his life), these errors, though they too, as I have said, are a result of the passage of Time, are not a social phenomenon but one of memory. And at that very moment I was presented with an example, of a different variety, it is true, but all the more impressive for that, of this forgetfulness which modifies for us our image of a human being. Long ago a young nephew of Mme de Guermantes, the Marquis de Ville-mandois, had behaved towards me with a persistent inso-lence which had obliged me to retaliate by adopting an equally insulting attitude towards him, so that tacitly we had become as it were enemies. This man, while I was engaged in my reflexions upon Time at the Princesse de Guermantes's party, asked someone to introduce him to me, saying that he thought that I had known some of his family, that he had read articles of mine and wanted to make, or re-make, my acquaintance. Now it is true to say that with age he had become, like many others, serious in-stead of rude and frivolous and that he had lost much of his former arrogance, and it is also true that I was a good deal talked about now, though on the strength of some very slight articles, in the circles which he frequented. But these motives for his cordiality, for his making advances to me, were only secondary. The principal motive, or at least the one which permitted the others to come into play, was that—either because he had a worse memory than I or because in the past, since I was then for him a much less important personage than he for me, he had

paid less attention to my ripostes than I to his attacks—
he had completely forgotten our feud. At most my name
recalled to him that he must have seen me, or some member of my family, in the house of one of his aunts. And
being uncertain whether he was being introduced to me
for the first time or whether we were old acquaintances,
he made haste to talk to me about the aunt in whose
house he was sure that we had met, remembering that my
name had often been mentioned there and not remembering our quarrels. A name: that very often is all that remains for us of a human being, not only when he is dead,
but sometimes even in his lifetime. And our notions about
him are so vague or so bizarre and correspond so little to
those that he has of us that we have entirely forgotten
that we once nearly fought a duel with him but remember
that, when he was a child, he used to wear curious yellow
gaiters in the Champs-Elysées, where he, on the contrary,
in spite of our assurances, has no recollection of ever having played with us.

Bloch had come bounding into the room like a hyena.
"He is at home now," I thought, "in drawing-rooms into
which twenty years ago he would never have been able to
penetrate." But he was also twenty years older. He was
nearer to death. What did this profit him? At close quarters, in the translucency of a face in which, at a greater
distance or in a bad light, I saw only youthful gaiety
(whether because it survived there or because I with my
recollections evoked it), I could detect another face, almost frightening, racked with anxiety, the face of an old
Shylock, waiting in the wings, with his make-up prepared,
for the moment when he would make his entry on to the
stage and already reciting his first line under his breath.

In ten years, in drawing-rooms like this which their own feebleness of spirit would allow him to dominate, he would enter on crutches to be greeted as "the Master" for whom a visit to the La Trémoïlles was merely a tedious obligation. And what would this profit him?

From changes accomplished in society I was all the better able to extract important truths, worthy of being used as the cement which would hold part of my work together, for the reason that such changes were by no means, as at the first moment I might have been tempted to suppose, peculiar to the epoch in which we lived. At the time when I, myself only just "arrived"—newer even than Bloch at the present day—had made my first entry into the world of the Guermantes, I must have contemplated in the belief that they formed an integral part of that world elements that were in fact utterly foreign to it, recently incorporated and appearing strangely new to older elements from which I failed to distinguish them and which themselves, though regarded by the dukes of the day as members of the Faubourg from time immemorial, had in fact—if not themselves, then their fathers or their grandfathers—been the upstarts of an earlier age. So much so that it was not any inherent quality of "men of the best society" which made this world so brilliant, but rather the fact of being more or less completely assimilated to this world which out of people who fifty years later, in spite of their diverse origins, would all look very much the same, formed "men of the best society." Even in the past into which I pushed back the name of Guermantes in order to give it its full grandeur—with good reason, for under Louis XIV the Guermantes had been almost royal and had cut a more splendid figure than they

did today—the phenomenon which I was observing at
this moment had not been unknown. The Guermantes of
that time had allied themselves, for instance, with the
family of Colbert, which today, it is true, appears to us in
the highest degree aristocratic, since a Colbert bride is
thought an excellent match even for a La Rochefoucauld.
But it is not because the Colberts, then a purely bourgeois
family, were aristocratic that the Guermantes had sought
them in a matrimonial alliance, it was because of this
alliance with the Guermantes that the Colberts became
aristocratic. If the name of Haussonville should be
extinguished with the present representative of that house,
it will perhaps owe its future renown to the fact that the
family today is descended from Mme de Staël, regardless
of the fact that before the Revolution M. d'Haussonville,
one of the first noblemen of the kingdom, found it gratifying to his vanity to be able to tell M. de Broglie that he
was not acquainted with the father of that lady and was
therefore no more in a position to present him at court
than was M. de Broglie himself, neither of the two men
for one moment suspecting that their own grandsons
would later marry one the daughter and the other the
grand-daughter of the authoress of *Corinne*. From the remarks of the Duchesse de Guermantes I realised that it
would have been in my power to play the role of the fashionable commoner in grand society, the man whom everybody supposes to have been from his earliest days
affiliated to the aristocracy, a role once played by Swann
and before him by M. Lebrun and M. Ampère and all
those friends of the Duchesse de Broglie who herself at
the beginning of her career had by no means belonged to
the best society. The first few times I had dined with

Mme de Guermantes how I must have shocked men like
M. de Beauserfeuil, less by my actual presence than by
remarks indicating how entirely ignorant I was of the
memories which constituted his past and which gave its
form to the image that he had of society! Yet the day
would come when Bloch, as a very old man, with recollections from a then distant past of the Guermantes
drawing-room as it presented itself to his eyes at this moment, would feel the same astonishment, the same ill-
humour in the presence of certain intrusions and certain
displays of ignorance. And at the same time he would no
doubt have developed and would radiate around him
those qualities of tact and discretion which I had thought
were the special prerogative of men like M. de Norpois
but which, when their original avatars have vanished from
the scene, form themselves again for a new incarnation in
those of our acquaintance who seem of all people the least
likely to possess them. It was true that my own particular
case, the experience that I had had of being admitted to
the society of the Guermantes, had appeared to me to be
something exceptional. But as soon as I got outside myself
and the circle of people by whom I was immediately surrounded, I could see that this was a social phenomenon
less rare than I had at first supposed and that from the
single fountain-basin of Combray in which I had been
born there were in fact quite a number of jets of water
which had risen, in symmetry with myself, above the liquid mass which had fed them. No doubt, since circumstances have always about them something of the
particular and characters something of the individual, it
was in an entirely different fashion that Legrandin
(through his nephew's strange marriage) had in his turn

penetrated into this exalted world, a fashion quite different from that in which Odette's daughter had married
into it or those in which Swann long ago and I myself had
reached it. Indeed to me, passing by shut up inside my
own life so that I saw it only from within, Legrandin's life
seemed to bear absolutely no resemblance to my own, the
two seemed to have followed widely divergent paths, and
in this respect I was like a stream which from the bottom
of its own deep valley does not see another stream which
proceeds in a different direction and yet, in spite of the
great loops in its course, ends up as a tributary of the
same river. But taking a bird's-eye view, as the statistician
does who, ignoring the reasons of sentiment or the avoid-
able imprudences which may have led some particular
person to his death, counts merely the total number of
those who have died in a year, I could see that quite a few
individuals, starting from the same social milieu, the portrayal of which was attempted in the first pages of this
work, had arrived finally in another milieu of an entirely
different kind, and the probability is that, just as every
year in Paris an average number of marriages take place,
so any other rich and cultivated middle-class milieu might
have been able to show a roughly equal proportion of men
who, like Swann and Legrandin and myself and Bloch,
could be found at a later stage in their lives flowing into
the ocean of "high society." Moreover, in their new surroundings they recognised each other, for if the young
Comte de Cambremer won the admiration of society for
his distinction, his refinement, his sober elegance, I myself
was able to recognise in these qualities—and at the same
time in his fine eyes and his ardent craving for social success—characteristics that were already present in his un-.

cle Legrandin, who in spite of his aristocratic elegance of
bearing had been no more than a typical middle-class
friend of my parents.

Kindness, a simple process of maturation which in the
end sweetens characters originally more acid even than
that of Bloch, is as widely disseminated as that belief in
justice thanks to which, if our cause is good, we feel that
we have no more to fear from a hostile judge than from
one friendly towards us. And the grandchildren of Bloch
would be kind and modest almost from birth. Bloch himself had perhaps not yet reached this stage of development. But I noticed that, whereas once he had pretended
to think himself obliged to make a two hours' railway
journey in order to visit someone who had scarcely even
asked him to come, now that he was flooded with invitations not only to lunch and to dine but to stay for a fortnight here and a fortnight there, he refused many of them
and did this without telling people, without bragging that
he had received and refused them. Discretion, both in action and in speech, had come to him with social position
and with age, with, if one may use the expression, a sort
of social longevity. No doubt in the past Bloch had lacked
discretion, just as he had been incapable of kindness and
devoid of good sense. But certain defects, certain qualities
are attached less to this or that individual than to this or
that moment of existence considered from the social point
of view. One may almost say that they are external to individuals, who merely pass beneath the radiance that they
shed as beneath so many solstices, varying in their nature
but all pre-existent, general and unavoidable. In the same
way a doctor who is trying to find out whether some
medicine diminishes or augments the acidity of the stom-

ach, whether it activates or inhibits its secretions, will obtain results which differ not according to the stomach from whose secretions he has removed a small quantity of gastric juice, but according to the more or less advanced stage in the process of ingestion of the drug at which he conducts the experiment.

To return to the name of Guermantes, considered as an agglomeration of all the names which it admitted into itself and into its immediate neighbourhood, at every moment of its duration it suffered losses and recruited fresh ingredients, like a garden in which from week to week flowers scarcely in bud and preparing to take the places of those that have already begun to wither are confounded with the latter in a mass which presents always the same appearance, except to the people who have not seen the newest blooms before and still preserve in their memories a precise image of the ones that are no longer there.

More than one of the men and women who had been brought together by this party, or of whose existence it had reminded me by evoking for me the aspects which he or she had in turn presented as from the midst of different, perhaps opposite circumstances one after another they had risen before me, brought vividly before my mind the varied aspects of my own life and its different perspectives, just as a feature in a landscape, a hill or a large country house, by appearing now on the right hand and now on the left and seeming first to dominate a forest and then to emerge from a valley, reveals to a traveller the changes in direction and the differences in altitude of the road along which he is passing. As I followed the stream of memory back towards its source, I arrived eventually at images of a single person separated from one another by

an interval of time so long, preserved within me by "I's"
that were so distinct and themselves (the images) fraught
with meanings that were so different, that ordinarily when
I surveyed (as I supposed) the whole past course of my
relations with that particular person I omitted these earliest images and had even ceased to think that the person to
whom they referred was the same as the one whom I had
later got to know, so that I needed a fortuitous lightning-
flash of attention before I could re-attach this latter-day
acquaintance, like a word to its etymology, to the original
significance which he or she had possessed for me. Mlle
Swann, on the other side of the hedge of pink hawthorn,
throwing me a look of which, as a matter of fact, I had
been obliged retrospectively to re-touch the significance,
having learnt that it was a look of desire; Mme Swann's
lover—or the man who according to Combray gossip occupied that position—studying me from behind that same
hedge with an air of disapproval which, in this case too,
had not the meaning which I had ascribed to it at the
time, and then later so changed that I had quite failed to
recognise him as the gentleman at Balbec examining a
poster outside the Casino, the man of whom, when once
every ten years I happened to remember that first image,
I would say to myself: "How strange! That, though I did
not know it, was M. de Charlus!"; Mme de Guermantes
at the marriage of Dr Percepied's daughter; Mme Swann
in a pink dress in my great-uncle's study; Mme de Cambremer, Legrandin's sister, so fashionable that he was terrified that we might ask him to give us an introduction to
her—all these images and many others associated with
Swann, Saint-Loup and others of my friends were like illustrations which sometimes, when I chanced to come

across them, I amused myself by placing as frontispieces on the threshold of my relations with these various people, but always with the feeling that they were no more than images, not something deposited within me by this particular person, not something still in any way linked to him. Not only do some people have good memories and others bad (without going so far as that perpetual forgetfulness which is the native element of such creatures as the Turkish Ambassadress, thanks to which—one piece of news having evaporated by the end of the week or the next piece having the power to exorcise its predecessor—they are always able to find room in their minds for the news that contradicts what they have previously been told), we find also that two people with an equal endowment of memory do not remember the same things. One of two men, for instance, will have paid little attention to an action for which the other will long continue to feel great remorse, but will have seized on the other hand upon some random remark which his friend let fall almost without thinking and taken it to be the key to a sympathetic character. Again, the fact that we prefer not to be proved wrong when we have uttered a false prophecy cuts short the duration of our memory of such prophecies and permits us very soon to affirm that we never uttered them. Finally, preferences of a more profound and more disinterested kind diversify the memories of different people, so that a poet, for example, who has almost entirely forgotten certain facts which someone else is able to recall, will nevertheless have retained—what for him is more important—a fleeting impression. The effect of all these causes is that after twenty years of absence where one expected to find rancour one finds often involuntary and unconscious forgiveness, but sometimes also we stumble upon a bitterness for which (because we have ourselves forgotten some bad impression that we once made) we can provide no reasonable explanation. Even where the people whom we have known best are concerned, we soon forget the dates of the various episodes in their lives. And because it was at least twenty years since she had first set eyes on Bloch, Mme de Guermantes would have sworn that he had been born in the world to which she herself belonged and had been dandled on the knees of the Duchesse de Chartres when he was two years old.

How often had all these people reappeared before me in the course of their lives, the diverse circumstances of which seemed to present the same individuals always, but in forms and for purposes that were shifting and varied; and the diversity of the points in my life through which had passed the thread of the life of each of these characters had finished by mixing together those that seemed the furthest apart, as if life possessed only a limited number of threads for the execution of the most different patterns. What, for instance, in my various pasts, could be more widely separated than my visits to my great-uncle Adolphe, the nephew of Mme de Villeparisis who was herself a cousin of the Marshal, Legrandin and his sister, and the former tailor who lived in our courtyard and was a friend of Françoise? And yet today all these different threads had been woven together to form the fabric, there of the married lives of Robert and Gilberte Saint-Loup, here of the young Cambremer couple, not to mention Morel and all the others whose conjunction had played a part in forming a set of circumstances of such a nature that the circumstances seemed to me to be the complete

unity and each individual actor in them merely a constituent part of the whole. And by now my life had lasted
so long that not infrequently, when it brought a person to
my notice, I was able, by rummaging in quite different
regions of my memory, to find another person, unlike
though with the same identity, to add to and complete the
first. Even to the Elstirs which I saw hanging here in a
position which was itself an indication of his glory I was
able to add very ancient memories of the Verdurins, the
Cottards, my first conversation with the painter in the
restaurant at Rivebelle, the tea-party in his studio at
which I had been introduced to Albertine, and a host of
other memories as well. Thus a connoisseur of painting
who is shown one wing of an altar-piece remembers in
what church or which museums or whose private collection the other fragments of the same work are dispersed
and, in the same way as by studying the catalogues of
sales and haunting the shops of the antique-dealers he
finds, in the end, some object which is a twin to one he
already possesses and makes a pair with it, he is able to
reconstruct in his mind the predella and the whole altar as
they once were. As a bucket hauled up on a winch comes
to touch the rope several times and on opposite sides, so
there was not a character that had found a place in my
life, scarcely even a thing, which hadn't turn and turn
about played in it a whole series of different roles. If after
an interval of several years I rediscovered in my memory
a mere social acquaintance or even a physical object, I
perceived that life all this while had been weaving round
person or thing a tissue of diverse threads which ended by
covering them with the beautiful and inimitable velvety
patina of the years, just as in an old park a simple runnel

of water comes with the passage of time to be enveloped in a sheath of emerald.

It was not merely the outward appearance of these people that made one think of them as people in a dream. In their inward experience too life, which already when they were young, when they were in love, had been not far from sleep, had now more and more become a dream. They had forgotten even their resentments, their hatreds, and in order to be certain that the person before them was the one with whom ten years earlier they had not been on speaking terms they would have had to consult some mnemonic register, but one which, unfortunately, was as vague as a dream in which one has been insulted one does not quite know by whom. All these dreams together formed the substance of the apparent contradictions of political life, where one saw as colleagues in a government men who had once accused each other of murder or treason. And this dreamlike existence became as torpid as death in certain old men on the days that followed any day on which they had chanced to make love. During those days it was useless to make any demands on the President of the Republic, he had forgotten everything. Then, if he was left in peace for a day or two, the memory of public affairs slowly returned to him, as haphazard as the memory of a dream.

Sometimes it was not merely in a single vivid image that the stranger so unlike the man or woman whom I had later come to know had first appeared before me. For years I had thought of Bergotte as the sweet bard with the snowy locks, for years my limbs had been paralysed, as though I had seen a ghost, by the apparition of Swann's grey top-hat or his wife's violet cloak, or by the mystery

with which, even in a drawing-room, the name of her race
enveloped the Duchesse de Guermantes; with all these,
and with others too, my relations, which in the sequel
were to become so commonplace, had had their origin almost in legend, in a delightful mythology which still at a
later date prolonged them into the past as into some
Olympian heaven where they shone with the luminous
brilliance of a comet's tail. And even those of my ac-
quaintanceships which had not begun in mystery, that for
instance with Mme de Souvré, so arid today, so purely social in its nature, had preserved among their earliest moments the memory of a first smile calmer and sweeter
than anything that was to follow, a smile mellifluously
traced in the fullness of an afternoon beside the sea or the
close of a spring day in Paris, a day of clattering carriages,
of dust rising from the streets and sunny air gently stir-
ring like water. And perhaps Mme de Souvré, had she
been removed from this frame, would have been of little
significance, like those famous buildings—the Salute, for
example—which, without any great beauty of their own,
are so well suited to a particular setting that they compel
our admiration, but she formed part of a bundle of memories which I valued "all in," as the auctioneers say, at a
certain price, without stopping to ask exactly how much
of this value appertained to the lady herself.

One thing struck me even more forcibly in all these
people than the physical or social changes which they had
undergone, and this was the modification in the ideas
which they possessed of one another. Legrandin in the
past had despised Bloch and never addressed a word to
him. Now he went out of his way to be civil. And this
was not because of the improvement which had taken

place in Bloch's social position—were this the case the fact would scarcely be worthy of mention, for social changes inevitably bring in their train a new pattern of relationships among those who have been affected by them. No: the reason was that people—and in saying "people" I mean "what people are for us"—do not in our memory possess the unvariability of a figure in a painting. Oblivion is at work within us, and according to its arbitrary operation they evolve. Sometimes it even happens that after a time we confuse one person with another. "Bloch? Oh yes, he was someone who used to come to Combray," and when he says Bloch, the speaker is in fact referring to me. Conversely, Mme Sazerat was firmly persuaded that it was I who was the author of a certain historical study of Philip II which was in fact by Bloch. More commonly, you forget after a while how odiously someone has behaved towards you, you forget his faults of character and your last meeting with him when you parted without shaking hands, and you remember on the other hand an earlier occasion when you got on excellently together. And it was to an earlier occasion of this kind that the manners of Legrandin adverted in his new civility towards Bloch, whether because he had lost the recollection of a particular past or because he thought it was to be deliberately eschewed, from a mixture of forgiveness and forgetfulness and that indifference which is another effect of Time. And then, as we have seen, the memories which two people preserve of each other, even in love, are not the same. I had seen Albertine reproduce with perfect accuracy some remark which I had made to her at one of our first meetings and which I had entirely forgotten. Of some other incident, lodged for ever in my head like a pebble flung with force, she had no recollection. Our life together was like one of those garden walks where, at intervals on either side of the path, vases of flowers are placed symmetrically but not opposite to one another. And if this discrepancy of memories may be observed even in the relation of love, even more understandable is it that when your acquaintance with someone has been slight you should scarcely remember who he is or should remember not what you used to think of him but something different, perhaps something that dates from an earlier epoch or that is suggested by the people in whose midst you have met him again, who may only recently have got to know him and see him therefore endowed with good qualities and a social prestige which in the past he did not possess but which you, having forgotten the past, instantly accept.

No doubt life, by placing each of these people on my path a number of times, had presented them to me in particular circumstances which, enclosing them finally on every side, had restricted the view which I had of them and so prevented me from discovering their essence. For between us and other people there exists a barrier of contingencies, just as in my hours of reading in the garden at Combray I had realised that in all perception there exists a barrier as a result of which there is never absolute contact between reality and our intelligence. Even those Guermantes around whom I had built such a vast fabric of dream had appeared to me, when at last I had first approached two of them, one in the guise of an old friend of my grandmother and the other in that of a gentleman who had looked at me in a most disagreeable manner one morning in the gardens of the Casino. So that it was in each case only in retrospect, by reuniting the individual to

the name, that my encounter with them had been an encounter with the Guermantes. And yet perhaps this in itself made life more poetic for me, the thought that the
mysterious race with the piercing eyes and the beak of a
bird, the unapproachable rose-coloured, golden race, had
so often and so naturally, through the effect of blind and
varied circumstances, chanced to offer itself to my contemplation, to admit me to the circle of its casual and
even of its intimate friends, to such a point that when I
had wanted to get to know Mlle de Stermaria or to have
dresses made for Albertine, it was to one or another of the
Guermantes, as being the most obliging of my friends,
that I had appealed for help. Admittedly I was bored
when I went to their houses, no less bored than I was in
the houses of the other society people whom I had later
come to know. And in the case of the Duchesse de Guermantes, as in that of certain pages of Bergotte, even her
personal charm was visible to me only at a distance and
vanished as soon as I was near her, for the reason that it
resided in my memory and my imagination. But still, in
spite of everything, the Guermantes—and in this respect
Gilberte resembled them—differed from other society
people in that they plunged their roots more deeply into
my past life, down to a level at which I had dreamed
more and had had more belief in individuals. Bored I may
have been as I stood talking this afternoon to Gilberte or
Mme de Guermantes, but at least as I did so I held
within my grasp those of the imaginings of my childhood
which I had found most beautiful and thought most inaccessible and, like a shopkeeper who cannot balance his
books, I could console myself by forgetting the value of
their actual possession and remembering the price which

had once been attached to them by my desire. But with other people I had not even this consolation, people however with whom my relations had at one time been swollen to an immense importance by dreams that were even more ardent and formed without hope, dreams into which my life of those days, dedicated entirely to them, had so richly poured itself that I could scarcely understand how their fulfilment could be merely this thin, narrow, colourless ribbon of an indifferent and despised intimacy, in which I could rediscover nothing of what had once been their mystery, their fever and their sweetness.

"What has become of the Marquise d'Arpajon?" inquired Mme de Cambremer. "She died," replied Bloch. "Aren't you confusing her with the Comtesse d'Arpajon, who died last year?" The Princesse d'Agrigente joined in the discussion; as the young widow of an old husband who had been very rich and the bearer of a great name she was much sought in marriage, and this had given her great self-assurance. "The Marquise d'Arpajon is dead too," she said, "she died nearly a year ago." "A year ago!" exclaimed Mme de Cambremer, "that can't be right, I was at a musical evening in her house less than a year ago." Bloch was as incapable as any young man about town of making a useful contribution to the subject under discussion, for all these deaths of elderly people were at too great a distance, from the young men because of the enormous difference in age and from a man like Bloch, because of his recent arrival in an unfamiliar society, by way of an oblique approach, at a moment when it was already declining into a twilight which was for him illumined by no memories of its past. And even for people of the same age and the same social background death had lost its strange significance. Hardly a day passed without their having to send to inquire for news of friends and relations *in articulo mortis*, some of whom, they would be told, had recovered while others had "succumbed," until a point was reached where they no longer very clearly remembered whether this or that person who was no longer seen anywhere had "pulled through" his pneumonia or had expired. In these regions of advanced age death was everywhere at work and had at the same time become more indefinite. At this crossroads of two generations and two societies, so ill placed, for different reasons, for distinguishing death that they almost confused it with life, the former of these two conditions had been turned into a social incident, an attribute to be predicated of somebody to a greater or lesser degree, without the tone of voice in which it was mentioned in any way indicating that for the person in question this "incident" was the end of everything. I heard people say: "But you forget that so and so is dead," exactly as they might have said "he has had a decoration" or "he has been elected to the Academy" or—and these last two happenings had much the same effect as death, since they too prevented a man from going to parties—"he is spending the winter on the Riviera" or "his doctor has sent him to the mountains." Perhaps, where a man was well known, what he left behind him at his death helped others to remember that his existence had come to an end. But in the case of ordinary society people of an advanced age it was easy to make a mistake as to whether or no they were dead, not only because one knew little about their past or had forgotten it but because they were in no way whatever linked to the future. And the difficulty that was universally experienced in these cases in choosing from among the alternatives of illness, absence, retirement to the country and death the one that happened to be correct, sanctioned and confirmed not merely the indifference of the survivors but the insignificance of the departed.

"But if she is still alive, why is it that one never sees her anywhere now, nor her husband either?" asked a spinster who liked to make what she supposed was witty conversation. "For the obvious reason," replied her mother, who in spite of her years never missed a party herself, "that they are old; when you get to that age you stay at home." Before you got to the cemetery, it seemed, there was a whole closed city of the old, where the lamps always glimmered in the fog. Mme de Saint-Euverte cut short the debate by saying that the Comtesse d'Arpajon had died in the previous year after a long illness and that more recently the Marquise d'Arpajon had also died, very rapidly, "in some quite unremarkable way," a death which, in virtue of this latter characteristic, resembled the lives of all these people (its unremarkableness explained too why it had passed unnoticed and excused those who had been in doubt). When she heard that Mme d'Arpajon really had died, the spinster cast an anxious glance at her mother, for she feared that the news of the death of one of her "contemporaries" might "be a blow" to her—indeed she already imagined people talking about her mother's death and explaining it in this way: "Madame d'Arpajon's death had been a *great blow* to her." But the old lady on the contrary, far from justifying her daughter's fears, felt every time someone of her own age "disappeared" that she had gained a victory in a contest against formidable competitors. Their deaths were the only fashion in which she still for a moment became agreeably conscious of her own life. The spinster noticed that her mother, who had seemed not displeased to remark that Mme d'Arpajon was one of those tired old people whose days are spent in homes from which they seldom emerge, had been even less displeased to learn that the Marquise had entered the city of hereafter, the home from which none of us ever emerges at all. This observation of her mother's want of feeling amused the daughter's sarcastic mind. And to make her own contemporaries laugh she gave them afterwards a comical account of the gleeful fashion in which her mother had said, rubbing her hands: "Gracious me, it appears to be true that poor Madame d'Arpajon is dead." Even the people who did not need this death to make them feel any joy in being alive, were rendered happy by it. For every death is for others a simplification of life, it spares them the necessity of showing gratitude, the obligation of paying calls. And yet this was not the manner in which Elstir had received the news of the death of M. Verdurin.

A lady left the room, for she had other afternoon parties to attend, and had also received the commands of two queens to take tea with them. It was the Princesse de Nassau, that great courtesan of the aristocratic world whom I had known in the past. Were it not that she had shrunk in height (which gave her, her head being now situated at a much lower elevation than formerly, an air of having "one foot in the grave"), one could scarcely have said that she had aged. She had remained a Marie-Antoinette with an Austrian nose and an enchanting glance, preserved, one might almost say embalmed, by a thousand cosmetics adorably blended so as to compose for

her a face that was the colour of lilac. Over this face there
floated that confused and tender expression which I remembered, which was at once an allusion to all the
fashionable gatherings where she was expected and an intimation that she was obliged to leave, that she promised
sweetly to return, that she would slip away without any
fuss. Born almost on the steps of a throne, three times
married, richly kept for years at a time by great bankers,
not to mention the countless whims in which she had permitted herself to indulge, she bore lightly beneath her
gown, mauve like her wonderful round eyes and her
painted face, the slightly tangled memories of the innumerable incidents of her life. As she passed near me,
making her discreet exit, I bowed to her. She recognised
me, took my hand and pressed it, and fixed upon me the
round mauve pupils which seemed to say: "How long it is
since we have seen each other! We must talk about all
that another time." Her pressure of my hand became a
squeeze, for she had a vague idea that one evening in her
carriage, when she had offered to drop me at my door
after a party at the Duchesse de Guermantes's, there
might have been some dalliance between us. Just to be
on the safe side, she seemed to allude to something that
had in fact never happened, but this was hardly difficult
for her since a strawberry tart could send her into an
ecstasy and whenever she had to leave a party before
the end of a piece of music she put on a despairing air
of tender, yet not final, farewell. But she was uncertain
what had passed between us in the carriage, so she did
not linger long over the furtive pressure of my hand and
said not a word. She merely looked at me in the manner which I have described, the manner which signi-

fied: "How long it is!" and in which one caught a momentary glimpse of her husbands and the men who had kept her and two wars, while her stellar eyes, like an astronomical clock cut in a block of opal, marked successively all those solemn hours of a so distant past which she rediscovered every time she wanted to bid you a casual good-bye which was always also an apology. And then having left me, she started to trot towards the door, partly so that her departure should not inconvenience people, partly to show me that if she had not stopped to talk it was because she was in a hurry, partly also to recapture the seconds which she had lost in pressing my hand and so arrive on time at the Queen of Spain's, where she was to have tea alone with the Queen. I even thought, when she got near the door, that she was going to break into a gallop. And indeed she was galloping towards her grave.

A stout lady came up to me and greeted me, and during the few moments that she was speaking the most diverse thoughts jostled each other in my mind. I hesitated an instant to reply to her, for I was afraid that possibly, recognising people no better than I did, she might have mistaken my identity, but then the assurance of her manner caused me on the contrary, for fear that she might be someone whom I had known extremely well, to exaggerate the amiability of my smile, while my eyes continued to scan her features for some trace of the name which eluded me. As a candidate for a degree fixes his eyes upon the examiner's face in the vain hope of finding there the answer that he would do better to seek in his own memory, so, still smiling, I fixed my eyes upon the features of the stout lady. They seemed to be those of Mme Swann, and there crept into my smile the appropriate shade of respect, while my indecision began to subside. But a moment later I heard the stout lady say: "You took me for Mamma, and it's quite true that I'm beginning to look very like her." And I recognised Gilberte.

We had a long talk about Robert, Gilberte speaking of him in an almost reverent tone, as though he had been a superior being whom she was anxious to show me that she had admired and understood. We recalled to one another the ideas which he had expounded in the past upon the art of war (for he had often repeated to her at Tansonville the theories that I had heard him develop at Doncières and elsewhere) and we marvelled how often, and on how many different points, his views had been proved correct by the events of the late war.

"I cannot tell you," I said, "how struck I am now by even the least of the things that I heard him say at Doncières and also during the war. Almost the last remark that he ever made to me, just before we said good-bye for the last time, was that he expected to see Hindenburg, a Napoleonic general, fight one of the types of Napoleonic battle, the one which aims at driving a wedge between two hostile armies—perhaps, he had added, the English and ourselves. Now scarcely a year after Robert was killed, a critic for whom he had a profound admiration and who manifestly exercised a great influence upon his military ideas, M. Henry Bidou, was saying that the Hindenburg offensive of March 1918 was 'the battle of separation fought by a single concentrated army against two armies in extended formation, a manoeuvre which the Emperor executed successfully in the Apennines in 1796 but in which he failed in Belgium in 1815.' In the course of the same conversation Robert had compared battles to plays in which it is not always easy to know what the author has intended, in which perhaps the author himself has changed his plan in mid-campaign. Now admittedly, to take this same German offensive of 1918, had Robert interpreted it in this fashion he would not have been in agreement with M. Bidou. But other critics believe that it was Hindenburg's success in the direction of Amiens, followed by his check there, then his success in Flanders and then another check, which, by virtue really of a series of accidents, made first of Amiens and then of Boulogne objectives which he had not fixed upon before the engagement began. And as every critic can refashion a play or a campaign in his own way, there are some who see in this offensive the prelude to a lightning attack upon Paris and others a succession of unco-ordinated hammer-blows intended to destroy the English army. And even if the orders actually given by the commander do not fit in with this or that conception of his plan, the critics will always be at liberty to say, as the actor Mounet-Sully said to Coquelin when the latter assured him that *Le Misanthrope* was not the gloomy melodrama that he wanted to make it (for Molière himself, according to the evidence of contemporaries, gave a comical interpretation of the part and played it for laughs): 'Well, Molière was wrong.' "

"And when aeroplanes first started"—it was Gilberte's turn now—"you remember what he used to say (he had such charming expressions): 'Every army will have to be a hundred-eyed Argus'? Alas, he never lived to see his prediction fulfilled!" "Oh! yes, he did," I replied, "he saw the battle of the Somme and he knew that it began with blinding the enemy by gouging out his eyes, by

destroying his aeroplanes and his captive balloons." "Yes,
that is true. And then," she went on, for now that she
"lived only for the mind" she had become a little pedantic, "he maintained that we return always to the
methods of the ancients. Well, do you realise that the
Mesopotamian campaigns of this war" (she must have
read this comparison at the time in Brichot's articles)
"constantly recall, almost without alteration, Xenophon's
*Anabasis*? And that to get from the Tigris to the Eu-
phrates the English command made use of the *bellum*, the
long narrow boat—the gondola of the country—which
was already being used by the Chaldeans at the very
dawn of history." These words did indeed give me a sense
of that stagnation of the past through which in certain
parts of the world, by virtue of a sort of specific gravity,
it is indefinitely immobilised, so that it can be found after
centuries exactly as it was. But I must admit that, because
of the books which I had read at Balbec at no great distance from Robert himself, I myself had been more impressed first in the fighting in France to come again upon
those "trenches" that were familiar to me from the pages
of Mme de Sévigné and then in the Middle East, apropos
of the siege of Kut-el-Amara (Kut-of-the-Emir, "just as
we say Vaux-le-Vicomte or Bailleau-l'Evêque," as the
curé of Combray would have said had he extended his
thirst for etymologies to the languages of the East), to see
the name of Baghdad once more attended closely by that
of Basra, which is the Bassorah so many times mentioned
in the *Arabian Nights*, the town which, whenever he had
left the capital or was returning thither, was used as his
port of embarkation or disembarkation, long before the
days of General Townshend and General Gorringe, when

the Caliphs still reigned, by no less a personage than Sindbad the Sailor.

"There is one aspect of war," I continued, "which I think Robert was beginning to comprehend: war is human, it is something that is lived like a love or a hatred and could be told like the story of a novel, and consequently, if anyone goes about repeating that strategy is a science, it won't help him in the least to understand war, since war is not a matter of strategy. The enemy has no more knowledge of our plans than we have of the objective pursued by the woman whom we love, and perhaps we do not even know what these plans are ourselves. Did the Germans in their offensive of March 1918 aim at capturing Amiens? We simply do not know. Perhaps they did not know themselves, perhaps it was what happened—their advance in the west towards Amiens—that determined the nature of their plan. And even if war were scientific, it would still be right to paint it as Elstir painted the sea, by reversing the real and the apparent, starting from illusions and beliefs which one then slowly brings into line with the truth, which is the manner in which Dostoievsky tells the story of a life. Quite certainly, however, war is not strategic, it might better be described as a pathological condition, because it admits of accidents which even a skilled physician could not have foreseen, such as the Russian Revolution."

Throughout this conversation Gilberte had spoken of Robert with a deference which seemed to be addressed more to my sometime friend than to her late husband. It was as though she were saying to me: "I know how much you admired him. Please believe that I too understood what a wonderful person he was." And yet the love which

she assuredly no longer had for his memory was perhaps
the remote cause of certain features of her present life.
Thus Gilberte now had an inseparable friend in Andrée.
And although the latter was beginning, thanks largely to
her husband's talent and her own intelligence, to penetrate, if not into the society of the Guermantes, at least
into circles infinitely more fashionable than those in which
she had formerly moved, people were astonished that the
Marquise de Saint-Loup should condescend to be her
closest friend. The friendship was taken to be a sign in
Gilberte of her penchant for what she supposed was an
artistic existence and for what was, unequivocally, a social
decline. This explanation may be the true one. But another occurred to me, convinced as I had always been that
the images which we see anywhere assembled are generally the reflexion, or in some indirect fashion an effect, of
a first group of different images—quite unlike the second
and at a great distance from it, though the two groups are
symmetrical. If night after night one saw Andrée and her
husband and Gilberte in each other's company, I wondered whether this was not because, so many years earlier,
one might have seen Andrée's future husband first living
with Rachel and then leaving her for Andrée. Very likely
Gilberte at the time, in the too remote, too exalted world
in which she lived, had known nothing of this. But she
must have learned of it later, when Andrée had climbed
and she herself had descended enough to be aware of each
other's existence. And when this happened she must have
felt very strongly the prestige of the woman for whom
Rachel had been abandoned by the man—the no doubt
fascinating man—whom she, Rachel, had preferred to
Robert. So perhaps the sight of Andrée recalled to

Gilberte the youthful romance that her love for Robert had been, and inspired in her a great respect for Andrée, who even now retained the affections of a man so loved by that Rachel whom Gilberte felt to have been more deeply loved by Saint-Loup than she had been herself. But perhaps on the contrary these recollections played no part in Gilberte's fondness for the artistic couple, and one would have been right to see in her conduct, as many people did, an instance merely of those twin tastes, so often inseparable in society women, for culture and loss of caste. Perhaps Gilberte had forgotten Robert as completely as I had forgotten Albertine, and, even if she knew that Rachel was the woman whom the man of many talents had left for Andrée, never when she saw them thought about this fact which had in no way influenced her liking for them. Whether my alternative explanation was not merely possible but true was a question that could be determined only by appeal to the testimony of the parties themselves, the sole recourse which is open in such a case—or would be if they were able to bring to their confidences both insight and sincerity. But the first of these is rare in the circumstances and the second unknown. Whatever the true explanation of this friendship might be, the sight of Rachel, now a celebrated actress, could not be very agreeable to Gilberte. So I was sorry to hear that she was going to recite some poetry at this party, the programme announced being Musset's *Souvenir* and some fables of La Fontaine.

In the background could be heard the Princesse de Guermantes repeating excitedly, in a voice which because of her false teeth was like the rattle of old iron: "Yes, that's it, we will forgather! We will summon the clan! I love this younger generation, so intelligent, so ready to join in! Ah!" (to a young woman) "what a mujishun you are!" And she fixed her great monocle in her round eye, with an expression half of amusement, half of apology for her inability to sustain gaiety for any length of time, though to the very end she was determined to "join in" and "forgather."

"But how do you come to be at a party of this size?" Gilberte asked me. "To find you at a great slaughter of the innocents like this doesn't at all fit in with my picture of you. In fact, I should have expected to see you any-where rather than at one of my aunt's get-togethers, be-cause of course she is my aunt," she added meaningly, for having become Mme de Saint-Loup at a slightly earlier date than that of Mme Verdurin's entry into the family, she thought of herself as a Guermantes from the begin-ning of time and therefore attainted by the misalliance which her uncle had contracted when he married Mme Verdurin, a subject, it is true, on which she had heard a thousand sarcastic remarks made in her presence by mem-bers of the family, while naturally it was only behind her back that they discussed the misalliance which Saint-Loup had contracted when he married her. The disdain that she affected for this pinchbeck aunt was not diminished by the fact that the new Princesse de Guermantes, from the sort of perversity which drives intelligent people to behave unconventionally, from the need also to reminisce which is common in old people, and in the hope lastly of confer-ring a past on her new fashionable status, was fond of saying when the name of Gilberte arose in conversation: "Of course I have known her for donkey's years, I used to see a lot of the child's mother; why, she was a great friend of my cousin Marsantes. And it was in my house that she got to know Gilberte's father. And poor Saint-Loup too, I knew all his family long before he married her, indeed his uncle was one of my dearest friends in the La Raspelière days." "You see," people would say to me, hearing the Princesse de Guermantes talk in this vein, "the Verdurins were not at all bohemian, they had always been friends of Mme de Saint-Loup's family." I was perhaps alone in knowing, through my grandfather, how true it was that the Verdurins were not bohemian. But this was hardly because they had known Odette. However, you can easily dress up stories about a past with which no one is any longer familiar, just as you can about travels in a country where no one has ever been. "But really," Gilberte concluded, "since you sometimes emerge from your ivory tower, wouldn't you prefer little intimate gatherings which I could arrange, with just a few intelligent and sympathetic people? These great formal affairs are not made for you at all. I saw you a moment ago talking to my aunt Oriane, who has all the good qualities in the world, but I don't think one is doing her an injustice, do you, if one says that she scarcely belongs to the aristocracy of the mind."

I was unable to acquaint Gilberte with the thoughts which had been passing through my mind for the last hour, but it occurred to me that, simply on the level of distraction, she might be able to minister to my pleasures, which, as I now foresaw them, would no more be to talk literature with the Duchesse de Guermantes than with Mme de Saint-Loup. Certainly it was my intention to resume next day, but this time with a purpose, a solitary life. So far from going into society, I would not even per-

mit people to come and see me at home during my hours
of work, for the duty of writing my book took precedence
now over that of being polite or even kind. They would
insist no doubt, these friends who had not seen me for
years and had now met me again and supposed that I was
restored to health, they would want to come when the
labour of their day or of their life was finished or interrupted, or at such times as they had the same need of me
as I in the past had had of Saint-Loup; for (as I had already observed at Combray when my parents chose to reproach me at those very moments when, though they did
not know it, I had just formed the most praiseworthy res-
olutions) the internal timepieces which are allotted to different human beings are by no means synchronised: one
strikes the hour of rest while another is striking that of
work, one, for the judge, that of punishment when already
for the criminal that of repentance and self-perfection has
long since struck. But I should have the courage to reply
to those who came to see me or tried to get me to visit
them that I had, for necessary business which required
my immediate attention, an urgent, a supremely important appointment with myself. And yet I was aware that,
though there exists but little connexion between our veritable self and the other one, nevertheless, because they
both go under the same name and share the same body,
the abnegation which involves making a sacrifice of easier
duties and even of pleasures appears to other people to be
egotism.

Was it not, surely, in order to concern myself with
them that I was going to live apart from these people who
would complain that they did not see me, to concern myself with them in a more fundamental fashion than would

have been possible in their presence, to seek to reveal them to themselves, to realise their potentialities? What use would it have been that, for a few more years, I should waste hour after hour at evening parties pursuing the scarcely expired echo of other people's remarks with the no less vain and fleeting sound of my own, for the sterile pleasure of a social contact which precluded all penetration beneath the surface? Was it not more worthwhile that I should attempt to describe the graph, to educe the laws, of these gestures that they made, these remarks that they uttered, their very lives and natures? Unfortunately, I should have to struggle against that habit of putting oneself in another person's place which, if it favours the conception of a work of art, is an obstacle to its execution. A habit this is which leads people, through a superior form of politeness, to sacrifice to others not only their pleasure but their duty, since from the standpoint of other people our duty, whatever it may be—and duty for a man who can render no good service at the front may be to remain behind the lines where he is useful—appears illusorily to be our pleasure.

And far from thinking myself wretched—a belief which some of the greatest men have held—because of this life without friends or familiar talk that I should live, I realised that our powers of exaltation are being given a false direction when we expend them in friendship, because they are then diverted from those truths towards which they might have guided us to aim at a particular friendship which can lead to nothing. Still, intervals of rest and society would at times be necessary to me and then, I felt, rather than those intellectual conversations which fashionable people suppose must be useful to writ-

ers, a little amorous dalliance with young girls in bloom
would be the choice nutriment with which, if with anything, I might indulge my imagination, like the famous
horse that was fed on nothing but roses. What suddenly I
yearned for once more was what I had dreamed of at Balbec, when, still strangers to me, I had seen Albertine and
Andrée and their friends pass across the background of
the sea. But alas! I could no longer hope to find again
those particular girls for whom at this moment my desire
was so strong. The action of the years which had transformed all the individuals whom I had seen today, and
among them Gilberte herself, had assuredly transformed
those of the girls of Balbec who survived, as it would have
transformed Albertine had she not been killed, into
women too sadly different from what I remembered. And
it hurt me to think that I was obliged to look for them
within myself, since Time which changes human beings
does not alter the image which we have preserved of
them. Indeed nothing is more painful than this contrast
between the mutability of people and the fixity of memory, when it is borne in upon us that what has preserved
so much freshness in our memory can no longer possess
any trace of that quality in life, that we cannot now, outside ourselves, approach and behold again what inside our
mind seems so beautiful, what excites in us a desire (a desire apparently so individual) to see it again, except by
seeking it in a person of the same age, by seeking it, that
is to say, in a different person. Often had I had occasion
to suspect that what seems to be unique in a person
whom we desire does not in fact belong to her. And of
this truth the passage of time was now giving me a more
complete proof, since after twenty years, spontaneously,

my impulse was to seek, not the girls whom I had known in the past, but those who now possessed the youthfulness which the others had then had. (Nor is it only the re-awakening of our old sensual desires which fails to correspond to any reality because it fails to take into account the Time that has been Lost. Sometimes I found myself wishing that, by a miracle, the door might open and through it might enter—not dead, as I had supposed, but still alive—not just Albertine but my grandmother too. I imagined that I saw them, my heart leapt forward to greet them. But I had forgotten one thing, that, if in fact they had not died, Albertine would now have more or less the appearance that Mme Cottard had presented in the Balbec days and my grandmother, being more than ninety-five years old, would show me nothing of that beautiful face, calm and smiling, with which I still imagined her, but only by an exercise of the fancy no less arbitrary than that which confers a beard upon God the Father or, in the seventeenth century, regardless of their antiquity, represented the heroes of Homer in all the accoutrements of a gentleman of that age.)

I looked at Gilberte, and I did not think: "I should like to see her again," I said merely, in answer to her offer, that I should always enjoy being invited to meet young girls, poor girls if possible, to whom I could give pleasure by quite small gifts, without expecting anything of them in return except that they should serve to renew within me the dreams and the sadnesses of my youth and perhaps, one improbable day, a single chaste kiss. Gilberte smiled and then looked as though she were seriously giving her mind to the problem.

Just as Elstir loved to see incarnate before him, in his

wife, that Venetian beauty which he had often painted in
his works, so I excused myself by saying that there was an
aesthetic element in the egotism which attracted me to the
beautiful women who had the power to make me suffer,
and I had a sentiment almost of idolatry for the future
Gilbertes, the future Duchesses de Guermantes, the future Albertines whom I might meet and who might, I
thought, inspire me as a sculptor is inspired when he
walks through a gallery of noble antique marbles. I ought
to have reflected, however, that prior to each of the
women whom I had loved there had existed in me a sentiment of the mystery by which she was surrounded and
that therefore, rather than ask Gilberte to introduce me to
young girls, I should have done better to go to places
where there were girls with whom I had not the slightest
connexion, those places where between oneself and them
one feels an insurmountable barrier, where at a distance of
three feet, on the beach, for instance, as they pass one on
their way to bathe, one feels separated from them by the
impossible. It was in this fashion that a sentiment of mystery had attached itself for me first to Gilberte, then to
the Duchesse de Guermantes, then to Albertine and to so
many others. (Later no doubt the unknown, the almost
unknowable, had become the known, the familiar, perhaps
painful, perhaps indifferent, but retaining still from an
earlier time a certain charm.) And to tell the truth, as in
those calendars which the postman brings us in the hope
of a New Year's gift, there was not one of the years of my
life that did not have, as a frontispiece, or intercalated between its days, the image of a woman whom I had desired
during that year; an image sometimes entirely arbitrary,
for the reason that, often, I had never seen the woman in

question, whether she were Mme Putbus's maid or Mlle d'Orgeville or some young woman or other whose name had caught my eye on the society page of a newspaper, amongst "the swarm of charming waltzers." I guessed her to be beautiful, I fell in love with her and I constructed for her an ideal body which towered above some landscape in the region of France where I had read in the *Annuaire des Châteaux* that the estates of her family were situated. In cases, however, where I had met and known the woman, the landscape against which I saw her was, at the very least, double. First she rose, each one of these women, at a different point in my life, with the imposing stature of a tutelary local deity, in the midst of one of those landscapes of my dreams which lay side by side like some chequered network over my past, the landscape to which my imagination had sought to attach her; then later I saw her from the angle of memory, surrounded by the places in which I had known her and which, remaining attached to them, she recalled to me, for if our life is vagabond our memory is sedentary and though we ourselves rush ceaselessly forward our recollections, indissolubly bound to the sites which we have left behind us, continue to lead a placid and sequestered existence among them, like those friends whom a traveller makes for a brief while in some town where he is staying and whom, leaving the town, he is obliged to leave behind him, because it is there that they, who stand on the steps of their house to bid him good-bye, will end their day and their life, regardless of whether he is still with them or not, there beside the church, looking out over the harbour, beneath the trees of the promenade. So that the shadow of, for instance, Gilberte lay not merely outside a church in

the Ile-de-France where I had imagined her, but also
upon a gravelled path in a park on the Méséglise way,
and the shadow of Mme de Guermantes not only on a
road in a watery landscape beside which rose pyramid-
shaped clusters of red and purple flowers but also upon
the matutinal gold of a pavement in Paris. And this second image, the one born not of desire but of memory,
was, for each of these women, not unique. For my friendship with each one had been multiple, I had known her at
different times when she had been a different woman for
me and I myself had been a different person, steeped in
dreams of a different colour. And the law which had governed the dreams of each year polarised around those
dreams my recollections of any woman whom I had
known during that year: all that related, for instance, to
the Duchesse de Guermantes in the time of my childhood
was concentrated, by a magnetic force, around Combray,
while all that concerned the Duchesse de Guermantes who
would presently invite me to lunch was disposed around a
quite different centre of sensibility; there existed several
Duchesses de Guermantes, just as, beginning with the
lady in pink, there had existed several Mme Swanns, separated by the colourless ether of the years, from one to
another of whom it was as impossible for me to leap as it
would have been to leave one planet and travel across the
ether to another. And not merely separated but different,
each one bedecked with the dreams which I had had at
very different periods as with a characteristic and unique
flora which will be found on no other planet; so much so
that, having decided that I would not accept an invitation
to lunch either from Mme de Forcheville or from Mme de
Guermantes, I was only able to say to myself—for in say-

ing this I was transported into another world—that one of these ladies was identical with the Duchesse de Guermantes who was descended from Geneviève de Brabant and the other with the lady in pink because a well-informed man within me assured me that this was so, in the same authoritative manner as a scientist might have told me that a milky way of nebulae owed its origin to the fragmentation of a single star. Gilberte, too, whom nevertheless a moment ago I had asked, without perceiving the analogy, to introduce me to girls who might be friends for me of the kind that she had been in the past, existed for me now only as Mme de Saint-Loup. No longer was I reminded when I saw her of the role which had been played long ago in my love for her by Bergotte, Bergotte whom she had forgotten as she had forgotten my love and who for me had become once more merely the author of his books, without my ever recalling now (save in rare and entirely unconnected flashes of memory) the emotion which I had felt when I was presented to the man, the disillusion, the astonishment wrought in me by his conversation, in that drawing-room with the white fur rugs and everywhere bunches of violets, where the footmen so early in the afternoon placed upon so many different consoles such an array of lamps. In fact all the memories that went to make up the first Mlle Swann were withdrawn from the Gilberte of the present day and held at a distance from her by the forces of attraction of another universe, where, grouped around a phrase of Bergotte with which they formed a single whole, they were drenched with the scent of hawthorn.

The fragmentary Gilberte of today listened to my request with a smile and then assumed a serious air as she gave it her consideration. I was pleased to see this, for it prevented her from paying attention to a group which it could hardly have been agreeable for her to observe. In this group was the Duchesse de Guermantes, deep in conversation with a hideous old woman whom I studied without being able to guess in the least who she was—she seemed to be a complete stranger to me. It was in fact to Rachel, that is to say to the actress, the famous actress now, who was going to recite some poems by Victor Hugo and La Fontaine in the course of this party, that Gilberte's aunt was talking. For the Duchess, too long conscious that she occupied the foremost social position in Paris and failing to realise that a position of this kind exists only in the minds of those who believe in it and that many newcomers to the social scene, if they never saw her anywhere and never read her name in the account of any fashionable entertainment, would suppose that she occupied no position at all, now scarcely saw—except when, as seldom as possible, and then with a yawn, she paid a few calls—the Faubourg Saint-Germain which, she said, bored her to death, and instead did what amused her, which was to lunch with this or that actress whom she declared to be enchanting. In the new circles which she frequented, having remained much more like her old self than she supposed, she continued to think that to be easily bored was a mark of intellectual superiority, but she expressed this sentiment now with a positive violence which turned her voice into a hoarse bellow. When, for instance, I mentioned Brichot, "Tedious man!" she broke in, "how he has bored me for the last twenty years!", and when Mme de Cambremer was heard to say: "You must re-read what Schopenhauer says about music," the

Duchess drew our attention to this phrase by exclaiming: "*Re-read* is pretty rich, I must say. Who does she think she's fooling?" Old M. d'Albon smiled, recognising in this outburst a sample of the Guermantes wit. In Gilberte, who was more modern, it evoked no response. Daughter of Swann though she was, like a duckling hatched by a hen she was more romantically minded than her father. "I find that most touching," she would say, or: "He has a charming sensibility."

I told Mme de Guermantes that I had met M. de Charlus. She found him much more "altered" for the worse than in fact he was, for people in society make distinctions, in the matter of intelligence, not only between different members of their set between whom there is really nothing to choose in this respect, but also, in a single individual, between different phases of his life. Then she went on: "He has always been the image of my mother-in-law, but now the likeness is even more striking." There was nothing very extraordinary in this resemblance: it is well known that women sometimes so to speak project themselves into another human being with the most perfect accuracy, with the sole error of a transposition of sex. This, however, is an error of which one can scarcely say: "*felix culpa*," for the sex has repercussions upon the personality, so that in a man femininity becomes affectation, reserve touchiness and so on. Nevertheless, in the face, though it may be bearded, in the cheeks, florid as they are beneath their side-whiskers, there are certain lines which might have been traced from some maternal portrait. Almost every aged Charlus is a ruin in which one may recognise with astonishment, beneath all the layers of paint and powder, some fragments of a beautiful woman preserved in eternal youth. While we were talking, Morel came in. The Duchess treated him with a civility which disconcerted me a little. "I never take sides in family quarrels," she said. "Don't you find them boring, family quarrels?"

If in a period of twenty years, like this that had elapsed since my first entry into society, the conglomerations of social groups had disintegrated and re-formed under the magnetic influence of new stars destined themselves also to fade away and then to reappear, the same sequence of crystallisation followed by dissolution and again by a fresh crystallisation might have been observed to take place within the consciousness of individuals. If for me Mme de Guermantes had been many people, for Mme de Guermantes or for Mme Swann there were many individuals who had been a favoured friend in an era that preceded the Dreyfus Affair, only to be branded as a fanatic or an imbecile when the supervention of the Affair modified the accepted values of people and brought about a new configuration of parties, itself of brief duration, since later they had again disintegrated and re-formed. And what serves most powerfully to promote this renewal of old friendships, adding its influence to any purely intellectual affinities, is simply the passage of Time, which causes us to forget our antipathies and our disdains and even the reasons which once explained their existence. Had one analysed the fashionableness of the young Mme de Cambremer, one would have found that she was the niece of Jupien, a tradesman who lived in our house, and that the additional circumstance which had launched her on her social ascent was that her uncle

had procured men for M. de Charlus. But all this combined had produced effects that were dazzling, while the
causes were already remote and not merely unknown to
many people but also forgotten by those who had once
known them and whose minds now dwelt much more
upon her present brilliance than upon the ignominy of her
past, since people always accept a name at its current val-
uation. So that these drawing-room transformations possessed a double interest: they were both a phenomenon of
the memory and an effect of Lost Time.

The Duchess still hesitated, for fear of a scene with
M. de Guermantes, to make overtures to Balthy and
Mistinguett, whom she found adorable, but with Rachel
she was definitely on terms of friendship. From this the
younger generation concluded that the Duchesse de Guermantes, despite her name, must be some sort of demi-rep
who had never quite belonged to the best society. There
were, it was true, a few reigning princes (the honour of
whose familiar friendship two other great ladies disputed
with her) whom Mme de Guermantes still took the trouble to invite to luncheon. But on the one hand kings and
queens do not often come to see you and their acquaintances are sometimes people of no social position, and
then the Duchess, with the superstitious respect of the
Guermantes for old-fashioned protocol (for while well-
bred people bored her to tears, she was at the same time
horrified by any departure from good manners), would
put on her invitation cards: "Her Majesty has commanded
the Duchesse de Guermantes," or "has deigned," etc.
And newcomers to society, in their ignorance of these for-
mulae, inferred that their use was simply a sign of the

Duchess's lowly situation. From the point of view of Mme de Guermantes herself, this intimacy with Rachel signified perhaps that we had been mistaken when we supposed her to be hypocritical and untruthful in her condemnations of a purely fashionable life, when we imagined that in refusing to go and see Mme de Saint-Euverte she acted in the name not of intelligence but of snobbery, finding the Marquise stupid only because, not having yet attained her goal, she allowed her snobbery to appear on the surface. But the intimacy with Rachel might also signify that the intelligence of the Duchess was no more than commonplace, but had remained unsatisfied and at a late hour, when she was tired of society, had driven her, totally ignorant as she was of the veritable realities of the intellectual life, to seek for intellectual fulfilment with a touch of that spirit of fantasy which can cause perfectly respectable ladies, thinking to themselves: "How amusing it will be!", to end an evening with a prank which is in fact deadly dull: you go off and wake up some acquaintance and then, when you are in his room, you don't know what to say, so, after standing awkwardly by his bed for a few moments in your evening clothes and realising how late it is, there is nothing left to do but go home to bed yourself.

One must add that the antipathy which the changeable Duchess had recently come to feel for Gilberte may have caused her to take a certain pleasure in receiving Rachel, a course of conduct which enabled her also to proclaim aloud one of the favourite Guermantes maxims, to wit, that the family was too numerous for its members to have to espouse one another's quarrels (or even, some

might have said, to take notice of one another's bereave-
ments), an independence, a spirit of "I can't see that I am
obliged" which had been reinforced by the policy that it
had been necessary to adopt with regard to M. de Charlus, who, had you followed him, would have involved you
in hostilities with all your acquaintances.

As for Rachel, if the truth was that she had taken
very great pains to form this friendship with the Duchesse
de Guermantes (pains which the Duchess had failed to
detect beneath a mask of simulated disdain and deliberate
incivility, which had put her on her mettle and given her
an exalted idea of an actress so little susceptible to snobbery), this was no doubt in a general fashion an effect of
the fascination which after a certain time the world of
high society exercises upon even the most hardened bohemians, a fascination paralleled by that which the same
bohemians themselves exercise upon people in society,
flux and reflux which correspond to—in the political order—the reciprocal curiosity, the desire to form a mutual
alliance, of two nations which have recently been at war
with each other. But Rachel's desire had possibly a more
particular cause. It was in Mme de Guermantes's house, it
was at the hands of Mme de Guermantes herself, that she
had in the past suffered the most terrible humiliation of
her life. This snub Rachel had with the passage of time
neither forgotten nor forgiven, but the singular prestige
which the event had conferred upon the Duchess in her
eyes could never be effaced.

The conversation from which I was anxious to divert
Gilberte's attention was, in any case, presently interrupted, for the mistress of the house came in search of the

actress to tell her that the moment for her recital had arrived. She left the Duchess and a little later appeared upon the platform.

Meanwhile at the other end of Paris there was taking place a spectacle of a very different kind. Mme Berma, as I have said, had invited a number of people to a tea-party in honour of her daughter and her son-in-law. But the guests were in no hurry to arrive. Having learnt that Rachel was to recite poetry at the Princesse de Guermantes's (which utterly scandalised Berma, who from her own lofty position as a great artist looked down on Rachel as still no more than a kept woman who, because Saint-Loup paid for the dresses which she wore on the stage, was allowed to appear in the plays in which she herself, Berma, took the leading roles—and scandalised her all the more because a rumour had run round Paris that, though the invitations were in the name of the Princesse de Guermantes, it was in effect Rachel who was acting as hostess in the Princess's house), Berma had written a second time to certain faithful friends to insist that they should not miss her tea-party, for she was aware that they were also friends of the Princesse de Guermantes, whom they had known when she was Mme Verdurin. And now the hours were passing, and still nobody arrived to visit Berma. Bloch, having been asked whether he meant to come, had ingenuously replied: "No, I would rather go to the Princesse de Guermantes's," and this, alas! was what everyone in his heart of hearts had decided. Berma, who suffered from a deadly disease which had obliged her to cut down her social activities to a minimum, had seen her condition deteriorate when, in order to pay for the luxurious existence which her daughter demanded and her son-in-law, ailing and idle, was unable to provide, she had returned to the stage. She knew that she was shortening her days, but she wanted to give pleasure to her daughter, to whom she handed over the large sums that she earned, and to a son-in-law whom she detested but flattered—for she feared, knowing that his wife adored him, that if she, Berma, did not do what he wanted, he might, out of spite, deprive her of the happiness of seeing her child. This child, with whom secretly the doctor who looked after her husband was in love, had allowed herself to be persuaded that these performances in *Phèdre* were not really dangerous for her mother. She had more or less forced the doctor to tell her this, or rather of all that he had said to her about her mother's health she had retained only this in her memory, the truth being that, in the midst of various objections of which she had taken no notice, he had remarked that he saw no grave harm in Berma's appearing on the stage. He had said this because he had sensed that in so doing he would give pleasure to the young woman whom he loved, perhaps also from ignorance and also because he knew that the disease was in any case incurable, since a man readily consents to cut short the agony of an invalid when the action that will have this effect will be advantageous to himself—and perhaps also from the stupid idea that acting made Berma happy and was therefore likely to do her good, a stupid idea which had appeared to him to be corroborated when, having been given a box by Berma's daughter and son-in-law and having deserted all his patients for the occasion, he had found her as extraordinarily charged with life on the stage as she seemed to be moribund if you met her off it. And indeed

our habits enable us to a large degree, enable even the organs of our bodies, to adapt themselves to an existence
which at first sight would appear to be utterly impossible.
Have we not all seen an elderly riding-master with a weak
heart go through a whole series of acrobatics which one
would not have supposed his heart could stand for a single minute? Berma in the same way was an old campaigner of the stage, to the requirements of which her
organs had so perfectly adapted themselves that she was
able, by deploying her energies with a prudence invisible
to the public, to give an illusion of good health troubled
only by a purely nervous and imaginary complaint. After
the scene in which Phèdre makes her declaration of love
to Hippolyte Berma herself might be conscious only of
the appalling night which awaited her as a result of her
exertions, but her admirers burst into tumultuous applause and said that she was more wonderful than ever.
She would go home in terrible pain, happy nevertheless
because she brought back to her daughter the blue banknotes which, with the playfulness of a true child of the
footlights, she had the habit of squeezing into her stock-
ings, whence she would draw them out with pride, hoping
for a smile, a kiss. Unfortunately these banknotes merely
made it possible for her son-in-law and her daughter to
make new embellishments to their house, which was next
door to Berma's own: hence constant hammering, which
interrupted the sleep of which the great actress was so
desperately in need. According to the latest change in
fashion, or to conform to the taste of M. de X—— or
M. de Y—— whom they hoped to attract to their house,
they altered every room in it. And Berma, realising that
sleep, which alone would have deadened her pain, had

gone for good, would resign herself to lying awake, not without a secret contempt for this determination to be smart which was hastening her death and making her last days an agony. That these were its consequences was no doubt in part the reason why she despised this social ambition, contempt being a natural form of revenge upon something that does us harm and that we are powerless to prevent. But there was another reason, which was that, conscious of her own genius and having learnt at a very early age the meaninglessness of all these decrees of fashion, she for her part had remained faithful to tradition, which she had always respected and of which she was herself an embodiment, and which caused her to judge things and people as she would have judged them thirty years earlier, to judge Rachel, for example, not as the well-known actress that she was today, but as the little tart that she had once been. Berma was, one must add, no better natured than her daughter, for it was from her mother that the young woman had derived, through heredity and through the contagion of an example which an only too natural admiration had rendered more than usually potent, her egotism, her pitiless mockery, her unconscious cruelty. But all this Berma had sacrificed to her daughter and in this way she had liberated herself from it. However, even if Berma's daughter had not incessantly had workmen in her house, she would have tired her mother out just the same, since inevitably youth with its powers of attraction, its ruthless and inconsiderate strength, tires out old age and ill health, which overtax themselves in the effort to keep up with it. Every day there was yet another luncheon party, and Berma would have been condemned as selfish had she deprived her daughter of this pleasure, or even had she refused to be present herself at entertainments where the prestige of the famous mother was counted upon as a means of drawing to the house, not without difficulty, certain recent acquaintances who needed to be coaxed. And even away from home her attendance at a social function might be "promised" to these same acquaintances as a way of doing them a civility. So that the poor mother, seriously engaged in her intimate dialogue with the death that was already installed within her, was compelled to get up early in the morning and drag herself out of the house. Nor was this enough. At about this time Réjane, in the full blaze of her talent, made some appearances on the stage in foreign countries which had an enormous success, and the son-in-law decided that Berma must not allow herself to be put in the shade; determined that his own family should pick up some of the same easily acquired glory, he forced his mother-in-law to set out on tours on which she was obliged to have injections of morphine, which might at any moment have killed her owing to the condition of her kidneys.

This same ambition to be smart, this longing for social prestige, for life, had on the day of the Princesse de Guermantes's reception acted in the manner of a suction-pump, drawing to the latter's house with the irresistible force of some such machine even Berma's loyalest friends, so that at the actress's party there was, in contrast and in consequence, an absolute and deathlike void. One solitary young man had come, thinking that possibly Berma's party might be just as fashionable as the other. When Berma saw the hour pass for which she had issued the invitations and realised that everybody had deserted her, she

ordered tea to be served and the four people in the room
sat down at the table as though it had been spread for a
funeral feast. Nothing now in her face recalled the countenance of which the photograph, one distant New Year's
Day, had so disturbed me. Death, as the saying goes, was
written all over her face, and she resembled nothing so
much as one of the marble figures in the Erechtheum.
Her hardened arteries were already almost petrified, so
that what appeared to be long sculptural ribbons ran
across her cheeks, with the rigidity of a mineral substance.
The dying eyes were still relatively alive, by contrast at
least with the terrible ossified mask, and glowed feebly
like a snake asleep in the midst of a pile of stones. But already the young man, who had sat down only because it
would have been rude to do anything else, was incessantly
looking at his watch, for he too felt the attraction of the
brilliant party in the Guermantes mansion. Berma uttered
not a word in reproach of the friends who had deserted
her and who were foolish enough to hope that she would
not discover that they had been to the Guermantes'. She
murmured only: "A Rachel giving a party in the Princesse
de Guermantes's house—that is something that could
only happen in Paris." And silently and with a solemn
slowness she continued to eat the cakes which the doctor
had forbidden her, still with the air of playing her part in
a funerary rite. The gloom of the tea-party was made
more intense by the vile temper of the son-in-law, who
was furious that Rachel, whom he and his wife knew very
well, had not invited them. To crown his indignation the
young man who had come told him that he knew Rachel
so well that, if he went off to the Guermantes party
straight away, he could even at this eleventh hour ask her

to invite the frivolous couple. But Berma's daughter was too well aware of the low level at which her mother placed Rachel, she knew that she would die of despair at the thought of her daughter begging for an invitation from the former prostitute. So she told the young man and her husband that what he suggested was impossible. But she took her revenge as she sat at the tea-table by a series of little grimaces expressive of the desire for pleasure and the annoyance of being deprived of it by her killjoy mother. The latter pretended not to see her daughter's cross looks and from time to time, in a dying voice, addressed an amiable remark to the solitary guest. But soon the rush of air which was sweeping everything towards the Guermantes mansion, and had swept me thither myself, was too much for him; he got up and said good-bye, leaving Phèdre or death—one scarcely knew which of the two it was—to finish, with her daughter and her son-in-law, devouring the funeral cakes.

My conversation with Gilberte was interrupted by the voice of the actress which now made itself heard. Her style of recitation was intelligent, for it presupposed the existence of the poem whose words she was speaking as a whole which had been in being before she opened her mouth, a whole of which we were hearing merely a fragment, as though for a few moments, as the actress passed along a road, she had happened to be within earshot of us.

The announcement that she was to recite poems with which nearly everybody was familiar had been well received. But when the actress, before beginning to speak, was seen to shoot searching and bewildered glances in every direction, to lift her hands with an air of supplication and then to utter each word as though it were a groan, the general reaction was to feel embarrassed, almost shocked by this display of sentiment. Nobody had said to himself that a recital of poetry could be anything like this. Gradually, however, each member of an audience grows accustomed to what is taking place before him, he forgets his first sensation of discomfort, he picks out what is good in a performance, he mentally compares different ways of reciting and passes judgment: "this is excellent, this is not so good." But for the first few moments, just as when, in a trivial case in a law-court, we see a barrister advance, raise a toga'd arm in the air and start to speak in a threatening tone, we hardly dare look at our neighbours. For our immediate reaction is that this is grotesque—but we cannot be sure that it is not in fact magnificent, so for the present we suspend judgment.

Nevertheless the audience was amazed to see this woman, before she had emitted a single sound, bend her knees, stretch out her arms to cradle an invisible body and then, to recite some very well-known lines of poetry, start to speak in a voice of entreaty. People looked at one another, not knowing what expression to put on their faces: a few bad-mannered young things giggled audibly; everyone glanced at his neighbour with that stealthy glance which at a smart dinner-party, when you find beside your plate an unfamiliar implement, a lobster-fork or sugar-grinder perhaps, of which you know neither what it is for nor how to use it, you cast at some more authoritative guest in the hope that he will pick it up before you and so give you a chance to imitate him—or with which, when someone quotes a line of poetry which you do not know but of which you do not wish to appear ignorant,

you turn towards a man better read than yourself and relinquish to him, as though it were a favour, as though you
were courteously letting him pass through a door before
you, the pleasure of naming the author. With just this
same glance, as they listened to the actress, each member
of the audience waited, his head lowered but his eyes
furtively prying, for others to take the initiative and decide whether to laugh or to criticise, to weep or to applaud. Mme de Forcheville, who had come back specially
for the occasion from Guermantes, whence, as we shall
see, the Duchess had been almost expelled, had assumed
an expression that was attentive, concentrated, almost
bad-tempered, either in order to show that she was a connoisseur of the drama and had not come merely for social
reasons, or to present a hostile front to people who were
less versed in literature and might have talked to her
about other things, or from the intensity with which with
all her faculties she strove to discover whether she "liked"
or "did not like" the performance, or perhaps because,
while she found it "interesting," she nevertheless "did not
like" the manner in which certain lines were recited. This
attitude might, one would have thought, have been more
appropriate to the Princesse de Guermantes. But as the
recitation was taking place in her house and as, having become as avaricious as she was rich, she had decided that
her payment to Rachel would consist of five roses, she
chose rather to act as claque and gave the signal for a
forced display of enthusiasm by a series of exclamations of
delight. And here alone could her Verdurin past be recognised, for she had the air of listening to the poems for her
own private enjoyment, of having felt a desire for someone to come and recite them to her alone, so that it

seemed to be mere chance that there were in the room five hundred people, her friends, whom she had permitted to come unobtrusively and share in her pleasure.

Meanwhile I observed—without any satisfaction to my vanity, for she was old and ugly—that the actress, in a somewhat restrained fashion, was giving me the glad eye. All the time that she was reciting she allowed to flutter in and out of her eyes a smile that was both repressed and penetrating and that seemed to be the first hint of an acquiescence which she would have liked to see come from me. Certain elderly ladies meanwhile, little accustomed to the recitation of poetry, were saying to their neighbours: "Did you see?", a question which had reference to the solemn, tragic miming of the actress, which they had no words to describe. The Duchesse de Guermantes sensed the slight wavering of opinion and turned the scale of victory with a cry of "Admirable!", ejaculated at a pause in the middle of the poem which perhaps she mistook for the end. More than one guest thought it incumbent upon him to underline this exclamation with a look of approval and an inclination of the head, less perhaps to display his comprehension of the reciter's art than his friendly relations with the Duchess. When the poem was finished, I heard the actress thank Mme de Guermantes, who was standing near her, as I was myself, and at the same time, taking advantage of my presence beside the Duchess, she turned to me and greeted me with charming civility. At this point I realised that she was somebody whom I ought to have known and that, whereas long ago I had mistaken the passionate glances of M. de Vaugoubert for the salutation of someone who was confused as to my identity, today on the contrary what I had taken in the actress to be a look of desire was no more than a decorous attempt to make me recognise and greet her. I responded with a smile and a gesture. "I am sure he does not recognise me," said the reciter to the Duchess. "Of course I do," I said confidently, "I recognise you perfectly." "Well then, who am I?" I had not the slightest idea and my position was becoming awkward. But fortunately, if throughout one of La Fontaine's finest poems this woman who was reciting it with such conviction had, whether from good nature or stupidity or embarrassment, thought of nothing but the difficulty of saying good-afternoon to me, throughout this same beautiful poem Bloch had been wondering only how to manoeuvre himself so as to be ready, the moment the poem ended, to leap from his seat like a beleaguered army making a sally and, trampling if not upon the bodies at least upon the feet of his neighbours, arrive and congratulate the reciter, perhaps from an erroneous conception of duty, perhaps merely from a desire to make people look at him. "How curious it is to see Rachel here!" he whispered in my ear. At once the magic name broke the enchantment which had given to the mistress of Saint-Loup the unknown form of this horrible old woman.[10] And once I knew who she was, I did indeed recognise her perfectly. "You were wonderful," Bloch said to Rachel, and having said these simple words, having satisfied his desire, he started on his return journey—but encountered so many obstacles and made so much noise in reaching his place that Rachel had to wait more than five minutes before beginning her second poem. This was *Les Deux Pigeons*, and at the end of it Mme de Morienval came up to Mme de Saint-Loup, whom she knew to be very well read without

remembering that she had inherited the oblique and sarcastic wit of her father. "That *is* La Fontaine's fable, isn't
it?" she asked, thinking that she had recognised it but not
being absolutely certain, since she did not know the fables
of La Fontaine at all well and in any case supposed them
to be childish things which no one would recite at a fashionable gathering. To have such a success the entertainer
had no doubt produced a pastiche of La Fontaine,
thought the good lady. Unintentionally Gilberte confirmed her in this idea, for, disliking Rachel and wanting
to say that with her style of diction there was nothing left
of the fables, she said it in that over-subtle manner which
had been her father's and which left simple people in
doubt as to the speaker's meaning: "One quarter is the invention of the actress, a second is lunacy, a third is meaningless and the rest is La Fontaine," a remark which
encouraged Mme de Morienval to maintain that the poem
which had just been recited was not La Fontaine's *Les
Deux Pigeons*, but an arrangement of which at most a
quarter was by La Fontaine himself. Given the extraordinary ignorance of all these people, this assertion caused no
surprise whatever.

Meanwhile, one of his friends having arrived after the
recital was over, Bloch had the satisfaction of asking him
whether he had ever heard Rachel and of painting for his
benefit an extraordinary picture of her art, exaggerating,
indeed suddenly discovering, as he described and revealed
this modernistic diction to another person, a strange pleasure of which he had felt nothing as he listened to it.
Then, with exaggerated emotion, he again congratulated
Rachel in a high-pitched voice which proclaimed his sense
of her genius and introduced his friend, who declared that

his admiration for her was unbounded. To this, Rachel, who was now acquainted with ladies of the best society and unwittingly copied them, replied: "Oh! I am most flattered, most honoured by your appreciation." Bloch's friend asked her what she thought of Berma. "Poor woman, it seems that she is living in the most abject poverty. She was once, I won't say not without talent, for what she possessed was not true talent—her taste was appalling—still, one must admit she had merit of a kind: she was more alive on the stage than most actresses, and then she had nice qualities, she was generous, she ruined herself for others. And as it is years now since she has earned a penny, because the public these days loathes the sort of thing she does . . . But of course," she added with a laugh, "I must admit that someone of my generation, naturally, only heard her right at the end of her career, and even then I was really too young to form an opinion." "She didn't recite poetry very well, did she?" hazarded Bloch's friend, to flatter Rachel. "Poetry!" she replied, "she had no idea how to recite a single line. It might have been prose, or Chinese, or Volapük—anything, rather than poetry."

In spite of Rachel's words I was thinking myself that time, as it passes, does not necessarily bring progress in the arts. And just as some author of the seventeenth century, who knew nothing of the French Revolution, or the discoveries of science, or the war, may be superior to some writer of today, just as perhaps Fagon was as great a doctor as du Boulbon (a superiority in genius compensating in this case for an inferiority in knowledge), so Berma was, as the phrase goes, head and shoulders above Rachel, and Time, when simultaneously it turned Rachel into a star and Elstir into a famous painter, had inflated the reputation of a mediocrity as well as consecrated a genius.

It was scarcely surprising that Saint-Loup's former mistress should speak maliciously about Berma. She would have done this when she was young, and even if she would not have done it then, she was bound to now. When a society woman becomes an actress, a woman even of the highest intelligence and the greatest goodness of heart, and in this unfamiliar occupation displays great talent and encounters nothing but success, one will be surprised, meeting her years later, to hear on her lips not her own individual language but that which is common to the theatrical profession, the special brand of obloquy that actresses have for their colleagues, those special qualities which are added to a member of the human race by the passage over him of "thirty years on the stage." These qualities Rachel inevitably had and her origin, as we know, was not in good society.

"You can say what you like, it was a wonderful performance, it had line, it had character, it was intelligent, one has never heard anyone recite poetry like that before," said the Duchess, for fear that Gilberte should make disparaging remarks. Gilberte wandered off towards another group, to avoid an argument with her aunt, whose comments upon Rachel were indeed of the most commonplace kind. But then, since even the best writers cease often, at the approach of old age or after producing too much, to have any talent, society women may well be excused if sooner or later they cease to have any wit. Swann already in the sharp-edged wit of the Duchesse de Guermantes found it difficult to recognise the gentle raillery of the young Princesse des Laumes. And now late in life, wearied by the least effort, Mme de Guermantes said a prodigious number of stupid things. It was true that at any moment, as happened more than once in the course of this party, she could re-become the woman whom I had known in the past and talk wittily on social topics. But alongside these moments there were others, and they were no less frequent, when beneath her beautiful eyes the sparkling conversation which for so many years, from its throne of wit, had held sway over the most distinguished men in Paris, shone, in so far as it still shone at all, in a meaningless way. When the moment came to make a joke, she would check herself for the same number of seconds as in the past, she would appear to hesitate, to have something within her that was struggling to emerge, but the joke, when at last it arrived, was pitifully feeble. But how few of her listeners noticed this! Because the procedure was the same they believed that the wit too had survived intact, like those people who, superstitiously attached to some particular make of confectionery, continue to order their petits four from a certain shop without noticing that they have become almost uneatable. Already during the war the Duchess had shown signs of this decay. If someone pronounced the word "culture," she would stop him, smile, kindle a light in her beautiful eyes and ejaculate: "Kkkkultur," which raised a laugh among her friends, who saw in this remark the latest manifestation of the Guermantes wit. And certainly the mould was the same, and the intonation and the smile, the same that had once enchanted Bergotte, who for his part too had preserved the individual rhythm of his phrases, his interjections, his aposiopeses, his epithets, but with all this rhetorical apparatus no longer had anything to say. But newcomers, who did not know her, were surprised and said sometimes, unless they had chanced to encounter her on a day when she was amusing and "at her best": "What a stupid woman this is!"

As her life drew to its close, Mme de Guermantes had felt the quickening within her of new curiosities. Society no longer had anything to teach her. The idea that she occupied the first place in it was as evident to her as the altitude of the blue sky above the earth, and she saw no need to strengthen a position which she deemed to be unshakeable. On the other hand she read and she went to the theatre, and enjoying these activities she would have been glad to prolong them; just as in the past, in the little narrow garden where she sipped orangeade with her friends, all that was most choice in the world of grand society would come familiarly, among the scented breezes of the evening and the gusts of pollen, to sustain in her the pleasure that this grand world gave her and her appetite for it, so now a different appetite caused her to want to know the reasons behind this or that literary controversy, to want to meet the authors whose books she had read, to make friends with the actresses whom she had seen on the stage. Her tired mind required a new form of food, and in order to get to know theatrical and literary people she now made herself pleasant to women with whom formerly she would have refused to exchange cards but who, in the hope of getting the Duchess to come to their parties, could boast to her of their great friendship with the editor of some review. The first actress to be invited to her house thought that she was the only one of her kind in an exotic milieu, which however appeared more commonplace to the second when she saw that she had a predecessor. The Duchess, because on certain evenings she received reigning monarchs, thought that there was no change in her social position. But the truth was that she who alone could boast of a blood that was absolutely without taint, she who had been born a Guermantes and who when she did not sign herself "La Duchesse de Guermantes" had the right to put "Guermantes-Guermantes," she who even to her husband's sisters seemed to be something more precious than they were themselves, like a Moses saved from the waters or Christ escaped into Egypt or Louis XVII rescued from his prison in the Temple, she the purest of the pure had now, sacrificing no doubt to that hereditary need for spiritual nourishment which had brought about the social decline of Mme de Villeparisis, herself become a Mme de Villeparisis, in whose house snobbish women were afraid of meeting this or that undesirable and of whom the younger generation, observing the *fait accompli* and not knowing what had gone before it, supposed that she was a Guermantes from an inferior cask or of a less good vintage, a Guermantes *déclassée*.

If, however, the Duchess indulged a taste for the society of her inferiors, she was careful to confine this activity within strict limits and not allow it to contaminate those members of her family from whom she derived the gratification of an aristocratic pride. If at the theatre, for instance, in order to fill her role of patroness of the arts, she had invited a minister or a painter and her guest had been so ingenuous as to ask whether her sister-in-law or her husband were not in the audience, the Duchess, with a superb assumption of lofty indifference which concealed her alarm, would haughtily reply: "I have not the slightest idea. As soon as I leave my house, I know nothing of what my family is doing. For politicians, for artists, who-ever they may be, I am a widow." In this way she sought to prevent the too eager social climber from drawing upon himself a snub and upon her a reprimand from Mme de Marsantes or from Basin.

"I can't tell you how pleased I am to see you," said the Duchess. "Good heavens, when was it that I saw you last?" "I believe it was at Mme d'Agrigente's—I was pay-ing a call and I found you there, as I often did." "But of course, I was constantly going there, my dear boy, since Basin was in love with her in those days. And calling on Basin's sweetheart of the moment was always where my friends were most likely to find me, because he used to say: 'I shall expect you to visit her without fail.' I must admit that there seemed to me to be a slight impropriety in these 'digestive visits' on which he used to send me to thank the lady for her entertainment of him. But I quite soon grew accustomed to them. The tiresome thing was, however, that I was obliged to continue my relations with his mistress after he had broken off his own. I was always reminded of the line in Victor Hugo:

Take away the happiness and leave the boredom to *me*.

Naturally—you remember how the poem goes on—'I en-tered smiling none the less,' but it really was not fair, he ought to have left me the right to be inconstant, for in the end I accumulated so many of his discards that I had not a single afternoon to myself. Still, compared with the pres-ent that epoch now seems to me relatively agreeable. That he has started to be unfaithful again is, of course, something that I can only find flattering, it almost makes me feel younger. But I preferred his old way of doing it. Unfortunately, he was so out of practice that he had forgotten how to set about it. However, in spite of it all we are on excellent terms, we talk to each other, we are even quite fond of each other"—this the Duchess added because she was afraid that I might think that she and her husband were completely separated, rather as one says apropos of someone who is desperately ill: "But he is still able to speak, I read to him this morning for an hour." "I will tell him you are here," she continued, "he will be delighted to see you." And she went towards the Duke, who was sitting on a sofa in conversation with a lady. I observed with admiration that, except that his hair was whiter, he had scarcely changed, being still as majestic and as handsome as ever. But seeing his wife approach to speak to him he assumed an air of such fury that she had no alternative but to retreat. "I can't interrupt him just now, I don't know what he is doing, we shall see presently," said Mme de Guermantes, preferring to leave me to form my own conclusions.

Bloch now came up to us and on behalf of his American inquired the identity of a young duchess who was at the party. I replied that she was a niece of M. de Bréauté, which caused Bloch, as this name meant nothing to him, to ask for further explanations. "Bréauté!" the Duchess exclaimed, turning to me. "You remember all that, of course. How ancient it seems now, how far away! Well,"—this to Bloch—"Bréauté was a snob. They were people who lived near my mother-in-law in the country. This couldn't possibly interest you, Monsieur Bloch— though it may amuse this young man, who knew all that

world long ago when I was in the midst of it myself."
This last remark referred to me, and by it Mme de Guermantes brought home to me in a number of different
ways how long was the time that had elapsed. First, her
own friendships and opinions had so greatly changed
since that period that now, in retrospect, she looked upon
her charming Babal as a snob. And then, not only was he
now seen at the other end of a great vista of time, but—
and of this I had been quite unaware when at my first entry into society I had supposed him to be one of the
quintessential notabilities of Paris, who would for ever remain associated with its social history as Colbert with the
history of the reign of Louis XIV—he too bore the stamp
of a provincial origin, he was a country neighbour of the
old Duchess and it was as such that the Princesse des
Laumes had made his acquaintance. Moreover this
Bréauté, stripped of his wit and relegated to a distant past
for which he himself provided a date (which proved that
between then and now he had been entirely forgotten by
the Duchess) and to the countryside near Guermantes,
was—and this too I would never have thought possible
that first evening at the Opéra, when he had appeared to
me in the guise of a marine deity dwelling in his glaucous
cavern—a link between the Duchess and myself, because
she remembered that I had known him and therefore had
been a friend of hers, if not of the same social origin as
herself at any rate an inhabitant of the same social world
for very much longer than a great many people who were
at the party today, she remembered this and yet remembered it so hazily that she had forgotten certain details
which to me on the contrary had then seemed to be of
prime importance, such as that I never went to Guer-

mantes and at the time when she came to Mlle Percepied's nuptial mass was merely a boy of a middle-class
Combray family, and that, in spite of all Saint-Loup's en-
treaties, throughout the year which followed her apparition at the Opéra she had never invited me to her house.
To me this seemed to be of supreme importance, for it
was precisely during this brief period that the life of the
Duchesse de Guermantes had appeared to me to be a paradise into which I should never enter. But for her, her life
then was merely a part like any other of her normal, commonplace life, and as from a certain moment onwards I
had dined often at her house and had also, even before
that date, been a friend of her aunt and of her nephew,
she no longer knew exactly at what period our friendship
had begun and was unaware of the grave anachronism
that she was perpetrating in supposing that we had become friends a few years earlier than in fact we had. For
this would have meant that I had known the Mme de
Guermantes of the name of Guermantes, whose essence it
was to be unknowable, that I had been permitted to enter
the name of the golden syllables, had been received into
the Faubourg Saint-Germain, whereas in fact I had
merely been to dine at the house of a lady who was already nothing more in my eyes than a very ordinary
woman and who had occasionally invited me, not to descend into the submarine kingdom of the Nereids, but to
spend an evening with her in her cousin's box. "If you
want to know anything more about Bréauté," Mme de
Guermantes continued, still speaking to Bloch, "though
there is no earthly reason why you should, ask our friend
here, who is a hundred times more interesting than
Bréauté ever was. He must have dined at my house with

him fifty times. It was at my house, was it not, that you
got to know Bréauté? In any case, it was there that you
met Swann." And I was just as surprised that she should
imagine that I might have met M. de Bréauté elsewhere
than at her house (which could only have happened had I
moved in that society before I became acquainted with
her) as I was to see that she believed that it was through
her that I had met Swann. Less untruthfully than
Gilberte, who had been in the habit of saying of Bréauté:
"He is an old country neighbour, I so enjoy talking to
him about Tansonville," whereas in fact in the past he
had never visited the Swanns at Tansonville, I might have
said of Swann: "He was a country neighbour who often
used to come round and see us in the evening," for indeed
the memories which he recalled to my mind had nothing
to do with the Guermantes. "I don't know how to describe him," she went on. "He was a man whose only
subject of conversation was people with grand titles. He
had a whole collection of curious anecdotes about my
Guermantes relations and about my mother-in-law and
about Mme de Varambon before she became a lady-in-
waiting to the Princesse de Parme. But does anybody today know who Mme de Varambon was? Our friend here,
yes, he knew all those people. But it is all ancient history,
they are not even names today, and in any case they don't
deserve to be remembered." And again it struck me that,
in spite of the apparent unity of that thing which we call
"society," in which, it is true, social relations reach their
maximum of concentration (for all paths meet at the top)
and in which there are no barriers to communication,
there exist nevertheless within it, or at least there are created within it by Time, separate provinces which after a

while change their names and are no longer comprehensible to those who arrive in society only when its pattern
has been altered. "Mme de Varambon was a good lady
who said things of an incredible stupidity," continued the
Duchess, who failed to appreciate that poetry of the incomprehensible which is an effect of Time and chose
rather to extract from every situation its element of ironic
humour, the element that could be transformed into literature of the type of Meilhac or into the Guermantes
brand of wit. "At one moment she had a mania for swallowing a certain kind of lozenge which people used to take
in those days for coughs and which was called" (and she
laughed as she pronounced a name that was so special, so
well known formerly and so unknown today to everyone
around her) "a Géraudel lozenge. 'Madame de Varambon,' my mother-in-law used to say to her, 'if you don't
stop swallowing a Géraudel lozenge every five minutes,
you will injure your stomach.' 'But Madame la Duchesse,'
replied Mme de Varambon, 'how can they possibly injure
the stomach when they go into the bronchial tubes?' And
then it was she who made the remark: 'The Duchess has
a most beautiful cow, so beautiful that it is always taken
for a bull!' " And Mme de Guermantes would gladly have
gone on relating anecdotes of Mme de Varambon, of
which she and I knew hundreds, but we realised that in
the ignorant memory of Bloch this name evoked none
of those images which rose up for us as soon as there
was mention of her or of M. de Bréauté or of the
Prince d'Agrigente, though perhaps for this very reason
all these names were endowed in his eyes with a glamour
which I knew to be exaggerated but which I found comprehensible—though not because I myself had at one

time felt its influence, for it is rarely that our own errors and absurdities, even when we have penetrated to the truth behind them, make us more indulgent to those of others.

The past had been so transformed in the mind of the Duchess (or else the distinctions which existed in my mind had been always so absent from hers that what had been an event for me had gone unnoticed by her) that she was able to suppose that I had first met Swann in her house and M. de Bréauté elsewhere, thus conferring upon me a past as man about town of which she exaggerated the remoteness from the present. For the notion of time elapsed which I had just acquired was something that the Duchess had too, and, whereas my illusion had been to believe the gap between past and present shorter than in fact it was, she on the contrary actually overestimated it, she placed events further back than they really were, a notable consequence of this being her disregard of that supremely important line of demarcation between the epoch when she had been for me first a name and then the object of my love and the utterly different epoch when she had been for me merely a society woman like any other. It was of course only during this second period, when she had become for me a different person, that I had been to her house. But to her own eyes these differences were invisible and she would have seen nothing in the least odd in my going to her house two years earlier, for how was she to know that she had then been a different woman and even her doormat a different doormat, since her personality did not present to her that break in continuity which it presented to me?

"All this reminds me," I said to her, "of that first

evening when I went to the Princesse de Guermantes's, when I wasn't sure that I had been invited to her party and half expected to be shown the door, and when you wore a red dress and red shoes." "Good heavens, how long ago all that was!" said the Duchesse de Guermantes, accentuating by her words my own impression of time elapsed. She seemed to be gazing into this remote past in a melancholy mood, and yet she laid a particular emphasis upon the red dress. I asked her to describe it to me, which she did most willingly. "One couldn't possibly wear a thing like that now. It was the sort of dress that was worn in those days." "But it was pretty, wasn't it?" I said. She was always afraid of giving away a point in conversation, of saying something that might depreciate her in the eyes of others. "Personally, I found it a charming fashion. If nobody wears those dresses today, it is simply because it isn't done. But they will come back, as fashions always do — in clothes, in music, in painting," she added with vigour, for she supposed there to be a certain originality in this philosophic reflexion. Then the sad thought that she was growing old caused her to resume her languid manner, which a smile, however, momentarily contradicted: "Are you sure that they were red shoes that I wore? I thought they were gold." I assured her that I had the most vivid recollection of the colour of her shoes, though I preferred not to describe the incident which made me so certain on this point. "How kind of you to remember that!" she said to me sweetly, for women call it kindness when you remember their beauty, just as painters do when you admire their work. And then, since the past, however remote it may be for a woman like the Duchess who has more head than heart, may nevertheless chance to have escaped oblivion, "Do you recall," she said, as though to thank me for remembering her dress and her shoes, "that Basin and I brought you home in our carriage? You couldn't come in with us because of some girl who was coming to see you after midnight. Basin thought it the funniest thing in the world that you should receive visits at such an hour." Indeed that was the evening when Albertine had come to see me after the Princesse de Guermantes's party and I recalled the fact just as clearly as the Duchess, I to whom Albertine was now as unimportant as she would have been to Mme de Guermantes had Mme de Guermantes known that the girl because of whom I had had to refuse their invitation was Albertine. (In fact, she was quite in the dark as to the identity of this girl, had never known it and only referred to the incident because of the circumstances and the singular lateness of the hour.) Yes, I recalled the fact, for, long after our poor dead friends have lost their place in our hearts, their unvalued dust continues to be mingled, like some base alloy, with the circumstances of the past. And though we no longer love them, it may happen that in speaking of a room, or a walk in a public park, or a country road where they were present with us on a certain occasion, we are obliged, so that the place which they occupied may not be left empty, to make allusion to them, without, however, regretting them, without even naming them or permitting others to identify them. Such are the last, the scarcely desirable vestiges of survival after death.

If the opinions which the Duchess expressed about Rachel were in themselves commonplace, they interested me for the reason that they too marked a new hour upon the dial. For Mme de Guermantes had no more com-

pletely forgotten than Rachel the terrible evening which
the latter had endured in her house, but in the Duchess's
mind too this memory had been transformed. "Of
course," she said to me, "it interests me all the more to
hear her, and to hear her acclaimed, because it was I who
discovered her, who saw her worth and praised her and
got people to listen when she was quite unknown and everybody thought her ridiculous. Yes, my dear boy, this
will surprise you, but the first house in which she recited
in public was mine! Yes, while all the so-called avant-
garde, like my new cousin," she said, pointing ironically
towards the Princesse de Guermantes, who for Oriane had
remained Mme Verdurin, "would have allowed her to die
of hunger rather than condescend to listen to her, I had
made up my mind that she was interesting and I offered
her a fee to come and act in my house in front of the
most distinguished audience that I could muster. I may
say, though the word is rather stupid and pretentious—
for the truth is that talent needs nobody to help it—that
I launched her. But I am not suggesting that she needed
me." I made a vague gesture of protest, and I saw that
Mme de Guermantes was quite prepared to accept the
contrary thesis. "You don't agree? You think that talent
needs a support, needs someone to bring it into the light
of day? Well, perhaps you are right. Curiously enough,
that is exactly what Dumas used to say to me. In this case
I am extremely flattered if I have done anything, however
little, to promote not of course the talent but the reputation of so fine an artist." Mme de Guermantes preferred
to abandon her idea that talent, like an abscess, forces its
way to the surface unaided, partly because the alternative
hypothesis was more flattering for her, but also because

for some time now, mixing with newcomers to the social scene and being herself fatigued, she had become almost humble, questioning others and asking them their opinion before she formed her own. "I don't need to tell you," she went on, "that that intelligent public which calls itself society understood absolutely nothing of her art. They booed and they tittered. It was no use my saying: 'This is strange, interesting, something that has never been done before,' nobody believed me, just as nobody has ever believed anything I have said. And it was exactly the same with the piece that she recited, which was a scene from Maeterlinck. Now, of course, it is very well known but in those days people merely thought it ridiculous — not I, however, I admired it. I must say I am surprised, when I think of it, that a mere peasant like myself, with no more education than all the other provincial girls around her, should from the very first moment have felt drawn to these things. Naturally I couldn't have said why, but I liked them, I was moved — indeed, even Basin, who can hardly be called hypersensitive, was struck by the effect that they had on me. 'I won't have you listening to these absurdities,' he said, 'it makes you ill.' And he was right, because although I'm supposed to be a woman without any feeling I'm really a bundle of nerves."

At this moment an unexpected incident occurred. A footman came up to Rachel and told her that the daughter and son-in-law of Berma were asking to speak to her. As we have seen, Berma's daughter had resisted the desire, to which her husband would have yielded, to ask Rachel for an invitation. But after the departure of the solitary guest the irritation of the young pair as they sat with their mother had increased. The thought that other people were enjoying themselves had become a torment to them and presently, profiting from a momentary absence of Berma, who had retired to her room spitting a little blood, they had thrown on some smarter clothes, called for a cab and come, without an invitation, to the Princesse de Guermantes's house. Rachel, guessing what had happened and secretly flattered, put on an arrogant air and told the footman that she could not be disturbed, the visitors must write a line to explain the object of their curious procedure. Soon the footman came back with a card on which Berma's daughter had scribbled a few words to the effect that she and her husband had not been able to resist the desire to hear Rachel—might they have her permission to come in? Rachel smiled at the naïvety of the pretext and at her own triumph. She sent back a reply that she was terribly sorry but she had finished her recital. In the anteroom, where the couple had now been waiting for an embarrassingly long time, the footmen were beginning to jeer at the two rejected petitioners.

But the ignominy of a rebuff, and the thought too of the worthlessness of Rachel in comparison with her mother, drove Berma's daughter to pursue to final victory an enterprise on which she had first embarked merely from an appetite for pleasure. She sent a message to Rachel, asking as a favour that, even if she had missed the privilege of hearing her, she should be allowed to shake her by the hand. Rachel was talking to an Italian prince, said to be not insensible to the attractions of her large fortune, the origin of which was now to some extent disguised by her partial acceptance in the world of society. And here at her feet were the daughter and the son-in-law of the illustrious Berma, a reversal of positions which she was able to savour to the full. After giving a ludicrous account of what had happened to everybody within earshot, she ordered the young couple to be admitted and in they came without waiting to be asked twice, thus at a single stroke ruining Berma's social position just as they had destroyed her health. Rachel had foreseen this; she knew that an amiable condescension on her part would do more than a refusal to win for herself a reputation in society for kindness of heart and for the young couple one for grovelling servility. So she welcomed them with a theatrical gesture of open arms and a few words spoken in the role of an exalted patroness momentarily laying aside her dignity: "Ah! here you are, it is so lovely to see you. The Princess will be delighted." Not knowing that in the world of the theatre it was generally believed that she had sent out the invitations herself, she had feared perhaps that, if she refused to let Berma's daughter and son-in-law come in, they might have doubts as to the extent, not so much of her good nature, which would scarcely have worried her, as of her influence. Instinctively the Duchesse de Guermantes drifted away, for in proportion as anyone betrayed a desire to seek out fashionable society, he or she sank in her esteem. At the moment she was uniquely impressed with Rachel's kindness, and had the daughter and son-in-law been presented to her she would have turned her back on them. Rachel meanwhile was already composing in her head the gracious phrase with which she would annihilate Berma when she saw her the following day backstage: "I was distressed and appalled that your poor daughter should be made to dance attendance on me. If I had only realised! She kept sending me card after card." Her spirits rose as she thought of this blow that she would deal to

Berma. Yet perhaps she would have flinched had she known that it would be mortal. We like to have victims, but without putting ourselves clearly in the wrong: we want them to live. Besides, in what way had she done wrong? A few days later she was heard to say, with a laugh: "It's a bit much. I try to be kinder to her children than she ever was to me, and now I'm practically accused of murdering her. The Duchess will be my witness." So died Berma. It seems that the children of actors inherit from their parents all their ugly emotions and all the artificiality of theatrical life, but not, as a by-product of these, the stubborn will to work that their father or mother possessed, and Berma is not the only great tragic actress who has died as the victim of a domestic plot woven around her, repeating in her own person the fate that she so many times suffered in the final act of a play.

In spite of her new interests the life of the Duchess was now very unhappy, for the reason to which she had briefly alluded in her conversation with me, a reason which had, as a further consequence, a parallel degradation of the society which M. de Guermantes frequented. The Duke was still robust, but with the advance of age his desires had grown less imperious and he had long ceased to be unfaithful to Mme de Guermantes, when suddenly, without anyone knowing quite how the liaison had begun, he had fallen in love with Mme de Forcheville. When one considered what her age must now be, this seemed extraordinary. But perhaps she had been very young when she started on her amatory career. And then there are women who, decade after decade, are found in a new incarnation, having new love affairs (sometimes long after one had thought they were dead) and causing

the despair of young wives who are abandoned for them
by their husbands. In any case, the Duke's liaison with
Mme de Forcheville had assumed such proportions that
the old man, imitating in this final love the pattern of
those that he had had in the past, watched jealously over
his mistress in a manner which, if my love for Albertine
had, with important variations, repeated the love of
Swann for Odette, made that of M. de Guermantes for
this same Odette recall my own for Albertine. He insisted
that she should lunch with him and dine with him and he
was always in her house, so that she was able to show him
off to friends who without her would never have made the
acquaintance of a Duc de Guermantes and who came
there to meet him rather as one might go to the house of
a courtesan to meet a king, her lover. It was true that
Mme de Forcheville had long ago become a society lady.
But starting again late in life to be kept, and to be kept by
an old man of such enormous pride who, in spite of the
situation, was the important person in her house, she was
herself not too proud to wear only those wraps which
pleased him, to serve only the dishes that he liked, and to
flatter her friends by telling them that she had spoken of
them to her new lover just as in the old days she would
tell my great-uncle that she had spoken of him to the
Grand Duke who sent her cigarettes; in a word, in spite
of all that she had accomplished in building up a social
position, she was tending under pressure of new circumstances to become once more, as she had first appeared to
me in my earliest childhood, the lady in pink. (It was, of
course, many years since my uncle Adolphe had died, but
the replacement of the old figures around us by new ones
does not necessarily prevent us from beginning our old

life again.) If Odette had yielded to the pressure of her
new circumstances, this was no doubt partly from greed,
but also because, having been much sought after in society as the mother of an eligible daughter and then ignored
once Gilberte had married Saint-Loup, she foresaw that
the Duc de Guermantes, who would have done anything
for her, would rally to her side a number of duchesses
who would perhaps be delighted to do an ill turn to their
friend Oriane; and perhaps too she warmed to the game
when she saw how it distressed the Duchess, in whose
discomfiture a feminine sentiment of rivalry caused her to
rejoice. Even among the Duke's relations she now had her
partisans. Saint-Loup up to his death had continued loy-
ally to visit her with his wife. Were not he and Gilberte
heirs both to M. de Guermantes and to Odette, who
would herself no doubt be the principal beneficiary of the
Duke's will? And even Courvoisier nephews with the
most exacting standards, even the Princesse de Trania and
Mme de Marsantes, came to her house in the hope of a
legacy, without worrying about the pain that this might
cause the Duchess, of whom Odette, stung by past af-
fronts, spoke in the most scurrilous fashion. As for the
Duke's own social position, his liaison with Mme de
Forcheville—this liaison which was merely a pale copy of
earlier affairs of the same kind—had recently caused him
for the second time in his life to lose his chance of the
presidency of the Jockey and a vacant seat in the
Académie des Beaux-Arts, just as the way of life of M. de
Charlus and his public association with Jupien had cost
him the presidency of the Union and that also of the So-
ciété des Amis du Vieux Paris when these were within his
grasp. Thus the two brothers, so different in their tastes,

had lost their reputations from a common indolence and a common lack of will, qualities already perceptible, but in a more agreeable fashion, in the Duc de Guermantes their grandfather, member of the Académie Française, but which, reappearing in his two grandsons, had permitted a natural taste in the one and what passes for an unnatural taste in the other to alienate their possessors from their proper social sphere.

The old Duke no longer went anywhere, for he spent his days and his evenings with Mme de Forcheville. But today, as he would find her here, he had come for a moment, in spite of the vexation of having to meet his wife. I had not seen him, and I would certainly have failed to recognise him, had he not been clearly pointed out to me. He was no more than a ruin now, a magnificent ruin—or perhaps not even a ruin but a beautiful and romantic natural object, a rock in a tempest. Lashed on all sides by the surrounding waves—waves of suffering, of wrath at being made to suffer, of the rising tide of death—his face, like a crumbling block of marble, preserved the style and the poise which I had always admired; it might have been one of those fine antique heads, eaten away and hopelessly damaged, which you are proud nevertheless to have as an ornament for your study. In one respect only was it changed: it seemed to belong to a more ancient epoch than formerly, not simply because of the now rough and rugged surfaces of what had once been a more brilliant material, but also because to an expression of keen and humorous enjoyment had succeeded one, involuntary and unconscious, built up by illness, by the struggle against death, by passive resistance, by the difficulty of remaining alive. The arteries had lost all suppleness and gave to the once expansive countenance a hard and sculptural quality. And though the Duke had no suspicion of this, there were aspects of his appearance, of his neck and cheeks and forehead, which suggested to the observer that the vital spirit within, compelled to clutch desperately at every passing minute, was buffeted by a great tragic gale, while the white wisps of his still magnificent but less luxuriant hair lashed with their foam the half submerged promontory of his face. And just as there are strange and unique reflexions which only the approach of a supreme all-foundering storm can impart to rocks that hitherto have been of a different colour, so I realised that the leaden grey of the stiff, worn cheeks, the almost white, fleecy grey of the drifting wisps of hair, the feeble light that still shone from the eyes that scarcely saw, were not unreal hues and glimmers—they were only too real but they were fantastic, they were borrowed from the palette and the illumination, inimitable in their terrifying and prophetic sombreness, of old age and the imminence of death.

The Duke stayed only for a few moments, long enough, however, for me to perceive that Odette, reserving her favours for younger wooers, treated him with contempt. But curiously, whereas in the past he had been almost ridiculous when he used to behave like a king in a play, he had now assumed an appearance of true grandeur, rather like his brother, whom old age, stripping him of all unessential qualities, caused him to resemble. And—in this too resembling his brother—he who had once been proud, though not in his brother's fashion, seemed now almost deferential, though again in a different fashion. He had not suffered quite the degradation of

M. de Charlus, he was not obliged by the unreliable memory of a sick man to greet with civility people whom he would once have disdained. But he was very old and when, wanting to leave, he passed laboriously through the doorway and down the stairs, one saw that old age, which is after all the most miserable of human conditions, which more than anything else precipitates us from the summit of our fortunes like a king in a Greek tragedy, old age, forcing him to halt in the *via dolorosa* which life must become for us when we are impotent and surrounded by menace, to wipe his perspiring brow, to grope his way forward as his eyes sought the step which eluded them, because for his unsteady feet no less than for his clouded eyes he needed support, old age, giving him without his knowing it the air of gently and timidly beseeching those near him, had made him not only august but, even more, suppliant.

Thus in the Faubourg Saint-Germain three apparently impregnable positions, of the Duc and the Duchesse de Guermantes and of the Baron de Charlus, had lost their inviolability, changing, as all things change in this world, under the action of an inherent principle which had at first attracted nobody's attention: in M. de Charlus his love for Charlie, which had enslaved him to the Verdurins, and then later the advent of senility; in Mme de Guermantes a taste for novelty and for art; in the Duke an exclusive amorous passion, of a kind of which he had had several in the course of his life, but one which now, through the feebleness of age, was more tyrannical than those that had gone before and of which the ignominy was no longer compensated by the opposing, the socially redeeming respectability of the Duchess's salon, where the

Duke himself no longer appeared and which altogether had almost ceased to function. Thus it is that the pattern of the things of this world changes, that centres of empire, assessments of wealth, letters patent of social prestige, all that seemed to be for ever fixed is constantly being re-fashioned, so that the eyes of a man who has lived can contemplate the most total transformation exactly where change would have seemed to him to be most impossible.

Unable to do without Odette, always installed by her fireside in the same armchair, whence age and gout made it difficult for him to rise, M. de Guermantes permitted her to receive friends who were only too pleased to be presented to the Duke, to defer to him in conversation, to listen while he talked about the society of an earlier era, about the Marquise de Villeparisis and the Duc de Chartres. At moments, beneath the gaze of the old masters assembled by Swann in a typical "collector's" ar-rangement which enhanced the unfashionable and "pe-riod" character of the scene, with this Restoration Duke and this Second Empire courtesan swathed in one of the wraps which he liked, the lady in pink would interrupt him with a sprightly sally: he would stop dead and fix her with a ferocious glance. Perhaps he had come to see that she too, like the Duchess, sometimes made stupid re-marks; perhaps, suffering from an old man's delusion, he imagined that it was an ill-timed witticism of Mme de Guermantes that had checked his flow of reminiscence, imagined that he was still in his own house, like a wild beast in chains who for a brief second thinks that it is still free in the deserts of Africa. And brusquely raising his head, with his little round yellow eyes which themselves had the glitter of the eyes of a wild animal, he fastened upon her one of those looks which sometimes in Mme de Guermantes's drawing-room, when the Duchess talked too much, had made me tremble. So for a moment the Duke glared at the audacious lady in pink. But she, unflinching, held him in her gaze, and after a few seconds which seemed interminable to the spectators, the old tame lion recollecting that he was not free, with the Duchess beside him, in that Sahara which one entered by stepping over a doormat on a landing, but in Mme de Forcheville's domain, in his cage in the Zoological Gardens, he allowed his head, with its still thick and flowing mane of which it would have been hard to say whether it was yellow or white, to slump back between his shoulders and continued his story. He seemed not to have understood what Mme de Forcheville was trying to say, and indeed there was seldom any very profound meaning in her remarks. He did not forbid her to have friends to dinner with him, but, following a habit derived from his former love-affairs which was hardly likely to surprise Odette, who had been used to the same thing with Swann, and which to me seemed touching because it recalled to me my life with Albertine, he insisted that these guests should take their leave early so that he might be the last to say good-night to her. Needless to say, the moment he was out of the house she went off to meet other people. But of this the Duke had no suspicion or perhaps preferred her to think that he had no suspicion. The sight of old men grows dim as their hearing grows less acute, their insight too becomes clouded and even their vigilance is relaxed by fatigue, and at a certain age, inevitably, Jupiter himself is transformed into a character in one of Molière's plays, and not even into the Olympian lover of Alcmène but

into a ludicrous Géronte. It must be added that Odette
was unfaithful to M. de Guermantes in the same fashion
that she looked after him, that is to say without charm
and without dignity. She was commonplace in this role as
she had been in all her others. Not that life had not frequently given her good parts; it had, but she had not
known how to play them.

On several occasions after the Guermantes party I attempted to see her again, but each time I was unsuccessful, for M. de Guermantes, in order to satisfy the requirements not only of his jealous nature but also of his
medical regime, allowed her to attend social functions
only in the daytime and even then placed an embargo
upon dances. This seclusion in which she was kept she
frankly avowed to me when at last we met, for several
reasons. The principal one was that, although I had only
written a few articles and published some essays, she
imagined me to be a well-known author, an idea which
even caused her naïvely to exclaim, recalling the days
when I used to go to the Allée des Acacias to see her pass
by and later visited her in her home: "Ah! if I had only
guessed that he would be a great writer one day!" And
having heard that writers seek the society of women as a
means of collecting material for their work and like to get
them to describe their love-affairs, she now, in order to
interest me, reassumed the character of an unashamed
tart. She would tell me stories of this sort: "And then
once there was a man who was mad about me, and I was
desperately in love with him too. We were having a heavenly life together. He had to go to America for some reason, and I was to go with him. The day before we were to
leave I decided that, as our love could not always remain

at such a pitch of intensity, it was more beautiful not to let it slowly fade to nothing. We had a last evening together—he of course believed that I was coming with him—and then a night of absolute madness, in which I was ecstatically happy in his arms and at the same time in despair because I knew that I should never see him again. A few hours earlier I had gone up to some traveller whom I did not know and given him my ticket. He wanted at least to buy it from me, but I replied: 'No, you are doing me a service by taking it, I don't want any money.'" Here was another: "One day I was in the Champs-Elysées and M. de Bréauté, whom I had only met once, began to stare at me so insistently that I stopped and asked him why he took the liberty of staring at me like that. He replied: 'I am looking at you because you are wearing a ridiculous hat.' This was quite true. It was a little hat with pansies, the fashions were dreadful in those days. But I was furious and said to him: 'I cannot allow you to talk to me like that.' At that moment it started to rain. I said to him: 'I would only forgive you if you had a carriage.' 'But I have one,' he replied, 'and I will accompany you.' 'No, I want your carriage but I don't want you.' I got into the carriage and he walked off in the rain. But the same evening he arrived on my door-step. For two years we were madly in love with each other. Come and have tea with me one day, and I will tell you how I made the acquaintance of M. de Forcheville. The truth is," she went on with a melancholy air, "that I have spent my life in cloistered seclusion because my great loves have all been for men who were horribly jealous. I am not speaking of M. de Forcheville, who was at bottom a commonplace man—and I have never really been able to love

anyone who was not intelligent. But M. Swann for one
was as jealous as the poor Duke here, for whose sake I renounce all enjoyment, because I know that he is so unhappy in his own home. With M. Swann it was different,
I was desperately in love with him and it seems to me
only reasonable to sacrifice dancing and society and all the
rest of it for a life which will give pleasure to a man who
loves you, or will merely prevent him from suffering.
Poor Charles, how intelligent he was, how fascinating, just
the type of man I liked." And perhaps this was true.
There had been a time when she had found Swann attractive, which had coincided with the time when she to him
had been "not his type." The truth was that "his type"
was something that, even later, she had never been. And
yet how he had loved her and with what anguish of mind!
Ceasing to love her, he had been puzzled by this contradiction, which really is no contradiction at all, if we consider how large a proportion of the sufferings endured by
men in their lives is caused to them by women who are
"not their type." Perhaps there are many reasons why this
should be so: first, because a woman is "not your type"
you let yourself, at the beginning, be loved by her without
loving in return, and by doing this you allow your life to
be gripped by a habit which would not have taken root in
the same way with a woman who was "your type," who,
conscious of your desire, would have offered more resistance, would only rarely have consented to see you, would
not have installed herself in every hour of your days with
that familiarity which means that later, if you come to
love her and then suddenly she is not there, because of a
quarrel or because of a journey during which you are left
without news of her, you are hurt by the severance not of

one but of a thousand links. And then this habit, not resting upon the foundation of strong physical desire, is a
sentimental one, and once love is born the brain gets
much more busily to work: you are plunged into a romance, not plagued by a mere need. We are not wary of
women who are "not our type," we let them love us, and
if, subsequently, we come to love them we love them a
hundred times more than we love other women, without
even enjoying in their arms the satisfaction of assuaged
desire. For these reasons and for many others the fact that
our greatest unhappinesses come to us from women who
are "not our type" is not simply an instance of that mockery of fate which never grants us our wishes except in the
form which pleases us least. A woman who is "our type"
is seldom dangerous, she is not interested in us, she gives
us a limited contentment and then quickly leaves us without establishing herself in our life, and what on the contrary, in love, is dangerous and prolific of suffering is not
a woman herself but her presence beside us every day and
our curiosity about what she is doing every minute: not
the beloved woman, but habit.

I was cowardly enough to say that it was kind and
generous of her to talk to me in this way, but I knew how
little truth there was in my remark, I knew that her frankness was mixed with all sorts of lies. And as she continued to regale me with adventures from her past life, I
thought with terror how much there was that Swann had
not known—though some of it he had guessed almost to
the point of certainty, merely from the look in her eyes
when she saw a man or a woman whom she did not know
and whom she found attractive—and how much the
knowledge of it would have made him suffer, because he

had fastened his sensibility to this one individual. And why was she now so outspoken? Simply in order to give me what she believed were subjects for novels. In this belief she was mistaken. It was true that from my earliest years she had supplied my imagination with abundance of material to work on, but in a much more involuntary fashion, through an act which originated with myself when I sought, unbeknown to her, to deduce from my observation of her the laws which governed her life.

M. de Guermantes now reserved his thunderbolts solely for the Duchess, to whose somewhat indiscriminate associations Mme de Forcheville did not fail to draw his wrathful attention. And so Mme de Guermantes was very unhappy. It is true that M. de Charlus, with whom I had once discussed the subject, maintained that the original transgressions had not been on his brother's side and that beneath the legendary purity of the Duchess there in fact lay skilfully concealed an incalculable number of love-affairs. But I had never heard any gossip to this effect. In the eyes of almost all the world Mme de Guermantes was a woman of a very different kind, and the idea that she had always been irreproachable went unchallenged. Which of these two ideas accorded with the truth I was unable to determine, the truth being almost always something that to three people out of four is unknown. I well recalled certain blue and wandering glances, which I had intercepted as they shot from the eyes of the Duchesse de Guermantes down the nave at Combray, but I could not really say that either of the two ideas was disproved by these glances, since both the one and the other could give them meanings which, though different, were equally acceptable. In my foolishness, child as I then was, I had for a moment taken them to be glances of love directed at myself. Later I had realised that they were merely the gracious looks that a sovereign lady, like the one in the stained-glass windows of the church, bestows upon her vassals. Was I now to suppose that my first idea had been correct and that, if in the sequel the Duchess had never spoken to me of love, this was because she had been more afraid to compromise herself with a friend of her nephew and her aunt than with an unknown boy encountered by chance in the church of Saint-Hilaire at Combray?

Perhaps the Duchess had been pleased for a moment to feel that her past had more substance because it had been shared by me, but certain questions which I put to her on the provincialism of M. de Bréauté, whom at the time I had scarcely distinguished from M. de Sagan or M. de Guermantes, caused her to resume the normal point of view of a society woman, the point of view, that is to say, of a woman who affects to despise society. While we were talking, she took me on a tour of the house. In one or two smaller sitting-rooms we came upon special friends of our hostess who had preferred to get away from the crowd in order to listen to the music. One of these was a little room with Empire furniture, where a few men in black evening clothes were sitting about on sofas, listening, while beside a tall mirror supported by a figure of Minerva a *chaise longue*, set at right angles to the wall but with a curved and cradle-like interior which contrasted with the straight lines all round it, disclosed the figure of a young woman lying at full length. The relaxation of her pose, from which she did not even stir when the Duchess entered the room, was set off by the marvellous brilliance of her Empire dress, of a flame-red silk be-

fore which even the reddest of fuchsias would have paled
and upon whose nacreous texture emblems and flowers
seemed to have been imprinted in some distant past, for
their patterns were sunk beneath its surface. To acknowledge the presence of the Duchess she made a slight bow
with her beautiful, dark head. Although it was broad daylight, she had asked for the curtains to be drawn as an aid
to the silence and concentration which the music required
and, to prevent people from stumbling over the furniture,
an urn had been lit upon a tripod and from it came a
faint, iridescent glimmer. I inquired of the Duchess who
the young woman was, and she told me that her name
was Mme de Saint-Euverte. This led me to inquire further how she was related to the Mme de Saint-Euverte
whom I had known. Mme de Guermantes said that she
was the wife of one of old Mme de Saint-Euverte's great-
nephews and appeared to think it possible that her
maiden name had been La Rochefoucauld, but denied
that she had ever herself known any Saint-Euvertes. I recalled to her the evening party (known to me, it is true,
only from hearsay) at which, when she was still Princesse
des Laumes, she had unexpectedly met Swann. Mme de
Guermantes assured me that she had never been at this
party. The Duchess had never been very truthful and now
told lies more readily than ever. For her Mme de Saint-
Euverte was a hostess—and one whose reputation, with
the passage of time, had sunk very low indeed—whom
she chose to disown. I did not insist. "No, someone you
may perhaps have seen in my house—because at least he
was amusing—is the husband of the woman you are talking about, but I never had anything to do with his wife."
"But she didn't have a husband." "That is what you

imagined, because they were separated. In fact he was much nicer than she was." At length it dawned upon me that an enormous man, of vast height and strength, with snow-white hair, whom I used to meet in various houses and whose name I had never known, was the husband of Mme de Saint-Euverte. He had died in the previous year. As for the great-niece, I do not know whether it was owing to some malady of the stomach or the nerves or the veins, or because she was about to have or had just had a child or perhaps a miscarriage, that she lay flat on her back to listen to the music and did not budge for anyone. Very probably she was simply proud of her magnificent red silks and hoped on her *chaise longue* to look like Mme Récamier. She could not know that for me she was giving birth to a new efflorescence of the name of Saint-Euverte, which recurring thus after so long an interval marked both the distance travelled by Time and its continuity. Time was the infant that she cradled in her cockle-shell, where the red fuchsias of her silk dress gave an autumnal flowering to the name of Saint-Euverte and to the Empire style. The latter Mme de Guermantes declared that she had always detested, a remark which meant merely that she detested it now, which was true, for she followed the fashion, even if she did not succeed in keeping up with it. To say nothing of David, whose work she hardly knew, when she was quite young she had thought M. Ingres the most boring and academic of painters, then, by a brusque reversal—which caused her also to loathe Delacroix—the most delectable of the masters revered by *art nouveau*. By what gradations she had subsequently passed from this cult to a renewal of her early contempt matters little, since these are shades of taste which the writings of an art critic reflect ten years before the conversation of clever women. After having delivered herself of some strictures upon the Empire style, she apologised for having talked to me about people of as little interest as the Saint-Euvertes and subjects as trivial as the provincial side of Bréauté's character, for she was as far from guessing why these things could interest me as was Mme de Saint-Euverte *née* La Rochefoucauld, seeking in her supine pose the well-being of her stomach or an Ingresque effect, from suspecting that her name—her married name, not the infinitely more distinguished one of her own family—had enchanted me and that I saw her, in this room full of symbolic attributes, as a nymph cradling the Infant Time.

"But how can I talk to you about this nonsense, how can it possibly interest you?" exclaimed the Duchess. She had uttered these words in an undertone and nobody had been able to hear what she was saying. But a young man (who interested me later when I discovered his name, which had been much more familiar to me at one time than that of Saint-Euverte) got up with an air of exasperation and moved away from us in order to listen undisturbed. For the Kreutzer Sonata was now being played, but having lost his place in the programme the young man thought that it was a piece by Ravel, which he had been told was as beautiful as Palestrina but difficult to understand. In his haste to move to another seat, he bumped violently against an escritoire which he had not seen in the half-dark, and the noise had the effect of slewing round the heads of several people, for whom the trifling physical exertion of looking over their shoulder was a welcome interruption to the torture of listening "religiously" to the Kreutzer Sonata. Mme de Guermantes and

I, who had caused this unfortunate little incident, hurriedly left the room. "Yes," she went on, "how can these inanities interest a man of your talent? That is what I asked myself just now, when I saw you talking to Gilberte de Saint-Loup. You should not waste your time on her. For me that woman is quite literally nothing—she is not even a woman, merely the most artificial and bourgeois phenomenon that I have ever encountered" (for even when she was defending intellectualism the Duchess did not divest herself of her aristocratic prejudices). "What, in any case, are you doing in a house like this? I can just see that you might want to be here today, because there was this recitation by Rachel and naturally that interests you. But wonderful though she was, she does not give of her best before a public like this. You must come and have luncheon alone with her in my house. Then you will see what an extraordinary creature she is. She is worth a hundred times more than all this riff-raff. And after luncheon she will recite Verlaine for you. You will be amazed! But otherwise your coming to a great omnium gatherum like this is something I simply cannot understand. Unless perhaps your interest is professional . . ." she added with a doubtful and mistrustful air and without venturing to follow this speculation too far for she had no very precise ideas as to the nature of the improbable operations to which she alluded. She went on to tempt me with the glittering prospect of her "afternoons": every day after luncheon there was X—— and there was Y——, and I found that her views on these matters were now those of all women who preside over a salon, those women whom in the past (though she denied it today) she had despised and whose great superiority, whose sign of election lay, according to her present mode of thinking, in getting "all the men" to come to them. If I happened to say that some great lady with a salon had spoken with malice of Mme Howland when she was alive, the Duchess burst out laughing at my simplicity: "But of course, she had all the men and Mme Howland was trying to get them away from her."

"Don't you think," I said to the Duchess, "that it must be painful for Mme de Saint-Loup to have to listen, as she has just been doing, to a woman who was once her husband's mistress?" I saw form in Mme de Guermantes's face one of those oblique bars which indicate that a train of thought is linking something a person has just heard to some disagreeable subject of reflexion. A train of thought, it is true, which usually remains unexpressed, for seldom if ever do we receive any answer to the unpleasant things that we say or write. Only a fool begs vainly ten times in succession for a reply to a letter which was a blunder and which he ought never to have written, for the only reply ever vouchsafed to this sort of letter is in the form of action: the lady whom you suppose to be merely an unpunctual correspondent addresses you as "Monsieur" when she next meets you instead of calling you by your Christian name. My reference to Saint-Loup's liaison with Rachel was, however, not seriously unpleasant and could only cause Mme de Guermantes a moment's annoyance by reminding her that I had been Robert's closest friend and that he had perhaps confided in me on the subject of the snubs which Rachel had suffered when she gave her performance at the Duchess's party. But Mme de Guermantes did not persist in these reflexions, the stormy bar faded from her face and she

replied to my question concerning Mme de Saint-Loup:
"Frankly, it is my belief that it can matter very little to
Gilberte, since she never loved her husband. She is a
quite dreadful young woman. She loved the social position
and the name and being my niece and getting away from
the slime where she belonged, but then having done this
her one idea was to return to it. I don't mind telling you
that I suffered a great deal for poor Robert, because,
though he was no genius, he saw this perfectly well, and a
lot of other things too. Perhaps I shouldn't say it, because
after all she is my niece and I have no absolute proof that
she was unfaithful to him, but there were any number of
stories. Oh! yes, there were, and I know for a fact there
was something between her and an officer at Méséglise.
Robert wanted to challenge him. It was because of all this
that Robert joined up—the war came to him as a deliverance from the misery of his family life: if you want my
opinion, he wasn't killed, he got himself killed. Do you
think she felt any grief? Not a scrap, she even astonished
me by the extraordinary cynicism with which she displayed her indifference, and this distressed me very much,
because I was really extremely fond of poor Robert. Perhaps this will surprise you, because people have a wrong
idea of my character, but even now I still think of him
sometimes—I never forget anybody. He never said a
word to me, but he saw very clearly that I guessed everything. Do you suppose, if she had loved her husband the
least little bit, that she could stoically endure like this to
be in the same drawing-room as the woman with whom
he was desperately in love for so many years—indeed one
may say 'always,' for I am quite certain that he never
gave her up, even during the war. Why, she would fly at

her throat!" exclaimed the Duchess, forgetting that she herself, in arranging for Rachel to be invited and so setting the stage for the drama which she judged to be inevitable if it were true that Gilberte had loved Robert, had perhaps acted cruelly. "No, in my opinion," the Duchess concluded, "she is a bitch." Such an expression on the lips of the Duchesse de Guermantes was rendered possible by the downward path which she was following, from the polished society of the Guermantes to that of her new actress friends, and came to her all the more easily because she grafted it on to an eighteenth-century mode of speech which she thought of as broad and racy—and then had she not always believed that to her all things were permitted? But the actual choice of the word was dictated by the hatred which she felt for Gilberte, by an irresistible wish to strike her at least in effigy if she could not attack her with physical blows. And at the same time the Duchess thought that somehow the word justified the whole manner in which she conducted herself towards Gilberte, or rather conducted hostilities against Gilberte, in society and in the family and even where pecuniary interests were concerned such as the succession to Robert's estate.

This savage attack on Gilberte struck me as quite unwarranted, but sometimes we pronounce a judgment which receives later from facts of which we were ignorant and which we could not have guessed an apparent justification, and Mme de Guermantes's tirade perhaps belonged to this category. For Gilberte, who had no doubt inherited certain family characteristics from her mother (and I had perhaps unconsciously anticipated some such laxness of principle in her when I had asked her to intro-

duce me to young girls), had now had time to reflect
upon my request and, anxious no doubt that the profit
should stay in the family, had reached a decision bolder
than any that I would have thought possible. "Let me
fetch my daughter for you," she said, "I should so like to
introduce her to you. She is over there, talking to young
Mortemart and other babes in arms who can be of no
possible interest. I am sure that she will be a charming
little friend for you." I asked whether Robert had been
pleased to have a daughter. "Oh! yes," she replied, "he
was very proud of her. But naturally," she went on, with
a certain naïvety, "I think that nevertheless, his tastes being what they were, he would have preferred a son."
Years later, this daughter, whose name and fortune gave
her mother the right to hope that she would crown the
whole work of social ascent of Swann and his wife by
marrying a royal prince, happening to be entirely without
snobbery chose for her husband an obscure man of letters.
Thus it came about that the family sank once more, below even the level from which it had started its ascent,
and a new generation could only with the greatest difficulty be persuaded that the parents of the obscure couple
had enjoyed a splendid social position. The names of
Swann and Odette de Crécy came miraculously to life
whenever anyone wanted to explain to you that you were
wrong, that there had been nothing so very wonderful
about the family, and it was generally supposed that Mme
de Saint-Loup had really made as good a match for her
daughter as could be expected and that the marriage of
this daughter's grandfather to Mme de Crécy had been no
more than an unsuccessful attempt to rise to a higher
sphere—a view of Swann's marriage which would have

astonished his fashionable friends, in whose eyes it had
been rather the product of an idealistic theory like those
which in the eighteenth century drove aristocratic disciples of Rousseau and other precursors of the Revolution
to abandon their privileges and live according to nature.

My surprise at Gilberte's words and the pleasure that
they caused me were soon replaced, while Mme de Saint-
Loup left me and made her way into another drawing-
room, by that idea of Time past which was brought home
to me once again, in yet another fashion and without my
even having seen her, by Mlle de Saint-Loup. Was she
not—are not, indeed, the majority of human beings?—
like one of those star-shaped crossroads in a forest where
roads converge that have come, in the forest as in our
lives, from the most diverse quarters? Numerous for me
were the roads which led to Mlle de Saint-Loup and
which radiated around her. Firstly the two great "ways"
themselves, where on my many walks I had dreamed so
many dreams, both led to her: through her father Robert
de Saint-Loup the Guermantes way; through Gilberte, her
mother, the Méséglise way which was also "Swann's
way." One of them took me, by way of this girl's mother
and the Champs-Elysées, to Swann, to my evenings at
Combray, to Méséglise itself; the other, by way of her father, to those afternoons at Balbec where even now I saw
him again near the sun-bright sea. And then between
these two high roads a network of transversals was set up.
Balbec, for example, the real Balbec where I had met
Saint-Loup, was a place that I had longed to go to very
largely because of what Swann had told me about the
churches in its neighbourhood, and especially about its
own church in the Persian style, and yet Robert de Saint-

Loup was the nephew of the Duchesse de Guermantes, and through him I arrived at Combray again, at the Guermantes way. And Mlle de Saint-Loup led to many other points of my life, to the lady in pink, for instance, who was her grandmother and whom I had seen in the house of my great-uncle. And here there was a new transversal, for this great-uncle's manservant, who had opened the door to me that day and who later, by the gift of a photograph, had enabled me to identify the lady in pink, was the father of the young man with whom not only M. de Charlus but also Mlle de Saint-Loup's father had been in love, the young man on whose account he had made her mother unhappy. And was it not Swann, the grandfather of Mlle de Saint-Loup, who had first spoken to me of the music of Vinteuil, just as it was Gilberte who had first spoken to me of Albertine? Yet it was in speaking of this same music of Vinteuil to Albertine that I had discovered the identity of her great friend and it was with this discovery that that part of our lives had commenced which had led her to her death and caused me such terrible sufferings. And it was also Mlle de Saint-Loup's father who had gone off to try and bring Albertine back. And indeed my whole social life, both in the drawing-rooms of the Swanns and the Guermantes in Paris and also that very different life which I had led with the Verdurins in the country, was in some sense a prolongation of the two ways of Combray, a prolongation which brought into line with one way or the other places as far apart as the Champs-Elysées and the beautiful terrace of La Raspelière. Are there in fact among all our acquaintances any who, if we are to tell the story of our friendship with them, do not constrain us to place them successively in all the most different settings of our own lives? A life of Saint-Loup painted by me would have as its background the various scenes of my own life, would be related to every part of that life, even those to which it was apparently most foreign, such as my grandmother and Albertine. And the Verdurins, though they might be diametrically opposed to these other characters, were yet linked to Odette through her past and to Robert de Saint-Loup through Charlie—and in the Verdurins' house too what a role, what an all-important role had not the music of Vinteuil played! And then Swann had been in love with Legrandin's sister, and Legrandin had known M. de Charlus, whose ward Legrandin's nephew, young Cambremer, had married. Certainly, if he was thinking purely of the human heart, the poet was right when he spoke of the "mysterious threads" which are broken by life. But the truth, even more, is that life is perpetually weaving fresh threads which link one individual and one event to another, and that these threads are crossed and recrossed, doubled and redoubled to thicken the web, so that between any slightest point of our past and all the others a rich network of memories gives us an almost infinite variety of communicating paths to choose from.

At every moment of our lives we are surrounded by things and people which once were endowed with a rich emotional significance that they no longer possess. But let us cease to make use of them in an unconscious way, let us try to recall what they once were in our eyes, and how often do we not find that a thing later transformed into, as it were, mere raw material for our industrial use was once alive, and alive for us with a personal life of its own. All round me on the walls were paintings by Elstir, that

Elstir who had first introduced me to Albertine. And it was in the house of Mme Verdurin that I was about to be presented to Mlle de Saint-Loup whom I was going to ask to be Albertine's successor in my life, in the house of that very Mme Verdurin whom I had so often visited with Albertine—and how enchanting they seemed in my memory, all those journeys that we had made together in the little train on the way to Douville and La Raspelière—and who had also schemed first to promote and then to break not only my own love for Albertine but, long before it, that of the grandfather and the grandmother of this same Mlle de Saint-Loup. And to complete the process by which all my various pasts were fused into a single mass Mme Verdurin, like Gilberte, had married a Guermantes.

I have said that it would be impossible to depict our relationship with anyone whom we have even slightly known without passing in review, one after another, the most different settings of our life. Each individual therefore—and I was myself one of these individuals—was a measure of duration for me, in virtue of the revolutions which like some heavenly body he had accomplished not only on his own axis but also around other bodies, in virtue, above all, of the successive positions which he had occupied in relation to myself. And surely the awareness of all these different planes within which, since in this last hour, at this party, I had recaptured it, Time seemed to dispose the different elements of my life, had, by making me reflect that in a book which tried to tell the story of a life it would be necessary to use not the two-dimensional psychology which we normally use but a quite different sort of three-dimensional psychology, added a new beauty to those resurrections of the past which my memory had effected while I was following my thoughts alone in the library, since memory by itself, when it introduces the past, unmodified, into the present—the past just as it was at the moment when it was itself the present—suppresses the mighty dimension of Time which is the dimension in which life is lived.

I saw Gilberte coming across the room towards me. For me the marriage of Saint-Loup and the thoughts which filled my mind at that date—and which were still there, unchanged, this very morning—might have belonged to yesterday, so that I was astonished to see at her side a girl of about sixteen, whose tall figure was a measure of that distance which I had been reluctant to see. Time, colourless and inapprehensible Time, so that I was almost able to see it and touch it, had materialised itself in this girl, moulding her into a masterpiece, while correspondingly, on me, alas! it had merely done its work. And now Mlle de Saint-Loup was standing in front of me. She had deep-set piercing eyes, and a charming nose thrust slightly forward in the form of a beak and curved, perhaps not in the least like that of Swann but like Saint-Loup's. The soul of that particular Guermantes had fluttered away, but his charming head, as of a bird in flight, with its piercing eyes, had settled momentarily upon the shoulders of Mlle de Saint-Loup and the sight of it there aroused a train of memories and dreams in those who had known her father. I was struck too by the way in which her nose, imitating in this the model of her mother's nose and her grandmother's, was cut off by just that absolutely horizontal line at its base, that same brilliant if slightly tardy stroke of design—a feature so individual that with its help, even without seeing anything else of a head, one could have recognised it out of thousands—and it seemed to me wonderful that at the critical moment nature should have returned, like a great and original sculptor, to give to the granddaughter, as she had given to her mother and her grandmother, that significant and decisive touch of the chisel. I thought her very beautiful: still rich in hopes, full of laughter, formed from those very years which I myself had lost, she was like my own youth.

The idea of Time was of value to me for yet another reason: it was a spur, it told me that it was time to begin if I wished to attain to what I had sometimes perceived in the course of my life, in brief lightning-flashes, on the Guermantes way and in my drives in the carriage of Mme de Villeparisis, at those moments of perception which had made me think that life was worth living. How much more worth living did it appear to me now, now that I seemed to see that this life that we live in half-darkness can be illumined, this life that at every moment we distort can be restored to its true pristine shape, that a life, in short, can be realised within the confines of a book! How happy would he be, I thought, the man who had the power to write such a book! What a task awaited him! To give some idea of this task one would have to borrow comparisons from the loftiest and the most varied arts; for this writer—who, moreover, must bring out the opposed facets of each of his characters in order to show its volume—would have to prepare his book with meticulous care, perpetually regrouping his forces like a general conducting an offensive, and he would have also to endure his book like a form of fatigue, to accept it like a discipline, build it up like a church, follow it like a medical

regime, vanquish it like an obstacle, win it like a friendship, cosset it like a little child, create it like a new world
without neglecting those mysteries whose explanation is to
be found probably only in worlds other than our own and
the presentiment of which is the thing that moves us most
deeply in life and in art. In long books of this kind there
are parts which there has been time only to sketch, parts
which, because of the very amplitude of the architect's
plan, will no doubt never be completed. How many great
cathedrals remain unfinished! The writer feeds his book,
he strengthens the parts of it which are weak, he protects
it, but afterwards it is the book that grows, that designates
its author's tomb and defends it against the world's clam-
our and for a while against oblivion. But to return to my
own case, I thought more modestly of my book and it
would be inaccurate even to say that I thought of those
who would read it as "my" readers. For it seemed to me
that they would not be "my" readers but the readers of
their own selves, my book being merely a sort of magnify-
ing glass like those which the optician at Combray used to
offer his customers—it would be my book, but with its
help I would furnish them with the means of reading
what lay inside themselves. So that I should not ask them
to praise me or to censure me, but simply to tell me
whether "it really is like that," I should ask them whether
the words that they read within themselves are the same
as those which I have written (though a discrepancy in
this respect need not always be the consequence of an error on my part, since the explanation could also be that
the reader had eyes for which my book was not a suitable
instrument). And—for at every moment the metaphor
uppermost in my mind changed as I began to represent to

myself more clearly and in a more material shape the task upon which I was about to embark—I thought that at my big deal table, under the eyes of Françoise, who like all unpretentious people who live at close quarters with us would have a certain insight into the nature of my labours (and I had sufficiently forgotten Albertine to have forgiven Françoise anything that she might have done to injure her), I should work beside her and in a way almost as she worked herself (or at least as she had worked in the past, for now, with the onset of old age, she had almost lost her sight) and, pinning here and there an extra page, I should construct my book, I dare not say ambitiously like a cathedral, but quite simply like a dress. Whenever I had not all my "paperies" near me, as Françoise called them, and just the one that I needed was missing, Françoise would understand how this upset me, she who always said that she could not sew if she had not the right size of thread and the proper buttons. And then through sharing my life with me had she not acquired a sort of instinctive comprehension of literary work, more accurate than that possessed by many intelligent people, not to mention fools? Already years ago, when I had written my article for *Le Figaro*, while our old butler, with that sort of commiseration which always slightly exaggerates the laboriousness of an occupation which the sympathiser does not practise himself and does not even clearly visualise— or even of a habit which he does not have himself, like the people who say to you: "How tiring you must find it to sneeze like that!"—expressed his quite sincere pity for writers in the words: "That's a head-splitting job you've got there," Françoise on the contrary both divined my happiness and respected my toil. The only thing that annoyed her was my speaking about the article to Bloch before it appeared, for she was afraid that he might forestall me. "You're too trustful," she would say, "all those people are nothing but copiators." And it was true that, whenever I had outlined to Bloch something that I had written and that he admired, he would provide a retrospective alibi for himself by saying: "Why, isn't that curious, I have written something very similar myself, I must read it to you one day," from which I inferred that he intended to sit down and write it that very evening.

These "paperies," as Françoise called the pages of my writing, it was my habit to stick together with paste, and sometimes in this process they became torn. But Françoise then would be able to come to my help, by consolidating them just as she stitched patches on to the worn parts of her dresses or as, on the kitchen window, while waiting for the glazier as I was waiting for the printer, she used to paste a piece of newspaper where a pane of glass had been broken. And she would say to me, pointing to my note-books as though they were worm-eaten wood or a piece of stuff which the moth had got into: "Look, it's all eaten away, isn't that dreadful! There's nothing left of this bit of page, it's been torn to ribbons," and examining it with a tailor's eye she would go on: "I don't think I shall be able to mend this one, it's finished and done for. A pity, perhaps it has your best ideas. You know what they say at Combray: there isn't a furrier who knows as much about furs as the moth, they always get into the best ones."

And yet in a book individual characters, whether human or of some other kind, are made up of numerous impressions derived from many girls, many churches, many sonatas, and combined to form a single sonata, a single church, a single girl, so that I should be making my book in the same way that Françoise made that *boeuf à la mode* which M. de Norpois had found so delicious, just because she had enriched its jelly with so many carefully chosen pieces of meat.

Thus it was that I envisaged the task before me, a task which would not end until I had achieved what I had so ardently desired in my walks on the Guermantes way and thought to be impossible, just as I had thought it impossible, as I came home at the end of those walks, that I should ever get used to going to bed without kissing my mother or, later, to the idea that Albertine loved women, though in the end I had grown to live with this idea without even being aware of its presence; for neither our greatest fears nor our greatest hopes are beyond the limits of our strength—we are able in the end both to dominate the first and to achieve the second.

Yes, upon this task the idea of Time which I had formed today told me that it was time to set to work. It was high time. But—and this was the reason for the anxiety which had gripped me as soon as I entered the drawing-room, when the theatrical disguises of the faces around me had first given me the notion of Lost Time—was there still time and was I still in a fit condition to undertake the task? For one thing, a necessary condition of my work as I had conceived it just now in the library was a profound study of impressions which had first to be recreated through the memory. But my memory was old and tired. The mind has landscapes which it is allowed to contemplate only for a certain space of time. In my life I had been like a painter climbing a road high above a lake, a view of which is denied to him by a curtain of rocks and trees. Suddenly through a gap in the curtain he sees the lake, its whole expanse is before him, he takes up his brushes. But already the night is at hand, the night which will put an end to his painting and which no dawn will follow. How could I not be anxious, seeing that nothing was yet begun and that though on the ground of age I could still hope that I had some years to live, my hour might on the other hand strike almost at once? For the fundamental fact was that I had a body, and this meant that I was perpetually threatened by a double danger, internal and external, though to speak thus was merely a matter of linguistic convenience, the truth being that the internal danger—the risk, for instance, of a cerebral haemorrhage—is also external, since it is the body that it threatens. Indeed it is the possession of a body that is the great danger to the mind, to our human and thinking life, which it is surely less correct to describe as a miraculous entelechy of animal and physical life than as an imperfect essay—as rudimentary in this sphere as the communal existence of protozoa attached to their polyparies or as the body of the whale—in the organisation of the spiritual life. The body immures the mind within a fortress; presently on all sides the fortress is besieged and in the end, inevitably, the mind has to surrender.

But—to accept provisionally the distinction which I have just made between the two sorts of danger that threaten the mind, and to begin with that which is in the fullest sense external—I recalled that it had often happened to me in the course of my life, in moments of intellectual excitement which coincided with a complete suspension of physical activity, as for example on those evenings when, half drunk, I had left the restaurant at Rivebelle in a carriage to go to some neighbouring casino, to feel very clearly within me the present object of my thought and at the same time to realise how much at the mercy of chance this intellectual activity was: how fortuitous it was that this particular thought had not entered my mind before, and how easily, through an accident to the carriage which was hurtling through the darkness, it might, along with my body, be annihilated. At the time this did not worry me. My high spirits knew neither forethought nor anxiety. The possibility that this joy might end in a second and turn into nothingness mattered to me scarcely at all. How different was my attitude now! The happiness which I was feeling was the product not of a purely subjective tension of the nerves which isolated me from the past, but on the contrary of an enlargement of my mind, within which the past was re-forming and actualising itself, giving me—but alas! only momentarily—something whose value was eternal. This I should have liked to bequeath to those who might have been enriched by my treasure. Admittedly, what I had experienced in the library and what I was seeking to protect was pleasure still, but no longer pleasure of an egotistical kind, or if there was egotism in it (for all the fruitful altruisms of nature develop in an egotistical manner and any human altruism which is without egotism is sterile, like that of the writer who interrupts his work to receive a friend in distress or to accept some public function or to write propaganda articles) it was an egotism which could be put to work for the benefit of other people. No longer was I indifferent to my fate as I had been on those drives back from Rivebelle; I felt myself enhanced by this work which

I bore within me as by something fragile and precious which had been entrusted to me and which I should have liked to deliver intact into the hands of those for whom it was intended, hands which were not my own. And this feeling that I was the bearer of a work made me think in a changed way of an accident in which I might meet with death, as of something much more greatly to be feared and at the same time, to the extent to which this work of mine seemed to me necessary and durable, absurd because in contradiction with my desire, with the flight of my thought, yet none the less possible for that, since accidents, being produced by material causes, can perfectly well take place at the very moment when wishes of a quite different order, which they destroy without being aware of their existence, render them most bitterly regrettable (at a trivial level of existence such accidents happen every day: at the very moment, for instance, when you are trying your hardest not to make a noise because of a friend who is asleep, a carafe placed too near the edge of his table falls to the ground and awakens him). I knew that my brain was like a basin of rock rich in minerals, in which lay vast and varied ores of great price. But should I have time to exploit them? For two reasons I was the only person who could do this: with my death would disappear the one and only engineer who possessed the skill to extract these minerals and—more than that—the whole stratum itself. Yet presently, when I left this party to go home, it only needed a chance collision between the cab which I should take and another car for my body to be destroyed, thus forcing my mind, from which life instantly would ebb away, to abandon for ever and ever the new ideas which at this moment, not yet having had time to place them within the safety of a book, it anxiously embraced with the fragile protection of its own pulpy and quivering substance.

But by a strange coincidence, this rational fear of danger was taking shape in my mind at a moment when I had finally become indifferent to the idea of death. In the past the fear of being no longer myself was something that had terrified me, and this had made me dread the end of each new love that I had experienced (for Gilberte, for Albertine), because I could not bear the idea that the "I" who loved them would one day cease to exist, since this in itself would be a kind of death. But by dint of repetition this fear had gradually been transformed into a calm confidence. So that if in those early days, as we have seen, the idea of death had cast a shadow over my loves, for a long time now the remembrance of love had helped me not to fear death. For I realised that dying was not something new, but that on the contrary since my childhood I had already died many times. To take a comparatively recent period, had I not clung to Albertine more tenaciously than to my own life? Could I at the time when I loved her conceive my personality without the continued existence within it of my love for her? Yet now I no longer loved her, I was no longer the person who loved her but a different person who did not love her, and it was when I had become a new person that I had ceased to love her. And yet I did not suffer from having become this new person, from no longer loving Albertine, and surely the prospect of one day no longer having a body could not from any point of view seem to me as sad as had then seemed to me that of one day no longer loving Albertine, that prospect which now was a fact and one which left me quite unmoved. These successive deaths, so feared by the self which they were destined to annihilate, so painless, so unimportant once they were accomplished and the self that feared them was no longer there to feel them, had taught me by now that it would be the merest folly to be frightened of death. Yet it was precisely when the thought of death had become a matter of indifference to me that I was beginning once more to fear death, under another form, it is true, as a threat not to myself but to my book, since for my book's incubation this life that so many dangers threatened was for a while at least indispensable. Victor Hugo says:

Grass must grow and children must die.

To me it seems more correct to say that the cruel law of art is that people die and we ourselves die after exhausting every form of suffering, so that over our heads may grow the grass not of oblivion but of eternal life, the vigorous and luxuriant growth of a true work of art, and so that thither, gaily and without a thought for those who are sleeping beneath them, future generations may come to enjoy their *déjeuner sur l'herbe*.

So much for the dangers from without; there were others, as I have said, that threatened me from within. Supposing that I were preserved from all accidents of an external kind, might I not nevertheless be robbed of the fruits of this good fortune by some accident occurring within myself, some internal catastrophe assailing me before the necessary months had passed and I had had time to write my book? When presently I made my way home through the Champs-Elysées, who was to say that I might not be struck down by that malady which had struck my grandmother one afternoon when she had gone there with me for a walk which, though of this she had no suspicion, was destined to be her last—so ignorant are we, as ignorant as the hand of a clock when it arrives at the point upon its dial where a spring will be released within the mechanism which will cause the hour to strike. And indeed perhaps the fear that I might already have traversed almost the whole of that last minute which precedes the first stroke of the hour, that minute during which the stroke is already preparing itself, perhaps the fear of the stroke that might already be moving into action within my brain was itself a sort of obscure awareness of something that was soon to happen, a sort of reflexion in the conscious mind of the precarious state of the brain whose arteries are about to give way, a phenomenon no more impossible than that sudden acceptance of death that comes to wounded men who, though the doctor and their own desire to live try to deceive them, say, realising the truth: "I am going to die, I am ready," and write their farewells to their wives.

Nor was anything so grave as a cerebral haemorrhage needed to hinder me in the execution of my task. Already the premonitory symptoms of the same malady, perceptible to me in a certain emptiness in the head and a tendency to forgetfulness thanks to which I now merely stumbled upon things in my memory by chance in the way in which, when you are tidying your belongings, you find objects which you had forgotten even that you had to look for, were making me resemble a miser whose strongbox has burst open and whose treasures little by little are disappearing. For a while there existed within me a self

which deplored the loss of these treasures, then I perceived that memory, as it withdrew from me, carried away
with it this self too.

And something not unlike my grandmother's illness
itself happened to me shortly afterwards, when I still had
not started to work on my book, in a strange fashion
which I should never have anticipated. I went out to see
some friends one evening and was told that I had never
looked so well, and how wonderful it was that I had not a
single grey hair. But at the end of the visit, coming downstairs, three times I nearly fell. I had left my home only
two hours earlier; but when I got back, I felt that I no
longer possessed either memory or the power of thought
or strength or existence of any kind. People could have
come to call on me or to proclaim me king, to lay violent
hands on me or arrest me, and I should passively have
submitted, neither opening my eyes nor uttering a word,
like those travellers of whom we read who, crossing the
Caspian Sea in a small boat, are so utterly prostrated by
seasickness that they offer not even a show of resistance
when they are told that they are going to be thrown into
the sea. I had, strictly speaking, no illness, but I felt myself no longer capable of anything, I was in the condition
of those old men who one day are in full possession of
their faculties and the next, having fractured a thigh or
had an attack of indigestion, can only drag on for a while
in their bed an existence which has become nothing more
than a preparation, longer or shorter, for a now ineluctable death. One of my selves, the one which in the
past had been in the habit of going to those barbarian fes-
tivals that we call dinner-parties, at which, for the men in
white shirt-fronts and the half-naked women beneath

feathered plumes, values have been so reversed that a man who does not turn up after having accepted the invitation—or merely arrives after the roast has been served—is deemed to have committed an act more culpable than any of those immoral actions which, along with the latest deaths, are so lightly discussed at this feast which nothing but death or a serious illness is an acceptable excuse for failing to attend—and then only provided that one has given notice in good time of one's intention to die, so that there may be no danger for the other guests of sitting down thirteen to table—this one of my selves had retained its scruples and lost its memory. The other self, the one which had had a glimpse of the task that lay before it, on the contrary still remembered. I had received an invitation from Mme Molé and I had learnt that Mme Sazerat's son had died. I determined therefore to employ one of those few hours after which I could not hope even to pronounce another word or to swallow a mouthful of milk, since my tongue would be tied as my grandmother's had been during her agony, in addressing my excuses to the one lady and my condolences to the other. But a moment or two later I had forgotten that I had these things to do—most happily forgotten, for the memory of my real work did not slumber but proposed to employ the hour of reprieve which was granted me in laying my first foundations. Unfortunately, as I took up a note-book to write, Mme Molé's invitation card slipped out in front of my eyes. Immediately the forgetful self, which nevertheless was able to dominate the other—is this not always the case with those scrupulous barbarians who have learnt the lore of the dinner-party?—pushed away the note-book and wrote to Mme Molé (whose esteem for me would no

doubt have been great had she known that I had allowed
my reply to her invitation to take precedence over my
labours as an architect). Then suddenly a word in my letter reminded me that Mme Sazerat had lost her son and I
wrote to her as well, after which, having sacrificed a real
duty to the factitious obligation to appear polite and sympathetic, I fell back exhausted and closed my eyes, not to
emerge from a purely vegetal existence before a week had
elapsed. During this time, however, if all my unnecessary
duties, to which I was willing to sacrifice my true duty,
vanished after a few moments from my head, the idea of
the edifice that I had to construct did not leave me for an
instant. Whether it would be a church where little by little a group of faithful would succeed in apprehending verities and discovering harmonies or perhaps even a grand
general plan, or whether it would remain, like a druidic
monument on a rocky isle, something for ever unfre-
quented, I could not tell. But I was resolved to devote to
it all my strength, which ebbed, as it seemed, reluctantly
and as though to leave me time to complete the periphery
of my walls and close "the funeral gate." Before very long
I was able to show a few sketches. No one understood
anything of them. Even those who commended my perception of the truths which I wanted eventually to engrave
within the temple, congratulated me on having discovered
them "with a microscope," when on the contrary it was a
telescope that I had used to observe things which were indeed very small to the naked eye, but only because they
were situated at a great distance, and which were each one
of them in itself a world. Those passages in which I was
trying to arrive at general laws were described as so much
pedantic investigation of detail. What, in any case, was I

hoping to achieve? In my youth I had had a certain facility, and Bergotte had praised as "admirable" the pages
which I wrote while still at school. But instead of working
I had lived a life of idleness, of pleasures and distractions,
of ill health and cosseting and eccentricities, and I was
embarking upon my labour of construction almost at the
point of death, without knowing anything of my trade. I
felt that I no longer possessed the strength to carry out
my obligations to people or my duties to my thoughts and
my work, still less to satisfy both of these claims. As for
the first, my forgetfulness of the letters I had to write and
of the other things I had to do, to some extent simplified
my task. But suddenly, at the end of a month, the association of ideas brought back the painful recollection of
these duties and I was momentarily overwhelmed by the
thought of my impotence. To my astonishment I found
that I did not mind, the truth being that, since the day
when my legs had trembled so violently as I was going
downstairs, I had become indifferent to everything, I
longed only for rest, while waiting for the great rest which
would come in the end. Amongst other things I was indifferent to the verdict which might be passed on my work
by the best minds of my age, and this not because I relegated to some future after my death the admiration which
it seemed to me that my work ought to receive. The best
minds of posterity might think what they chose, their
opinions mattered to me no more than those of my contemporaries. The truth was that, if I thought of my work
and not of the letters which I ought to answer, this was
not because I attached to these two things, as I had during my years of idleness and later, in that brief interval
between the conception of my book and the day when I

had had to cling to the banister, very different degrees of importance. The organisation of my memory, of the pre-occupations that filled my mind, was indeed linked to my work, but perhaps simply because, while the letters which I received were forgotten a moment later, the idea of my work was inside my head, always the same, perpetually in process of becoming. But even my work had become for me a tiresome obligation, like a son for a dying mother who still, between her injections and her blood-lettings, has to make the exhausting effort of constantly looking after him. Perhaps she still loves him, but it is only in the form of a duty too great for her strength that she is aware of her affection. In me, in the same way, the powers of the writer were no longer equal to the egotistical demands of the work. Since the day of the staircase, nothing in the world, no happiness, whether it came from friendship or the progress of my book or the hope of fame, reached me except as a sunshine unclouded but so pale that it no longer had the virtue to warm me, to make me live, to instil in me any desire; and yet, faint though it was, it was still too dazzling for my eyes, I closed them and turned my face to the wall. When a lady wrote to me: "I have been *very surprised* not to receive an answer to my letter," I must, it seemed, to judge from the sensation of movement in my lips, have twisted an infinitesimal corner of my mouth into a little smile. Nevertheless, I was reminded of her unanswered letter and I wrote her a reply. Not wishing to be thought ungrateful, I tried hard to raise my tardy civilities to the level of those which I supposed that other people, though I had forgotten it, had shown to me. And I was crushed by the effort to impose upon my moribund existence the superhuman fatigues of life. The loss of my memory helped me a little by creating gaps in my obligations; they were more than made good by the claims of my work.

The idea of death took up permanent residence within me in the way that love sometimes does. Not that I loved death, I abhorred it. But after a preliminary stage in which, no doubt, I thought about it from time to time as one does about a woman with whom one is not yet in love, its image adhered now to the most profound layer of my mind, so completely that I could not give my attention to anything without that thing first traversing the idea of death, and even if no object occupied my attention and I remained in a state of complete repose, the idea of death still kept me company as faithfully as the idea of my self. And, on that day on which I had become a half-dead man, I do not think that it was the accidents characterising this condition—my inability to walk downstairs, to remember a name, to get up from a chair—that had, even by an unconscious train of thought, given rise to this idea of death, this conviction that I was already almost dead; it seems to me rather that the idea had come simultaneously with the symptoms, that inevitably the mind, great mirror that it is, reflected a new reality. Yet still I did not see how from my present ailments one could pass, without warning of what was to come, to total death. Then, however, I thought of other people, of the countless people who die every day without the gap between their illness and their death seeming to us extraordinary. I thought also that it was only because I saw them from within—rather than because I saw them in the deceptive colours of hope—that certain of my ailments, taken singly, did not seem to me to be fatal although I believed

that I would soon die, just as those who are most convinced that their hour has come are, nevertheless, easily
persuaded that if they are unable to pronounce certain
words, this is nothing so serious as aphasia or a stroke,
but a symptom merely of a local fatigue of the tongue, or
a nervous condition comparable to a stutter, or the lassitude which follows indigestion.

No doubt my books too, like my fleshly being, would
in the end one day die. But death is a thing that we must
resign ourselves to. We accept the thought that in ten
years we ourselves, in a hundred years our books, will
have ceased to exist. Eternal duration is promised no more
to men's works than to men.

In my awareness of the approach of death I resembled
a dying soldier, and like him too, before I died, I had
something to write. But my task was longer than his, my
words had to reach more than a single person. My task
was long. By day, the most I could hope for was to try to
sleep. If I worked, it would be only at night. But I should
need many nights, a hundred perhaps, or even a thousand. And I should live in the anxiety of not knowing
whether the master of my destiny might not prove less indulgent than the Sultan Shahriyar, whether in the morning, when I broke off my story, he would consent to a
further reprieve and permit me to resume my narrative
the following evening. Not that I had the slightest pretension to be writing a new version, in any way, of the *Arabian Nights*, or of that other book written by night,
Saint-Simon's *Memoirs*, or of any of those books which I
had loved with a child's simplicity and to which I had
been as superstitiously attached as later to my loves, so
that I could not imagine without horror any work which

should be unlike them. But—as Elstir had found with Chardin—you can make a new version of what you love only by first renouncing it. So my book, though it might be as long as the *Arabian Nights*, would be entirely different. True, when you are in love with some particular book, you would like yourself to write something that closely resembles it, but this love of the moment must be sacrificed, you must think not of your own taste but of a truth which far from asking you what your preferences are forbids you to pay attention to them. And only if you faithfully follow this truth will you sometimes find that you have stumbled again upon what you renounced, find that, by forgetting these works themselves, you have written the *Arabian Nights* or the *Memoirs* of Saint-Simon of another age. But for me was there still time? Was it not too late?

And I had to ask myself not only: "Is there still time?" but also: "Am I well enough?" Ill health, which by compelling me, like a severe director of conscience, to die to the world, had rendered me good service (for "except a corn of wheat fall into the ground and die, it abideth alone: but if it die, it bringeth forth much fruit"), and which, after idleness had preserved me from the dangers of facility, was perhaps going to protect me from idleness, that same ill health had consumed my strength and as I had first noticed long ago, particularly when I had ceased to love Albertine, the strength of my memory. But was not the re-creation by the memory of impressions which had then to be deepened, illumined, transformed into equivalents of understanding, was not this process one of the conditions, almost the very essence of the work of art as I had just now in the library conceived it? Ah! if only I

now possessed the strength which had still been intact on
that evening brought back to my mind by the sight of
*François le Champi*! Was not that the evening when my
mother had abdicated her authority, the evening from
which dated, together with the slow death of my grandmother, the decline of my health and my will? All these
things had been decided in that moment when, no longer
able to bear the prospect of waiting till morning to place
my lips upon my mother's face, I had made up my mind,
jumped out of bed and gone in my night-shirt to post
myself at the window through which the moonlight entered my room until I should hear the sounds of
M. Swann's departure. My parents had gone with him to
the door, I had heard the garden gate open, give a peal of
its bell, and close . . .

While I was asking myself these questions, it occurred to me suddenly that, if I still had the strength to
accomplish my work, this afternoon—like certain days
long ago at Combray which had influenced me—which in
its brief compass had given me both the idea of my work
and the fear of being unable to bring it to fruition, would
certainly impress upon it that form of which as a child I
had had a presentiment in the church at Combray but
which ordinarily, throughout our lives, is invisible to us:
the form of Time.

Many errors, it is true, there are, as the reader will
have seen that various episodes in this story had proved to
me, by which our senses falsify for us the real nature of
the world. Some of these, however, it would be possible
for me to avoid by the efforts which I should make to
give a more exact transcription of things. In the case of
sounds, for instance, I should be able to refrain from al-

tering their place of origin, from detaching them from
their cause, beside which our intelligence only succeeds in
locating them after they have reached our ears—though
to make the rain sing softly in the middle of one's room
or, contrarily, to make the quiet boiling of one's tisane
sound like a deluge in the courtyard outside should not
really be more misleading than what is so often done by
painters when they paint a sail or the peak of a mountain
in such a way that, according to the laws of perspective,
the intensity of the colours and the illusion of our first
glance, they appear to us either very near or very far
away, through an error which the reasoning mind subsequently corrects by, sometimes, a very large displacement.
Other errors, though of a more serious kind, I might continue to commit, placing features, for instance, as we all
do, upon the face of a woman seen in the street, when instead of nose, cheeks and chin there ought to be merely
an empty space with nothing more upon it than a flicker-
ing reflexion of our desires. But at least, even if I had not
the leisure to prepare—and here was a much more important matter—the hundred different masks which ought
properly to be attached to a single face, if only because of
the different eyes which look at it and the different meanings which they read into its features, not to mention, for
the same eyes, the different emotions of hope and fear or
on the contrary love and habit which for thirty years can
conceal the changes brought about by age, and even if I
did not attempt—though my love-affair with Albertine
was sufficient proof to me that any other kind of representation must be artificial and untruthful—to represent
some of my characters as existing not outside but within
ourselves, where their slightest action can bring fatal dis-

turbances in its train, and to vary also the light of the moral sky which illumines them in accordance with the variations in pressure in our own sensibility (for an object which was so small beneath the clear sky of our certainty can be suddenly magnified many times over on the appearance of a tiny cloud of danger)—if, in my attempt to transcribe a universe which had to be totally redrawn, I could not convey these changes and many others, the needfulness of which, if one is to depict reality, has been made manifest in the course of my narrative, at least I should not fail to portray man, in this universe, as endowed with the length not of his body but of his years and as obliged—a task more and more enormous and in the end too great for his strength—to drag them with him wherever he goes.

Moreover, that we occupy a place, always growing, in Time is something everybody is conscious of, and this universality could only make me rejoice, it being the truth, the truth suspected by each of us, that I had to seek to elucidate. Not only does everybody feel that we occupy a place in Time, but the simplest of us measures this place approximately, as he would measure the one we occupy in space. People with no special perspicacity, seeing two men whom they do not know, both perhaps with black moustaches or both clean-shaven, will say that of the two one is about twenty and the other about forty years old, for the face of a young man cannot possibly be confused with that of a man of middle age, which in the eyes even of the most ignorant beholder is veiled by a sort of mist of seriousness. Of course, this evaluation of age that we make is often inaccurate, but the mere fact that we think ourselves able to make it indicates that we conceive of age as an entity which is measurable. And the second of the two men with black moustaches has, in effect, had twenty years added to his stature.

This notion of Time embodied, of years past but not separated from us, it was now my intention to emphasise as strongly as possible in my work. And at this very moment, in the house of the Prince de Guermantes, as though to strengthen me in my resolve, the noise of my parents' footsteps as they accompanied M. Swann to the door and the peal—resilient, ferruginous, interminable, fresh and shrill—of the bell on the garden gate which informed me that at last he had gone and that Mamma would presently come upstairs, these sounds rang again in my ears, yes, unmistakably I heard these very sounds, situated though they were in a remote past. And as I cast my mind over all the events which were ranged in an unbroken series between the moment of my childhood when I had first heard its sound and the Guermantes party, I was terrified to think that it was indeed this same bell which rang within me and that nothing that I could do would alter its jangling notes. On the contrary, having forgotten the exact manner in which they faded away and wanting to re-learn this, to hear them properly again, I was obliged to block my ears to the conversations which were proceeding between the masked figures all round me, for in order to get nearer to the sound of the bell and to hear it better it was into my own depths that I had to redescend. And this could only be because its peal had always been there, inside me, and not this sound only but also, between that distant moment and the present one, unrolled in all its vast length, the whole of that past which I was not aware that I carried about within me.

When the bell of the garden gate had pealed, I already existed and from that moment onwards, for me still to be able to hear that peal, there must have been no break in continuity, no single second at which I had ceased or rested from existing, from thinking, from being conscious of myself, since that moment from long ago still adhered to me and I could still find it again, could retrace my steps to it, merely by descending to a greater depth within myself. And it is because they contain thus within themselves the hours of the past that human bodies have the power to hurt so terribly those who love them, because they contain the memories of so many joys and desires already effaced for them, but still cruel for the lover who contemplates and prolongs in the dimension of Time the beloved body of which he is jealous, so jealous that he may even wish for its destruction. For after death Time withdraws from the body, and the memories, so indifferent, grown so pale, are effaced in her who no longer exists, as they soon will be in the lover whom for a while they continue to torment but in whom before long they will perish, once the desire that owed its inspiration to a living body is no longer there to sustain them. Profound Albertine, whom I saw sleeping and who was dead.

In this vast dimension which I had not known myself to possess, the date on which I had heard the noise of the garden bell at Combray—that far-distant noise which nevertheless was within me—was a point from which I might start to make measurements. And I felt, as I say, a sensation of weariness and almost of terror at the thought that all this length of Time had not only, without interruption, been lived, experienced, secreted by me, that it

was my life, was in fact me, but also that I was compelled
so long as I was alive to keep it attached to me, that it
supported me and that, perched on its giddy summit, I
could not myself make a movement without displacing it.
A feeling of vertigo seized me as I looked down beneath
me, yet within me, as though from a height, which was
my own height, of many leagues, at the long series of the
years.

I understood now why it was that the Duc de Guermantes, who to my surprise, when I had seen him sitting
on a chair, had seemed to me so little aged although he
had so many more years beneath him than I had, had
presently, when he rose to his feet and tried to stand firm
upon them, swayed backwards and forwards upon legs as
tottery as those of some old archbishop with nothing solid
about his person but his metal crucifix, to whose support
there rushes a mob of sturdy young seminarists, and had
advanced with difficulty, trembling like a leaf, upon the
almost unmanageable summit of his eighty-three years, as
though men spend their lives perched upon living stilts
which never cease to grow until sometimes they become
taller than church steeples, making it in the end both difficult and perilous for them to walk and raising them to
an eminence from which suddenly they fall. And I was
terrified by the thought that the stilts beneath my own
feet might already have reached that height; it seemed to
me that quite soon now I might be too weak to maintain
my hold upon a past which already went down so far. So,
if I were given long enough to accomplish my work, I
should not fail, even if the effect were to make them resemble monsters, to describe men as occupying so consid-

erable a place, compared with the restricted place which is reserved for them in space, a place on the contrary prolonged past measure, for simultaneously, like giants plunged into the years, they touch the distant epochs through which they have lived, between which so many days have come to range themselves—in Time.

# NOTES · SYNOPSIS

# Notes

1 (p.   9)  Proust's manuscript adds at this point: "Cruelty on the death of her father (copy from the note-book where it is described)."

2 (p.  12)  Legrandin has earlier been described in almost identical terms (see Vol. V, *The Fugitive*, pp. 904, 905).

3 (p.  14)  Another chronological inconsistency. Bergotte's death was reported long before the marriage of Gilberte and Saint-Loup.

4 (p.  39)  From Victor Hugo's *Les Contemplations*.

5 (p. 101)  Quotation from Baudelaire's *Le Balcon*.

6 (p. 150)  "Le moi est haïssable" (Pascal).

7 (p. 339)  Eponymous hero of a novel by the Comtesse de Ségur.

8 (p. 354)  And yet the narrator does not meet her until more than 70 pages later, failing to recognise her at first (see p. 427).

9 (p. 381)  The remark occurs later: see preceding note.

10 (p. 460)  This passage is also rather surprising, since Rachel has been identified several pages before. All such inconsistencies are attributable to Proust's endless additions to his original text. He died before he had time to resolve the resulting confusions.

*Tansonville*. Walks with Gilberte (1). Disenchantment with the scenes of my childhood (2). Gilberte shows me that the Guermantes and the Méséglise ways are not irreconcilable (3–4; cf. **I** 188) and reveals the meaning of the sign she made to me years ago (4; cf. **I** 199).

Scene from the window of my room at Tansonville (10). Effects of Saint-Loup's vice on his behaviour (12). His lies (13). Françoise's esteem for him (14–5). His feelings towards Gilberte (16). The Guermantes type in Robert (18–9). The Guermantes' amatory tastes (20). Conversation with Gilberte about Albertine (24).

The Goncourt journal (26). Its description of the Verdurin salon (27–38). My lack of a bent for literature (39).

*M. de Charlus during the war*. My return to Paris in 1916 (47). Wartime Paris: changes in fashions and in society (47–55). News of the war in the Verdurin salon (55. The new "faithful"; Morel, a deserter, and "I'm a wash-out," Andrée's husband (57–8). Mme Verdurin's overtures to Odette (59–60).

Aircraft in the sky at nightfall (63). Walks in night-time Paris, reminiscent of Combray (64).

Meeting with Saint-Loup in 1914 (67); his secret efforts to get to the front (69). Bloch passed fit for military service (70). Bloch and Saint-Loup (70–1). Ideal of virility among homosexuals (78–81). The manager of the Grand Hotel and the lift-boy (81–2); the lift-boy and the rich young man (82). Françoise and the war (84); tormented by the butler (85–7).

Return to the sanatorium (88). A letter from Gilberte: German occupation of Tansonville (88–9). A letter from Robert (89).

Second return to Paris: another letter from Gilberte, with news of the fighting round Combray (93–4). A visit from Saint-Loup, in Paris on leave (96). Beauty of nocturnal air-raids (98–9); reflexions on strategy (101).

shocked by his mumbling voice (250). Jupien speaks of the
Baron's health, his Germanophilia, his persistent randiness
(251).

The uneven paving-stones in the Guermantes courtyard
(255); sensation of felicity similar to that of the madeleine, etc.
(255); resurrection of Venice (256). Further exhilarating sensations (256-7). "The true paradises are the paradises that we
have lost" (261). Impressions "outside time" (262). Reflexions
on time, reality, memory, artistic creation (262 et sqq.). Futility
of literary theories (277). Absurdity of popular art or patriotic
art (279). *François le Champi* (281). Bibliophilia (286). Celibates
of Art (293). Aberrations of literary criticism (295).

Further reflexions on literary and artistic creation (297 et
sqq.). The raw material for literature: my past life (304). A Vocation? (304). The importance of dreams (322). The influence of
Swann (328). The role of jealousy (330). Chateaubriand, Nerval
and Baudelaire (334-5).

Back to the Guermantes reception: a *coup de théâtre*
(336-7). M. d'Argencourt as an old beggar (338). Bloch (347).
The Duchesse de Guermantes (349). The meaning of old age
(354). M. de Cambremer (356). Legrandin (358). The Prince
d'Agrigente (359). Various effects of Time (361). Odette: a challenge to the laws of chronology (377); "a rose that has been ster-
ilized" (380). Bloch's English chic (384); I introduce him to the
Prince de Guermantes (385). Mme Verdurin has become the
Princesse de Guermantes (387). Society and the chemistry of
Time (389 et sqq.). Following the stream of memory back to its
source (412 et sqq.). "Who's dead?" (422-5).

The Princesse de Nassau (425). Gilberte: "You took me for
Mamma" (428). Conversation about Robert (428) and the art of
war (429). Her friendship with Andrée (432). My determination
to avoid social life (435-6). The Duchesse de Guermantes and
Rachel (444).

Berma's tea-party (450). Her daughter and son-in-law
(451). Rachel's performance (456). She runs down Berma (462).
Mme de Guermantes in old age: her social decline (464).
Berma's daughter and son-in-law received by Rachel (478).

The Duke's liaison with Odette (481). "A magnificent

# A GUIDE TO PROUST

## Foreword

This is intended as a guide through the 4,300-page labyrinth of *In Search of Lost Time* not only for readers who are embarking on Proust's masterpiece for the first time but for those too who, already under way, find themselves daunted or bewildered by the profusion of characters, themes and allusions. It also aims to provide those who have completed the journey with the means of refreshing their memories, tracking down a character or an incident, tracing a recurrent theme or favourite passage, or identifying a literary or historical reference. Perhaps, too, the book may serve as a sort of Proustian anthology or bedside companion.

The task of compiling the *Guide* would have been infinitely more laborious without the pioneering work of P. A. Spalding, whose *Reader's Handbook to Proust* (that is, to the twelve-volume translation of the novel then current) was published by Chatto & Windus in 1952 and reissued, in a revised edition edited by R. H. Cortie, by George Prior in 1975. I must also acknowledge a debt to the editors of the Pléiade edition (1954) of *À la recherche du temps perdu*, whose very detailed index was an indispensable aid, especially in identifying historical personages and literary allusions.

The *Guide* consists of four separate indexes: of Proust's characters; of real or historical persons; of places; and of themes. Since the places index is comparatively short, it includes both the real and the fictional, the latter being indentified by the symbol (f). The present edition of the translation contains a synopsis at the end of each volume, and so I have not included one here. Page references are to the six volumes, as indicated by Roman bold numerals.

I have referred to the narrator throughout by the initial M, for Marcel. Proust is careful, almost from the beginning to the end of the novel, to avoid giving the narrator a name. But twice he allows his guard to slip: first, teasingly, early in *The Captive*,

when Albertine on awakening murmurs "My darling——" and
the blank is then filled in with the name Marcel, "if we give the
narrator the same name as the author of this book" (Vol. V, p.
91), and the second time, later in the same volume, when Albertine addresses him unequivocally as "My darling dear Marcel"
in her note from the Trocadéro (p. 202).

# Index of Characters

ACTRESS (from the Odéon). Forms an exclusive group at Balbec with her rich young lover and two aristocratic friends: **II** 352–55. Invites M to dinner: 726. Her lover an invert, according to Charlus: **V** 411 (cf. **VI** 82–83)

ACTRESS-SINGER (novice), "tortured" by Rachel: **III** 229–30.

ACTRESS (ex-) with whom Bloch's sister causes a scandal in the Casino at Balbec: **IV** 326–27, 337–38. (Not to be confused with Léa.)

ADOLPHE, Uncle. His sanctum at Combray and his study in Paris: **I** 99. M visits him and meets the "lady in pink," thereby precipitating a breach with the family: 104–10. Swann visits him to talk about Odette, who provokes a quarrel between them: 444. The pavilion in the Champs-Elysées recalls his room at Combray: **II** 91. After his death, his photographs of actresses and courtesans brought to M by Charles Morel, son of his former valet: **III** 357–61. His generosity: **IV** 418. Morel's devotion to his memory; his house in the Boulevard Malesherbes: 620–22.

AGRIGENTE, Prince d' ("Grigri"). Visits the Swanns: **II** 130, 239–40, 246. At the Guermantes dinner-party; introduced to M, on whom he makes a bad impression: **III** 592–93. Unable to disguise his ignorance of Flaubert: 671. Drinks M's fruit-juice: 703. Discusses genealogy with the Duc de Guermantes: 735–36. Related to the Duke of Modena: 743. Invited to the Saint-Euverte garden-party: **IV** 96–97. In Mme Swann's box: 198. Regarded as a flashy foreigner by a club servant to whom he owes money: 410. Gilberte's interest in him; his illness: **V** 794–96. The nickname Grigri: **VI** 56, 61. Did he marry Mlle X?: 326. At the Guermantes *matinée*, "embellished" by age: 359.

AIMÉ. Headwaiter at the Grand Hotel, Balbec: **II** 347–48, 363, 366–67, 373–74. Charlus sends for him at night: 473–74. His views on the Dreyfus Case: 527–28. Headwaiter at a restaurant in Paris: **III** 201; waits on M, Saint-Loup and Rachel; his attractive and distinguished looks; Rachel's interest in him, and

Robert's jealousy; Charlus's ploy: 218–25. Back in Balbec: **IV** 233; the Princesse de Parme's tip: 254–55; his appreciation of moneyed clients: 306–7. His role in Nissim Bernard's relations with a young waiter: 330–31, 343–44. Conversations with M; relations with clients ("business first"); his letter from Charlus: 527–34. His familiarity with the chauffeur: 536–37, and interest in the chauffeur's tip: 576. His pleasure in M's special dinners: 658. His remembered remarks about Albertine exacerbate M's jealousy; M sends him a photograph of Esther Lévy for identification: **V** 103–7, 491–92. Sent by M to Balbec to make inquiries about Albertine's behaviour in a bathing establishment: 664; his letter: 692–702. Sent by M to Touraine; second letter with revelations concerning Albertine's relations with the laundry-girls: 706–8, 714. His revelations concerning Saint-Loup: 926–28.

A.J. *See* Moreau, A. J.

ALBARET, Céleste. Lady's-maid in the Grand Hotel, with whom M strikes up a friendship during his second visit to Balbec: **IV** 331–37. Brichot gives the etymology of her name: 448. Her grief at M's departure: 716. Her strange linguistic genius: **V** 12–13, 167.

ALBERT. *See* Guastalla, Albert, Duc de.

ALBERTINE Simonet. Niece of M. and Mme Bontemps; at school with Gilberte; "the famous Albertine": **II** 116. Her insolence, according to her aunt: 237–38. M misses the opportunity of meeting her: 277–78. Her first appearance among the "little band" at Balbec—"a girl with brilliant, laughing eyes and plump, matt cheeks, a black polo-cap . . . pushing a bicycle": 503–12. The name "Simonet": 520–21, 528, 540–41, 579–80. Is she the girl M sees with an English governess?: 557–58. M sees her from a window of Elstir's studio; her beauty spot; Elstir identifies her; her social position: 577–82. The different Albertines: 596–98. M introduced to her at Elstir's: 614–22. Location of the beauty spot: 618, 622, 624–25. Conversation with her on the esplanade; her jaunty slang: 623–29. Encounters with Andrée, Octave, the d'Ambresacs; her taste and intelligence: 631–36. Plays "diabolo": 637 (cf. 695). Her attitude to Gisèle: 637–40. Her hair: 641. Cycling in the rain: 645 (cf. **V** 658–59). Her craze for amusement: 647. Discusses dress with Elstir:

653–55. Her attitude to Bloch's sisters: 659. Her voice and vocabulary: 666–68. Her note to M: "I like you very much": 670. Her reaction to Gisèle's essay: 670–73. The game of "ferret": 680–85. Her hands: 680–81. Her ringing laughter, "somehow indecent" like the cooing of doves or certain animal cries: 681 (cf. IV 243, 264, 348, 705; V 152, 165, 226). Her kindness: 687–88. "I knew now that I was in love with Albertine": 689–94. In her room at the hotel; the rejected kiss: 697–701. Her charm and attraction and social success: 702–7. "The multiple utilisation of a single action": 707. Explains her refusal to allow M to kiss her; the little gold pencil: 710–11. The moral esteem she inspires in M, and the consequences thereof: 712–13. Her changing face: 718–20. Her abrupt departure from Balbec: 724. Visits M in Paris; changes in her appearance and vocabulary; allows him to make love to her; her frankness and simplicity: III 479–506. Second visit; accompanies M to the island in the Bois and to Saint-Cloud: 529–33. M gives her a box for *Phèdre* and arranges to meet her after the Prince de Guermantes's party: IV 61, 138, 148, 168–70. He anxiously awaits her return: 174–77; her telephone call: 177–81; her visit: 181–87. Denies knowing Gilberte Swann: 186 (cf. V 20, 506–7). At Balbec again; sends word to M asking to see him: 220; M refuses: 227. The manager's annoyance with her: 237. Françoise's dislike of her: 239, 253. M at last decides to see her: 243–44. Recrudescence of M's desire for her: 246–47. He sends Françoise and the lift-boy to fetch her: 252–62. Dances with Andrée in the Casino at Incarville; Cottard's remarks: 262–66. Her secret life, unknown to M: 267–68. The visit to Infreville; her lies: 268–72 (cf. V 137). Observes Bloch's sister and cousin in a mirror: 273–74. M's changed attitude towards her: 274–76. Introduced to the Cambremers: 279. Her admiration for Elstir: 283–84. Reveals a knowledge of Amsterdam: 289 (cf. V 518, 529, 580). M "has things out" with her; his spurious confession of love for Andrée; accusations, denials, reconciliation: 302–17. Picnics with M near Balbec: 320; and further afield: 324. His suspicions and her reassurances: 324–26. Her attitude towards young women: 338–42. Flirts with Saint-Loup at Doncières station: 348–49. Reproaches and reconciliation: 350–51, 355–58. M's mother raises the question of his marriage to Albertine: 442–43. Invited (as M's cousin) to La Raspelière: 501–2, 505. Expeditions with M; paints the church of Saint-Jean-de-la-Haise: 534–35. The toque and veil: 536. Motor-car drives; visit to the Verdurins: 537–51. The church of Marcouville-l'Orgueilleuse: 561–62. Amorousness after drinks at a farm: 562–63. Lunch at Rivebelle; her interest in the waiter: 563–65. Further outings; nights on the beach; M's growing jealousy and anxiety: 565–71. Reputed intimacy with Morel: 586 (cf. **V** 810–11). Visits to the Verdurins; the little train; her make-up: 590–95, 675. Her clothes admired by Charlus: 618–19 (cf. **V** 290–95). How she gives herself away when lying: 677–78. Avoids Saint-Loup: 692. M's decision to break with her: 698–99. Sudden reversal on hearing of her friendship with Mlle Vinteuil and her friend; M persuades her to spend the night in the Grand Hotel and return to Paris with him next day: 701–16. "I absolutely must marry Albertine": 724. Living with M in Paris: **V** 1–2. Sings in her bath: 3–4. Mamma's disapproval: 6–9. Changes in her vocabulary and appearance: 12–14. Outings with Andrée; the Buttes-Chaumont: 15–16 (cf. 524, 740, 822–23). M's feelings for her—jealousy without love: 16–30. Admits having known Gilberte: 20. Her fastidious taste in clothes: 32–33. The syringa incident: 63–65. Her dissimulation: 66–74. Her elegant clothes; her gold ring; her intelligence: 75–76. Memories of her at Balbec: 81–84. Her sleep: 84–90, and awakening: 90–91 (cf. 521–22). Visits M in his bedroom; her love play; her good-night kiss; makes him promise to work: 91–99. Aimé's ambiguous remarks about her; a new access of jealousy: 103–7. Her plan to visit Mme Verdurin; renewed suspicions; "a fugitive being"; lying a part of her nature: 108–22. Visits to aerodromes: 132–33. Her lie about Infreville exposed: 137 (cf. **IV** 268–72). Denies knowing Bloch's cousin: 140 (cf. 460–61). M kisses her while she sleeps the sleep of a child: 141–46. Her morning visit; plans to go to the Trocadéro instead of the Verdurins' after a ride with Andrée; M warns her of the danger of riding accidents: 151–53. Her fondness for the streetcriers and their wares: 160–63. Rhapsody on ice-creams: 165–66. Visit to Versailles with the chauffeur: 167–71. Journey to Balbec with the chauffeur: 174 (cf. 448–50). Her contradictory lies:

186–88. Léa at the Trocadéro; M's frenzy of jealous suspicion; sends Françoise round with a note requesting Albertine to return home: 188–98; she complies, and sends an affectionate note ("What a Marcel!"): 201–3. Her new ring: 214. Her knowledge of painting and architecture: 217–18. Expedition to the Bois de Boulogne: 219–28. Feels herself a prisoner; her desire to escape: 228–31. Her technique in lying: 231–35, 247–52. M visits the Verdurins without her: 252. Charlus regrets her absence: 290, 293–95. Vinteuil's music revives M's love for her: 235–37, 344–45, 353, 408, 441–42. Her lighted window: 444–45. Her attitude to M's jealousy: 445–46. Her annoyance on learning of his visit to the Verdurins: 447. Admits that her trip to Balbec with the chauffeur was an invention: 448–50. Denies having been intimate with Mlle Vinteuil and her friend: 451–2. Her interrupted phrase ("get myself b . . .") of which M finally discovers the meaning: 453–58. Crushed by M's feigned decision to break with her there and then: 458–60. Her intimacy with Bloch's cousin Esther: 460–61. Her three-week trip with Léa: 470–73, and her visit to Léa's dressing room: 480. Reconciliation: 482–84. M visits her in her room and finds her already asleep: 485–86. Does she want to leave him?: 486–89. Attempts to dispel his suspicions: 491. Fears of her departure: 494–95. Her interest in old silver and Fortuny gowns: 496–501 (cf. 237–38, and her plans with M to acquire a yacht). Plays the pianola: 501–3, 513–16. Revelation about Gilberte: 506–7. Conversation about literature: 506–14. Watching her sleep once more: 521–22. Why she had returned to Paris with M; her relations with Andrée; her lie about the Buttes-Chaumont: 523–29. The Fortuny gown: 530–31 (cf. 237–38). Quarrel with M about Andrée; refusal to kiss him: 532–41. Noise of her window being opened during the night: 541–42. Visit to Versailles: 545–48. Makes eyes at a woman in a pastry-cook's: 548–50. Her sudden departure: 558–59. "Mademoiselle Albertine has gone!": 563–64. Her farewell letter: 565–66. Her behaviour just before her departure: 574–76. M learns that she has gone to Touraine: 580–81. How to get her back; plan to send Saint-Loup in search of her; Saint-Loup's reaction to her photograph: 584–96. Her letter from Touraine and M's reply: 610–21. Her forgotten rings:

623–27. Her third letter: 630–33. Saint-Loup's report: 635–41. Her death in a riding accident: 641–42. Her two posthumous letters: 643–44. She continues to live in M after her death; his memories and regrets: 645–94. Aimé's revelations about the bathing establishment at Balbec: 694–702. His inquiries in Touraine and revelations about the laundry-girl: 706–15. Fragmentation into many different Albertines: 713–21. She appears in M's dreams: 725–28. Andrée denies having had illicit relations with her: 737–41. M's love for her survives in his pursuit of women of her type and background: 743–52. Stages on the road to indifference: 754, 801–6. Andrée's revelations—her own relations with Albertine; Albertine and Morel; the syringa incident: 809–13. Albertine's reason for leaving M; the Buttes-Chaumont; her relations with Octave: 821–43. M nearing total indifference, in Venice: 844, 848–50. Brief and fortuitous reawakenings of her memory: 866–69. A telegram which M believes to be from her accelerates his return to indifference: 869–74. The Austrian girl who resembles her: 879–81. M's "reflex" memory of her at Tansonville: **VI** 11. He discusses her with Gilberte: 24–25. He no longer thinks of her: 117–18. Retrospectively, her exclamation on being caught by Françoise *in flagrante delicto*: 192. Linked with Saint-Loup in M's memory: 227–28. Had been of use to him by causing him unhappiness: 319–20. The inspiration of his books: 328.

ALBON, Old M. d'. Smiles at a remark by Mme de Guermantes: **VI** 444–45.

ALIX, the "Marie-Antoinette of the Quai Malaquais," one of the "three Parcae"; at Mme de Villeparisis's reception: **III** 260–70.

AMBASSADRESS, Turkish. At the Guermantes': **III** 732–40, why she irritates M: **IV** 80–81; her social utility: 82.

AMBRESAC, M., Mme and Mesdemoiselles d'. At Balbec; related to Mme de Villeparisis, despised by Albertine; Saint-Loup engaged to one of the girls?: **II** 633–36 (cf. **III** 37). Mme d'Ambresac at the Opéra: **III** 43–44. Saint-Loup denies the engagement rumour: 133–34. Competition for the hand of Daisy d'Ambresac: 553–54. Saint-Loup talks to her at the Princesse de Guermantes' reception: **IV** 133.

AMONCOURT, Mme Timoléon d'. Offers the Duchesse de Guermantes some Ibsen manuscripts; her wit, beauty and obligingness: **IV** 89–91.

ANDRÉE. The eldest of the "little band" of girls at Balbec, the "tall one." Jumps over the old banker: **II** 508 (cf. 631). Plays golf: 625–27. Introduced to M by Albertine: 631. Complexity of her character; lies to M; quarrels with Gisèle: 636–40. In the Casino; her sympathetic disposition; her friendship with Albertine: 646–49. Her comments on Gisèle's essay: 670–75. Her hands; the game of "ferret": 680–81. M's doubts as to her kindness: 687–88. M pretends to prefer her to Albertine; her jealousy: 692–94. Her mother and Albertine: 703–6. M finds her a neurotic, sickly intellectual like himself: 714. "A camellia in the night": 717. Dances with Albertine in the Casino at Incarville: **IV** 263–66. Expresses abhorrence of Sapphic behaviour: 272–73. Her tender ways with Albertine: 274–75. M pretends to be in love with her: 308, 311–14. She and Albertine avoid each other: 326. M prefers her to Albertine: 699–700. Albertine's chaperone in Paris: **V** 12, 15, 20–21. The syringa incident: 63–65. Intensification of her defects; denounces Octave; M's suspicions of her: 69–74 (cf. 128, 943–44). Her voice on the telephone: 124–27. Albertine murmurs her name while asleep: 144. Her lies dovetail with Albertine's: 233–34, 298, 448–49. Her secret life with Albertine: 523–28. M quarrels with Albertine over her: 534–36. M invites her to come and live with him after Albertine's departure: 632–33, 643–44. M jealous of her: 717–18. Visits M after Albertine's death; admits to her own Sapphic tastes but denies having had illicit relations with Albertine: 735–41. Her second visit: 805–28; confesses her relations with Albertine; new version of the syringa incident: 809–15; her defamatory remarks about Octave, whom she later marries: 816–18; her explanation of Albertine's departure: 821–28. Third visit to M; further revelations about Albertine and a new explanation for the latter's departure (a plan to marry Octave): 830–33, 838–39. During the war, now married to Octave, remains M's friend: **VI** 58–59. Her friendship with Gilberte: 432–33.

ANDRÉE'S mother. Mentioned by Albertine at Balbec: **II** 632,

704. Her social position and attitude to Albertine: 703–6. Her hair: 717. Her "horses, carriages, pictures": **V** 12.

ANTOINE, the Guermantes' butler. Françoise's opinion of him and his "Antoinesse": **III** 21; his arrogant air: 27; his anti-Dreyfusism: 402–3.

ARCHIVIST, encountered *chez* Mme de Villeparisis: *See* Vallenères.

ARGENCOURT, Comte d', later Marquis d'. Belgian Chargé d'Affaires in Paris. At Mme de Villeparisis's reception: **III** 284–88, 300–301; speaks of Maeterlinck's *Seven Princesses*: 308–10, 336–37; his anti-semitism: 316; his rudeness to Bloch: 329–33. Meets M and Charlus in the street; Charlus's opinion of him: 395–97. "A terrible snob": 613. At Mme Verdurin's musical soirée; his changed attitude to Charlus: **V** 362–63. During the war, arrested and released: **VI** 235–36. After the war, at the Guermantes reception, has become an amiable old dotard: 338–44.

ARGENCOURT, Dowager Comtesse d' (*née* Seineport), mother of the above. Bluestocking hostess: **III** 613.

ARPAJON, Vicomtesse or Comtesse d'. At the Guermantes dinner-party (one of the "flower maidens"): **III** 586–87. Mistress of the Duke: 656, 660. Conversation with M about the archives in her château: 669. Her opinion of Flaubert: 670–71, and of Victor Hugo: 673–76. Quotes Musset for Hugo: 680. Ridiculed by Mme de Guermantes: 680, 684. Addressed by the latter as "Phili": 691. At the Princesse de Guermantes's, declines to introduce M to the Prince: **IV** 67–70. Jealous of Mme Surgis-le-Duc, who has succeeded her in the Duke's affections: 70. Drenched by the Hubert Robert fountain: 77–78. Cultivates Odette: 199–201. Her brilliant tea-parties: 542. Doubts the existence of M. Verdurin: **V** 363. In her old age, seems at once unknown and familiar: **VI** 362–63. Her death discussed at the Guermantes reception: 422–25.

AUBERJON, Duchesse Gisèle d'. Summoned by Mme de Villeparisis to help with her theatricals: **III** 289.

AYEN, Duchesse Jane d'. Charlus deplores the conversation at her house: **V** 413.

BABAL. *See* Bréauté-Consalvi.

BALLEROY, Mme de. Great-aunt of a niece of Mme de Guermantes: **V** 250.

BASIN. *See* Guermantes, Basin, Duc de.

BARRISTER (*see* Blandais), president of the Cherbourg bar. Staying at the Grand Hotel, Balbec: **II** 346–47. Entertains the Cambremers to lunch: 361–63. Orders trout from Aimé: 366. Irritated by Mme Blandais: 382. Visits Féterne: 388. M learns of his death: **IV** 205.

BAVENO, Marquise de. Comments on Oriane's "Teaser Augustus" pun: **III** 638.

BEAUSERFEUIL, General de. Overhears Swann's Jewish witticism at the Guermantes' reception: **IV** 132. The Prince de Guermantes consults him about Dreyfus: 143, 146–47.

(*See* Monserfeuil: it is clear that the two names apply interchangeably to the same general.)

BEAUSERGENT, Marquis de (Mme d'Argencourt's brother). In Mme de Cambremer's box at the Opéra: **III** 65–66. At the final Guermantes party, now an aged colonel: **VI** 364–65.

BEAUTREILLIS, General de. At the Guermantes dinner party: **III** 674. His anti-Dreyfusism: 681.

BELLOEUVRE, Gilbert de. Young golfer at Balbec, remembered by M: **V** 821.

BERGOTTE. Distinguished writer recommended to M by Bloch, who lends him one of his books: **I** 124. His style, and its effect on M: 129–34. Swann speaks of him; an admirer of Berma: 135. A great friend of Gilberte: 137–38, 192. His booklet on Racine presented to M by Gilberte: 572, 582–83. Quotations from this concerning *Phèdre*: **II** 18. Norpois's unfavourable opinion of him—"a deliquescent mandarin": 60–65 (cf. **III** 299). Luncheon party at the Swanns'; the man with the goatee beard and snail-shell nose and the gentle bard with the snowy locks: 164–83. His voice and style; "Bergottisms"; his family: 168–77. Vices of the man and morality of the writer: 178–83. Speaks of Berma and Racine: 185–85. His opinion of Norpois: 186–87. Favourably impressed by M; they leave together; his medical advice and malicious remarks about Cottard and the Swanns: 196–200. M's parents change their opinion of him: 201–4, 209–13. Sought after by Mme Verdurin: 239. M receives a letter

from him at Balbec: 400. Charlus lends M one of his books:
472. M. Bloch's opinion of him: 477–83. Legrandin's opinion of
him—"gamy stuff for the jaded palates of refined voluptuaries":
**III** 203. Admired by the Duchesse de Guermantes: 283–84, 299.
Dr du Boulbon speaks of him to M's grandmother: 409, 415.
His visits to M during his grandmother's illness; his own illness,
his increasing fame, his indifference to the new: 442–47. Reputed to have written a satirical one-act play about the Prince de
Guermantes: **IV** 101–2, 138. Mme Swann's salon crystallises
round him: 194–97. Reported to be seriously ill: 503. M still
reads him: **V** 65–66, 728–29. His death; "the little patch of yellow wall": 238–46. His instinctive attraction towards inferior
women: 281. Charlus visits him on behalf of Morel: 289–90. M
gives Albertine one of his manuscripts: 483. His one-time belief
in table-turning: 713. His reaction to the *Figaro* article in M's
dream: 799. His influence on Morel's style: **VI** 113. M's even-
tual disillusionment with his books: 286. The intricacy of his
style now out of fashion: 295. The role he had played in M's
love for Gilberte: 443.

BERMA. Her rank as an actress: **I** 102. Admired by Bergotte:
135, 137. M's desire to see her perform: 559, 572. Her
performance in *Phèdre*: **II** 10–11; M's disappointment: 20–29.
Norpois's opinion of her: 36–38. "What a great artist!": 72. M
buys a photograph of her; her face and her loves: 80–83.
Bergotte's opinion of her: 183–85. Swann's view: 193. M sees
her again in *Phèdre*; an interpretation "quickened by genius": **III**
39, 49–67. Rachel's patronising comments: 221–22. Françoise
compared to her in histrionic virtuosity: **IV** 182. Gives a party
in honour of her daughter and son-in-law; their selfishness and
cruelty; failure of the party: **VI** 240, 450–56. Rachel's malicious
remarks about her: 477. Her daughter and son-in-law beg
Rachel to receive them: 478–79. Rachel's cruel disclosure of this
proves a mortal blow to her: 479–80.

BERNARD, Nissim. Rich great-uncle of Bloch. At dinner *chez*
the Blochs at Balbec; the family butt; his lies: **II** 482–86; but he
really did know M. de Marsantes: **III** 374–75. Grows mannered
and precious with advancing age: 393. His relations with a
young waiter at the Grand Hotel: **IV** 327–31, 337, and with the

tomato-faced waiters at the "Cherry Orchard": 342–44. Allusion to his death (?): 682. Incurs Morel's enmity by lending him five thousand francs: **V** 62 63. Leaves money to the young waiter from the Grand Hotel, now manager of a restaurant: **VI** 67.

BERTHE. Friend of Albertine: **V** 738.

BIBI. Friend of the Prince de Foix, announces his engagement to Daisy d'Ambresac: **III** 553–54.

BICHE ("Master"). *See* Elstir.

BLANDAIS (*see* Barrister), M. Notary from Le Mans on holiday at Balbec: **II** 345–48, 362–63, 383, 463.

BLANDAIS, Mme. Wife of the above: **II** 348–49. Impressed by M. de Cambremer: 356. Annoys the president: 382–83. Not invited to the Cambremers' at Féterne: 388, 462. M tells a funny story about her: **III** 132.

BLATIN, Mme. Apparent friend of Gilberte; reads the *Journal des Débats* in the Champs-Elysées: **I** 565–66. Her affectation: 576–77. M's mother's poor opinion of her: 587–88. Mme Swann dreads her visits: **II** 110. Resembles a portrait of Savonarola: 147. "Me nigger; you old cow!": 149.

BLOCH, Albert. Schoolfriend of M's. Recommends Bergotte to him; despises Racine and Musset, admires Leconte de Lisle: **I** 124. His neo-Homeric jargon: 124–25 (*see also* **II** 442–47, 478, 484–88; **III** 328; **IV** 319, 682). Antagonises M's family: 107–10. His likeness, according to Swann, to Gentile Bellini's portrait of Sultan Mahomet II: 115. Unwittingly helps M to gain access to the Swanns: **II** 102. Greets Mme Swann in the Bois; she mistakes his name: 159 (cf. 489). Alters M's notions about women, and takes him to a brothel: 205–8, 396–97. His affectation of anti-semitism: 433 (cf. 445–46). His absurdity, his snobbery; his family; his ill breeding: 434–37, 442–48. M and Saint-Loup dine with him and his family: 474–89. His gaffe about Charlus: 488–89. Claims to have had carnal relations with Odette: 489. Sees Saint-Loup off at the station; his tactlessness: 609–11. Albertine's antipathy to him: 627–29. His Dreyfusism: **III** 134 (*see also* 402–3). Dislike of Stendhal: 136. At Mme de Villeparisis's reception, now a rising dramatist: 252–336. His exotic Jewishness: 253–55. Knocks over a glass of water: 289. His ambivalent remarks about Saint-Loup: 292–93 (cf. 306–7). His rudeness:

293–96. Introduced to Norpois: 296–98; discusses the Dreyfus Case with him: 313–16, 323–33. Snubbed by M. d'Argencourt and the Duc de Châtellerault: 333–34. Takes leave of Mme de Villeparisis, who feigns sleep: 335–36. His friendliness towards Saint-Loup, who invites him to dinner: 373 (cf. 546). Charlus's interest in him: 389–91. Snubbed by Charlus on being introduced to him by M: 523–24. Regular meetings with his Jewish friends to discuss the Zola trial in the restaurant where M and Saint-Loup dine one foggy night: 547–49. Behaviour on being introduced to Mme Alphonse de Rothschild: 693. His petition on behalf of Colonel Picquart: **IV** 152–53. His fondness for authentic Greek spelling: 319. Pretends not to recognise his sister: 337–38. Offended by M's reluctance to leave the little train to meet his father: 682–86. Charlus questions M about him: 686–92. Calls on M in Paris, without knowing that Albertine is in the house: **V** 1–2. Arranges a loan for Morel and thereby incurs his enmity: 62–63. Sends M a photograph of his cousin Esther Lévy: 105–7, 140, 461. His taste in furniture: 229–30. Charlus wants to invite him to his house: 282–83. A poet "in my idle moments": 285–86. Fails to recognise Albertine dressed as a man: 450. Visits M after Albertine's departure and incurs his anger: 596–97. Ignores M's *Figaro* article: 797–98. His noisy ostentation and pretentiousness in a Balbec restaurant: 925–26. During the war, chauvinistic before being passed fit for service, thereafter anti-militarist; "at once coward and braggart": **VI** 67–73, 77. Marries one of his daughters to a Catholic: 192. Bored by society novels: 277. After the war, M recognises him in spite of his having aged: 347–48. His cult of his dead father: 353–54. Has adopted the name Jacques du Rozier; his English chic; his physical transformation: 384–85. Questions M about society figures of the past: 385–88. His own position in society; his fame as a writer: 392–93, 403–9. His new discretion: 411. Refuses Berma's invitation: 450. Compliments Rachel: 460–61. His interest in M. de Bréauté: 468–72. Steals M's ideas for articles: 510.

BLOCH, M. Salomon, father of the above. Impressed by his son's acquaintanceship with Saint-Loup: **II** 447. His stereoscope: 448. M and Saint-Loup dine with him; his preposterous stories;

his opinion of Bergotte; his avarice: 474–87. His admiration for Léa: 660. Impressed by Sir Rufus Israels: **III** 293. Charlus declines to be introduced to him; greets Mme Sazerat: 332. His post-chaise with postilions: **IV** 682. His Stock Exchange connexions: **VI** 72. Dies of grief during the war: 347.

BLOCH'S cousin. *See* Lévy, Esther.

BLOCH'S sisters. At Balbec, introduced to M: **II** 434–35. Their admiration for their brother: 435, and imitation of his jargon: 477–78, 482. Their vulgarity: 459–60. One of them, with her cousin, attracts Albertine's attention in the Casino at Balbec: **IV** 272–74, and causes a scandal in the Grand Hotel by her behaviour with an ex-actress: 326–27, 337–38.

BONTEMPS, M. Albertine's uncle. Chief Secretary to the Minister of Public Works: **II** 114–16. Dines with the Swanns: 128–30. At an official dinner with M's father: 277. Supports Albertine but anxious to be rid of her: 703. Considered somewhat "shady": 703, and a political opportunist: 705. Once a counsellor in Vienna: **IV** 708. A "lukewarm" Dreyfusard: **V** 316. His election committee: 594. Chauvinist and militarist during the war, his Dreyfusism forgotten: **VI** 51–55. Mme Verdurin's telephone conversations with him: 61–63.

BONTEMPS, Mme. Albertine's aunt. Her visits to Odette; her vulgarity and snobbishness: **II** 109, 114–19, 235–37, 242–50. Albertine's attitude towards her: 632. M's desire to meet her at Balbec: 693–94. Albertine conceals her assignation with M from her: 697. Her influence on Albertine: **III** 487, 503. Her anti-Dreyfusism: 798. Takes a villa at Epreville: **IV** 244. Calls at the Grand Hotel to take Albertine home: 313. M's fears about her disreputable friend: 341–42. Strongly in favour of his marrying Albertine: 442. Her lunch party, attended by Bloch, at which M is praised: 685–86. Her influence on Albertine's taste in music: **V** 3–4. Raises no objection to Albertine's living *chez* M: 7, 54–55. Her pronunciation of "Béarn": 35. Gives Albertine a ring?: 75, 214. Placed on the Index by Charlus: 315–16. Unwittingly reveals to M one of Albertine's lies: 523–24. Saint-Loup's mission to persuade her to send Albertine back: 587, 594–95, 608–9, 635–36. Telegraphs M to inform him of Albertine's death: 641–42. Her schemes for Albertine to marry Octave:

830–33. Entertained by Gilberte: 908. One of the queens of war-time Paris: **VI** 47, 51. Firmly established in the Faubourg Saint-Germain: 55.

BORANGE. Grocer, stationer and bookseller at Combray: **I** 115–16.

BORODINO, Prince de. Cavalry captain at Doncières: **III** 90. Allows M to sleep in barracks: 97–98. Saint-Loup's poor opinion of him: 98. Refuses Saint-Loup leave: 161, then changes his mind at the instance of his hair-dresser: 165. His aloofness from Saint-Loup and his friends; his Imperial background; his social attitudes; differences between the two aristocracies: 167–73. He rides majestically by: 182. Mme de Villeparisis denounces him: 292. His invitations to M: **IV** 682.

BOUILLON, Cyrus, Comte de. Father of Mme de Villeparisis: **II** 392. His literary acquaintances: 394–95. Chateaubriand and the moonlight: 410–11. Visited by the Duc de Nemours: 415. (Somewhat confusingly, in *The Guermantes Way* Mme de Villeparisis's father is called Florimond de Guise: **III** 727, cf. **III** 255.)

BOUILLON, Comtesse de. Mother of Mme de Villeparisis. The Duchesse de Praslin's armchair: **II** 416.

BOUILLON, Duc de. Outside the Duc de Guermantes's library; his timid, humble appearance: **III** 786–87. Identified as the only genuine surviving member of the princely La Tour d'Auvergne family, Oriane's uncle and Mme de Villeparisis's brother: **IV** 109.

BOULBON, Doctor du. Admirer of Bergotte: **I** 130–31. His likeness to a Tintoretto portrait: 315. Recommended to M by Bergotte: **II** 199. At M's grandmother's bedside: **III** 407–18. Provokes Cottard's jealousy at Balbec: **IV** 264–65, 510–11. Compared with Louis XIV's physician, Fagon: **VI** 462.

BOURBON, Princesse de. *See* Mme de Charlus.

BRÉAUTÉ-CONSALVI, Marquis (or Comte) Hannibal de ("Babal"). At Mme de Saint-Euverte's; his monocle: **I** 464. Reputed lover of Odette: 506, 513 (cf. **VI** 489). Less witty than Bergotte: **III** 282–83. At the Guermantes'; his curiosity about M and extravagantly affable salutations: 588–90. His social assiduity although he claims to loathe society; reputation as an intellectual:

618, 666, 671, 690–91. Discusses botany with Mme de Guermantes 707–9. His mother a Choiseul and his grandmother a
Lucinge: 735. Introduces M to the Prince de Guermantes: **IV**
73–74. His "improvements" to the Hubert Robert fountain: 79.
His explanation for the alleged quarrel between Swann and the
Prince de Guermantes: 101–2, 109. His malicious amusement at
Mme de Guermantes's plan to avoid the Saint-Euverte garden
party: 113–14. In Mme Swann's box: 169. An habitué of her salon; a changed man: 198. Regular visitor at Mme de Guermantes': **V** 40. Repeats Cartier's *mot* about Zola; his voice and
pronunciation: 44–47. Refuses to know Odette and Gilberte:
780. Gilberte's interest in him: 794. "Dead!": **VI** 249. Oriane's
reminiscences about him—"Bréauté was a snob": 468–72 (cf. **III**
618). Odette's account of her love affair with him: 489. His
"provincialism": 493, 496.

BRÉQUINY, Comte de. Father of the ladies with the walking
sticks, Mme de Plassac and Mme de Tresmes: **III** 785, 788;
**IV** 1.

BRETEUIL, Quasimodo de. Friend of Swann and of Mme de
Guermantes: **V** 794.

BRETONNERIE, Mme de la. Lady of Combray with whom Eulalie had been in service: **I** 93.

BRICHOT, Professor at the Sorbonne. Dines at the Verdurins':
**I** 356. His pedantic witticisms: 357–59, 369–70. Admired by
Forcheville: 358, 365. Swann's antipathy to him: 375–77.
Bergotte's *mot* concerning him: **II** 172. His anti-Dreyfusism: **III**
799 (*see also* **IV** 385). In the little train: **IV** 359–98. His near-
blindness 360–62. His liaison with his laundress torpedoed by
Mme Verdurin: 360–62. His spectacles: 369–70. His affected
mode of nomenclature: 371–72, 380–81. His etymological dissertations: 387–93. Announces the death of Dechambre: 396–407.
M. Verdurin's irony at his expense: 407–8. Introduced to the
Cambremers: 426. More etymology: 434–36, 439–41, 445–51,
456–58. His opinion of Favart: 453. Criticised by Mme Verdurin: 472–76. Compliments Charlus: 478. His tirade against
the new poetry: 481–83. Compared with Swann by Mme Verdurin and by M: 503–4. His denunciation of Balzac: 611–16,
619. Speaks of Norpois: 619. His love for the young Mme de

Cambremer: 668–70. More etymology: 678–81, 688–89. M meets him on the way to the Verdurins' new house in Paris; his new glasses: **V** 260. Recalls the Verdurin salon of the old days, in the Rue Montalivet: 264–67 (*see also* 378–81). His attitude towards Charlus: 268–70. Admires Albertine: 290. At the Verdurin soirée: 301–3, 317, 324. His complicity in Mme Verdurin's plot against Charlus: 372–78. Conversation with Charlus about sodomy: 381–413 *passim*. Praised by Charlus, who attends his lectures: 386–90. Sums up Charlus on the way home in M's carriage: 440–44. Referred to in the pastiche of the Goncourt Journal: **VI** 29. Attends Mme Verdurin's war-time receptions: 62. Delighted with Morel's satirical pieces at Charlus's expense: 112–13. His war-time journalism; criticised by Charlus: 125, 127–30, 141. His relations with Mme Verdurin during the war; his fame as a pundit; his style: 145–51. His fondness for the phrase "a lively pen": 283.

BRISSAC, Mme de. Her opinion of Victor Hugo: **III** 681.

BURNIER. One of Charlus's footmen: **III** 766.

BUTCHER'S ASSISTANT. Reminiscent of a handsome angel on the Day of Judgment: **V** 176–77.

BUTCHER'S BOY. Protégé of Françoise: **VI** 87, 96.

BUTLER, M's family's. *See* Victor.

BUTLER, the Guermantes'. *See* Antoine.

BUTLER, the Swanns'. Walks the dog; his white whiskers: **I** 591. His words make clear to M that all is over with Gilberte: **II** 221–22.

CALLOT, "Mother." Vegetable-seller of Combray: **I** 74.

CAMBREMER, Dowager Marquise Zélia de. At Mme de Saint-Euverte's soirée; her social obscurity and her passion for music: **I** 466–67, 470–72. Declares that her daughter-in-law is an "angel": 489. At Balbec, hit in the face by a diabolo ball: **II** 696. Ceases to attend Mme de Saint-Euverte's parties: **IV** 94. Her social life in the neighbourhood of Balbec: 223–27. Sends M notice of her cousin's death: 251–52. Calls at the Grand Hotel; her elaborate attire; her salivation; her worship of Chopin: 276–302. The lift-boy's mispronunciation of her name: 276, 304. Her children: 424. Her relationship with her gardener: 429–30. Her letter to M; the rule of the three adjectives: 468–69 (*see also*

663). Her influence throughout her family: 663–64. "Queen of the Normandy coast": 670–71. Her grandson takes after her: **V** 915. Lives to a very advanced age: **VI** 357–58.

CAMBREMER, Marquis de. Married to Legrandin's sister: **I** 92, 174. Calls at the Grand Hotel, Balbec, to collect guests for his wife's weekly "garden party": **II** 355. Lunches with the barrister: 361–62. Nicknamed "Cancan": **IV** 294. Invited to dinner by the Verdurins: 383–86. His appearance, his nose, his character; explanation of his nickname: 421–24. His two fables: 426–27, 439–41. Introduced to M: 428–29. His deference to Charlus: 430, 465–66, 469–70. Impressed by Brichot's etymological expertise: 434–36, 439–40, 446. His interest, not to say delight, in M's fits of breathlessness: 441–42, 570, 676. Criticises the Verdurins' taste in furniture: 467. His admiration for Cottard: 487–88. Talks to him about drugs: 489–91. Explains a point in heraldry to Mme Verdurin: 492–93. His anti-Dreyfusism: 496–97 (cf. **V** 312–13). Fails to appreciate a Cottard pun: 508. Tips the Verdurin coachman: 511–12. His ignorance of his native countryside: 540. He and his wife quarrel with the Verdurins: 664–75. Tries to persuade M to remain at Balbec: 716–17. His opinion on the Dreyfus Case: **V** 312–13. Saint-Loup's favourable opinion of him during the war: **VI** 70–71 (cf. **III** 644). M meets him at the Guermantes reception after the war, unrecognisably aged: 356.

CAMBREMER, Marquise Renée de. Wife of the above and sister of Legrandin. Lives near Balbec: **I** 92. Legrandin avoids giving M and his family a letter of introduction to her: 182–85. At Mme de Saint-Euverte's soirée; a Wagnerian, despises Chopin: 472. The candle incident: 478. Admired by Froberville: 479. Her name discussed by Swann and the Princesse des Laumes: 485. Introduced to Froberville by Swann: 488–89. Swann follows her to Combray: 541–42. Said to have been "mad about" Swann: **II** 146–47. Aunts Céline and Flora refuse to mention her name: 305. Her weekly "garden party" at Féterne: 355. Lunches with the barrister at Balbec: 361–62. At the Opéra: **III** 64–68. Ridiculed by Mme de Guermantes: 271–72, 311–13. Recommended to M by Saint-Loup: **IV** 207. Her rudeness and arrogance: 224–25. Introduced to M; her social and intellectual snobbery; contempt for her mother-in-law; avant-garde tastes in art and music: 279–94. Her pronunciation of Chenouville: 294–95. Her relations with Robert: 296. Invited to La Raspelière by the Verdurins: 383–87, 421–514 *passim*. Her contempt for them; her "haughty and morose" demeanour; her pleasure at meeting Charlus; her irritating habits: 424–28. Criticises the Verdurins' alterations at La Raspelière: 436–37, 466–68. Conversation with M; his reflexions on her intellect, her aesthetic tastes, her snobbery, her vocabulary: 437–45. Her enthusiasm for Debussy and Scarlatti: 480–81. Her affected good-bye to M; mispronounces "Saint-Loup"; her impertinent teasing: 512–14. Her social preoccupations; invitations to Morel and Cottard resented by Mme Verdurin: 664–66. Brichot in love with her; Mme Verdurin intervenes: 669–70. Dinner party for M and Mme Féré at which Charlus fails to appear: 670–72. Quarrel with the Verdurins: 672–75. Reaction to her son's engagement to Jupien's niece: **V** 892–94, 899–901. Becomes indifferent to the friendly overtures of the Duchesse de Guermantes: 907. Criticised by Saint-Loup: **VI** 71. At the Verdurin reception after the war: 357.

CAMBREMER, Léonor de. Son of the above. Marries Jupien's niece (Mlle d'Oloron): **V** 892–94. An invert: 900. Deserts the minor nobility for the intelligent bourgeoisie: 901. His resemblance to his uncle Legrandin: **VI** 373, 410–11.

CAMILLE. Servant of the Swanns: **II** 114.

CAMUS. Grocer at Combray: **I** 76–77, 93; his packing cases: 114; his pink sugar biscuits: 196.

CANCAN. *See* Cambremer, Marquis de.

CAPRAROLA, Princesse de. Visits Mme Verdurin: **IV** 195. Visits Odette and mentions the Verdurins: 364–65.

CARTIER. Brother of Mme de Villefranche and intimate friend of the Duc de la Trémoïlle. His *mot* about Zola recounted by Bréauté, to the irritation of Mme de Guermantes: **V** 44–45. His later obscurity: 262.

CASHIERS. At the Rivebelle restaurant, "two horrible cashiers" like a pair of witches: **II** 533. At the Grand Hotel, Balbec, the cashier "enthroned beneath her palm": **IV** 329. Hideous one in an unnamed hotel, regarded by the staff as a "fine-looking" woman: **V** 250.

CÉLESTE. *See* Albaret.

CÉLINE and FLORA. Sisters of M's grandmother. Share her nobility of character but not her intelligence; their aesthetic interests; their ingenious circumlocution: **I** 20, 27–34. Swann's present of wine: 28, 32–34, 45–46. Their provincial dogmatism; 135. Pupils of Vinteuil: 156. Disapproval of M's artistic taste: 206. Their revenge for Legrandin's insult: **II** 305. Refusal to leave Combray to see their dying sister: **III** 442, 468. M's mother goes to visit one of them at Combray: **IV** 699, 711–12; **V** 7–8.

CHANLIVAULT, Mme de. Sister of "le vieux Chaussepierre," lives in the Rue La Pérouse: **I** 488–89. Aunt of M. de Chaussepierre, who later ousts M. de Guermantes from the Presidency of the Jockey Club: **IV** 98–99.

CHARLUS, Baron de (Palamède, nicknamed "Mémé"). At Combray; reputed lover of Mme Swann: **I** 45, 137. Seen by M at Tansonville: "a gentleman in a suit of linen 'ducks' . . . stared at me with eyes which seemed to be starting from his head": 199–200. Friend of Swann: 272, 441. Go-between with Odette: 442, 449, 456. Chaperones her at Swann's request: 458. Suspected by Swann of writing an anonymous letter: 506–7. Expected at Balbec: **II** 448. Saint-Loup's account of him; his social position; his arrogance, his reputation for womanising: 449–52. Visual encounter with M outside the Casino: 452–53. Mme de Villeparisis introduces him: 455. Studied sobriety of his clothes: 454–55. A Guermantes: 456. His title explained: 457–58. His intelligence and sensibility, aesthetic taste, obsession with virility, attitude to the nobility: 458–61; delights M's grandmother: 458, 467–70. Invites M to tea: 462. His strange behaviour and enigmatic stare: 463–66. His voice: 469. Comes to M's bedroom and lends him a Bergotte novel: 471–72. Strange behaviour on the beach next day: 473–74. Bloch's derisive remarks about him: 487–88. Comes to call on Aimé at the restaurant where M is lunching with Saint-Loup and Rachel: **III** 223. At Mme de Villeparisis's; attaches himself to Odette; his relations with his aunt: 361–66. Invites M to accompany him after the party: 376.

Mme de Villeparisis seems upset by this: 384. Strange conversation with M; his views on high politics, the Jews, the Duchesse de Guermantes, Mme de Villeparisis; his sudden departure in a cab: 386–402. Mme de Guermantes pronounces him "a trifle mad": 520–21. His attitude to Bloch: 523–24 (cf. 389–92; **IV** 683–84; **V** 282–83). Through Saint-Loup, invites M to call on him: 564. "Teaser Augustus": 636–40, 665. "Knows it all by heart": 673. How he mourned his wife: 695–96. M's visit to him after dining at the Guermantes'; his strange welcome, violent rage followed by affectionate melancholy: 757–72. Accompanies M home: 772–76. His meeting with Jupien; his true nature suddenly revealed: **IV** 1–20, 36–44. At the Princesse de Guermantes's soirée; talks to the Duke of Sidonia: 52–54. His greetings to the guests: 65–66. Pretends to play whist: 70–71. Decline of his influence in society: 72–73. Refuses to introduce M to the Prince de Guermantes: 73, but talks to him about the gardens and the Hubert Robert fountain: 78–79. His conversation with M. de Vaugoubert: 86–89, 100–1 (cf. 57–58). Enveloped in the Comtesse Molé's skirt: 100 (cf. 123). In the card-room, gazes at the young Comte de Surgis: 119–20. Saint-Loup speaks of his womanising: 123–26. His attentiveness to Mme de Surgis, who introduces her two sons to him: 127–34, 140–45. His outrageous diatribe against Mme de Saint-Euverte: 135–38 (*see also* 729–30). Swann's view of his sexual proclivities: 146. The Princesse de Guermantes's secret passion for him: 154–57 (*see also* 608, 730–40). Brotherly exchange with the Duc de Guermantes: 158–61. His first meeting with Morel at Doncières station: 351–55. His visit to La Raspelière announced by M. Verdurin: 407. Confused in artistic circles with another Charlus: 408–10. Arrives at La Raspelière with Morel; his mincing manner with the Verdurins: 414–28. Misinterprets Cottard's winks: 430–34. Impresses Mme Verdurin with a reference to the Comtesse Molé: 454–55. M. Verdurin's gaffe, Charlus's contemptuous laugh; he enumerates his titles: 463–64. Declines in a lordly manner M. de Cambremer's offer of his chair: 465–66. Expatiates on his family's heraldic situation: 469–72, 477–78. Accompanies Morel in a Fauré sonata; link between his artistic gifts and his nervous weaknesses: 479–80. Proposes a pilgrimage

creet behaviour with the footmen: 345. Conversation with Mme de Mortemart and other guests after the concert: 353–64. Condescending remarks to Mme Verdurin; the Queen of Naples's fan; Mme Molé again; Mme Verdurin's fury: 364–71. Approaches General Deltour about Morel's decoration: 371–72. Conversation in an ante-room with Brichot and M; his comments on Morel's performance and his lock of hair: 381–84. His attendance at Brichot's lectures: 385–90. A discussion of homosexuality: 395–413. Rupture with Morel and the Verdurins; the Queen of Naples; his illness and (temporary) moral improvement: 423–36. Brichot's affectionate remarks about him: 440–44. Recites poetry to Morel during a visit to M: 808–9. Adopts Jupien's niece and gives her the title Mlle d'Oloron: 893 (cf. 417). Approves her marriage to young Cambremer: 903–4, 915. Meets Legrandin: 903–6. Compared and contrasted with Saint-Loup during the war: **VI** 80–81, 102–4. M meets him on the boulevards—"a tall, stout man with a purplish face" following two *zouaves*: 106–7. His social isolation; continued hostility of Mme Verdurin and Morel: 107–13. Acquires a taste for little boys: 116. Corresponds with soldiers at the front: 117. Germanophilia; unorthodox views about the war: 121–44, 151–65. Anxious for a reconciliation with Morel: 130–32, 164–65. Morel's fear of him; the posthumous letter: 166–68. Likens war-time Paris to Pompeii; his admiration for British, French and in particular German soldiers: 169–73. Later the same evening M discovers him in Jupien's brothel, chained to a bed being whipped by a soldier called Maurice: 181–86. Conversation with the "gigolos": 195–201. The snobbery of the gutter: 203. A dilettante in the sphere of art: 205. The poetry beneath his madness: 215–18. Arrested at Morel's instigation but soon released: 235. M meets him, greatly aged, on his way to the Princesse de Guermantes's reception; his Lear-like appearance; his salute to Mme de Saint-Euverte; his dead friends: 244–49. Jupien describes him in his dotage: "just a big baby now": 251–53. His resemblance to his mother: 445.

CHARMEL. Footman to M. de Charlus: **III** 766. Charlus proposes that Morel should adopt the name: **IV** 628.

COIGNET. One of Charlus's valets: **III** 758.

CONDUCTOR (of a tram or a bus) with whom Charlus has a rendezvous: **IV** 157, 732–34 (*see also* 13–16).

COTTARD, Doctor. Member of the Verdurins' "little clan": **I** 265–67. His artificial smile, naïve thirst for knowledge, obsession with figures of speech; his puns and his literal-mindedness: 281–86, 288, 357–60, 370. Failure to understand either Vinteuil's sonata or M. Biche's painting: 300–1. His stupidity and social inexperience: 304–7. Conversation with Forcheville: 371–74. Becomes "Professor Cottard": **II** 1–3. His fame, prestige and diagnostic gifts: 4–5. His newly acquired air of glacial impassivity: 5. Called in to attend M; his prescriptions; "we realised that this imbecile was a great physician": 95–97. Speaks favourably of M to Mme Swann: 102. Invited to dinner at the Swanns': 128–30. Bergotte's "mannikin in a bottle": 172, 197–98. Called in to attend M's grandmother: **III** 404–5; has "something of the greatness of a general" in deciding on the right course of treatment: 438. "The most unfaithful and most attentive of husbands": 448. Meets M at Incarville; his remark about Albertine and Andrée dancing together: **IV** 262–64. His professional jealousy and his failure to cure a grand-duke: 265–66. Narrowly misses the little train: 361–63. His new self-assurance: 366–67. Has a passenger ejected from the "little clan's" compartment: 371. The importance of the Verdurin Wednesdays in his life: 372, 377–80. Excited by the idea of meeting the Cambremers: 382–85. Introduces M to Princess Sherbatoff: 393–95. Loses his ticket: 396–98. Introduced to Charlus: 421, who momentarily misinterprets his winks: 430–34. Criticises M. de Cambremer's clichés: 436. Questions M about his fits of breathlessness: 441. Discusses Charlus with Ski: 450–51. Plays a game of cards with Morel, interspersed with puns and witticisms: 485, 491–94, 507–9. Mme Verdurin sings his praises for the benefit of M. de Cambremer: 487–88, 492. Teases his wife when she dozes off, and discusses drugs with M. de Cambremer: 488–92. His hand-rubbing and shoulder-shaking: 508. Criticises Dr du Boulbon: 510–11. With Charlus in the little train—his confused attitude to the Baron: 593–94, 612–16. Invited by Charlus to be his second: 635, 641–44. Refuses, on Mme Verdurin's instructions, an invitation to dine at the Cambremers': 665–67. His death referred to prematurely: **V** 321. Looks after Saniette, and informs M of the Verdurins' generosity to him: 436–39. Mentioned in the Goncourt pastiche: **VI** 29, 34–37. At the Verdurins' during the war, in a colonel's uniform with a sky-blue sash: 115. Dies from overwork: 116.

COTTARD, Mme Léontine. Wife of the above. At the Verdurins': **I** 265, 281, 286; her homely taste in painting and music: 300–1; the Japanese salad in *Francillon*: 362–66. Meets Swann in a bus; discusses painting with him; assures him of Odette's affection: 532–36. Entertains her husband's colleagues and pupils: **II** 4. Her visits to Odette: 109. Her modesty and good nature: 121. Her stately language: 235, 243–51. Her devotion to her husband: 237, 249–50. Calls on M's family during his grandmother's last illness, and offers to lend her a "waiting-woman": **III** 448. Her effeminate nephew: **IV** 415. At La Raspelière: 434–36, 458–59; falls asleep after dinner: 488–92; small talk with M. de Cambremer: 495. With Charlus in the little train; her mistake about his religion: 594–98. Accused by her husband of being neurotic: 613–14. Charlus's rudeness to her: 643–44. Invited by an unsuspecting guest of the Verdurins to the luxury brothel at Maineville: 647–49.

COURGIVAUX, M. de. M takes him for his son at the Princesse de Guermantes's reception: **VI** 371.

COURVOISIER, Vicomte Adalbert de. Nephew of Mme de Gallardon, "a young man with a pretty face and an impertinent air," introduced to Charlus at the Prince de Guermantes's soirée: **IV** 71. An invert but a good husband: **VI** 20. Frequents Jupien's brothel: 194.

COURVOISIERS, The. Relations and rivals of the Guermantes clan; their social ethos compared and contrasted with the latter's: **III** 604–19, 631–32, 639–43, 651–55.

COUSIN (female) by whom M is initiated into "the delights of love" on Aunt Léonie's sofa: **II** 208–9.

COUSIN of M's nicknamed "No flowers by request": **III** 465.

COUSIN (of Bloch). *See* Lévy, Esther.

CRÉCY, Pierre de Verjus, Comte de. Impoverished nobleman

with a taste for good food and wine, cigars and genealogy, be-friended by M at Balbec: **IV** 657–61. His patronym is Saylor, hence the family motto *Ne sçais l'heure*: 661. Invites himself to dinner: 695. M learns from Charlus that he was Odette's first husband, and lives on an allowance from Swann: **V** 402.

CRÉCY, Mme de. *See* Odette.

CRIQUETOT, M. de. "How goes it?": **IV** 698.

CRIQUETOT, Comtesse de. Cousin of the Cambremers; M receives notice of her death at Balbec: **IV** 251.

CURÉ of Combray. His asparagus: **I** 74. His brother a tax-collector at Châteaudun: 78. His visits to Aunt Léonie; his knowledge of etymology: 94, 142–47, 165. "Touches the Princesse des Laumes for 100 francs a year: 485. Transferred to Criquetot for a time; his pamphlet on the place-names of the Balbec district: **IV** 282. Brichot's criticisms of this work: 387–93, 434–35, 534–36. Knew what was "right and proper": **V** 9–10.

DAIRYMAID who brings M a letter at the Grand Hotel, Balbec: **II** 400.

DAIRYMAID. "Startling towhead" glimpsed by M at the dairy: **V** 178–79. Brought in by Françoise to run an errand: 181–85, 189–90.

DALTIER, Emilie. Pretty girl—"a good golfer"—known to Albertine: **V** 551.

DANCER, back-stage in the theatre, admired by Rachel: **III** 235–41.

DECHAMBRE. Pianist patronised by Mme Verdurin. Brichot announces his death; discussion about his age: **IV** 396–97. Effect of his death on the Verdurins: 399–407, 445–46. M. Verdurin speaks of him to Charlus: 463.

(*See* Pianist (young) patronised by the Verdurins.)

DELAGE, Suzanne. Mistakenly believed by Albertine and Mme Bontemps to have been a childhood friend of M's: **III** 503–5.

DELTOUR, General. Secretary to the Presidency of the Republic. Approached by Charlus in connexion with Morel's decoration: **V** 371–72.

DIEULAFOY, Professor. *See* Index of Persons.

DRAWING-MASTER (of M's grandmother), who never saw his mistress without a hat: **II** 598–99.

DUCRET. One of Charlus's valets: **III** 758.

DURAS, Duc de. Mentioned by the Duc de Guermantes in connexion with Saint-Loup's election to the Jockey Club: **III** 322. Marries the widowed Mme Verdurin; dies two years later: **VI** 387.

DURAS, Duchesse de. At the Verdurins' musical soirée; praised by Charlus: **V** 366–70; resented by Mme Verdurin: 416, 420–21.

DURAS, Duchesse de. *See* Verdurin, Mme.

DUROC, Major. Lecturer on military history admired by Saint-Loup: **III** 97–98, 135–38; his Dreyfusism: 139–40.

E——, Professor. Distinguished doctor whom M persuades to examine his grandmother after her stroke; his bad grace and his pessimistic (and accurate) verdict: **III** 426–27, 430–32. M meets him again at the Princesse de Guermantes's soirée: **IV** 54–57.

EGREMONT, Vicomtesse d'. Assumes the role of parlour-maid *chez* the Princesse d'Epinay: **III** 634.

ELSTIR. Painter, habitué of the Verdurin salon, where he is known as "Master Biche": **I** 266, 281. His love of match-making: 285. Invites Swann and Odette to visit his studio; his portrait of Cottard: 286. His painting too advanced for the Cottards: 300–1. Swann finds him pretentious and vulgar, but admires his intelligence: 351, 355. His flashy dissertation on a fellow-painter: 361–62 much admired by Forcheville: 365. His (perhaps deliberate) gaffe in front of Swann: 403–4. Reputed lover of Odette: 506 (cf. 602; **V** 592–93). Goes on a cruise with the Verdurins after an illness: 531–32. Appears in Swann's dream: 538–40. His art compared to that of Mme de Sévigné: **II** 315. M and Saint-Loup meet him in the restaurant at Rive-belle—"the famous painter Elstir": 553–57. M's visit to his studio; his seascapes; visual "metaphors"; Balbec church; his friendship with Albertine; the portrait of "Miss Sacripant"; Mme Elstir, "my beautiful Gabrielle!"; his ideals as a painter: 564–89. Walks with M along the front; meets the "little band"; is revealed as "M. Biche": 592–607. "We do not receive wisdom, we must discover it for ourselves": 605–6. His revelation to M of the poetry of "still lifes": 613. Gives a party at which M meets Albertine: 613–16. His good taste in dress; his influence on Albertine: 634–35 (*see also* **IV** 617–18). Speaks of race-meetings, regattas, landscapes and seascapes, Venice, costume (Fortuny): 652–58. His influence on M's way of seeing things, and on his attitude to Berma's art: **III** 27, 39, 51, 59. Saint-Loup's high opinion of his intelligence: 135. M's passion for his work—"my favourite painter": 162–64. Mme de Guermantes's Elstirs: 162–64, 185. Norpois and *The Bunch of Radishes*: 299. M sees the Guermantes' Elstirs at last: 573–78. Swann's attitude to him recalled ("an oaf," "balderdash"): 631. His work criticised by the Duc and Duchesse de Guermantes: 685–88. His portrait of Oriane: 717. His work disliked by the Kaiser: 717, 721 (cf. **IV** 470–71). Admired by Albertine and Mme de Cambremer: **IV** 283–84. Compared with Ski: 367–68. His breach with the Verdurins: 458–65. His opinion of the church of Marcouville-l'Orgueilleuse: 561–62 (cf. **V** 217–18). M visits the scene of two of his landscapes: 581–82. His austere taste in women's clothes: 617–18. His paintings of a little boy on the sands at Saint-Pierre-des-Ifs: 692–93. His passion for violets: **V** 178, 181. In contradiction with his own impressionism: 217 (cf. **IV** 562). Brichot describes his "buffooneries" in the old days at the Verdurins': 266. The uniqueness of his art: seeing the universe through other eyes: 339, 343. His views on the furnishing of yachts, on old silver, on Fortuny gowns: 237–38, 496–97 (cf. **II** 653–54). Compared to Dostoievsky and Mme de Sévigné: 510. Two of his pictures sold to the Luxembourg by Mme de Guermantes: 545. Significance of his portrait of Odette: had he been her lover?: 592–93. His intellectual charm: 668, 670. His paintings of naked girls in a wooded landscape remind M of Albertine and the laundry-girls: 710–11. His work becomes fashionable: 787–88. Mentioned in the Goncourt pastiche; Mme Verdurin claims to have taught him how to paint flowers ("he was always known simply as Monsieur Tiche"): **VI** 33–35, 42–43. His grief at M. Verdurin's death: 116–17.

ELSTIR, Mme. M meets her in the artist's studio at Balbec; "My beautiful Gabrielle!": **II** 586–88. Albertine admires her taste in clothes: 634. Denounced by Mme Verdurin as a "trollop": **IV** 460–61. Embodies the kind of "heavy" "Venetian" beauty Elstir sought to capture in his painting: **VI** 116, 439–40.

ENTRAGUES, Mlle d'. Daughter of the Duc de Luxembourg, sought in marriage by Saint-Loup and by the Duc de Châtellerault: **V** 898.

EPINAY, Victurnienne, Princesse d'. Entertains the Duc and Duchesse de Guermantes; admires Oriane's witticisms ("Teaser Augustus"): **III** 633–40.

EPINOY, Princesse d'. Astonished at the brilliance of Odette's salon: **IV** 195–96.

EPORCHEVILLE, Mlle d'. Name wrongly thought by M to be that of the girl of good family recommended by Saint-Loup as a frequenter of brothels: **V** 760–65, 772–74.

(*See* Orgeville, Mlle de l'; Gilberte.)

ESTHER. *See* Lévy, Esther.

EUDOXIA, Queen. Wife of King Theodosius: **V** 327–28.

EUDOXIE, Grand Duchess. Friend of Princess Sherbatoff: **IV** 372–74.

EUGÈNE, M. Deputy of the Liberal Action party, an habitué of Jupien's brothel: **VI** 183. Re-elected after the war: 237.

EULALIE. Retired domestic servant at Combray; confidante of Aunt Léonie: **I** 93–96. Visits Aunt Léonie with the Curé: 141–48. Her rivalry with Françoise: 148–51, 162–65 (cf. **V** 475–76, 486). Praised by Françoise after her death: **III** 24. M remembers a week spent in her room in early childhood: **VI** 276.

FAFFENHEIM-MUNSTERBURG-WEININGEN, Prince von. German Prime Minister. Visits Mme de Villeparisis; poetry of his name belied by his persona; his efforts to persuade Norpois to get him elected to the *Institut*: **III** 345–56. Introduced to M by Norpois: 370. Praises Mme de Villeparisis's painting: 372. At the Guermantes' dinner-party; his vise-like German handclasp; his nickname "Prince Von": 591. Speaks to M about Rachel, and invites him to come home with him: 697–99. His ironical praise of the Kaiser's intelligence and taste in art: 721–22. His hatred of the English: 722–23. A Dreyfusard: **IV** 105.

FARCY, Mme de. American wife of the Comte de Farcy, an

obscure relation of the Forchevilles; friend of Bloch: **VI** 296–97, 468.

FATHER of the narrator. His interest in meteorology: **I** 12 (*see also* 127, 233; **V** 95–96). Annoyed by the "good-night kiss": 15, and by his wife's pleas on behalf of Swann's wife and daughter: 29–30. His arbitrariness; his unexpected indulgence; his resemblance to Benozzo Gozzoli's Abraham: 46–49. His fondness for chocolate cream: 97. M resembles him, according to Uncle Adolphe: 105. The "lady in pink" (Odette) finds him "exquisitely charming," to M's surprise: 106. Quarrels with Uncle Adolphe: 109. Irritated by Bloch: 127. Evening walks round Combray: 159–60. Doubts about Legrandin: 166–67, and vain efforts to elicit from him information about his relations at Balbec: 182–86. His influential position: 244. Discusses M's proposed visit to Venice: 557–59. Unaware of M's passion for Gilberte Swann: 586–88. Dismisses Swann as a "pestilent" fellow: **II** 1. His relations with Norpois: 7–10, and their effect on his attitude to M's career: 12–13. Invites Norpois to dinner: 21, discusses M's career with him: 29–36, and talks to him about international affairs: 41–48. Proposed trip to Spain with Norpois: 48 (cf. 304). Resigns himself to M's abandonment of diplomacy for literature: 73–74. His opinion of Norpois: 75–77. Discusses restaurants with Françoise: 78–79. His reactions on hearing of M's meeting with Bergotte: 201–3. Mme de Villeparisis speaks of him and his trip with Norpois; his admiration for El Greco: 381–82. His naïvety: 710. His liking for thin toast exasperates Françoise: **III** 25–26. His relations with the Duc de Guermantes: 34, 195–97. His candidature for the *Institut*; will Norpois support him?: 199 (*see also* 301–4). "Cut" by Mme Sazerat because of his anti-Dreyfusism: 199–200. Norpois speaks about him to M: 302–4. During the illness of M's grandmother: 464–70. Appears in M's dreams about his grandmother: **IV** 216–18, 241–42. M's increasing resemblance to him: **V** 93–97, 112–13, 135–37. His sensibility concealed behind a cold exterior: 136–37. His brusque manner: 137–38.

FÉRÉ, M. and Mme. Fashionable friends of the Cambremers, who give a dinner in their honour: **IV** 670–72. M plays chess with them: 697.

FIERBOIS, Marquis de. His "complicated and rapid capers" condemned as ridiculous by Charlus: **III** 611. His illness: **IV** 2.

FISHER-GIRL approached by M at Carqueville: **II** 402–4.

FLORA. *See* Céline and Flora.

FOGGI, Prince Odo. Discusses Italian politics with Norpois in Venice: **V** 857–62.

FOIX, Prince de. *Habitué* of the restaurant where M dines with Saint-Loup; his wealth, arrogance and secret sodomy: **III** 551–57. Saint-Loup borrows his cloak: 561–63. At the Guermantes': 591, 697–99. Inherits his sexual tastes from his father: **VI** 200.

FOIX, Prince de. Father of the above. *Habitué* of Jupien's brothel, where his death is regretted: **VI** 199–200.

FOOTMAN (young). Favourite of Françoise. *See* Périgot.

FOOTMAN at the Guermantes'. *See* Poullein.

FOOTMAN of Mme de Chevregny. Invited to dinner at the Grand Hotel, Balbec, by Charlus: **IV** 524–27.

FOOTMAN at the Verdurins'. Object of Charlus's attention: **V** 300–1.

FOOTMEN (other). At the Guermantes': **III** 35–37; Georges: 663; Saint-Loup gives one of them some cynical advice: **V** 633–35.

FOOTMEN at the Swanns': **II** 113–37.

FOOTMEN of M. de Charlus. *See* Burnier; Charmel.

FOOTMEN at Mme de Saint-Euverte's: **I** 459–61.

FORCHEVILLE, Comte (later Baron) de. Introduced to the Verdurin circle by Odette; his snobbery and vulgarity: **I** 355–77. Becomes one of the "faithful": 383. Brutally insults Saniette (his brother-in-law): 392–93. Letter addressed to him by Odette deciphered through its envelope by Swann; his intimacy with Odette and Swann's jealousy: 400–5, 406–8, 422–31, 451, 505–6, 526–27. Swann dreams of him: 538–41. Marries Odette and adopts Gilberte: **V** 775–77, 787.

FORCHEVILLE, Mme de. *See* Odette.

FORCHEVILLE, Mlle de. *See* Gilberte.

FORESTELLE, Marquis de. Friend of Swann, who visits him at his house near Pierrefonds: **I** 417–18. At Mme de Saint-Euverte's; his monocle: 465–66.

FORESTIER, Robert. Playmate of M in the Champs-Elysées: **III** 503–5.

FRANÇOISE. Aunt Léonie's cook at Combray: **I** 12, 22. Her code: 37–38. Takes a note from M to his mother: 39–40. Her devotion to M's family; her qualities as a servant; her family; conversations with Aunt Léonie: 69–80, 139–42. Her artistry and largesse as a cook: 96–98. Her kitchen-maid: 110–13. Conversation with the gardener on war and revolution: 122–23. Her attitude to money; hatred of Eulalie; relations with Aunt Léonie; her Saturday routine: 148–54, 162–65. In her kitchen; cruelty and sentimentality; policy towards other servants; harshness to the kitchen-maid: 168–73 (cf. 151). Resembles the figures in the porch of Saint-André-des-Champs—a "mediaeval peasant": 212. Her wild grief at the death of Aunt Léonie: 215–17. Her malapropisms: 217, and her colourful idiom: 233. Enters into service with M's family after Aunt Léonie's death; takes M to the Champs-Elysées: 546, 559–62, 565, 575–76, 580–81, 584, and accompanies him in pursuit of the Swanns: 591, 594–96. Prepares dinner for Norpois; compared to Michelangelo: **II** 21–22, 39–40. Her views on Norpois and on Paris restaurants: 76–77. Visits the water-closet in the Champs-Elysées; the "Marquise": 88–89. Reactions to M's illness: 93, 98. Praised by Odette: "your old nurse": 110. Her "simple but unerring taste" in clothes; her natural distinction; "the élite of the world of the simple-minded": 308–10. Her social connexions in the Grand Hotel, Balbec: 369–71. Her pride; attitude towards the aristocracy; forgives Mme de Villeparisis for being a marquise: 373–77. Her opinion of Bloch and of Saint-Loup: 489–91. M mocks her sentimentality: 500. Her resentment of M's reproaches, discontent with Balbec and dislike of the "little band": 649–51. Wants to leave Balbec: 724. In the family's new flat in Paris; regrets at leaving Combray: **III** 1–2. Her preoccupation with the Guermantes: 11. Holds court below stairs; invocation to Combray: 12–14. Relations with Jupien ("Julien"): 14–18. Reflexions on the Guermantes: 20–22, and further reminiscences of Combray, Méséglise, Aunt Léonie: 22–25. Conversations with the Guermantes footmen; cult of the nobility: 35–37. Her relations with M; disapproval of his pursuit of Mme de Guermantes; her intuition, her moods and idiosyncrasies: 76–82. "The very language of Saint-Simon": 84. Visits to her relations: 193–94. Her sympathy for the Guermantes' lovesick footman: 193, 202, 417. During M's grandmother's illness; her irritating reflexions at the bedside: 408; her devoted care for the patient despite her tactlessness and insensitivity: 434–37, 449–56, 468–70. Interrupts M and Albertine making love; her knowledge of M's doings: 489–93. Her peasant sense of propriety: 502. Admires Charlus and Jupien: **IV** 41–42. Entertains her daughter; her highly individual French; her dialect: 170–73. Refuses to use the telephone: 176–77 (see also **V** 126, 200–1). Her dislike of Albertine: 182–85. Reveals to M the circumstances that had caused his grandmother to have her photograph taken by Saint-Loup: 237–38. The servant's lot; M's pity and affection for her: 238–40. Prophesies that Albertine will make M unhappy: 252–53. Complaints about money-grubbers: 257. Disapproves of Céleste and Marie: 335. Shocked at seeing Charlus arm in arm with a servant: 527. With M and Albertine in Paris; makes Albertine observe the rules of the house: **V** 2–3, 4, 6, 10–11. Her regrets at not having said good-bye to the housekeeper at Balbec: 10–11. Her hatred of Albertine: 122–23 (see also 198–99). Listens to M's telephone conversations: 126. Fetches a dairymaid to run an errand for M: 178–81. Sent to bring back Albertine from the Trocadéro; her vocabulary contaminated by her daughter's slang; her inability to tell the time correctly: 196–202. How Aunt Léonie thwarted her secret plans for an outing: 475–76. Unable to contain her jealousy of Albertine: 486. Her innuendoes; her curiosity about money: 492–94. Announces Albertine's departure: 558–59. Discovers the rings left behind by Albertine: 622–25. Alarmed at the possibility of Albertine's return: 629–30 (cf. 596). Makes no pretence of sorrow at Albertine's death: 648–49. Her attitude to her "masters"; despises them so as not to feel despised herself: 765–66. Her persistent errors in grammar and pronunciation: 774–75. Her attitude to liaisons between men: **VI** 14–16. In 1914, tormented by the butler about the war news: 83–87 (see also 219–26); her concern to get the butcher's boy exempted from military service: 96. Unimpressed by Saint-Loup's bravery: 219; her pacifism: 223–24. Her nephew killed at Berry-au-Bac; the noble behaviour of her cousins, the Larivières: 225–26. Her grief at Saint-Loup's death: 229–31. Speaks of M's "paperies": 319; M compares his work with hers: 509–11.

FRANÇOISE'S cousins. *See* Larivières.

FRANÇOISE'S daughter. *See* Marguerite.

FRANÇOISE'S nephews. One of them tries to get exempted from military service during the war: **VI** 83–84, 225; another killed at Berry-au-Bac: 225.

FRANÇOISE'S niece. "The butcheress": **III** 193–194; **IV** 171–72.

FRANÇOISE'S son-in-law. *See* Julien.

FRANQUETOT, Vicomtesse de. Cousin of the dowager Marquis de Cambremer. At Mme de Saint-Euverte's: **I** 466–78; **IV** 94.

FRÉCOURT Marquis de. Owner of a coach-house with red-tiled turret: **III** 785; **IV** 1.

FROBERVILLE, General de. At Mme de Saint-Euverte's; his monocle: **I** 464–65. Conversation with the Princesse des Laumes; admires the young Mme de Cambremer: 478–83, who is introduced to him by Swann: 488–89. Exchanges ironical looks with Swann at the Elysée Palace: **V** 906.

FROBERVILLE, Colonel de. Nephew of the above. At the Princesse de Guermantes's: **IV** 100–3; his social position; ingratitude and envy vis-à-vis Mme de Saint-Euverte: 103–4; hopes for the failure of her garden-party and is delighted to hear that Mme de Guermantes will not attend: 112–15. Described as "gaga" by the Duc de Guermantes: 189.

G——. Writer; visits Mme de Villeparisis; frequently invited to the Guermantes': **III** 276.

GALLARDON, Marquise de, *née* Courvoisier. At Mme de Saint-Euverte's; her obsession with the Guermantes family: **I** 467–69. Unrewarding exchange with her cousin the Princesse des Laumes; snide remarks about Swann's Jewishness: 473–77. Her Courvoisier snobbery and conventionality: **III** 604–5, 652–53. Despised by Mme de Guermantes: 688. Introduces her nephew to Charlus, in spite of her doubts as to the latter's morals: **IV** 71 (*see also* 408). Encounter with Oriane on the staircase at the Princesse de Guermantes's: 161–62, 164–65.

GALLARDON, Dowager Duchesse de, mother-in-law of the Princesse de Gallardon. Her Courvoisier ignorance of literature: **III** 612.

GALOPIN. Pastrycook at Combray: **I** 76; his dog: 79.

GARDENER at Combray. Aligns the garden paths too symmetrically for M's grandmother: **I** 12, 87, 119. His views on war and revolution: 122–23.

GARDENER at La Raspelière. Groans beneath the Verdurins' yoke; his mixed feelings about Mme de Cambremer: **IV** 429–30.

GAUCOURT, Mme de. Sister of M. de Cambremer. Suffers from fits of breathlessness: **IV** 441–42, 510, 512, 676, 694; **VI** 356–57.

GIBERGUE. Friend of Saint-Loup at Doncières: **III** 136–37.

GILBERT. *See* Guermantes, Gilbert, Prince de.

GILBERTE. Daughter of Swann and Odette. (Later Mlle de Forcheville, then, through her marriage to Robert, Marquise de Saint-Loup.) Remembered by the narrator (as Mme de Saint-Loup): **I** 6. Worshipped by her father; M's mother speaks to him about her: 29–31. Bergotte "her greatest friend"; M's reflections on learning this: 137–8, 192. M's first sight of her, at Tansonville; her indelicate gesture; the name Gilberte: 197–200. M's obsession with her: 202–5. In the Champs-Elysées, the little girl with reddish hair playing battledore and shuttlecock: 560. M's love for her; games of prisoner's base; the agate marble and Bergotte's monograph on Racine; her indifference, her absences; waiting for a letter from her: 561–87. Before her parents' marriage, Odette would blackmail Swann by refusing to let him see his daughter: **II** 51–52. Swann's ambition to present her to the Duchesse de Guermantes: 57–58. Norpois's opinion of her: 65–66. New Year's Day; M writes her a letter which remains unanswered: 80–85. She returns to the Champs-Elysées: 85. Her parents "can't stand" M: 85–86. Amorous wrestle behind the clump of laurels: 90–91. Writes to the convalescent M inviting him to tea; her signature: 98–101. Her tea-parties: 103–10, 114–16. Her kind-heartedness and apparent devotion to her father: 149–50. Her strange behaviour to him: 162–63. Her resemblance to both her parents; the two Gilbertes: 188–92. M's doubts as to her true character: 195–96. Why he dare not invite her to his home: 204. Beginnings of the rupture with M; her sulks; M writes her mutually contradictory letters to which she does not reply; his feigned indifference: 211–27, 235–36. Another New Year's Day; M's efforts to extinguish his love; his letters: 251–60, 269–71. The two walkers in the Elysian gloom: Gilberte and a young man—later identified as Léa in male costume (**VI** 7): 272–77. M's dream about her: 281–82. Further progress towards forgetting her: 284–86. Brief recrudescence of his love for her, extinguished by habit: 299–301. Later, M declines Swann's invitation to meet her again: **IV** 153–54. He gives the turquoise-studded book-cover she had had made for him to Albertine: 186–87 (*see* 175). He writes to her, without emotion; her name depoeticised: 187–88. She inherits a fortune; the Faubourg Saint-Germain begins to take an interest in her and her mother: 199. M interrogates Albertine about her: **V** 20 (cf. **IV** 186–87). He learns from her maid that at the time when he used to visit her every day, she was in love with another "young man": 173–74. Albertine admits to having kissed her: 506–7. Her resemblance to Albertine: 677–78. M meets her without recognising her; she gives him a furtive glance that arouses him; he wrongly identifies her as Mlle d'Eporcheville: 758–65. Reintroduced to M at Mme de Guermantes's; she has become Mlle de Forcheville: 773–77. Responds with alacrity to Mme de Guermantes's advances; lunches at her house: 780–86; prefers to forget her father; conceals her origins; her snobbery: 786–97. Failure to fulfil her father's hopes: 799–801. Sends M a telegram in Venice which he imagines to be from Albertine: 869–74 (cf. 889–90). Her marriage to Robert de Saint-Loup: 889, 895–97, 900–3. Changes in her attitude to society after her marriage: 907–12. M renews his friendship with her, and visits her at Tansonville: 920–21. Robert's infidelity: 921–25. Her pregnancy: 925–26. Jealous of Rachel, whom she seeks to imitate: 928–30. Her avarice: 931–33. Walks with M at Combray; her surprising revelations about the two "ways": **VI** 1–4. Confesses her love for him as a child; the meaning of her indelicate gesture: 4–5. It was with Léa that she had been walking in the Champs-Elysées: 6–7 (cf. **II** 272–73). Her love for Robert: 9, and her relations with him at Tansonville: 11–18. Discusses Al-

bertine with M: 22–25. Reads Balzac's *La Fille aux yeux d'or*:
23, 26. Lends M a volume of the Goncourt Journal: 26. In
September 1914, leaves Paris for Combray; writes to M about
the German invasion: 88–89. In 1916, writes him another letter
with a new interpretation of her departure: 93–96. Her face becomes a perfect replica of Odette's: 361. At the Princesse de
Guermantes's, M takes her for her mother: 427–28. Conversation about Robert: 428–32. Her friendship with Andrée: 432–33.
Her disdain for the new Princesse de Guermantes (Mme Verdurin) and even for Oriane: 434–35. Her ironic and fanciful
reply to Mme de Morienval: 461. Vilified by Mme de Guermantes: 476–500. Introduces her daughter to M: 501–7.

GINESTE, Marie. Sister of Céleste Albaret; lady's-maid at
Balbec: **IV** 265, 331–33. Her friendship with M; her colourful
language: 333–36. Her grief at M's departure: 716.

GIRL (tall and handsome) admired by M as she serves *café au
lait* to the passengers on the train to Balbec: **II** 317–18.

GIRL ("glorious") with the cigarette who joins the little train
at Saint-Pierre-des-Ifs: **IV** 381–82.

GIRL (with blue eyes) whom Swann meets in a brothel: **I**
530–31.

GIRL (blonde) who gazes at M in the restaurant at Rivebelle:
**II** 541; his obsession with her: 549.

GIRL resembling Albertine getting into a car in the Bois: **V**
758.

GIRL (little poor) taken home by M after Albertine's departure: **V** 583. Her parents bring a charge against him: 597–99.

GIRL (little) with a bicycle in the Bois: **V** 224.

GIRL (little) with the sharp voice, a friend of Gilberte's, in the
Champs-Elysées: **I** 560–61, 567, 577.

GIRLS (two), friends of Léa, whom Albertine stares at in the
mirror in the Casino at Balbec. In vol. **IV** they are identified as
Bloch's sister and cousin (pp. 272–74); in vol. **V** they are differentiated from the Bloch girls: 105. M fears that Albertine may
meet them with Léa at the Trocadéro: **V** 185–86, 190–93. Said
to frequent the bathing establishment of the hotel: 663.

GIRLS (three) in the Bois, sitting beside their bicycles; how Albertine stares at them: **V** 220–21.

GIRLS at Balbec (the little band). First appearance on the esplanade: **II** 502–16, 519–20, 529, 540. M sees a photograph of them as little girls, an amorphous, undifferentiated group: 549–52. M's anxiety to meet them: 558–62. Elstir knows them; their social background: 578–82. M sees them with Elstir on the front—"a few spores of the zoophytic band"—but his hopes of being introduced to them are disappointed: 593–96, 606–8. Hopes of making their acquaintance through Albertine; her reluctance: 622–25, 635–40. M finally gets to know them all; their flowering-time: 642–46. Games in the Casino: 645–46. Excursions and picnics: 649–51, 660–61. Their faces: 662–63. Their conversation, voices, mannerisms: 665–66. A subject for French composition: 670–75. M's collective love for them; the confrontation of memory with an ever-changing reality: 675–80. The game of "ferret": 680–84. Their faces differentiated: 716–19. From fabulous beings to ordinary girls: 721–24. On his second visit to Balbec, M longs to see them again: **IV** 243. That summer, he enjoys the "ephemeral favours" of thirteen of them, not counting Albertine: 255–56. The picnics resumed: 320. Still a race apart: 699. A grove of budding girls: **V** 82–83. Their impenetrable solidarity as liars: 233–35. M's love divided among them all: 681–82. Andrée denies that any of them had Sapphic tastes: 738–39. Their attitude to Albertine: 821–23.

GISÈLE. Member of the little band at Balbec. Makes a sarcastic remark in a rasping voice when Andrée jumps over the old gentleman: **II** 508 (cf. 637–39). "The cruel one": 512. Joins M and Albertine on the beach: 637–39. Hated by Andrée (cf. 649) and considered "boring" by Albertine: 639. Leaving Balbec to "swot" for her exams: 640. M attempts to accompany her: 641. Andrée speaks of her with affection: 648–49. A letter from her: her French composition: 670–75. Mistakenly referred to as the girl who jumped over the old gentleman: **III** 496. M meets her in Paris; her lies: **V** 231–35. Accused by Andrée of treachery: 740. Andrée's "best friend": 807–8.

GLASS-VENDOR (young Venetian). M's liaison with her and plan to take her back to Paris: **V** 867–68. A "new Albertine": 873.

GOUPIL, Mme. At Combray: Did she get to Mass before the

Elevation?; has company for lunch: **I** 74–77, 93, 151. Her new silk dress: 139–40. Gossips with M's family after Mass: 174. Writes to congratulate M on his article in the *Figaro*: **V** 797–99.

GOVERNESS (Gilberte's). In the Champs-Elysées; her blue feather: **I** 561, 566. Goes shopping with Gilberte: 576, 586. Goes to a concert with Gilberte: **II** 161.

GRANDFATHER of the narrator (Amédée). His house in Combray: **I** 6. Encouraged by his cousin to take a sip of brandy, though forbidden to do so: 13. A great friend of Swann's father: 17–18. His interest in Swann's social contacts: 26–35. His refusal to answer a letter from Swann about his relations with Odette: 45 (cf. 273–74). Disapproval of Uncle Adolphe's philandering: 103; violent "words" with him: 109. Distrusts M's Jewish friends: 125–26. Walk by Swann's way with M and his father: 188–201. Refuses to further Swann's amatory intrigues: 273–74, or to introduce him to the Verdurins, with whom he was acquainted: 281. Invites Swann to his daughter's wedding: 441. Suspected by Swann of writing an anonymous letter: 509. Appears in Swann's dream: 538–39. His daughter has inherited something of his cast of mind: **II** 120. His love of the Army: **III** 200. During his wife's last illness: 464–70. Mme Verdurin speaks contemptuously of him and his father: **IV** 418–19. His social rigidity, passed on to his daughter: 579. His loathing for the Germans: **V** 135.

GRANDMOTHER of the narrator (Bathilde or Mme Amédée). Evenings at Combray; her walks in the garden; her love of fresh air and of naturalness; her worries (M's lack of will-power and delicate health, her husband's brandy-drinking); her sweetness and humility: **I** 12–15, 16. Visits Mme de Villeparisis, a childhood friend of hers (cf. 144); finds the Jupiens charming and the Prince des Laumes "common": 24–25. Admires Swann's taste: 28. Her principles in the matter of upbringing: 48–49. Her ideas on literature; gives M the pastoral novels of George Sand: 52–53. Her choice of presents: 52–55. Her love for the steeple of Saint-Hilaire: 86–87. Her opinion of Legrandin: 92–93 (cf. 177). Begs M to go out of doors: 114–15. Displeased by Bloch: 127. Criticised by Françoise—"slightly batty": 141. Her remark about Mlle Vinteuil: **I** 157–58. Plan for her to accompany M to

Balbec: 182–85. Concern for M's health: **II** 12. Accompanies him to see Berma in *Phèdre*: 20, 27, 37–38. During M's illness, her loving care; her anxiety about his taking alcohol, even as medicine: 93–95 (cf. 310–13). Reproaches M for not working: 211–12. Accompanies M to Balbec: 299, 304–5; her "beloved Sévigné": 305, 308–15 (*see also* **I** 25; **II** 372, 375–76, 467–68; **III** 408–9, 423; **IV** 229–31; **V** 11, 892); her concern about M's drinking: 311–12. Arrival at Balbec: 325–30. Her loving tenderness; the knocking on the wall: 334–37. Opens the dining-room window: 345. Meets Mme de Villeparisis, whom she avoids at first, then resumes her friendship with her: 358–61, 371–82. Excursions with Mme de Villeparisis: 386; sings her praises: 418. M tells her that he couldn't live without her: 418–19. Introduced to Saint-Loup: 425, who makes a conquest of her: 428–30. Introduced to Charlus: 456, whom she finds delightful: 458–73. Photographed by Saint-Loup: 500–1. Her concern for M's moral and physical welfare: 509, 516–17, 530. Reproaches M for not visiting Elstir: 559, 564. Her nature and M's: 589. Presents Saint-Loup with a collection of Proudhon's letters: 608. Moves to a flat in the Hôtel de Guermantes for the sake of her health: **III** 3. Her voice on the telephone: 173–80. Her changed appearance on M's return from Doncières: 183–85. Refuses invitations from Mme de Villeparisis on the grounds of health: 197–98. Her attitude to the Dreyfus Case: 200. Her health deteriorates; Cottard called in; Dr du Boulbon's visit: 403–18. Goes to the Champs-Elysées with M and has a stroke: 419–24. M takes her to see Professor E——: 427–31. Her last illness and death: 433–41, 452–58, 462–71. Professor E—— seeks confirmation of her death: **IV** 54–57. Her resurrection in M's memory on his second arrival at Balbec—"the intermittencies of the heart": 210–16. M dreams of her: 216–20. Memories and meditations concerning her; the truth about the Saint-Loup photograph: 237–43, 246, 249–50. M's mother talks to him about her; her literary purism: 318–19. Would have thought M. de Cambremer "very common": 423. Her life in her daughter's memory, like "a pure and innocent childhood": 711–12. Their resemblance: 721–22, 724. Her influence on her daughter: **V** 8, 11–12; and on M: 95–96, 136–38. M wakes up thinking of her:

157–58. He has inherited from her a lack of self-importance: 387. Her death juxtaposed with Albertine's; "a double murder": 669–70, 676. Appears with Albertine in a dream: 726–28. Invoked by M's mother in the train from Venice apropos of the marriages of Gilberte and Jupien's niece: 892–94, 916–17.

GREAT-AUNT of the narrator. Cousin of M's grandfather and mother of Aunt Léonie: I 66. Reads the "accompanying patter" of the magic lantern: 10. Teases M's grandmother: 13–14. Underestimates Swann and misconstrues his social position: 18–23. A trifle "common": 21. Her ideas on *déclassement*: 24–28. Finds Swann aged: 45. Her "indictment" of M's grandmother: 54. Leaves her fortune to a niece from whom she had been estranged for years: 128. Slandered by Bloch: 129. Her ideas on Sunday observance: 139. Her concern for her invalid daughter: 166. Her straightforwardness: II 199–200.

GREAT-GRANDFATHER of the narrator. Referred to contemptuously by Mme Verdurin; his stinginess: IV 418–19.

GREAT-UNCLE of the narrator. Pulls M's curls: I 3.

GRIGRI. *See* Agrigente, Prince d'.

GROUCHY, M. de. Late for dinner with the Guermantes: III 594. Offers Mme de Guermantes some pheasants: 662.

GROUCHY, Mme de. Daughter of the Vicomtesse de Guermantes: III 594, 662.

GUASTALLA, Albert, Duc de. Son of the Princesse de Parme: III 581–82, 710; Charlus's cousin: 773–74.

GUASTALLA, Duc de. Son of the Princesse d'Iéna: III 710–11. Visited on his sick-bed by Mme de Guermantes: 713–14. His title ridiculed by Charlus: 774.

GUERMANTES, The. Legrandin suffers from not knowing them: I 178–80. The Guermantes way: 188–89, 233–62. Mme de Gallardon's obsession with them: 467–69. The "witty Guermantes set" as represented by the Princesse des Laumes: 475, 479–87. Odette adopts some of their verbal mannerisms through Swann: II 113–14, 129, who has imbibed their combination of taste and snobbishness: 116–20, 194. The magic of the name Guermantes: III 6–11. Françoise's interest in them: 11–12, 19–22. Their position in the Faubourg Saint-Germain: 27–32. Their characteristic features: 99, 274–75 (*see also* 591). Their at-

titude to distinguished commoners: 276–79, 339. Charlus speaks
of "these powerful Guermantes": 388–89, 397. Their reliance on
Dr Dieulafoy in grave cases: 459–60. Their house "forbidden
territory" to M; his invitation to dinner: 512–17. Vulgar arrogance and ancient grandeur: 569, 572–73, 596. Their physical
characteristics: 600–602. The family genie; the Guermantes and
the Courvoisiers; the wit of the Guermantes: 602–20, 627–44,
652–56. Their earthiness, as exemplified by the Duchess: 677.
M. de Bréauté follows the Guermantes style: 691. Poetry and reality; family history; cousins galore: 720–21, 726–32, 744–44,
750, 778–83, 785. The Guermantes style as exemplified by
Swann: 793–99, and by Charlus: IV 2–4 (see also 596, 624–25,
628–29, 642–44, 666–67; V 273–74, 345, 353). Party-giving à la
Guermantes: 64–65, 72–74, 82–84. M earns credit from the
Guermantes for his discreet bow: 84–85. Mme de Saint-Euverte
tries to emulate them: 93–97, 102–4, 113–15. People beginning
to lose interest in them: 198–99. Cottard's low estimate of them:
377–79. The noblest family in France, according to Charlus: 666
(see also V 56–57, 309–10). Discussed by the Cambremers: 673.
Their contempt for the opinion of commoners: V 274. The
Guermantes tone: 345. Attitude to Mme de Villeparisis: 391–92.
Adopt a German style: 829 (cf. VI 89). Indifference to wealth:
867. Inherited characteristics—Saint-Loup, Charlus and the
Duke: 934–36; VI 15, 18–19. Gilberte adopts something of the
Guermantes spirit: 88–89. Saint-Loup a true Guermantes:
231–32. The old magic of the name Guermantes revived for M:
240–41, 282–83, 286–87. A profound transformation: 389–91,
407–12. Their roots deeply embedded in M's past life: 420–22.
Their superstitious respect for old-fashioned protocol: 447. Oriane epitomises the decline of the Guermantes: 463–64, 499–500.
Time and the Guermantes "way": 502–7.

GUERMANTES, Basin, Duc de. (Prince des Laumes before in-
heriting the dukedom on the death of his father.) M's grandmother finds him "common": I 25. Consistently unfaithful to
his wife: 481. Suspected by Swann of writing an anonymous letter: 506–10. Brother of M. de Charlus: II 449. Present owner of
the Château de Guermantes: 456. His ducal habits; his appearance; his horses; his affability to M's father: III 32–35 (cf.

300–1). At the Opéra: 62. Praised by Norpois: 196–97. Plays a joke on Mme de Villeparisis: 257–58, 281. His entry *chez* Mme de Villeparisis: 300–1; his looks, his wealth and vanity: 301 (*see also* 385); his weird vocabulary: 305 (cf. 317–23); acts as "feed" to his wife: 311–12, 321–23; deplores Saint-Loup's Dreyfusism: 316–17. Calls on M's family during his grandmother's illness: 458–62. Rumour of a separation between him and his wife: 507, 513. Vulgar arrogance and ancient grandeur: 569. M dines at his house; his old-world courtesy: 570–73, 578–83, 593–98. A bad husband but a trusty friend in Oriane's social activities: 620–21, 633–37, 646–47. Member of Parliament when Prince des Laumes; his political flair: 648–49. His mistresses: 656–61, 675. Conversation at dinner: 664–702; his views on literature, art and music: 672–73, 685–88, 718; genealogical talk—"But he's Oriane's cousin!": 727–55 *passim*. M's visit to ask him about an invitation from the Princesse de Guermantes; Amanien's illness and the fancy dress ball; his "Velazquez"; Swann's view of him; more genealogy; the Duchess's red shoes: 783–819. Breaks off his liaison with Mme d'Arpajon: **IV** 70. Compared unfavourably by M with his cousin the Prince: 74–75. Appreciates M's discreet bow: 84–85. His suspicion of authors: 89–90. Reproaches his wife for snubbing Mme de Chaussepierre: 98–99. Deplores Swann's Dreyfusism and his marriage: 104–8. His furious bow to M. d'Herweck—"Jupiter Tonans": 111–12. His relationship with Mme de Surgis: 116, 143–44. Affectionate but gaffe-ridden exchange with his brother Charlus: 157–61. His bad French: 162, 168–69, (cf. 479). His impatience to get to the ball; reaction to the news of Amanien's death ("They're exaggerating"): 169–70. His change of mind on the Dreyfus Case: 188–90. Fails to be elected President of the Jockey Club: **V** 42–43. Irritated by any mention of the Dreyfus Case (two years after): 43–46. The world of the arts closed to him: 271. Encourages his wife to see Gilberte: 784–87. Reads M's *Figaro* article: 788; his qualified compliments: 796. Hints that Mlle d'Oloron is the natural daughter of Charlus: 905. Physical mannerisms similar to Charlus's: 934–35. Rumours of his being sued for divorce in 1914; "a dreadful husband," in Saint-Loup's opinion: **VI** 69. Anglophile and anti-Caillautist during the war: 134–136. At the

Prince de Guermantes's reception, "as majestic and handsome as ever": 468. His liaison with Odette, now Mme de Forcheville: 481–83. His appearance in old age—"a magnificent ruin": 483–88, 531.

GUERMANTES, Oriane, Duchesse de. Married to her cousin; M refuses to believe that she is related to Mme de Villeparisis: **I** 143–44. Having caught a glimpse of her, M asks Legrandin if he knows her: 178. M's daydreams about her along the Guermantes way: 243, 257. Her appearance in Combray Church: 245–51. A friend of Swann's: 383, 396. As Princesse des Laumes, at Mme de Saint-Euverte's; snubs Mme de Gallardon; conversations with Froberville and with Swann; a preliminary sketch of her character: 470–88. Swann's longing to present his wife and daughter to her: **II** 57–58 (cf. **III** 341). Swann adopts some of her social attitudes: 117–19. Niece of Mme de Villeparisis and aunt of Saint-Loup: 456–57. Her Elstirs: 565–66 (cf. **III** 162–63, 185–86). The magic and mystery of her name: **III** 3–9. "The highest position in the Faubourg Saint-Germain": 28. M speculates about her life: 28–38. At the Opéra: 61–69. Her morning walks, and M's obsession with her: 69–76; "I was genuinely in love with Mme de Guermantes": 82–85. Her photograph in Saint-Loup's room at Doncières: 92, 98–100. M speaks of her to Robert, and asks him in vain for the photograph: 127–31. M's longing for her: 154–56. Robert agrees to persuade her to show M her Elstirs: 162–64; she fails to do so: 185–86. Her clothes and her appearance out walking: 189–90. At Mme de Villeparisis's tea-party: 266–356. Her chilly demeanour on being introduced to M and the historian of the Fronde: 267. Ridicules Mme de Cambremer: 270–72, 311–13. M's reflections on her appearance, her eyes and voice, her "smiling, disdainful, absent-minded air," her manner of treating intellectuals and other distinguished commoners: 273–78. Her witticisms on the subject of the Queen of Sweden: 282. Refers appreciatively to Bergotte: 283–84, 299. Ridicules Rachel: 299–301, 305–10. Her views on the Dreyfus Case: 316–22. Refuses to meet Odette: 341–42, 356–57. Addresses M for the first time: 344; offers him tea and cake: 356. Charlus's view of her: 397–98. The end of M's love for her: 507–12. Change in her attitude towards him; a new friendliness and an invitation to dinner: 512–22. Dinner at her house: 570–750. M takes her in to dinner: 595; her character as a Guermantes; the family genie; her social style, studied unconventionality, wit, imitations: 599–634. "Teaser Augustus": 637–40. Her perverseness of judgment: 642–46. Relations with her husband: 647: "Oriane's latest": 652–55. Relations with her husband's mistresses: 657–61. Hypocritical cruelty to her servants (the lovesick footman): 661–63 (cf. 193, 202, 417, 578, 805–6). Conversation at dinner: 663–702; views on Wagner: 672; Victor Hugo: 676–77; Zola: 683–85; Elstir: 685–88 (cf. 711; **V** 887–88); Mme de Villeparisis: 691–94; Charlus: 695–96; Saint-Loup: 696–98. Refuses to intercede on Saint-Loup's behalf with General de Monserfeuil: 701, 705. Views on botany: 707–9; on the Empire style: 709–15 (cf. **I** 480–81; **VI** 496); on Manet and Frans Hals: 716–21. Her "musical moments": 748–49. Her red dress and her rubies admired by Swann; her views on the Prince and Princesse de Guermantes; her "card" for Mme Molé; Swann's illness; the red shoes: 800–19. At the Princesse de Guermantes's reception: **IV** 79–119; her party expression: 82–83, 91; snubs Mme de Chaussepierre: 98–99; her refusal to meet Swann's wife and daughter: 108–9; intends to avoid Mme de Saint-Euverte's garden-party: 111–16; her unexpected politeness to Mme de Gallardon: 161–66. In the carriage on the way home, indignantly refuses to introduce M to Mme Putbus: 166–68. Her gradual withdrawal from the social scene brings Mme Molé to the fore: 196–97. Her opinion of Mme de Montmorency: 201–3 (cf. **III** 780–81). M consults her about Albertine's clothes; more attractive than in the days when M was in love with her; the purity of her speech; her anecdotes; her views on the Dreyfus Case: **V** 30–48. Gives M some syringa: 63–64. Her attitude to the Dreyfus Case in its social aspects: 312–13. Fails to turn up at the Verdurins' musical soirée: 369. Her Fortuny dresses: 497–98 (*see also* 34–35). M calls on her and meets Gilberte, now Mlle de Forcheville: 772–74. Her change of attitude towards Gilberte after Swann's death: 777–83; invites her to lunch and talks to her about Swann: 783–85. Repeats some of her anecdotes, with variations: 788–90, 793–96. Becomes friendly with Mme de Cambremer: 907. Rumours of her suing for divorce in 1914: **VI** 68–69. Her unexpected grief at the death of Saint-Loup: 233–34. Her sympathy for the Russian imperial family after the Revolution: 234–35. Greets M at the Prince de Guermantes's reception, as her "oldest friend": 346, 349–50; dyes her hair: 359; her cheeks, "like nougat": 363; her new position in society: 394–96; would have sworn that Bloch had been born in her world: 415; friendship with Rachel; antipathy to Gilberte: 444–49. Decay of her wit and social decline: 464–67. Speaks to M and Bloch hazily about the past; her husband and his mistresses: 467–68; Bréauté and Mme Varambon: 468–71; her red dress: 474. Claims to have discovered Rachel: 476 (cf. **III** 300–310). Her unhappiness with her husband, because of his liaison with Odette: 481–82, 492. Her legendary chastity called into question by Charlus: 492. Her lies and changeability: 494–95. Savage attack on Gilberte: 499–500.

GUERMANTES, Gilbert, Prince de. Cousin of the Duc de Guermantes: **III** 36. Violently anti-semitic, according to Oriane: 316. Described as "feudal" by the Duke: 321. His contempt for M. de Grouchy as husband for a Guermantes: 594. Allusion to his future marriage to Mme Verdurin: 594 (cf. **VI** 387–88). His antiquated ideas: 602. His grave and measured paces: 611. Mocked by his aunt, Mme de Villeparisis: 616. An "animated gravestone," in Oriane's words: 716–17. His obsession with rank and birth: 726–27, 782 (*see also* 802–3). Swann talks of his anti-semitism: 797 (cf. 791–92; **IV** 92). The soirée at his house; M introduced to him; his stiff and haughty greeting (but M detects a genuine simplicity beneath his reserve): **IV** 74–75. Leads Swann off to the far end of the garden, reputedly "to show him the door": 75, 97–98, 101–2. Swann's account of their conversation: how the Prince, and his wife, had become persuaded of Dreyfus's innocence: 138–43, 146–52. Revealed as an invert: 525–26. Spends a night with Morel at Maineville: 650; failure of subsequent assignations: 655–56. Charlus gossips about his homosexuality: **V** 410–11. Referred to by the name of his country house, Voisenon: 785. Gives an afternoon party in his new house in the Avenue du Bois: **VI** 242. A bibliophile: 286. Aged almost beyond recognition: 336–37. Bloch introduced to him by M: 385–86. His marriage to Mme Verdurin: 387–88.

GUERMANTES, Princesse Marie de, *née* Duchesse en Bavière, known as Marie-Gilbert or Marie-Hedwige (cf. **III** 309). Wife of the above, sister of the Duke of Bavaria: **III** 36. In her box at the Opéra; her beauty and her finery: 45–49. Her elegance compared to that of her cousin the Duchesse: 62–67. Her name: 309. Her beauty and distinction praised by Charlus: 775. M invited to her house: 779. Her royal birth; the exclusiveness of her salon: 782–83. Oriane's description of her: 801–2. Her grandeur compared to that of her husband: 802, 808–9. The soirée at her house: **IV** 45; her style as hostess: 47–48. Her beauty: 48–49. Her friendly welcome to M: 51–52. Conversation with M: polite banal remarks characteristic of society people: 79–80. "The kindest of women": 117–18. Her secret Dreyfusism: 146–50 (cf. 143). Her unrequited passion for Charlus: 155–57, 431 (*see also* Charlus and the bus conductor: 730–39). Lack of innovation in her soirées: 198–99. Her death: **VI** 387.

GUERMANTES, Baron de. Friend of the Duc de Châtellerault. At Mme de Villeparisis's: **III** 285.

GUERMANTES-BRASSAC, Mlle de. Niece of the Princesse de Guermantes. Rumoured to be engaged to Saint-Loup: **IV** 444, 673; **V** 596. Saint-Loup denies the rumour: **VI** 68–70.

HAIRDRESSER at Doncières; persuades the Prince de Borodino to grant leave to Saint-Loup: **III** 165–66.

HERWECK, M. d'. Bavarian musician introduced by Oriane to her husband at the Princesse de Guermantes's soirée: **IV** 111–12.

HEUDICOURT, Zenaïde d'. Cousin of Oriane's, discussed at dinner by the Guermantes, the Princesse de Parme and M. de Bréauté; her meanness: **III** 661–68.

HISTORIAN of the Fronde. *See* Pierre, M.

HOWSLER. The Verdurins' head coachman; an "excellent fellow," but melancholic: **IV** 398–99. Tipped by M. de Cambremer: 511–12. Victim of the machinations of Morel and the chauffeur; sacked by the Verdurins: 583–86.

HOWSLER, The elder. Brother of the above, hired as a footman by the Verdurins: **IV** 398–99, 583–84.

HUNOLSTEIN, Mme de, nicknamed "Petite" because of her enormous size: **III** 726 (cf. Montpeyroux, Comtesse de).

IÉNA, Prince and Princesse d'. Friends of Basin de

Guermantes, but not of Oriane, who affects to despise their taste in furniture: **I** 480–81. Oriane extols them, their son and their Empire furniture to the Princesse de Parme: **III** 710–16. Charlus ridicules their pretensions to nobility: 774.

IMBERT, Mme, of Combray. Her asparagus: **I** 74–75.

ISRAELS, Sir Rufus. Jewish financier, married to Swann's aunt: **II** 123–24. Owner of a house with a Le Nôtre park that had belonged to Charlus's family: 470–71. M. Bloch claims acquaintance with him: 477, 481–82, 486. Bloch tells a story about his son: **III** 292–93.

ISRAELS, Lady. Wife of the above, aunt of Swann. Norpois refers (without naming her) to her campaign to ostracise Odette socially: **II** 51. Her wealth; Swann presumed to be her heir; jealous of Swann's social position: 123–24. Meets, and ignores, Odette *chez* Mme de Marsantes: 124 (*see also* **II** 735–36). Her social position: 295. Mme de Marsantes turns against her, on account of the Dreyfus Case: **III** 342. Her nephew "Momo": 519. Gilberte denies knowing her: **V** 790.

JOURNALISTS in the theatre: **III** 236; Saint-Loup strikes one of them: 239–41.

JULIEN. Françoise's son-in-law; lives near Combray: **I** 72–73.

JULOT. One of the men M overhears in Jupien's brothel: **VI** 170.

JULOT ("Big"). Another habitué of Jupien's brothel, now at the front, of whom there has been no news; is he or isn't he a ponce?: **VI** 178–79.

JUPIEN. Tailor (or waistcoat-maker) who keeps a shop in the courtyard of Mme de Villeparisis's house; praised by M's grandmother: **I** 25. A new friend for Françoise: **III** 14–18 (*see also* 450, 464; **IV** 527). M's unfavourable first impression of him, later dispelled; his appearance, his cultured speech: 17–18. Claims compensation from the Duc de Guermantes for damage to his shop-front: 32–34. His indiscretion; reveals to M Françoise's criticism of him: 81. His fits of ill-humour: 186. His respect for the laws of syntax: 418. Expands his shop: 508–10. His meeting with Charlus in the courtyard: **IV** 1–18, 37–41. Charlus engages him as his secretary: 41. Accompanies Charlus to the brothel at Maineville to spy on Morel: 651–56. Morel asks him for his niece's hand: **V** 59–60. An ex-convict, according to Mme Verdurin: 373–74. Tells Charlus of Morel's mal-treatment of his niece: 417–18. Odette's first cousin: 915. Informs M in indignant terms of Saint-Loup's relations with Morel: 922–23. M comes across him during the war in a brothel which he has bought on behalf of Charlus; his conversation with the latter: **VI** 182–85. His astonishment at finding M in his establishment: 193. His dealings with the "gigolos," whom he encourages to be "more perverse": 195–201. Explains his position to M: 202–5. His intelligence and sensibility: 214. Looks after the Baron in his old age: 244–47, 251–53.

JUPIEN, Marie-Antoinette. Niece of the above (although M's grandmother takes her for his daughter, and Proust occasionally makes the same mistake): **I** 25. Seamstress in Paris: **III** 16. Introduced to Morel; their mutual attraction: 360–61. Recommended by Charlus to the aristocracy: **IV** 41. Seems to be enamoured of Morel: 353, 554. His sadistic plans in relation to her: 553–54 Attitude towards her of Charlus; "stand you tea"; her charming manners; received in society; had once been "in trouble": **V** 49–59. Morel asks Jupien for her hand: 59–60. Alters her opinion of Morel and Charlus: 80. Brutally insulted by Morel: 212–13; his guilt and shame, and his decision to break with her: 253–59. Adopted by Charlus under the title of Mlle d'Oloron: 417–18. Marries the young Léonor de Cambremer: 892–95. Her death, a few weeks after her marriage: 912–13.

"KING" of a South Sea island, staying with his mistress at the Grand Hotel, Balbec: **II** 247–48, 356.

KITCHENMAID at Combray. Her resemblance to Giotto's "Charity": **I** 110–13; her confinement: 151–72; Françoise's cruelty to her; allergic to asparagus: 170–73.

LAMBRESAC, Duchesse de. At the Princesse de Guermantes's; her way of greeting people: **IV** 109–10.

LARIVIÈRES, the. Rich cousins of Françoise; their self-sacrificing behaviour during the war; "the only real people in the book": **VI** 224–26 (cf. **III** 381).

LAU D'ALLEMANS, Marquis du. Mme de Guermantes speaks of his informality with the Prince of Wales: **V** 38, 793–94. A friend of Swann; Gilberte's desire to meet him: 794–96.

LAUMES, Prince and Princesse des. *See* Guermantes, Duc and Duchesse de.

LAUNDRESS, Brichot's mistress; Mme Verdurin breaks up his relationship with her: **IV** 361–62; he has a daughter by her: 670 (cf. **V** 374).

LAUNDRY-GIRL in Touraine; her relations with Albertine, reported by Aimé: **V** 709–14.

LAUNDRY-GIRLS (two) whom M brings to a house of assignation; their love-making: **V** 741–42.

LAVATORY ATTENDANT. *See* "Marquise."

LAWYER, "eminent barrister from Paris," friend of the Cambremers. His passion for Le Sidaner: **IV** 278, 284–86. His wife and son: 298. Invites M to see his collection in Paris and to meet Le Sidaner: 298–99.

LÉA, Mlle. Actress; Elstir speaks of her elegance at the races: **II** 654. Admired by Bloch's cousin: her Gomorrhan tastes: 660. Lives with Bloch's cousin: **IV** 272–73. Mme de Cambremer alludes to her obliquely in connexion with Albertine: 677. Billed to appear at the Trocadéro on the occasion of Albertine's visit: **V** 185. M's anxiety about her possible relations with Albertine: 185–96. Her letter to Morel: 280–82, 502–3. Albertine admits to having visited her in her dressing-room: 479–81, and to having gone on a three-week trip with her: 470–73. It was she who, dressed as a man, had been walking with Gilberte in the Champs-Elysées (cf. **II** 273): **VI** 7.

LEBLOIS DE CHARLUS, Comte. Confused with the Baron de Charlus in professional and artistic circles: **IV** 409.

L'ÉCLIN, Mme de. Nicknamed "Hungry belly": **III** 592.

LEGRANDIN. Engineer and man of letters; his character and appearance; tirades against the nobility; flowery speech: **I** 92–93. Strange behaviour to M's father: 166–67. His snobbery and affectation; his wink; M dines with him: 174–82. His lyrical descriptions of Balbec; refuses to introduce his sister, Mme de Cambremer: 182–86 (*see also* 547–48). M meets him in Paris, and is rebuked for his social zeal: **III** 202–3. At Mme de

Villeparisis's; obsequious to her, furious with M: 267–73, 286–87, 371. Raises his hat to M's grandmother as she drives back with M from the Champs-Elysées after her stroke: 427–29. His sister's displeasure when M claims acquaintance with him: **IV** 297–98. Assumes the name Legrand de Méséglise: 660. His kindness to M's great-aunt: **V** 7–8. Discussed by Charlus and the Princesse de Parme in connexion with his nephew's marriage to Jupien's niece; the Princess invites him to call; changes in his appearance and sexual proclivities; of his two vices, snobbery now giving way to the other: 903–7. Becomes Comte de Méséglise: 913–14. His relations with Théodore: **VI** 14–15. A journalist during the war: 125. In old age, ceases to use cosmetics, becomes gloomy and taciturn: 358–59. Resemblance to his nephew: 372–73. His new civility towards Bloch: 418–19.

LÉON, Prince de. Nephew of Mme de Guermantes, brother-in-law of Saint-Loup. Mme de Guermantes's anecdote about him: **V** 37–38.

LÉONIE, Aunt (Madame Octave). Her habit of giving M a piece of madeleine dipped in tea or tisane: **I** 63–64. Bedridden since her husband's death; her bedroom, her way of life: 66–71. Relations with Françoise: 72–80, and with Eulalie: 93–96. Conversations with Françoise, Eulalie and M. le Curé: 139–51. Her "little jog-trot": 151. Occasional longing for change; her "counterpane dramas"; plays Françoise and Eulalie off against one another; terrorises Françoise: 160–65. Vague plan to visit Tansonville: 201–2. Her death: 215–17. Leaves her fortune and her furniture to M: **II** 33. M gives some of her furniture to a brothel-keeper; sells her silver to buy flowers for Mme Swann: 209–10, and her Chinese vase to buy flowers for Gilberte: 272. Françoise sings her praises: **III** 24–25. M begins to resemble her more and more: **V** 95–96. Analogy between one of her ploys with Françoise and M's with Albertine: 475–77.

LEROI, Mme Blanche. A snob; "cuts" Mme de Villeparisis: **III** 247, 250. Her superior social position: 251, compared to Mme de Villeparisis: 258–60. Her witticism about love: 259–60. The daughter of rich timber merchants; Mme de Villeparisis affects to despise her: 370–71. After the war, her name is all but forgotten: **VI** 400–1.

LÉTOURVILLE, Duchesse de. Meets the aged Charlus with M in the Champs-Elysées and is shocked by his appearance: **VI** 249–50.

LÉTOURVILLE. Young relative of the above; M meets him on his way into the Princesse de Guermantes's afternoon party; just out of Saint-Cyr; regards M as an elderly gentleman: **VI** 346–47.

LÉVY, ESTHER. Cousin of Bloch; her unconcealed admiration for Léa: **II** 660, 712. Lives with Léa; she and Bloch's sister attract Albertine's attention in the Casino at Balbec: **IV** 272–74. Her amorous intrigue with a young married woman whom she meets in the Grand Hotel: 339–40. M's suspicions as to her relations with Albertine; he asks Bloch for her photograph: **V** 105–7. Albertine denies knowing her: 140, but later confesses to having given her a photograph of herself: 460–61, 491–92.

LIFT-BOY at the Grand Hotel, Balbec. M's first introduction to him and his esoteric craft: **II** 331. M puzzled by his vocabulary: 518–19. A know-all: 521. The manager gives M his opinion of him: **IV** 209–10. Glows with pleasure on seeing M again: 221. Go-between with Albertine; his inability to shut doors, his verbal mannerisms, false veneer of intelligence, democratic pride, physical appearance: 256–62. "Camembert" for "Cambremer": 276–77, 304, 347. His anxiety over his tip: 303–7. Cycles to Doncières station with a telegram for M: 344. His whooping cough: 576–78. Saint-Loup had made advances to him, according to Aimé: **V** 926–28. Joins the air force in 1914; his "virtuous declarations": **VI** 81–83. M's conversation with him about "Charlism": 82–83.

LOISEAU, Mme. Her house beside the church at Combray; her fuchsias: **I** 85.

LONGPONT, Mme Barbe de. Star attraction at one of Mme Verdurin's Wednesdays at La Raspelière: **IV** 503.

LOREDAN. Nickname of Swann's coachman. *See* Rémi.

LUXEMBOURG, Grand Duke of. Formerly Comte de Nassau, nephew of the Princesse de Luxembourg. His high qualities; writes to M during his grandmother's illness: **III** 448–49. Malicious stories about him retailed by the Prince de Foix and his friends: 562, and the Guermantes and their friends, including Oriane and the Turkish Ambassadress: 731–32, 737–39.

LUXEMBOURG, Princesse de. At Balbec; her stately appearance; introduced to M and his grandmother by Mme de Villeparisis; her presents; her little negro page: **II** 377–80. Mme Poncin takes her for an elderly tart: 383–84. Saint-Loup describes her as "an old trout": 492. In the restaurant at Rivebelle: 537. Presents her negro page to her nephew the Grand Duke: **III** 731–32.

MAMA. *See* Osmond, Amanien, Marquis d'.

MAMMA (M's mother). Her good-night kiss at Combray: **I** 15–16, 35–48 (*see also* 257–58, 260–61). Speaks to Swann about his daughter: 29–31. Spends a night in M's room; reads him *François le Champi*: 50–58 (cf. **VI** 281–89). Her practical wisdom tempers the ardent idealism of her mother: 56–57. Gives M a madeleine soaked in tea: 60–61. Holidays at Combray; her relations with Françoise: 71–73. Her resemblance to M, according to the "lady in pink": 140. Her kindness to M. Vinteuil: 156–57. Her admiration for her husband: 159–60. Amused by Legrandin's snobbery: 181. Finds M in tears on the little path near Tansonville: 204. Pities Mlle Vinteuil after her father's death: 225–26. Swann invited to the wedding: 441. Her black hair and beautiful plump white hands: 575. Her unfavourable opinion of Mme Blatin: 487–88. Meets Swann at the Trois Quartiers: 588–90. Disapproves of make-up: **II** 3–4. Her opinion of Norpois, a reflection of her own modesty, delicacy and wifely devotion: 9–11. Entertains Norpois to dinner: 21, 35, 39–41, 48–50. Her doubts about M's literary career: 73. Discusses Norpois with her husband: 75–76. Talks to Françoise about cooking and restaurants: 77–79. Quarrels with Cottard's prescriptions; her concern for M: 96–97. Ridicules Odette and her friends: 120. Her reaction to M's acquaintance with Bergotte: 201–3. Refuses to meet Mme Swann: 204 (cf. **I** 589). Remains in Paris when M and his grandmother go to Balbec: 304; sees them off at the station: 307–11. Incapable of rancour, and absolutely unspoiled: 445. "Cut" by Mme Sazerat: **III** 199–200; her impartiality over the Dreyfus Case: 200. Her deference to Dr du Boulbon: 411. At her mother's death-bed; her grief and devotion: 432–35, 440, 449, 454–69. Her respect for her mother's

memory: 474. Cures M of his obsession with Mme de
Guermantes: 507–8. Joins M at Balbec; her cult of grief for her
mother, and her increasing resemblance to her, including her
veneration for Mme de Sévigné: **IV** 227–31, 236–37, 242–43.
Avoids M's visitors: 280. Reminiscences of her mother; gives M
both French versions of *Arabian Nights*: 317–19. Her views on
Albertine's suitability as a wife: 442–43, and her anxiety about
M's intimacy with her: 567–68. Congenitally attached to the
rule of caste; the "Combray spirit": 579–80. Gratified to learn
that M has decided not to marry Albertine: 699. Plans to visit
Combray to look after one of her aunts: 711–12. M mistakes her
for his grandmother: 721–23. He informs her of his decision to
return to Paris and marry Albertine: 723–24. Writes daily to M
from Combray; disapproves of his living with Albertine; quotes
Mme de Sévigné: **V** 6–12, 180–81, 490. Teaches M to distinguish between sensibility and sentimentality: 135–36. Reserves
her love and generosity for those close to her: 432. Brings M *Le
Figaro* containing his article: 765–66. Lunches with Mme Sazerat: 806. Visits the Princesse de Parme, who ignores her: 807.
The Princess returns her visit next day: 829–30. Takes M to
Venice: 844–47, 851–52. Invites Mme Sazerat to dinner: 853. In
the baptistery of St Mark's; compared to the old woman in
Carpaccio's *St Ursula*: 874–76. Refuses to postpone their departure from Venice; M rebels, but joins her in the train at the last
minute: 883–88. Her views on the marriages of Jupien's niece
and Gilberte: 891–97, 916–18.

MANAGER of the Grand Hotel, Balbec. Receives M and his
grandmother; his appearance and character, alien ancestry,
malapropisms: **II** 327–32, 355–56, 376, 517, 609, 724–26. Wel-
comes M on his second visit to Balbec; more malapropisms: **IV**
204–5. Complains of his staff: 209–10. Brings M a message
from Albertine 220–23. Displeased with Albertine and her
friends: 237. Tells M of his grandmother's "sincups": 240–41.
Carves the turkeys himself: 659–60. Interned as a "Boche" in
1914: **VI** 81.

MANCHESTER, Consuelo, Duchess of. Takes Oriane shopping
in London; now dead: **V** 48.

MARIE-AYNARD. *See* Marsantes, Comtesse de.

MARIE-GILBERT or MARIE-HEDWIGE. *See* Guermantes, Princesse Marie de.

MARGUERITE. Françoise's daughter. Lives near Combray: **I** 72. Moves to Paris; Françoise's visits to her; her trendy slang and contempt for the country: **III** 194, 464. Recommends a "radical" cure for M's grandmother: 451. Entertained by Françoise; more Parisian slang: **IV** 172–73. Her deplorable influence on Françoise's vocabulary: **V** 199–200; **VI** 86.

"MARQUISE," the. Keeper of the water-closets in the Champs-Elysées. Françoise regards her as "a proper lady"; her partiality towards M: **II** 88–89. Discusses her customers with the park-keeper; her exclusiveness; M's grandmother compares her to the Guermantes and the Verdurins: **III** 420–23.

MARSANTES, Comte or Marquis de. Saint-Loup's father; contrasted with Robert: **II** 426–27. Nissim Bernard claims to have been a friend of his: 484–86 (cf. **III** 374–75). Was President of the Jockey Club for 10 years: **III** 317. Killed in the war of 1870–71: **IV** 673.

MARSANTES, Comtesse de (Marie-Aynard). Widow of the above. Saint-Loup's mother, and sister of Basin de Guermantes and Charlus. Her relations with Mme Swann and Lady Israels: **II** 124 (cf. 51: a possible allusion in Norpois's conversation with M's family: 735, and **III** 342). Niece of Mme de Villeparisis: 424. How she brought up her son: 425. Anti-Dreyfusist: **III** 217 (cf. 318–19, 321, 342, 798). *Mater semita*: Rachel's anti-semitic etymology of the name Marsantes: 237 (cf. 321–22; **V** 902–3). At Mme de Villeparisis's; her character and looks: 337–41 (cf. 560). Her joy at seeing Robert: 343–45, 365–66, and possessive love and concern for him: 375, 379–84. Her deference to M: 374, 384 (cf. 339). Hypocritical and mercenary (finding a rich wife for Robert): 559–60, 340 (cf. 617; **IV** 133; **V** 898–99). Old-fashioned purity of her vocabulary: 678 (cf. **V** 35). Furthers Odette's social ascent: **IV** 197–99 (cf. **V** 778–79). Charlus's resemblance to her: 416. Brings off the marriage of Robert and Gilberte: **V** 898–99. Condescends to dine with the Cottards and the Bontemps *chez* Gilberte: 908. Brings about a reconciliation between Robert and Gilberte: 923–94. Robert resembles her more and more: **VI** 18–19.

MAURICE. One of the "gigolos" in Jupien's brothel. Flogs Charlus: **VI** 177, 180–82. His resemblance to Morel: 185–86. His kindheartedness: 189–90. His virtuous principles disappoint Charlus: 197–99.

MÉMÉ. Charlus's nickname (Palamède).

MOLÉ, Comtesse. Leaves an envelope instead of a card on Mme de Guermantes: **III** 808, who replies in kind: 814. Envelops Charlus in her huge skirt; his professed admiration for her: **IV** 100, 123. Goes to the Swanns': 102. In Odette's box at the theatre: 197. Her exalted position in society: 197. Mme Verdurin's interest in her: 454–55, 499–500 (cf. **V** 310–11). The object of slanderous newspaper articles by Morel inspired by Charlus (an allusion to her death that does not accord with subsequent references to her): **V** 288. The mystery of Charlus's furious rancour against her: 310; he denounces her to Mme Verdurin: 310–11, 367–69. During the war, defends Charlus against Mme Verdurin: **VI** 109. Admires Brichot but disowns him: 148–49. M refuses an invitation to dine with her: 519–20.

MONK, brother-in-law of M's grandmother. Surreptitiously observes M while praying by her death-bed: **III** 462.

MONSERFEUIL, General de. Mme de Guermantes refuses to speak to him on behalf of Saint-Loup; his failures at the polls: **III** 701–2, 705–6.

(*See* Beauserfeuil.)

MONTERIENDER, Comtesse de. At Mme de Saint-Euverte's; her absurd remark about Vinteuil's sonata: **I** 501.

MONTMORENCY-LUXEMBOURG, Duchesse de. Contrasted by M, as a friend, with Mme de Guermantes: **III** 780–81; her opinion of Oriane, and Oriane's of her: **IV** 202–3. M's pleasure in visiting her; her town-house: 203. Charlus's response to an invitation from her: **V** 354–55.

MONTPEYROUX, Comtesse de. Sister of the Vicomtesse de Vélude; nicknamed "Petite" because of her stoutness: **III** 591–92 (cf. Hunolstein, Mme d').

MONTPEYROUX, Marquis de. Comes to meet the little train at Incarville; recommends his son to M: **IV** 694–95.

MOREAU, A. J. Friend and colleague of M's father. Provides a ticket for Berma at the Opéra: **III** 38–39. Gives M's father some information about Norpois: 195. Referred to by Norpois: 299.

MOREL, Charles. Violinist, son of Uncle Adolphe's valet. Calls on M at his father's instigation; his conceit and ambition; attracted to Jupien's niece: **III** 357–61. His first meeting with Charlus, at Doncières station: **IV** 352–55. Mme Verdurin's favourite violinist: 382–83, 395, 407. Arrives with Charlus at La Raspelière: 414. His obsequious request to M, followed by rudeness towards him: 417–20. His vile nature and his gifts as a musician: 420–21. Plays Fauré's violin sonata, followed by Debussy and Meyerbeer: 478–80. Plays cards with Cottard: 485–86, 492–98, 507–9. Motor-car trips with Charlus; his friendship with the chauffeur; conversation with the Baron in a restaurant at Saint-Mars-le-Vêtu: 550–58. Pursuit of young girls: 557–58. His machinations with the chauffeur to displace Mme Verdurin's coachman: 582–86. Was he on friendly terms with Albertine?: 586 (cf. **V** 810–11). His contradictory character: 586–89. The nature of Charlus's relations with him: 606–11, 615–17, 623–30. His affectionate allusions to M's Uncle Adolphe: 621–22. His attitude to M; his cruelties to Charlus; pride in his musical career: 625–30. His behaviour over Charlus's sham duel: 630–45. His requests for money: 645–46. The bogus algebra lessons: 649–50. His assignations with the Prince de Guermantes in the Maineville brothel; spied upon by Charlus and Jupien: 648–56. Takes Charlus's social precepts too literally: 665–67. Declines an invitation to dine with the Cambremers: 667; on another occasion accepts, but turns up without the Baron: 670–72. His hostility to Bloch: 691. Tea with Charlus at Jupien's: **V** 48–54. His ambivalent feelings vis-à-vis Jupien's niece and cynical intentions towards her: 55–60 (cf. **IV** 553–55). Asks for her hand in marriage: 59–61. Borrows money from Nissim Bernard through Bloch and fails to repay it; his anti-semitism: 61–63. Jupien's niece becomes aware of his malevolence and perfidy: 80. The algebra lessons: 210–11. Neurotic outburst against his fiancée (*grand pied de grue*): 211–13. His madness: 236–37. His remorse, and his decision to break with the Jupiens: 253–59. His relations with Léa: 279–83 (*see also*

502). Charlus admires his successes with women and his talents as a writer: 283–87; the lampoons against Mme Molé: 288. Refuses to perform for Mme Verdurin's friends; she resolves to separate him from Charlus: 303–6, 324–26. Plays Vinteuil's septet: 330–35, 342. Reactions to his performance: 357–65, 366–67, 372, 383–84. Refuses to play Bizet: 385. The Verdurins persuade him to break with Charlus: 414–33. Charlus recites poetry to him: 808–9. His illicit relations with Albertine, according to Andrée: 810–11. His liaison with Saint-Loup (the letter signed "Bobette"): 922–23, 928–29, 931–32; **VI** 15–21, 98. A deserter during the war: 57. Pursues Charlus with a venomous hatred; attacks him in newspaper articles; his Bergottesque style: 111–13. Joins up at last: 113–14. Meets Charlus in the street and teases him; the latter threatens revenge: 130–31. Turns heterosexual: 132. His justified fear of Charlus; the latter's posthumous letter: 164–68. Arrested as a deserter, sent to the front, decorated for bravery: 235–36. After the war, a distinguished and respected public figure; M meets him at the Guermantes reception: 391–92, 446.

MORIENVAL, Baronne de. At the Opéra, compared unfavourably to the Princesse and the Duchesse de Guermantes ("eccentric, pretentious and ill-bred"): **III** 46, 64. Her ignorance of La Fontaine: **VI** 461.

MORTEMART, Duchesse de. Conversation with Charlus at the Verdurins': **V** 354–61.

MUSICIAN (eminent), friend of Ski's, invited to La Raspelière; furthers Morel's career and his relations with Charlus: **IV** 606–8.

NASSAU, Comte de. *See* Luxembourg, Grand Duke of.

NASSAU, Princesse de. Aged society courtesan; greets M at the Princesse de Guermantes's reception: **VI** 425–26. (She and the Princesse d'Orvillers (q.v.) are clearly the same person.)

NIÈVRE, Princesse de. Cousin of Mme de Guermantes; has designs on Gilberte for her son: **V** 782.

NOÉMIE, Mlle. Attendant in the "house of pleasure" at Maineville; arranges for Charlus and Jupien to spy on Morel: **IV** 652–55.

NORPOIS, Marquis de. Ex-Ambassador; his career and character: **II** 5–12. Dines with M's family; his physical appearance, manner and voice; advice on M's career and investments: 29–36. His opinion of Berma: 37–39. Appreciates Françoise's cooking: 39–40. King Theodosius's visit: 41–47. Opinions on Balbec and the Swanns: 48–53; on the Comte de Paris, Odette, Bergotte, M's prose poem, Gilberte: 58–66. Reasons for his failure to inform the Swanns of M's admiration for them: 70–71 (cf. **III** 367–69). Reactions to his visit of M's parents: 75–76, and of Françoise: 76–77. His views (in the matter of art) compared with Bergotte's; the latter's opinion of him, and those of Swann and Odette: 185–88. Allusion to his liaison with Mme de Villeparisis: 187. Visits Spain with M's father: 304 (cf. 48, 381–82). His social diplomacy: the art of "killing two birds with one stone": 708–9. Likened by M to Mosca in *La Chartreuse de Parme*: **III** 136. M's father's discovery of his friendship with Mme de Villeparisis: 195–96. M's father's hopes of his support as a candidate for election to the *Institut*: 198–99. His relations with Mme de Villeparisis: 244–45, 294–98. At Mme de Villeparisis's reception; introduced to Bloch; views on art: 296–99. Declines to support M's father's candidacy: 302–4. Discusses the Dreyfus Case with Bloch: 313–16, 323–33. His tortuous diplomatic manoeuvrings with Prince von Faffenheim: 345–55. Calls M "a hysterical little flatterer": 367 (cf. 724–25). Attends M's grandmother's funeral: 468. Meets M in the street and gives him no sign of recognition: 510. In favour of an Anglo-French rapprochement: 722–24. Mme de Guermantes talks about him (and his liaison with Mme de Villeparisis) at dinner: 725–26 (*see also* **III** 828–29). Widower of a La Rochefoucauld: 727. Fails to introduce any of his *Institut* colleagues to Mme de Villeparisis: **IV** 620. His amnesia about his false prognostications: **V** 41. In Venice with Mme de Villeparisis: 854–66 (cf. 947–50). His war-time articles: **VI** 60, 125, ridiculed by Charlus: 129–38, 156, 172.

NORPOIS, Baron and Baronne de. Nephew and niece of the Marquis: **III** 33–34.

NOTARY from Le Mans. *See* Blandais, M.

OCTAVE. Young toff at Balbec, consumptive, dissipated, gambling son of an industrialist: **II** 348, 356–57. Friend of

Albertine and the little band; his golf-playing; "I'm a wash-out": 625–27. Related to the Verdurins: 632–33. His views on Mme de Villeparisis and Mme de Cambremer: 695–97. Maligned by Andrée: **V** 71 (cf. 816). His liaison with Rachel: 816–17; marries Andrée: 817–18. His artistic genius: 818–21. Previously in love with Albertine: 830–33 (cf. 122—a vague allusion by Françoise *also* 817; **VI** 57–58). His friendliness towards M: 840–41. One of the stars of Mme Verdurin's wartime salon: **VI** 57–58. His illness; a poor friend: 58–59.

OCTAVE, Madame. *See* Léonie, Aunt.

OCTAVE, Uncle. Husband of Aunt Léonie; already dead when M used to spend his holidays at Combray: **I** 66, 75, 141, 152.

ODETTE (Mme de Crécy, then Mme Swann, and finally Mme de Forcheville). M's family refuse to receive her at Combray: **I** 16; "a woman of the worst type": 26; Charlus's mistress, according to Combray gossip: 45 (cf. 137–38, 200). The "lady in pink" at Uncle Adolphe's: 104–8 (cf. **III** 360–61). The "lady in white" at Tansonville: 199. As Odette de Crécy, a member of the Verdurins' "little clan": 266. Beginnings of her liaison with Swann; introduces him to the Verdurins; her looks; "I'm always free": 268–69, 275–81. The little phrase of Vinteuil, "the national anthem of their love": 299, 308–9, 335–37. Her house in the Rue La Pérouse; entertains Swann to tea: 309–13. Resemblance to Botticelli's Zipporah: 314–18. The letter from the Maison Dorée: 319. Swann's anguished search for her through the night: 321–28. The cattleyas; becomes Swann's mistress: 328–38. Her discomfiture when she lies: 339–40 (cf. 398–99). Her vulgarity and bad taste: 341–50. Introduces Forcheville to the Verdurins: 355, 359–60, 369–76. Her money troubles; Swann's presents; a "kept woman": 378–82. Swann's jealous suspicions: 386–91. A cruel smile of complicity with Forcheville: 393. Lies to Swann: 394–99. Her letter to Forcheville, which Swann reads: 400–2. Acquiesces in Swann's exclusion from the Verdurins': 404–5. Expeditions with the Verdurins; progress of Swann's jealousy: 411–22. Her soothing words: 423–24. The trip to Bayreuth: 427–31. Her confidence in Swann's devotion to her: 433–39. Friendship with Charlus: 441, 448–49, 456–58 (cf. **II** 458; **V** 400–2). Quarrels with Uncle Adolphe: 443–44. Swann's jealousy, and her feelings towards him: 447–57. The little phrase reminds Swann of the early days of their love: 490–95. An anonymous letter about her love life: 506. Swann's suspicions; he interrogates her about her illicit relations with women and dealings with procuresses; her admissions: 511–26. Confesses to having been with Forcheville on the evening of the cattleyas: 526–27. Her suspect effusions: 529–30. Cruises with the Verdurins; thinks constantly of Swann, according to Mme Cottard: 531–35. Proof that she had indeed been Forcheville's lover: 538. "A woman who wasn't even my type": 543. Married to Swann; Gilberte's mother; still not received by M's family: 587–88. Walks or drives in the Allée des Acacias: 592–98, 601–6. Her social position as Swann's wife: **II** 1–2. Norpois reports on a dinner-party in her house: 49–52. Scenes she made to Swann before their marriage; has now become "angelic": 51–58. Receives M at last; her house, her "at home" days, her social mannerisms, development of her salon: 103–30. Her Anglomania: 125 (cf. **I** 107, 269, 276, 314; **II** 134–36, 148, 151, 160, 164, 212, 215, 230, 293, 297; **III** 250, 251; **VI** 144–45, 380–81). Change in Swann's feelings towards her: 130–34. Plays Vinteuil's sonata: 139–47. Walks in the Zoological Gardens: 155–64. Invites M to lunch with Bergotte: 164. Criticises Norpois: 186–88 (cf. **III** 367). M's visits to her after his breach with Gilberte; her flowers, her "tea"; her indoor elegance: 230–33. Entertains Mmes Cottard, Bontemps and Verdurin: 234–51. Changes in her furniture and clothes: 261–64. Her new style of beauty; "an immortal youthfulness": 264. The embodiment of fashion; "a period in herself": 265–69. Walks in the Bois: 290–98. Bloch claims to have enjoyed her favours in a train: 489. Her portrait as "Miss Sacripant" by Elstir: 583–85, 600–4 (*see also* **III** 360; **V** 400, 592–93). Oriane's view of her: **III** 307. Gains an entrée into aristocratic society through anti-Dreyfusism: 341. At Mme de Villaparisis's: 356–57; Charlus pays court to her: 361–66; she and Oriane ignore one another: 369–70. Her salon crystallised round Bergotte; her social rise: **IV** 194–96. Denies and then admits her former intimacy with the Verdurins: 364–65. Photographs of her—"touched-up" portraits and Swann's snapshot: **V** 267 (cf. **II** 264). Charlus's account of her life before meeting

Swann; his own relations with her; her lovers; *was* married to M. de Crécy: 400–2 (cf. **IV** 661). Said to have been Elstir's mistress: 592–93 (cf. **II** 604). Sincerely grieved by Swann's death; marries Forcheville: 776–78. A first cousin of Jupien: 915. Changed attitude to Gilberte's marriage; finds a generous protector in her son-in-law Saint-Loup: 930–31. During the war, Mme Verdurin fails to win her back: **VI** 59–61. Her remarks about the war; admiration for the English: 144–45. Her appearance in old age "defies the laws of chronology": 377–81; less than three years later "a bit gaga": 382–83. Her love for Gilberte: 383. M mistakes Gilberte for her: 427–28 (cf. 381–82). Listens to Rachel's poetry recital: 458–59. Her liaison with the Duc de Guermantes: 480–88. Regales M with anecdotes about her former lovers; had been "desperately in love" with Swann: 488–93.

OLORON, Mlle d'. *See* Jupien, Marie-Antoinette.

ORGEVILLE, Mlle de l'. Girl of good family said by Saint-Loup to frequent brothels: **IV** 126–27. M's desires focus on her: 166; **V** 106, 693. Confused with Mlle de Forcheville (Gilberte): 760–65, 772–74.

(*See* Eporcheville, Mlle de.)

ORIANE. *See* Guermantes, Oriane, Duchesse de.

ORSAN, M. d'. Friend of Swann, suspected of having written an anonymous letter: **I** 506–8.

ORVILLERS, Princesse d' (Paulette). Makes advances to M in the street: **III** 510. Late arrival at the Princesse de Guermantes's soirée; said to be a natural daughter of the Duke of Parma; her ambiguous social position: **IV** 162–64. "Rather straight-laced," according to Oriane and her husband: 168.

(*See* Nassau, Princesse de.)

OSMOND, Amanien, Marquis d' ("Mama"). Cousin of the Guermantes; his imminent death and its potential effect on the Guermantes' social arrangements: **III** 788–89, 792–93, 805–8; **IV** 83. The Duc de Guermantes's reaction to his death: "They're exaggerating": 169. Ran off with Odette, according to Charlus: **V** 402.

PAGES at the Grand Hotel, Balbec.

pleasure at moving house: **III** 1–2; his deference to Françoise: 12–13, 22–27; his taste for poetry; "borrows" M's books: 437, 754; his letter: 776–77.

PERUVIAN (young). Conceives a violent hatred for Mme de Mortemart: **V** 360.

PHILOSOPHER, Norwegian. Guest of the Verdurins at La Raspelière; his deliberation of thought and diction and rapidity of departure: **IV** 446–48, 453–54. Mystery of his disappearance: 509. Quotes Bergson on soporifics; his belief in the immortality of the soul: 520–22.

PIANIST (young) patronised by the Verdurins: **I** 265–66; his aunt: 266–67, 287–88, 368, 414–15; plays Vinteuil's sonata: 290–91, 297–302, 308–9, 373–74. (Is this pianist Dechambre? q.v.)

PIERRE, M. Historian of the Fronde. Visits Mme de Villeparisis; "solemn and tongue-tied": **III** 252; his insomnia: 257, 289; his ignorance of social customs and of botany: 285–88; mocked by the Duc de Guermantes: 319–22 (*see also* 265–67, 304, 308–11).

PIERRE. Club doorman, writes M. de Charlus an intimate letter: **V** 51.

PIPERAUD, Dr. Combray doctor: **I** 75.

PLASSAC, Walpurge, Marquise de. Her town-house: **III** 785. Calls on her cousin the Duc de Guermantes, with her sister Mme de Tresmes, to report on Amanien d'Osmond's state of health; her walking-stick: 788–90. Brings news of Amanien's death: **IV** 169.

POICTIERS, Duchesse de. Cousin of Saint-Loup, who recommends her to M as a substitute for his aunt Oriane—"a very good sort": **III** 192–93.

POIRÉ, Abbé. Dreyfusist priest confided in by both the Prince and the Princesse de Guermantes: **IV** 147–50.

POIX, Princesse de. Intimate friend of Oriane de Guermantes, attends Alix's "Fridays": **III** 261. Visits Gilberte de Saint-Loup: **V** 909.

POMMELIÈRE, Marquise de la. Nicknamed "la Pomme"; the Princesse de Guermantes's inane remark about her: **IV** 80.

PONCIN, M. Senior judge from Caen, on holiday at Balbec: **II**

345–48, 362, 382–83. Becomes Commander of the Legion of Honour: **IV** 205. His delight on hearing of M's arrival at Balbec: 209, 221–22. Condoles with M's mother: 230. His mistake as to the identity of the Princesse de Parme: 252. Doffs his hat to the Marquise de Cambremer: 276. His frustrated snobbery: 299–302, 591–92 (cf. Toureuil, Judge).

PONCIN, Mme. Wife of the above. Her social resentment and disapproval: **II** 348–49, 361–62. Her misapprehensions about Mme de Villeparisis and the Princesse de Luxembourg: 383–84. Observes the passers-by on the esplanade: 503–4. Regards M. de Cambremer as a man of supreme aristocratic distinction: **IV** 423.

PORTEFIN, Berthe, Duchesse de. Helps Mme de Villeparisis with her theatricals: **III** 289–90. Admired by Morel: **V** 423.

POULLEIN. Guermantes footman, prevented from going to see his fiancée; Françoise's sympathy for him: **III** 193, 202, 417, 510, 578. Mme de Guermantes changes his day off out of jealousy and spite: 662–63, 675, and insists on his staying in when the Duke allows him a night out: 805–6.

POUSSIN, Mme. Lady from Combray on holiday at Balbec with her daughters; nicknamed "Just You Wait"; her absconding son-in-law: **IV** 231–32.

PUBLISHER from Paris. Visits La Raspelière; "not smart enough for the little clan": **IV** 411.

PUPIN, M., daughter of. Schoolgirl at Combray: **I** 76.

PUTBUS, Baroness. Patient of Dr Cottard: **I** 373–74. Described by Mme de Guermantes as "the dregs of society": **IV** 167–68. Invited to La Raspelière: 206–8. Friend of Princess Sherbatoff: 375. No longer expected at La Raspelière: 449. Extremely prudish: **V** 266. Arrives in Venice on the day of M's departure: 883.

PUTBUS, Maid of Mme. Said by Saint-Loup to frequent brothels, to be partial to women, and to be "wildly Giorgionesque": **IV** 127, 129. M's desire for her: 166–67, 206–8. M dreads her arrival in Balbec, because of Albertine: 325, 345. Sister of Théodore, of Combray: **V** 411.

RACHEL. M meets her in a brothel and nicknames her "Rachel when from the Lord": **II** 206–7. Mme de Villeparisis's allusion to her liaison with Saint-Loup: 420. Saint-Loup's love for her:

430; he telegraphs her every day: 448; her influence over him; her mercenariness; their quarrels: 492–97. Her performance *chez* Oriane: 498–99 (cf. **III** 299–300 et sqq.; **VI** 475–76). Rupture and reconciliation with Saint-Loup: **III** 156–62. Saint-Loup invites M to meet her; her house on the outskirts of Paris; M's stupefaction on discovering that Robert's mistress is "Rachel when from the Lord": 201–13. Her two different selves: 213–16. In the restaurant; her literary talk; her Dreyfusism; ogles the waiters and other customers; Robert's jealousy; her maliciousness; quarrel and reconciliation: 216–28. In the theatre; her appearance on the stage: 231–33; the ballet-dancer; Robert's jealousy; the promised necklace: 235–40. Remarks about her at Mme de Villeparisis's reception: 291–322 *passim*. Robert's gloom and remorse about their quarrel; she refuses the necklace; her generosity; Robert's ignorance of her infidelities: 376–83. Final breach: 475–77. Prince Von talks to M about her: 697. She and her friends make fun of Robert: **IV** 129. Robert's dialect borrowed from her: 296. Her liaison with Octave: **V** 816, and her despair when he leaves her to marry Andrée: 817. Her continued influence over Robert: 924–26, 932–33; Her resemblance to Morel: 928–29, 934. Gilberte tries to look like her: 929–30; **VI** 16–17. After the war, becomes a famous actress and an intimate friend of the Duchesse de Guermantes; invited to recite poetry at the Princesse de Guermantes's: 447–50. Berma's low opinion of her: 450–53. Her recital and its reception: 456–59. Makes eyes at M, who fails to recognise her: 459–60. Her malicious remarks about Berma: 462–63. Oriane's opinion of her: 475–77, 497. Her reception of Berma's daughter and son-in-law: 477–80.

RAMPILLON, Mme de. At Mme de Saint-Euverte's—"that appalling Rampillon woman," says Oriane: **I** 487. At the Princesse de Guermantes's—"old mother Rampillon" ridiculed by Oriane: **IV** 114–15.

RAPIN, M. Chemist at Combray: **I** 20, 85.

RÉMI. Swann's coachman: **I** 308. His resemblance to Rizzo's bust of the Doge Loredan: 315. Helps Swann in his nocturnal search for Odette: 324–27. Odette takes against him: 455–57. Suspected by Swann of writing an anonymous letter: 508–9.

RESTAURATEUR. Proprietor of restaurant in Paris where M dines with Saint-Loup; his rudeness and servility: **III** 549–51, 556–58, 561.

RICH YOUNG MAN. An invert, whose mistress "flushed out the game": **II** 352–55; **VI** 82–83 (cf. **V** 396–97, 411–12).

(See Vaudémont, Marquis Maurice de.)

ROSEMONDE. Member of the little band at Balbec: **II** 641, 644, 651. Her "incessant japing"; her northern face and voice: 668. Games on the cliff: 669–70, 676, 684, 691. Her mother: 703. Her features and colouring—"a geranium growing by a sunlit sea": 717. Her parents take Albertine "en pension" at Incarville: **IV** 244, 248. Her remark to M about his attitude towards Albertine: 276, 302–3. Albertine kisses her on the neck: 705 (cf. **V** 738).

ROUSSEAU, Mme. Her death at Combray: **I** 75–76.

SAINT-CANDÉ, M. de. At Mme de Saint-Euverte's; his monocle: **I** 465.

SAINT-EUVERTE, Marquise de. Gives a musical soirée attended by Swann, the Princesse des Laumes and others: **I** 457–501. Gives a dinner-party attended by the Guermantes: **III** 804, 817, which is followed by the reception at the Princesse de Guermantes's, to which she comes to recruit guests for her garden-party next day: **IV** 93. Changes in the composition of her salon: 93–97. Colonel de Froberville's ambivalent attitude to her garden-party: 103–4. Oriane announces her intention not to go, much to Froberville's delight: 112–15. Overhears Charlus's scatological remarks about her; her craven reaction: 135–38. Mme de Surgis's portrait in her house: 145. Mme d'Arpajon declines to introduce her to Odette: 200. Further Charlus insults: 729–30. During the war, her salon "a faded banner": **VI** 51. After the war, greeted with obsequious respect by Charlus: 245–47. At the Guermantes reception: 424. Oriane denies ever having known her: 494.

SAINT-EUVERTE, Mme de. Wife of a great-nephew of the above, *née* La Rochefoucauld; M comes across her at the Guermantes reception listening to music in a Mme Récamier pose: **VI** 494–96.

SAINT-FERRÉOL, Mme de. Mme de Guermantes proposes to

visit her; Saint-Loup pretends not to know who she is: **III** 345, 356. (Françoise claims that the lavatory attendant "marquise" in the Champs-Elysées belongs to the Saint-Ferréol family: **II** 88.)

SAINT-FIACRE, Vicomtesse de. At the Guermantes *matinée*; prematurely aged from drug addiction: **VI** 371.

SAINTINE. Once "the flower of the Guermantes set," now *déclassé* through marriage: **V** 306–8.

SAINT-JOSEPH, General de. Saint-Loup hopes Mme de Guermantes will use her influence with him to get a transfer from Morocco: **III** 564, 706. Françoise despairs of his help in getting her nephew exempted from war service: **VI** 83–84.

SAINT-LOUP-EN-BRAY, Marquis Robert de. Son of Aynard and Marie de Marsantes. Comes to Balbec on leave to visit his great-aunt Mme de Villeparisis: **II** 420. His dashing aristocratic elegance; his apparent coldness and arrogance, then his immediate friendship and regard for M; his intellectual tastes and advanced ideas: 420–33. His tact with Bloch: 434–37. He and M invited to dinner by Bloch: 446–47. Speaks to M of his uncle Charlus: 448–52, and of the Guermantes: 456–58 (cf. **III** 8–10). His fashionably slangy vocabulary: 451, 459. Regards genealogy and heraldry as "rather a joke": 456–58. Prefers modern furniture: 460 (cf. **III** 755). Dinner with the Blochs: 474–87. His egalitarianism, contempt for high society, gift for friendship: 490–91. His liaison with Rachel; her influence on his character and behaviour; their quarrels: 492–500. Photographs M's grandmother: 500–1. Dinners with M at Rivebelle: 529–31, 535–38, 542–44, 553–55. His departure from Balbec; writes to M: 608–14. Rumours of his engagement to Mlle d'Ambresac: 634 (cf. **III** 37, 133–34). M visits him at Doncières: **III** 85–182. His welcome; his idiomatic turns of phrase; his contempt for the Prince de Borodino (cf. 167–71); his resemblance to his aunt Oriane: 99. His solicitude for M: 112–14. His popularity: 116–20. Conversation about Oriane; agrees to recommend M to her but refuses to give him her photograph: 127–31, 162–64. Dinners with his messmates; conversations on military strategy; his Dreyfusism: 139–54. His unhappiness because of Rachel: 156–62. His relations with the Prince de Borodino; the two aristocracies: 165–73. His strange salute: 180–81 (cf. 233–34). Brief visit to Paris; of-

fers to introduce M to his cousin Mme de Poictiers instead of
Oriane as being a more "liberal" representative of the aristocracy: 192–93. Invites M to lunch with Rachel: 201. His tender
feelings for her and illusions about her: 205–16 (cf. 231–33). In
the restaurant; his jealousy; quarrel and reconciliation: 215–28.
In the theatre; another quarrel; he hits a journalist and an "im-
passioned loiterer": 234–43. Remarks about him and his mistress
at Mme de Villeparisis's: 292–322 *passim*. Arrives *chez* Mme de
Villeparisis: 343–45. Refuses to be introduced to Mme Swann:
357. Irritation with his mother: 364–66, 378–80. His friendship
with Bloch: 373. His remorse about Rachel; the promised necklace: 377–78. His ignorance of Rachel's life: 382–83. Writes M a
letter of bitter reproach: 417 (cf. 475–76). Calls on M's family
during his grandmother's illness: 460–61. Posted to Morocco;
writes to M about Mme de Stermaria. Final breach with Rachel:
475–77. Calls on M in Paris and takes him out to dinner:
539–69; his tactless remark concerning M and Bloch: 546–47;
borrows the Prince de Foix's cloak for M; his nimble circum-
ambulation of the restaurant; his physical grace and effortless
good breeding—epitome of the best qualities of the aristocracy:
559–69. Oriane mocks his mannerisms of speech and refuses to
speak to General de Monserfeuil or General de Saint-Joseph on
his behalf: 696–701, 705–6. Elected to the Jockey Club in spite
of his Dreyfusism: 798–800. At the Princesse de Guermantes's;
speaks to M about Charlus, recommends brothels and Mlle de
l'Orgeville and Mme Putbus's maid; no longer interested in literature: **IV** 123–30. No longer Dreyfusist: 133, 151. Recommends M to the Cambremers: 207. Mme de Cambremer-
Legrandin adopts his vocabulary (borrowed from Rachel); alleged to have been Mme de Cambremer's lover: 296–97. Meets
M and Albertine at Doncières station; ignores Albertine's
flirtatious advances: 348 (cf. 682–85, 692). Albertine discusses
him with M: 355–57. Rumour of his engagement to the Princesse de Guermantes's niece: 443–44 (cf. 673; **VI** 68–70).
M's fear of his meeting Albertine at Balbec or *chez* the Verdurins; Saint-Loup has no wish to meet the latter: 571–72.
His Dreyfusism discussed by the Cambremers: 673. Visits M on
the little train; Albertine avoids him: 682–85, 692. M employs

him to search for Albertine after her flight: **V** 584–96, 596–604, 608–10. Strange conversation with a Guermantes footman overheard by M: 633–35. Reports on his abortive mission: 635–41. Consulted by M about Mlle d'Eporcheville (de l'Orgeville): 762–65. His marriage to Gilberte: 889–91, 895–902, 911–12. Turns out to be "one of those": 900. Unfaithful to Gilberte; Jupien's revelations; his liaison with Morel: 922–25. Visit to Balbec with Gilberte; Aimé's revelations; the development of his inversion; Rachel's influence still visible; her resemblance to Morel; gives her an enormous income: 925–30. Bribes Odette with expensive presents to obtain her complicity: 930–31. M's reflexions on the new Robert; when did it date from?: 931–36. At Tansonville; his relations with his wife; changes in his personality; his love for Charlie: **VI** 12–26. During the war, dines with M one evening while on leave: 64. Feigns cowardice but secretly does everything he can to be sent to the front; comparison with Bloch; his undemonstrative courage and patriotism: 67–81. His "delightful" letter from the front: 88–93. Visits M on leave from the front; discussion about aeroplanes at night; opinions on the war; compared with Charlus: 96–104. M sees him emerging from Jupien's brothel: 175. The lost *croix de guerre*: 189, 219. Killed in action: 226. M's grief; memories of him, linked to those of Albertine; effect of his death on Françoise and on Oriane; buried at Combray: 226–34. "If he had lived . . .": 236–37. M talks to Gilberte about him at the Guermantes reception: 428–32.

SAINT-LOUP, Mlle de. Daughter of Robert and Gilberte. Introduced to M by her mother at the Guermantes reception; memories and reflexions she awakens in M; her beauty; her resemblance to her parents and grandparents: **VI** 501–7.

SANIETTE. Palaeographer; member of the Verdurins' "little clan"; his shyness, simplicity and good nature: **I** 286–87. Forcheville's brother-in-law: 355. Scolded by Mme Verdurin: 369. In an endeavour to amuse, makes up a story about the La Trémoïlles: 370–71. Attacked by Forcheville and driven from the house: 393. Dreyfusist, in spite of being a practising Catholic: **III** 799. His social awkwardness aggravated by his efforts to correct it: **IV** 366–67. Upset by Cottard's behaviour in the little train: 371. The Verdurins' whipping-boy: 405–6, 446, 449–57. His failed witticisms: 455–59. Unable to play whist: 485. Mme Verdurin's views on him: 506–11. M's analysis of his social deficiencies: 573–76. His pedantic phraseology: **V** 298–99, 302–3 (*see also* 945–46). His bankruptcy and his stroke; the Verdurins' generosity to him; M attends his funeral some years later: 436–39. (cf. 945–46)

SANILON. Surname of Théodore (q.v.).

SANTOIS, Bobette. Proust's original name for the violinist Charlie Morel: *see* **II** 741–43; **V** 922.

SAUMOY, Guy. Friend of the "little band" at Balbec, retrospectively evoked by M: **V** 821.

SAXONY, Prince of. Is he the blond young man who joins the Princesse de Guermantes in her box at the Opéra?: **III** 40–41, 61–62.

SAYLOR. Patronym of M. de Crécy (q.v.).

SAZERAT, Mme. Neighbour of M's family at Combray: **I** 76. Her dog: 79. In church: 81. Eulalie's belief that her name is Sazerin: 95–96. Comments on Odette's make-up: 137. Her son: 244. Her mauve scarf: 246. Her attitude to servants: **III** 79. Her Dreyfusism separates her from M's family: 199–201, 442. Meets Bloch *père*: 392–93. M's mother's opinion of her lunch-parties: **V** 11, 806. Her Wednesday voice; her restricted life, the result of her father's indiscretions with a duchess: 806–7. M's mother invites her to dinner in Venice: 853. Her emotion on hearing the name Villeparisis; reveals that Mme de Villeparisis was the duchess who ruined her father: 858–60. Death of her son: **VI** 519.

SERVING-GIRL seduced by M in an inn at Doncières: **III** 542.

SHERBATOFF, Princess. In the little train at Balbec; M's mistake as to her identity: **IV** 347–48. A model member of the Verdurins' "faithful"; impresses her fellow-members of the "little clan"; reality of her social position; her three friends: 369–80. M recognises her as the fat, vulgar lady he had seen alone on the train: 393–94. Her pronunciation: 394–96. Her obligingness: 397–98. Her concern about the effect of Dechambre's death on Mme Verdurin: 400, 403–4. Mme Verdurin uses her as a screen to hide her mock laughter: 482. Rebuffed by Cottard in the little train: 598. Her proclaimed anti-snobbery the result of wounded snobbery; quarrels with M: 602–6. Appreciates a Cottard pun: 613. Her death announced by Saniette: **V** 302. Mme Verdurin's indifference to the event: 317–20. Referred to in the Goncourt pastiche as having perhaps been the murderer of the Archduke Rudolf: **VI** 29.

SIDONIA, Duke of. Spanish grandee and formidable talker; competes with Charlus at the Princesse de Guermantes's: **IV** 52–53.

SILISTRIE, Princesse de. Calls on the Guermantes to discuss Amanien d'Osmond's illness: **III** 788. Seeks to marry her son to Gilberte: **V** 897–98.

SIMONET. *See* Albertine.

SKI, diminutive of Viradobetski. Polish sculptor, friend of the Verdurins. In the little train: **IV** 360–61; his character and appearance; superficially gifted in all the arts; his affectations: 367–69. His opinion of Mme de Cambremer: 386–87. Warns Mme Verdurin against Charlus: 408–10. Teases Brichot about his "eye for the ladies": 434–36. Reveals Charlus's vice to Cottard: 450–51. His affected flight of fancy about the colour of food: 459–60. Mistaken about Charlus's background: 481–84. His witticisms at the Baron's expense: 599. Discusses Bizet with Morel; his affected laugh: **V** 384–85. Charlus ridicules Brichot's suggestion that he might be homosexual: 403–4. Fascinated by Morel's tears: 429–30. In old age, has become like a dried fruit or flower: **VI** 361.

SOUVRÉ, Marquise de. Friend of the Princesse de Parme, but not received by Oriane de Guermantes: **III** 620–21. Her social manner: **IV** 66–67. Half-hearted attempt to introduce M to the Prince de Guermantes: 67–69, 70, 73. Conversation with Odette about the Verdurins: 365. Evoked by M at the Guermantes reception: **VI** 418.

STERMARIA, Mlle (later Mme, and finally Vicomtesse Alix) de. At Balbec with her father, a Breton squire: **II** 351–52. Her aristocratic looks: 357. M's dream of love on a Breton island with her: 363–65 (cf. **III** 528–29). Saint-Loup meets her in Tangier (divorced after three months of marriage) and arranges for M to dine with her in Paris: **III** 475–78. A letter from her agreeing to dine on the island in the Bois: 506. M's pleasurable anticipation; she cries off at the last moment: 525–39.

STERMARIA, M. de. Breton squire, father of the above, on holiday at Balbec: **II** 351. His contemptuous arrogance: 352, 357. Introduces himself to the barrister as a friend of the Cambremers: 363.

SÛRETÉ, Director of the. M receives a summons from him for having corrupted a little girl; his cynicism: **V** 597–99.

SURGIS-LE-DUC, Marquise or Duchesse de. Mistress of the Duc de Guermantes: **III** 675. At the Princesse de Guermantes's; her statuesque beauty: **IV** 70, reproduced in her two sons: 116–17, 120–21. Charlus's unwonted friendliness towards her; her portrait by Jacquet; introduces her sons to the Baron: 127–46. Swann gazes concupiscently at her bosom: 142, 146. Origin of her name; her social position: 143–44. Later, forbids her sons to visit Charlus: **V** 269.

SURGIS-LE-DUC, Victurnien and Arnulphe de. Sons of the above; their "great and dissimilar" beauty derived from their mother: **IV** 116–17. Admired by Charlus: 120–21. Introduced to him by their mother: 130–31. Conversation with him: 131–35, 140–41. Their subsequent visits to him, eventually forbidden by their mother: **V** 269.

SWANN, Charles. His evening visits at Combray; his brilliant social life unsuspected by M's family: **I** 16–35. Why he might have understood M's anguish at having to go to bed without a good-night kiss from his mother: 39–41. His habit, inherited from his father, of rubbing his eyes and drawing his hand across his forehead in moments of stress: 45 (cf. 381, 420, 452, 493, 510, 537, 588). "Giotto's Charity": 110. His Jewish origin: 125. Speaks to M about Bergotte and Berma: 134–37. "Swann's Way" (the Méséglise way); his estate at Tansonville: 188 et sqq. Meets Vinteuil in Combray: 209–11 (cf. 302). *Swann in Love*: 265–543. His womanising: 269–75. Introduced to Odette; his initial indifference to her: 275–80. His essay on Vermeer: 279 (cf. 340–41, 423, 502; **II** 54, 146–47; **IV** 145). Introduced by Odette to the Verdurins: 280. His social ease and courtesy: 285–87. Hears Vinteuil's sonata: 294; the "little phrase":

296–300, "the national anthem of their love": 308–9 (cf. 335–37, 374–75). Visits to Odette's house: 309–13. His penchant for comparing people to figures in the old masters: 314–17 (cf. 110, 134, 459–62, 465; **II** 148; **V** 516–17). His nocturnal search for Odette: 323–26. The cattleyas; Odette becomes his mistress: 328–32. Progress of his love: 332–50. His enthusiasm for the Verdurins: 350–54. Dines at the Verdurins' with Forcheville: 355–75. The beginnings of his jealousy; he taps on the wrong window: 387–92. Odette lies to him: 394–99. He reads her letter to Forcheville: 400–1. Rejected by the Verdurins; his tirade against them: 403–10. Progress of his jealousy: 411–53. At Mme de Saint-Euverte's: 458–501; conversation with the Princesse des Laumes: 483–87; the little phrase again, reminding him of the early days of his love for Odette: 490–501. Abandons hope of happiness with Odette: 502–5; hopes for her death: 504 (cf. **V** 641–43). The anonymous letter: 506–10, and the suspicions it arouses in him: 510–14. Interrogates Odette: 514–27. Visits brothels: 530–31. Conversation with Mme Cottard on a bus: 532–36. Dreams of Odette and Forcheville: 538–43. "A woman who wasn't even my type": 543. Speaks to M of Balbec church: 547. His need for gingerbread: 571. Comes to fetch his daughter from the Champs-Elysées; his prestige and glamour in M's eyes: 576–79, 586–88. Meets M's mother in the Trois Quartiers: 588–90. His new persona as Odette's husband: **II** 1–3. Norpois's remarks about the Swann *ménage*: 49–52. How the marriage came about: 52–58. His suspicions of M: 85–87. M becomes a regular visitor to his house: 103–4. His library: 111–13. His changed attitude to society: 117–31. His indifference to Odette; in love with another woman (Mme de Cambremer?): 130–34 (cf. 146–47; **I** 541–42; **IV** 426). His love for his daughter: 192–93. Bergotte's remarks about him: 199–200. Relations with Mme Verdurin: 239–40. Has "a separate life of his own": 246. His photograph of the Botticellian Odette: 264 (cf. **V** 267). Persuades the Guermantes to buy Elstirs: **III** 685–87. Oriane recalls her botanical expeditions with him: 708–9. Inculcates in her a taste for Empire furniture: 711, 715. His researches into the Templars: 787. M meets him at the Guermantes'; his changed appearance; his illness; his Dreyfusism; his comment on the

Duke's "Velazquez"; has only three or four months to live: 792–819. At the Princesse de Guermantes's; said to have quarrelled with the Prince: **IV** 75, 98, 101–2, 138–39. His grandmother, a Protestant married to a Jew, was the Duc de Berry's mistress: 92. The Duc de Guermantes, supported by his wife, deplores his Dreyfusism and his marriage—a double betrayal of the Faubourg Saint-Germain: 104–8. His desire to introduce his wife and daughter to Oriane before he dies: 108–9 (cf. **II** 57–58; **V** 776–80). His face grotesquely changed by illness; his Jewishness more pronounced: 121–22, 134. His preoccupation with the Dreyfus Case: 132–33, 150–54; but nevertheless desires to be buried with military honours: 152–53. Talks to M about jealousy: 139–40. Concupiscent gaze at Mme de Surgis-le-Duc's bosom: 142, 146. Reports to M his conversation with the Prince de Guermantes: 142–52. Effect of his Dreyfusism on his wife's social aspirations: 199–200. Casual allusion to his death: 364. Vilified by Mme Verdurin: 503–4. Charlus cites his views on Balzac: 611, 614, 623. His death in retrospect: **V** 260–64. Allusion to the Tissot picture of Charles Haas, of whom there are "some traces in the character of Swann": 262–63. Charlus's reminiscences concerning him; madly attractive to women; fought a duel with d'Osmond; had been the lover of Odette's sister: 399–403. Recalled patronisingly by the Duc and Duchesse de Guermantes in conversation with Gilberte: 783–87. How mistaken he had been in pinning his hopes of survival on his daughter: 799–801 (cf. **II** 192–93). Referred to in the Goncourt pastiche: **VI** 29, 36–37. The many different Swanns: 441–42. How the raw material of M's experience, and of his book, came from Swann: 328–30.

SWANN *père*. Stockbroker; close friend of M's grandfather; his behaviour on the death of his wife ("often, but a little at a time"); his familiar gesture when faced with a perplexing problem: **I** 17–19. Recalled by M's mother apropos of his granddaughter's marriage: **V** 894–95, 917–18.

SWANN, Mme. *See* Odette.

SWANN, Gilberte. *See* Gilberte.

TAORMINA, Princess of. Hears Morel play at the Verdurins': **V** 383.

TELEGRAPH-BOY. Protégé of a colleague of Brichot's, then of M. de Charlus, who finds him a post in the colonies: **V** 442–43.

THÉODORE. Choirboy and grocer's boy at Combray: **I** 76, 79. He and his sister show visitors the crypt of the church: 84, 146. His encyclopaedic knowledge of local affairs: 93. A scapegrace, but nevertheless helps Françoise to tend Aunt Léonie; the spirit of Saint-André-des-Champs: 212–13. Coachman to a friend of Charlus; his sexual misbehaviour; his sister is Mme Putbus's maid: **V** 411. Writes to M to congratulate him on his *Figaro* article; his surname is Sanilon: 799; **VI** 15. Gilberte's revelations about his escapades with the girls; becomes chemist at Méséglise: 5. His liaison with Legrandin: 15.

THEODOSIUS II. East European sovereign on a state visit to Paris: **I** 580, 588–89. His conversation with Norpois: **II** 9, 41. Norpois's comments on his speech at the Elysée: 41–47. Charlus and Vaugoubert discuss his possible inversion: **IV** 88–89. Return visit to Paris with Queen Eudoxia: **V** 327–28.

THIRION, M. Second husband of Mme de Villeparisis: **III** 398–99.

TICHE (Monsieur). *See* Elstir.

TOUREUIL, Judge. Presumably the senior judge from Caen, elsewhere referred to as Poncin (q.v.): **IV** 442.

TOURS, Vicomtesse de (*née* Lamarzelle). At the Princesse d'Epinay's; remarked by the Duc de Guermantes: **III** 633–34.

TRANIA. Princesse de. Visits Odette at the time of her liaison with the Duc de Guermantes: **VI** 482.

TRESMES, Mme Dorothée de. Cousin of the Duc de Guermantes: **III** 785. Calls on the Duke, with her sister Mme de Plassac, with news of Amanien d'Osmond; her walking-stick: 788–89. She and her sister bring news of Amanien's death: **IV** 169.

TROMBERT, Mme. Regular visitor to Odette's salon: **II** 109; M's mother's joke at her expense: 120; her hats: 245.

USHER (or "barker") at the Princesse de Guermantes's. His adventure with the Duc de Châtellerault: **IV** 46, 49–50.

VALCOURT, Mme Edith de. At the Verdurins'; excluded from Mme de Mortemart's musical evening: **V** 359–60.

VALET, M's father's. *See* Victor.

VALET, Uncle Adolphe's: **I** 103–4. Charlie Morel's father; his veneration for Uncle Adolphe's memory: **III** 357–59. Described to the Verdurins, at Charlie's request, as "steward" in M's family: **IV** 417–18, 425. Charlie has inherited his conviction of Uncle Adolphe's grandeur: 621–22.

VALLENÈRES, M. Archivist, occasional secretary to Mme de Villeparisis: **III** 252, 256–58; helps with the management of her estates: 287–88. A strong Nationalist and anti-Dreyfusard: 294–95, 319, 334–35. The "daughter of the house": 310. Explains the word "mentality" to M. de Guermantes: 319. His influence over Mme de Villeparisis: 335–36.

VARAMBON, Mme de. Lady-in-waiting to the Princesse de Parme. Her stupidity; insists that M is related to Admiral Jurien de La Gravière: **III** 681–83. Irritates the Princess: 747, 749–50. Mme de Guermantes's anecdote about her: **VI** 471–72.

VATRY, Colonel the Baron de. Tenant of M's Uncle Adolphe: **IV** 621.

VAUDÉMONT, Marquis Maurice de. One of two young noblemen who, with an actress and her lover, form an exclusive group at Balbec: **II** 352–55. Invites M to dinner: 727. M and Charlus discuss him and his friends in the context of sexual inversion; the actress's lover an invert: **V** 411–12; **VI** 83.

(*See* Actress from the Odéon; Rich Young Man.)

VAUGOUBERT, Marquis de. Ambassador of France at the court of King Theodosius; praised by Norpois: **II** 42–44, 47. Has the same tastes as Charlus: **IV** 57–58. His mediocrity does not prevent him from being one of the best representatives of the French Government abroad: 58–60. Introduces M to his wife at the Princesse de Guermantes's: 60–61. Manifestations of his vice; conversation with Charlus: 86–89, 100. His excessive politeness: 100, 102–3. Further homosexual exchanges with Charlus: **V** 51. Forcibly retired from the service: 327–28. Loses his son in the war; his extreme grief: **VI** 91–92.

VAUGOUBERT, Mme de. Wife of the above. Her masculine air; her considerable intelligence: **IV** 61–63. Brings about her husband's disgrace: **V** 327–28.

VÉLUDE, Vicomtesse de. Sister of the Comtesse de Montpeyroux (q.v.), nicknamed "Mignonne" on account of her stoutness: **III** 591–92.

VERDURIN, M. The "little clan": **I** 265–68. His subordinate role vis-à-vis his wife: 269. M's grandfather knew his family: 281. His laugh and his pipe: 290, 303, 372–73. His opinion of Swann and Odette: 321–22, 354–55. His hostility to Swann: 376–77. Organises a Mediterranean cruise for the "faithful": 532. Despised by Octave, who is a relative of his—"an old fellow in a frock coat": **II** 632–33 (cf. **IV** 365–66). At La Raspelière; his attitude towards the death of one of the "faithful": **IV** 399–400, 403–7. Uses Saniette as a whipping-boy: 405–6 (cf. 446, 449 et sqq., 511). His irony at Brichot's expense: 408 (cf. 473–77). His enthusiasm for La Raspelière: 412–13. His ignorance of the hierarchy of social rank: 428 (cf. 462–64). Bullies Saniette: 451–56, 459, 485, 506–7. His ineptitude with Charlus ("one of us"): 462–64. Pride in his intimacy with Cottard: 486–88. The evening of the concert organised by Charlus; further brutality to Saniette: **V** 302–3 (*see also* 945–46). Abets his wife's despotic behaviour towards the "faithful": 304–5. Reaction to Princess Sherbatoff's death: 318–19. Takes Morel aside to warn him against Charlus: 414–15. His name is Gustave: 423 (cf. **VI** 33–34). His generosity to the sick and penurious Saniette: 436–40. His contradictory nature: 439–40. Eulogised in the Goncourt Journal; art critic in his younger days and author of a book on Whistler: **VI** 27–30. Praises Morel's satires: 112. Dies soon after Cottard; mourned by Elstir, who saw him as the man who had had "the truest vision" of his painting: 116–17.

VERDURIN, Mme. "Mistress" of the "little clan": **I** 265–69. Reactions to music: 266, 290–91, 299–300. Dislocates her jaw from laughing so much: 266–67. Her new, less dangerous way of showing her hilarity: 289–90. Distressing effect on her of the discovery of Swann's grand connexions: 307 (cf. 354, 366–69). Attitude to Swann and Odette: 321–22, 354. Gives a dinner-party attended by Swann, Odette, Forcheville, Brichot and others: 355–75. Her hostility to Swann: 376–77; breaks with him: 403–10. Excursions with Odette: 414–19. Her strange behaviour with Odette (*Les Filles de marbre*): 512–14. Mediterranean cruise with Odette and the "faithful": 531–35. Her relations with Odette after her marriage to Swann; their rival salons; entertains the idea of "society" as her final objective: **II** 239–49. Instals electricity in her new house: 249–50. M "makes a conquest" of her: 251. M unintentionally pursues her in the street: 399. Her latent bourgeois anti-semitism awakened by the Dreyfus Case [this is entirely inconsistent with what follows]: **III** 341. An extreme Dreyfusard and anti-clerical: 799. Successful development of her salon; the Russian Ballet: **IV** 193–94 (cf. **V** 311–15). The little clan an active centre of Dreyfusism: 194–95, 198–99 (cf. 383–86). Rents La Raspelière from the Cambremers: 206–7. Her "Wednesdays": 344–47. Compels Brichot to break with his laundress: 361–62. Evolution of her salon towards Society; a Temple of Music: 362–66. Her recruits to the little clan—Ski (replacement for Elstir) and Princess Sherbatoff (the ideal member of the "faithful"): 367–79. Ambivalent attitude to the Cambremers; plays down her Dreyfusism: 383–86 (cf. **V** 312–13). Her attitude to the death of one of the faithful: 399–401, 403–6. Her delight in La Raspelière: 411–13. Physical changes produced in her by years of listening to music: 413–14 (cf. **V** 304, 331). Hatred of family life; anecdote about M's great-grandfather: 418–19. The changes she has made at La Raspelière: 428–30. Impressed by Mme Molé, on whom she bestows a nobiliary particle: 454–55. Disparages Elstir and eulogises Ski: 458–62. Shows M Elstir's flowers: 464–65. Disparages Brichot: 472–76 and Saniette: 476–77. Her new technique for showing her amusement: 481–82 (cf. **I** 289–90). Attempts to annex Charlus to the little clan; suppresses her outraged anti-clericalism: 484–85. Praises Cottard: 492. Her first skirmish with Charlus: 497–99. Her advances to M; disparages the Cambremers and Féterne; vilifies Swann: 499–50. Jeers at Saniette: 507, then coaxes him to return: 511. Her assiduity as a hostess; excursions with her guests; knows the neighbourhood better than the Cambremers: 539–40. Her Monday tea-parties: 542–44. Visited by M and Albertine: 544–48. Charlus becomes for her "the faithfullest of the faithful"; her tolerance of his relations with Morel: 601–4. Deterioration of her relations with the Cambremers: 664–66. Compels Brichot to forswear his passion for Mme de

Cambremer: 669–70. M goes to a musical party organised by Charlus at her new house in the Quai Conti; Brichot describes to him her former salon in the Rue Montalivet: **V** 260, 265–67. Infuriated by Charlus's dictatorial attitude, determines to separate him from Morel: 303–11. Social development of her salon; influence of the Dreyfus Case; her genuine love of art; the Russian Ballet: 310–11 (cf. **IV** 193–94). Her indifference to the death of Princess Sherbatoff: 317–19. Takes rhino-gomerol to counteract the effects of Vinteuil's music: 320–21. Rudeness of Charlus's guests to her, apart from the Queen of Naples: 326–30, 353–65. How she listens to the music: 331, 334. Enraged by Charlus's insolence: 364–71. Persuades Brichot to co-operate in her plan of revenge: 372–76. Her slanderous attack on Charlus convinces Morel: 414–25. Humiliated by the Queen of Naples: 430–33. Supports her husband's generosity to Saniette: 436–39. Wanted Albertine to meet her nephew Octave: 832–33. Her salon described in the Goncourt pastiche; Fromentin's "Madeleine": **VI** 27–37. One of the queens of war-time Paris: 47. Visits Venice during the war: 51. Thoroughly at home with the Faubourg Saint-Germain; no longer dreads "bores"; constant mention of GHQ: 55–57. Overtures to Odette: 59–61. Her telephonings, her receptions: 61–63. Her aversion to Charlus: 107–10. Tries to persuade the faithful not to join up: 115. Her life changed by the war; her croissants and the sinking of the *Lusitania*: 120–21. Her relations with Brichot; ridicules his articles: 145–51. After the war, and M. Verdurin's death, marries first the Duc de Duras and then the Prince de Guermantes: 387–88. At her reception; her false teeth and monocle; still as indefatigable as ever: 433. Reaction to Rachel's recital: 458.

VICTOR. Butler to M's family (sometimes referred to as valet). Peppers his conversation with the latest witticisms: **III** 19. His cynical view of politicians: 26. Purloins writing-paper from M's bedroom: 27 (cf. 437). A Dreyfusard: 402–3. Quarrels with Françoise: **V** 153. His mispronunciation of *pissotière* (Charlus's yellow trousers): 249 (cf. **VI** 86–88). Teases Françoise by pretending to read unpleasant news in the newspaper: 630. His familiarity with the nicknames of sovereigns: **VI** 56. Terrifies

Françoise during the war with tales of disasters and atrocities: 84–85, 219–26, 230–31.

VILLEBON, Mme de. A Courvoisier and stickler for social distinctions: **III** 604–7.

VILLEMANDOIS, Marquis de. Asks to be introduced to M at the Princesse de Guermantes's reception, having totally forgotten their old feud: **VI** 405–6.

VILLEMUR, Mme de. Introduced to the painter Detaille at the Princesse de Guermantes's: **IV** 47–48.

VILLEPARISIS, Marquise de, *née* Mlle de Bouillon, aunt of the Duc and Duchesse de Guermantes. Visited by M's grandmother, a friend from convent days: **I** 24–25 (cf. 144). Likened by Odette to an "usherette": 345. Allusion to her by Norpois: **II** 50. Allusion by Swann to her liaison with Norpois: 187. At the Grand Hotel, Balbec; her entourage; ridiculed by the barrister and his friends: 348–51. Pointed out to M's grandmother; "the fiction of a mutual incognito": 358–61. Their accidental meeting and renewed friendship; her kindness to M and his grandmother: 371–78. Introduces them to the Princesse de Luxembourg: 378–80. Her knowledge of the movements of M's father: 381 (cf. **III** 244). Takes M and his grandmother for drives; her aristocratic erudition, "liberal" views, literary anecdotes, acquaintance with the great: 386–87. Introduces her great-nephew Saint-Loup: 424. Introduces her nephew Charlus: 455–56. A Guermantes!—transformed in M's eyes: 456 (cf. 736–39; **V** 391–92). Tea with Charlus in her room at the hotel; critical of Mme de Sévigné: 462–66, 467–68 (cf. 375–76). Complains about diabolo: 695–96. Neighbour of M's family in Paris: **III** 10, 35. M. de Norpois's regular visits; he speaks of her in glowing terms to M's father: 195–96. Her "School of Wit": 197–98. Her intimacy with Norpois: 244–46, 295–98. Her "at home": 244–385. Vicissitudes of her social situation; her salon; her *Memoirs*: 244–61. Her rivalry with the three Parcae: 260–70. Her flower painting: 252, 272, 286–88, 371–72. Her *grande dame* act with Bloch: 336. Receives Mme Swann: 341. Her relations with her nephew Charlus: 362–64. Alarmed by his interest in M: 384–85. Origin of the Villeparisis name explained by Charlus: 398–99.

Gives a reception at which M arrives late; invites him to dinner: 507, 512–13. Influenced by the Guermantes family genie: 603–4, 615–16. Discussed by Oriane; the horrors of her dinner-table; her morals; known as "aunt Madeleine": 691–94. Oriane ridicules the idea of her marrying Norpois: 725 (cf. 829–29). Praised by the Turkish Ambassadress: 740. Charlus calls on her at an unusual hour: **IV** 2–5. M talks to her on the little train, to the disgruntlement of Princess Sherbatoff: 604–5. Premature allusion to her death: **V** 391. Her true social situation: 391–92 (cf. **III** 244–52; **II** 456). In Venice with M. de Norpois in old age: 854–60 (cf. 947–50). Had been the ruin of Mme Sazerat's father: 858–60 (cf. 806). Dies in isolation: **VI** 108, survived by Norpois: 133–34.

VINTEUIL. Musician, former piano-teacher to M's grandmother's sisters; living in retirement at Montjouvain, near Combray: **I** 32. His prudishness and modesty; his passion for his daughter: 155–57. Pain which she causes him: 206–9. Meets Swann: 209–10. His death; his compositions: 225–26. His daughter's sacrilegious gesture: 226–30. His sonata played at the Verdurins': 290–303. The "little phrase" becomes the "national anthem" of Swann's love for Odette: 308–9, 335–36, 374–75. Swann hears the sonata again at Mme de Saint-Euverte's, and it reminds him of his lost happiness: 489–500. Odette plays the little phrase to M; M's reflections on the work, Swann's comments on it: **II** 139–46. Vinteuil the pianist: **III** 54. His extraordinary prestige—"the greatest of contemporary composers": **IV** 363–64. M mentions his name to Albertine: 701–2. M plays his sonata; reflections on artistic creation; Vinteuil and Wagner: **V** 204–9. Effect of his music on Mme Verdurin: 320–21. His septet played at the Verdurins': 330–46. His work transcribed by his daughter's friend: 347–53. Albertine plays his music on the pianola: 502–6. "Expressing the inexpressible": 502–6, 513–14. The little phrase and Albertine: 755–56.

VINTEUIL, Mlle. Daughter of the above. Her boyish appearance: **I** 157–58. Her bad reputation; causes her father unhappiness: 206–9. Scene of sadism with her friend at Montjouvain; profanes her father's memory: 224–32. Gilberte's disapproval of her: **II** 150. Shattering revelation of Albertine's intimacy with her and her friend: **IV** 701–24. She and her friend expected at the Verdurins' (in fact they fail to appear): **V** 295–98. M interrogates Mme Verdurin and Morel about her: 321. Her penitence and veneration for her father; her sadism merely a pretence of wickedness: 348–49. M interrogates Albertine, who denies being on terms of intimacy with her and her friend: 447–48, 451–52 (cf. 533–34). The truth concerning her relations with Albertine, according to Andrée: 831–33.

VINTEUIL, Friend of Mlle. Comes to live at Montjouvain; her bad reputation; Vinteuil regards her as "a superior woman," with great musical gifts: **I** 206–8. Her part in the scene at Montjouvain: 226–32. Albertine reveals that she had been a mother or a sister to her: **IV** 701–3, 707–13, 722–23. Expected at the Verdurins': **V** 295–98, 321. Her patient and dedicated labour transcribing Vinteuil's works: 347–53. Albertine denies having been more or less brought up by her: 451–53. Andrée's version of the story: 831–33.

VIRADOBETSKI. *See* Ski.

VIRELEF, Mme de. Invites the Guermantes to the Opéra with Gilberte: **V** 782.

VLADIMIR, Grand Duke. His delighted amusement at the inundation of Mme d'Arpajon: **IV** 76–78.

VON, Prince. *See* Faffenheim.

WAITERS at the "Cherry Orchard." Twin brothers resembling tomatoes; Nissim Bernard's relations with them: **IV** 342–43.

WAITERS in the hotel at Doncières; their breathless speed; the "reserve of cherubim and seraphim": **III** 125–26.

WAITERS in the restaurant at Rivebelle; their gyrations round the "astral tables": **II** 532–34; one of them fascinates Albertine: **IV** 563–65; two of them, transferred to the Grand Hotel, Balbec, whom M fails to recognise: 528.

WAITERS in Aimé's restaurant in Paris, like superannuated actors: **III** 218, 222.

WAITERS in the restaurant in Venice: **V** 854.

WARWICK, Lady. English friend of Mme de Guermantes: **V** 48.

YOURBELETIEFF, Princess. Sponsor of the *Ballets russes*; appears at the theatre in the company of Mme Verdurin: **IV** 193; **V** 315.

WOMAN ("beautiful young") with the flashing eyes who seems to recognise Albertine and strikes up a Gomorrhan relationship with Bloch's cousin: **IV** 338–40.

WOMAN (young Austrian) who attracts M in Venice because of her resemblance to Albertine: **V** 879–81.

# Index of Persons

ADAM, Adolphe, French composer (1803–56). Allusions to his operettas *Le Chalet*: **III** 673 and *Le Postillon de Longjumeau*: **V** 205.

ALENÇON, Duchesse d', sister of Elisabeth, Empress of Austria, and of Maria, Queen of Naples. Allusion to her accidental death (in a fire) in 1897: **III** 700. Referred to in connexion with the Queen of Naples' visit to the Verdurin musical soirée: **V** 328, 414.

ALENÇON, Emilienne d'. Famous Belle Epoque courtesan: **IV** 661.

ALFONSO XIII, King of Spain. "Fonfonse" to M's family's butler: **VI** 56.

ALLEMANS, Armand du Lau, Marquis d', "nobleman of Perigord" (1651–1726). His portrait by Saint-Simon: **V** 794–95 (cf. Lau, Marquis du, in the *Index of Characters*).

AMAURY (Ernest-Félix Socquet), 19th-century French actor who had his moment of celebrity: **III** 167.

AMÉLIE, daughter of the Comte de Paris, Queen of Portugal from 1889 to 1908. Referred to familiarly by Françoise: **II** 491.

AMPÈRE, André, French physicist and mathematician (1775–1836). Invoked by Swann in connexion with Vinteuil's creative genius: **I** 499. His son Jean-Jacques, historian (1800–64): **VI** 408.

ANGELICO, Fra, Italian painter (*c.* 1387–1455): **I** 549.

ANNUNZIO, Gabriele d', Italian writer (1863–1938). Admirer of the Duchesse de Guermantes: **IV** 89.

APOLLONIUS OF TYANA, neo-Pythagorean philosopher: **VI** 150.

ARBOUVILLE, Mme Césarine d'. Hostess, woman of letters, and friend of Sainte-Beuve: **V** 769–70.

ARISTOTLE, Greek philosopher: **I** 212; **III** 257, 285, 612.

ARLINCOURT, Vicomte d', French historical novelist (1789–1856): **IV** 110.

ARNAULD, Antoine, Jansenist theologian (1612–94): **V** 918.

AROUET. *See* Voltaire.

ARVÈDE BARINE (Mme Charles Vincens), French writer (1840–1908). Saint-Loup reads a book of hers on a train, and mistakes the author's sex and nationality: **II** 611.

ASSURBANIPAL, King of Assyria 668–626 BC: **II** 68.

AUBER, Esprit, French composer (1782–1871). References to his operettas, *Les Diamants de la Couronne, Le Domino noir* and *Fra Diavolo*: **I** 101; **III** 615, 673; **VI** 244.

AUDIFFRET-PASQUIER, Duc d', French politician (1823–1905): **I** 26.

AUGIER, Emile, French playwright (1820–89): **II** 485; **III** 277; Oriane de Guermantes ascribes to him a line of Musset's: 308.

AUGUSTUS III of Poland, Elector of Saxony (1696–1763): **VI** 152.

AUMALE, Henri d'Orléans, Duc d', French general and historian, fourth son of Louis-Philippe (1822–97). Cottard's euphemism for lavatory: **I** 372–73. M. Bloch *père* referred to as his double: **II** 480. The Guermantes visit him at Chantilly: **III** 35 (cf. 803–4). In a box at the Opéra: 43; frequents Mme de Villeparisis's salon: 259. He and Princesse Mathilde brought together by Oriane: 642, 710. His liaison with Mme de Clinchamp: **IV** 672.

AVENEL, Vicomte Georges d', French historian and economist (1855–1939): **III** 286.

BACH, Johann Sebastian, German composer (1685–1750). Conversation of the inhabitants of Françoise's native village has the "unshakeable solidity of a Bach fugue": **IV** 172. Charlus's laugh and Bach's "small high" trumpets: 463–64. Morel plays a Bach air and variations on a walk with the Verdurins: 584. A "sublime aria" by Bach: **V** 862.

BAGARD, César, sculptor and cabinet-maker from Nancy (1639–1709). Executed the panelling in the apartments of Mme de Villeparisis's father in the Hotel de Bouillon: **II** 415, and in Charlus's apartments: **III** 770.

BAKST, Léon, Russian painter and designer (1866–1924). His

decors for the *Ballets russes:* **II** 718; **IV** 193; **V** 497. Andrée disapproves of his decoration of the Marquis de Polignac's house: **VI** 59.

BALTHY, music-hall singer (1869–1925), whom Mme de Guermantes hesitates to cultivate, though finding her "adorable": **VI** 447.

BALZAC, Honoré de, French novelist (1799–1850). His "tigers" now "grooms": **I** 459. Disparaged by Mme de Villeparisis: **II** 394, 395, 412. Parodied by Saint-Loup: 418. "Adored" by the Duc de Guermantes, who attributes to him a novel by Dumas, *Les Mohicans de Paris:* **III** 673. Charlus "knows it all by heart": 673. Discussed by Charlus with Victurnien Surgis-le-Duc, who has the same Christian name as d'Esgrignon in *Le Cabinet des Antiques:* **IV** 132. Charlus reads him in the little train: 594–97. The Baron's favourite volumes of *La Comédie humaine:* 611. Discussed by Charlus and Brichot: 611–16. The Princesse de Cadignan: 617–19, 622–23. The Cambremers as Balzac characters: 668. Clothes of his heroines: **V** 34 (cf. **IV** 617–18). Retrospective unity of the *Comédie humaine:* 207–8. The "spoken newpaper" of Paris: 288. Construction of his novellas: 675. The marriage of Mlle d'Oloron and the young Cambremer a "marriage from the end of a Balzac novel": 893. Gilberte reads *La Fille aux yeux d'or:* **VI** 23. His genius, in spite of his vulgarity: 42.

BARBEDIENNE, Ferdinand, bronze founder (1810–92): **IV** 430; **V** 229–30.

BARBEY D'AUREVILLY, French novelist (1808–89): **II** 443; "key-phrases" in his work: **V** 506.

BARRÈRE, Camille, French diplomat, Ambassador in Rome from 1897 to 1924: **V** 863.

BARRÈS, Maurice, French writer (1862–1923): **II** 7. Swann revises his opinion of his work in the light of the Dreyfus Case, comparing him unfavourably to Clemenceau: **III** 799. His denunciation of parliamentary corruption: **V** 398. His views on art and the nation: **VI** 153–55, 280.

BARRY, Mme du, mistress and favourite of Louis XV (1743–93): **V** 378, 496–97, 755; **VI** 30.

BARTOLOMMEO, Fra, Florentine painter (1469–1517). Mme Blatin resembles his portrait of Savonarola: **II** 147.

BAUDELAIRE, Charles, French poet (1821–67). Allusion to his poem *L'Imprévu*—the epithet "delicious" applied to the sound of the trumpet: **I** 251. Allusions to poems about the sea: **II** 343, 372, 391. The antithesis of the kind of writer approved of by Mme de Villeparisis and her like: 394, 418, and of Mme de Guermantes's type of mind: **III** 689, 781 (cf. **V** 35). Mme de Cambremer quotes a line from *L'Albatros*: **IV** 289. Denounced by Brichot: 483. Quotation from *Les Fleurs du Mal* XLI ("like a dulcimer"): 521. Quoted by M on murder: **V** 511. Allusion to *La Lune offensée*—the "yellow and metallic" moon: 550–51. Saint-Loup quotes from *Le Balcon*: **VI** 101. M finds in his work reminiscences, transposed sensations, which for him are the foundation of art; quotations from *La Chevelure* and *Parfum exotique*: 335.

BEETHOVEN, Ludwig van (1770–1827). The Ninth Symphony one of Mme Verdurin's "supreme masterpieces": **I** 361. The Moonlight Sonata in the Bois: 403–4, 407. The late quartets: **II** 142–43 (cf. 451–52; **IV** 51, 482, 555–56). Allusion to one of the Razumovsky quartets by Mme de Guermantes: **III** 715. The Pastoral Symphony played in Charlus's house: 771. Charlus's ogling glances at Jupien likened to Beethoven's "questioning phrases": **IV** 7. Mme de Citri finds him "a bore": 119. Mme de Cambremer inhales the sea air like the prisoners in *Fidelio*: 293. Invoked by Brichot in connexion with Dechambre's death: 400–1. Charlus on the piano transcription of Quartet No. 15: 555–56. The "Bonn Master": **V** 416. His "terrible ravaged face": **VI** 314–15. The Kreutzer Sonata played at the Princesse de Guermantes's reception: 496.

BELLINI, Gentile, Venetian painter (1429–1507). Bloch resembles his portrait of the Sultan Mahomet II: **I** 134 (cf. 505). His painting of the portico of St Mark's: 234.

BELLINI, Giovanni, Venetian painter (c. 1430–1516). The "little band" play upon their vocal instruments "with all the application and ardour of Bellini's angel musicians": **II** 666. Vinteuil's music evokes "a grave and gentle Bellini seraph strumming a theorbo": **V** 347.

BENOIS, Alexander, Russian painter and ballet designer (1870–1960): **IV** 193; **V** 497.

BERGSON, Henri, French philosopher (1859–1941). On the effect of soporific drugs on the memory: **IV** 520–22.

BERLIOZ, Hector, French composer (1803–69). The *Childhood of Christ*: **IV** 688; as a writer: **V** 288.

BERNARD, Samuel, French financier (1651–1739): **II** 445; **III** 356.

BERNARDIN DE SAINT-PIERRE, French writer, author of *Paul et Virginie* (1737–1814). Cited by Charlus: **V** 369.

BERNHARDI, General Friedrich von, German military historian (1849–1930): **III** 144.

BERNHARDT, Sarah, French actress (1844–1923): **I** 102, 283; **IV** 639, 659; **V** 311; **VI** 197, 396.

BERRY, Duc de, grandson of Louis XIV (1686–1714). Cited by Saint-Simon as living his life among his lackeys: **VI** 203.

BERRY, Duc de, son of Charles X (1778–1820): **III** 735. Swann's grandmother said to have been his mistress, hence the legend (subscribed to by the Prince de Guermantes) that Swann was his natural grandson: 792; **IV** 92.

BEYLE, Henri. *See* Stendhal.

BIDOU, Henry, French writer, military commentator of *Le Journal des Débats* during World War I: **VI** 428–29.

BILLOT, General, French Minister of War between 1896 and 1898: **III** 402.

BING, Siegfried. Franco-German art collector, pioneer of Art Nouveau (1838–1905): **III** 756.

BISMARCK, Prince Otto von (1815–98). Rates Norpois's intelligence highly: **II** 9, 60 (cf. **III** 298, 303). Struck by the Prince de Borodino's resemblance to Napoleon III: **III** 168.

BIZET, Georges, French composer (1838–75). Disliked by Morel: **V** 384–85.

BLACAS, Duc de, Restoration politician (1771–1839). Contrasted by Mme de Villeparisis with Chateaubriand: **II** 411.

BLANCHE DE CASTILLE, wife of Louis VIII and mother of Saint Louis (1188–1252). Subject of one of Brichot's rodomontades: **I** 357.

BOIELDIEU, François-Adrien, French composer (1775–1834): **II** 427; **III** 672.

BOIGNE, Mme de (1781–1866). Friend of Sainte-Beuve, famous for her salon and for her *Memoirs*: **III** 569; **V** 769.

BOILEAU, Nicolas, French poet and critic (1636–1711): **II** 7; quotation from *L'Art poétique* in Gisèle's essay: 672.

BOISDEFFRE, General de, French Army Chief of Staff 1893–98: **III** 134, 326; **VI** 128.

BOISSIER, Gaston, antiquarian and permanent secretary of the *Académie Française* (1823–1908): **IV** 620; **V** 443.

BONAVENTURE, Saint (1221–74). Quoted by Charlus: **III** 764.

BORELLI, Vicomte de, society poet of the late 19th century: **I** 341; **III** 286, 337; **V** 109.

BORNIER, Vicomte Henri de, French writer, author of *La Fille de Roland* (1825–1901): **III** 570–72.

BORODIN, Alexander, Russian composer (1833–87). Allusion to the Polovtsian Dances from *Prince Igor*: **V** 315. Albertine plays *In the Steppes of Central Asia* on the pianola: 514.

BOSSUET, Jacques-Bénigne, French prelate, writer and orator (1627–1704): **I** 408; **V** 399; **VI** 247.

BOTHA, General (1862–1919). Boer leader, quoted by Prince Von on the subject of English ineptitude: **III** 722–23, 751–52, 776.

BOTTICELLI (Sandro di Mariano), Italian painter (c. 1445–1510). Odette's resemblance to the figure of Zipporah in *The Life of Moses* in the Sistine Chapel: **I** 314–18, 330, 337–38; and to the women in some of his other paintings, including the *Madonna with the Pomegranate*: 398; the *Primavera*, the *Vanna*, and the *Venus*: 445; the Virgin in the *Magnificat*: **II** 264.

BOUCHARD, Charles, French physician (1837–1915): **IV** 487, 614.

BOUCHER, François, French painter (1703–70): **II** 459; **III** 9; **V** 124, 263–64.

BOUFFE DE SAINT-BLAISE, French obstetrician: **IV** 488.

BOUFFLERS, Duc de, Marshal of France (1644–1711). One of Charlus's list of alleged 17th-century inverts: **V** 405.

BOULLE, André-Charles, French cabinet-maker (1642–1732). The Guermantes' "marvellous Boulle furniture": **III** 755.

BOURGOGNE, Duc de, grandson of Louis XIV and father of Louis XV (1682–1712): **III** 598; **IV** 477.

BOUTROUX, Emile, French philosopher (1845–1921). Quoted by the Norwegian philosopher: **IV** 447–48, 520–21.

BRESSANT, 19th-century French actor. Swann adopts his hair-style: **I** 17; **VI** 102.

BREUGHEL the Elder, Peter, Flemish painter (c. 1520–69). Soldiers in the streets of Doncières resemble Breughel peasants: **III** 124.

BRISSAC, Henri-Albert de Cossé, Duc de, brother-in-law of Saint-Simon (1644–99). One of Charlus's 17th-century inverts: **V** 405.

BROGLIE, Victor-Claude, Prince de (1757–94). Posthumous connexion with Mme de Staël: **VI** 408.

BROGLIE, Duc Victor de (son of the above), French statesman (1785–1870): **I** 26; **III** 259; his daughter marries the Comte d'Haussonville, 783; he himself had married the daughter of Mme de Staël: **VI** 408.

BROGLIE, Duc Albert de (son of the above), French statesman and historian (1821–1901). Author of *Le Secret du Roi*: **V** 731.

BROGLIE, Duchesse de, daughter of Mme de Staël and wife of Duc Victor de Broglie; her letters: **III** 373, 674, 679; her daughter and son-in-law: **VI** 408.

BRONZINO, Angiolo, Florentine painter (1503–63). Morel "so beautiful," according to Charlus, "he looks like a sort of Bronzino": **V** 284.

BRUANT, Aristide, Montmartre *chansonnier* (1851–1925): **V** 327.

BRUNETIÈRE, Ferdinand, French literary critic, Professor at the Sorbonne (1849–1906): **III** 338; **IV** 295; **VI** 295.

BRUNSWICK, Duke of, German prince and soldier (1624–1705). Another of Charlus's alleged inverts of the 17th century: **V** 405.

CAILLAUX, Joseph, French politican (1863–1944). His foreign policy "severely trounced" in the *Echo de Paris*: **IV** 205. His trial for treason: **VI** 135.

CALLOT, dress designer. Approved of by Elstir: **II** 655–56, and by Mme de Guermantes: **V** 47.

CAPET, Lucien, French violinist (1873–1928): **V** 383.

CAPUS, Alfred, French dramatist (1858–1922). Reference to his *La Châtelaine*: **IV** 662.

CARNOT, Lazare, mathematician and revolutionary, "the organiser of victory" (1753–1823): **III** 803.

CARNOT, Sadi, President of the French Republic from 1887 until his assassination in 1894: **II** 360; **III** 802–3.

CARO, Elme Marie, French philosopher (1826–87): **IV** 295.

CARPACCIO, Vittore, Venetian painter (1450–1525). Tender sweetness in pomp and joy expressed in certain of his paintings: **I** 251. San Giorgio degli Schiavoni: **II** 14 (cf. **V** 868–69). Elstir on his paintings of regattas on the Grand Canal: 652–54 (cf. **V** 497). "Speaking likenesses" of his friends or patrons: **III** 575. His reliquaries: 735. His courtesans: **V** 508. M and his mother admire his pictures in Venice; his *St Ursula* and *The Patriarch of Grado* (Albertine's Fortuny cloak): 876–77. War-time Paris as exotic as his Venice: **VI** 106.

CARRIÈRE, Eugène, French painter (1849–1906). Admired by Saint-Loup (portrait of his Aunt Oriane at Guermantes): **II** 457 (cf. **III** 755).

CARVALHO, Mlle, French opera singer (1827–95): **III** 638.

CASTELLANE, Mme de, Mme de Villeparisis's Aunt Cordelia (*née* Greffulhe). Admired by Chateaubriand, married Colonel (later Marshal) Comte Boniface de Castellane: **III** 372.

CAVAIGNAC, Jacques Godefroy, French politician, extreme anti-Dreyfusard, twice Minister of War during the Dreyfus Case (1853–1905): **III** 326.

CELLINI, Benvenuto, Italian sculptor and metalsmith (1500–71). A Saint-Euverte footman resembles his statue of an armed watchman: **I** 460; his *Perseus*: **II** 29.

CHABRIER, Emmanuel, French composer (1841–94). Quoted by Mme Verdurin: **V** 420.

CHAIX D'EST-ANGE, French lawyer and politician (1800–76): **III** 813.

CHAMBORD, Comte de, Pretender to the throne of France under the name Henri V (1820–83): **III** 389; **IV** 691; **V** 37 (allusion to Frohsdorf, where he lived in exile from 1841 until his death).

CHAMISSO, German writer (1781–1838), author of *Peter Schlemihls wundersame Geschichte*: **II** 482.

CHAPLIN, Charles Josuah, French society portrait-painter (1825–91): **VI** 45.

CHARCOT, Dr Jean Martin, French neurologist (1825–93): **III** 408; **IV** 378, 487, 663.

CHARDIN, Jean-Baptiste, French painter (1699–1779): **II** 309. Elstir and Chardin: **III** 574–75 (cf. **VI** 525); **V** 848.

CHARLES VI, King of France (1368–1422): **I** 81.

CHARLES X, King of France (1757–1836): **IV** 144, 691; **V** 42.

CHARTRES, Duc de, grandson of Louis-Philippe and younger brother of the Comte de Paris (1840–1910). Friend of Swann: **I** 441; **II** 125 (cf. **IV** 104, 106). His attitude to the Dreyfus Case: **III** 327–28. M. de Bréauté lunches with him: 590. Charlus his cousin: **IV** 691.

CHATEAUBRIAND, François-René de, French writer and statesman (1768–1848). His genius; "marvellous pages of Chateaubriand": **II** 72, 127. Bergotte's opinion of him: 177. Mme de Villeparisis's reminiscences of him: 394, 410–11. Quoted by M: 410–11. His ready-made speech on moonlight: 411 (cf. **V** 550). *Chez* Mme Récamier at L'Abbaye-aux-Bois: **IV** 373. Attacked by Brichot, defended by Charlus: 612–14. Local legends related in the *Mémoires d'Outre-tombe*: **V** 36. His writings "insufficiently confidential" (Sainte-Beuve quoted by Brichot): 442. The moon in Chateaubriand: 550. M. de Guermantes finds traces of his "antiquated prose" in M's *Figaro* article: 796. Reflexions on the *Mémoires d'Outre-tombe*; examples of involuntary memory such as will inspire M's own book: **VI** 54, 334–35.

CHÂTELET, Mme du, friend and patroness of Voltaire (1706–49): **IV** 373.

CHERBULIEZ, Victor, French novelist and Academician (1829–99). Norpois compares him favourably to Bergotte: **III** 299.

CHEVREUSE, Marie de Rohan, Duchesse de (1600–79), formerly married to the Connétable de Luynes: **III** 269.

CHEVREUSE, Charles-Honoré d'Albert, Duc de (1646–1712), son of the Duc de Luynes and grandson of the Connétable: **III** 597 (cf. 741).

CHOISEUL, Duchesse de. *See* Praslin.

CHOPIN, Frédéric, Polish composer (1810–49). A prelude and a polonaise played at Mme de Saint-Euverte's; Mme de Cambremer's delight in his "long, sinuous" phrases: I 471, 476 (cf. II 507). Once played in Mme de Villeparisis's father's château: II 392. Despised by Mme de Cambremer-Legrandin, and worshipped by her mother-in-law: IV 288–94, 301, 468, 509. Charlus missed hearing him play: 554–55.

CLAPISSON, Louis, French composer (1808–66): I 428.

CLAUDEL, Paul, French poet and diplomat (1868–1955): II 7, 475; III 444.

CLAUSEWITZ, General Karl von, German military theorist (1780–1831): VI 150.

CLEMENCEAU, Georges, French statesman (1841–1929): III 332, 402; praised by Swann: 798–99; his Dreyfusism unknown to the younger generation: VI 391.

CLÉMENTINE, Princesse, daughter of Louis-Philippe, mother of Ferdinand of Bulgaria by her marriage to the Duke of Saxe-Coburg-Gotha: III 328.

CLERMONT-TONNERRE, Duchesse Émilie de. Author of a book on country food: III 690; IV 557.

COMBES, Emile, French politician (1835–1921) who introduced anti-clerical laws when Prime Minister between 1902 and 1905: VI 149.

CONDÉ, Louis II, Prince de (known as "the Great") (1621–86): III 780; IV 483. Charlus and Brichot on his alleged homosexuality: V 405–6.

CONSTANTINE, King of Greece 1913–22, known familiarly as "Tino": VI 56, 117, 142, 224.

CONTI, Louis-Armand de Bourbon, Prince de, nephew of the Great Condé (1661–1685). His marriage to a bastard daughter of Louis XIV (Mlle de Blois) cited in connexion with the marriage of Mlle d'Oloron and the young Cambremer: V 905.

CONTI, François-Louis de Bourbon, Prince de, brother of the above (1664–1709). Echoes of Saint-Simon's portrait of him in Charlus's treatment of his menservants: III 758. An invert?: V 406. Saint-Simon praises his "marvellous intelligence," and in particular his knowledge of genealogy: VI 398.

COPPÉE, François, French poet (1842–1908): **III** 692.

COQUELIN, Constant, French actor (1841–1909): **I** 102. Seen in the Bois de Boulogne: **I** 595–96. His mulatto friend: **II** 149. M. Bloch senior's irony at his expense: 486. Plays beginners' roles in gala performances: **IV** 659. His view of Molière's *Le Misanthrope*: **VI** 429.

CORNEILLE, Pierre, French dramatist (1606–84). Quotation from *La Mort de Pompée*: **I** 35; **II** 485. Quotation from *Polyeucte*, attributed by Bloch to Voltaire: **II** 628. Françoise uses the word *ennui* in the Cornelian sense: **III** 15. Political dissertations in his tragedies: 260. His "intermittent, restrained" romanticism: 753.

CORNÉLY, Jean-Joseph, French journalist (1845–1907). Although a monarchist, campaigned for the revision of the Dreyfus trial: **III** 799.

COROT, Jean-Baptiste-Camille, French painter (1796–1875). Swann owns one of his paintings: **I** 28, 33.

COUTURE, Thomas, French painter (1815–79). Allusion to his picture *Les Romains de la Décadence*: **V** 382.

COYSEVOX, Antoine, French sculptor (1640–1720): **III** 264.

CRÉBILLON *fils*, licentious novelist (1707–77): **III** 371.

DAGNAN-BOUVERET, academic French painter (1852–1929) admired by Norpois: **III** 299.

DANTE (Dante Alighieri), Italian poet (1265–1321). Strainings and contortions of water-lilies in the Vivonne reminiscent of the "peculiar torments" of the damned in the *Inferno*: **I** 238. The Verdurins and their "little clan" the "nethermost circle of Dante" (Swann): 408. Reading-room of the Grand Hotel alternately the *Paradiso* and the *Inferno*: **II** 329; **III** 270; **VI** 158.

DARIUS, King of Persia: **II** 107, 483; **III** 254; **V** 53.

DARU, Pierre Bruno, Quartermaster-General of Napoleon's Grand Army and later Academician (1767–1829): **II** 395.

DARWIN, Charles, British scientist (1809–82): **III** 486, 709; **IV** 40–41; **VI** 133.

DAUDET, Alphonse, French writer (1840–97). Mention of *Tartarin de Tarascon*: **V** 257.

DAUDET, Léon, French journalist and novelist, son of the

above (1867–1942): **II** 8; **V** 398; **VI** 183. (*See* the dedication to *The Guermantes Way*.)

DAUDET, Mme Léon. *See* Pampille.

DAVID, Jacques-Louis, French painter (1748–1825): **VI** 295, 495.

DAVIOUD, Gabriel (1823–81), architect of the Trocadéro: **V** 217.

DEBUSSY, Claude, French composer (1862–1918). Mme de Cambremer's enthusiasm for *Pelléas*: **IV** 285–93 (cf. 300, 467, 481). Debussy and Wagner: 290–91. On the "wrong" side in the Dreyfus Case: 384. Morel plays Meyerbeer for Debussy: 481. M. de Chevregny finds *Pelléas* trivial: 662. The street-criers' cadences remind M of *Pelléas*: **V** 147.

DECAMPS, Alexandre-Gabriel, French orientalist painter (1803–60). Bloch as exotic-looking as a Jew in a Decamps painting: **III** 253. War-time Paris reminds Charlus of the Orient of Decamps: **VI** 173.

DECAZES, Duc, minister and favourite of Louis XVIII. Mme de Villeparisis's grandfather reluctant to invite him to a ball: **III** 256.

DEFFAND, Mme du (1697–1780). Famous for her salon: **II** 232.

DEGAS, Edgar, French painter (1834–1917). Mme de Cambremer's enthusiasm for him: **IV** 285. His admiration for Poussin: 287. Nissim Bernard's type of "dancer" still lacks a Degas: 328–30.

DELACROIX, Eugène, French painter (1798–1863). War-time Paris reminds Charlus of his oriental scenes: **VI** 173. Loathed by Mme de Guermantes: 495.

DELAROCHE, Paul, French painter (1797–1856). Reference by M. de Guermantes to his *Princes in the Tower*: **III** 686.

DELAUNAY, Comédie-Française actor (1826–1903): **I** 102; **VI** 102.

DELCASSÉ, Théophile, French statesman, architect of the Entente Cordiale (1852–1923): **V** 487.

DELTOUR, Nicolas-Félix, Inspector-General of Secondary Education, author of *Principles of Style and Composition* (1822–1904). Recommended by Andrée as an authority to quote in exams: **II** 675.

DERBY, Lord (Edward Henry Smith Stanley), British statesman (1826–93). Cited on the Irish question: **III** 238.

DÉROULÈDE, Paul, ultra-nationalist French politician and poet (1846–1914): **VI** 154.

DESCARTES, René, French philosopher (1596–1650): **V** 465 (cf. **II** 437).

DESCHANEL, Paul, French statesman (1855–1922): **II** 8; **III** 286; **IV** 197; **VI** 111.

DESHOULIÈRES, Mme, French poetess (1638–94): **III** 674.

DESJARDINS, Paul, French critic and philosopher (1859–1940). Quoted by Legrandin: **I** 167–8.

DETAILLE, Edouard, painter of military scenes (1848–1912): **III** 588; **IV** 47–48.

DETHOMAS, Maxime, French painter (1867–1929). His "superb studies" of Venice: **V** 848.

DIAGHILEV, Serge (1872–1929). Impresario of the Russian Ballet: **IV** 194, 420–21.

DIANE DE POITIERS, favourite of Henri II: **IV** 15.

DIANTI, Laura, Italian Renaissance beauty, second wife of Alfonso d'Este, Duke of Ferrara. Albertine's hair compared to hers during the game of "ferret" (Proust was evidently thinking of Titian's *Young Woman at her Toilet* in the Louvre, for which Laura was then thought to have been the sitter): **II** 683.

DIEULAFOY, Professor Georges, French physician (1839–1911). Called in to attend M's grandmother on her death-bed: **III** 459–60, 466–68.

DIEULAFOY, Mme Jeanne, French archaeologist (1851–1916): **II** 483.

DOSTOIEVSKY, Feodor, Russian novelist (1821–81). "Abominated" by Bergotte: **II** 177. The Dostoievsky side of Mme de Sévigné: 315 (cf. **V** 508–10). His novels "hoarded" by Albertine: **V** 432. His "new kind of beauty": 508–13. Charlus and Dostoievsky: **VI** 126–27. Rasputin's murder a Dostoievsky incident in real life: 126–27. His way of telling a story: 366.

DOUCET, Dress designer. Approved of by Elstir: **II** 655; and by Mme de Guermantes: **V** 47, 76.

DOUDAN, Ximenès, French writer, secretary to the Duc de Broglie (1800–72): **II** 418; **III** 372.

DOYLE, Sir Arthur Conan, British writer (1859–1930). "It's pure Sherlock Holmes": **V** 615.

DREYFUS, Alfred. *See under* Dreyfus Case *in* Index of Themes.

DRIANT, Colonel, right-wing politician and military commentator (under the pseudonym *Capitaine Danrit*) during the Dreyfus Case: **III** 332.

DRUMONT, Edouard, anti-semitic politician and journalist (1844–1917): **III** 393; **V** 46.

DU CAMP, Maxime, French man of letters (1822–94): **II** 7.

DUGUAY-TROUIN, Rene, French sailor (1673–1736). His statue in Balbec: **II** 330; **IV** 232.

DUMAS *fils*, Alexandre, French novelist and playwright (1802–70). Reference to his play *Les Danicheff*: **I** 304; and to *Francillon*: 363–64; **II** 157. Admired by Mme de Guermantes: **III** 679 (cf. **VI** 476).

DUMONT D'URVILLE, Jules, French navigator (1790–1842): **I** 488.

DUPANLOUP, Monseigneur, French prelate, orator and polemicist (1802–78): **III** 259; **IV** 162; **VI** 349.

EDWARD VII, King of England (1841–1910). Mme de Guermantes gives a reception for him and his wife: **III** 588, 619. Reviled by Prince Von, defended by Mme de Guermantes: 723–24. At Guermantes: **V** 794.

ELEANOR OF AQUITAINE, wife of Henry II Plantagenet, King of England (1122–1204): **II** 683.

ELIOT, George, English novelist (1819–80). Disliked by Bergotte: **II** 177. Andrée translates one of her novels: 714. Her name crops up in M's dreams: **V** 155.

ELISABETH, Madame, sister of Louis XVI: **III** 770.

ELISABETH, Empress of Austria, daughter of Maximilian-Joseph, Duke of Bavaria, sister of Sophie, Duchesse d'Alençon and Maria, Queen of Naples: **III** 252. Allusion to her death (in a riding accident) in 1898: 698. Referred to in connexion with the Queen of Naples' visit to the Verdurins' musical soirée: **V** 328, 414.

EMERSON, Ralph Waldo, American philosopher (1803–82). Subject of conversation at lunch with Rachel: **III** 377.

FEYDEAU, Georges, French playwright (1862–1921). Allusion to *La Dame de chez Maxim* ("*ce n'est pas mon père*"): **II** 478; **III** 19; Allusion to *L'Hôtel du libre échange*: **VI** 100.

FLAUBERT, Gustave, French novelist (1821–80): **II** 157. "Bourgeois through and through," according to Mme de Guermantes: **III** 643. His letters superior to his books, according to Mme d'Arpajon, who forgets his name: 670–71. Phrases of Flaubert in Montesquiou: **IV** 291. Morel and *L'Education sentimentale*: **V** 210. It was not affection for the bourgeoisie that made him choose the themes of *Madame Bovary* and *L'Education sentimentale*: **VI** 280.

FLORIAN, Jean-Pierre Claris de (1755–94). Author of one of the two fables which M de Cambremer knows: **IV** 427, 441.

FOCH, Marshal (1851–1929), Generalissimo of the Allied armies in 1918: **VI** 90.

FOIX, Catherine de, Queen of Navarre (1470–1517): **III** 568.

FONTANES, Louis, Marquis de, French writer and politician, friend of Chateaubriand (1757–1821): **II** 395; **IV** 587.

FORTUNY, Venetian dress designer. Elstir speaks of him to M and Albertine: **II** 653. Mme de Guermantes wears his dresses: **V** 37, 48 (cf. 497). Albertine covets them; how they evoke the Venice of Carpaccio and Titian: 497–500. M plans to buy one for Albertine: 237, and orders six: 531, 537–38. Albertine's Fortuny dressing-gown and two coats: 499–500, 546. Reawakens M's nostalgia for Venice: 555. M sees the original of one of Albertine's Fortuny coats in a Carpaccio in the Accademia: 877.

FOUCHÉ, Joseph (1759–1820), Minister of Police under Napoleon and Louis XVIII: **III** 711.

FOULD, Achille, French politician (1844–1924), Minister of Finance under Napoleon III: **III** 171.

FRAGONARD, French painter (1732–1806): **V** 124.

FRANCE, Anatole, French writer (1844–1924). Quoted by Legrandin on the subject of the Normandy coast: **I** 183. A star of Mme Verdurin's salon?: **V** 314. Sylvestre Bonnard cited by Brichot: 444. "Our sweet master of delicious scepticism" (Brichot): **VI** 149–50.

FRANCK, César, Franco-Belgian composer (1822–90): **IV** 119,

479. M asks Morel to play some Franck, causing acute pain to Mme de Cambremer-Legrandin: 480; **V** 860.

FRANÇOIS I, King of France (1494–1547): **I** 1; **III** 640.

FRANZ-JOSEF, Emperor of Austria-Hungary (1830–1916). His "cousinly relations" with Charlus: **III** 389. Charlus's thoughts about him during the war: **VI** 103, 139–40.

FREDERICK THE GREAT, King of Prussia (1712–86): **III** 144.

FREGOLI, Leopoldo, Italian mime (1867–1936): **VI** 375.

FROMENTIN, Eugène, French painter and writer (1820–76): **III** 445; **VI** 27, 173.

GABRIEL, Jacques-Ange, architect of the palaces in the Place de la Concorde and of the Petit Trianon (1698–1782): **II** 83–84, 471.

GALLAND, Antoine, translator of the *Arabian Nights* (1646–1715): **IV** 318.

GALLÉ, Emile, artist in glass (1846–1904): **II** 522; **III** 537.

GALLIFET, General Marquis de, Minister of War 1899–1901: **III** 166; **V** 263; **VI** 55, 90.

GALLI-MARIÉ, French opera singer (1840–1905): **IV** 486.

GAMBETTA, Léon, French statesman (1838–82). His funeral: **I** 304. Mme de Guermantes admires his letters: **III** 671.

GARNIER, Robert, French playwright (1544–90), author of *Les Juives*: **II** 673.

GARROS, Roland, French aviator (1888–1918): **V** 879.

GASQ-DESFOSSÉS, author of text-books for *baccalauréat* candidates published between 1886 and 1909: **II** 675.

GAUTIER, Théophile, French poet (1811–82). Allusion to his novel *Le Capitaine Fracasse*: **IV** 455; **VI** 27.

GENLIS, Mme de, woman of letters; governess to the future Louis-Philippe (1746–1830): **V** 511.

GEOFFRIN, Mme (1699–1777). Famous for her salon: **III** 569.

GÉRAULT-RICHARD, Socialist Deputy and Dreyfusard activist: **III** 330.

GÉRÔME, Jean-Léon, French painter and sculptor (1824–1904): **II** 109.

GHIRLANDAIO, Florentine painter (1449–98): Swann identifies M. de Palancy's nose in one of his pictures: **I** 315.

GIOLITTI, Giovanni, Italian statesman (1842–1928). His name

invoked by Norpois in conversation with Prince Foggi in Venice: **V** 861–62. Norpois calls Caillaux "the Giolitti of France": **VI** 135.

GIORGIONE, Italian painter (c. 1478–1510): **I** 556–58; **III** 584. Mme Putbus's maid "wildly Giorgionesque": **IV** 129, 206; **V** 516–17.

GIOTTO, Italian painter (c. 1266–1337). The Vices and Virtues in the Arena Chapel in Padua; Swann gives M photographs of them; the pregnant housemaid resembles the figure of "Charity": **I** 110–13, 169–72. M. de Palancy and his monocle remind Swann of the figure of "Injustice": 465. M identifies Florence with the genius of Giotto: 554. The procession of the "little band" recalls Giotto: **II** 528. Albertine playing diabolo resembles his "Idolatry": 637. The allegorical figures appear in M's sleep: **III** 192. M and his mother visit the Arena Chapel: **V** 878–79.

GLEYRE, Charles, Swiss painter (1806–74): **I** 206.

GLUCK, Christoph Willibald von, German composer (1714–87): **III** 644; **IV** 694. Quotation from his *Armide* attributed to Rameau: **V** 148.

GOETHE, Johann Wolfgang von, German poet (1749–1832): **III** 346; **V** 819; **VI** 129, 320.

GOGOL, Nikolai, Russian writer (1809–52): **V** 509.

GONCOURT, the brothers Edmond (1822–96) and Jules (1830–70), novelists, critics and diarists. M reads a newly published volume of their Journal: **VI** 26–27; pastiche of a passage therefrom: 27–38; M's reflections on it: 38–43, 130, 238, 281.

GONDI, Paul de. *See* Retz, Cardinal de.

GORRINGE, General. Commander of the Relief Force that failed to rescue Kut-el-Amara in 1916: **VI** 430.

GOT, French actor (1822–1901): **I** 102.

GOYA, Francisco de, Spanish painter (1746–1828): **I** 462.

GOZZOLI, Benozzo, Florentine painter (1420–97). M's father in his night-clothes resembles Abraham in a Gozzoli picture: **I** 49. Prominent members of the Medici family depicted in *The Procession of the Magi*: **II** 148; **V** 83.

GRANDMOUGIN, Charles, French playwright and librettist (1850–1930): **III** 619.

GRANIER, Jeanne, French actress (1852–1939): **III** 678.

GRECO, El, Spanish painter (c. 1541–1614). Admired by M's father: **II** 382. Charlus resembles a Grand Inquisitor by El Greco: **V** 272. Paris during an air-raid compared to *The Burial of Count Orgaz*: **VI** 100.

GREGORY THE GREAT, Pope. Paris street-criers echo Gregorian chant: **V** 162, 176.

GRÉVILLE, Henry (Alice Fleury), French romantic novelist (1842–1902): **II** 233.

GRÉVY, Jules, President of the Republic 1879–87: **I** 304–6; **V** 906.

GRIBELIN, Registrar in the Bureau des Renseignements; testified against Dreyfus: **III** 324.

GRIGNAN, Mme de, daughter of Mme de Sévigné (1646–1705): **II** 467; **V** 11–12.

GUILBERT, Yvette, music-hall singer (1868–1944): **IV** 663.

GUILLAUMIN, Art Nouveau furniture-maker: **II** 460.

GUISE, Henri, Duc de (1550–88): **II** 167, 333; **V** 894.

GUIZOT, François, French statesman and historian (1787–1874): **III** 389.

GUTENBERG, Johannes, 15th-century inventor of printing by movable type: **III** 178; **VI** 63.

GUYS, Constantin, French graphic artist (1802–92): **I** 595.

HAAS, Charles. Friend of Proust. Wears the same hat as Swann: **III** 794. Identified with Swann: **V** 263.

HADRIAN, Roman emperor: **IV** 541.

HAHN, Reynaldo, French composer, friend of Proust (1875–1947). Allusion to Pierre Loti's *L'Île du Rêve*, for which Hahn wrote the music: **VI** 115.

HALÉVY, Fromental, French composer (1799–1862). M's grandfather hums passages from his opera *La Juive*: **I** 125; "Rachel when from the Lord": **II** 207; another quotation from *La Juive*: **IV** 331.

HALÉVY, Ludovic (nephew of the above), novelist, playwright and librettist, collaborator of Meilhac (1834–1908). Admired by Mme de Guermantes: **I** 475; **III** 278, 678. Quotation from *La Belle Hélène*: **V** 909.

HALS, Frans, Dutch painter (c. 1580–1666). Allusion to one

of his masterpieces, *The Women Regents of the Haarlem Almshouse*: **I** 361. Discussed at the Guermantes dinner-party: **III** 717–21, 745, 752.

HANDEL, George Frideric, German composer (1685–1759): **V** 284.

HANSKA, Comtesse. Balzac's "l'Etrangére," whom he married in 1850: **IV** 614.

HARCOURT, Alphonse-Henri-Charles de Lorraine-Elbeuf, Prince d' (1648–79). His familiarity with his lackeys deplored by Saint-Simon: **VI** 203.

HARDY, Thomas, English novelist and poet (1840–1928). The "stonemason's geometry" in his novels (cf. Vinteuil's "key-phrases"): **V** 507.

HARUN AL-RASHID, Caliph of Baghdad 786–809: **VI** 173.

HAUSSONVILLE, Louis-Bernard, Comte d' (1770–1840). Denies knowing Necker, father of Mme de Staël; subsequent connexion of his family with Mme de Staël through the Broglies: **VI** 408 (cf. **III** 783–84; **VI** 55).

HÉBERT, Ernest, academic French painter (1817–1908) admired by Norpois: **III** 299.

HEGEL, Georg Wilhelm Friedrich, German philosopher (1770–1831): **VI** 90.

HELLEU, Paul, French painter and engraver (1859–1927) (said to have been one of the models for Elstir): **IV** 459.

HELVÉTIUS, Claude-Adrien, one of the *philosophes* of the French Enlightenment (1715–71): **V** 315.

HENRI IV, King of France 1589–1610: **III** 43, 689; **V** 895. Allusion to his father, Antoine de Bourbon: **III** 744.

HENRI V, *See* Chambord, Comte de.

HENRY VIII, King of England 1509–47. Allusion to his encounter with François I on the Field of Cloth of Gold: **III** 640 (cf. **I** 567).

HENRY, Colonel, one of the principal actors in the Dreyfus Case whose suicide on 31 August 1898 was its most dramatic episode: **III** 315, 325–26; **IV** 147; **VI** 128.

HÉRÉDIA, José-Maria de, French poet (1842–1905): **II** 447.

HERVEY DE SAINT-DENIS, Marquis d', French sinologist and man of letters (1823–92): **IV** 159.

HERVIEU, Paul, French dramatist (1857–1915). An outspoken Dreyfusist: **V** 313.

HINDENBURG, Field-Marshal von, Chief of the German General Staff 1916–18: **VI** 101–3, 428–29.

HIRSCH, Baron, German Jewish banker and philanthropist (1831–96): **IV** 92.

HOGARTH, William, English painter and engraver (1697–1764). Albertine's English "Miss" resembles a portrait of Judge Jeffreys by Hogarth: **II** 557.

HOHENFELSEN, Countess, morganatic wife of the Russian Grand Duke Paul: **VI** 234.

HOMER, Greek epic poet: **III** 259, 346, 446, 571, 684. Bloch's archaic Greek names for Homer's gods, borrowed from Leconte de Lisle: **IV** 319 (cf. **I** 124–25; **II** 444–46, 478). References to the *Odyssey*: **VI** 370, 381.

HOOCH, Pieter de, Dutch painter (1630–81). Vinteuil's "little phrase" recalls effects in his interiors: **I** 308.

HORACE, Roman poet. Reasons for the pleasure of reading his odes: **II** 460–61. His sycophancy to Maecenas, according to Brichot: **IV** 478. Brichot recites to himself a Horatian ode: **V** 443.

HOYOS, Count, Austrian Ambassador in Paris: **III** 670; **V** 372.

HUGO, Victor, French poet, novelist and dramatist (1802–85): **I** 108; **II** 7, 144. Disparaged by Mme de Villeparisis; M quotes to her a line from *Booz endormi*: 394, 395, 410–12, 418. His dramatic works compared unfavourably to Racine's by Charlus; Saint-Loup finds this "a bit thick": 469. The Comtesse de Noailles's verse compared to his: **III** 137–38. Quotation from *Ultima verba* (*Les Châtiments*): 607. Discussed at the Guermantes' dinner-table: 674–75. Mme d'Arpajon's opinion of him; reference to *Lorsque l'enfant paraît* . . . : 674 (cf. **IV** 68). Mme de Guermantes' opinion of him; quotes lines from *Les Contemplations* and *Les Feuilles d'automne*: 679–80; quotes *Booz endormi*: 726 (cf. 279, 680, 752). The earlier and the later Hugo; the former supplies "thoughts" (*pensées*) instead of food for thought: 752–53. M re-reads him; Françoise's footman has purloined his copy of *Les Feuilles d'automne*: 754. Charlus quotes *Booz endormi*: 770. Allusion to *Tristesse d'Olympio*: **IV** 611, 615–16. Charlus quotes from *Les Chants du Crépuscule*: 730. *La*

*Légende des Siècles* an example of the retrospective unity imposed on their works by great writers of the 19th century: **V** 207 (cf. 351). Reference to *Hernani* (Doña Sol): 382. Surrounds himself with disciples in his old age: 386. The moon in his work; M recites *Booz endormi* to Albertine: 551. A line from *Les Contemplations* quoted: **VI** 39. Rachel to recite some of his poems at the Princesse de Guermantes's reception: 444. Mme de Guermantes quotes a line from *Les Contemplations*: 467. Allusion to a line from *Tristesse d'Olympio* ("fils mystérieux"): 504. A line from *À Villequier* quoted: 516. Quotation from *Le Tombeau de Théophile Gautier* ("la porte funéraire"): 520.

HULST, Monseigneur d', founder and Rector of the Institut Catholique de Paris (1841–96): **V** 441.

HUXELLES, Nicolas du Blé, Marquis d', Maréchal de France (1652–1730). Charlus impersonates him, after the portrait of him in Saint-Simon's *Memoirs*: **IV** 499. Charlus quotes the Saint-Simon portrait in the context of his dissertation on 17th-century inverts: **V** 407.

HUXLEY, Aldous, English writer (1894–1964). Mentioned parenthetically in connexion with T. H. Huxley (*see below*): **IV** 50.

HUXLEY, Thomas Henry, English scientist (1825–95). Anecdote concerning one of his patients: **IV** 50.

HUYSUM, Jan van, Dutch flower painter (1682–1749): **III** 286.

IBSEN, Henrik, Norwegian dramatist (1828–1906). Disliked by Bergotte: **II** 177. Subject of conversation at lunch with Rachel: **III** 377. Presents the manuscripts of three of his plays to Mme Timoléon d'Amoncourt, who offers two of them to Mme de Guermantes: **IV** 89.

INDY, Vincent d', French composer (1851–1931): **IV** 384, 444.

INGRES, Dominique, French painter (1780–1867). Shrinking of the "unbridgeable gulf" between him and Manet: **III** 575 (cf. 716: Mme de Guermantes's view). M. de Guermantes cites *La Source* as against Elstir: 686. His orientalism: **VI** 173. Vicissitudes of Mme de Guermantes's attitude to his work: 495.

IRVING, Sir Henry, English actor (1838–1905). Françoise's "stage effects" compared to his: **III** 492.

LABICHE, Eugène, French playwright (1814–88). Swann, in his tirade against the Verdurins, suggests that the "little clan" are like characters in a Labiche comedy: **I** 406. Saint-Loup's intellectually snobbish attitude to his father suggests the possible attitude of a son of Labiche to his: **II** 427. Names that might have come out of Labiche: **IV** 99. Drinks no longer to be found except in his plays: 643. M. d'Argencourt in old age like a character from a Regnard farce rewritten by Labiche: **VI** 339.

LABORI, Maître Fernand, counsel for Dreyfus and Zola. His oratorical style: **III** 529. Frequents Mme Verdurin's salon during her Dreyfusard period: **IV** 199 (cf. 384; **V** 315–16).

LA BRUYÈRE, Jean de, French writer and moralist, author of *Les Caractères* (1645–96). Quotation from *Du coeur*: **II** 274, 462. Quotation by Charlus from *Du coeur*: 468. Françoise uses the verb *plaindre* in the same sense as La Bruyère: **III** 25. Loose quotation from *De la mode*: **V** 270. Quotation from *Du coeur*: **VI** 297.

LACHELIER, Jules, French philosopher (1832–1918): **IV** 438.

LACLOS, Choderlos de, French writer, author of *Les Liaisons dangereuses* (1741–1803). The "ultra-respectable" author of the "most appallingly perverse" book: **V** 511 (cf. **VI** 280).

LA FAYETTE, Mme de, French writer, author of *La Princesse de Clèves* (1634–92): **II** 670; letter from Mme de Sévigné about her death: **III** 408–9; **IV** 32; **VI** 35.

LAFENESTRE, Georges, French poet and critic (1837–1919): **III** 720.

LA FONTAINE, Jean de, French poet (1621–95). Allusion by Charlus to *The Two Friends* and *The Two Pigeons*: **II** 467. Reference to *The Miller and his Son*: **III** 737. M. de Cambremer knows only one of his fables: **IV** 427; this is *The Man and the Snake*: 440; but he also seems to know *The Camel and the Floating Sticks*: 493 (cf. **V** 312). Quoted by Brichot: **V** 443. Rachel recites his *Two Pigeons*: **VI** 459–62.

LAMARTINE, Alphonse de, French poet and statesman (1790–1869). Recited poems in Mme de Villeparisis's father's château: **II** 392. A subject for the literary ladies of the aristocracy: **III** 263: Occasionally quoted by Mme de Guermantes: 279. Sneered at by Bloch: 328; **IV** 319.

LAMBALLE, Princesse de, friend of Marie-Antoinette, victim of the September massacres (1792): **III** 770.

LANDRU, famous French murderer: **V** 269.

LANNES, Marshal, general in the Napoleonic armies (1769–1809): **III** 146.

LA PÉROUSE, French navigator (1741–88): **I** 488.

LA ROCHEFOUCAULD, François VI, Duc de, Prince de Marcillac, author of the *Maxims* (1613–80). Legrandin finds a resemblance to him in Mme de Villeparisis: **III** 269. Brichot refers to him as "that Boulangist de Marcillac": **IV** 372. An apocryphal maxim quoted by Charlus: **V** 407–8.

LA ROCHEFOUCAULD, François VII, Duc de, Master of the Royal Hounds, son of the above. Saint-Simon appalled to find him hobnobbing with his lackeys: **VI** 203.

LA TOUR, Quentin de, French portraitist (1704–88). Albertine resembles one of his pastels: **V** 470. His works destroyed by the revolutionaries: **VI** 280.

LAVOISIER, Antoine, French scientist (1743–94). His name invoked by Swann apropos of Vinteuil's creative genius: **I** 499.

LAWRENCE, Sir Thomas, English painter (1769–1830). Referred to in the Goncourt pastiche: **VI** 32.

LAWRENCE O'TOOLE, Saint, Archbishop and patron of Dublin (c. 1127–1180). Referred to in one of Brichot's etymological dissertations: **IV** 392.

LE BATTEUX, Abbé, French grammarian (1713–80): **V** 302.

LEBOURG, Art Nouveau furniture-maker: **II** 460.

LEBRUN, Pierre-Antoine, French poet (1785–1873): **II** 395; **III** 372; **VI** 408.

LECONTE DE LISLE, French poet (1818–94). Revered by Bloch ("my beloved master, old Leconte"): **I** 124 (cf. **II** 447, 475, 659). Quoted on the sea: **II** 391, 659. His authentic Greek spelling, copied by Bloch: **IV** 319. The moon in his poetry: **V** 551. (Passages inspired by his translation of Homer: **IV** 319; and by Hesiod's *Orphic Hymns*: **IV** 324.)

LEGOUVÉ, Ernest, Permanent Secretary of the *Académie Française* (1807–1903): **II** 7.

LEIBNIZ, Gottfried Wilhelm, German philosopher (1646–1716): **III** 356. The salons of the Faubourg Saint-Germain likened to his monads: 656. Not modern enough for Mme de Cambremer: **IV** 437–38.

LELOIR, Maurice, 19th-century *Salon* painter. Mme Cottard compares him to Machard (q.v.): **I** 534.

LEMAIRE, Gaston, French composer (1854–1928): **III** 619.

LEMAÎTRE, Frédérick, French actor (1800–1876). Françoise's "stage effects" compared to his: **III** 492.↑

LENIN, Russian revolutionary and statesman (1870–1924): **VI** 147.

LE NÔTRE, André, French garden designer (1613–1700). Charlus speaks of a house with a park laid out by Le Nôtre which has been destroyed by the Israels: **II** 470–71.

LEO X, Pope (1513–21): **V** 395.

LEONARDO DA VINCI (1452–1519). His *Last Supper*: **I** 54, 234. Quoted on painting (*cosa mentale*): **II** 99. Gilberte's plaits a work of art more precious than a sheet of flowers drawn by Leonardo: 103. Dark glaze of shadows among rocks as beautiful as Leonardo's: 689. Albertine's face hook-nosed as in one of his caricatures: **V** 97.

LEROI-BEAULIEU, Anatole, economist and member of the *Académie des Sciences morales et politiques* (1842–1912). Advises M's father to stand for election to the *Institut*: **III** 199. Presses M's father's candidacy with Norpois: 302–3. His "stern Assyrian profile": 303. Norpois seeks his support on behalf of Prince Von: 355.

LE SIDANER, French painter (1862–1939). Favourite artist of the Cambremers' lawyer friend from Paris: **IV** 278, 284–86, 299.

LESPINASSE, Mlle de (1732–76). Famous for her salon, which rivalled that of her former patron Mme du Deffand (q.v.): **II** 232.

LEVERRIER, Urbain, French astronomer (1811–77): **V** 398.

LISZT, Franz, Hungarian composer (1811–86). His "St Francis preaching to the Birds" played at Mme de Saint-Euverte's: **I** 466; Oriane has come up from Guermantes specially to hear it: 484. Once played at Mme de Villeparisis's father's château: **II** 392. Mme de Villeparisis and "Alix" both claim acquaintance with him: **III** 266.

LLOYD GEORGE, David, British statesman (1863–1944): **VI** 134.

LOMÉNIE, Louis de, French man of letters, frequenter of Mme Récamier's salon (1815–78): **II** 63, 417.

LONGUEVILLE, Duchesse de, sister of the Great Condé: **III** 744, 780.

LOTI, Pierre, French novelist (1850–1923): **III** 286. Mention of *Pêcheur d'Islande*: **V** 257. Allusion to his *L'Île du Rêve*: **VI** 115.

LOUBET, Emile, President of the Republic during the revision of the Dreyfus Case: **IV** 132; **V** 315; **VI** 401.

LOUIS VI, the Fat, King of France (1081–1137): **II** 416; **III** 717.

LOUIS IX (Saint Louis), King of France (1214–70): **I** 82–83, 212; **III** 725; **IV** 690.

LOUIS XI, King of France (1423–83): **III** 788, 793.

LOUIS XIII, King of France (1601–43): **III** 610, 755, 779; **IV** 690; **V** 310.

LOUIS XIV, King of France (1638–1715). Aunt Léonie's routine resembles the "mechanics" of life at his court: **I** 165. Allusion to Racine's fall from grace: **II** 188. Incidental allusions: 204, 476; **III** 391, 571, 580. The Duc de Guermantes's rules of social behaviour compared to those of Louis XIV; anecdotes from Saint-Simon: 597–98. Further allusions: 719, 728, 740, 779, 782; **IV** 63, 78, 234. Charlus's views on him; compared to the Kaiser: 471–72. Charlus's great-great-grandmother at the Court of Versailles: 477–78 (cf. 666; **VI** 407). Further incidental allusions: **V** 405, 496, 905. His ignorance of genealogy, according to Saint-Simon: **VI** 398.

LOUIS XV, King of France (1710–74): **III** 719, 734; **IV** 111; **V** 671, 746–47, 755; **VI** 29.

LOUIS XVI, King of France (1754–93): **III** 120; **IV** 691.

LOUIS XVII, uncrowned king of France (1785–?1795): **VI** 466.

LOUIS XVIII, King of France (1755–1824): **III** 255–56. Shows his faculty for forgetting the past by appointing Fouché (q.v.): 711.

LOUIS THE GERMANIC, son of Louis I ("the Pious") and grandson of Charlemagne (804–76): **I** 83; **III** 347.

LOUIS-PHILIPPE, King of France (1773–1850): **I** 26, 144. His architectural "excretions": 415. His conversational talent: **II** 394. The "pinchbeck age" of Louis-Philippe: **III** 719. Genealogical connexions: 735–36; **IV** 111. The Citizen King: **V** 392.

LOUIS BONAPARTE, Prince, nephew of the Princesse Mathilde. Officer in the Russian Imperial Guard: **II** 160.

LOUIS, Baron, Minister of Finance under Louis XVIII and Louis-Philippe (1755–1837). Quoted by Norpois: **II** 45 (cf. **VI** 134).

LOZÉ, French diplomat, Ambassador in Vienna 1893–7: **V** 856.

LUCINGE, Mme de, illegitimate daughter of the Duc de Berry: **III** 735 (cf. **V** 893).

LUINI, Bernardino, Milanese painter (c. 1475-c. 1533). Swann once resembled one of the three kings in his *Adoration of the Magi*: **II** 201. Swann compares a woman to a Luini portrait: **V** 516.

LULLY, Jean-Baptiste, Franco-Italian composer (1632–87). His "shrewd avarice and great pomp," according to Saint-Simon: **I** 439.

LUTHER, Martin, German religious reformer (1483–1546): **III** 347.

MACHARD, Jules-Louis, French painter (1839–1900). Mme Cottard speaks to Swann of one of his portraits which "the whole of Paris is rushing to see": **I** 533–34.

MACK, General, Austrian commander against Napoleon. His defeat at Ulm: **III** 149.

MACMAHON, Marshal (1808–93), President of the Republic 1873–79. Mme de Villeparisis related to him: **I** 26 (cf. **II** 360).

MADAME. *See* Orléans, Charlotte-Elisabeth of Bavaria, Duchesse d'.

MAECENAS, patron of Virgil and Horace. Cited by Brichot; Charlus describes him as "the Verdurin of antiquity": **IV** 478, 481.

MAES, Nicolaes, Dutch painter (1632–93). A painting attributed to him by the Mauritshuis in reality a Vermeer, in Swann's view [subsequently confirmed by the experts]: **I** 502.

MAETERLINCK, Maurice, Belgian poet and playwright (1862–1949). His *Les Sept Princesses* discussed at Mme de Villeparisis's and ridiculed by Mme de Guermantes: **III** 308–9. Mme de Guermantes and M. d'Argencourt discuss him: 336–37. Mme de Guermantes comes to admire him, in deference to fashion: **V** 35 (cf. **VI** 477). The "vague sadness" of Maeterlinck; quotations from *Pelléas*: 148.

MAHOMET II, Sultan of Turkey 1451–81. Bloch resembles his portrait by Gentile Bellini: **I** 134. Stabbed his wife to death: 505.

MAILLOL, Aristide, French sculptor (1861–1944): **VI** 91.

MAINTENON, Mme de (1635–1719), mistress, confidante and finally morganatic wife of Louis XIV: **I** 439; **II** 389.

MALHERBE, François de, French poet (1555–1628): **IV** 51.

MALLARMÉ, Stéphane, French poet (1842–98). "Alarm and exhaustion" induced in M's grandmother by his later verse: **III** 674. Sneered at by Brichot: **IV** 483. Mocked by Meilhac: **V** 35. Poems of his to be engraved on Albertine's yacht and Rolls-Royce: 614.

MANET, Edouard, French painter (1832–83). Elstir's portrait of Odette contemporary with Manet's portraits: **II** 604. His *Olympia* once regarded as a "horror" by society people, but now accepted: **III** 575. Elstir once modelled himself on him: 685. Mme de Guermantes's view of his *Olympia*—"just like an Ingres": 716. Admired by Mme de Cambremer, though she prefers Monet: **IV** 285.

MANGIN, General Charles (1866–1925). A genius, according to Saint-Loup at Doncières: **III** 145. Cited by Saint-Loup again during the Great War: **VI** 103.

MANSARD, Jules Hardouin, French architect (1646–1708): **III** 587.

MANTEGNA, Andrea, Italian painter (c. 1430–1506). A Saint-Euverte footman resembles a soldier in one of his paintings: **I** 460. The roof of the Gare Saint-Lazare recalls one of his menacing skies: **II** 303. Isabella d'Este and Mantegna: **III** 719–20. The Trocadéro reminds Albertine of the background of his *St Sebastian*: **V** 218. Vinteuil's septet conjures up "some scarlet-clad Mantegna archangel sounding a trumpet": 347. The Marquis de

Beausergent in old age resembles a portrait study by Mantegna: **VI** 364.

MARDRUS, Dr Joseph-Charles-Victor, translator of the unexpurgated *Arabian Nights*, published 1898–1904: **IV** 318–19.

MARGUERITE D'AUTRICHE, daughter of the Emperor Maximilian and wife of Philibert le Beau of Savoy (1480–1530). Her tomb at Brou: **I** 420.

MARIE-AMÉLIE, Queen, wife of Louis-Philippe. Once said to Mme de Villeparisis, "You are just like a daughter to me": **III** 250. Her portrait: 251, 519, 736. M's grandmother shocked by her behaviour: **V** 895.

MARIE-ANTOINETTE, Queen of France (1755–93): **II** 470–71. Charlus has her hats: **III** 770; **VI** 141.

MARIVAUX, Pierre de Chamberlain de, French playwright and novelist (1688–1763): **III** 356. Characters known by their titles alone: **IV** 380.

MARY STUART, Queen of Scotland (1542–87): **II** 470.

MASCAGNI, Pietro, Italian composer (1863–1945). Reference to *Cavalleria Rusticana*, admired by Albertine: **II** 632, 635.

MASPÉRO, Gaston, French Egyptologist (1846–1916): **II** 68; **V** 441.

MASSÉ, Victor, French composer (1822–84). Odette's delight at the prospect of his operetta *La Reine Topaze*: **I** 348. The Verdurins take her to his *Une Nuit de Cléopâtre*; Swann's diatribe against him: 411–13.

MASSÉNA, Marshal, Napoleonic general (1758–1817): **III** 171.

MASSENET, Jules, French composer (1842–1912). Compared with Debussy: **IV** 291. Albertine sings his *Poème d'amour*: **V** 3–4. Quotations from *Manon*: 609–10.

MATERNA, Mme, Austrian singer (1847–1918): **I** 32.

MATHILDE, Princesse, daughter of Jérôme Bonaparte (1820–1904). Entertained by the Princesse des Laumes: **I** 468, 473. M meets her in the Bois de Boulogne with the Swanns: **II** 156–60. Not at all royal in her ways: 380–81. Her relations with the Faubourg Saint-Germain: **III** 642–44. Mme de Guermantes invites her with the Duc d'Aumale: 710.

MAUBANT, French actor (1821–1902): **I** 32. Seen by M emerging from the Théâtre-Français: 102.

MAULÉVRIER, Marquis de, French Ambassador in Madrid 1720–23. Swann quotes Saint-Simon's description of him: **I** 34.

MAUREL, Victor, French opera-singer (1848–1923): **III** 775.

MAURRAS, Charles, right-wing writer and publicist (1868–1952): **II** 8. His novel *Aimée de Coigny*: **VI** 156–57. Reference to his newspaper *L'Action Française*: 183.

MAYOL, Félix, music hall singer (1876–1941). Morel sings his *Viens Poupoule*: **IV** 632. Discussed by Charlus and the bus conductor: 735.

MEILHAC, Henri, French playwright and librettist (1831–97), collaborator of Ludovic Halévy (q.v.). Admired by Mme de Guermantes: **I** 475 (cf. **III** 278, 678–79; **VI** 472). Imagined dialogue between the Princesse de Guermantes and her guests in her box at the Opéra suggests a scene from *Le Mari de la Débutante*: **III** 48. His Cleopatra: **IV** 387. Mallarmé mocked by him: **V** 35. Quotation from *La Belle Hélène*: 909.

MÉLINE, Jules, French statesman (1838–1925). Prime Minister during the Dreyfus Case; friend of M's father: **III** 200.

MEMLING, Jan, Flemish painter (c. 1433–94). Allusion to his St Ursula reliquary in Bruges: **III** 735.

MENANDER, Greek poet and dramatist: **II** 485.

MENDELSSOHN, Felix, German composer (1809–47). Charlus refers to him as "the virtuoso of Berlin": **IV** 556; **V** 860.

MENDÈS, Catulle, French poet (1841–1909). Referred to familiarly by Bloch's sister: **II** 482.

MENIER, Gaston, Chocolate manufacturer. Allusion (by Bloch) to his powerful and luxurious yacht: **II** 446.

MERCIER, General, Minister of War at the outset of the Dreyfus Case: **III** 653.

MÉRIMÉE, Prosper, French writer (1803–70). His style and influence: **I** 475 (cf. **III** 48, 277–78, 678–79). Admired by Mme de Villeparisis: **II** 395. Mme de Guermantes has his type of mind: **III** 278 (cf. **I** 475; **III** 781); her favourite writer, together with Meilhac and Halévy: 678–79. He and Baudelaire despise one another: 781 (cf. **V** 35). His travels in Spain: **V** 441.

MERLET, Gustave, French literary academic (1829–91): **II** 675.

MÉTRA, Olivier, French composer and conductor (1830–89).

His *Valse des Roses* one of Odette's favourite pieces: **I** 335, 341, 349.

METTERNICH, Princess Pauline von (1836–1921), wife of Metternich's son Richard, for several years Austrian Ambassador in Paris. Introduces Bergotte to Norpois in Vienna: **II** 64–65. A passionate Wagnerian: **III** 775; **V** 365.

MEULEN, van der, Flemish painter (1634–94): **III** 527.

MEURICE, Paul, writer and friend of Victor Hugo: **V** 386.

MEYER, Arthur, French journalist, ultra-Nationalist and anti-Dreyfusard (1844–1924): **VI** 103, 236.

MEYERBEER, Giacomo, Franco-German composer (1791–1864). Morel plays him instead of Debussy: **IV** 481.

MICHELANGELO Buonarotti, Italian painter, sculptor, architect and poet (1475–1564). Globes of mistletoe like the sun and moon in his *Creation*: **I** 601–2. Françoise "the Michelangelo of our kitchen"; her search for the best cuts of meat compared to his care in choosing marble for the monument to Julius II: **II** 21, 39. Albertine's face in bed at Balbec, as M approaches to kiss it, seems to rotate like a Michelangelo figure: 701. Vinteuil's creative fury compared to Michelangelo's in the Sistine Chapel: **V** 339. Brichot acquits him of homosexuality: 395. "Grimacing immobility" of a portrait study: **VI** 364.

MICHELET, Jules, French historian (1798–1874). Charlus quotes him on the Guermantes clan: **III** 388. Reference to his aesthetic approach to natural history: **IV** 36. Personifies the 19th century; his greatest beauties in his prefaces: **V** 207.

MIGNARD, Pierre, French portrait painter (1612–95). His portrait of Charlus's uncles: **III** 770. The Duc de Guermantes's "Mignard": 795–97.

MILL, John Stuart, British philosopher and economist (1806–73): **IV** 438.

MILLET, Jean-François, French painter (1814–75): **IV** 438.

MISTINGUETT, popular singer and dancer (1875–1956). Mme de Guermantes hesitates to make overtures to her, though finding her "adorable": **VI** 447.

MOLIÈRE, French dramatist (1622–73): **I** 36. Norpois avoids his word *cocu*: **II** 52 (as does Cottard: **IV** 493–94). Meeting between M's grandmother and Mme de Villeparisis compared to a scene in Molière: 371–72. Reference to *Le Misanthrope*—exam question on Alceste and Philinte: 640. Quoted by M's grandmother: **III** 423–25. Conversation between Charlus and the Duke of Sidonia recalls a Molière comedy: **IV** 52. Allusion to *Le Médecin malgré lui*: 56. Charlus as Scapin: 130. The only writer's name known to Céleste Albaret: 333–34. Reference to *Le Malade imaginaire*: 393. Reference to *L'Avare*: 434. Allusion to *La Comtesse d'Escarbagnas*: 556. Charlus's imitation swordsmanship reminiscent of Molière: 539–40. An invert, according to Charlus: **V** 405. Differing views of *Le Misanthrope*: **VI** 429.

MOLTKE, General von, Prussian Chief of Staff during the Franco-Prussian war: **VI** 77.

MONALDESCHI, Jean de, Italian nobleman assassinated at Fontainebleau in 1657 at the instigation of Queen Christina of Sweden: **IV** 93.

MONET, Claude, French painter (1840–1926). Admired by Mme de Cambremer: **IV** 283–85. Mentioned: **V** 411; **VI** 117.

MONSEIGNEUR, son of Louis XIV (1661–1711): **III** 597–98.

MONSIEUR (Philippe, Duc d'Orléans), brother of Louis XIV (1640–1701). Anecdotes from Saint-Simon: **III** 597; **IV** 78, 477, 666. Called "Monsieur" because he was such an "old woman" (Charlus): 691. His homosexuality: **V** 405–7.

MONTALAMBERT, Charles, Comte de, French politician and publicist (1810–70). Frequented Mme de Villeparisis's salon: **III** 259.

MONTESPAN, Mme de, mistress of Louis XIV: **IV** 234.

MONTESQUIEU, Charles de Secondat, Baron de, French writer and political philosopher (1689–1755). Anticipates Flaubert: **IV** 291. Brichot refers to him as "Monsieur le Président Secondat de Montesquieu": 372.

MONTMORENCY, Duchesse de, *née* des Ursins (1601–66). Mme de Villeparisis has inherited a portrait of her: **III** 252, 265–66, 270, 298.

MORAND, Paul, French writer (1888–1976). Allusion to his novel *Clarisse*: **VI** 152.

MOREAU, Gustave, French painter (1826–98). The idea of a "kept woman" suggests to Swann some fantasy by Moreau: **I** 380. Allusion to his portrayal of Jupiter: **II** 382. Some "stunning pictures" by him at Guermantes, according to Saint-Loup: 457. Mme de Guermantes talks about his *Death and the Young Man*: **III** 713–14.

MORGHEN, Raphael, Italian engraver (1758–1833). His engraving of Leonardo's *Last Supper*: **I** 54.

MOTTEVILLE, Mme de, memorialist (c. 1621–1689): **III** 743.

MOUNET-SULLY, French tragedian (1841–1916): **IV** 639; **V** 275. His approach to Molière's *Le Misanthrope*: **VI** 429.

MOUSSORGSKY, Modest, Russian composer (1839–81). The street criers' cadences remind M of *Boris Godunov*: **V** 147–48.

MOZART, Wolfgang Amadeus (1756–91). Reference to his clarinet quintet: **I** 474. "Mischievous unexpectedness" with which the piano takes over in his concertos: **II** 36.

MURAT, Princesse, Queen of Naples: **II** 480; **III** 711; **V** 365–66. (To be distinguished from Maria-Sophia-Amelia, wife of Francis II, last king of the two Sicilies—*see* Naples, Queen of.)

MUSSET, Alfred de, French poet and dramatist (1810–57). M's grandmother's choice of Musset's poems as a present for her grandson disapproved of by his father: **I** 52–53. Despised by Bloch, apart from one "absolutely meaningless line": 124. Arrives "dead drunk" to dine with the Princesse Mathilde: **II** 158. Mme de Villeparisis's poor opinion of him: 411–12. The Musset admired by the likes of Bloch: 475. A line of his attributed by Oriane to Emile Augier: **III** 308. Critical opinions of him: 645. Mme d'Arpajon quotes a line from his *La Nuit d'Octobre* thinking it to be by Hugo: 679–80. Quoted in Joseph Périgot's letter: 777. His notion of "hope in God": **V** 792. Quotation by Charlus from *La Nuit d'Octobre*: 808–9 (cf. 323; **VI** 321, 324). Rachel to recite *Le Souvenir* at the Princesse de Guermantes's reception: **VI** 433.

NANTES, Mlle de, daughter of Louis XIV and Mme de Montespan; married the grandson of the Great Condé: **V** 905.

NAPLES, Queen of. Maria-Sophia-Amelia, daughter of Maximilian-Joseph, Duke of Bavaria. Her reaction to her sister's death discussed at the Guermantes' dinner-table: **III** 699–700. Her graciousness to Mme Verdurin: **V** 328–29, 375, 419–20; forgets her fan: 364–66; Charlus intends to present Morel to her: 402–3, 414; returns to fetch her fan, and takes Charlus under her protection: 429–33. Accused of espionage by Mme Verdurin during the war: **VI** 109.

NAPOLEON Bonaparte (1769–1821): **II** 157–59. His strategy and tactics discussed by Saint-Loup at Doncières: **III** 142–51. The Prince de Borodino's possible descent from him and points of resemblance with him: 167–72. His place in Balzac: 736. Napoleonic titles: 774, 813. Discussion of whether he chewed tobacco or not, in the Goncourt pastiche: **VI** 37–38. His strategy and tactics discussed by Saint-Loup in 1914: 101–2. Compared by Charlus to the Kaiser: 157.

NAPOLEON III (1808–73). Appears in Swann's dream: **I** 538–40. Mentioned: **II** 9, 157. Captain de Borodino's relationship and resemblance to him: **III** 167–72. The Duc de Guermantes objects to his handing out of titles: 812–13. Features in Norpois's article on the eve of the Franco-Prussian war: **V** 865–66.

NATTIER, Jean-Marc, French portrait-painter (1658–1766). Jacquet's portrait of Mme de Surgis compared to his *Duchesse de Châteauroux*: **IV** 145; **V** 796.

NÉGRIER, General de (1839–1913). Discussed at Doncières: **III** 166 (cf. **VI** 90).

NEMOURS, Duc de, son of Louis-Philippe (1814–96). Mme de Villeparisis tells an anecdote about him: **II** 415.

NERO, Roman emperor. Quoted by Brichot: **IV** 400. Cited by M's mother as being probably "highly-strung": **V** 135.

NERVAL, Gérard de, French poet (1808–55). Illustrated editions of his books remind M of a "personal share" in the Water Company: **II** 35. His *Sylvie*, "one of the masterpieces of French literature," figures a sensation of the same order as the taste of the madeleine: **VI** 335.

NICHOLAS II, Tsar (1868–1918). Visits Paris: **II** 159. Françoise ashamed of France's treatment of him: **III** 450. Charlus speaks of him: **VI** 142, 158.

NIETZSCHE, Friedrich Wilhelm, German philosopher (1844–1900): **II** 4. Admired by Saint-Loup: 426. His attitude to friendship and his relationship to Wagner: **III** 540 (cf. **V** 205). Quoted in Saint-Loup's letters to M during the war: **VI** 93. Charlus ridicules Cottard's denigration of him: 129.

NIJINSKY, Vaslav, Russian ballet dancer (1890–1950): **IV** 193.

NOAILLES, Anna de, French poetess (1876–1933). Alluded to as "an Eastern princess," said to write poetry "quite as fine as Hugo's or Vigny's": **III** 137. A "poet of genius": **VI** 44.

NOAILLES, Duc de, friend of Sainte-Beuve: **V** 769–70.

NOAILLES, Duchesse de, *née* Champlâtreux, mother-in-law of Anna de Noailles. Sainte-Beuve's poem about her as a little girl: **VI** 44.

OFFENBACH, Jacques, Franco-German composer (1819–80): **II** 361–2. Quotation from his *Les Brigands*: **IV** 331. Quotation from *La Belle Hélène*: **V** 909.

OHNET, Georges, French novelist and playwright. References to his *Matîre de Forges* and *Serge Panine*: **I** 364–65.

OLLIVIER, Emile, French statesman (1825–1913): **III** 320.

ORLÉANS, Louis d'. Assassinated by Jean sans Peur in 1407: **IV** 691.

ORLÉANS, Duc d', the Regent (1674–1723): **IV** 691. Married one of Louis XIV's bastards, Mlle de Blois, daughter of Mme de Montespan: **V** 905.

ORLÉANS, Duc d', eldest son of Louis-Philippe (1810–42): **III** 519, 735–36.

ORLÉANS, Philippe, Duc d', son of the Comte de Paris and grandson of the above (1869–1926): **II** 125, 491.

ORLÉANS, Charlotte-Elisabeth of Bavaria, Duchesse d', "the Princess Palatine" (1652–1722). Wife of Monsieur, and known as "Madame." Her correspondence: **II** 157; **III** 743 (cf. **IV** 62–63; **V** 407). Her masculine ways. **IV** 62–63. The "Wife of an Auntie": **V** 407.

ORLÉANS, Duchesse d', mother of Louis-Philippe. Betrayed by Mme de Genlis: **V** 511.

ORLÉANS, Prince Henri d', eldest son of the Duc de Chartres (1867–1901). Publicly embraces Esterhazy after the Zola trial: **III** 327–28.

OSSIAN, legendary Scottish bard impersonated by James Macpherson. A "mediocre mystifier": **III** 572.

OVID, Roman poet: **II** 457. "That holy terror" (Brichot): **IV** 614. Quoted by Cottard: 643; **VI** 150.

PADEREWSKI, Ignace, Polish pianist and prime minister (1860–1941). Dechambre compared to him: **IV** 400, 407.

PAILLERON, Edouard, French playwright (1834–99). Allusion to Oriane's "Pailleronism": **III** 679.

PALATINE, Princess. *See* Orléans, Charlotte-Elisabeth of Bavaria, Duchesse d'.

PALÉOLOGUE, Maurice, French diplomat. Ambassador in St Petersburg during the 1914–18 war. Veiled allusion: **IV** 62. "Notoriously inadequate" in Serbia, according to Norpois: **V** 856. Pestered with telegrams from the Duchesse de Guermantes after the Russian Revolution: **VI** 234.

PALESTRINA, Italian composer (1525–94): **IV** 485; **V** 176; **VI** 496.

PALISSY, Bernard, French ceramic artist and scientist (c. 1510–90). Platter of seafood at Doncières resembles one of his ceramic dishes: **III** 152.

PAMPILLE (Mme Léon Daudet); published cooking recipes in *L'Action Française*. Her "delightful" books referred to by Mme de Guermantes: **III** 688. Her "incomparable recipe" (M. Verdurin): **IV** 407. "That true poet": **V** 38.

PAQUIN, dress designer. Approved of—"sometimes"—by Elstir: **II** 655. Mme de Guermantes recommends him: **V** 47.

PARIS, Comte de, eldest grandson of Louis-Philippe (1838–94). Swann "a particular friend" of his: **I** 19, 33, 578. Referred to as Philippe VII: 579. Favourably impressed by Odette, according to Norpois: **II** 59, 75, 125, 127.

PARNY, Evariste-Désiré de, French poet (1753–1814): **III** 617.

PASCAL, Blaise, French philosopher and scientist (1623–62): **I** 33; **III** 20: Quoted by Saint-Loup: 130. Charlus and the Duc de Guermantes recall their tutor's lessons on him: **IV** 159. "We can make discoveries no less precious than in Pascal's *Pensées* in an advertisement for soap": **V** 732. Gulf between M and Gilberte as imaginary as Pascal's: **VI** 8. Quoted by Brichot (*le moi est haïssable*): 150.

PASQUIER (*le chancelier*), French statesman (1767–1862); **I** 26, **II** 395. Friend of Mme de Boigne: **V** 769.

PATY DE CLAM, Colonel du. One of the principal actors in the Dreyfus Case. Norpois's views on him: **III** 325–26, 330, 334. Quotes lines from an adversary, the Dreyfusard poet Pierre Quillard, at the Zola trial: **VI** 93. His "disguises and strategies": 128.

PAU, General (1848–1932): **III** 166. Quoted by Charlus on the declaration of war in 1914: "I have been waiting forty years for this day. It is the most glorious day of my life": **VI** 157.

PAUL, Saint. The "unforgivable sin": **I** 92.

PÉLADAN, Sâr, French writer and occultist (1858–1918): **III** 308.

PÉRIER, Jean-Alexis, French singer, creator of the role of Pelléas: **IV** 662.

PERRONNEAU, Jean-Baptiste, French painter (1715–83). Admired by Elstir: **III** 574.

PÉTAIN, General (1856–1951): **VI** 90.

PETRONIUS, Roman writer: **V** 377.

PHIDIAS, classical Greek sculptor. The Duc de Guermantes likened to the statue of Olympian Zeus said to have been cast in gold: **III** 385. Inscribed the name of the athlete he loved on the ring of his Olympian Zeus: **V** 442. Anglo-Saxon soldiers "like living statues by Phidias" to Charlus: **VI** 126.

PHILIBERT LE BEAU (1480–1504), Duke of Savoy. His initials intertwined with those of Margaret of Austria in the church of Brou: **I** 420.

PHILIPPE VI, de Valois, King of France (1293–1350): **III** 597.

PHILIPPE LE HARDI, King of France (1245–85): **III** 716.

PHILIPPE-ÉGALITÉ, Duc d'Orléans (1747–93): **III** 803.

PICCINNI, Niccoló, Neapolitan composer (1728–1800). His *Iphigenia* compared to Gluck's: **III** 644.

PICQUART, Georges-Marie, Colonel, later General and Minister of War (1854–1914). One of the principal actors in the Dreyfus Case: **III** 139. Discussed by Norpois and Bloch: 315–16, 323–25. Minister of War: 402 (cf. **VI** 156). Bloch's appeal on his behalf: **IV** 152, 154. Frequents Mme Verdurin's salon: 198–99 (cf. 384; **V** 315); **VI** 156.

PINDAR, Greek poet: **III** 259.

PIRANESI, Giambattista, Italian architect and engraver (1720–78): **I** 90.

PISANELLO, Antonio, Italian painter and medallist (c. 1380–1456). Patterns of foam in Balbec bay etched with the delicacy of a Pisanello: **II** 522. His flower drawings compared unfavourably with Mme de Villeparisis's by Legrandin: **III** 286. Queen Victoria's profile on English pennies might have been drawn by him: **VI** 48.

PIUS IX, Pope (1792–1878). Françoise buys a photograph of him: **II** 80, 360.

PLANTÉ, Francis, French pianist (1839–1934): **I** 265; **IV** 400.

PLATO, Greek philosopher: **I** 408. Françoise distorts Mme de Villeparisis's words as Plato distorts Socrates': **II** 376. Françoise's mistakes due, like the fables in which Plato believed, to a false conception of the world and to preconceived ideas: **III** 490. Plato and homosexuality: **V** 270 (cf. 290; **IV** 479; **VI** 170). Allusion to the *Symposium*: 376. Brichot in Charlus's company feels like Plato with Aspasia: 443. Analogous ideas may differ according to whether they have been expounded by Xenophon or Plato: **VI** 81.

PLAUTUS, Roman comedy writer: **II** 485.

PLINY the Younger, Roman writer: **III** 610.

PLOTINUS, 3rd-century philosopher: **IV** 521.

POE, Edgar Allan, American writer (1809–49): **II** 418.

POINCARÉ, Henri, French mathematician (1854–1912): **III** 149.

POINCARÉ, Raymond, President of the Republic 1913–20: **VI** 86, 159.

POLIGNAC, Prince Edmond de. Rents the Prince of X's castle for the Bayreuth festival: **III** 736. Figures in Tissot's picture of the Rue Royale club: **V** 262–63.

POMPADOUR, Mme de (1721–64), mistress of Louis XV: **III** 780; **V** 746–47; **VI** 46.

PONSARD, François, French poet and dramatist (1814–67). Allusion to his comedy *Le Lion amoureux*: **III** 644.

POREL, Director of the Odéon 1884–91: **IV** 449, 454.

PORPHYRY, neo-Platonist philosopher: **IV** 521.

POTAIN Dr, French physician (1825–1901). Cottard compared to him: **I** 265 (cf. **IV** 378). Despairs of Vinteuil's life: 302.

POURTALÈS, Comtesse Edmond de, Second Empire beauty and hostess. The Prince de Borodino dines with her: **III** 172. Her ignorance of the Dreyfus Case: 549. "Mélanie Pourtalès arranged things far better" (Oriane): **IV** 97.

POUSSIN, Nicolas, French painter (1594–1665). Gilberte's name, floating through the air, compared to a little cloud in a Poussin landscape: **I** 561. To destroy a park by Le Nôtre as bad as slashing a Poussin painting: **II** 470–71. Discussed by M. and Mme de Cambremer; "an old hack" in her view, but Degas's admiration for him gives her pause: **IV** 284–87, 291.

PRADON, Nicolas, French poet and playwright, rival of Racine (1632–98): **III** 644.

PRASLIN, Duchesse de (Choiseul), daughter of General Sebastiani, murdered by her husband in 1847. Friend of Mme de Villeparisis's mother: **II** 415–16; **III** 735.

PRAXITELES, classical Greek sculptor: **V** 270.

PROUDHON, Pierre-Joseph, French philosopher (1809–65). Admired by Saint-Loup: **II** 426. M's grandmother gives Saint-Loup a collection of autograph letters by him: 608 (cf. **III** 90).

PUCCINI, Giacomo, Italian composer (1858–1924): **V** 284.

PUGET, Loïsa, French poetess (1810–89): **IV** 110.

QUILLARD, Pierre, French poet, Hellenist and journalist (1864–1912). Violent Dreyfusard; his encounter at the Zola trial with Colonel du Paty de Clam, who quotes from his symbolist play *La Fille aux mains coupées*: **VI** 93.

RABELAIS, François, French writer (c. 1494–1553). Quoted by Norpois: **III** 332. Quoted by Brichot: **IV** 612; who prefers him to Balzac: 614.

RACINE, Jean, French dramatist (1639–99). Bloch quotes a famous line from *Phèdre*, which has "the supreme merit of meaning absolutely nothing": **I** 124. Bergotte's essay on him: 137. Quotation from *Athalie*: 150. Indirect quotation from *Phèdre*: 204. Gilberte gives M Bergotte's monograph: 572. M reads a passage on the old myths from which Racine drew his inspiration: 582. Quotation from *Phèdre*: **II** 14, 17–18. Phrases from Bergotte: 18. Berma in *Phèdre*: 20–29. M discusses *Phèdre* with

Bergotte: 183–86. Racine and Louis XIV: 187–88. Quotation from *Esther*: 362. Charlus on Racine: 469. Allusion to a line from *Athalie*: 519. Gisèle's essay, "Letter from Sophocles to Racine": 670–75 (cf. **III** 482; **V** 513). Berma in *Phèdre* again: **III** 58–61. Quotation from *Esther*: 517. Quotation from *Andromaque*: 607. M. de Vaugoubert's behaviour at the Princesse de Guermantes's recalls passages from *Esther*: **IV** 87–88. Pages at the Grand Hotel suggest the chorus from *Athalie*: 235–36 (cf. 524–25). Nissim Bernard's young waiter likened to an Israelite in *Athalie*: 327–29. *Esther* quoted by Charlus: 524–25. Quotation from *Esther*; Albertine compares M to Assuerus: **V** 13–14 (cf. 532). "Albertine-Esther": 123. Another scene from *Esther*: 151–52. Charlus's transition from violence to Christian meekness compared to the change of tone between *Andromaque* and *Esther*: 434. More quotations from *Esther*: 555. M sees the declaration scene in *Phèdre* as a sort of prophecy of the amorous episodes in his own life: 617–19. Quotation from *Phèdre*: 873. Phèdre as a Jansenist: **VI** 321. Berma identified with Phèdre: 456.

RAMBUTEAU, Claude-Philibert Berthelot, Baron de, French politician and administrator, *préfet* of the Seine in 1833; introduced public urinals with individual compartments: **V** 249; **VI** 86–87.

RAMEAU, Jean-Philippe, French composer (1683–1764). Quotation from Gluck's *Armide* attributed to him: **V** 148. Albertine plays him on the pianola: 514.

RAPHAEL, Italian painter (1483–1520): **II** 459; **V** 208. Silhouettes of trees in Paris reminiscent of those in the backgrounds to his paintings: **VI** 66. Goncourt elevates Watteau above him: 130.

RASPAIL, François, French politician and scientist (1794–1878). Françoise buys a photograph of him: **II** 80, 360.

RASPUTIN, Gregory (c. 1871–1917). His murder a Dostoievsky incident in real life: **VI** 126.

RAUDNITZ. Dress-designer. Mme Cottard swears by him: **II** 238.

RAVEL, Maurice, French composer (1875–1937): **VI** 496.

RÉCAMIER, Mme: **III** 569. Her salon at l'Abbaye-aux-Bois: **IV** 373, 612 731; **VI** 46, 495.

REDFERN, Dress-designer: **II** 238.

REDON, Odilon. French painter (1840–1916). His "subtlety of expression" (Elstir): **II** 575.

REGENT, The. *See* Orléans, Duc d'.

REGNARD, Jean-François, French playwright (1655–1709): **VI** 339.

RÉGNIER, Mathurin, French satirist poet (1573–1613). Quoted by the president at Balbec: **II** 384.

REICHENBERG, Suzanne, French actress (1853–1924), for thirty years the principal *ingénue* at the Comédie-Française. The Duc de Guermantes persuades her to recite for Edward VII: **III** 589. Mme Molé's attempt to emulate both the Duchesse and the Princesse de Guermantes like someone trying to be at once Reichenberg and Sarah Bernhardt: **V** 311.

REINACH, Joseph, French writer and politician (1856–1921). Dreyfusard activist: **III** 326, 334. His achievement in the Dreyfus Case "the most astonishing victory for rational politics the world has ever seen": 402. Frequents Mme Verdurin's salon: **IV** 198–99 (cf. 384). Mentioned: **V** 313; **VI** 325, 401.

RÉJANE, French actress (1856–1920): **III** 678; **VI** 454.

REMBRANDT, Dutch painter (1606–69). Odette's "Rembrandt hat": **I** 340–41. His *Night Watch* "the supreme masterpiece" in Mme Verdurin's view: 361. The Swann dining-room as dark as "an Asiatic temple painted by Rembrandt": **II** 107. Interior of the Grand Hotel seen from the lift reminiscent of a Rembrandt: 519. A little curio shop in Doncières at night like a composition by Rembrandt: **III** 122–23. Charlus's two Rembrandts: 771. The "gentle gravity" of certain of his portraits: **IV** 107. His Jewish scenes admired by Charlus: 690. His portraits of women compared to Dostoievsky: **V** 508. The fantastic world of the *Night Watch*: 511–12. Unique rays that still reach us from the world of Rembrandt: **VI** 299. The "terrible ravaged face" of the aged Rembrandt: 314–15.

RENAN, Ernest, French historian (1823–92): **II** 107; **V** 352, 441.

RENOIR, Auguste, French painter (1841–1919). It took a great deal of time for him to be hailed as a great artist: **III** 445. His painting of the publisher Charpentier at home: **VI** 45, 116.

RETZ, Paul de Gondi, Cardinal de (1613–79). "That *struggle for lifer* de Gondi" (Brichot): **IV** 372.

RIBOT, Alexandre, French statesman (1842–1923): **II** 8; **III** 589.

RIGAUD, Hyacinthe, French portrait-painter (1659–1743): **III** 795.

RIMBAUD, Arthur, French poet (1854–91): **II** 418; **V** 819.

RIMSKY-KORSAKOV, Nicolai, Russian composer (1844–1908). Reference to *Sheherazade*: **V** 315.

RISLER, Edouard, French pianist (1873–1929): **IV** 400.

RISTORI, Mme, Italian tragic actress (1821–1906). Recites *chez* "Alix": **III** 264, 270.

RIZZO, Antonio, Italian architect and sculptor (1430–98). Swann's coachman Rémi resembles his bust of the Doge Loredan: **I** 315, 324.

ROBERT, Hubert, French painter (1735–1808). M's grandmother gives him a photograph of the "fountains of Saint-Cloud" after Hubert Robert: **I** 54. His art stimulated by moonlight on Combray gardens: 159. The Hubert Robert fountain in the Prince de Guermantes's garden: **IV** 75–77; Mme d'Arpajon inundated by it: 77; Charlus's opinion of it: 79.

RODIN, Auguste, French sculptor (1840–1917): **VI** 91.

ROETTIERS, Joseph, 18th-century jeweller: **V** 496–97.

ROLLAND, Romain, French writer and pacifist (1866–1944). Quoted by Saint-Loup in his letters to M during the war: **VI** 93.

RONSARD, Pierre de, French poet (1524–85): **IV** 408–9. Line from one of his *Sonnets pour Hélène*: 738; **V** 590.

ROQUES, General, Minister of War in 1916: **VI** 327.

ROSTAND, Edmond, French poet and playwright (1868–1918), author of *Cyrano de Bergerac* and *L'*Aiglon: **III** 286; **IV** 639.

ROTHSCHILDS, The. Sir Rufus Israels' family compared to them: **II** 124. The Prince de Guermantes allows a wing of his château to be burnt down rather than ask the help of his Rothschild neighbours: **III** 797. The Duchesse de Guermantes entertains them: **V** 42. Baron de Rothschild: **II** 477. Baronne Alphonse de Rothschild: **III** 399; Bloch's gaffe when introduced to her by Mme de Villeparisis: **III** 693; constantly *chez* Oriane:

**IV** 92; a rose named after her: 551; at the La Trémoïlles': **V** 45. Edmond de Rothschild: **III** 585.

ROUHER, Eugène, Minister of Napoleon III (1814–84): **III** 171.

ROUJON, Henry, French Academician (1853–1914), author of a book (*Au milieu des hommes*) which Mme Verdurin offers to Charlus: **IV** 604.

ROUSSEAU, Jean-Baptiste, French poet (1671–1741): **III** 328.

ROUSSEAU, Jean-Jacques, French-Swiss writer and philosopher (1712–78). M's father disapproves of his being given a volume of Rousseau as a birthday present: **I** 52–53.

ROUSSEAU, Théodore, French painter (1812–67): **V** 383.

ROUVIER, Maurice, French politician (1842–1911), Prime Minister during the Moroccan crisis between France and Germany in 1905: **V** 779.

RUBENS, Peter Paul, Flemish painter (1577–1640). Swann's Rubens: **II** 155. M. Bloch's bogus Rubens: 487. Made goddesses out of women he knew: 724.

RUBINSTEIN, Anton, Russian pianist (1829–94): **I** 265. M's grandmother has a weakness for his discords and wrong notes: **II** 428.

RUSKIN, John, English writer and artist (1819–1900). Quotations (unattributed) from *Stones of Venice*: **I** 556–59. Quoted by M's mother: **II** 308. "A tedious old proser," according to Bloch, who calls him Lord John Ruskin: 436. M's work on Ruskin: **V** 874. Jupien's allusion to M's translation of *Sesame and Lilies*: **VI** 206.

SABRAN, Mme de. One of the mistresses of the Regent: **III** 735.

SAGAN, Prince de. Greets Odette in the Bois: **II** 297. His dashing style: **III** 689. His hats: 794. His last appearence in society: **IV** 162. References to the Princesse de Sagan: **I** 265–66; **III** 276, 328–29. Friend of Swann: **VI** 397.

SAINT-LÉGER LÉGER, Alexis, French poet and diplomat, better known under his pseudonym Saint-John Perse (1887–1975). "Is it poetry, or just riddles?" asks Céleste: **IV** 336.

SAINT-MÉGRIN. Favourite or "mignon" of Henri III: **VI** 141.

SAINT-SAENS, Camille, French composer (1835–1921). Allusion to his *Samson et Dalila* ("Israel, break thy chains"): **I** 125.

SAINT-SIMON, Duc de, author of the *Memoirs* (1675–1755). Quoted by Swann on Maulévrier: **I** 33–35. The "mechanics" of life at Versailles: 162 (cf. 439). One of Swann's favourite authors: 439. Françoise's class attitudes compared to Saint-Simon's: **II** 88. His portrait of Villars quoted to illustrate the unforeseeableness of the language of great writers: 170. Cited in illustration of the superiority of creation to observation: 475–76. Françoise uses his language: **III** 84. Mme de Villeparisis has a portrait of him: 399. The Duc de Guermantes's punctilious courtesy as a host reminiscent of an ancestor of his described by Saint-Simon; quoted on the ethos of Louis XIV's court and its similarity to the behaviour of the Duc de Guermantes: 597–98. "Admirable but fearsome": 628. Quoted by Charlus on the validity of a Guermantes title: **IV** 471. Charlus's Saint-Simonian tableaux-vivants; the Maréchal d'Huxelles: 499. The caste system of Combray as rigid as Saint-Simon's: 579. Mme de Guermantes's style of reminiscence recalls Saint-Simon: **V** 38. His euphemism for homosexuality: 280. "That old pest" (Brichot): 405. Quoted on the Maréchal d'Huxelles: 407 (cf. **IV** 499). Albertine enjoys talking about him to M: 714, 750. His portrait of the Marquis d'Allemans: 794–95. Quoted on the subject of noblemen who (like Charlus) associate with their inferiors: **VI** 206. Quoted on Louis XIV's ignorance of genealogy: 398; and the intelligence of the Prince de Conti: 398–99. M's book "the *Memoirs* of Saint-Simon of another age": 525.

SAINT-VALLIER (father of Diane de Poitiers): **VI** 141.

SAINTE-BEUVE, Charles-Augustin, French writer (1804–69). Quoted by Norpois on Alfred de Vigny: **II** 63. Admired by Mme de Villeparisis: 395. Approved by Andrée: 675. In describing the subtle distinctions between salons unwittingly betrays the vacuity of salon life: **III** 569. Preferred alternatively as critic and poet: 645. Depravity of taste shown in his prose style: **IV** 663. Charlus's scandal-mongering "enough to supply all the appendixes of the *Causeries du Lundi*" (Brichot): **V** 442. The original flaw in the type of literature represented by his *Lundis*: 769. Allusion to his poem *La Fontaine de Boileau*: **VI** 44, 46.

The grimacing smile that accompanies and disfigures his "spoken phrases": 302.

SAINTINE, Xavier, French novelist (1798–1865): **I** 206.

SALVANDY, Comte de, French writer and politician (1795–1856): **II** 395; **III** 372.

SAMARY, Jeanne, French actress (1857–90): **I** 102; **IV** 455.

SAND, George, French novelist (1804–76). M's grandmother gives him the four pastoral novels: **I** 53 (cf. **V** 8). His mother reads *François le Champi* to him: 55–57. Saniette's story about the duke who didn't know that George Sand was a woman: 370–71. Attractive compromise between the provincial and the literary in *La Petite Fadette*: **V** 36. The marriage of Mlle d'Oloron and the young Cambremer "a marriage from the last chapter of a George Sand novel": 893. On opening *François le Champi* in the Prince de Guermantes's library, M finds his whole childhood restored to him: **VI** 281–86, 526.

SAPPHO, Greek poetess. M compares Albertine to her: **IV** 272.

SARCEY, Francisque, French drama critic (1827–99): **IV** 393.

SARDOU, Victorien, French playwright (1831–1908). All the notabilities of Paris "walk on" in one of his plays: **II** 148, 485. Queens in his plays: **III** 583.

SARRAIL, General. Commander of the Salonika expeditionary force in 1916: **VI** 327.

SAUSSIER, General. His role in the Dreyfus Case: **III** 134–35.

SAVONAROLA, Girolamo, Italian preacher (1452–98). Mme Blatin the image of his portrait by Fra Bartolommeo: **II** 147.

SAXE, Maréchal de, French general (1696–1750): **III** 589.

SCARLATTI, Domenico, Italian composer (1685–1757). Mme de Cambremer requests Morel to play a "divine" Scarlatti piece: **IV** 481.

SCARRON, Paul, French poet and playwright (1610–60). Husband of Mme de Maintenon (q.v.): **II** 188.

SCHILLER, Johann Friedrich von, German poet and dramatist (1759–1805): **III** 674. Allusion to his comedy *Uncle and Nephew*: **IV** 128; **VI** 147, 210.

SCHLEGEL, Wilhelm von, German naturalist (1767–1845). Taught Mme de Villeparisis botany in her childhood: **III** 372.

SCHLIEFFEN, Field-Marshal von, Chief of the German General

Staff 1891–1905. Saint-Loup refers to his famous "plan": **III** 144.

SCHLUMBERGER, Gustave, French historian (1844–1929): **III** 286.

SCHOPENHAUER, Arthur, German philosopher (1788–1860). Mme de Cambremer's knowledge of him: **VI** 70, 444.

SCHUBERT, Franz, Austrian composer (1792–1828). M celebrates the renunciation of his love for Mme de Guermantes by singing Schubert's *Farewell*: **III** 508.

SCHUMANN, Robert, German composer (1810–56). M hears him being played from his hotel room: **IV** 255. Fauré's Schumannesque sonata: 479–80. "Hushed serenity" of *Kinderszenen*: **V** 337. Sudden dénouements of some of his ballads: 675. Mentioned in Saint-Loup's letters to M during the war: **VI** 93. Last words which M hears on Saint-Loup's lips the opening lines of a Schumann song: 226.

SCOTT, Sir Walter, Scottish writer (1771–1832). References to Rob Roy and Diana Vernon: **IV** 32.

SCRIBE, Eugène, French playwright and librettist (1791–1861). Wrote the librettos of *Les Diamants de la Couronne*: **I** 100–1; **III** 615, 673; *Le Domino noir*: **I** 101; *La Juive*: **II** 207; **IV** 331; *Fra Diavolo*: **III** 673; *Le Chalet*: 673; *Robert le Diable*: **IV** 481.

SERT, Jose Maria, Catalan painter (1876–1945). Designer for the *Ballets russes*: **V** 497; *The Legend of Joseph*: 876–77.

SÉVIGNÉ, Mme de, author of the famous *Letters* (1626–96). "Sévigné would not have put it better!": **I** 25 (cf. **III** 449). A "worthy old snob" (Brichot): 370. M's grandmother's "beloved Sévigné"; her plan to follow her itinerary to Normandy: **II** 305, 308. Quoted by M's mother: 310. M's grandmother gives him a volume of the *Letters* to read in the train to Balbec: 313. Reflexions on her style; her Dostoievsky side: 314–15 (cf. **V** 509). Quoted by M's grandmother on the food in the Grand Hotel: 372, 376. Criticised by Mme de Villeparisis: 376. Defended by Charlus against Mme de Villeparisis: 467–68. Françoise's Sévigné vocabulary: **III** 21. Quoted on Mme de La Fayette's death: 408–9. Quoted by M's grandmother apropos of the "Marquise" in the Champs-Elysées: 423. Charlus has a rare edition of the *Letters* bound for M: 772. M's grandmother's devotion to Sévigné inherited by her daughter, who reads and quotes her constantly in letters to M: **IV** 229–31 (cf. 252, 280, 318, 443, 567; **V** 11–12, 180, 490). The name Sévigné draws a grimace from Mme de Cambremer-Legrandin: 301. M's mother scorns "hackneyed" Sévigné: **V** 892 (cf. **II** 314–15).

SHAKESPEARE, William (1564–1616). Allusion to *A Midsummer Night's Dream* apropos of asparagus: **I** 169. Effects of reading Shakespeare: **II** 198. Transvestism in his comedies: **IV** 29. Allusion to *Romeo and Juliet* apropos of Charlus and Jupien: 37. *Hamlet* quoted by Saint-Loup: 572. Reference to *Hamlet*: 591. Lear-like majesty of Charlus in old age: **VI** 245, 339. The face of an old Shylock detectable in Bloch at close quarters: 406.

SILVESTRE, Armand, French writer (1837–1901). Quoted by Charlus to Morel: **V** 808.

SIMIANE, Pauline de, granddaughter of Mme de Sévigné (1674–1737). Quotations from her letters: **II** 314; **III** 610.

SOCRATES, Greek philosopher. His words distorted by Plato: **II** 376. Inverts take pleasure in recalling that he was one of them: **IV** 22 (cf. 480). Quoted by Cottard: 613–14. His jokes about young men: **V** 270. Jupien on Socrates: **VI** 205.

SODOMA (Giovanni Bazzi), Italian painter (c. 1477–1549): **V** 290.

SOPHOCLES, Greek dramatist. Gisèle's essay—"Letter from Sophocles to Racine": **II** 670–75 (cf. **III** 482). Reference to Oedipus: **VI** 246.

SPARTACUS, Roman slave leader: **I** 482.

SPINOZA, Baruch, Dutch philosopher (1632–77). Admired by Charlus: **IV** 690.

SPITTELER, Karl, Swiss novelist (1845–1924). Brichot praises his anti-militarism: **VI** 128.

STAEL, Mme de, French woman of letters (1766–1817). The Haussonville family descended from her, through her daughter and granddaughter: **VI** 408.

STAMATI, Franco-Greek pianist (1811–70). Charlus took lessons from him: **IV** 555.

STENDHAL (Henri Beyle), French novelist (1783–1842). "Stendhalian sweetness" of the name Parma: **I** 552 (cf. **III**

584–85). Mme de Villeparisis recalls her father's personal reminiscences of him: **II** 395. Discussed with Saint-Loup at Doncières; Bloch "can't stand" him; Norpois compared to Mosca: **III** 136. Mme de Guermantes's invitation to dine with the Princesse de Parme evokes for M Fabrice and Count Mosca: 514–15. Far from being a Sanseverina, the Princess turns out to be excessively un-Stendhalian: 584–85. Reference to la Sanseverina: **IV** 549. Symbols in his work discussed by M with Albertine: **V** 507–8 (cf. 734). Allusion to the preface of *La Chartreuse de Parme*: 742.

STEVENSON, Robert Louis, British writer (1850–94). "A very great writer," according to Swann, quoted in the Goncourt pastiche: **VI** 37.

STRAUSS, Richard, German composer (1864–1949). "Vulgar motifs" of *Salome*: **III** 614. A "great composer": **V** 315. Allusion to *The Legend of Joseph*: 876–77.

STRAVINSKY, Igor, Russian composer (1882–1972). Flowering of the Russian Ballet reveals his genius: **IV** 193. A "great composer": **V** 315.

SUGER, Abbé de Saint-Denis, minister and counsellor of Louis VI and Louis VII (1081–1151): **I** 358.

SULLY-PRUDHOMME, French poet (1839–1907). His *Ici-bas tous les lilas meurent* the only poem Céleste and her sister know: **IV** 336, 716. His *Aux Tuileries* recited by Charlus to Morel: **V** 808.

SYLVA, Carmen, pen-name of Elisabeth, Queen of Romania (1843–1916): **III** 270.

SYVETON, Gabriel, Nationalist Deputy who died in mysterious circumstances in 1904: **VI** 157.

TACITUS, Roman historian. Françoise would have written like him: **III** 491.

TAGLIAFICO, Franco-Italian singer and composer (1821–1900). One of Odette's favourite musicians; his *Pauvre Fou* to be played at her funeral: **I** 335.

TAINE, Hippolyte, French critic, philosopher and historian (1828–93). The Princesse Mathilde offended by an article of his on Napoleon: **II** 157. He and Charlus agree about Balzac: **IV** 614–15. His name floats through M's dreams: **V** 155.

TALLEMANT DES RÉAUX (1619–92). Author of *Les Historiettes*. Anecdote about the Chevalier de Rohan: **III** 731–32.

TALLEYRAND, Charles-Maurice, French statesman (1754–1838): **III** 171. Dr du Boulbon quotes his phrase *"bien portant imaginaire"*: 416. Quoted by Brichot: **IV** 371–72, who refers to him as "Charles-Maurice, Abbé de Périgord": 380–81; **VI** 103.

TALLIEN, Mme, wife of the revolutionary Jean-Lambert Tallien and leader of fashion under the Directory (1773–1835). Her "fine and flowing hair": **III** 735. War-time Paris compared to the Directory; Tallien styles in dress: **VI** 47. Mme Verdurin and Mme Bontemps "old and ugly" versions of Mme Tallien: 51.

TALMA, François-Joseph, French actor (1763–1826): **VI** 47.

THIBAUD, Jacques, French violinist (1880–1953). Compared to Morel: **V** 63, 383.

THIERRY, Augustin, French historian (1795–1856). M reads him in the garden at Combray: **IV** 319.

THIERS, Adolphe, French statesman and historian (1797–1877): **III** 259, 277; **V** 866.

THIRON, French actor (1830–91): **I** 102; **II** 76; **III** 167.

THUREAU-DANGIN, French historian (1837–1913), Permanent Secretary of the Académie Française: **IV** 620.

TIEPOLO, Giovanni Battista, Venetian painter (1696–1770). The Duchesse de Guermantes's cloak "a magnificent Tiepolo red": **IV** 83, 161. Albertine's Fortuny gown lined in "Tiepolo pink": **V** 531.

TINTORETTO, Venetian painter (1518–94): Dr du Boulbon resembles one of his portraits: **I** 315.

TISSOT, James, French painter (1836–1902). Allusion to his picture of the Rue Royale club: **V** 262–63.

TITIAN, Venetian painter (c. 1487–1576): **I** 54, 556–57. The "Frari Titian" (the *Assumption of the Virgin*): **II** 14. Mme de Villeparisis's family Titians: 396. Mentioned: 588; **V** 497, 531, 794; **VI** 44. M's Venetian girlfriend compared to a Titian: **V** 868. Barrès on Titian: **VI** 280.

TOLSTOY, Count Leo, Russian writer (1828–1910): "Abominated" by Bergotte: **II** 177. Discussed at lunch with Rachel: **III** 377. Mme de Guermantes's "sally" in his defence: 612–13.

Mme de Cambremer and Tolstoy's mujiks: **IV** 438. Reference to *War and Peace*: **V** 509. Tolstoy and Dostoievsky: 513.

TOURVILLE, Maréchal de, French sailor (1642–1701): **II** 49.

TOWNSHEND, General Sir Charles, Commander of the expeditionary force in Mesopotamia during World War I: **VI** 430.

TSCHUDI, Hugo von, German art historian, Director of the National Gallery in Berlin: **IV** 471.

TURNER, J. M. W., English painter (1775–1851): **I** 54. Charlus's Turner rainbow: **III** 771. Turneresque view from the Hôtel de Guermantes: 786. Anticipated by Poussin: **IV** 291. Turner and Venice: **V** 884.

VACQUERIE, Auguste. Writer and friend of Victor Hugo: **V** 386.

VAN DYCK, Sir Anthony, Flemish painter (1599–1641). Allusion to his portrait of Charles I in the Louvre: **V** 755.

VAULABELLE, Achille de, French historian (1799–1879): **I** 108; **III** 359.

VELAZQUEZ, Diego, Spanish painter (1599–1660). Saint-Loup compares a Carrière to a Velazquez: **II** 457, 459. M. de Charlus alludes to the *Surrender of Breda* in the Prado: **III** 762. The Duc de Guermantes's putative Velazquez: 792, 795. Albertine's hair done up like a Velazquez Infanta's: **V** 501.

VENDÔME, Louis-Joseph, Duc de. Great-grandson of Henri IV and Gabrielle d'Estrées and one of Louis XIV's generals (1654–1712). An invert?: **V** 405–6.

VENIZELOS, Greek statesman, Prime Minister during World War I: **VI** 141.

VERLAINE, Paul, French poet (1844–96): **II** 418. Anathematised by Brichot: **IV** 483. Mme de Guermantes offers M a Verlaine recital by Rachel: **VI** 497.

VERMANDOIS, Comte de, son of Louis XIV and Mlle de la Vallière (1667–83). An invert?: **V** 405.

VERMEER, Jan, Dutch painter (1632–75). Swann's essay on him: **I** 279, 340–41, 423, 502; **II** 54, 146–47 (cf. **IV** 145). The Duc de Guermantes uncertain of having seen the *View of Delft* in The Hague: **III** 718. Swann's favourite painter; Charlus compares Jacquet to him: **IV** 145. "Do you know the Vermeers?"

asks Mme de Cambremer; Albertine thinks they are living people: 289. Bergotte gets up from his sickbed to go and look at the *View of Delft*; the little patch of yellow wall: **V** 244–45. His pictures fragments of an identical world: 508. Unique radiance that still reaches us from his world: **VI** 299.

VERNE, Jules, French writer (1828–1905): **IV** 576.

VERONESE, Paul, Venetian painter (1528–88). Roof of the Gare Saint-Lazare recalls one of his skies, "of an almost Parisian modernity": **II** 303. Albertine's profile less beautiful than those of Veronese's women: 597. His paintings of Venetian revels: 652–54 (cf. **IV** 66). Fruit and wine "as luscious as a beautiful Veronese" (Ski): **IV** 460. Mentioned: **V** 271, 848.

VIBERT, Jehan-Georges, French painter (1840–1902). M. de Guermantes prefers him to Elstir: **III** 687 (cf. 720).

VIGNY, Alfred de, French poet (1797–1863). Swann recalls a passage from his *Journal d'un Poète*: **I** 522–23. Norpois's opinion of him: **II** 63. Quoted by M to Mme de Villeparisis: 410; her low opinion of him: 411 (cf. **III** 256). Anna de Noailles compared to him: **III** 137. Quotations from *La Colère de Samson*: **IV** 21. M quotes two lines from *La Maison du Berger* to Albertine: 357. Quotations from *Eloa* applied to Princess Sherbatoff: 374. "Manly reticence"—an echo of *Servitude et Grandeur militaires*: **VI** 79.

VILLARS, Duc de, Maréchal de France (1653–1734). His portrait by Saint-Simon: **II** 170. An invert?: **V** 406.

VILLIERS DE L'ISLE-ADAM, French Symbolist writer (1840–89). Referred to familiarly by Bloch's sister: **II** 482.

VIOLLET-LE-DUC, Eugène, French architect and writer (1814–79). Allusion to his restorations apropos of Combray: **I** 233–34. Denounced by Swann: 415. Restorations by pupils of his often give "the most potent sensation of the Middle Ages": **IV** 380.

VIRGIL, Roman poet. Allusion to Book IV of the *Georgics*: **I** 22. Anecdotes from Virgil in the porch of Saint-André-des-Champs: 212. In Dante's *Inferno*: 238. "Virgil's Leucothea" (a Proustian error—the "white goddess" is not mentioned in Virgil): **II** 721. Cited by Brichot: **IV** 448, 478. Charlus and Virgilian shepherds: 479; **V** 270 (cf. 443).

VOISENON, Abbé de, licentious novelist, friend of Voltaire (1708–75): **III** 371.

VOLTAIRE (François-Marie Arouet), French writer and philosopher (1694–1778). Bloch attributes to him ("Master Arouet") two lines from Corneille's *Polyeucte*: **II** 628. Andrée quotes him on Racine: 674. Allusion to *Zaïre*: **III** 49. Brichot at La Raspelière sees himself as the equivalent of "M. de Voltaire" *chez* Mme du Châtelet: **IV** 381. Further allusion by Brichot: 614.

WAGNER, Richard, German composer (1813–83). "Solemn sweetness" of a joyful celebration characteristic of *Lohengrin*: **I** 215 (cf. **III** 5). Odette's projected visit to Bayreuth: 428. Vinteuil's "little phrase" compared to a theme in *Tristan*: 498. Saint-Loup deplores his father's indifference to Wagner: **II** 427–28. Plaintive whine of a closing door reminds M of the overture to *Tannhäuser*: **III** 536. Nietzsche and Wagner: 540 (cf. **V** 205). Mme de Guermantes's glib views on Wagner: 643, 645, 672; he sends the Duke to sleep: 672. His later manner compared to Victor Hugo's: 753. Allusion to the March in *Tannhäuser*: **IV** 66. The sound of the telephone compared to the shepherd's pipe in *Tristan*: 177. Odette a "Wagnerian": 201. Mme de Cambremer compares *Pelléas* and *Parsifal*: 288. Reflexions on Debussy and Wagner: 290–91. Mme Verdurin and Wagner: 384, 413, 444. The Princesse de Guermantes a passionate Wagnerian: 731. Vinteuil's sonata and *Tristan*; M's reflexions on Wagner's themes, the mystery of creativity, the retrospective unity of the *Ring*, etc.: **V** 205–9 (cf. 219, 655). Early and late Wagner compared: 350 (cf. 927–28). Princesse von Metternich's reaction to the hissing of Wagner: 365. Allusion to Beckmesser by Charlus: 367. Wagnerian leitmotifs: 597–98. Saint-Loup's reference to the wood-bird in "that sublime *Siegfried*": **VI** 93. "The music of the air-raid sirens like the Ride of the Valkyries" (Saint-Loup): 99 (cf. 127: "the only German music to have been heard since the war").

WATTEAU, Antoine, French painter (1684–1721). Swann's memories of Odette's smiles recall sheets of sketches by Watteau: **I** 340. Odette's "Watteau *peignoir*": **II** 262. Dancer in the theatre with cheeks chalked in red "like a page from a Watteau album": **III** 235. Elstir a Watteau *à vapeur* (Saniette's pun): **IV** 459. Goncourt elevates him above Raphael: **VI** 130. His works destroyed by the revolutionaries: 280.

WEDGWOOD, Josiah, Staffordshire potter (1730–95): **III** 710.

WELLS, H. G., English writer (1866–1946). Allusion to *The Invisible Man*: **III** 257.

WHISTLER, James McNeill, American painter (1834–1903). Carrière portrait of Mme de Guermantes "as fine as Whistler" (Saint-Loup): **II** 457. Balbec seascape reminiscent of a Whistler "Harmony in Grey and Pink": 526. Elstir's portrait of Odette compared to a Whistler: 604. Balbec Bay the "gulf of opal painted by Whistler" (Elstir): **III** 27. Quoted by Charlus: 773. Charlus's evening coat a "Harmony in Black and White": **IV** 71. Charlus cites him as an arbiter of taste: **V** 403. Skyline in Carpaccio's *Patriarch of Grado* reminiscent of Whistler: 876. M. Verdurin has written a book about him, according to the Goncourts: **VI** 27 (cf. 117).

WIDAL, Fernand, French physician (1862–1929): **III** 405.

WIDOR, Charles, French composer and organist (1845–1937): **III** 589.

WILDE, Oscar, Irish writer (1854–1900). Allusion to his downfall in the dissertation on the plight of inverts: **IV** 21.

WILLIAM II, the Kaiser, Norpois's views on him: **II** 46–47. Charlus hints that he is an invert: **III** 394 (cf. **IV** 471; **VI** 143) Saint-Loup on his intentions over Morocco: 565. Discussed at the dinner-table by Prince Von and Oriane; dislikes Elstir's work; Prince Von's irony apropos of his aesthetic judgment: 717, 721–24, 751, 776. Mme Verdurin's claims on the "faithful" compared to his claims on his subjects: **IV** 372–74. Charlus's opinion of him; the Eulenburg affair: 471. During the war, M. Bontemps wants him to be put up against a wall and shot: **VI** 55. Discussed by Bloch and Saint-Loup; rumours of his death; Saint-Loup and the Guermantes insist on referring to him as "the Emperor William": 71–73. Charlus describes him as "a complete upstart": 140, but defends him against French chauvinists: 157–59 (cf. Saint-Loup's view: 226).

*Index of Places*

ABBAUE-AUX-BOIS. Disused convent in Paris where Mme Récamier lived and held her salon and where Chateaubriand was a regular visitor: **IV** 373, 612.

ACACIAS, Allée des. *See* Bois de Boulogne.

AGRIGENTO, Sicily. Evoked by M on being introduced to the Prince d'Agrigente: **III** 593.

ALENÇON, capital of the Orne department. Eating habits that are considered unacceptable in "the best society of Alençon": **II** 347; the "high society" of Alençon: **IV** 423.

AMSTERDAM. Visited by M: **III** 718. Visited by Albertine; the gulls in Amsterdam: **IV** 289 (cf. **V** 518, 529, 580).

ANDELYS, Les, town on the lower Seine. A house there contains one of Elstir's finest landscapes: **III** 163.

BADEN-BADEN. Odette once led a gay life there: **I** 445.

BAGATELLE (f). Farm-restaurant near Balbec: **II** 660; **IV** 320.

BALBEC (f). Remembered by the narrator: **I** 9. Legrandin's sister lives in the neighbourhood: 92. Described by Legrandin: 182–86. M's room in the Grand Hotel: 545. M's imagined Balbec; "the land of the Cimmerians"; its "Persian" church; the poetry of its name: 545–54. Norpois's opinion of Balbec and its church: **II** 48–49. M goes there with his grandmother: 299–308. Old Balbec, Balbec-en-Terre; M's disappointment with the church: 322–24. The "little train": 325–26. Arrival at the Grand Hotel; the manager; the lift; M's room: 327–34. Views of the sea: 342–44 (*see also* 387, 523–24; **IV** 247–48). Clientele of the hotel: 345–56. The countryside round Balbec; landscapes and seascapes: 389–92, 395–409. The Casino: 434–35, 486, 502; behaviour of the "little band" there: 631–32, 645. The sea-front: 502–4. The cliffs of Canapville: 557, 580. Gimcrack splendour of Balbec's architecture: 564. Elstir's studio and his Balbec seascapes: 564–72. His enthusiasm for the "Persian" church: 573–76 (cf. **III** 484). The Mayor, the dentist, and other personalities of Balbec identified by Albertine: 631–32. Farms in the neighbourhood; picnics on the cliffs: 660–62. End of the season

685

at Balbec; M's memories of his stay: 724–30. Balbec bay the "gulf of opal painted by Whistler": **III** 27. M's desire for Albertine confused with his desire for Balbec: 479–81, 483–84. M's second visit: **IV** 204–724. The manager of the Grand Hotel and his malapropisms: 204–10, 220–21. Life at the hotel; the lift-boy, the pages; a Racinian stage-set: 233–36 (cf. 327–28). Views of the sea: 247–49. The little train and its nicknames: 249. At the Casino Albertine stares at Bloch's sister and cousin in the mirror: 272–74. Girls on the beach: 321–24. A scandal at the Grand Hotel: 326–27. Nissim Bernard and the fledgling waiter: 327–31. Gomorrhan behaviour there: 337–41. Etymology of the name Balbec: 456–58. Roads near Balbec and their associations for M: 558–60. Corrupting effect of the country round Balbec— "this too social valley": 697–98. The two pictures of Balbec; Albertine's sleep evokes nights of full moon on the bay: **V** 81–86. Albertine's trip to Balbec with the chauffeur: 174 (cf. 449–50). Bathing establishment at the Grand Hotel: 663. M's retrospective musings about the Albertine of Balbec and her possible Gomorrhan activities: 673–703 *passim*. Aimé's report on his investigative mission to Balbec: 694–96. "My Hell was the whole region of Balbec": 699. The Grand Hotel a stage-set for the different dramas of M's life: 730–31. M visits Balbec with the Saint-Loups: 925–27. M's memories of Balbec and the sea revived by a starched napkin: **VI** 258–59, 265–68. (*See also* Rooms *in* Index of Themes)

BAYEUX. One of the stops on the 1.22 train: **I** 548–49. What its name evokes: 554. A stained glass window in its cathedral decorated with the arms of the Arrachepels: **IV** 282.

BAYREUTH. Odette's proposed trip: **I** 427–28. The Prince of X lets his castle during the festival: **III** 736. Visitors to Bayreuth: **IV** 201, 290–91.

BÉARN. Correct way of pronouncing: **V** 35.

BEAUMONT (f). Hill near Balbec with a view of the sea through woods: **IV** 548–50 (cf. **II** 391).

BEAUVAIS. Mme Verdurin's Beauvais tapestry settee: **I** 292. Its cathedral: 415; **II** 321; **III** 7. Captain de Borodino posted there: 172. Mme de Villeparisis's Beauvais chairs: 251, 275, 366. Charlus's Beauvais chairs: 770. A Beauvais armchair illustrating the Rape of Europa: **IV** 191.

BENODET. One of the stops on the 1.22 train: **I** 548–49. What its name evokes: 553.

BERLIN. The Wilhelmstrasse: **II** 44. The Spree: **III** 331. Prince Von's wife a leading light in the most exclusive set in Berlin: 348. Unter den Linden (Norpois): **V** 864; Unter den Linden (Charlus): **VI** 171.

BOIS DE BOULOGNE, Paris. Verdurin dinner-parties in the Bois: **I** 373, 381–83, 403–4. Odette's encounter with a woman on the Island in the Bois: 519–21. The Swanns live near it: 586, 590. What it represents for M; Mme Swann's walks and drives there; the Allée des Acacias: 592–98. The Bois in autumn; the Allée des Acacias; "the Elysian Garden of Woman": 598–606. Associated with Swann's memory of Vinteuil's "little phrase": **II** 144–46. M. Bloch drives through it in a hired victoria: 481. M. invites Mme de Stermaria to dine with him on the Island in the Bois; visits it with Albertine: **III** 525–33. "Improper things" happen there at night: 709. M. de Charlus wants to admire the moonlight in the Bois: 771 (cf. **IV** 3). M goes for a walk there with Albertine and contemplates the girls: **V** 219–28. M walks there alone one Sunday in autumn; its charm and melancholy; "aflower" with girls: 754–59.

BONNÉTABLE, in the Perche region. Norpois went shooting there with Prince Foggi: **V** 858.

BOURGES. The cathedral: **II** 321; its soaring steeple in a Book of Hours: **V** 790.

BRABANT. Its "old-gold, sonorous" name: **I** 10. The lords of Guermantes were Counts of Brabant: 143, 242, 246; **II** 456 (cf. **III** 711, 808, 811–12). Charlus claims to be Duke of Brabant: **IV** 464, 477.

BRITTANY. Evoked by Legrandin: **I** 183, 185 (cf. **II** 576–77). Towns of Brittany served by the 1.22 train: 548–49, 552–53. The Stermarias, an ancient Breton family: **II** 351, 357–58; M imagines a life of poetry and romance in Brittany with Mlle de Stermaria: 364–66. The Island in the Bois evokes for M the "marine and misty" atmosphere of Mlle de Stermaria's Breton island: **III** 529, 546. Mme de Guermantes's Breton anecdotes: **V** 38. The Breton postal system: 174.

BROU. Tombs of Philibert le Beau and Marguerite d'Autriche in its church: **I** 420.

BRUGES. Visited by Rachel every year on All Souls' Day: **III** 162–65.

BUTTES-CHAUMONT, public park in Paris. Andrée proposes to take Albertine there since she has never been before: **V** 15; M advises against: 16. Mme Bontemps reveals that Albertine used to go there constantly: 524. M is painfully reminded of this: 732. Andrée admits to having frequently made love to Albertine in the Buttes-Chaumont: 823 (cf. 740).

CALIFORNIE (f), farm restaurant near Balbec: **II** 660.

CARQUETHUIT (f), a small port near Balbec. Subject of an Elstir picture: **II** 567–69, 576. Reminiscent of Florida, according to Elstir: 592.

CARQUEVILLE (f), mediaeval village with an ivy-covered church which M visits with Mme de Villeparisis: **II** 391, 401–2.

CHAMPS-ELYSÉES, Paris. "Melancholy neighbourhood" where Gilberte lives: **I** 201. Françoise takes M for daily walks there: 546, 559–60. M's first meeting with Gilberte there: 560–62. The importance it assumes in his life; games with Gilberte: 562–81; **II** 80–89. The little pavilion and the "Marquise": 87–89 (cf. **III** 419–22). Its bad reputation as regards children's health: 91, 97–98. M sees Gilberte walking along the Avenue des Champs-Elysées with a young man: 272–73 (cf. **VI** 6–7). Dr du Boulbon advises M's grandmother to go there for her health: **III** 411. M takes his grandmother there; her stroke: 419–24. M's nostalgic memory of the streets in the neighbourhood of the Champs-Elysées: **VI** 243–44.

CHANTEPIE, Forest of (f), near Balbec. M. de Cambremer shoots there; etymology of the name: **IV** 434–39, 489. M and Albertine drive through it: 535 (cf. **V** 649, 659).

CHANTILLY. Residence of the Duc d'Aumale, where M. de Guermantes used to go and dine every week: **III** 803–4. The Poussins at Chantilly: **IV** 287.

CHARLUS (f). Little village in the heart of Burgundy: **III** 742. The Château de Charlus: 759.

and voice remind M of Combray countryside: 677. Rue de Sain-trailles: 728. The Curé's magnum opus on the parish: **IV** 282, 387–88. The "Combray spirit"—the rule of caste: 579–80 (cf. **V** 867, 894); order and propriety: **V** 8–10. Françoise's Combray "customary": 648. Venice compared to Combray: 844–48, 874–75. Combray's reaction to Gilberte's marriage: 919–20. M's disillusionment on revisiting the neighbourhood: **VI** 1–5, 9–10, 24. Occupied during the war: 88, 94–96; the church destroyed: 153–54. A memory of Combray the point of departure for M's exploration of Time: 526–32.

COMMANDERIE, La (f). House near Balbec rented by Bloch's father: **IV** 682; Charlus's anti-semitic observations on the sub-ject: 687–88.

COMPIÈGNE. The Verdurins take Odette there without Swann to watch the sunsets in the forest: **I** 415–17. The Marquis de Forestelle has a house in the neighbourhood: 417. Napoleon III's residence: **V** 866 (cf. **II** 159–60).

COULIVILLE (f). Village near Balbec. Sacrilegious subject rep-resented on the capitals of its old church: **IV** 652. Morel takes Albertine to a brothel there: **V** 811.

COUTANCES. One of the stops on the 1.22 train: **I** 548–49. What its name evokes: 553.

COWES, Isle of Wight. Albertine wants to go there for the re-gatta: **II** 655.

CREUNIERS, Les (f). Rocks near Balbec, reminiscent of a cathe-dral: **II** 656–57. Andrée takes M there: 684, 689.

CROIX D'HEULAND, La (f). Farm-restaurant near Balbec: **II** 660; **IV** 320.

DELFT. Home of Vermeer: **I** 279, 341. His *View of Delft*: **III** 718 (cf. **V** 244). Tulip-gardens in Delft: 784 (cf. **V** 881). The Master of Delft: **IV** 145.

DONCIÈRES (f). Garrison town not far from Balbec. Remem-bered by M: **I** 9. Saint-Loup on military service there: **II** 420, 478, 502, 528, 609–10, 663. Description: **III** 86. M visits Saint-Loup there: 86–183. First impressions; the barracks, the Cap-tain's house in the Place de la République: 91–92. First morning there; the view from Saint-Loup's room; mist, frost and hot chocolate: 100–101. The Hôtel de Flandre: 102–5. Walks through the town: 116, 120–22; Doncières by night: 122–25. The hotel where Saint-Loup and his friends dine, the Faisan Doré: 124–27 (cf. **IV** 681–82); military comradeship: 131–54 *passim*. M's memories of "mornings at Doncières": 472–73, 534, and of evenings there (the inn, the panelled dining-room, the serving-girl): 542–43. M and Albertine meet Saint-Loup at Doncières station: **IV** 344–45, 348–50; meeting between Charlus and Morel, who is doing his military service there: 351–55 (cf. 382). Brichot gives the etymology of the name: 681. Meetings at Doncières station; invitations from Saint-Loup's friends; meeting with Bloch: 682–86. Depoeticisation of the name: 695–96; its association with Albertine: **V** 730. Recollections of Doncières during the war: **VI** 75–76, 89, 100, 164, 428.

DOUVILLE (f). Station on the little local railway: **II** 326, and the stop for Féterne and La Raspelière: **IV** 248–49, 361. Its etymology: 390–91. The village and its surroundings: 398–99; the toll-house: 401–2. Beauty spots round Douville: 539; the "view of Douville": 544. Painters from Paris spend their holidays there: 589.

DRESDEN. Swann needs to go there for his study of Vermeer: **I** 502. Odette surrounded by Dresden pieces: **II** 262. Mme de Guermantes "a statuette in Dresden china": **III** 10. The women at the Guermantes dinner party "like Dresden figures": 599. Dresden china plates: **IV** 66 (cf. **VI** 35–36). The art gallery: 659; **V** 75.

ECORRES, Les (f). Farm-restaurant near Balbec: **II** 660. Françoise's young footman born there: **III** 777. Remembered by M: **V** 646.

EGYPT. Odette's projected trip there with Forcheville on Whitsun: **I** 506. Norpois was Controller of the Egyptian Public Debt: **II** 5. "Doubles" of the dead in ancient Egypt: **III** 39. Napoleon's Egyptian expedition: 711, 715.

EPREVILLE (f). Watering-place near Balbec where Mme Bontemps takes a villa: **IV** 244. M sends the lift-boy there to fetch Albertine: 256, 262, 267. Etymology: 534.

FERNEY, Hermitage of. Residence of Voltaire: **IV** 614.

FÉTERNE (f). The Cambremer estate near Balbec. The notary goes there on Sundays: **II** 362. Hired cabs wait at the Grand

Hotel for the Féterne guests: 388. Its marvellous gardens; its position overlooking the sea: **IV** 223–26. Compared with La Raspelière: 282–83. The Dowager Mme de Cambremer talks of her little back garden and of her roses: 287–88. M invited there, but not the judge: 299–302. "Féterne is starvation corner" (Mme Verdurin): 505. A dinner-party at Féterne: 663–72.

FLORENCE. Poetry of the name; M conjures it up in his imagination ("a supernatural city"); abortive plan to visit it at Easter: **I** 549–59. Resurgence of M's desire to go there: **II** 287. His memory of this desire makes it the paschal city: **III** 187, 195.

FLORIDA. Carquethuit reminds Elstir of certain aspects of Florida: **II** 592.

FONTAINEBLEAU. Albertine on the Fontainebleau golf club: **III** 485. The forest of Fontainebleau: 732. Doncières has a spurious look of Fontainebleau: **IV** 681. Water-grapes from Fontainebleau: **V** 163.

FROHSDORF. Austrian residence of the Comte de Chambord, pretender to the French throne: **V** 37.

GAETA, port in southern Italy. Its siege and capitulation in 1861 put an end to the Kingdom of the Two Sicilies: **V** 329, 364–65, 432–33.

GOURVILLE (f). Village near Balbec: **IV** 538; the plain of Gourville: 558; the château of Gourville: 664; etymology: 680.

GRAINCOURT-SAINT-VAST (f). First station after Doncières on the little local railway; Cottard catches the train there: **IV** 358, 366. Cottard and Ski nearly miss the train there: 369, 435.

GRATTEVAST (f). On the little local railway, in the opposite direction from Féterne: **IV** 534; M. de Crécy's sister has a house there: 657.

GUERMANTES (f). Seat of the Guermantes family, not far from Combray. The ultimate goal of the "Guermantes way"—"a sort of abstract geographical term"; surrounded by river scenery (the Vivonne): **I** 188–89, 233–36. M and his family never reach it on their walks: 241–43. M's longing to go there: 243, 250, 257–62. Permanent significance of the Guermantes way for him: 258–62. Swann reminded of Guermantes and its countryside on meeting the Princesse des Laumes: 483. Saint-Loup talks about the château: **II** 456–57. M imagines the château: **III** 7–10. Françoise talks about it: 20–22, 35–36. Mme de Guermantes stays on there late into the season: 67. "Shadowy, sun-splashed coolness" of the woods of Guermantes: 273. The Duchess's lunch-parties: 276–79. She and Charlus had played there together as children: 518. Carnations from Guermantes: 747. The Guermantes visitors' book: 753. Life there remembered by the Duke and his brother: **IV** 158. The Duchess tells an anecdote about a shooting party (the Marquis du Lau and the Prince of Wales): **V** 38 (cf. 794). Gilberte reveals that it can be reached in a quarter of an hour from Combray: **VI** 3; the Guermantes way and the Méséglise way not irreconcilable: 3–4.

HAARLEM. The Frans Halses there discussed at the Guermantes dinner-party: **III** 717–18. Tulip gardens in Haarlem: 784 (cf. **V** 881).

HARAMBOUVILLE (f). One of the stopping places on the little local railway: **II** 326. A farm labourer gets into the little clan's compartment and is ejected by Cottard: **IV** 371. Mme Verdurin plans an outing there: 501. The Cambremers lunch with friends there: 668. Its etymology (Herimbald's town): 693.

HERMENONVILLE (f). M. de Chevregny's station: **IV** 662. Etymology of the name (Herimund's town): 680, 682, 693–95.

HAGUE, The. Swann needs to go there for his study of Vermeer; the Mauritshuis: **I** 502. M has been there: **III** 717–18. Its art gallery lends Vermeer's *View of Delft* for an exhibition in Paris: **V** 244.

HOLLAND. Swann's fondness for it; Odette imagines it to be ugly: **I** 350. M has once been there: **III** 718. Albertine has been there: **IV** 289. Her excursions in the Dutch countryside: **V** 518. M anxious to prevent her from returning: 557. (*See* Amsterdam; Delft; Haarlem; Hague, The.)

HUDIMESNIL (f), near Balbec. M's experience with the three trees near there: **II** 404–7 (cf. **V** 347).

INCARVILLE (f), near Balbec. Stopping place on the little local railway: **II** 326. Albertine "en pension" there with Rosemonde's family: **IV** 244, 248–50. M meets Cottard there and they go to the Casino: 262–63, where they see Albertine and Andrée dance together: 263–66. Albertine meets Mme Bontemps's friend with the "bad name" there: 341–42. M and Albertine drive through it: 549. Brichot refers to Balbec as Incarville: 617 (cf. **V** 301). M. de Crécy's old castle perched above Incarville: 661. Etymology of the name (the village of Wiscar): 680. Its cliff: 693. The Marquis de Montpeyroux and M. de Crécy visit the little train at Incarville station: 694–95. The arcades of Incarville where Albertine would wait for M: **V** 593. (Sometimes confused with Parville (q.v.).)

INFREVILLE (f), near Balbec. Albertine proposes to call on a lady there: **IV** 268–70. Later, she denies ever having been near the place: **V** 137; its associations with Albertine: 730.

ITALY. Swann brings back photographs of old masters from his visits to Italy: **I** 22. M's parents promise him a holiday in the north of Italy: 549. Dreams of Italy: 549–50. Evocations of Florence, Venice, Parma, etc: 549–60 (cf. **II** 299; **III** 195); "Precious lustre" of streets in old Italian towns: **III** 190–91. Mme de Guermantes invites Swann to go with her to Italy: 813–16. Trip to Venice: **V** 844–88. (*See* Florence; Milan; Orvieto; Padua; Parma; Pisa; Rome; Siena; Trieste; Venice.)

JARDIES, Les. Balzac's house on the outskirts of Paris: **IV** 614.

JOSSELIN. Residence of the Rohans in Brittany: **V** 38.

JOUY-LE-VICOMTE (f). Town near Combray where M's grandmother buys books for him: **I** 53. M. Pupin's daughter goes to boarding school there: 76. Its canals can be seen from the top of the steeple of Combray; its etymology: 147–48. Operations in the neighbourhood during the Great War: **VI** 88.

LAGHET, Notre Dame de. Place of pilgrimage in the Alpes-Maritimes; Odette has a medal from there: **I** 313, 516.

LAMBALLE. One of the stops on the 1.22 train: **I** 548–49. What its name evokes: 553.

LANNION. One of the stops on the 1.22 train: **I** 548–49. What its name evokes: 553.

LAON. Gilberte Swann often goes to spend a few days there: **I** 205. Its cathedral: **III** 7.

LAUMES, Les (f). Village in Burgundy. The Duc de Guermantes is Prince des Laumes: **V** 790.

LONDON. Visited by the Verdurins: **II** 117. Visited by Mme de Cambremer-Legrandin; the British Museum: **III** 271. Prince

Von has a house there: 347. Mme de Guermantes goes shopping there: **V** 48. (*See* Chelsea; Twickenham.)

MAINEVILLE (f). Last stop before Balbec on the little local railway: **II** 326. M and the little band hire a couple of two-seater "governess-carts" there: 691. Its cliffs visible from the Grand Hotel: 700. Its luxury brothel: **IV** 250. Princess Sherbatoff catches the train there: 370, 380, 393–94. An unsuspecting newcomer takes the luxury brothel for a grand hotel: 647–48. Morel's assignation with the Prince de Guermantes: 648–51. Experiences in the brothel of Charlus and Jupien: 651–56. Albertine leaves the train there on fine evenings: 696.

MANS, LE. The notary staying in the Grand Hotel comes from there: **II** 345. The "high society" of Le Mans: 356. Albertine buys a ring left in a hotel there: **V** 214.

MARCOUVILLE-L'ORGUEILLEUSE (f). On the little local railway: **II** 326. Just visible from Rivebelle: 385. M and Albertine visit its church; "I don't like it, it's restored" (Albertine): **IV** 561 (cf. **V** 217). Its etymology: 679.

MARIE-ANTOINETTE (f). Farm-restaurant near Balbec adopted by the "little band": **II** 660; **IV** 320; **V** 648.

MARIE-THÉRÈSE (f). Farm-restaurant near Balbec: **II** 660.

MARTINVILLE-LE-SEC (f), near Combray. One of the fiefs of Guermantes: **I** 236. The twin steeples of its church and the sketch they inspire M to write in Dr Percepied's carriage: 253–57. M reminded of them by the three trees near Hudimesnil: **II** 404–5. The article on the steeples sent to *Le Figaro*: **III** 544 (cf. **V** 6, 766–72, 788). M reminded of the steeples in a carriage on the way to dine with Saint-Loup: 544, and in a carriage on the way to visit Charlus: 751. Symbolic importance of the impression produced by the steeples: **V** 347, 505; **VI** 255, 273.

MÉSÉGLISE-LA-VINEUSE (f), near Combray. One of the two "ways" for walks round Combray (also known as "Swann's way"): **I** 188–89. Méséglise "as inaccessible as the horizon" for M: 188. Itinerary of the Méséglise walks: 189–97, 204–5. Its climate somewhat wet: 211–12, 214–16. What M owes to the Méséglise way: 218. His desire for a peasant-girl bound up with his desire for Méséglise: 219–23 (cf. **II** 317–18, 395–96; **III** 71,

123; **IV** 208). Permanent significance of the Méséglise way for M: 258–62. Swann yearns after his park near Méséglise: 383. Françoise sings its praises: **III** 23–24. Françoise's daughter reluctant to go back there ("the people are so stupid"): 194. The Prince des Laumes is Deputy for Méséglise: 648. Its dialect: **IV** 173. Legrandin becomes Comte de Méséglise: **V** 913–14. Staying with Gilberte at Tansonville—back to the Méséglise way: **VI** 1. Not irreconcilable with the Guermantes way: 3–4. Théodore now the chemist there: 5. The battle for Méséglise during the Great War: 95–96.

MEUDON, near Paris. The natural heights of Meudon: **III** 527. Presbytery of Meudon (reference to Rabelais): **IV** 614.

MILAN. The Curé of Combray impressed by the number of steps in the cathedral: **I** 146. The Ambrosian Library: **V** 531. A church in Milan: **VI** 215.

MIROUGRAIN (f), near Combray. Aunt Léonie has a farm there: **I** 149. One of her tenant farmers buys it: **V** 914.

MONTE-CARLO. Admired by Odette: **I** 350. Féterne like a garden in Monte-Carlo: **IV** 286. "Superb," according to the lift-boy at the Grand Hotel: 577.

MONTFORT-L'AMAURY, near Paris. Mme de Guermantes proposes to go and see the famous stained-glass windows of its church on the day of Mme de Saint-Euverte's garden-party: **IV** 113–15.

MONTJOUVAIN (f), near Combray. M. Vinteuil's house there: **I** 157–59, 206–7. M's walks in the vicinity: 218. Scene of sadism witnessed there by M: 224–33 (cf. **IV** 10). The scene revived in M's memory by Albertine's revelation about Mlle Vinteuil: **IV** 701–24 (cf. **V** 17, 94, 166, 353, 451, 820, 871).

MOROCCO. Saint-Loup posted there; writes to M: **III** 475. He talks about it to M ("Interesting place, Morocco"); hopes to get a transfer: 565 (cf. 697, 701, 706).

NEW YORK. How Françoise pronounces it: **II** 21–22.

NICE. Odette once lived there: **I** 313, and enjoyed a sort of amorous notoriety there: 444–46. Her mother said to have sold her to a rich Englishman there: 522. Nissim Bernard dined there with M. de Marsantes: **II** 485–86 (cf. **III** 374).

NORMANDY. 18th-century houses in a quaint Norman town: **I**

89. Charm of the plains of Normandy: 138. Normandy skies evoked by Legrandin: 182–83. "Celestial geography" of Lower Normandy: 186. Its towns different in reality from what their names suggest: 550–52. Its architecture and landscapes: 553. Apple-trees in Normandy flower later than in the region of Paris: III 287. Albertine associated with Normandy: V 137, 704, 744. (*See also* Balbec.)

NORWAY. Mme de Guermantes goes on a cruise in the Norwegian fjords: III 654.

ORLEANS. Its cathedral the ugliest in France, according to Charlus: IV 15.

ORVIETO. The Creation of Woman in one of the sculptures of its cathedral: V 512.

PADUA. Giotto's Vices and Virtues in the Arena Chapel: I 111–13, 169; Swann a fervent admirer of them: 465. Mantegna altarpiece in the church of San Zeno and frescoes in the Eremitani chapel: 460. St Anthony of Padua: II 113. Mentioned in a quotation from Alfred de Musset: 475. The life of Fabrice del Dongo related to Stendhal by a Canon of Padua: V 742. Visited by M and his mother: 878–79.

PARIS. Swann's house on the Quai d'Orléans: I 20–21 (cf. 346). The dome of Saint-Augustin seen across a jumble of roofs—a Piranesi view of Paris: 90. "Melancholy neighbourhood" of the Champs-Elysées where Gilberte lives: 201. Swann scours the boulevards in search of Odette: 322–28. Odette walks in the Rue Abbattucci (now Rue de la Boétie): 340. Odette's idea of the smart places in Paris: 344–45. The frozen Seine from the Pont de la Concorde: 565. M's plan of Paris and obsession with the Swanns' neighbourhood: 586, 590–92. M's mother meets Swann in the Trois Quartiers: 588–90. Paris in autumn: 598–601. The Sainte Chapelle "the pearl among them all" (Norpois): II 49. Restaurants of Paris: 77–79. M's reactions to Parisian architecture; Gabriel's palaces compared unfavourably to the Trocadéro: 83–84. Paris "darker than today"; indoor and outdoor lighting; Parisian "winter-garden": 228–29. Spring in Paris; Mme Swann's walks in the Avenue du Bois de Boulogne (now Avenue Foch): 288–98. The Gare Saint-Lazare: 303. Paris street names: 360. Rue d'Aboukir, in the Jewish quarter: 433.

The Hôtel de Guermantes, a palace in the heart of Paris: **III** 9–10. Streets of Paris aflower with unknown beauties: 71. Suburbs of Paris: 204, 207. Rachel and her professional friends—another Paris in the heart of Paris (Place Pigalle, Boulevard de Clichy): 215. Paris in the late afternoon: 275. The Europe district: 585. Poor quarters of Paris reminiscent of Venice; roof-top views: 784. Place de la Concorde on a summer evening: **IV** 45. A populous, nocturnal Paris brought miraculously close to M by the telephone: 177, 181. M. de Chevregny sees all the shows in Paris: 662–63. Charlus's dissertation on the ecclesiastical background of Paris street names; the Judengasse: 687–90. Andrée to take Albertine to the Buttes-Chaumont (q.v.): **V** 15–16. Street cries of Paris: 146–51, 160–63, 174–77. Charm of the old aristocratic quarters lies in the fact that they are also plebeian: 147. M's drive through Paris with Albertine: 216–29; houses in the boulevards and avenues "a pink congelation of sunshine and cold": 216; girls in shop-doors, in the streets, in the Bois (q.v.): 216–24; Albertine on the Trocadéro (q.v.): 217–18; charm of the new districts: 218; full moon over Paris: 228. M meets Gisèle in Passy: 231–32. The "spoken newspaper" of Paris: 288. Albertine spends three days in Auteuil: 449–50. Paris by moonlight, seen from the Porte Maillot: 550. Long summer evenings in Paris: 649–51. Paris in war-time: **VI** 47–237 *passim*. Fashion and pleasure, in the absence of the arts; comparison with the Directory: 47–63. The blackout: 63–67. Zeppelin raids: 98–100. Nightfall over Paris; comparison with 1815: 104–6, 161–62. Paris as Pompeii: 169–70 (cf. 209–10); or as Harun al-Rashid's Baghdad: 173. Hotels and shops closed: 174. M walks through Paris in an air-raid: 207–8, 218. The catacombs of the Métro: 208–9. The Prince de Guermantes's new house in the Avenue du Bois: 242. The streets near the Champs-Elysées: 243. (*See* Abbaye-aux-Bois; Bois de Boulogne; Buttes-Chaumont; Champs-Elysées; Trocadéro.)

PARMA. Poetry of the name: **I** 552. Parma violets: **II** 231, 291 (cf. **III** 584). Evoked for M on meeting the Princesse de Parme: **III** 584–85. The Duc de Guermantes spends a winter there: 656. The Princess's palace there: **IV** 255.

PARVILLE-LA-BINGARD (f). Station on the little local railway:

**IV** 348. View of Parville from La Raspelière: 541. Etymology: 549. M drops Albertine there after their outings: 566, 569. The cliffs of Parville: 572, 722. Albertine's revelation about her relationship with Mlle Vinteuil occurs as the train enters Parville station: 700–4. (Sometimes confused with Incarville (q.v.).)

PIERREFONDS. The Verdurins take Odette to see the château: **I** 415–16. The Marquis de Forestelle has a house in the neighbourhood; Swann considers inviting himself to stay in order to intercept Odette at the château: 417–18.

PISA. One of the Italian towns that M imagines visiting: **I** 555–56 (cf. **V** 223).

POMPEII. "Arrested in an accustomed movement," as at the destruction of Pompeii: **II** 667. "Like a hearse on some Pompeian terracotta": **III** 432. War-time Paris compared to Pompeii: **VI** 169–70, 210.

PONT-À-COULEUVRE (f). On the little local railway: **II** 326. The manager of the Grand Hotel meets M there: **IV** 204, 210. M. de Cambremer has seen no snakes there: 440; Brichot gives its etymology: 440–41.

PONT-AVEN. One of the stops on the 1.22 train: **I** 548–49. What its name evokes: 553 (cf. **II** 324, 622).

PONTORSON. One of the stops on the 1.22 train: **I** 548–49. What its name evokes: 553.

QUESTEMBERT. One of the stops on the 1.22 train: **I** 548–49. What its name evokes: 553.

QUETTEHOLME (f), near Balbec. Goal of some of M's excursions with Mme de Villeparisis; its rocks: **II** 387. M and Albertine drive through it on the way to the church of Saint-Jean-de-la-Haise: **IV** 534–38, 558–60. Albertine sends M telegrams and postcards from there: 570.

QUIMPERLÉ. One of the stops on the 1.22 train: **I** 548–49. What its name evokes: 553 (cf. **II** 324, 622).

RASPELIÈRE, LA (f). Cambremer house rented for the season by the Verdurins: **II** 3; **IV** 206–7, 226. Its situation and view; etymology of the name: 280–82. Compared to Féterne: 283, 287–88. Mme Verdurin's "Wednesdays" there: 346–47. M takes the train with the "little clan" to go and dine there: 358–59. The dinner-party: 404–514. M's first impressions; the Verdurins' en-

thusiasm for the place: 411–13. The changes they have made
and the Cambremers' reactions to them: 425, 428–30, 436–37,
467–68, 474. M calls there with Albertine; its garden and its
"views"; excursions in the neighbourhood: 538–47. Similarities
between La Raspelière and Quai Conti: **V** 378–81.

RHEIMS. The cathedral: **I** 84–85. Mme Swann and her daughter go there: 191. "A positive jewel in stone" (Norpois): **II** 49.
The statues at Rheims: 435 (cf. 656). Biscuits of Rheims: **III**
627. Destruction of the cathedral: **VI** 154, 215.

RIVEBELLE (f), near Balbec. The summer lasts longer there
than at Balbec: **II** 346. Splendours of Rivebelle almost wholly
invisible from Marcouville: 385. Dinners with Saint-Loup there:
523–57 *passim*. The restaurant and its garden; the waiters and
the diners; M gets drunk: 529–42. The women in the restaurant:
541–44 (cf. **III** 535). M and Saint-Loup meet Elstir: 553–57.
Seen across the bay: 729 (cf. **IV** 300). M remembers getting
drunk there: **III** 226. Further memories of evenings at Rivebelle:
535, 541, 545 (cf. **IV** 590). Its islands and indentations seen
from the coach on the way to La Raspelière: **IV** 399. Denigrated
by Mme Verdurin: 502. Waiters from Rivebelle at the Grand
Hotel: 528. The "view of Rivebelle" at La Raspelière: 541–42.
M takes Albertine to lunch there; her interest in the waiter:
563–65. M returns alone, and again drinks too much: 565. Les-
bian dinner-party there: **V** 111. Final evocation of Rivebelle: **VI**
261.

ROBINSON. Restaurant-cabaret in the suburbs of Paris: **III** 594.

ROME. Piranesi views of Rome: **I** 90. The Rome embassy (will
Vaugoubert get the post?): **II** 43–46. Norpois was counsellor
there: 187. M has never been there: **IV** 659.

ROUEN. Bookstall at one of the doors of the cathedral: **V** 147.
British soldiers based there during the war; it has become "another town"; beauty of the emaciated saints of the cathedral: **VI**
170.

ROMANIA. Status of the Jews there: **II** 434 (cf. **III** 253). Ronsard known there as a nobleman rather than a poet: **IV** 409.

ROUSSAINVILLE-LE-PIN (f), near Combray. Its castle keep visible from the little closet smelling of orris-root: **I** 14. Françoise

buys a turkey in Roussainville market: 97, where she goes every Saturday: 153, (cf. 164). Its etymology: 144. Roussainville woods: 211, 218–23. Its white gables carved in relief against the sky: 211. M has never been there: 214, though he longs to do so: 220, and yearns for a village girl: 219–23 (cf. II 317). Gilberte used to play with little boys in the castle keep: VI 4, 9. Fought over during the war: 95.

RUSSIA. Status of the Jews there: II 434. The pogroms: III 139.

SAINT-ANDRÉ-DES-CHAMPS (f), near Combray. Its twin spires: I 205. M and his family shelter under the porch; its Gothic sculptures and their living models: 212–13, 216–17 (II 573; III 560–61). "An old church, monumental, rustic, and golden as a haystack": 260. The ethos of Saint-André-des-Champs, as illustrated by Françoise: III 193–94, 502 (cf. V 774–75); by Albertine: 502, 506 (cf. V 815); by Andrée: V 815; by Saint-Loup: VI 70; by the butler: 220; by Françoise's cousins, the Larivières: 224–26.

SAINT-CLOUD. Open-air restaurants there patronised by the Verdurins: I 381–84. M's mother moves to a house there during his absence at Balbec: II 307, 310. M goes there with Albertine: III 533. He advises her to go there rather than to the Buttes-Chaumont: V 16. Seen from the Bois de Boulogne: 227. Visited by the Duc and Duchesse de Guermantes: 782–83.

SAINT-FRICHOUX (f), near Balbec. M sends the lift-boy to find Albertine there: IV 256. Last station before Doncières: 348. Etymology: 449.

SAINT-JEAN-DE-LA-HAISE (f). Isolated church in the neighbourhood of Balbec, painted by Albertine: IV 534–39. Buried in foliage: 558–59. "All pinnacles"; its stone angels: 560.

SAINT-MARS-LE-VÊTU (f), near Balbec. Goal of some of M's excursions with Mme de Villeparisis: II 387. Charlus and Morel have lunch in a restaurant there: IV 551–52. Albertine curious as to its etymology: 562 (cf. V 700). Its piscine steeples: 562. Remembered by M: V 647, 700, 730.

SAINT-MARS-LE-VIEUX (f). Station on the little local railway: II 326; IV 393. M drives there: 538, 558.

SAINT-MARTIN-DU-CHÊHNE (f). Charlus takes a house near there: **IV** 449. Brichot gives the etymology of the name: 451. Charlus takes the train there: 599.

SAINT-PIERRE-DES-IFS (f). One of the stations on the little local railway. Glorious girl with a cigarette gets into the train there: **IV** 381. Charlus takes a house near there: 449; the name associated with him: 692–93.

SICILY. Charlus's ancestors Princes of Sicily: **II** 448. The Guermantes plan to go there: **III** 813. Prince Foggi has an estate there: **V** 862. (*See also* Agrigento.)

SIENA. "Seductive charms" of: **II** 206. Balbec "as beautiful as Siena" (Swann): 324. M has not yet been there: **IV** 659.

SOGNE, La (f), near Balbec. Albertine goes to the races there: **II** 623. M sends the lift-boy to find Albertine there: **IV** 256. Stop on the little railway; Brichot gives the etymology of the name: 397. The Cambremers' station: 512.

SPAIN. Norpois plans to take M's father there: **II** 48 (cf. 304, 381; **III** 244). Spain "all the rage" (Cottard): 96.

SUSA, capital of ancient Elam (now part of W. Iran) and residence of Darius and later Kings of Persia. Nissim Bernard like a figure from Susa restored by Mme Dieulafoy: **II** 483. Bloch's appearance likewise evokes reflexions on monuments from Susa: **III** 254. The throne-room at Susa: **IV** 87.

TANGIER. Saint-Loup meets Mme de Stermaria there: **III** 475.

TANSONVILLE (f), the Swanns' place near Combray. M remembers his stay there with Mme de Saint-Loup (Gilberte): **I** 6 (cf. **VI** 1 et sqq.). Description of Swann's park; the white fence; the lilacs, the ornamental pond and the water plants; the hawthorns: 190–7, 201–4, 215, 218. Swann yearns after it in the spring in Paris: 325; **II** 288, 289. Remembered by Françoise: **III** 23. The Saint-Loups settle in there: **V** 917–18. M goes to stay: 921; **VI** 1–27; the house and park: 9–10. Tansonville during the war (Gilberte's letters): 88, 93–96.

TARN. Correct way of pronouncing: **V** 35.

THIBERZY (f), near Combray. M's cousins come over from Thiberzy for lunch on Sundays: **I** 88. Etymology: 146. Françoise goes there to fetch a midwife: 151.

TOURAINE. Mme Bontemps has a house there: **V** 482. M

hopes that Albertine has gone there: 580. Saint-Loup sent down to find her: 587, 636–41. Albertine's death: 642–44. M sends Aimé there to investigate: 706; his report on Albertine and the laundry-girl: 706–8.

TOURS. Minced pork (*rillettes*) of Tours: **III** 627. Horror of the name for M: **V** 729.

TRIESTE. Albertine has spent "the happiest years of my life" there with Mlle Vinteuil's friend: **IV** 701. It becomes, for M, no longer "a delightful place" but "an accursed city": 707–11.

TROCADÉRO, Paris. M finds more style in it than in Gabriel's palaces: **II** 83–84. The Trocadéro museum: 322–23. M persuades Albertine to go to a gala matinée there instead of calling on the Verdurins: **V** 134, 151. Léa due to appear there: 185. M sends Françoise to recall Albertine: 196–203. M and Albertine discuss its architecture: 217–18. The towers of the Trocadéro: **VI** 105.

TWICKENHAM, London. Residence of the exiled Comte de Paris. Swann invited there: **I** 23; **II** 2 (cf. **VI** 403–4).

VENICE. Remembered by M: **I** 9. M's first idea of Venice gleaned from a reproduction of a Titian drawing with the lagoon in the background: 54. The "Staircase of the Giants" in the Doges' Palace: 461. Potency of the name: 550. Plan for a spring holiday there; the Venice of M's imagination: 554–59 (cf. **II** 161, 287–88). The Frari Titian and the Carpaccios of San Giorgio degli Schiavoni: **II** 14. Bloch's pronunciation of the name in English (Ruskin's *Stones of Venice*): 436. Mentioned in a quotation from Musset: 475. The Venice of Carpaccio and Veronese evoked by Elstir: 652–53. M's dream of Venice: **III** 191–92 (cf. **V** 237). Blend of softness and brittleness of Venetian glass: 474. Perspectives in Venice: 498–99. Its poor quarters resemble those of Paris: 784. Mme de Cambremer-Legrandin detests the Grand Canal: **IV** 286–87. M's persistent longing for Venice: **V** 27, 137, 220–22, 229. Albertine's Fortuny gowns conjure up the Venice of the Doges: 497–98, and seem to be the "tempting phantoms" of the invisible Venice M has dreamed of for so long: 531, 538. Evocation of Venice in the spring: 555–59. M visits Venice with his mother: 844–88, impressions of the city: 844–50; M's solitary excursions; Venetian women: 848–50, 879–84; its social life:

852–53; the baptistery of St Mark's: 877–79; Carpaccio: 876–77. Evening in Venice: 881–82. *O sole mio*; the vision crumbles: 883–87. Mme Verdurin visits Venice during the war: **VI** 51. M's unsatisfactory "snapshots" of Venice: 253–56. The uneven paving-stones; resuscitation of his real memory of Venice: 257, 260–61, 264, 270.

VERSAILLES. Swann's liking for it; Odette finds it boring: **I** 350. M crosses the Bois de Boulogne on his way to Trianon: 598; its chestnut-trees and lilacs: 602. Rachel takes a little house in the neigbhourhood: **III** 160. The view from the terrace of the palace: 527. The Princess de Guermantes's garden, with its Hubert Robert fountain, is "Versailles in Paris": 801; **IV** 75. Doncières has a spurious look of Versailles: 681. Albertine visits Versailles with the chauffeur: **V** 168–74. M takes Albertine there: 545–47. Nude statues of goddesses among its groves and fountains: 711–12.

VICHY. Bloch thinks of taking a cure there: **III** 296. Mme Cottard declines to go there on the grounds that "it's too stuffy": **IV** 495. Albertine once knew a woman of ill repute there: 677–78. Albertine on the subject of Vichy water: **V** 166.

VIEUXVICQ (f), near Combray. Relationship of its steeple to the twin steeples of Martinville: **I** 254–56.

VITRÉ. One of the stops on the 1.22 train: **I** 548–49. What its name evokes: 553.

VIVONNE (f). River near Combray. Its water-lilies recalled with the rest of Combray and its surroundings by the taste of the madeleine dipped in tea: **I** 64. The apse of Saint-Hilaire seen from its banks: 90. Its course visible from the top of the steeple: 147. Meeting with Legrandin on its banks: 182. Runs along the "Guermantes way"; description of its course: 235–38. Its unattainable source: 241–42. M's dreams of a life of pleasure by the Vivonne; its association with Guermantes: 257, 260 (cf. **III** 7, 13, 28). Seeing it again, M finds it "narrow and ugly": **VI** 1–2; he discovers its source: 3.

VOISENON (f). The Prince de Guermantes's country seat: **V** 785.

# Index of Themes

AEROPLANES. Freemasonry of aviation enthusiasts: **III** 548 (cf. **V** 132–33). M sees an aeroplane for the first time: **IV** 582 (cf. **V** 209–10). M and Albertine visit aerodromes: **V** 132–33. "One of those 120 horse-power machines—the Mystère model": 209–10. An aeroplane high in the sky above Versailles—beauty of the sound of "that little insect throbbing up there": 547–48. Albertine's lie about a visit to an aerodrome with Andrée: 828. Flying angels in Giotto's Padua frescoes reminiscent of airmen looping the loop: 878–79. Aeroplanes at evening over war-time Paris: **VI** 63 (cf. 161–62). Saint-Loup's opinion of aeroplanes in war: 82; his discussion with M about the beauty of war-planes at night: 98–100. Air raids: 161–62, 207–10.

ALCOHOL. M's doctor prescribes alcohol for his suffocations, to the distress of his grandmother, who sees him "dying a drunkard's death": **II** 93. M's drunken euphoria on the train to Balbec: 311–14. His sensations after drinking too much champagne and port at Rivebelle: 531–35. Charm that alcohol gives to the present moment; inebriation brings about for a while "a state of subjective idealism, pure phenomenalism": 538–41 (cf. **VI** 513). Alcoholic slumbers: 544–47. M gets drunk in Aimé's restaurant; different kinds of intoxication; he sees himself in a mirror: **III** 227. M drinks seven or eight glasses of port to overcome his diffidence with girls: **IV** 321–22. Effect of cider on Albertine: 562–63. At Rivebelle again; M's solitary drinking; the pattern on the wall: 565.

AMERICANS. Swann's liaison with an American: **I** 275. American lady and her daughter at Balbec: **II** 726. American lady whose only book is a copy of Parny's poems: **III** 617. American multi-millionairess married to a French prince: 734. American lady bursts into M's room at the Grand Hotel: **IV** 260. An American called Charles Crecy marries a niece of Mme de Guermantes: 661. American Jewesses in their night-dresses in Paris hotels during air-raids: **VI** 100. Charlus on the Americans

705

during the war: 153. American hostesses: 242, 246. Bloch's American friend in the new context of Parisian society: 396–403.

ANTI-SEMITISM. *See* Dreyfus Case; Jews.

APPLE-TREES. On the "Méséglise way"—their circular shadows on the sunlit ground: **I** 205. Seen from the road near Balbec: **II** 390. M's night-long contemplation of a branch of apple blossom: 390–91 (cf. 582). Mme de Villeparisis's painting of apple blossom: **III** 286–88. "Dazzling spectacle" of apple-trees in spring: **IV** 244–45. Compared to hawthorns: 250–51 (cf. 740).

AQUARIUM. M. de Palancy's monocle a "symbolical fragment of the glass wall of his aquarium": **I** 465 (cf. **III** 48). Berma in *Phèdre* like a branch of coral in an aquarium: **II** 185. Dining-room in the Grand Hotel, Balbec "an immense and wonderful aquarium" at night: 353 (cf. **V** 702–3). Garden of the Rivebelle restaurant like "an aquarium of gigantic size lit by a supernatural light": 536. Subaqueous domain of the Princesse de Guermantes's box at the Opéra: **III** 41–49. The lover separated from the outside world as though he were in an aquarium: 383. Charlus lives like a fish in an aquarium, unaware of his own visibility: **IV** 609–10.

ARABIAN NIGHTS. Swann's secret life as mysterious as Ali Baba's: **I** 21–22. Aunt Léonie's *Arabian Nights* plates: 77, 96; **II** 660–61. Jews at Balbec suggest illustrations to the *Arabian Nights*: 435. Quoted apropos of a Paris restaurant proprietor: **III** 557. Oriane de Guermantes pictured as someone more wonderful than Princess Bedr-el-Budur: 613. M's mother gives him both French translations, Galland and Mardrus: **IV** 318–19. M obliged to show the ingenuity of a Sheherazade to keep Albertine amused: **V** 167. Mendacious but none the less charming tales: 187–88. M imagines himself a character in the *Arabian Nights*: 331 (cf. **VI** 258). Purlieus of Venice like a city in the *Arabian Nights*: 849, 881. War-time Paris reminds M of the *Arabian Nights*: **VI** 173. M compares the scene in Jupien's brothel to one of the tales: 206. The name Basra recalls Bassorah and Sinbad the Sailor: 430–31. M's book the *Arabian Nights* of another age?: 524–25.

ART. *See* Literature; Music; Painting.

ASPARAGUS. Discussed by Aunt Léonie and Françoise: **I**

74–75. M enraptured by their iridescent colours: 168–69. The kitchen-maid allergic to their smell: 173. Elstir's *Bundle of Asparagus*: **III** 686. The Duc de Guermantes on green asparagus; E. de Clermont-Tonnerre (q.v.) quoted on the subject: 690.

BALLET. Bakst's decors for the Russian Ballet: **II** 718 (cf. **V** 3). Dancer admired by Rachel: **III** 235–36. The impact of the Russian Ballet: **IV** 193–94 (cf. **V** 314–15). Charlus's influence on Morel as an artist compared to Diaghilev's: 420–21. Mme Verdurin "an aged Fairy Godmother" to the Russian dancers: **V** 313–15. Theatrical designs of Sert, Bakst and Benois: 497–98. Reference to the "dazzling" *Legend of Joseph* by Sert, Strauss and Kessler: 876–77.

BEAUTY. Element of novelty essential to beauty: **II** 318. "The complementary part that is added to a fragmentary and fugitive stranger by our imagination, over-stimulated by regret"; "a sequence of hypotheses which ugliness cuts short": 398–99. Youth in pursuit of Beauty: 502. "Fluid, collective and mobile beauty" of the girls of the "little band"; "noble and calm models of human beauty": 505–6. Elstir's ideal of beauty: 586–88. Beauty is "ordered complexity": **III** 61. "True beauty is so individual, so novel always, that one does not recognise it as beauty": 341. "The mysterious differences from which beauty derives": **V** 157. Perverse notion that true beauty is represented by a railway carriage rather than Siena, Venice or Granada: 173–74. "The possibility of pleasure may be a beginning of beauty": 180. The identity of the woman we love is far more important than her beauty: 593–94.

BELIEF. Our beliefs are neither engendered nor destroyed by facts: **I** 208–9. A fetishistic attachment to things survives the disappearance of our belief in them: 603. The part played by belief in the image we form of a person: **II** 595–96. Our beliefs of more importance to our happiness than the person we see, since it is through them that we can see the person: 720. Only imagination and belief can "create an atmosphere": **III** 32. "Irreducible essence" which, when we are young, our beliefs confer on a woman's clothes: 528–29. Invisible and variable atmosphere created around us by our beliefs: **V** 191. "Invisible belief that sustains the edifice of our sensory world": 600. Belief engendered by desire: 690–92, 692–94, 823–25. Dubious belief which leaves room for the possibility of what we wish to be true: 792. A large part of what we believe "springs from an original mistake in our premises": 890.

BICYCLES. Albertine pushing a bicycle: II 509; "spinning through the showers": 645 (cf. V 658–59). The lift-boy on his bicycle: IV 344. "Winged messengers of variegated hue"—hotel messengers on bicycles: V 175. "Fabulous coursers"—girls and their bicycles in the Bois de Boulogne: 220; "half-human, half-winged, angel or peri"—another girl cyclist: 224. Albertine at the pianola revives M's memories of her cycling at Balbec: 515, 518; speeding through Balbec bent over her "mythological wheel": 658–59.

BIRDS. M's bedroom in winter—building a nest like a sea-swallow: I 7. Pigeons in the Champs-Elysées—"the lilacs of the feathered kingdom": 575, 579. Birdsong in the forests near Balbec, to which M listens like Prometheus to the Oceanides: II 408 (cf. IV 535). The "little band" at Balbec like "a flock of gulls": 503; "an assembly of birds before taking flight": 508 (cf. V 225). Cooing of pigeons: III 186–87 (cf. V 539–40). Blue-tits in the blossoming apple-trees near Balbec: IV 244. Gulls on the sea at Balbec—like water-lilies: 280, 284; admired by Albertine: 289, 308, 311. Unknown bird chanting matins in the Lydian mode: V 522. "Melancholy refrain" of the pigeons: 539–40.

BODY. The body's memory more enduring than the mind's: I 5–6 (cf. VI 11). We localise in a person's body all the potentialities of his or her life: III 38. Touching prescience of women for what will give pleasure to the male body: 221. Illness makes us aware of that unknown being, our body: 404. Albertine's naked body: V 97–98 (cf. 710–12). The body's "terrible capacity for registering things": 571. "Possession of a body . . . the great danger to the mind": VI 512.

BRITISH. See English.

BROTHELS. Odette's dealings with procuresses: I 525–26. Swann's visits to brothels; the girl with the blue eyes: 530–31. Bloch takes M to a house of assignation; "Rachel when from the Lord": II 205–8. Uninterestingness of women met in brothels: III 209, 496 (cf. V 181–83, 222–23). Saint-Loup's enthusiasm for brothels; Mme Putbus's maid and Mlle d'Orgeville: **IV** 127. Luxury brothel at Maineville: 250; mistaken for a grand hotel: 647–48; the Prince de Guermantes's assignation with Morel, and the experiences of Charlus and Jupien with Mlle Noémie: 650–56. Women of the "closed houses": **V** 181–83, 222–23. M and two laundry-girls in a house of assignation: 741. Morel, Albertine and a fisher-girl in a brothel at Couliville: 810–11. Social gossip in the Maineville brothel: 899–900. Jupien's brothel in war-time Paris: **VI** 174–212. The Métro in war-time like a Pompeian brothel: 208–9.

CLASS. "Hindu" view of society at Combray—a rigid caste system: **I** 19 (cf. **IV** 579–80). For M's grandmother, distinction of manners independent of social position: 25. M's great-aunt disapproves of Swann for associating with people outside his "proper station": 26. For Aunt Céline, "one man is as good as the next": 34. Françoise's "class" pessimism: **II** 98. Social mobility of Swann: 118–19. Intermediate class between the Faubourg Saint-Germain and the world of the merely rich: 294–95. Mutual misunderstanding between the aristocracy and the middle classes: 383–85. Distinctions in middle-class life even more stupid than in "society": 480. Physiognomical variety of the French middle class: 579. Similarities between people of the same generation more evident than those between people of the same class: **IV** 109–11. M makes no class distinctions: 579, but his mother is imbued with the "Combray spirit" in the matter of caste: 579–80. "Every social class has its own pathology": **V** 11. "The classes of the intellect take no account of birth": **VI** 61.

DEATH. Swann *père*'s behaviour on the death of his wife: **I** 17–18. The Celtic belief in metempsychosis: 59. The "seamy side," as opposed to the abstract idea, of death: 112–13. Françoise's reaction to Aunt Léonie's death: 215–16. Love and death and the mystery of human personality: 438. Our unconscious resistance to the oblivion death will bring: **II** 338–39. Resurrection of the soul after death perhaps a phenomenon of memory (q.v.): **III** 111. Unpredictability of the hour of death; the sick person's first acquaintance with the Stranger that has taken up residence in him: 427–30 (cf. **VI** 517–18). M's grandmother's death: 470–71. Signs of death on Swann's face: **IV** 121–22. "The dead exist only in us": 214–15. "The dead annex the living"; true and false sense in which we may say that death is not in vain: 228–30. Our indifference towards the dead: 230–31. Diversity of the forms of death: 359 (cf. **V** 260–61). Mme Verdurin's reaction to the deaths of the "faithful": 399–400, 404–7 (cf. **V** 317–20). "Each alteration of the brain is a partial death"; the phenomena of memory and life after death: 522–23. Imminence of death makes us appreciate life: **V** 101–2 (cf. 651–52). Bergotte's death; "Dead forever? Who can say?": 238–46. Swann's death; "There are almost as many deaths as there are people": 260–64. "The death of others is like a journey one might oneself make": 264. Presentiments of death: 538, 540, 543–44. In good health we imagine we are not afraid of death: 569–70. Albertine's death: 641–42. "The idea that one will die is more painful than dying, but less painful than the idea that another person is dead": 686. Our fear of the dead as judges: 689 (cf. 836–37). M's hopes of being reunited with Albertine in death: 690–92. Our inability to picture the reality of death: 700–1. Death little different from absence; a person may go on living after death as a sort of cutting grafted on to the heart of another: 706. "It is not because other people are dead that our affection for them fades; it is because we ourselves are dying": 805. "Nobody really believes in a future life": 836–37. "Death merely acts in the same way as absence": 872. Death cures us of the desire for immortality: 874. The abyss of death between us and the women we no longer love: **VI** 6. Saint-Loup's death: 226. Death subject to certain laws; accidental death may be predetermined: 231–32. Charlus's roll-call of the dead: 249. Beatific visions of Combray and Venice make death a matter of indifference to M: 254, 262 (cf. 526). Death as a deliverance: 319. Old age is like death, in that some face them both with indifference, not because they have more courage than others but because they have less imagination: 350. Ubiquity and familiarity of death: 422–24. "Every death is for others a simplification of life": 425. Berma's dialogue with death: 454. The last and least enviable forms of survival after death: 475. M's renewed fear of death not for himself but for his book: 514–15. The idea of

death takes up permanent residence within him: 523. Men's
works will die as well as men: 524.

DOCTORS. *See* Medicine.

DREAMS. M's dreams of a woman: I 3. Swann's dream of leaving Odette: 503–4. Swann's dream of Odette and Forcheville:
538–43. M's dream about Gilberte: II 281–82. M's dreams after
dining at Rivebelle: 545–46. Beauty of the dream-world; nightmares and their fantastic picture-books: III 105–10. Saint-
Loup's dream of Rachel's infidelity: 160. M's dream of Venice:
191–92. M dreams of his dead grandmother; he speaks of her to
his father; dream language: IV 216–19, 241–42, 246. Pleasures
experienced in dreams: 518–20. A dream may have the clarity of
consciousness: 523–24. The stuff of dreams: V 153–55; inven-
tiveness in dreams: 156–60; M's dream of a woman carriage-
driver: 158. Bergotte's nightmares: 241–42. M's bad dreams:
664. The "reprises" or "da capos" of one's dreams; seeming reality of dreams; Albertine's constant presence in M's dreams; he
speaks to her in a dream, in the presence of his grandmother:
725–28. The importance of dreams; tricks they play with Time
(q.v.); the "nocturnal muse": VI 322–27.

DRESS. Legrandin's bow-ties: I 92, 167. Unbecoming fashion
prevailing at the time of Swann's meeting with Odette: 278;
Odette's cape trimmed with skunk, and her Rembrandt hat:
340–41. Head-dress of the Princesse des Laumes: 471, 484.
Mme Cottard "in full fig": 532. Gilberte's governess's macin-
tosh and blue-feathered hat: 561. Gilberte's fur-trimmed cap:
566. Odette's costumes in the Bois: 494–95, 603–6. M deplores
the new (1913) fashions in the Bois: 603–6. M's Charvet tie and
patent leather boots: II 135. Odette's indoor clothes: 138–39,
155, 230–33, 262–69. Mme Cottard's Raudnitz dress: 238.
Changes in fashion; Odette adapts the new fashions to the old
("Mme Swann is quite a period in herself"): 263–69. Odette's
splendour in the Avenue du Bois; exquisite details of her (typi-
cally mauve) outfit; the apotheosis of fashion: 290–96. Swann's
tall hat lined with green leather: 296. Françoise's simple good
taste in dress: 308–9. Saint-Loup's white suit: 421; "relaxed and
careless elegance" of his clothes appreciated by M's grandmother: 428 (cf. III 117–18). Studied sobriety of Charlus's

clothes: 454–55. Simple but expensive elegance of Mme Elstir's clothes: 586, 634. Elstir's unerring taste in dress, appreciated by Albertine: 634–35. Yachting and racing dress; Mlle Léa's costume at the races: 651–58. Costumes of Veronese's and Carpaccio's Venice; their secret rediscovered by Fortuny: 652–54. Elstir on Paris couturiers: 655. The art of the milliner: 659. Costumes of the Princesse and Duchesse de Guermantes at the Opéra: **III** 45–49, 61–64, 68–69, and Mme de Cambremer's comparative dowdiness: 64. The Duchesse de Guermantes's street clothes: 74, 189–90. Saint-Loup's style in dress: 117–19. Mme de Guermantes's blue pekin skirt and straw hat trimmed with cornflowers: 274. Mme de Marsantes's white surah dress: 338. Françoise's mourning dress: 456. Role of costume in love: 529. Low-necked dresses of the "flower-maidens": 579–80. Swann's elegance; his pearl-grey frock-coat, white gloves and flared topper: 793–94. The Duchess's red satin dress, ostrich feather and tulle scarf: 800, and her black shoes: 818–19. Her Tiepolo evening cloak: **IV** 83, 161. Sartorial elegance of the Balbec liftboy: 257–58. The dowager Mme de Cambremer's get-up: 277–78. Albertine's motoring toque and veil: 536, 561–62 (cf. **V** 70). Albertine's clothes, inspired by Elstir; her grey outfit with plaid sleeves: 617–18. Charlus on dress; the Princesse de Cadignan: 618–19. The Princesse de Guermantes's eccentricity of dress; her Gainsborough hat: 730–31. Albertine's delight in the accessories of costume: **V** 32, 74–76. Mme de Guermantes's elegance; "the best-dressed woman in Paris"; her Fortuny gowns: 33–34. M discusses clothes with her: 39–40, 47–48, 75–76. Different attitudes towards clothes of rich and poor women: 75–76. Albertine's black satin dress: 127–28. The dairymaid's sweater: 184–85. Charlus's interest in women's clothes, and his views on Albertine's: 291–94. Albertine and Fortuny; reminders of Venice: 497–500, 531, 538, 546, 555 (cf. 877). Paris fashions in war-time: **VI** 47–48. Young Mme de Saint-Euverte's Empire dress: 493–94.

DREYFUS CASE. Its effect on Society: **II** 122–23 (cf. **III** 252–53; **IV** 107–8; **V** 312–14). Aimé persuaded of Dreyfus's guilt: 527. Saint-Loup a Dreyfusard; the Case discussed at Doncières: **III** 134–40, 153. Mme Sazerat ("alone of her kind at Combray") a

Dreyfusard: 200 (cf. 392). M and his father take opposite sides: 200. Rachel's view: 217. Mme de Villeparisis's aloofness: 253 (cf. 319, 335). Bloch and Norpois discuss the Case: 313–16, 323–24. Views of the Duc and Duchesse de Guermantes: 316–23; of Mme Swann 341 (cf. 357); of Mme Verdurin ("a latent bourgeois anti-semitism"—but cf. **IV** 194–95): 341; of Mme de Marsantes: 342; of Prince Von: 346 (cf. **IV** 105); of Charlus: 390–93; of the two butlers: 402–3. Reinach's achievement; Dreyfusism and heredity; France divided from top to bottom: 403. Dreyfusism in a Paris café: 548–49. Mme de Guermantes's ambivalence: 653 (cf. 704; **V** 45–46). Swann's Dreyfusism: 792–800 (cf. **IV** 122, 132–33, 151–53). Saniette a Dreyfusard: 799. The Duc de Guermantes deplores Swann's "treachery": **IV** 104–8. Saint-Loup changes his tune: 132–33, 151–52. The Prince de Guermantes and his wife converted to Dreyfusism: 142–54 (cf. 731). The Duc de Guermantes converted (temporarily) to Dreyfusism by three Italian ladies: 188–90. Influence of the Case on the salons of Mme Verdurin ("the active centre" of Dreyfusism) and Mme Swann: 194–99 (cf. 384–85; **V** 312–14). Brichot's anti-Dreyfusism: 384–85 (cf. **III** 799). M. de Cambremer's anti-Dreyfusism: 496–97 (cf. **V** 312–13). The Duc de Guermantes, the Jockey Club and the Dreyfus Case: **V** 41–46. Complex influence of the Case on Society: 312–14; continuing social anti-semitism: 776 et sqq. The Dreyfus Case in retrospect (1916): **VI** 52–55; after the war: 391.

DRINK. *See* Alcohol.

ENGLISH, ENGLISHMEN. "Our friends across the Channel" (Odette): **I** 107. English visitors to Combray: 146. Affectation of British stiffness in Odette's handwriting: 314. Odette as a child sold by her mother to a rich Englishman in Nice: 522. M's ignorance of English: **II** 110, 161. Odette's Anglomania: 125, 136, 148, 164; speaks to Gilberte in English: 215; her English accent: 230. Bloch's mispronunciation of English: 436. English visitors "athirst for information" about Elstir: 554. "Positively British stiffness" of the Duchesse de Guermantes's get-up at the Opéra: **III** 63. "In France we give to everything that is more or less British the one name that it happens not to bear in England" (*smoking*): 659 (cf. **II** 87–88: *water-closets*). Prince Von on the ineptitude of the British army ("the English are so *schtubid*"): 722–23. The Duc de Châtellerault poses as an Englishman: **IV** 46, 49. English soldiers during the war—like Greek statues, "unimaginable marvels" (Charlus): **VI** 126, 170; "Our loyal allies," English fair play, "the brave tommies" (Odette): 144–45. The Duc de Guermantes's anglophilia: 135. Change in English attitude towards the Germans: 135–36. Bloch's English *chic*: 385.

FAUBOURG SAINT-GERMAIN. Swann's position in the aristocratic world of the Faubourg Saint-Germain: **I** 19, 269, 304–5. *Noli me tangere* of the Faubourg: 408. Psychology of the women of the Faubourg: 476. Odette's detachment from the Faubourg: **II** 124–27 (cf. 294–96). The Faubourg Saint-Germain has no more to do with the mind of a Bergotte than "with the law of causality or the idea of God": 179. Its barriers: 294–95. Nine-tenths of the men of the Faubourg appear to the middle classes as crapulous paupers: 384. Not lavish with tips: 389. Excess of politeness as a professional "bent": 414. The Guermantes' position in the Faubourg; M's romantic notions about it; "the well-trodden doormat of its shore": **III** 28–29. Its attitude to the Imperial nobility: 169 (cf. 641–42). Jews in the Faubourg: 252–54. Mme de Marsantes's edifying influence on it: 337–38. Nicknames in the Faubourg: 591–92. Relations of the Princesse Mathilde with the Faubourg: 642–43. Party ritual in the Faubourg; "the prime and perfect quality of the social pabulum": 704–5. Its silliness, aggravated by malice: 737–38. Its mysterious life: 745. Walking-sticks common in a certain section of the Faubourg: 789. Odette taken up by certain elements of the Faubourg: **IV** 194–202; also Gilberte when she suddenly becomes rich through a legacy: 199 (cf. **V** 898–99, 909–10). Mme de Montmorency's old house in the Faubourg: 202–3. Mme Verdurin and the Faubourg: 363–66 (cf. **V** 312–14). Charlus's morals unknown to the Faubourg: 408–9. How the Faubourg speaks to any bourgeois about other bourgeois: **V** 784. During the war, Mme Verdurin and Mme Bontemps firmly installed in the Faubourg: **VI** 55–56. Brichot's success with the Faubourg: 146–51. Mme Verdurin becomes Duchesse de Duras and then Princesse de Guermantes and occupies a "lofty position" in the

Faubourg: 387–88. Its decline—"like some senile dowager now": 390.

FLOWERS. Lime-blossom from the trees in the Avenue de la Gare at Combray used for Aunt Léonie's infusions: **I** 64, 69–70. Mme Loiseau's fuchsias: 85. Legrandin's evocation of spring flowers: 176–77. Lilacs at Tansonville: 190–91, 262. M falls in love with hawthorn in Combray church: 155–56, 158 (cf. **II** 685; **IV** 739–40). Hawthorn blossom at Tansonville: 193–97. M bids farewell to his hawthorns: 204. Flowers in Swann's park: 190–92, 197. Poppies and cornflowers in the fields beyond Tansonville: 194–95. Spring flowers by the Vivonne; "blue flame of a violet": 235. Buttercups: 236–37. Water-lilies: 237–40. Odette gives Swann a chrysanthemum picked from her garden: 310. Chrysanthemums in Odette's house: 311; chrysanthemums, and cattleyas, her favourite flowers; "a fleshy cluster of orchids": 312. The cattleyas: 328–32; "do a cattleya" = "make love": 331–32, 386, 528, 529. Odette wears violets in her bosom: 340–41, 604; or in her hair: 594–95. Gilberte and Odette like a white lilac beside a purple: **II** 189. The "winter-garden"; Mme Swann's flowers; Parma violets, chrysanthemums: 228–34 (cf. **I** 594–95; **V** 216); guelder-roses: 289. Cornflowers near Balbec: 395–96. Human kindness blossoms like a solitary poppy: 437–38. Geranium cheeks of one of the girls at Balbec (Rosemonde?): 505, 659, 717–18. The "little band" like a bower of Pennsylvania roses: 516. Elstir's flower-piece: 583–85 (cf. **III** 162–63). Albertine's cheeks like rose petals; M's "passionate longing for them such as one feels sometimes for a particular flower": 639 (*see also* **III** 497). Hawthorn near Balbec: 685. Cherry-blossom, pear-blossom and lilac in Parisian suburbs: **III** 204–8. Mme de Villeparisis's flower painting: 286–87. Her knowledge of botany: 372. Albertine "a rose flowering by the sea": 480. Scarlet geraniums in the Bois: 528. Botanical discussion at the Guermantes': 706–9. The fertilisation of flowers; the orchid and the bee; an analogy with the conjunction of inverts: **IV** 2–4, 8–9, 36–44. Apple-blossom in sun and rain: 244–45. Hawthorn and apple-blossom: 250–51, 739–40. Albertine's laugh, "pungent, sensual and revealing as the scent of geraniums": 263. The garden at La Raspelière: 429. Elstir's roses:

464–65. Albertine's hair like black violets: **V** 14. The syringa incident: 63–64, 811–13, 827–28. Elstir's passion for violets: 178, 181. Honeysuckle and white geraniums in Vinteuil's sonata: 332–33; his music has "the perfumed silkiness of a geranium": 505.

FOOD. Stewed beef at Combray: **I** 11. Coffee-and-pistachio ice: 45. Lunch at Combray; Françoise's culinary largesse: 96–98. Almond cake: 158. Françoise's preparations for dinner: 168–70. Asparagus: 168–69. Françoise's roast chicken: 170, 187. Swann's gingerbread: 571. Dinner for Norpois; Françoise's *boeuf à la gelée*: **II** 21, 39; pineapple and truffle salad: 41; Nesselrode pudding: 51. Chocolate cake for tea *chez* Gilberte: 107 (cf. 660). Lobster *à l'Américaine*: 152. "A blackish substance which I did not then know to be caviare": 168. Soles for lunch at Balbec: 343. Mme de Villeparisis orders *croque-monsieurs* and creamed eggs: 370. Hotel dining-room at Doncières; Flemish profusion of victuals: **III** 125–26; exquisite dishes presented like works of art: 152. Chicken *financière* at the Guermantes dinner party: 690. The Duke's leg of mutton with *béarnaise* sauce: 807. Dinner at La Raspelière; bouillabaisse: **IV** 405; grilled lobsters (*demoiselles de Caen*): 407; strawberry mousse: 460. Tea at La Raspelière—"pancakes, Norman puff pastry, trifles, boat-shaped tartlets . . .": 543. The street cries of Paris—winkles: **V** 148; snails: 149; artichokes: 150; fish: 160–63; fruit, vegetables and cheese: 161–63. Albertine's rhapsody on ice cream: 164–66. Display in a butcher's shop: 176–77. Mme de Villeparisis and Norpois dine in Venice—red mullet and risotto: 856 (cf. 949). Dinner party at the Verdurins described by the Goncourts: **VI** 29–32.

FRIENDSHIP. Among the bourgeoisie, as opposed to the aristocracy, "always inseparable from respect": **I** 440. M's friendship with Saint-Loup; melancholy reflexions on the subject: **II** 430–31; his inability to find spiritual nourishment elsewhere than in himself makes him (in contrast with Saint-Loup) incapable of friendship: 491. Friendliness of a great artist superior to that of a nobleman: 556. Friendship an abdication of self and thus fatal to an artist; M prepared to sacrifice its pleasures to that of playing with the "little band" of girls: 664–65 (cf. **III** 540–41). The stuff of friendship: **III** 129–31. Mystery of instinctive, non-physical liking between men: 133. Our relations with friends "as eternally fluid as the sea itself": 364. Further reflexions on friendship; its superficiality; "halfway between physical exhaustion and mental boredom"; yet even so deadly a brew can sometimes be precious and invigorating; from the realm of ideas M "thrown back upon friendship": 540–45. Virtues of friendship enshrined in Saint-Loup: 565–68. Friendship and love: **V** 478–79. Necessity of lying between two friends one of whom is unhappy in love: 595. Friendship and treachery: 840–41. Revival of old friendships: 920 (cf. **VI** 60). M's tarnished friendship with Saint-Loup: 935–36. Recollections of their friendship after Saint-Loup's death: **VI** 227. A great friendship does not amount to much in society: 234. A "simulacrum," an "agreeable folly": 268, which leads nowhere: 434.

FURNITURE. Aunt Léonie's rooms at Combray; her prie-dieu and velvet armchairs with antimacassars: **I** 66–68. Mme Verdurin's high Swedish chair of waxed pinewood: 289; her Beauvais settee and chairs: 292–93. Furnishings of Odette's house in the Rue La Pérouse: 310–13. Odette's taste in furniture: 346–47 (cf. **II** 105–6, 153–55, 261–63). The Iénas' Empire furniture: 481 (cf. **III** 710–13). "Henri II" staircase in Swann's house: **II** 105–6. Furniture in the Swanns' drawing-room: 153–55, 261–63. Aunt Léonie's sofa, on which M makes love to one of his girl cousins, and which he later presents to the madam of a brothel: 208. Saint-Loup's Art Nouveau furniture: 460 (cf. **III** 755). Furniture of the hotel at Doncières: **III** 103–5. Mme de Villeparisis's Beauvais tapestry settees and chairs: 251, 366. Mme de Guermantes on Empire furniture: 709–15. The Guermantes's Boulle and Saint-Loup's Bing furniture: 755–56. Charlus's Louis XIV *bergère* and Directory *chauffeuse*: 759–61; his Bagard panelling and Beauvais chairs: 770. Furniture at La Raspelière: **IV** 429–30, 436–37, 467. M's Barbedienne bronze: **V** 229–30. Furniture from La Raspelière at Quai Conti: 378–80. (*See* Rooms.)

GAMES. Gilberte and her friends play battledore and shuttlecock in the Champs-Elysées: **I** 560–61. Prisoner's base in the Champs-Elysées: 562. Golf at Balbec; Andrée's "record" round; Octave, "I'm a wash-out": **II** 625. Albertine plays diabolo: 637,

695–96. "Ferret" (hunt-the-slipper) with the little band: 680–84. "Golf gives one a taste for solitary pleasures": 696. Cottard and Morel play écarté at La Raspelière: **IV** 485 et sqq.

GERMAN, GERMANS. "Straightforward bluntness" of the Princess Mathilde, inherited from her Württemberger mother, recalls the Germany of an older generation: **II** 157–58. The name Faffenheim-Munsterburg-Weinigen expresses "the energy, the mannered simplicity, the heavy refinements of the Teutonic race": **III** 346. "The vice of a German handclasp" (Prince Von's): 591. Charlus's "German habit" of fingering M's muscles: **IV** 422. M's mother's admiration for the German language despite her father's "loathing for that nation": **V** 135. Gilberte impressed by the "perfect breeding" of the German officers billeted at Tansonville: **VI** 89. Charlus's pro-Germanism: 121–26; "that splendid sturdy fellow, the Boche soldier": 171. Saint-Loup's respect for the bravery of the Germans: 219, and for German culture: 226–27. M's reflexions on his own attitude towards the Germans: 324–26.

HABIT. "That skilful but slow-moving arranger" who helps us to adapt to new quarters: **I** 8–9 (cf. **II** 339–41). Suffering caused by the interruption or cessation of habit: 10–11. The force of habit blunts one's sensitivity to a work of music: **II** 141. Contradictory effects of habit: 319. "Our faculties lie dormant because they can rely upon habit": 319. The analgesic effect of habit: 340–41. Without habit, life would seem continually delightful: 398. We prefer to friends we have not seen for some time people who are the mirror of our habits: 412–13. Habit dispenses us from effort: **III** 103–4. Modification in our habits makes our perception of the world poetic: 106. Habit the hardiest of all plants of human growth: 159. The many secretaries employed by Habit: **IV** 187–88. A second nature that prevents us from knowing our first: 208. Effect of habit on M's view of the Grand Hotel: 221. Sleep and habit: 517–18. "The regularity of a habit is usually in direct proportion to its absurdity": **V** 48–49. Habit prevents us from appreciating the value of life: 101–2. "In love, it is easier to relinquish a feeling than to give up a habit": 479. A new aspect of Habit—a "dread deity" that can be as cruel as death itself: 564–65. The "immense force of Habit"

lacking in M's love for Gilberte and Mme de Guermantes: 577.
Habit produces the illusion of necessity in love: 679–80. Laws of
habit as applied to the idea of Albertine's infidelities: 720–22.
"The heavy curtain of habit . . . which conceals from us almost
the whole universe": 732–33. Force of habit infinitely outweighs
the hypnotic power of a book: 757–58. Our habits in love
survive even the memory of the loved one: 921. Our habits
develop independently of our moral consciousness: **VI** 213.
What is dangerous in love . . . is not the beloved, but habit:
491.

HAWTHORN. See Flowers.

HEREDITY. Arbitrary laws of filial resemblance; Gilberte and
her parents: **II** 190–92. Saint-Loup's hereditary virtues: 432.
"We take from our family . . . the ideas by which we live as
well as the malady from which we shall die": 644. Inheritance of
mannerisms of speech, etc. (the "little band"); "the individual is
steeped in something more general than himself": 667. Andrée's
hair inherited from her mother: 717. Heredity gives uncles the
same faults as they censure in their nephews: **IV** 124, 128–29.
Hereditary resemblance of M's mother and grandmother; "the
dead annex the living": 227–29, 711–12, 720–22. "The souls of
the dead from whom we sprang . . . shower upon us their
riches and their spells"—M comes to resemble all his relatives:
**V** 95–97, 135–37, 474–76. Heredity and bad habits: 201–2.
"We do not create ourselves of our own accord out of nothing"; hereditary accumulation of egoisms: 791–92. Atavistic wisdom of Mme de Marsantes: 923–24. Moral cells of which an
individual is composed more durable than the individual himself: **VI** 352. Berma's daughter inherits her mother's defects:
453. Hereditary need for spiritual nourishment in the Duchesse
de Guermantes: 466.

HISTORY. M's grandfather's interest in history: **I** 26, 31.
Swann's curiosity about Odette's occupations comes from the
same thirst for knowledge with which he had once studied history: 388–90. Charlus's aristocratic prejudices reinforced by his
interest in history: **II** 459–61. The Duc de Guermantes's politeness a survival from the historic past: **III** 571. Aristocratic
names bring history to life: 734–44. The wisdom of families in-

spired by the Muse of History: **V** 918–19. History and Society: **VI** 403–8.

HOMOSEXUALITY. See Inversion.

INTOXICATION. See Alcohol.

INVERSION. "What is sometimes, most ineptly, termed homosexuality": **IV** 9. The race of inverts: 19–44, their predicament; "a race upon which a curse is laid"; an extensive freemasonry: 20–24; "improperly" called a vice: 24 (cf. 18: "we use the term for linguistic convenience"); types of invert—the gregarious, the solitaries, the zealots, the gynophiles, the affected, the guilt-ridden backsliders: 24–34; typical career of a solitary invert: 31–36; subvarieties of invert; those who care only for elderly gentlemen; the miracle of their conjunction: 36–40 (cf. 9); botanical analogy: 38–41; inversion can be traced back to a primeval hermaphroditism: 40–41. Numerous progeny of the exiles from Sodom: 42–43. M. and Mme de Vaugoubert: a case of reversal of roles: 57–63. Characteristic voice of the invert: 86. Discussion between Charlus and Vaugoubert: 87–89 (cf. **V** 51–52). A "diplomatic Sodom": 100–1. Bloch's sister and an actress cause a scandal: 326–27, 337–38. Nissim Bernard and the waiters: 327–31, 342–44. "Astral signs" by which the daughters of Gomorrah recognise one another (as do also "the nostalgic, the hypocritical, sometimes the courageous exiles of Sodom"): 338–40. Instinctive behaviour of inverts on entering a strange drawing-room: 414–16. "By dint of thinking tenderly of men one becomes a woman": 417. The cold shoulder of the invert on meeting his kind; rivalry among inverts; speed of mutual recognition: 431–34. Connexion between inversion and aesthetic sensibility: 479–80 (cf. **V** 291–92). Giveaway signs—voice, gestures, manner of speech: 497–99. Charm of unfamiliarity in the conversation of an invert: 598–99. Gomorrah disseminated all over the world: **V** 20. Gomorrah of today a jigsaw puzzle made up of unexpected pieces: 111. Distinction between conventional (classical) homosexuality and the "involuntary, neurotic" homosexuality of today: 269–73. Charlus's "camping": 275–77. Significance of the term "one of them" or "one of us": 280–81 (cf. **IV** 462–63). Jealousy among inverts; attitude towards relations with women: 283–85. Paternal feelings of inverts: 322–23. Furtive party conversation among inverts: 323–24. Charlus and Brichot discuss the statistics of "what the Germans call homosexuality"; historical examples, present-day trends: 395–413. Recognition between daughters of Gomorrah in a crowd; a typical Gomorrhan encounter: 472–73. "Physiological evolution" of Saint-Loup: 922–36; **VI** 11–12. Homosexuals make good husbands: **V** 929–30; **VI** 20 (cf. **V** 409–10). "The phenomenon, so ill-understood and so needlessly condemned, of sexual inversion": 321. Inverts as readers: 321–22.

(*For references to homosexuality, male and female, related to specific individuals, see the* Index of Characters *under* Albertine; Andrée; Argencourt; Bernard, Nissim; Bloch's sister(s) and cousin(s); Cambremer, Léonor; Charlus; Châtellerault; Foix; Gilberte; Guermantes, Prince de; Jupien; Léa; Legrandin; Lévy, Esther; Morel; Odette; Saint-Loup; Théodore; Vaugoubert; Vinteuil, Mlle).

JEALOUSY. Swann's jealousy: **I** 385–457 *passim*, 505–43 *passim*. Inquiries of the jealous lover compared to the researches of the scholar: 388–90, 445. Jealousy compared to physical pain: 391. Jealousy as it were the shadow of love: 392. Jealousy composed of an infinity of different, ephemeral jealousies: 529. Swann's jealousy in retrospect; "that lamentable and contradictory excrescence of his love" revives for another woman: **II** 130–34. A certain kind of sensual music the most merciless of hells for the jealous lover: 534–35. Saint-Loup's jealousy of Rachel: **III** 157–61, 217–24, 223–43, 476–77. Jealousy cannot contain many more ingredients than other products of the imagination; it outlives love: 476. Jealousy among inverts: **IV** 29–31 (*see also* **V** 283). Swann speaks of his jealousy to M: 139. Jealousy a resource that never fails: 270–71. "Jealousy belonging to that family of morbid doubts which are eliminated by the vigour of an affirmation far more surely than by its probability": 314–15. "Every impulse of jealousy is unique and bears the imprint of the creature . . . who has aroused it": 708. Arbitrary localisation of jealousy: 709–10. M's jealousy: **V** 16–30, 63–252 *passim*; 445–585 *passim*; retrospective jealousy: 563–752 *passim*. An intermittent and capricious disease: 28–30 quickly detected, and regarded, by the person who is its object, as justifying deception: 73–74, 111–12. Delayed-action jealousy: 106–7. Jealousy a form of tyranny: 112–13. "The demands of our jealousy and the blindness of our credulity are greater than the woman we love could ever suppose": 119. "Revolving searchlights" of jealousy; "a demon that cannot be exorcised": 129. Jealousy may perish for want of nourishment: 131–32. Jealousy like a historian without documents, "thrashes around in the void": 188–89. Jealousy is "blindfold"; like the torture of the Danaides or Ixion: 195. A social form of jealousy (Mme Verdurin): 370–71. Blind ignorance of the jealous lover: 400–1. Albertine on M's jealousy: 445–47. Jealousy lacks imagination: 585. For jealousy there can be neither past nor future, but invariably the present: 662. To the jealous man reality a "dizzy kaleidoscope": 699–700. Retrospective jealousy proceeds from the same optical error as the desire for posthumous fame: 701. In jealousy we choose our own sufferings: 735. Retrospective jealousy a physical disease: 872–73. "Jealousy is a good recruiting-sergeant": **VI** 330.

JEWS. M's grandfather distrusts M's Jewish friends (Bloch): **I** 125–26. Mme de Gallardon on Swann's Jewishness: 475–77. Swann illustrates all the successive stages in social behaviour through which the Jews have passed: **II** 2–3. Jews in society: 122–24, 127. A brothel-keeper offers M a Jewess as a special treat (Rachel): 206–7. Bloch affects anti-semitism: 433–34 (cf. 442, 445–46; **III** 334). Jewish colony at Balbec: 433–35. The Bloch family: 474–87. Albertine's anti-semitism: 629, 659 (cf. **III** 487). *Mater Semita*: **III** 237 (cf. 321–22). Jews in a French drawing-room; racial atavism: 253–55. The "Syndicate": 319 (cf. **IV** 132). Mme de Marsantes's anti-semitism: 342, 346 (cf. 217, 237). Charlus and the Blochs: 389–93. Mme Sazerat both Dreyfusist and anti-semitic: 392. Jewishness and Dreyfusism (Reinach and Bloch): 402–3. Reflections on Jews in a Paris restaurant: 559–60. Swann returns to "the spiritual fold of his fathers": 796. Jews compared with inverts: **IV** 21–22. M. de Guermantes on the Jews: 105. Swann's Jewishness; "certain Jews, men of great refinement and delicacy, in whom there remain in reserve . . . a cad and a prophet": 122; "that stout Jewish race": 141–42. Charlus's tirade against the Jews: 687–91. Jews discussed by the Duc and Duchesse de Guermantes: **V**

45–46. Morel's anti-semitism, the effect of a loan from Nissim Bernard through Bloch: 62–63 (cf. **IV** 691). Anti-semitism in society; Gilberte changes her name from Swann to Forcheville: 775–77 (cf. 790–92). Strong family feeling among Jews; Bloch's devotion to his father's memory: **VI** 353.

(*See* Dreyfus Case.)

LANGUAGE. Hereditary transmission of speech characteristics: **II** 667–68. The two laws of language—"we should express our-selves like others of our mental category and not of our caste"; the ephemeral vogue for certain modes of expression: **III** 317–18. The term "mentality": 319. Refined expressions used in a given period by people of the same intellectual range: **IV** 438–39, 445. Expressions peculiar to families: **V** 437–38. Invol-untary, give-away expressions blurted out under the impact of sudden emotion: **VI** 192. Quality of language rather than aes-thetic theory the criterion for judging intellectual and moral value of a work: 278.

*Language of individual characters.* Albertine's slangy speech: **II** 509, 631–34; her voice and vocabulary: 666–68; significant changes in her vocabulary: **III** 482–88; **V** 13.

Voices and speech mannerisms of the "little band": **II** 666–68.

Bergotte's mannerisms of speech and vocabulary: **II** 168–79.

Bloch's affected style of speech and mock-Homeric jargon: **I** 124–25; **II** 443–44, 477–78, 489; **III** 328; **IV** 319, 682.

Bréauté's voice and pronunciation: **V** 44–47.

Brichot's pedantic language: **I** 357–60; **IV** 371–72, 380–81, 481–83, 611–14.

Mme de Cambremer-Legrandin's pretentious vocabulary and pronunciation: **III** 271; **IV** 294–97, 437–45, 512–13.

Colourful language of Céleste Albaret and her sister: **IV** 331–35; Céleste's strange linguistic genius: **V** 12–13, 167.

Cottard's puns: **I** 283 et sqq.

Mme Cottard's stately language: **II** 234–35, 242–51.

Françoise's malapropisms: **I** 217; her colourful idiom: 233; her language, "like the French language," thickly strewn with errors: **III** 20–21; speaks the language of Mme de Sévigné: 21; of La Bruyère: 25; of Saint-Simon: 84; her speech traditional and local, "governed by extremely ancient laws": 77 (cf. **IV** 171–72); her vocabulary contaminated by her daughter's slang: **V** 199–200; **VI** 86 (cf. **III** 194, 464; **IV** 172–73).

Verbal mannerisms of the Guermantes set: **I** 475, 479–87; **II** 113–14, 129. The Duke's odd vocabulary: **III** 305, 317–22, 570; his bad French: **IV** 162, 479 (cf. **V** 43). Old-fashioned purity of the Duchess's language; her richly flavoured vocabulary; voice and accent that betray "a rudeness of the soil": **III** 677–78, 688–89, 781, **V** 34–39.

Jupien's cultured speech: **III** 17–18, 418.

Legrandin's flowery speech: **I** 92–93, 177–86.

The idiom of Norpois: **II** 9, 29–71 *passim*; **III** 302–55 *passim*; **V** 855–66.

Rachel's language, "the jargon of the coteries and studios": **III** 220–21.

Saint-Loup's mannerisms of speech; cultivates up-to-date expressions: **II** 451, 468–69; **III** 87–88, 698; **IV** 207.

Saniette's pedantic phraseology: **V** 298–99, 301–3.

Swann's verbal mannerisms: **I** 134–36, 483–84; **II** 104, 113–14.

Mme de Villeparisis affects "the almost rustic speech of the old nobility": **III** 265.

LAUGHTER. Not a well-defined language: **II** 217. "Let us show all pity and tenderness to those who laugh": **IV** 262. Verbal descriptions incomplete without the means to represent a laugh (Charlus): 463–64.

*Laughter of individual characters.* Albertine's laughter—"indecent in the way that the cooing of doves or certain animal cries can be": **II** 681; M longs to hear it again: **IV** 243, "pungent, sensual and revealing": 263; "deep and penetrating": 264; "provoking": 348; "that laugh in which she gave utterance as it were to the strange sound of her pleasure": 705; "that laugh that I always found so disturbing": **V** 152, 165; "insolent" laughter on the beach at Balbec: 226–27; "blithe and tender" laugh on awakening: 522.

Bloch's braying laugh which echoes his father's: **II** 476.

M. de Cambremer's laugh and its possible meanings: **IV** 440–41, 513–14.

Charlus's laughter, expressing his "lordly insolence and hysterical glee": **IV** 78; his tinkling laugh with its ancestral sonorities: 463–64.

Mme Cottard's "charming, girlish" laugh: **I** 363.

Gilberte's laugh which seems to be tracing an invisible surface on another plane: **II** 86, 217.

Insolent and coquettish laugh of the Princesse des Laumes: **I** 473–74, 477.

Odette's little simpering laugh: **I** 311.

"Merry angelus" of Ski's laugh: **V** 384–85.

Mme Verdurin dislocates her jaw from laughing too much: **I** 266–67; symbolical dumb-show as a substitute for laughter: 289–90 (cf. **IV** 482).

M. Verdurin's dumb-show of "shaking with laughter": **I** 372–73, and his laugh like a smoker's choking fit: **V** 385.

LETTERS. Note from M to his mother at Combray: **I** 37–39. Letters from Odette to Swann: 276, 314, 319. Swann's letter of feigned disappointment and simulated anger to Odette: 319. Odette's letter to Forcheville: 400–2. Anonymous letter to Swann about Odette's infidelities: 506–7. Express letter (*pneu*) from M to Gilberte: 572–73. Norpois's promptness in answering letters: **II** 11. M's New Year letter to Gilberte: 80–81. M's self-justifying letter to Swann: 86–87. Gilberte's letter of invitation to M; her signature: 98–101; her writing-paper: 104–5. M's letters to Gilberte during the crisis of his love: 219–23, 258–60. The pain of hostile letters from the beloved: 278. Correspondence between M and Gilberte concerning the imaginary "misunderstanding" between them: 285–87. Saint-Loup's letter from Doncières: 611–12. Charlus's violent letter to Mme de Villeparisis: **III** 263–64. Saint-Loup's vituperative letter to M: 417. The footman's letters, peppered with quotations from the poets: 437; example of these: 776–77. Saint-Loup writes to M from Morocco: 475: Note to M from Mme de Stermaria: 536. Letter to Charlus from the Princesse de Guermantes: **IV** 157 (cf. 732–33). M's unemotional letter to Gilberte: 187. The charm of first letters from women: 322–23. Mme de Cambremer's letter inviting M to dinner; the rule of the three adjectives: 468–69 (cf. 663–64). Charlus's letter to Aimé: 530–33. Charlus's letter to

Morel announcing his imaginary duel: 631–35. Charlus's letter from a club doorman: **V** 51. M's mother writes to him, quoting Mme de Sévigné: 180. Albertine's note to M after leaving the Trocadéro: 202–3. Letter from Léa to Morel intercepted by Charlus: 279–80. Albertine's farewell letter: 565–66. Letter which M receives from a niece of Mme de Guermantes: 606. Letter from Albertine after Saint-Loup's *démarche*; M's reply: 610–15. "How little there is of a person in a letter": 611–12. Albertine's second letter and M's reply: 630–33. M's letter to Andrée: 632. Albertine's posthumous letters: 643–44. Aimé's letter from Balbec; his grammatical eccentricities: 694–96. Aimé's letter from Touraine: 707–8. Letters congratulating M on his article in the *Figaro*: 797–99. Bourgeois conventionality in letters: 798–99. M receives a letter from his stockbroker: 866–88. Letters announcing marriages: 888–93. Letters from Gilberte at Tansonville during the war: **VI** 88–89, 93–96. Saint-Loup's letter from the front: 88–92. Charlus's posthumous letter: 167–68.

LIFTS. Lift in the Grand Hotel, Balbec; M's sensations on going up in it: **II** 331, 519. Professor E——'s lift and his mania for working it: **III** 430–31. Lift in M's flat; sentence of solitary confinement represented by the sound of its not stopping at his floor: 478–79 (cf. **V** 703).

LITERATURE. Reflexions on reading; the art of the novelist: **I** 55–57, 114–20. Style and genius of Bergotte: 124–25, 129–38, **II** 165–75 (cf. **III** 443–47); the nature of originality in literature: 168–69; relation between speech and writing: 168–75; "unforeseeable beauty" of the work of great writers: 170; style of the writer and character of the man: 179–80. A good book is something special and unforeseeable: 318. Mme de Villeparisis's literary judgments; her incomprehension of great writers: 394–95 (cf. **III** 247). Creation in a writer superior to observation: 476. Literature and fashionable society: **III** 246–52; literary talent the living product of a certain moral conformation that conflicts with purely social duties: 248. Vagaries of literary reputation; problems of appreciating new original writers; does art, after all, progress like science?: 444–46. Depravity of taste in literary criticism: 644–46. Profit which a writer can derive from the conversation of aristocrats: 751–56. The same people are interesting in a book and boring in life: 780. Practical men wrong to despise the pursuit of literature: **IV** 591. Incompleteness a characteristic of the great works of the nineteenth century; their retrospective unity; the importance of prefaces: **V** 207–8. Sensual pleasure helpful to literary work: 239–40. Literature and music—is literature, which analyses what we feel about life, less true than music, which recomposes it?: 503–4; unique identity underlying the works of a great writer; M's observations on Dostoievsky, Barbey d'Aurevilly, Hardy, Tolstoy, Baudelaire: 506–13. Certain novels bring us into temporary contact with the reality of life— "the almost hypnotic suggestion of a good book": 757–58. Discrepancy between the thoughts of author and reader; basic flaws in literary journalism: 767–72. Objections against literature raised by M's reading of the Goncourt Journal: **VI** 39–46. Relation of literature to life: 126. Reflexions on literary creativity: 274–335; falsity of realism in literature; absurdity of popular or patriotic literature: 277–85; "the function and the task of a writer are those of a translator": 291; aberrations of literary criticism: 294–96; "real books . . . the offspring not of daylight and casual talk but of darkness and silence": 302; in literary creation, imagination and sensibility are interchangeable: 307; writing is for the writer a wholesome and necessary function comparable to exercise, sweat and baths for a man of more physical nature: 308; "a book is a huge cemetery": 310; our passions inspire our books, and intervals of repose write them: 317; futility of trying to guess an author's models: 317–18; a writer's works "like the water in an artesian well": 318; a work of literature a kind of optical instrument enabling the reader to see himself more clearly: 344–45.

*The narrator and his work.* M's first efforts to express himself in writing; the impact of Bergotte: **I** 132–34. His desire to translate his sensations and impressions: 218–19. His wish to be a writer; despair at his lack of talent and the "nullity" of his intellect; renounces literature for ever: 243–45, 251–52. The steeples of Martinville inspire him to composition: 253–57. Norpois advocates a literary career for M: **II** 13, but in such terms as to make him doubly determined to renounce the idea: 31–33; his "prose poem" fails to impress Norpois: 35, who sees in it the malign influence of Bergotte: 60–63 (cf. **III** 298–99). Bergotte restores his confidence: 196–97. Inability to settle down to work; writing and social life: 209–12, 530; M is distracted from work by the "unknown beauties" who throng the streets of Paris: **III** 70–71, and by his pursuit of Mme de Guermantes: 82–83. "If only I had been able to start writing!": 196. He sends an article to *Le Figaro*: 474, 544. "The invisible vocation of which this book is the history": 544. Trees near Balbec seem to warn him to set to work before it is too late: **IV** 560. He scans *Le Figaro* in vain for his article: **V** 6, 151. Continued procrastination; changes in the weather an excuse for not working: 100–2. Musings on art and literature while listening to Wagner; is there in art a more profound reality than in life, or is great art merely the result of superior craftsmanship?: 204–10, 259–60. Vinteuil's septet restores his faith in art and in his vocation: 347–51 (cf. 503–5, 513–14). Appearance of his article in *Le Figaro* at last; a boost to his self-confidence as a writer; the pleasure of writing incompatible with social pleasures: 766–72. Renewed discouragement during a visit to Tansonville: **VI** 1–2, and after reading an unpublished passage from the Goncourt Journal which convinces him not only of his own lack of talent but of the vanity and falsehood of literature: 26, 38 (cf. 239, 254). Renunciation, for several long years, of his project for writing: 46. Salvation at last; the uneven paving-stones; M's doubts suddenly dissipated; involuntary memory the key: 255–60. Reflexions on the work he has now decided to undertake: 262–336, 505–31; deciphering "the inner book of unknown symbols": 274; "this most wonderful of all days": 287; the work of art "the only means of rediscovering Lost Time"; the materials for his work stored up inside him: 304; "my whole life . . . might and yet might not have been summed up under the title: A Vocation": 304; Albertine, by causing him to suffer, more valuable to him than a secretary to arrange his "paperies": 320 (cf. 511); Swann the inspiration for his book: 328; his discovery of the destructive action of Time at the very moment of conceiving the ambition to intellectualise extra-temporal realities in a work of art: 351, 355; his duty to his work more important than that of being polite or even kind: 435–36; the readers of his book will be the readers of their own selves: 508; a church or a druid monument?: 520; his indifference to criticism: 521; the *Arabian Nights* or the *Memoirs* of Saint-Simon of another age?: 524–25; the dimension of Time: 526–32 (cf. 505–12). "In this book . . . there is not a single incident which is not fictitious, not a single character who is a real person in disguise . . . everything has been invented by me in accordance with the requirements of my theme": **VI** 225.

LOVE. Prerequisite of love, that it should win us admission to an unknown life: **I** 139. Love may come into being without any foundation in desire: 277. Modes of production of love; "the insensate, agonising need to possess exclusively": 327. The illusion that love exists outside ourselves: 569–70. Love creates "a supplementary person": **II** 54. "No peace of mind in love"; "a permanent strain of suffering": 213–14. Love "radiates towards the loved one," then returns to its starting-point, oneself: 252–53. "Not like war": 275. Effects of absence and the passage of time; sufferers from love's sickness are "their own physicians": 279–83. Effects of Habit: 301 (cf. **V** 478–79, 577; **VI** 490). "Those who love and those who enjoy are not always the same": 304. Features of our first love attach themselves to those that follow: 561–62 (cf. 647–48; **V** 921; **VI** 317–18). "The most exclusive love for a person is always a love for something else": 563. The women we love are "a negative of our sensibility": 647. "Loving helps us to discern, to discriminate": 666. Silence is "a terrible strength in the hands of those who are loved": **III** 157–58. The illusion on which the pains of love are based: 210–11. Mme Leroi on love: "I make it often but I never talk about it": 260. "A charming law of nature," that we live in ignorance of those we love: 382. Memories are accompaniments to carnal desire: 493–95. "The moment preceding pleasure" restores to Albertine's features "the innocence of earliest childhood": 501. Self-deception and subjectivity of love: 507. Role of costume in love: 529. Intimacy creates social ties which outlast love: 530–31. "This terrible need of a person": **IV** 179–80. Role of pity in love: the human need to "repair the wrongs" we do to the loved one: 313. Love makes us "at once more distrustful and more credulous": 315. Those who love us and whom we do not love seem insufferable: 431. The "invisible forces" within the woman we love to which we address ourselves "as to obscure deities": 718–19. "The possession of what we love is an even greater joy than love itself": **V** 58. Apostrophe to girls—to define them we need to cease to be sexually interested in them: 77–80. "O mighty attitudes of Man and Woman": 97. "Beneath any carnal attraction that goes at all deep, there is the permanent possibility of danger": 100. "Love is an incurable malady": 105. More than any others, "fugitive beings" inspire love: 113–17. The object of our love is "the extension of that being to all the points in space and time that it has occupied and will occupy": 125; the "revolving searchlights of jealousy": 129; love is "kept in existence only by painful anxiety," "we love only what we do not wholly possess": 133. Love is "reciprocal torture": 137. "To be harsh and deceitful to the person whom we love is so natural!": 139. All love "evolves rapidly towards a farewell": 474–75. "In love, it is easier to relinquish a feeling than to give up a habit": 519. "Love is space and time made perceptible to the heart": 519. The unknown element in Albertine "formed the core" of M's love: 580–81 (cf. 669–70). "There is not a woman in the world the possession of whom is as precious as that of the truths which she reveals to us by causing us to suffer": 669 (cf. 834–36; **VI** 300–2, 310–19). "One wants to be understood because one wants to be loved, and one wants to be loved because one loves": 670. Natural to love "a certain type of woman"; "unique, we suppose? She is legion": 677–82. "Death does not make any great difference": 705–6. "We fall in love for a smile, a look, a shoulder": 715. Love is "a striking example of how little reality means to us": 764. "A mistake to speak of a bad choice in love, since as soon as there is a choice it can only be a bad one": 825–26. Reasons for love remaining platonic: **VI** 186–88. Love is "a portion of our mind more durable than the various selves which successively die within us," a portion of the mind which gives the understanding of this love "to the universal spirit": 301. Value of love and grief to the writer; "ideas come to us as the substitutes for grief"; "had we not been happy . . . the unhappinesses that befall us would be without cruelty and therefore without fruit"; the painful dilemmas consequent on love "reveal

to us, layer after layer, the material of which we are made":
311–19.

LYING. Odette's lies; fragment of truth that gives her away: **I**
394–96; signs of distress that accompany her lying: 398–99,
413–14, 421. Nissim Bernard's perpetual lying: **II** 485–86. Andrée's lying; people who lie once will lie again: 636–37. Albertine's polymorphous lies prompted by a desire to please
everybody: 706–8. Unconscious mendacity: **III** 80. A complete
lie more easily believed than a half-lie: **IV** 156. Albertine's lies;
the Infreville story: 268–70 (cf. **V** 137); how she gives herself
away when lying: 677–78; how to decipher her lies; jealousy
multiplies the tendency to lie in the person loved: **V** 72–74,
111–12; a liar by nature: 122–23; her contradictory lies; we fail
to notice our mistress's first lies: 186–98; her aptitude for lying;
her "charming skill in lying naturally": 232–36, 246–52. A lie
"the most necessary means of self-preservation": 221–22. "Impenetrable solidarity" of the little band as liars: 233–34. Lovers'
lies to a third person: 277–79. Value of lies and liars to literary
men; "the perfect lie . . . is one of the few things in the world
that can open windows for us on to what is new and unknown":
281–82. Disparity between the truth which a lying woman has
travestied and the idea which the lover has formed of that truth:
448–49. Perseverance in falsehood of those who deceive us: 517.
Lying formulas that turn out to have been prophetic truths:
621–22, 684–85. "Lying is essential to humanity"; we lie to protect our pleasure or our honour; "one lies all one's life long,
even, especially, perhaps only, to those who love one": 823–25
(cf. 943). Lying is a trait of character as well as a natural defence: 834–37. "One ruins oneself, makes oneself ill, kills oneself
all for lies"—a lode from which one can extract a little truth: **VI**
320.

MARRIAGE. Swann's marriage: **II** 1–2, 50–58, 126–34. "Igno-
minious marriages are the most estimable of all": 56. The "sub-
servience of refinement to vulgarity" the rule in many marriages:
126. Marital schemes of the Prince de Foix and his friends: **III**
553–54. Skin-deep Christianity of the Guermantes set invariably
leads to "a colossally mercenary marriage": 560. Happy marriages arranged by inverts for their nieces: **IV** 129. Reflexions on

the marriage of Gilberte to Saint-Loup and of Jupien's niece to young Cambremer: **V** 891–905; effects of these marriages: 905–20. An "unfortunate" marriage may be the only poetical action in a man's life: 923. Advantage for a young husband of having kept a mistress: 925–26. Homosexuals make good husbands: 929–30; **VI** 20.

MEDICINE. Mysterious flair of the diagnostician; "we realised that this imbecile [Cottard] was a great physician": **II** 97. Bergotte's views on the sort of doctor needed by an artist: 197–99. M's grandmother's illness—rival prescriptions of Cottard and du Boulbon: **III** 404–16; Professor E——'s diagnosis: 426–31 (cf. **IV** 55–57); Cottard has "something of the greatness of a general" when deciding on a course of treatment: 438; the specialist X——, nose expert: 441–42; Professor Dieulafoy: 466–67. Medicine is "a compendium of the successive and contradictory mistakes of medical practitioners": 405. "To believe in medicine would be the height of folly, if not to believe in it were not a greater folly still": 405. Doctors create illness by making patients believe they are ill (du Boulbon): 410–11. "A great part of what doctors know is taught them by the sick": 411–12. Du Boulbon on nervous disorders: 410–16. "Doctors, like stockbrokers, employ the first person singular": 559 (cf. **IV** 405). Innumerable mistakes of doctors; "medicine is not an exact science"; "medicine has made some slight advance in knowledge since Molière's day, but none in its vocabulary": **IV** 55–57. Cottard and his rivals at Balbec: 264–66. Toxic actions "a perilous innovation in medicine": 265. Medicine "busies itself with changing the sense of verbs and pronouns": 405. Cottard on sleeping draughts and on the digestion: 489–91. Medicine has developed the art of prolonging illnesses, but cannot cure the illnesses it creates: **V** 238. Bergotte and his doctors: 241–43.

MEMORY. The body's memory more enduring than that of the mind: **I** 7–10 (cf. **VI** 11). Voluntary memory preserves nothing of the past itself: 59. The madeleine; taste and smell alone bear "the vast structure of recollection": 60–64 (cf. **VI** 255–56). The three strata of memory: 262–64. The "terrible re-creative power" of memory: 523. A mistake to compare the images stored in one's memory with reality: 606. Role of memory in our gradual assimilation of a new piece of music: **II** 140–42. Memory presents things to us in reverse: 208. Memory's conflicting photographs: 621–22, 642 (cf. 678; **V** 644–45). Process of recapturing a line of verse: **III** 41–42 (cf. **IV** 521–23). Resurrection of the soul may be conceived as a phenomenon of memory: 111. Sleep and memory: 115–16 (cf. **IV** 521–23; **V** 154). Influence of the atmosphere in stimulating memory: 187 (cf. **V** 23, 645–62). Process of recapturing a name; advantages of an imperfect memory: **IV** 67–70. Arbitrariness of the images selected by memory: 205–6. M's "complete and involuntary recollection" of his grandmother; "with the perturbations of memory are linked the intermittencies of the heart"; restoration of the self that experienced the resuscitated sensations: 210–12. Soporifics and memory: 520–23. Poor memories of men and women of action: **V** 40–41. Resuscitation of memory after the amnesia of sleep; "the goddess Mnemotechnia": 154–57. Memory "a void from which at odd moments a chance resemblance enables one to resuscitate dead recollections": 188. Microscope of the disinterested memory more powerful and less fragile than that of the heart: 233. "Translucent alabaster of our memories": 379–81. Process of unravelling Albertine's interrupted sentence: 454–58. Memory a sort of pharmacy or laboratory in which we find "a little of everything": 526 (cf. 701–2). Memories of Albertine: 644–72 *passim*, 731–34; fortuitous memories more potent than deliberate ones: 732–33; "memory has no power of invention": 748; the cruelty of memory: 753–54; "our legs and our arms are full of torpid memories": **VI** 11. Apotheosis of involuntary memory; three analogous sensations (cf. **I** 60–64) and their significance: 256–74; examples from literature: 334–35. Vagaries in our memories of people; "the memories which two people preserve of each other, even in love, are not the same": 406, 412–15, 419–21. Mutability of people and fixity of memory; "if our life is vagabond our memory is sedentary": 438–43.

MONOCLES. Swann's monocle, which delights Odette: **I** 348–49, and which he removes "like an importunate, worrying thought": 493. Variety of monocles at Mme de Saint-Euverte's party: 463–65. Saint-Loup's fluttering monocle: **II** 421; **III** 87–89. The Duc de Guermantes's "quizzical" monocle: 33; "gay

flash" of his monocle: 62. M. de Palancy's monocle, like a fragment of the glass wall of an aquarium: 48 (*see* I 465). Charlus's
monocle: 365. Bréauté's: 590; IV 74; V 40 (*see also* I 464–65).
M. de Cambremer's: IV 513–14. Bloch's "formidable" monocle
which alters "the significance of his physiognomy": VI 384–85.
Large monocle sported by the Princesse de Guermantes (Mme
Verdurin): 433–34.

MOON. Moonlight in a bedroom in summer: I 8. Moonlight in
the garden at Combray: 43. Walks round Combray by moonlight: 159–60. Long ribbon of moonlight on the pond at Combray: 187. Moon in daylight (cf. II 690); images of the moon in
books and paintings: 205–6. Bright moon on clear, cold nights
which Swann compares to Odette's face: 334, 338. Moonlight on
one of Gabriel's palaces: II 84. M reads a description of moonlight in Mme de Sévigné: 315. Moonlight on a village seen from
the train: 317. Moon near Balbec inspires M to quote poetic
descriptions of it; Mme de Villeparisis's anecdote about Chateaubriand: 410–11. Opalescent moonlight in a fountain at Doncières: III 120–21. Charlus's desire to look at the "blue light of
the moon" in the Bois with M: 771–72. Crescent moon at twilight over Paris: IV 45 (cf. 568–69). Moon through the oaks at
La Raspelière: 494–95, and over the valley: 507. Full moon over
Paris: V 227–28. Albertine asleep by moonlight: 521. Moonrise
over Paris; the moon in poetry: 550–51. Venetian *campo* by
moonlight: 882. Effects of moonlight in war-time Paris: VI
65–66; "cruelly and mysteriously serene": 162; "like a soft and
steady magnesium flare": 164; "narrow and curved like a sequin": 172.

MOTOR-CARS. M hires a motor-car for Albertine: IV 536–39.
Effect of the motor-car on our ideas of topography and perspective; difference between arrival by car and by train (cf. II
301–2); the charm of motoring: 546–50. A drive through Paris:
V 216–28. M's delight in the sound of motor-cars and the smell
of petrol: 554–55. Albertine's Rolls-Royce, her favourite car:
566, 613–14.

MUSIC. Vinteuil's sonata; the ineffable character of a first musical impression; the "little phrase": I 294–300. Insanity diag-

nosed in Vinteuil's sonata: 302–3. The "little phrase" becomes the "national anthem" of Swann's love for Odette: 308; its effect on Swann: 335–37, 374–75, 489–91, 493–501 (*see also* **II** 144–46). The music of the violin, "the sapient, quivering and enchanted box": 494. Great musicians reveal to us a new world in the depths of the soul: 497. "Inexorably determined" language of music: 500. Role of memory in our gradual assimilation of a new composition; originality of Vinteuil's sonata; "great works of art do not begin by giving us the best of themselves"; works such as Beethoven's late quartets create their own posterity: **II** 140–46. M's attempts to grasp the truths expressed by music: 378. Intoxicating and sensual effect of music enhanced by that of alcohol: 534–35. A great pianist is "a window opening upon a great work of art": **III** 54–55. People feel justified in enjoying vulgar music if they find it in the work of a good composer (such as Richard Strauss): 614–15. Conversation about music with Mme de Cambremer; Debussy and Wagner; reflexions on theories, schools, fashions and tastes: **IV** 288–94. Music evoked by Paris street cries—*Boris, Pelléas,* Palestrina, Gregorian chant: **V** 146–51, 161–62, 176. Rhythms of sleep compared to those of music; it is the lengthening or shortening of the interval that creates beauty: 153–54, 160. Music helps M to "descend into himself" and discover new things; it also enables us to know the essential quality of another person's sensations: 206. Vinteuil's septet: 330–54. Tone colour: 337–39. Unique, unmistakable voice of a great composer is proof of "the irreducibly individual existence of the soul": 340–42. "The transposition of creative profundity into terms of sound": 342. Music "the unique example of what might have been . . . the means of communication between souls": 344. Inferior compositions may prepare the way for later masterpieces: 350–51. Albertine at the pianola; M's pleasure in elucidating the structure of musical compositions; "a piece of music the less in the world, perhaps, but a truth the more": 501–2. Is music, which recomposes what we feel about life, truer than literature, which analyses it?: 503–4. Great music must correspond to some definite spiritual reality: 503–6; or is this an illusion?: 513–14. Visual images evoked by music: 514.

Bird singing in the Lydian mode: 522. Melancholy refrain of pigeons compared to phrases in Vinteuil: 539–40. The "little phrase" and M's love for Albertine: 755–56.

(See also Bach; Beethoven; Chopin; Debussy; Schumann; Wagner under Index of Persons.)

NAMES. By pronouncing a name one secures a sort of power over it (Guermantes): I 178. The name "Gilberte" heard for the first time by M at Tansonville: 199–200; and later in the Champs-Elysées: 560–62. Poetry of place-names: 545–60. Imaginative difference between words and proper names: 551–52. Images evoked by names of Italian, Norman and Breton towns: 552–53; (see also II 326). Effect on M of Gilberte calling him by his Christian name for the first time: 573–74. "Names are whimsical draughtsmen": II 166. Names of the cathedral towns: 321. Place-names on the way to Balbec; contrast between place-names with and without personal associations: 326. Pleasures of collecting old names: 448–49. The name Simonet: 520–21, 528; importance of the single "n": 579–80 (cf. III 504). "The names which designate things correspond invariably to an intellectual notion, alien to our true impressions"; Elstir re-creates things by renaming them: 566. Affective content of names and how it decays; changing connotations of the name Guermantes: III 4–9. M incapable of integrating the name Guermantes into the living figure of the Duchess: 28–29. Poetic German landscape evoked by the name Faffenheim-Munsterburg-Weinigen: 346–47. We hate our namesakes: 504. Nicknames in society: 591–93. Poetry of the name Isabella d'Este: 719. Names change their meaning for us more in a few years than words do in centuries: 728–29. The nobility are the etymologists of the language of names, but are oblivious of its poetry: 730. M's aesthetic pleasure in historic names: 743–44. The name Surgis-le-Duc stripped of its poetry: IV 143–44. Noble names of Normandy: 251–52. Depoeticisation of place-names in the region of Balbec: 693–98. Bitter-sweet charm in the possessive use of a Christian name: V 124–25. Albertine after her departure scarcely exists for M save under the form of her name, which he repeats to himself incessantly: 581. Place-names near Balbec become impregnated with baleful mystery: 699. Habit strips names of their charm and significance:

722–23. Venomous overtones of the name of Tours: 729. Succession to a name is a melancholy thing: **VI** 338–39. "A name: that very often is all that remains for us of a human being . . . even in his lifetime": 406.

OLD AGE. The "great renunciation" of old age as it prepares for death: **I** 201–2. Disillusionment of old age; the futility of writing letters: **II** 82. The day when one feels that love is too big an undertaking for the little strength one has left: **IV** 382. "Old age makes us incapable of doing but not, at first, of desiring": **V** 860–61. Charlus in old age: **VI** 244–53. Metamorphoses due to old age seen at the Guermantes reception: 336–81. We see our age in a mirror: 350. Old age is of all the realities of life "the one of which we preserve for longest a purely abstract conception": 354–55. The phenomenon of old age seems, in its different modes, to take into account certain social habits: 372. The Duc de Guermantes in old age: 480–87. Norpois and Mme de Villeparisis in old age: **V** 947–50 (cf. 854–55).

PAINTING. Swann's penchant for finding likenesses to real people in the old masters: **I** 314–16, 459–61; **II** 147–48. Elstir at work: 565–89; metaphors in his works: 567; description of his *Carquethuit Harbour*: 567–72; painting and photography: 570–71. Reflexions on portrait-painting: 601–4. Profundities of "still life": 613 (cf. **III** 152). Race-courses and regattas as subjects for painting: 651–58. "The original painter proceeds on the lines of the oculist"—the visual world is created afresh: **III** 445. M's reflexions on painting while studying the Guermantes's Elstirs; Elstir's relation to earlier painters; analysis of a waterside carnival; the painter's eye; the immortalisation of a moment: 572–78. Conversation about painting with Mme de Cambremer at Balbec: **IV** 280–87. The "little patch of yellow wall": **V** 244–45. Aesthetic truth and documentary truth in portraits: **VI** 40–41. "The artist may paint anything in the world that he chooses"; the artist of genius may be inspired by commonplace models: 44–46.

(*See also* Botticelli; Carpaccio; Giotto; Greco; Hooch; Leonardo; Manet; Mantegna; Michelangelo; Monet; Poussin; Rembrandt; Renoir; Turner; Vermeer; Veronese; Watteau; Whistler *under* Index of Persons.)

PARTIES. Dinner-party at the Verdurins' at which Swann hears the Vinteuil sonata: **I** 281–304. Dinner-party at the Verdurins' at which Forcheville is present: 355–75. Musical soirée at Mme de Saint-Euverte's: 457–501. Elstir's afternoon party to introduce Albertine: **II** 613–20. Afternoon party at Mme de Villeparisis's: **III** 251–385. Theatrical soirée at Mme de Villeparisis's for which M arrives too late: 507–23. Dinner-party at the Duchesse de Guermantes's: 569–750. Evening party at the Princesse de Guermantes's: **IV** 45–165. Dinner-party at La Raspelière: 404–514. Musical soirée at the Verdurins' (Quai Conti): **V** 299–307. Afternoon party at the Princesse de Guermantes's: **VI** 332–507.

PHOTOGRAPHY. Swann studies photographs of Odette: **I** 414, but prefers an old daguerreotype to more recent photographs: **II** 264 (*see also* **V** 267). M's photograph of Berma, which he studies in bed: **II** 80, 82–83. Charlus on photography: "A photograph acquires something of the dignity which it ordinarily lacks when it ceases to be a reproduction of reality and shows us things that no longer exist": 470. Saint-Loup photographs M's grandmother: 500 (cf. **IV** 214, 237–43). An old photograph of the "little band": 549–50. Influence of photography on painting: 570. Saint-Loup's photograph of Mme de Guermantes seems to M like a "supplementary prolonged encounter" with her: **III** 99. By "a cruel trick of chance," M sees his grandmother as a photograph: 183–85. Similar effects produced by photography and kissing: 498–99. Contrasting photographs of Odette, "the earlier a photograph the older a woman looks in it": **V** 267. Saint-Loup's stupefaction on seeing M's photograph of Albertine: 588–92.

POLITICS. Diplomacy and politics; the "governmental mind" (Norpois): **II** 7. M discovers to his surprise that, in politics, to repeat what everyone else is thinking is the mark not of an inferior but of a superior mind: 40. Mme de Villeparisis's "advanced" but anti-socialist opinions: 393–94. Saint-Loup's "socialistic spoutings": 426, 490–91. Elusiveness of truth in politics: **III** 325–26. Subtlety of politicians, a perversion of the science of "reading between the lines," accounts for the behaviour of the Guermantes circle and in particular the Duchess's paradoxical judgments; the Duke as politician: 646–51.

RAILWAYS. Arrival by train at Combray: **I** 65, 85, 159. The railway timetable "the most intoxicating romance in the lover's library": 415–16; timetables minister to M's longing for aesthetic enjoyment; the "wizard's cell": 556–57. The "fine, generous" 1.22 train to Normandy and Brittany: 548–49; **II** 305–6. Reflexions on rail travel; railway stations "marvellous" but "tragic" places; the Gare Saint-Lazare: 301–3 (cf. **IV** 549–50). Journey to Balbec: 312–25. Concomitants of long railway journeys: sunrise, hard-boiled eggs, illustrated papers, packs of cards, rivers: 316. Whistling of locomotives at Doncières: **III** 179. Difference between arrival by train and by motor-car: **IV** 549–50 (cf. **II** 301–2). Return journey from Venice to Paris: **V** 887–88. Halt by a sunlit line of trees on M's train-journey back to Paris from the sanatorium: **VI** 238–39. M's memory of the hooting of the trains at night at Combray: 276.

*The "little train."* M's first journey on it; names of stations: **II** 326. Various colloquial names for it—"crawler" (Saint-Loup): 609, "tram," "rattletrap" (Albertine): 623. Service suspended in winter: 725–26. Further nicknames: **IV** 249. Breakdown at Incarville: 262–63. Leisurely arrival at Balbec station: 345–46. M travels with Albertine to Doncières: 347–58. M travels with the "faithful" to Douville: 358–98, 589–622. Stations on the little railway: 647–48, 657, 662, 674–75, 682, 692–98. Halts on the little railway a setting for social intercourse: 694–98. M's last journey on the little train—Albertine's shattering revelation as it enters Parville station: 699–704.

ROOMS. M remembers various bedrooms in which he has slept: **I** 4–10, 263–64. His bedroom at Combray: 9–11. The little room at the top of the house smelling of orris-root: 14, 122. Aunt Léonie's rooms; the charm of country rooms, reflecting "a whole secret system of life": 66–67. Uncle Adolphe's sanctum: 99 (cf. **II** 91). M's room in summer: 113–14. Rooms in Odette's house in the Rue La Pérouse: 310–12. M's bedroom in the Grand Hotel, Balbec: 545; **II** 332–34, 340–43, 690–91, 727–30. Waiting-room in Swann's house: **II** 136–38. Mme Swann's

drawing-room: 153–55, 230–34, 288. Dining-room of the Grand
Hotel: 343–45, 351–52, 613 (cf. **IV** 181). M's grandmother's
room in the Grand Hotel: 386–87. Saint-Loup's room at Doncières: **III** 91–92. "Unbreathable aroma" of every new bedroom:
102. Silent but alive and friendly rooms in the hotel at Doncières: 103–12. Dining-room at Doncières: 125–26. Mme de
Villeparisis's drawing-room: 251–52. M's bedroom in Paris:
472–73, 534–35; **V** 1–4, 482, 501, 514–15, 553–54. Card-room
at the Princesse de Guermantes's—"magician's cell": **IV** 119.
Drawing-room at La Raspelière: 411–12 (cf. **V** 378–80). Verdurin drawing-rooms at Rue Montalivet and Quai Conti: **V**
265–67, 378–80. Room in Andrée's grandmother's apartment:
527. M's bedroom at Tansonville: **VI** 10. Eulalie's room at
Combray: 276.

SADISM. Scene of "sadism" at Montjouvain between Mlle
Vinteuil and her friend: **I** 226–33. Sadists of Mlle Vinteuil's sort
are "purely sentimental, naturally virtuous": 231. Real sadism—
"pure and voluptuous cruelty"—uncommon: **III** 230. The
sadism in Charlus—a medium: **IV** 555. Irresistible sadism as a
motive for crime: **V** 269. Sado-masochistic scene in Jupien's
brothel: **VI** 181–82, and reflexions thereon: 195.

SEA. The sea reflected in the glass of the book-cases in M's
room at Balbec: **I** 545. M's longing to witness a stormy sea: 546.
The sea seen from M's window at Balbec; variety of seascapes:
**II** 341–44, 386–87, 521–26 (*see also* **IV** 221, 247–48). Sea
glimpsed from high ground through trees: 391 (cf. **IV** 558–59).
The "little band" inseparable from the sea: 562 (cf. **III** 481; **V**
81–84, 611). The sea in Elstir's pictures: 567–71, 657–58. M's
efforts to see the sea through Elstir's eyes: 658. "Perpetual re-
creation of the primordial elements of nature which we contemplate when we stand before the sea": 663. M's pleasure in
returning to the sea: **IV** 221, 243. The "rural" sea: 247–48.
Sight and sound of the sea from a hill near Douville: 283–84.
The sea from La Raspelière: 540–42. "The plaintive ancestress
of the earth": 559. M and Albertine lie on the beach at night
listening to the sea: 569 (cf. **V** 85). Albertine asleep reminds M
of the sea: **V** 83–86.

SELF. "Our social personality is a creation of the thoughts of other people": **I** 23. Mystery of personality: 438. Revival of an old self can make us experience feelings long dead: **II** 299–301 (cf. **III** 367–69). "Fragmentary and continuous death" of our successive selves: 340. Oneself: a subject on which other people's views are never in accordance with one's own: 437–42 (cf. **IV** 211–13). Uses of self-centredness: 478–79. Eclipse of one's old self at a social gathering: 615–16. Friendship an abdication of self: 664. M's "Self" which he rediscovers periodically when he arrives in a new place: **III** 102. Recovery of one's own self after sleep: 109–11. Ephemeral personalities of characters in a play make one doubt the reality of the self: 228–29. Contrast between one's own picture of one's self and that seen by others: 367–69. Our body "a vase enclosing our spiritual nature": **IV** 211–13. Our unfaithfulness to our former selves: 349. "Experience of oneself which is the only true experience": 434. "We lack the sense of our own visibility": 609–10. M's several "selves", notably the philosopher and "the little barometric mannikin": **V** 5–6. "We detest what resembles ourselves": 136. We do not see our own bodies, which other people see, while the object of our thoughts is invisible to them: 237. Our ignorance of ourselves: 563–64 (cf. 641). The "innumerable and humble 'selves' that compose our personality": 578–79 (cf. 660: "a composite army," and 713–14). Self-plagiarism: 586–87. "Man is the creature who cannot escape from himself, who knows other people only in himself": 607. "Our ego is composed of the superimposition of our successive states": 733–34. Other people are "merely showcases for the very perishable collections of one's own mind": 751. "Spare selves" that are substituted for a self "that has been too seriously wounded": 803–5. Death of one's former self no more distressing than the continuous eclipse of the various incompatible selves that make up one's personality: 869–70. "Through art alone are we able to emerge from ourselves": **VI** 299 (cf. 276–77; **V** 205).

SERVANTS. Françoise's tyranny over other servants: **I** 173. Servants must be actuated by different motives from ours: 509. Servants observe and misinterpret the behaviour of their employers as human beings do animals: **II** 374. Lunch below stairs, Françoise holds court: **III** 11–27. Françoise less of a servant than others: 77. "Monstrous abnormality" of the life led by servants 78. Defects of his servants reveal to M his own shortcomings: 79. M's pity for servants: **IV** 239–40. Power of divination in servants: 303. Servants recognise their own kind, as do convicts and animals: 526–27. Servants only make clearer the limitations of their caste the more they imagine they are penetrating ours: **VI** 85. Clichés in the servants' hall as in social coteries: 230.

SLEEP. Depersonalisation due to sleep; the sleep of things; disorientation in time and space: **I** 1–9. Distortion in sleep of the sleeper's real perceptions: 540–41. Sleep in a train: **II** 315–16. Sleep after evenings at Rivebelle; mysteries into which we are initiated by deep sleep; a form of intoxication; a potent narcotic; the body measures time in sleep: 544–47. Sleep at Doncières; poetic landscape of sleep; the "secret garden" in which different kinds of sleep grow "like unknown flowers"; "sleeping like a log": **III** 105–11; "organic dislocations" produced by sleep after great fatigue take us back to our earlier selves; "a charming fairy-tale": 115–16. Remains of waking thoughts subsist in sleep; diminutions that characterise sleep reflected symbolically in dreams: 191–92. The act of awakening is one of forgetting: 457. Insomnia helps us to appreciate sleep: **IV** 69. The world of sleep; an "inward Lethe": 216. Mme Cottard falls asleep at La Raspelière; Cottard on soporifics: 488–90. Sleep like a second dwelling, a different world in which we lead another life; distortion of time during sleep; sensual pleasure enjoyed in sleep a positive waste: 516–20. Sleep itself the most powerful soporific; Bergson on soporifics; sleep and memory: 520–24. Albertine's sleep: **V** 84–91, 142–46, 485–86, 494–95, 521–22. Refreshing quality of heavy sleep; changing rhythms of sleep; varieties of sleep; images of pity in sleep: 153–60. Insomnia and narcotics (Bergotte): 242–44. "That curiously alive and creative sleep of the unconscious": 456. Sleep and the memory of Albertine: 604, 658–59. After all these centuries we still know very little about sleep: **VI** 38.

SMELL. Taste and smell alone bear "the vast structure of recollection": **I** 63–64.

*Evocative smells*: Scent of the lilacs of Tansonville: **I**

190–91, 262; bitter-sweet almond fragrance of hawthorn blossom: 158, 194 (cf. **IV** 739); musty smell of the little trellised pavilion in the Champs-Elysées recalls Uncle Adolphe's sanctum at Combray: **II** 87–88, 91 (cf. **I** 99–100); smell of a log fire and the paper of one of Bergotte's books linked in M's memory with the names of villages round Combray: 326; evocative power, for M, of a smell of leaves: 409–10; scent of twigs which Françoise throws on the fire revives memories of Combray and Doncières: **V** 24–25; smell of petrol reawakens memories of motoring at Balbec: 554–55.

*Isolated smells*: Smell of vetiver in an unfamiliar room: **I** 8; (*see also* **II** 334); smell of orris-root in the little closet: 14, 222; smell of varnish on the staircase at Combray: 36; smell of cooking from the Oiseau Flesché: 65–66; country smells concentrated in Aunt Léonie's rooms: 66–68; "glutinous, insipid, indigestible and fruity" smell of her bedspread: 68; odour of unbleached calico in the draper's shop: 88; balmy scent of the lime-trees on evening walks: 159; M's chamber-pot "a vase of aromatic perfume" after eating asparagus: 169; aroma of roast chicken the "proper perfume" of one of Françoise's virtues: 169; smell of asparagus gives the kitchen-maid asthma: 173; fragrance of Odette's chrysanthemums: 311; fragrance of acacias in the Bois: 593; Odette's scent, whose "fragrant exhalations" perfume the whole apartment: **II** 103, 113; lemon fragrance of guelder-roses: 288; Odette's drawing-room permeated with the scent of flowers: 289; the smell of Albertine's cheeks: 639, 701; (*see also* **III** 497). Coarse, stale, mouldy smell of the barracks at Doncières: **III** 91–92; "peculiar odour" of the soap in the Grand Hotel, Balbec: **IV** 222; M compares his desires for different girls to the perfumes of antiquity: 323–24; smell of rhino-gomenol exuded by Mme Verdurin on musical evenings: **V** 320; smells evoked by a spring morning: 553–54; "cool smell" of a forest: **VI** 257.

SNOBBERY. Legrandin's tirades against snobbery—"the unforgivable sin": **I** 92; his own snobbery: 177–82 (cf. **V** 8, 906–7). Princes "know themselves to be princes, and are not snobs": **II** 128. Bloch taxes M with snobbery: 437, 442 (cf. **IV** 686–87). Snobbish distinctions among the lower classes more surprising because more obscure: 579. Offensive snobbishness of the Prince de Foix and his friends: **III** 551–52. "Evangelical snobbery" of the Princesse de Parme: 585. Bréauté's hatred of snobs derives from his own snobbishness: 691 (cf. 618). Craven snobbishness of Mme de Saint-Euverte: **IV** 137–38. Artistic snobbery (Mme de Cambremer-Legrandin) and its effect on reputations: 288–94 (cf. 480–81). "Congenital and morbid" snobbery (of Mme de Cambremer) which renders its victim immune to other vices: 438. "Snobbery is a grave disease, but it is localised and so does not utterly corrupt the soul": **V** 8. Gilberte's snobbery, which has "something of Swann's intelligent curiosity": 790–94. Element of sincerity in snobbery: 795. The snobbery of the gutter: **VI** 203. How snobbery changes in form: 393–95.

SOLITUDE. M's exhilaration in the solitude of autumn walks: **I** 217–20. M can be truly happy only when alone: **II** 430–31. Reasons for Elstir's life of solitude; the practice of solitude engenders a love for it: 556–57. "An artist, if he is to be absolutely true to the life of the spirit, must be alone": 605. The "solitary work of artistic creation": 664. "Each of us is indeed alone": **III** 432. Ideas are like goddesses who appear only to the solitary mortal: 545. "Exhilarating virtues of solitude": **V** 22–23. M's fears that marriage will deprive him of "the joys of solitude": 25–26. "The fortifying thrill of solitude": 265. Impression of solitude in Venice: 884. Solitude can be preserved in the midst of social life: **VI** 332–33; but M proposes to return to a solitary life to write his book: 435–37.

SPEECH. *See* Language.

STOCK EXCHANGE. M's stocks and shares; Norpois's advice on his portfolio: **II** 33–34 (cf. **V** 866–67). Peculiar credulity of the Stock Exchange—sensational war-time rumours: **VI** 71–72.

SUN. Afternoon sun behind closed shutters at Combray: **I** 113–14. Rays of the setting sun in Aunt Léonie's room: 187. Sunlight on a balcony: 563 (cf. **III** 418); on the snow in the Champs Elysées: 567; in M's classroom: 575. Sunlight in the train to Balbec: **II** 312; sunrise from the train: 316–17. Morning sun on the roof of the Grand Hotel annex: 337; on the sea: 342; in M's and his grandmother's rooms: 342–43, 386, 729–30. Balbec sunsets: 522–26. Exaltation of sunlight at Doncières: **III** 101–2. Desolating sunrise on M's last day at

Balbec, symbolising "the bloody sacrifice I was about to have to make of all joy, every morning until the end of my life": **IV** 720–23. Play of sunlight on bathroom windows: **V** 3–4. Sunset and painful memories: 646–47. The evening sun in Venice: 881.

TEARS. M's childhood tears; sobs that still echo in the silence of evening; "a manumission of tears": **I** 49–52. "Quite half the human race in tears": **III** 509. Lowering of temperatures caused by a certain kind of tears: 539. Effect of tears on Françoise: **IV** 239–40 (cf. **V** 648–49). Upper-class people pretend not to notice tears whereas simple people are distressed by them: 480. Our own (suppressed) tears in other people's eyes are infuriating: **V** 136. "People are not always very tolerant of the tears which they themselves have provoked": 417–18. .

TELEPHONE. Mme Cottard's wonder at the novelty of the telephone: **II** 250. M considers it improper that the telephone should play pander between Saint-Loup and his mistress: **III** 160–61. M's abortive conversation with his grandmother; magic of the telephone; the "Vigilant Virgins"; "convulsions of the vociferous stump": 173–80. "Purposeless smiles" of people on the telephone: 786 (cf. **V** 124). Françoise's resistance to the telephone: **IV** 176–78 (cf. **V** 126, 200–1). M's call from Albertine; the "top-like whirr" of the telephone: 177–78. Familiarity of a "supernatural instrument before whose miracles we used to stand amazed": **V** 31– 32. M invokes the "implacable deities" (telephone call to Andrée); genre scene for a modern painter: "At the Telephone": 124. "A flying squadron of sounds" (M's conversation with the telephonist speaking for Françoise): 200–1. Mme Verdurin's war-time telephoning: **VI** 61.

THEATRE. M's platonic love for the theatre as a child; his classification of actors: **I** 100–2. Swann advises him to go and see Berma in *Phèdre*: 135; he does so at last: **II** 11–29; expectations before seeing Berma; preconceptions about the art of acting: 14–20; first impressions on entering a theatre: 23–24; disappointment with Berma: 25–29; retrospective reappraisal, influenced by (1) Norpois's opinion: 36–39; (2) an enthusiastic newspaper review: 71–72; (3) Bergotte's views: 183–86; (4) Swann's views: 193. Waning of M's enthusiasm for the art of acting: **III** 39, 50–53. Second experience of Berma; a gala night at the Opéra: 40–69. M recognises and appreciates Berma's dramatic genius, and realises why he had failed to do so before; reflexions on the art of acting; interpretative genius transcends mediocre material: 53–61. Rachel on theatre: 220–22. Reflexions on actors: 228–29. A case of theatrical bitchiness: 229–30. Backstage at the theatre: 231–41. The language of the theatrical profession: **VI** 463. Unpleasant aspects of theatrical life (Berma and Rachel): 479–80.

TIME. Distortion of time during sleep: **I** 4–10 (cf. **II** 545–48; **IV** 516–18; **V** 153–55). Time the fourth dimension of Combray church: 83. Imaginary Time of the armchair traveller: 558. M's realisation that he is not situated somewhere outside Time but subject to its laws: **II** 74. Time is elastic, the passions we feel expand it, those we inspire contract it: 257. Life is careless of chronology, "interpolating so many anachronisms into the sequence of our days": 299. Time accurately measured by the body during sleep: 546–47. For M, far from Mme de Guermantes, the arithmetical divisions of time assume "a dolorous and poetic aspect": **III** 156. Lengthening of time in solitude: 478, or while waiting for a rendezvous: 524–25. Reappearance of Albertine "like an enchantress offering me a mirror that reflected time": 479. Phenomena of memory make Time appear to consist of a series of different parallel lines: **IV** 212. We take account of minutes, the Romans scarcely of hours: 303. "We can sometimes find a person again, but we cannot abolish time": 381–82. Sleep has its own time different from waking time—or perhaps is outside time: 516–20 (cf. **V** 153–55). Albertine "a mighty goddess of Time": **V** 520. "As there is a geometry in space, so there is a psychology in time": 751 (cf. **VI** 505–6). Time brings forgetfulness, which in turn alters our notion of time; "there are optical errors in time as there are in space": 802–3. Man an "ageless creature" who floats between the walls of time "as in a pool the surface-level of which is constantly changing": 830. Recapturing Lost Time; extra-temporal sensations; "a fragment of time in the pure state"; "a minute freed from the order of time" re-creates "the man freed from the order of time": **VI** 262–65; a work of art "the sole means of rediscovering Lost Time": 304 (cf. 350–55); dreams, in spite of "the extraordinary effects which they achieve with Time," cannot enable us to rediscover it: 323. Guests at the Guermantes reception "puppets which exteriorised Time"; M. d'Argencourt a revelation of Time made visible; "the distorting perspective of Time": 341–44; re-creative power of Time; "Time, the artist": 360–61, 367–68; variations in the tempo of Time: 371–73; "balancing mechanism of Time": 378–79; "the chemistry of Time . . . at work upon society": 389–411, 446–47. The young Mme de Saint-Euverte a symbol of Time's continuity: 495. Time, "colourless and inapprehensible," materialised in Mlle de Saint-Loup: 506. Time a spur to M: 506–12; fundamental importance of Time in his book; he will describe men as "occupying so considerable a place . . . prolonged past measure . . . in Time": 526–32.

TRAINS. *See* Railways.

TREES. Trees in the Bois de Boulogne (Allée des Acacias): **I** 592–93; autumn in the Bois: 598–602 (cf. **III** 533). The three trees of Hudimesnil: **II** 404–8 (cf. **VI** 255). Trees on the roads round Balbec seem to M to be silently warning him to get down to work: **IV** 559–60. Row of sunlit trees by a railway line: **VI** 238–39, 257.

(*See* Apple-trees; Flowers; Hawthorns.)

TRUTH. The search for truth the "vague but permanent" object of the young M's thoughts: **I** 116. "The truth which one puts into one's words is not irresistibly self-evident": **II** 257. Fortuitous stumblings on the truth give some support to the theory of presentiment: 600–1. "Truth has no need to be uttered to be made apparent": **III** 79–80. Elusiveness of truth in politics: 326. Truth in the context of diplomacy: 351–52. Under the stress of exceptional emotion, people do sometimes say what they think: 693. Truth a current which flows from what people say rather than the actual thing they say: **IV** 677. The truth comes to us, unexpectedly, from without: 701. Truth, even if logically necessary, not always foreseeable as a whole: **V** 1–2. "The truth is so variable for each of us . . .": 15. A single small fact may be enough to reveal the truth about a whole category of analogous facts: 693. "How difficult it is to know the truth in this world": 839. "Truth and life are very difficult to fathom": 843. Truths which the intellect apprehends directly less profound and necessary than those received through intuition: **VI** 273, 275–76, 303–4. Truth for the writer: 289–90. Truth unknown to three people out of four: 492.

VICE. "Perhaps it is only in really vicious lives that the problem of morality can arise in all its disquieting strength"; vice can arise from hypersensitiveness as much as from the lack of it; vice in a writer not incompatible with morality in his books (Bergotte): **II** 180–81. "The variety of our defects is no less remarkable than the similarity of our virtues": 438. The bad habit of denouncing our own defects in others: 441. "Every vice, like every profession, requires and develops a special knowledge which we are never loath to display": 441. Sexual inversion "improperly" called a vice: **IV** 23–25. People with the same vice recognise each other instinctively: 52. Nothing so isolates us as an inner vice: **V** 275. There is no one we appreciate more than a person who places his virtues at the service of our vices: 283. Nothing is more limited than vice: **VI** 199. Internal and external signs of vice: 211. The greatest vice of all—lack of will-power: 212.

(*See* Inversion; Sadism.)

VIRTUE. "The impassive, unsympathetic, sublime face of true goodness": **I** 113. Our virtues are not free and floating qualities but closely linked to the actions in conjunction with which we exercise them: **II** 2–3. "The frequency of the virtues that are identical in us all is not more wonderful than the multiplicity of the defects that are peculiar to each one of us": 437. It is not common sense, but kindness, that is "the commonest thing in the world": 437. Other people more capable of kind acts than we suppose: **V** 439–40. "Kindness, a simple process of maturation": **VI** 411.

WAR. Françoise and the gardener at Combray discuss the possibility of war: **I** 121–23. Discussions at Doncières on the art of war; Saint-Loup's theories: **III** 140–51 (cf. **VI** 101–2, 428–31). Françoise's reaction to the Russo-Japanese war: 450. Saint-Loup on the possibility of a Franco-German war; his predictions as to the cosmic nature of a future war: 565. M's interest in the Boer

War: **IV** 11. Preparations for war provoke war: **V** 487–89. The 1914–18 war: **VI** 46–104 *passim*; war-time Paris: 53–54; profound changes brought about by the war in inverse ratio to the quality of the minds it touched: 53–54; the misery of the soldier: 63–64; patriotism, courage and cowardice, heroism of the *poilu*; the ethos of the soldier (Saint-Loup): 69–80, 91–92; the butler "puts the wind up" Françoise; "a good blood-letting is useful now and again": 84–85; relation of 1914–18 war to previous wars: 101–4; the war considered as a struggle between two human bodies: 118–19; "scum of universal fatuousness" which the war left in its wake: 236. Saint-Loup's theories about war vindicated: 429–31. War "is something that is lived like a love or a hatred and could be told like the story of a novel": 431.

WEATHER. M's father's meteorological preoccupations: **I** 12, 127 (inherited by M: **V** 95–96). Sonorous atmosphere of hot weather: 114. Atmospheric variations provoke changes of key in M's sensibility: 550. Importance of weather for M's hopes of meeting Gilberte in the Champs-Elysées: 563. Cold weather at Doncières: **III** 124. Profound and unpredictable psychological effect of atmosphere: 187. "A change in the weather is sufficient to create the world and ourselves anew": 472. Evocation of a spring day: **IV** 243–45. Hot weather at Balbec and its effect on M's love affairs: 320–21 (cf. 534). Changes in the weather fill M with joy since they herald changes in his own life: 509. M in bed reads the weather from the quality of street sounds: **V** 1. The "barometric mannikin": 5–6. Moments of inspiration and elation due to the weather: 23. Various kinds of weather and their interest for the idle man: 100–3. A spring day in winter: 147. Fine spring weather reawakens M's desire for women and travel: 544–45, 553–56. Atmospheric changes provoke other changes in the inner man, awaken forgotten selves: 663.

A COMPREHENSIVE MODERN LIBRARY

READING GROUP GUIDE FOR

# In Search of Lost Time

## VOLUMES I–VI

*is available online at*

*www.modernlibrary.com/rgg*

# MODERN LIBRARY IS ONLINE AT
## WWW.MODERNLIBRARY.COM

MODERN LIBRARY ONLINE IS YOUR GUIDE
TO CLASSIC LITERATURE ON THE WEB

## THE MODERN LIBRARY E-NEWSLETTER

Our free e-mail newsletter is sent to subscribers, and features sample chapters, interviews with and essays by our authors, upcoming books, special promotions, announcements, and news.

To subscribe to the Modern Library e-newsletter, send a blank e-mail to: **sub_modernlibrary@info.randomhouse.com** or visit **www.modernlibrary.com**

## THE MODERN LIBRARY WEBSITE

Check out the Modern Library website at
**www.modernlibrary.com** for:

- The Modern Library e-newsletter
- A list of our current and upcoming titles and series
- Reading Group Guides and exclusive author spotlights
- Special features with information on the classics and other paperback series
- Excerpts from new releases and other titles
- A list of our e-books and information on where to buy them
- The Modern Library Editorial Board's 100 Best Novels and 100 Best Nonfiction Books of the Twentieth Century written in the English language
- News and announcements

Questions? E-mail us at **modernlibrary@randomhouse.com**
For questions about examination or desk copies, please visit
the Random House Academic Resources site at
**www.randomhouse.com/academic**